Climbing the Ranks 2

A Tower Climber Epic Fantasy

By

Tao Wong

Copyright

This is a work of fiction. Names, characters, businesses, places, events, and incidents are either the products of the author's imagination or used in a fictitious manner. Any resemblance to actual persons, living or dead, or actual events is purely coincidental.

No part of this publication may be reproduced, distributed, or transmitted in any form or by any means, including photocopying, recording, or other electronic or mechanical methods, without the prior written permission of the publisher, except in the case of brief quotations embodied in critical reviews and certain other non-commercial uses permitted by copyright law.

Climbing the Ranks 2
Copyright © 2024 Tao Wong. All Rights reserved.
Copyright © 2024 Sarah Anderson
Copyright © 2024 BadMoon Studios

Published by Starlit Publishing
PO Box 30035
High Park PO
Toronto, ON
M6P 3K0
Canada
www.starlitpublishing.com

Ebook ISBN: 9781778551727
Paperback ISBN: 9781778552175
Hardcover ISBN: 9781778552168

Books in the Climbing the Ranks Series

Climbing the Ranks 1
Climbing the Ranks 2
Climbing the Ranks 3

Other Series by Tao Wong
A Thousand Li
Adventures on Brad
Dating Evolution
Eternal Night
Magic Kingdom at War
Power, Masks and Cape

The System Apocalypse Universe
The System Apocalypse
System Apocalypse: Australia
System Apocalypse: Kismet
System Apocalypse: Liberty
System Apocalypse – Relentless

The Hidden Universe
Hidden Dishes
Hidden Wishes

Table of Contents

Chapter 1 15
Chapter 2 23
Chapter 3 28
Chapter 4 33
Chapter 5 37
Chapter 6 42
Chapter 7 47
Chapter 8 52
Chapter 9 56
Chapter 10 61
Chapter 11 65
Chapter 12 71
Chapter 13 76
Chapter 14 81
Chapter 15 87
Chapter 16 92
Chapter 17 97
Chapter 18 103
Chapter 19 108
Chapter 20 114
Chapter 21 118
Chapter 22 123
Chapter 23 129
Chapter 24 134
Chapter 25 139
Chapter 26 143
Chapter 27 149

Chapter	Page
Chapter 28	155
Chapter 29	160
Chapter 30	165
Chapter 31	169
Chapter 32	173
Chapter 33	179
Chapter 34	186
Chapter 35	190
Chapter 36	195
Chapter 37	200
Chapter 38	205
Chapter 39	210
Chapter 40	215
Chapter 41	220
Chapter 42	225
Chapter 43	229
Chapter 44	234
Chapter 45	239
Chapter 46	243
Chapter 47	247
Chapter 48	251
Chapter 49	255
Chapter 50	259
Chapter 51	264
Chapter 52	268
Chapter 53	272
Chapter 54	277
Chapter 55	282

Chapter 56 287
Chapter 57 293
Chapter 58 300
Chapter 59 305
Chapter 60 310
Chapter 61 315
Chapter 62 319
Chapter 63 325
Chapter 64 331
Chapter 65 337
Chapter 66 343
Chapter 67 349
Chapter 68 357
Chapter 69 362
Chapter 70 370
Chapter 71 374
Chapter 72 379
Chapter 73 383
Chapter 74 389
Chapter 75 393
Chapter 76 397
Chapter 77 402
Chapter 78 407
Chapter 79 413
Chapter 80 419
Chapter 81 425
Chapter 82 429
Chapter 83 434

Chapter 84	439
Chapter 85	444
Chapter 86	450
Chapter 87	455
Chapter 88	461
Chapter 89	467
Chapter 90	472
Chapter 91	477
Chapter 92	483
Chapter 93	487
Chapter 94	493
Chapter 95	500
Chapter 96	507
Chapter 97	511
Chapter 98	517
Chapter 99	521
Chapter 100	525
Chapter 101	530
Chapter 102	535
Chapter 103	541
Chapter 104	546
Chapter 105	551
Chapter 106	556
Chapter 107	560
Chapter 108	565
Chapter 109	570
Chapter 110	576
Chapter 111	582

Chapter 112	589
Chapter 113	595
Chapter 114	601
Chapter 115	605
Chapter 116	610
Chapter 117	615
Chapter 118	622
Chapter 119	628
Chapter 120	634
Chapter 121	639
Chapter 122	644
Chapter 123	649
Chapter 124	654
Chapter 125	659
Chapter 126	665
Chapter 127	671
Chapter 128	676
Chapter 129	681
Chapter 130	686
Chapter 131	693
Chapter 132	698
Chapter 133	704
Chapter 134	709
Chapter 135	714
Chapter 136	721
Chapter 137	729
Chapter 138	735
Chapter 139	741

Chapter 140 747
Chapter 141 753
Chapter 142 760
Chapter 143 766
Chapter 144 771
Chapter 145 776
Author's Note 782
About the Author 783
About the Publisher 785

Chapter 1

Arthur finished binding his wounds, his backpack splayed out beside him. Movement hurt, everything from the damaged disc in his lower back to the numerous and significant cuts all across his body making him wince. That he was doing a mostly slipshod job of wrapping his wounds did not escape the Tower climber, mostly because his healing technique would eventually clot up the wounds and bring him to full health.

If the Tower gave him enough time. As it was, it did not seem to mind his delay in the liminal space between Tower floors. About the only thing it seemed particularly upset with Arthur about was how he continued to ignore the pressure on his mind coming from the notifications it wanted to push to him.

Of course, he had a good reason for that.

"Can't be reading, if I'm bleeding…" Arthur said, automatically attempting to rhyme. It was a silly little thing that he did, a mental tic that kept his mind from worrying about things he could not control, like how the rest of his team had done. For that matter, he kind of liked the challenge. On long days outside the Tower, running errands and working odd jobs, filling his head with silly patter kept him sane when going over forms or when information from Tower wikis no longer kept his interest.

Now he was in the Tower, after years of preparation. He had even reached the second floor, though it had taken him longer than he'd have liked. Still, there was no timetable that he had to hit for the outside world. There might be a few people he might wish to visit—the batch of fellow students under his master that had gone ahead of him—but that was it.

Another breath, and Arthur pushed himself to pack his backpack again. Movements were slow, the weird omni-directional light of the liminal space throwing his spatial judgment off a little. If not for the fact that the walls and ceiling were just a tad differently coloured, he might have been truly disoriented.

End of the day though, all that hesitating and stalling had to end.

"Time to look at the kind of book? Rook? Mook?" Arthur trailed off, shaking his head. He was not doing well with the rhyming right now. He knew the loss of blood was part of it. Energy was being drained constantly from his core as his body tried to heal him.

Best get this over with now, then start cultivating and healing.

Just then, golden lines of text appeared in his mind's eye.

First floor final test completed.
Results are being graded.
Please wait...
Tests have been graded.
Would you like to review your results now?

Arthur blinked, then grinned. Yes, he definitely would want to see his results.

First Floor Final Test
Type: Gauntlet
Time Taken: 00:07:09
Number of Enemies Defeated: 17
Bonus: Alpha Jenglot Defeated
Overall Grade: B+

"B! B!" Arthur leapt to his feet, then collapsed back, clutching his chest with a wince. "I'm never living that down."

Never mind what his *sifu* would think if the man ever learned about the horrible grade. If someone like Jan or Mel—or worse, the Chin family—heard he'd done so badly, he would have no mien at all. How could he dare show his face, with a grade like this.

Of course, a small portion of him—the one that had grown up watching Western television—knew that such expectations were a little warped. Not everyone could get an A, especially if they were grading on a curve. Someone, somewhere, had to get a B. Or a C or D. Probably not a fail. In the Tower, after all, a fail likely meant death and there was no point in grading that.

In fact, that thought actually cheered Arthur up. If this entire grading system was just grading survivors, then the grade was actually better than it looked. After all, he was being graded against survivors and not the entire Tower population that had tried the first floor.

Grim and a little morbid, but he would take it.

Would you like to review your rewards?

"Reward? Oh, right. There was something like that," Arthur muttered to himself. He'd forgotten that passing each floor often saw a boon given. Of course, the boons were often minor and varied so greatly that he'd mostly just forgotten about it. After all, he did not need a fire-starter or an enchanted tent. Well, an enchanted tent might be nice...

Assessing results.
Verifying current reward list.
Reward options:

- *Attribute Increase (+1)*
- *Core Rewards (17 enemies defeated)*
- *Cultivation Technique*

"*Celaka!* Bloody cheaters. Isn't that just paying me for what I killed?" Arthur groused when he read the second option. He found himself crossing his arms as he stared at the words. It also told him a little about the other option for completing the trial.

It'd have been insane for someone to actually wipe out all those monsters in the test, but if they had taken out a good portion of the monsters, they might actually come out of the trial laughing at the riches they'd accumulated. After all, the sheer volume of cores for doing so and passing the test would make them rich beyond easy belief.

Pretty nice, but not particularly useful for him.

The +1 attribute increase was actually better, though it seemed to be a touch stingy. Two points would have made a much bigger difference for him. Then again, this was the first floor of the Tower. Couldn't expect too much from the rewards.

If so, that suggested what kind of cultivation technique they had to offer. It would certainly be a technique, not a cultivation method which might have been vaguely better. Cultivation techniques covered all manner of skills both offensive and defensive, while cultivation methods were approaches to drawing Tower energy into one's body.

The problem with getting a technique as a reward was that he already have it. Or, worse, he might receive something new but utterly useless. After all if it was, for example, a fire creation technique, with his Yin Body he'd struggle to deal with all that.

Arthur sighed. "Never easy, when you're as good as me, eh?"

He didn't even bother to rhyme that one. Instead, he flicked his hand sideways, pulling up his status sheet. About time to see how that was doing.

Cultivation Speed: 1.237 Yin
Energy Pool: 3/17 (Yin) (Yang – unusable 0.9)
Refinement Speed: 0.0387
Refined Energy: 0.031 (6) (Yang – unusable 0.1712)

Attributes and Traits
Mind: 5 (Multi-Tasking)
Body: 8 (Enhanced Eyesight, Yin Body)
Spirit: 5 (Sticky Energy)

Techniques
Yin Body – Cultivation Technique
Focused Strike
Accelerated Healing – Refined Energy (Grade III)
Heavenly Sage's Mischief

Refined Energy Dart

Partial Techniques
Simultaneous Flow (13.1%)
Yin-Yang Energy Exchange (36.1%)
Bark Skin (0.02%)

Not much change since the last time he had reviewed it, which was no surprise. It wasn't as though he'd had a lot of time to practise before they had to attempt the ascent to the second floor.

He needed to pull—or cultivate, as they called it—more energy from his surroundings in the Tower and process it into the refined energy that half his techniques used. Refined energy was also the only way he could increase his attributes, which would in turn increase everything else like the capacities of his cultivated energy pool and refined energy pool.

Supposedly, there were more energies and elements he'd yet to encounter—beyond refined energy—but that was so far away he'd barely paid attention to those things. Never had been his plan to push that far ahead, after all. Survival and doing well for himself only required him to clear this Tower. Everything after that was just a bonus.

At least, that was the plan. Now he had a clan seal and headed a clan. That meant he had to climb much further unless he wanted to be a pawn.

The entire point of climbing this Tower was to get out of being a pawn of forces he could not control. In the real world, of course, that had been the circumstances of his birth, the technological changes that had swept across the planet, and a government that just didn't care.

Now he was drawn into another game, of forces much more powerful than he: other clans and guilds, other Tower climbers, who'd want to make use of his clan. On that thought, he could not help but pull up information on his clan, reviewing it again.

The Benevolent Durians Clan

Organizational Ranking: 182,771
Number of Towers Occupied: 1
Number of Clan Buildings: 1
Number of Clan Members: 98
Overall Credit Rating: F-
Aspect: Guardianship
Sigil: The Flame Phoenix

A quick query pulled up the Aspects and Sigil details.

Aspect Bonuses

- *Minor increase in effectiveness of protective, healing, and shielding cultivation techniques.*
- *Trivial increase in effectiveness of precision, speed, and bonding cultivation techniques.*
- *Variable increase in cultivation and refinement speed, dependent upon the number of Clan members within close proximity.*
- *Tower quest types have been expanded.*

Sigil Bonuses

- *Sigil Bonuses (Clan Head): Accelerated Healing – Refined Energy (Grade I) improved to Accelerated Healing – Refined Energy (Grade II)*
- *Sigil Bonuses (Clan): Cultivation Exercise – Accelerated Healing – Refined Energy (Grade I) has been imparted to all Clan members.*

Nope. No real change there either.

Arthur sighed. Well, he'd been avoiding it for a while now, but it was fast becoming clear that he needed to make a decision. What would he take as his reward?

As though there really were a choice.

Chapter 2

Simple solutions were the best. Attributes were what linked everything together, from offering new Traits that helped differentiate one Tower climber from another to providing larger energy pools and more refined energy points. All of which was to say: If he had a choice, he'd always grab at more attributes.

It also helped that with the Yin Body, he was already ahead of the game. The increased in his attributes of the Yin Body by itself meant that he had done less work to build himself up than others of the same level of refined energy. It also let him keep cool, his mind calmer and clearer than ever before. Of course, in the greater context of the Tower, he was still a baby—not even having reached the second transformation yet.

Oh, he was looking forward to that. Ten points in each attribute. It was the easiest transformation to make—not counting the one you received when you first entered a Tower—and after which, things got complicated. But that was a common enough refrain that he could ignore it.

"I'll take the Attribute point," Arthur announced out loud.

A tad slow, a tad tired. He forgot that he actually should have chosen which attribute he was putting the point into. He felt the energy pour into him, into his refined energy core, urgent in its desires as though it refused to stay there.

A part of Arthur wondered why the Tower couldn't just give them that refined energy all the time. Another part of him urged Arthur to figure out what he was dedicating that energy point to right now, damn it. Otherwise, he felt, he was going to burst like a balloon.

Mind, Body, or Spirit? Respectively, those improved energy refinement, energy pool capacity, and cultivation speed. And each attribute, when increased, came with many more subtle benefits, whether it was comprehending techniques, being physically more imposing and robust, or even just mentally and emotionally more resilient.

A thought flickered across his mind: Even if the Spirit attribute did provide resiliency, it did not seem to necessarily make people better. He forced it aside, not wanting to delve into those thoughts, though he knew there were significant philosophical debates about the role of the spirit or soul, the way the Tower improved individuals, and what, if anything, that meant about the initial and intrinsic qualities of humanity.

It was one of those late-night conversations that you had with friends while sipping a drink at the *mamak* stall and the *teh tarik* was flowing strong. The hours were long and your body was aching, but you had no better job to do because all the good work was already handled by the machines.

None of those conversations were particularly useful right this moment.

Mind, Body, or Spirit? He'd most recently increased his Body attribute, getting him to 8 points. That meant he was two off from obtaining another Body Trait. Important and highly useful, those traits. It was the way cultivators differentiated themselves. Whether it was by gaining an Iron Body or Cat Reflexes or a Malleable Soul, it was the traits that dictated the long-term growth path of a cultivator. It also could mean a significant difference between two fighters with equally matched attribute stats.

It almost made Arthur consider putting the point there without thought. After all, another point in Body meant he only had to dedicate a small amount of time—but a lot of resources—into gaining that tenth point. Also, a higher Body attribute meant he could, in most cases, fight on a much more equal level. Considering he was going in weaker than most people, having rushed his way through the first floor, that would be important.

Then again, he was now an ally of Casey Chin. The powerful Chin family were not likely to just let him get himself killed, which meant his direct conflicts with other groups and individuals were likely to decrease. Didn't mean he was safe, just safer from random attacks.

On the other hand, he had a lot of other areas to improve in. Refinement speed was important; if nothing else, to help increase the rate he was going to improve at. Same with cultivation speed, though to a lesser extent. More importantly, an increased Mind attribute would help him understand more quickly the three techniques he had been practising. That, compared to a higher Body attribute, was more likely to save him.

Traits might be the flourish to an attribute, but it was techniques that were the wide strokes in the painting of their souls. If he had to choose, and he did, he might as well make sure those flourishes were broad and numerous.

Mind made up, he poured the power through his Mind meridian, guiding the choice that the Tower was imposing upon him. Arthur felt the energy enter his head, the pain of his body that he'd forgotten about intensifying briefly. Agony washed over him, bright lights flickered through his closed eyes, and he swore he tasted pink for a moment and heard *laksa*. Which, of course, made no sense.

Then again, the Tower was rewiring his brain or something similar to it. So what made sense, anyway?

Pain flowed through him and exited, leaving Arthur panting. After a few minutes, running his tongue along the back of his teeth, smacking his lips and pinching his body, he ascertained that the brief moment of disorientation was over.

All for the best.

"Now that that's over, let's see… the differential of two thousand, nine hundred, and forty three is…" Arthur paused, then snorted. "So much *lalang*. I still have no idea. I hate math."

He flopped back onto the ground, starfishing on the flat and rather uncomfortable surface. At least it wasn't stone or marble. Both had the tendency to suck all your body warmth away. Great for hot days, which was why so many floors in KL—Kuala Lumpur, the Malaysian capital—were made of stone or marble rather than wood.

For that matter…

He frowned, turning a little to stare at the ground. His cheek pressed against the firm flooring, he eyed the white material. It was as hard as stone or marble, but it didn't draw heat as fast. Maybe the floor itself was warm? It didn't feel warm; in fact, it was a little chilly.

Not metal. That was even worse for sucking away heat. And not wood, because it was both harder than wood and also colder. Something in between then.

Arthur paused, wondering why the hell he was thinking of these matters when he had more important things to do. So far, the Tower had not seemed intent on kicking him out of this space, but there was no guarantee it wasn't going to do that.

With a groan, he pushed himself upwards into cycling position. He crossed his legs, placed his hands together and straightened his back, then hesitated. He breathed slowly and began the process of drawing in Tower energy. He was critically low on energy, and if he were suddenly forced out of this liminal space, he'd need more of it.

Never know what world you'll be pushed into.

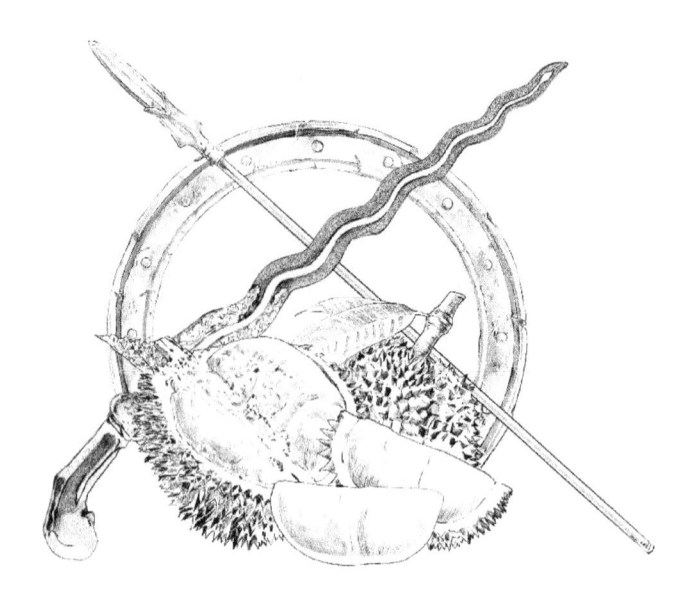

Chapter 3

Thirty minutes later and Arthur eyed his cultivation pool. It was not halfway full, but close enough that it would do. It was weird, having a fractional cultivation speed. The Tower did not care; it simply pulled energy from him in whole numbers, though even he understood that those were approximations. It was not as though when he triggered a technique he was portioning things out in perfectly whole numbers. In fact, that was the point of practice. In time, one could, theoretically, lower the amount of energy being used at any one time, such that a technique could be wielded at fractions of what it was meant to use.

Of course, many techniques had a minimum amount of energy required, like the Refined Energy Dart that required the majority of a point since the dart itself needed to do damage. If anything, refinement in that case was about speed and accuracy rather than saving energy.

Pushing that thought aside, Arthur now had enough Tower energy that he didn't feel half-drained. Next up on the list of things to do to stay alive was healing some of those nasty wounds. A half hour of passive healing layered on top of a Tower body's accelerated healing meant that he was no longer bleeding at a steady rate.

But he could do better than that.

Gritting his teeth, pulling at the refined energy that lay in his core—called the *dantian* in some teachings—he poured that concentrated lightning in a bottle through his meridians, guiding them through the necessary movements to trigger his healing technique before he sent them towards the portions that ached. Some energy leaked out, of course, but that was fine. The Accelerated Healing technique was meant to heal all of him, so whatever healing energy leaked out to other parts of the body would do good there too.

And Arthur was very, very careful not think about cancers and tumours and anything else that rampant growth might cause.

Healing was never a pleasant process. It wasn't necessarily painful—he didn't have bones that were out of place, oh wait, there was one—but it was uncomfortable. This time, however, it was painful to feel torn skin connect to skin, dislocated bones and ligaments reattach, and inflammation decrease.

Ten minutes later, Arthur was panting, his body covered with light sweat. He grimaced and wiped himself clean, taking the time to wipe himself down with a wet cloth after unwinding all his bandages. He made sure to store those in a ziplock bag for washing later.

Sure, he could buy more cloth and bandages from the Tower on the second floor, but it made no sense to be profligate like that. Why spend cores or credits on mere cloth? Cores were valuable for growing stronger, while credits could buy techniques and enchanted items.

Anyway, decades of being a cheapskate and saving everything he could were not going to be washed away by suddenly becoming rich. Or, if not rich, at least connected to the Chins.

"Ugh. I hate when the scabs peel off. Either come off properly or don't!" He prodded at a deep cut on his chest, portions of skin still stuck to the scab. He reached sideways, grabbing at a knife only to pause, realising that what he held wasn't just a plain knife but a kris.

The cursed kris.

Cursed Kris of the Lost Warrior

Enchantments: Applies an instance of Toxic Yin Chi when blood is drawn. Effects of Toxic Yin Chi vary depending on resistances and the individual but include clouding of senses, numbness, paralysis, and respiratory or cardiac arrest.

Staring at the details showing up before his eyes—or technically his mind, since even blind people saw Tower notifications—he sighed. Right. No stabbing himself accidentally with the cursed kris. Careful not to nick himself with its wavy-shaped blade, he sheathed the dagger-sword, then searched his belt for a pocket knife.

"Celaka! I must have lost it," he grumbled. Frustrated, he pinched the scab on his chest and tugged, wincing as it ripped, and ignored the new bleeding. He finished wiping the rest of his body off.

Clean at last and unlikely to bleed much more, he stuffed everything back into his pack. The pressure from the Tower had been growing silently as he worked, indicating that his quiet time in this liminal space was coming to an end.

It'd be too easy after all, for other Tower climbers to quietly cultivate in between floors, gathering strength and power without any risk.

Whoever, or whatever, had dropped the Towers onto Earth must be sadistic *sei baat gung*—bastards in Cantonese, his family's dialect—who liked to see people fight and struggle. No peaceful transition to a higher power for them, no cooking or baking or flower arrangement contests.

Only the strong and determined got to climb a Tower, the kind of people who didn't mind murdering another person. And boy was that a whole can of repressed worms there, what with the recollection of his most recent fights still lingering and the kinds of problems those created.

A small part of Arthur was curious what it would be like in another fifty years. Already, the Towers had altered the entire global economy. They had changed the course of lives for an entire generation, his generation. They were studying for jobs that were low paying and almost guaranteed to be automated in their lifetime, and so now being a Tower climber was the profession they looked up to.

What happened when Tower climbers who were, for the most part immortal, started showing back up in the real world in larger numbers? Sure, they had to go back into the Towers eventually, climbing up harder Towers and getting even stronger. But some of the smarter ones were already using commerce to bypass the need to keep climbing.

More and more Tower climbers coming out of the Towers were feeding their betters with monster cores—also called beast stones by some—so they could extend the amount of time these ex-climbers could stay in the real world. At some point, all the governments would start helping them along, trying to keep their people happy.

After all, anyone in the Top 100 was worth an army all by themselves.

"Top 100. Heh. I don't even know why I'm thinking of that," Arthur snorted to himself. He was so far from those people, he might as well be an ant. Or a mortal.

He was only one floor done, and already thinking—vaguely—that he might one day join their ranks. Fool's hope. Better to focus on what he needed to do next. Simple enough to make sure he had everything ready, slip the pack over his shoulders, and grab his black spear with the other hand. Then, he focused his attention on the next notification that the Tower was trying to push on him, letting it unroll.

Time to see who had survived and what the second floor had to offer him.

Assessment completed.
Rewards distributed.
Teleportation commencing to second floor.
Please wait.

. . .

Chapter 4

Arthur's world lurched as he was teleported, the Tower twisting and throwing him through time and space. He fought the disorientation that threatened to empty his stomach, his body feeling no more stable than a leaf in a monsoon, tossed and turned and torn apart by pelting rain.

Still, for all that, it was significantly less painful than the last time he had been teleported to a new floor. He could still remember how helpless he had been, whereas this time, his eyes were open, his grip on his spear still firm. And while he might still throw up, it'd be in the direction of his enemies.

A win, all things considered.

Hard stone beneath his feet—the teleportation platform with all its requisite enchantments—and a slight chill in the air were the first things Arthur noticed. Then, his vision informed him of the lack of trouble. A second later, the teleportation platform did its thing, disappearing from under his feet and leaving him stumbling a little.

A good thing that the teleportation platforms didn't appear in the same spot all the time. If not, it would be a simple thing for other cultivators to wait for newcomers' arrival and conduct some leveraged trading—as they did on the first floor.

Unfortunately, Arthur was going to be alone for a little bit, without any idea or clue as to how his friends were doing. There were, however, a few rules about transportation that the Tower generally kept to that were well known.

Firstly, they were all within around five kilometers or so of the mini Tower-built town on each floor. While the number of individuals on the second floor was smaller than the first floor, there was still a need for basic services, from the Tower exchange center to quest registration. And, of course, hotels—which were one of the few truly safe areas.

Secondly, teleportations were only done if individuals were no closer than a few hundred meters from one another. The exact specifications of timing were hard to confirm; it seemed the Tower took into account things like line of sight and hearing, but Arthur knew he was, for the most part, safe from being discovered.

Lastly, teleportations by the Tower could not be tracked. No one thus far had publicly declared they could locate or track individuals being teleported in. Made it difficult to keep groups together, but it also meant that enemies could not wait to ambush an entire group of arrivals all at once.

In another time and place, with more money, simple solutions like signal stones might be used. However, Arthur's team had nothing that extravagant to wield. As such, they had chosen a much simpler method of gathering: they were to meet in town within three days.

All that was to say: Arthur had two days to rest up and heal if he wanted to. And he had to admit that was definitely high on his want-to list. If nothing else, he needed to get a better idea about this new floor, how it worked, and the energy that coursed through the surroundings.

Of course, being Yin-bodied, his best time to cultivate would be at night. And looking up through the trees—weird ones with broad flat leaves that looked spiky but large branches which made them perfect for climbing—he noted that the sun was two-thirds across the horizon.

No idea, of course, if it was setting or rising. No way to tell until more time had passed.

Another look around, noting the small patch of clear ground he was in. Not enough to be called a clearing, just a space between trees. The trees themselves were mostly the usual mixture of dark brown and black, though a few were paler towards white.

Weird.

More importantly, this seemed to be a primary growth forest. Not much brush or shrubbery under the trees, what with the thick canopy blocking out the sunlight. It was pretty dark around here, and extending his senses and touching upon the energy around him, Arthur noted that the Yin energy was pretty thick.

Decent enough to spend time cultivating if he wanted.

On the other hand, it would be even better if he could find a monster to slay. Each monster core here was twice as strong as the ones on the first floor. As such, a single monster core here would mean a significant increase to his cultivation speed.

It'd also mean that he could test himself against them.

For a moment, Arthur debated the best course of action. Then hurrying over to a nearby tree, he began the slow process of climbing it, first slinging his spear across his back using one of the straps that was built to hold it.

Up and up he climbed till he reached the thick canopy. He kept going, making sure he was hidden from sight before he carefully unslung his backpack. He strapped it to the tree trunk, which was thinner at this altitude, then paused long enough to listen for monsters and look around for problems. Other than a lizard that he had to smack across the head and send scurrying away, nothing too concerning.

No sign of his friends either, but that was not surprising.

Then, with his spear still attached to the straps over his vest, Arthur began to make his way down.

It was probably the worst idea he'd had in a while. There might be other cultivators hanging around out of sight and possibly looking to rob him. But he needed to know exactly how well he stacked up against the monsters here. And if he was going to embarrass himself in a fight, he'd rather have it happen when he was alone.

Anyway, there was no way the jump between the first floor and second floor was as bad as they said, right?

Right?

Chapter 5

Arthur was never certain if it was a good or bad thing that finding monsters was easy. Previous Tower climbers had even noted an increase in the volume of monsters on the first three floors before the numbers leveled out.

Once you left the "safety" of town, you had to be ready to fight at any time. It was also why safe zones like clan buildings were vastly more important on higher floors, if there were any. Long nights camping alone was going to become a problem soon enough.

As it stood, for the first three floors, Arthur knew there was not going to be a significant change in the general variety of monsters. The Tower would reuse monsters from previous floors but make them larger, stronger, and more skilled, such that something as simple as the *kuching hitam* that Arthur was currently struggling with was the size of an actual puma now rather than a merely large tabby cat. And it was better at hiding in treetops.

Arthur knew that if he had not had a trait boosting his ability to spot things—so-called Enhanced Eyesight, hah!—he would have been surprised by the *kuching*. Well, more surprised. He literally caught sight of the creature moments before it chose to pounce, launching itself at him with claws extended. Bringing his spear haft up, he caught the creature just before it hit. Swinging the haft shed the cat-like monster aside, but only for a moment.

Then the fight was on.

The kuching hitam had struck the ground and bounced sideways, dodging Arthur's follow-up stab. It countered by lashing out with a claw. He jerked his hand back, tried another stab, watched the monster dodge and swing at him again.

Arthur growled as the pair kept feinting and lashing out at one another, each dancing back and forth as they struck at one another. The creature was fast, faster than the first-floor version, but it didn't seem that much smarter. In fact, if Arthur recalled, creatures like that had a tendency to run soon after their initial surprise attack. Which meant…

The cat leapt backwards after another feint. Then it jumped sideways towards a nearby bush and up to a broken branch. It was there that Arthur was waiting for the creature, shuttling his spear to his front hand with a surge and pouring chi into a Focused Strike. The attack caught the creature just as it landed, piercing through hardened fur and striking its heart.

The creature twisted, pulling away as blood ran from its side. It leapt again even as blood pulsed from its wound, before it stumbled and fell, landing in a nearby bush. Arthur brought the base of the spear down, cracking its back. Legs splayed out, the monster cried out in pain as a leg and chest cracked next.

Then another step and Arthur stabbed it once more. Spear tip plunged, exited, and then he swung the spear around, eyeing his surroundings.

Simple. Quick. Not that hard, unless it had caught him by surprise. Then those couple-of-inches-long claws would have rent him apart.

Nasty.

Bending down, carefully using the kris to break open its chest, Arthur pulled the body apart and took out the beast's core. He grunted as he eyed the core, noting how it pulsed with energy. He put it in a pouch next to his belt and then stored the kris, scanning the surroundings again for trouble.

Not long after that, he was back up the tree he had kept his backpack on. Thankfully, no other kuching hitam or malevolent cultivator met him on his ascent, allowing Arthur to quickly secure his spear and then himself to the tree trunk with a quick-release tumble hitch knot before pulling his legs close in.

One last check for monsters, then Arthur cycled his breathing down as he extracted the monster core from his pouch. Time to see if all the information he'd read about second-floor cores and cultivation was true.

An hour later, Arthur's eyes opened as he felt the core he had been holding crumble away in his hand, dispersing into motes of light. He watched them drift away, a slight wry smile on his face, and then called up his status. He didn't actually need the notification, and there was something to be said about not relying on the Tower entirely since Tower notification screens were significantly curtailed in the real world, but he figured he might as well check. After all, he was only interested in one thing.

Refined Energy: 0.041 (6) (Yang – unusable 0.1717)

There it was. A 0.02 point increase in his refined energy pool. A small amount of increase in Yang energy too, though he knew he bled that out as time went along. At some point, he'd get good enough at Yin cultivation that he would no longer be forced to take in the literally scalding-hot Yang energy.

Perhaps when he got his new cultivation method from Casey.

That, of course, raised the question of what was best. Even as he scanned the surroundings yet again to make sure nothing had tried to sneak up on him, paused contemplation long enough to unstrap himself, hop over a few trees and kill a snake that had been slowly making its way up, snatch the core from it and then return to his seat, he considered his options.

He needed to finish healing up, which meant at least another ten minutes. But he was rather low on energy overall, which was not a great spot to be. He needed to conserve this energy for some of his techniques, as well as to increase his attributes.

Arthur really wanted some time alone to just cultivate, but he had a feeling that was not going to happen. And while he had three days to wait for his team to arrive, he didn't want to flounce in at the last second. That would just be rude. Never mind the increased danger of sitting out here by himself.

On the other hand, going into town first, alone and injured, was a bad idea. Same with going into town without filling up his energy pools. Even in town, if he was hanging out by himself, the longer he was alone, the more danger he'd be in. He wasn't like Casey, who might be his best bet to meet up with first. After all, she could head off most trouble just by dropping names—her own family name, that is.

Dropping his own name would just be asking for trouble.

Well, put that way, it kind of made sense. He should heal up, fill up more of his energy stores, and then go into town. He didn't need to have full stores of energy, but he certainly could do better than what he had right now.

Of course, the question was how long it would take to fill them up. A quick glance at his cultivation pool showed he had four points out of a maximum of fifteen. Each ten minutes of cultivation added 1.2 points in his cultivation pool, and ten points of Tower energy could be refined down to 0.01 points of refined energy. It was almost doubly more efficient to simply draw energy from a second-floor beast core.

Problem was finding those cores, of course. Which was why some people preferred to just cultivate energy from Tower surroundings. Not a problem if you were doing that on the first floor, but the second floor onward saw increased danger from monsters.

Thus, quests.

Quests got you contribution points, they put you moving through the floor, meaning you'd be fighting and acquiring cores and, hopefully, leapfrog ahead with the question completion rates.

Something that he had not done much of, what with all his other concerns. Still, with the sheer volume of monsters hanging around, hunting was generally a better idea than merely cultivating in the wilds. There was a good chance of finding herds of *babi ngepet*, as sounders could usually be found trotting around—at least on the first floor, where he could kill half a dozen devil pigs in one battle.

Still, ignoring all that: He needed, say, 0.1 points worth of refined energy or about four more cores, before he felt comfortable going anywhere. And a full cultivation pool. So about an hour and a half worth of cultivating to fill up his pool.

And hunting for another three monster cores, which would require another three hours of cultivating those cores at least. So, total timeline of at least five and a half hours, probably closer to eight, before he was ready to head into town. Add another half day of travel, and he'd be arriving nearly a full day later. More than enough time for others to get there before him.

Mind resolved, Arthur got down to work, of which the first part was just healing up.

Chapter 6

Everything had been going so well. By the time Arthur had finished healing, poured another half hour into cultivating just to refill his normal cultivation pool and then climbed back down, the heat of the afternoon had begun to fade. He'd arrived in the early morning, so at least that question had been answered.

Of course, Arthur left his backpack up in the tree. No point hunting with it strapped to him, especially considering how heavy that thing was. On the first floor he'd already survived one harrowing battle with it strapped on, and his back was still protesting from falling, rolling, and getting slammed into the ground repeatedly on top of one of his cooking pots.

He wasn't even sure why he had a cooking pot in there, other than the fact that it helped make tea. And the occasional warm meal was nice, especially if you managed to find enough meat to cook. Not that he needed to eat—no one in the Tower did. They survived off Tower energy, which bled out of them at increasing rates as they increased in strength.

That energy drain was one of the few negatives of a Tower body, but a simple one to fix if you just cultivated. Of course, being a Malaysian, he felt that missing out on actual good food was a crime against humanity. Which was why, even now, one of the courier jobs for new climbers was bringing foodstuff to higher floors.

All that said, he was still in a good mood until about fifteen minutes ago, when he realised that someone might be stalking him. Confirming that fact took him another five minutes of careful movement, including picking some routes that no one in their right mind would go through, not if they had a choice or disliked having thorns in their nethers.

What gave the game away was the fact that his stalker had a camouflage technique that had trouble keeping up with them when they moved fast. Since Arthur was now hunting for trouble, or actively avoiding it, it meant the stalker had to keep up.

And the shifting branches, the flickering of leaves as their shade of colour shifted from dark to lighter, was all too telling. Arthur debated what to do.

Kill them and he might set off a feud.

Leave them alone and he might get backstabbed.

Any fight he'd have to finish fast. Figure out if this stalker was just an opportunistic robber or someone he had to bury, damn the consequences.

He wondered how to bring his opponent in close. Whoever it was, they were careful to stay a good distance away, such that Arthur couldn't strike them with his spear.

He needed bait.

And lucky for him, he'd found some.

Bending down low, he ran his fingers along the ground where the earth had been torn up and nearby bushes destroyed or eaten. Clear sign of travel, and travel by more than just a single boar for sure. Not a full sounder at a dozen babi or whatever, but at least three or four.

Of course, that was rather worrying. The babi ngepet down on the first floor had been one of the tougher enemies to deal with. And while he'd grown significantly stronger, he still wasn't exactly looking forward to taking them on when they had received an upgrade in strength too.

However, if there was a way to draw in his stalker, this was it. Especially if he was under pressure. But wasn't that a pleasure?

Humming the aforementioned rhyme to himself under his breath, Arthur stood up and followed the trail. He moved a little faster than normal, though he kept his head lowered and the spear by his side, ready for use.

Finding the trio of monstrous pigs was not hard. In fact, Arthur found himself literally stumbling upon them, for he came up over a rise at a light jog and noticed the shifting mass of bodies beneath him. His mind spun through a variety of options before he leapt, twisting in mid-air to stab his spear downward and sideways.

Waking the babi ngepet that he targeted in this manner led to quite a bit of confusion. The earth that he had thought was firm gave way beneath his foot as he landed, tough flesh and bone compressing. Without thought, he flipped himself upwards, spinning all the way around so that he was upside down even as he stabbed down at the monster that was raising its head, intent on throwing off the irritating fly that had landed on it.

Spear impacted, its sharp tip skimming off and tearing deep into the jowls before slipping into the eye socket. The spear head jammed in the flesh there, and the monster twisted and threw him sideways, sending him flying away into a nearby thicket.

Hitting a bush and rolling, he cracked one shoulder on a tree trunk, which sent him twirling around. He rolled a few more times before he finally managed to get his sense of balance and momentum bled off, a part of him cursing at the surprise factor that left him unable to use any of his cultivation techniques.

Mostly though, his attention was focused on the monsters that had roused themselves from the mud pit they'd dug into the side of the hill, a resting place they'd carved from a small spring that bubbled down the slope.

These babi were twice as large as the ones he had fought on the first floor. Unlike wild boars from Europe or those that infested the northeast of North America these days, these creatures were about the size of a Perodua Kancil—the Malaysian-made tiny hatchback car they'd re-released recently in electronic engine format as a more luxurious alternative to electronic scooters. Probably weighed twice as much as a Kancil, though, as they had plenty of muscle beneath that fat.

The first monster he'd stuck was bleeding a little from a wound along the side, mostly superficial from what Arthur could tell. The second, the closest to him and the one getting ready to charge, was untouched. And the last one was busy throwing a tantrum, what with being blinded and streaming blood.

And, of course, somewhere along the way, he'd lost track of his stalker who might have scampered off or was still on the other side of the hill.

"Where's my bubbles, when there's troubles?" Arthur cried, even as he flicked a glance back to check his rear. By the time he looked back though, the babi ngepet that had been getting ready to charge him had covered half the ground.

Rather than panicking, Arthur continued to watch the monster close on him. He knew better than to jump too early. Panicking that way meant the monster could change direction and strike him. No, instead he readied himself, leaning sideways a little as he surreptitiously drew out his kris. The monster's narrowed, beady black eyes promised pain.

Quickly, Arthur took a series of quick sidesteps rather than a full leap.

He would never have dared this before, but with a Body attribute of 8, he was significantly faster than he had been. And while the babi were much bigger and stronger, they were no faster than before. Which meant that even as it tried to turn to follow him, it failed, scrambling on muddy ground. All its desperate turning did was drive Arthur's cursed kris deeper into its side, leaving a trail of poisonous Yin chi in its body.

One poisoned.

Three more to go.

And, of course, his stalker.

"Got to say, this is no easy play."

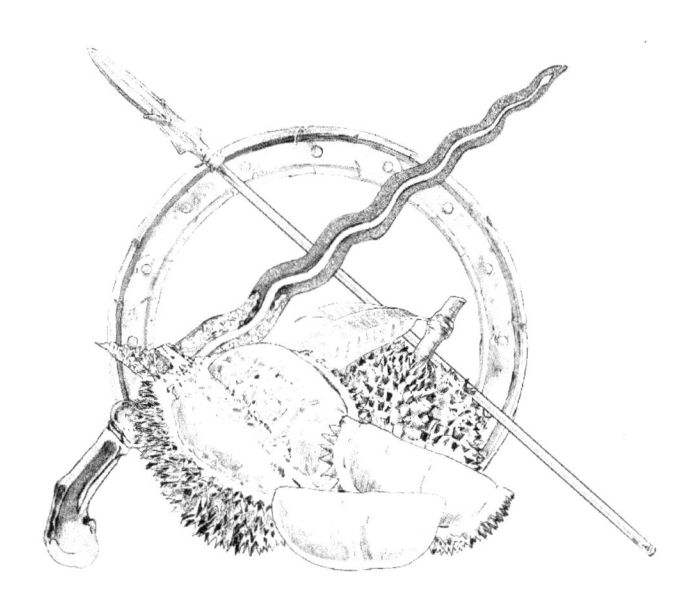

Chapter 7

Mind splintering and running down different tracks, Arthur kept shuffling to the side in the dense primary forest. Not a lot of light down here, but that was fine with his Enhanced Eyesight trait. An advantage of increasing his Body attribute had been an overall increase in that ability too. Along with that, the trait allowed him to pay attention to multiple areas and develop ideas at the same time.

Which was why, when he was sufficiently far away from his initial attacker, he chose to plant his feet, twist, and launch his spear one-handed at the injured creature even as he sunk as much energy as he could into a Focused Strike. The spear flew through the air, embedded in the charging creature's body, and sunk deep within, even as the cultivation technique faded. It was not, after all, meant to work as a ranged attack but rather in contact with Arthur's body. Still, the additional sharpening of intent and the energy carried through the spear tip as it flew through the air was enough to pierce the monster's thick hide.

The long-tusked babi ngepet roared in anger and yet barely flinched. The spear remained embedded, bobbing with each movement. Lowering its head, the devil boar prepared to charged. Arthur, now feeling the thunder of incoming hoofs from both behind and ahead leapt up, using his now-free hand to grab the branch above and haul himself up a tree.

Beneath, the pair of monsters ran into one another. With great bulk came great momentum. Unable to steer themselves aside, the thundering crash shook the surroundings and sent leaves and branches shaking. The impact even sent ripples through bunched muscles and hardened skin. Arthur watched as his spear haft bent, nearly snapping as the monster stumbled and drove the tip further in and additional blood spurted from the wound.

He noted that the third monster boar was still pawing the ground, in misery at its missing eye. Whether wisdom or distraction kept it from the skirmish, it didn't matter to Arthur. More importantly, he had something insane to try.

He let himself drop, landing on shifting flesh beneath his feet, letting his legs bunch up beneath him as he crouched and jammed the kris into flesh below. Then, having found momentary purchase, he thrust himself away, hopping over to the next monster and using his kris as a piton that stabbed deep into flesh as he rode the bucking, oinking creatures.

For a few glorious seconds he managed to bounce back and forth, stabbing and throwing himself upon them, the monsters crashing into one another again and again in attempts to strike him. They twisted their massive bodies but were unable to reach him as he stuck to their backs.

Until a mistimed jump, a blood-slicked body, and bucking made him miss his grab. Even the kris sunk into flesh was not enough this time to give him the purchase to throw himself away and he found himself sliding down, between both the pigs.

Eyes widened in fear as he forecast a rather messy and painful future. Rather than keep hold of his kris that was slowing his fall, he let go, leaving it impaled in the fleshy body. Falling, his head bounced off the ground and he tried to flatten himself as best he could.

Above him, two heavy bodies crashed together, feet scrabbling on muddy earth to find purchase and stomp on him. One foot came down hard on his calf, tearing skin and punching through half his flesh before he jerked away reflexively. It left a gaping wound there, nearly as bad as the wound caused by the foot that came down next on his forearm, cracking one half of the bones.

His hand found a swinging tail, and gripping it tight as it twisted and the bodies pulled away, Arthur was pulled along. At the same time, one fleshy wall of monstrous pork gave way and collapsed, the kris having punctured a lung and leaked cursed energy that drained strength.

The other boar twisted and spun round and round, trying to shake Arthur off, like a cat chasing its own tail, but much less cute and far more murderous.

His blood- and mud-slicked hand lost grip as centrifugal forces threw Arthur aside. He was airborne briefly before he crashed into a tree and then bounced off it to land on the ground and slide down a hill.

"That went a lot better in my head." Arthur spat dirt from his mouth, pushing himself to his feet. Motion caught in his peripheral vision had him duck low. A dart passed over his head, parting his hair as it passed.

Energy poured into his hand as Arthur threw himself into a roll towards a nearby tree. Another dart crossed the ground he just was on—this time he saw that it was a real dart, not an energy-made one like his. He managed to make himself scarce behind the thin trunk moments before a third dart arrived. Then he burst out in the direction he had come from, anticipating correctly that the fourth dart would come streaking towards the opposite direction.

Hand raised and finger pointed, Arthur released the Refined Energy Dart he had formed, the cultivation technique striking his stalker even as they scrambled to grab another throwing dart from their chest. Unusual weapon, Arthur noted; these darts were translucent in the center where a liquid sloshed within.

Poison or a toxin of some form. It didn't matter as Arthur had no desire to find out yet. However, it did mean that he shifted his attacker from "annoyance" to "lethal danger," and he now aimed his Energy Dart at the stalker's face rather than limb or torso.

Bursting through the air, the dark blue formation of energy struck his opponent before they could react properly. Arthur was not, of course, intending to stop with a single attack. However, pounding hoofs came. Two steps into Arthur's charge-turned-desperate-leap, an angry babi thundered down the slope, nearly clipping his heel as it passed by beneath.

Hand flailing, Arthur only just managed to snag a branch. He let his weight pull it down, then yanked himself upwards, using the branch as a springboard and feeling it crack under his movement as he thrust himself higher. Moments later, the entire tree shook as the pig slammed into it, attempting to knock the climbing monkey of a human off its perch. Soon, the other pig arrived.

Caught below, the stalker—a man—was struggling to recover after being struck in the face by the energy dart that had burned through his skin. To Arthur's surprise, the man's camouflage ability worked fast, fading the cultivator into the shadows and blending into the greenery.

The problem was: the pigs were not particularly gentle. They smashed across the ground all around the tree that Arthur perched upon, inadvertently knocking over the retreating stalker. And once the man was down, extracting his own dagger was no use; it was all but over as the creatures stomped, crushed, and gored him.

Rather than watch the poor man's demise, Arthur scurried off to the first beast's corpse, extracting his cursed kris from its body.

Then he returned to the battle, and saw that—for all the futility of fighting—before dying his stalker had managed to stab one of the pigs to death, the same one that Arthur had buried his spear into.

Leaving only one creature, the one missing an eye and whose rage did it little good against its faster, more dexterous, and only partly banged up opponent.

A few minutes later, Arthur was done prying cores from bodies. He retrieved the spear and rolled a babi corpse off the trampled body of the other cultivator, curiosity driving him to peruse the remains.

After all, you never knew what goods you might find.

Chapter 8

"There's never anything more disgusting.
than sorting through the corpse
of one who was recently hustling
all in search of a torque."

Silently, Arthur worked his way through his stalker's corpse, pulling apart fragments of skin and clothing. The smell of blood and innards was overpowering, overwhelming the clean odour of mud and trashed vegetation all around him. It sucked.

And still, he persisted.

A good five minutes later, Arthur scurried away with his looted goods further uphill. He kept a close eye for trouble, but their battle had, luckily, failed to attract attention from the other denizens of the forest. Good thing too, since his body still ached from being thrown around. If he had been an ordinary mortal, he would have likely picked up a number of nasty fractures.

As it was, he was only badly bruised and might have torn a few muscles. Nothing a few rounds of cultivation wouldn't fix.

Near the spring that had created the mud pit, Arthur bent to wash himself quickly. He stripped his shirt and wiped down his body with the bloody cloth, rinsing out mud and dirt with quick swipes. The act got rid of the most of the mud and made him hiss as water and rough cloth went over open wounds, but it did not stop him. Rather, he focused on washing the wounds down even more, trying to remove as much of the sand and other foreign objects from the open wounds as he could.

Thankfully, the passive healing that the Tower offered seemed to take into account the down and dirty circumstances of cultivator life. It did a decent job at getting rid of the majority of these foreign objects, pushing them out of the body as the cultivator healed and cultivated. Of course, that added its own taxation of energy, so getting rid of dirt the old-fashioned way before cultivating was preferred.

Also, wounds just itched and hurt more if you left dirt in them.

Once Arthur was clean, he bent his focus to the few items he had found that were not a complete mess. One of which was a pair of boots. A little too large for his own feet and a little damaged. However, the stitching on the bottom had caught Arthur's attention, and the slight glow and flow of energy in the quiescent boots told him something was up.

Too bad the Tower didn't provide detailed information on this pair. He'd have to get the boots identified first. Still, after washing and tossing out a separated human toe, Arthur figured this was a definite win.

Now, figuring out how to store the boots was going to be interesting. He didn't want to put them in his backpack, but hanging them off the end like any good hiker would just attract attention. Maybe he could wrap them in some leaves? While there weren't any banana trees around, some of the broader palms would work just as well, he figured.

Next up, the pouch. There was a hole in it, which was why the entire thing was wrapped up in a big, leaky sappy leaf that made the entire thing sticky. The slight itching sensation that he felt while handling the leaf made him take note. Probably something to avoid touching in the future if he had any choice.

Pouring the contents of the pouch out, Arthur grinned, his greedy little inner pig rising up. While he would never hunt other cultivators like his stalker, he could see the appeal. Five new cores, all of them decently sized and one significantly larger than the others, had him smiling. There was also a small grey token, which made him frown. Still, added to his three cores, he'd increased his store of earnings quickly.

That did raise a little concern, about exactly how strong his stalker would have been if the babi ngepet had not interrupted their fight and trampled the man to death.

On that note, Arthur might have gotten a touch overconfident after kicking the ass of both the black cat on this floor and herds of babi ngepet on the first floor. And on hindsight, jumping on the moving bodies of the babi to stab them had not been his smartest idea, even if it was the fastest way of slowing them down with kris poison.

"Maybe I should change tactics?" Arthur mused out loud as he touched the hilt of his kris. The ability to poison someone and drain them of energy meant that, in a battle of attrition, he would win. Perhaps he should look for camouflage skills like his stalker had, allowing him to strike quickly and fade into shadows.

"Rogue build for the win? Or put it in the bin?"

That brought him to the other piece of loot. One poison dart left, fallen on the wayside when Arthur had initially attacked his opponent with a Refined Energy Dart. The rest of the stalker's vials and darts had been smashed apart on the body itself, so he considered it lucky that he even managed to find a single one intact.

Arthur picked up the dart, eyeing the simple green and black fletching from some unknown bird, then the glass vial and the dark yellow liquid within. He sniffed at the dart tip, noted the small wax plug that had been placed on the needle tip to ensure the liquid did not leak out and, eventually, shook his head.

No clues about what, exactly, was within. Again, something else to have inspected.

He let out a long sigh, then sifted through the rest of the items. Dagger, plain and simple and not at all enchanted. Bent a little on the blade from being stabbed into the thick hide of devil pigs. Still decent and workable. Much like the sheath that it came with and the set of skinning knives he found rolled up. Unfortunately, half of those thin sharp blades had been bent.

Retrieving the small grey token from his pouch, he bounced it up and down in his hand. He had a guess that it was this floor's credit marker. Just a guess. For all he knew, it might be a tracker or a clan seal, allowing others to find him if he took it. For that matter, it might be both.

He bounced the token further, debating quietly whether to keep it or let it go. The question, as always, was whether the risk was worth it. Potential untold riches or extra trouble? Or, as was his luck, a little of both?

Chapter 9

It did not take long for Arthur to return to the tree where he'd stored his backpack. Climbing the tree, on the other hand, was an exercise of agony and patience, as strained muscles reported in varying volumes and quantity as he scrambled up. Still, he eventually found himself at the top, strapped to the tree trunk by rope once again. He dabbed and cleaned up some of the bandages that had started leaking blood, making his nose wrinkle before he settled in to cycle his healing technique.

Ten minutes later, his eyes flew open and he grabbed at the rope and kris with separate hands. Instinct had him shifting to the side, just a moment before a kuching hitam launched itself at him, claws tearing at a shoulder that he'd hunched. Battered armour barely held together while the attack tore deep into his deltoids. Still, having drawn his kris, the cat could not help but impale itself on the weapon after its leap.

Furious scrabbling with back feet had the cat throw itself backwards, tearing up Arthur's pants and legs even as the cultivator tumbled out of the tree, the quick slip knot releasing as he pulled it hard and fell. Down five feet, before his turning body hit the bigger branch he'd aimed for, breath slamming out of him. Still, Arthur managed to sling one foot over the tree branch and roll himself up so that he didn't fall off entirely.

Head turning sideways, he spotted the damn cat leaping at him, claws extended. Releasing his grip on one side, Arthur swung free and twisted himself such that he was now underneath the branch, the cat missing its attack as it landed on the branch, claws snatching and only tearing at clothing. Rather than jump away, the cat repositioned itself to tear into Arthur's limbs that were still gripping the tree branch.

Rather than wait for that attack, Arthur pulled himself up again so that his body was pressed right against the tree limb. He could not see from this angle, but he only needed a moment to swing his kris up, sinking the wavy-bladed sword into the side of the creature. It missed the main body but it still scored a deep cut in the flank.

A burning pain along Arthur's arms had his hand open reflexively, swinging him sideways as he let go. Holding on only by one slung leg, he pivoted and found his grip sliding. Rather than wait for the inevitable, Arthur released himself and twisted, grabbing at another branch with his free hand as he dropped. A couple of smaller branches broke against his body, slowing his motion as he managed to pivot far enough to get his feet on another branch and turn, swinging his kris blindly.

The kuching hitam had chosen to stay on the first branch rather than chase him. It glared at Arthur who stared right back as he settled his weight. The animal snarled a little, pacing and watching the kris that tracked its motion. The cat moved with a little limp as it did so, and Arthur could have sworn that there was a slightly dazed look to its eyes.

The kris's poison was once again taking effect, slowing down his enemy. On the other hand, not at all to Arthur's surprise, the cat chose the better part of valour: it turned to jump away, almost mockingly. Rather than release a Refined Energy Dart that he was uncertain would hit, especially with foliage in the way, Arthur chose to climb back up to his backpack.

Healing himself had mostly finished by the time that damn cat had arrived, but now he sported new bleeding wounds. More importantly, it seemed his current perch was not the best place to hang out in. He doubted he'd be lucky enough for the poison to kill the cat, which meant that at least one monster would know where he was.

Better to find a new place to hide.

Forty-five minutes, one snake, and a snuffling small babi later, Arthur was burrowed deep into the side of a hill under what he could only describe as a hollow. He'd woven a simple cover in the front of leaves and tree branches to hide the entrance and then placed a series of spikes driven behind the artificial cover as a surprise for unwelcome visitors. Then he began the process of cleaning himself again.

Surprising how few movies and TV shows showed this. Oh, you sometimes got the bandaging and cleaning parts in movies, but only to make a point about how damaged the hero or villain was. Mostly in shows that were trying for something a little more realistic.

In reality, all this running, jumping, and fighting meant that you ended up sweaty, injured, and bleeding more often than not. Add in dirt, mud, and sap from the various plants around and staying clean was at best a losing proposition. The best one could do was clean regularly, wipe down, and wrap any open wounds—and then heal.

None of which was new to Arthur, but the increased volume of monsters was now rather off-putting. He could almost swear that they were more aggressive too, and part of the reason it had taken Arthur so long to find a place to rest was because he thought he was being stalked again.

At some point, he had to take a break and night was falling. This hole in the corner was the best he could do. At least, with the sun set and the moon high above, a new kind of monster was in play, which meant his previous problems were gone.

Grateful that he was for the moment safe from being attacked, Arthur returned to the process of healing. Cycling energy from his dantian into the rest of his body, watching the refined energy that was in the center of his being flow through meridians before pushing into the appropriate paths, caused him to shiver a little and grit his teeth as the crazed itching ran through him, but he mostly managed to keep his complaints to his mind.

Twenty minutes later—plus a full core's worth of energy and an hour's worth of time basically wasted—
and Arthur got back to his initial plan. Which was, in this case, getting both his basic energy and refined energy cores up to speed.

He did debate holding off for a little longer, just enough for him to cycle the full extent of everything he had through his body and increase his attributes once more. It might even have been a good option, if he didn't have to meet up with his team soon.

Resolved to stop playing around on the outskirts, Arthur pushed those considerations aside and focused on channelling the beast cores through his body. The faster he managed to refill his energy pools, the faster he could enter the town and meet up with his friends. Then, maybe he could actually get on with clearing this floor.

Chapter 10

By the time Arthur managed to make it to the outskirts of town, it was nearly the evening of the next day. He was moving a little slow, having only caught a few hours of sleep the night before, concentrated as he was on both filling his dantian with energy from the monster cores and being watchful about any attackers. As it was, when he finally left, he had to deal with a replay of the kuching hitam that had stalked him all the way to his burrow and waited for him to leave.

This time around, though, he managed to catch the cat on his spear as it leapt at him, stabbing the monster clear through the body and then shedding its weight aside. He dropped a knee on the body while prying the spear out, which allowed him to finish the monster off before it could escape again.

Even so, he managed to pick up another long scratch from a flailing backfoot on his chest, which had to be bandaged. And then, it had taken him nearly half a day to make his way into town, having to dodge three different cultivators on the way in. Some, he thought, were just like him: newcomers to the floor. Arthur figured that at least one was—the one carrying a large backpack like he did.

The other two cultivators looked to be predators, armed with minimal gear and carefully scanning the surroundings. One had even set themselves up in a hunting blind, watching for trouble from high above with his recurve bow, while the other was prowling the forest like Arthur's first stalker.

Spotting all three had been a simple enough thing, though getting past the hidden hunter had only been a matter of chance. Someone in the east had set off a flare and firecracker combo, alerting everyone to their position. A call for help perhaps, or a signal that they had arrived. In either case, while the hunter had moved to the other side of the hunting blind to watch, Arthur had scrambled across the forest floor and hidden again.

Now, here he was, near the outskirts of town, lurking in the underbrush and trying to spot additional trouble. Theoretically, the area right around town was mostly safe. The ground was cleared of foliage regularly by the dominant power in charge, and the safety of those arriving guaranteed. Last he heard, the second floor was being run by TG Inc., a former rubber manufacturing conglomerate that had some rather dodgy ties to groups like the Double Sixes and the Ghee Hin triads. Or at least, their subsidiary gangs. Still, TG Inc.'s façade was said to be all charm and welcoming smiles, even if they ran a rather large company store.

In fact, peering into town, Arthur was quite certain he could tell which was theirs. The three-storey building was made entirely of cross-cut wood timbers and loomed over everything else, even the two-storey Tower-built stone buildings in the center of the clearing.

Still, for all the reassurances that entering town was supposed to have, Arthur continued to hesitate. He did so long enough to watch another individual, weighed down with a backpack, break out from the forest.

The fellow made it a dozen feet towards town, before a pair of men emerged from either side. They weren't running; in fact, Arthur would call it sauntering the way they made their way over. The poor Tower climber, caught between the two, glanced at them and the town entrance before picking up speed a little. But even if the pair weren't running, their higher Body attributes meant that they covered the ground faster. Thirty or so feet away from the buildings, one of the men laid a hand on the newcomer.

Arthur watched as the newcomer threw a punch that was easily deflected. The second thug came along, but to his surprise, rather than lay a beatdown on the newcomer, what ensued was a rather lengthy and aggressive discussion. He couldn't hear what was said, but there certainly was a lot of arm-waving, stamping of feet, and other aggressive movements.

More importantly, he also noted two bystanders: a pair of cultivators dressed in button-down shirts and slacks had appeared, carrying truncheons and taking up post near the entrance to town. They watched the shakedown—it had to be a shakedown—with some quiet amusement and made no move to interfere.

"So the question is: are they bribed or are they just lousy hires?" Arthur muttered to himself. "Or is this how things go here?"

Corruption was always a good guess when it came to how people did things in Malaysia, but he was not entirely certain that was the case here. It could be that they were just letting the conversation continue because the other cultivator had taken a swing to begin with. Or maybe, they actually did know one another and the new Tower climber was trying to shirk some duty. That backpack was definitely larger than normal.

Before Arthur could draw any more conclusions, another couple of figures broke from the foliage. The first was another stranger, though a memorable one. She looked to be in her late teens but was tiny, barely five feet tall, and must have poured a significant amount of energy into her Body attribute since she carried a backpack that was quadruple her size with little problem.

Walking by her side, chatting amiably with the young woman, was a familiar if surprising figure. Which, when he thought about it, was just about right. Because that's what Arthur's luck was like, running into the one "friendly" face he's rather not meet first.

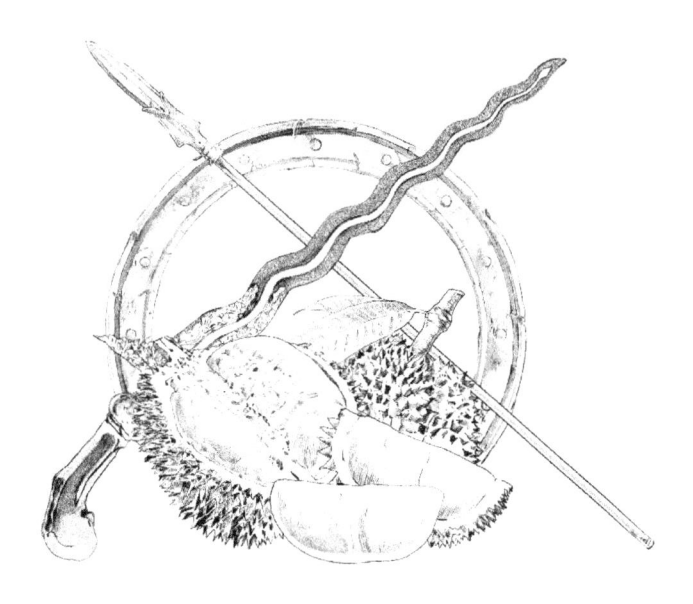

Chapter 11

Arthur could have sworn that woman knew only how to bite, chew, or otherwise curse him out. Even in the gloom he could tell it was her, alright. There was just a set to her shoulders that marked her off from all the other Malaysian Chinese women in his life with a bob cut.

"If it had to be anyone, it had to be Jan, eh?" Arthur sighed, pushing himself to his feet.

Well, no reason to delay, not anymore. And not when four figures emerged from different parts of the surrounding forest and moved towards Jan and the teenage girl. Now that he was moving too, one of those watchers changed direction to come after him, a big wide smile on his face.

Now, wasn't there a warning about people who smiled too much being the least trustworthy of all? Arthur was sure he remembered a saying like that. And if there wasn't, there really should be. Perhaps add "and is too handsome for his own good" to that list of other untrustworthy things.

No, there was no jealousy there at all. Even if the one coming to him was a lot taller than Arthur, had a good head of hair that looked like it had actually seen proper shampoo and conditioning and a non-student hairstylist, and nicely bronzed skin which likely meant he didn't actually burn in the damn sun. No reason to be jealous at all.

"*Apa khabar?*" the man greeted Arthur, raising a hand as he neared.

"*Khabar baik,*" Arthur returned the ritual Malay greeting reflexively. How's things? Good. You'd think that humanity would come up with more interesting conversation starters, especially just before robbing someone, but nope. Here they were, with the prosaic.

Then again, they were trying to rob him in broad daylight. Perhaps asking for originality might have been a tad too much.

"So, boss, need someone to help walk you inside? You know how things are, right?" A big grin, wide and without guile.

Arthur tipped his spear, which he had been using as a walking stick. With its sharp point aimed at the man, he replied breezily, "I think I can walk well enough."

"*Ei*, it can get real dangerous, you know," the man said, shaking his head. "You don't know the kind of trouble you can get here. No guide, *susah*; It's gonna be tough for you. Me, I'm honest, not like those guys."

Arthur's eyes narrowed, eyeing the tall Malay. Now that they were closer, he noted a few things. One, the other man was staying a good distance away, far enough that it would take Arthur a good lunge to hit him with his spear. The other was that he might have good hair and clean clothes, but the clothes themselves were looking a little frayed at the edges. There was even a stain on the lower right of the man's shirt that spoke of blood washed out in cold water, leaving its rather unique trace behind.

So, not as well off as he tried to present himself at first sight.

"Look, I don't have time to play with you. So why don't you explain what is going on, before my short-tempered friend there causes real trouble," Arthur jerked his head towards Jan ahead of him.

He could see avarice and calculation fly across the man's face as he took in the other three men. Two of the three had already reached Jan, but the third hesitated, debating between coming over to where Arthur was or going to the women.

Weird. They weren't all working together?

"Okay, okay. No need to hurry," the man said placatingly. "This just a small bribe, *lah*. You don't want, then no need. But then again, maybe someone tries to steal your stuff. Maybe they find you outside." He shrugged.

"Oh, you mean *you're* going to do that?" Arthur said, eyeing the man up and down. It was never easy to tell exactly how strong someone else was just from looks, but he wouldn't put the other man at much tougher than himself.

"Me? What are you thinking, *lah*. I'm just a guide."

Arthur sighed. "What's your name, guide? And who do you work for?"

He started walking towards Jan again, waving the man to follow him. He could see that she'd spotted him too and was gesturing vigorously, even while keeping a hand on her parang rather than the spear she had slung over her back. Of course, he knew she preferred the machete; but personally, he thought the added reach of a spear was hard to beat.

"Raahim." The man grinned. "And I'm from the Double Sixes."

"Oh." Recognition flickered through Arthur's psyche at the name. The Double Sixes, or the 66, were a large underworld gang that had taken a significant interest in the Tower. Really, most of the triads and gangs had. Any place the law could not reach properly the underworld had extended their reach to. And Arthur knew it was not just in their own Malaysian Tower but in Towers all over the world.

Between the lack of legal employment in the real world, the boredom caused by not having anything useful to do, restrictions put in place by mega-corporations that made even basic entrepreneurial craft work more difficult, and the sheer plethora of designer drugs, the underworld had flourished before the arrival of the Towers.

The Towers were just a shot in the arm they needed to become major players. For the most part gangs still kept their heads down, but most legal corporations and even a few governments used them for their dirty work.

"Does TG Corp know?"

"They do. They got their own people from the Suey Ting," Raahim said, jerking his chin towards the group around Jan and her friend. "But if you work with me, they won't bother you."

Arthur was getting a quick idea of what was happening. A double-dipping, if you would. After all, not everyone was going to shop at the TG Inc.'s big store. And even if they were, why not increase demand by stealing goods from newcomers? Made sure it was harder for rivals to form another store. Explained why they had so many people around the short teenager. Carrying so much on her back it almost screamed competitor.

"Your protection, does it cover them too?" Arthur wondered why Mohammad Osman hadn't mentioned anything like this to him on the first floor. He'd had a proper alliance with Osman's Double Sixes. Or at least, he thought they had.

"Them who?" Raahim said.

"My friends." They were within ten feet now and the closest member of the trio was turning to Arthur and Raahim. Arthur idly noted that the very first newcomer—the one who had been shaken down—finally managed to get into town with little more fanfare, though the guards watching at the border had increased to four now.

"Those two? Okay, can."

"Then, it's just a matter of price."

Now Raahim's gaze flicked between the three Suey Ting thugs. The one approaching them, a singlet-wearing, hairy South Indian man was stalking forward with fists curling and uncurling as he glared at Raahim.

"Three cores," Raahim said.

"Done," Arthur replied immediately.

"*Kawan*, you're too late," Raahim said, grinning and stepping in front of the other man. "This one—and the ladies—are with me."

"That one too?" A jerk of the head at the girl with the backpack. "No way."

"That one too," Raahim said, stepping forward confidently so that he was now only inches away from the girl. "Unless you want another fight. Heard you did bad on the first floor. Want to make it two floors?"

"You don't dare."

Raahim just grinned, and the other man looked between Raahim, the big backpack, his friends, and then the guards. His gaze lingered on one of the guards, and Arthur caught a slight shake of the head from that man. The Indian man took a step back. But puffing his chest out, he growled, "Whatever. You 66 push too hard, we push back. Then you'll see."

"Yeah, yeah," Raahim waved the man away. Arthur's group stayed silent as they watched the trio of thugs blend back into the forested surroundings. They heard, in the distance, voices engaged in argument—probably other newcomers, or even second-floor residents, being accosted in similar shakedowns. As the sun finally set and darkness arrived, more and more second-floor residents were streaming into town. All of them gave their small group a wide berth, though.

"So, boss, just to check. You not opening a store, are you?" Raahim said, suddenly looking a little nervous as he eyed the girl's backpack. She looked hesitant, unsure of what to do. Jan placed an assuring hand on her arm.

"Me? Hell no," Arthur said. Then inclined his head to the backpack girl. "Though I don't know about her."

"*Celaka*," Raahim swore.

Chapter 12

Three pairs of eyes locked on the girl carrying the large backpack as they stood in the middle of the cleared ground between forest and makeshift town. Light faded from the sky. Arthur was, as usual, doing his best not to think about how the "sun" worked in the Tower, since it would make no scientific sense. Then again, very little in the Tower made scientific sense. There were entire departments in universities that were churning out new papers on Tower science, three quarters of which were invalidated the next month by new studies. That things worked in the Tower was enough for Arthur, for now. Let someone else figure out the underpinnings of "reality" under Tower rule.

"What's your name?" Arthur interrupted, the moment she tried to speak.

"Uh... Su Mei." The petite Chinese girl ducked her head. Arthur noted her eyes were strikingly slanted, even for your typical Chinese Malaysian. A Mainland Chinese perhaps. Or Japanese or Korean. Mixed race babies were more common these days, especially after the major immigration waves in the second quarter of the twenty-first century.

"Well, Su Mei, you starting a store? Or just feeding an army?" Arthur asked.

"What army? Why would I feed them? We don't need to eat?" Su Mei replied, looking confused.

Jan snorted, letting go of Su Mei's arm to run a hand through her hair in frustration. When she spoke, her voice dripped with barely contained venom. "*Oi*, idiot. Don't confuse her, *lah*."

"Fine. Just answer the question. What's the bag for?"

"It's mine," Su Mei said, hunching down a little. "I'm a courier. I got to deliver this."

"*Celaka*," Raahim swore yet again. "Deliver where?"

"And why you?" Arthur said, cocking his head to the side. "For that matter, how'd you get through the trials carrying all that?"

"What trials?" Su Mei said, looking confused. "I was just given a Level Up token."

Stunned silence from the group greeted her words. All three of them looked at one another, before Jan shifted slightly away from Su Mei as she asked, "Who you working for?"

"The Tower. It's my quest." She looked between the wary trio and could not help but ask, "What's wrong?"

"You know those tokens are incredibly rare?" Arthur said, slowly.

"No?" Su Mei replied, puzzled.

"Fools and idiots," Jan swore.

"The last one that was taken out of a Tower and resold raked in tens of millions. US dollars," Arthur said. He watched as her eyes widened, a hand flying to her mouth as she let out a startled little cry. He kind of felt bad for her. She'd had no idea that she'd blithely spent a fortune by using that Level Up token. "They can be used in any Tower." He paused a beat and then stressed again, "Any Tower."

"Oh shit. Oh shit. Ma always said I'd forget my own name... shit, shit, shit."

"They didn't give you another, did they?" Raahim asked, all too casually. Jan shot him a look, her hand clutching her parang hilt, but she ended up relaxing when Su Mei answered.

"No. Just one. They said I should use it once I was ready. And I was! So I did. And then I had to hike here and that was hard and I... shit."

"I wonder what they're having you deliver that's so precious," Arthur said, eyeing her bag. He was not a greedy man by most margins, content to make his way through life with hard work. Desiring what others had was a good way to get beaten down or end up spending what little money you had on "luxuries" that the corpos pushed on you. Better to just be content with what you had, so you didn't end up in debt. All that said, he was still a rather curious person and he wouldn't be human if he was not a little curious about what she had within that bulging pack.

"Don't know," Su Mei said.

Raahim was looking both contemplative but also wary, for Jan was wielding her patented "I will stab you and enjoy it" look on him. Having been subject to that look more often than he liked, Arthur knew how intimidating it was.

On top of that, while the majority of second-floor residents were ignoring them as they headed back into town, with most giving no more than a glance to the rather good-looking Raahim, a few cultivators were throwing more than cursory glances.

Rather than have a repeat of his own first-floor entrance, Arthur chose to still his curiosity for now. "Let's go. Inside. We help Su Mei deliver her goods, maybe we get an answer to all our questions, eh?" When Raahim looked to object, he added, "Her employer, whoever they are, has been so generous already; who knows, maybe they'll be generous again, eh?"

"Uh... why?" Su Mei began to say, but Jan had put her hand on the girl's backpack and given it a little shove and the girl started walking, momentum doing all the work. Now that he was closer to her, Arthur could not help but confirm that she really was as strong as she seemed, the bulky backpack doing little to slow her down even as her feet sank noticeably into the turf with each step.

"You know, my Master used to say: There are three kinds of successful people in this world," Arthur said, taking the left flank while waving Raahim to go ahead of them. The Malay man looked a little unhappy at first, but greed—and his own word—won out as he took position, waving others away as he strode in front of the group.

"You gonna finish or not?" Jan snapped at Arthur after he had fallen silent for too long.

"Oh, right. Sorry. Three types." Arthur idly spun his spear around his hand as he walked, letting his voice run. "The rich, who are born into success. The hardworking, who push until they succeed. And the best of all..." He paused for dramatic effect to tease her.

"I can still stab you, you know," Jan growled impatiently.

"I've really missed your loving conversation and threats of bodily harm. Really." Arthur grinned, then ducked his head as she pulled her parang out. Of course, that also meant that she had it on hand, in case any of the people who had started to drift closer to them decided to try anything. He could be imagining things; perhaps people were just moving closer because it was more crowded in here than outside the town border.

Arthur continued, "But the last one is what I think you are, Su Mei."

"What's that?"

"The heaven-blessed lucky."

Chapter 13

For all the precautions he might have to take and did take, Arthur was grateful that they managed to get into town with minimal violence. Raahim waved at the guards as he came through, hurried forward, and then surreptitiously dropped a monster core into one hand as he bribed the guards to look the other way and give them a little space. He did it so smoothly that, if Arthur had not been watching so closely, he might even have missed it.

On the other hand, the walk past wooden buildings on the outer circle of town was rather tense. Without a cheap source of electricity, the only lighting available came in one of three forms. Generators and batteries that came from mortal Earth—that is, outside the Tower—which had to be carefully watched over in case someone stole them. These were hooked up to electric lights. Next there were burn barrels full of wood that gave off warmth and light and allowed people to cook game from the forest. And for the high-class establishments, also known as anything owned by TG Inc., there were spirit lamps powered by monster cores.

What that all meant was that the group moved through pools of darkness splashed with sudden explosions of light, as windows were thrown open or they arrived at a crossroads, where burn barrels were often set in place. The main thoroughfares were well lit, with external lights from TG-owned buildings comfort and protection; guards were present here too. Of course, that also meant it was more crowded on these streets. All in all, smart marketing.

But for Arthur's purposes, slightly less crowded and darker streets were optimal. With Raahim guiding them, they were, hopefully, headed in the right direction.

"Who built these streets? It's curvier than a…" Arthur trailed off, eyes still sweeping for trouble. But the denizens of the second floor were mostly keeping away from the armed group, offering only glimpses of avarice.

"Than what?" Jan said, challengingly.

Arthur knew better than to finish that sentence. There was a reason he'd stopped; he couldn't think of a suitable ending that wasn't going to get him poked. But under the glare she had turned on him, he scrambled for a word. "Durian."

"Durian." Skepticism deep in her voice.

"But durians aren't curvy. They're spiky!" Su Mei said.

"I know, why do you think I stopped?" Arthur said, glaring at Su Mei. "It's not as though I've got a writer penning things for me to say. Sometimes I just get it wrong!"

"Still…" Su Mei shook her head. "Wheels? The old highway? Mountains. Maybe even noodles? All a lot curvier than durians."

"Oh, great. Any suggestions?" Arthur said to Jan, who snorted.

Bickering good-naturedly, the quartet kept walking. The talk helped take their minds off the oppressive darkness, the encroaching fear as they passed unfriendly-looking residents and disappeared deeper and deeper into town. If not for the fact that Arthur could glimpse the three-storey, lit-up beacon of the TG Inc. shop and use it as their guidepost for travel, he'd have been more worried.

As it was, rather than taking a single, easy-to-travel direct route, they'd snaked back and forth a few times. But eventually the buildings they passed began to change. Although a minority were quite shabby, the majority now looked less makeshift and more like permanent structures of stone and wood. A testimony to the slapdash earlier construction of the first Tower climbers, Arthur assumed, and then the slow gentrification of the Tower floor as more and more people arrived.

"About time," Jan groused.

"It's not easy, you know," Raahim said, stopping. He turned back, putting a hand on his hip. "Got to watch for the stupid ones and the aggressive ones. Got to take the right routes to avoid roads the Suey Ting control."

"Fine, fine," Jan waved the man's protests away.

Raahim opened his mouth to protest more, but Su Mei kept trudging on and almost bowled him over. He skipped aside, glaring at her. "Anyway, that's—"

"My destination. I know. I have a marker," Su Mei said.

All three stared at the girl again, who seemed to not notice their looks. Her head bent low as she carried the heavy bag. For the first time, Arthur noted the way her feet dragged a little, the hesitation in her steps. Perhaps she might have been strong, but carrying all that could not have been easy.

"Right, let's get this done." Arthur kept scanning around, only slowing when Raahim drifted over to his side. "What?"

"*Duit.*" Raahim held out his hand for payment.

"At the door," Arthur said, hedging their bets. Raahim looked unhappy but said nothing, waiting until they were close enough to the Tower administrative center that was Su Mei's destination before he stuck his hand out. He relaxed a little when he saw Arthur digging around his belt at the pouch he had strapped on but also tucked in his pants. No comment at all, since pickpockets were certainly a thing.

Three monster cores, two from the first floor and one from the second, came out. Arthur could tell the difference just from their size and the pulse of energy within them, which was good as he handed over the cores and Raahim glared at him.

"*79p aini?*" Raahim stared at the three cores on his palm unhappily but pulled his hand away to make it harder for Arthur to grab them back.

"Three cores. Your payment," Arthur said.

"No, no, no. *Tak boleh!* Second-floor cores." He closed his fist around the cores and waved it. "This isn't enough!"

"To guide us through? You're joking. I even paid extra for Su Mei," Arthur said.

Speaking of the girl, she had left the two arguing men behind, stepping right through the double doors of the Tower office without a word and past the faceless Tower guards that stood in front. The only place, Arthur assumed, that these guards would do anything. Jan looked between the two, but at Arthur's gesture, hurried after Su Mei.

After all, he didn't lead her all the way in just to miss finding out what she carried in her backpack.

"You cheater!" Raahim growled, stepping close.

"I don't like being shaken down. You provided a service, I'll grant you that. But I don't get shaken down." Arthur paused, then added as an afterthought, "If you have a problem, tell your boss. In fact, tell your boss that Arthur Chua of the Benevolent Durians is here."

"Durian? More like durian-brained," Raahim spat, but Arthur just grinned, stepping swiftly around the man. He went past the Tower guards swiftly, ignored the yelp from behind which quickly enough turned to grumbling. No point in hiding his presence anymore, he figured.

If he was right, he was about to make a big splash anyway.

Chapter 14

The inside of the second-floor Tower office that dealt with quests was very similar to the first-floor one. Wide open hallway, counters all along one wall with one waist-high swinging doorway. The majority of staff were human, though a few humanoid alien-like creatures stood taking orders.

Other than a few benches for people to take a seat upon while waiting and tables lining the opposite wall, the room was fairly empty. There were only four Tower climbers, all being attended to, and Su Mei was one of them.

Her backpack sat on the floor beside her while Jan stood a short distance away, watching as packet after packet was drawn from the backpack's mouth. Each packet was wrapped in green cloth and tied off with brown twine. Only a few hints of their contents could be picked up. Smell was one of them, the aroma of dried herbs unmistakeable now that the bag was open. The way some of those packets shifted, their density and distribution spoke of cloth or heavier but malleable objects within. Others were irregularly shaped as bumps from tight packaging showed up. Sadly, it was hard for Arthur to guess their weight, since Su Mei handled them all with the same ease as before.

Arthur took all this in within seconds as he stepped within the administrative room. He crossed over to Jan and Su Mei, the young girl giving him a quick grin before turning back to her work. There was a giant cork board on the wall by them with pinned notices of quests.

"Any trouble?" Arthur asked Jan.

"Nope. She walked in, gave her token, unpacked." While one attendant remained with them, other attendants were taking the packets and bringing them behind the counter and into some other room, leaving their group none the wiser.

"So, pretty boring, eh?"

"*Ya lah*," Jan sighed.

Su Mei looked at the pair, ducked her head a little and whispered. "You don't have to watch over me anymore, sis. I should be fine."

"Oh, you think you so big already, *ah*?" Jan put her hands on her hips, glaring at the younger girl. "What's your plan now?"

"I... find a place to rest? Cultivate?" Su Mei said sheepishly. "I'll have a few credits with the store after this."

"We do not speak about our quest rewards with those who are not part of the process." The attendant's voice was cool, cutting Su Mei off before she could speak further. She blushed and ducked her head. The attendant glared at the rest of them. She looked mostly human, all but for the slight shine of scales along her temples and the top of her hands. Emerald green scales, pale and almost not there. You'd have to pay close attention to notice.

"We aren't enemies. In fact... we might be able to offer the girl a more attractive option than wasting her credits on a hotel," Arthur said, holding his hands up placatingly.

"It is not a waste," the attendant said immediately.

"But it is expensive," Arthur looked around, spotted a free attendant and walked over. He cut ahead of another cultivator, who had just entered the room. He flashed the man a grin and got a glare in return, but since another Tower climber had finished up just then, the man chose not to make a thing of it.

"Yes, sir?" the attendant asked, leaning forward as Arthur approached.

Jan had drifted over to Arthur, having guessed what was happening.

"I'm here to register my arrival on this floor," Arthur said.

The human attendant, whose most recognizable quality was a rather big and punchable nose, could not help but let out a long sigh. "We do not do that on the second floor, sir."

"Normally you don't." Arthur nodded as he spoke, then held out his own token. "But if you check that, I think you'll find I'm not your normal case."

Stifling another sigh, the attendant took the token rather than argue with Arthur, not even bothering to look at it. He was speaking even before he had even swiped it down his tablet, "As you see sir, this is not..." The attendant trailed off as light bloomed on the tablet. His hand stilled as he still clutched the seal, eyes reading over the information now before him. "Oh. Oh my."

"Yes, that's about right. Thanks," Arthur said, leaning back against the counter now as he felt the Tower pushing notifications to him. He was not going to shunt these aside.

The moment he let the Tower's energies flow through, he saw a wireframe diagram appear: a map of the second-floor town. Unlike the first-floor village, the number of buildings on offer here was a lot smaller. In fact, there were literally only two options, both on opposite corners of the map.

Not much to choose from. Poking at both buildings had their display increase in size, but he could not help but sigh because they were both almost exactly the same—long, rectangular buildings. Single-storey only, but thankfully long enough that he assumed there would be space for multiple rooms.

Figuring he might as well choose the one closer to where they were, he tapped on the southward-facing one and watched as it highlighted itself. Another quick tap confirmed his choice, and then he watched as more notifications spiralled out.

Second Floor Clan Building Selected
Building Type: Residential
Residential Bonus: Security – One Tower Guard assigned

Arthur grinned, leaning back, but a moment later more notifications streamed in. Because of course they would.

Update: The Benevolent Durians Clan Status
Organizational Ranking: 182,769
Number of Towers Occupied: 1
Number of Clan Buildings: 2
Number of Clan Members: 104
Overall Credit Rating: F-
Aspect: Guardianship
Sigil: The Flame Phoenix

"Yes!" Arthur hissed.

"What?" Jan asked.

"We went up by two on the organizational rankings," Arthur said.

"That good, ah?" she could not help but ask, though she sounded half-distracted. Arthur assumed she was looking up her own clan details too.

"Can't be bad, right?" Arthur considered and eyed the data once more, before he added, "Seems like Amah Si is recruiting."

"Shouldn't she?" Jan asked.

"Well, yes." He hesitated, then remembered that Jan was once part of the Thorned Lotuses, the now-defunct group of women who had banded together to safeguard themselves. Rather than continue to discuss his own hesitation at being, basically, surrounded by people he did not personally recruit, Arthur went on. "We should check out the clan building."

"Clan?" Su Mei looked Arthur up and down and then Jan. She was carrying the large bag which had been folded down a lot, straps tugged tight to make it a lot more manageable.

"The Benevolent Durians," Arthur said.

"Ooooh! That one. The funny-named one."

Jan glared at Arthur, who just grinned at Su Mei. "That's us!" Then, growing serious, he added, "Want to join?"

"What? Me?" Su Mei frowned. "Why me?"

"Why not?" Arthur said. "I could use the luck."

"You just want to use me like a lucky charm?" The girl frowned at Arthur.

"Also, because you're trustworthy." He gestured at the pack she had and then the area around them. "You never thought to look into the packets, or skip out on the quest. You just did your job, because that's what you promised."

"Maybe I was too stupid to think about that. Maybe that's why you want me," Su Mei said.

Arthur just stared back at the girl. She flushed a little under his regard, but she refused to take her words back and chewed on her bottom lip as she met his gaze. He found himself snorting and looking away first. Jan was watching the entire interaction with her arms crossed.

"You found her. You convince her," Arthur said, exasperated. A quick glance around and he sighed, realizing there was more than just one problem to deal with.

Of course there was.

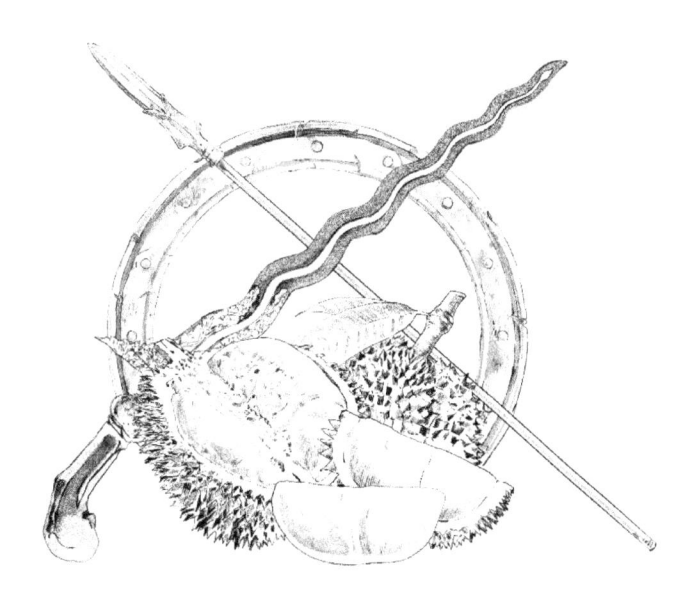

Chapter 15

The man walking over to Arthur's group with a small smile had just finished his own business with an attendant. Arthur gave him a flat look. He wasn't trying for unwelcoming; he was just tired and wanting to crash at his new residence. As it stood, getting through the town would be a pain and a half, even if he could make use of the main thoroughfares now.

The scruffy-looking newcomer did not hesitate. A mix of Caucasian and Indian or Malay, Arthur presumed. The man's khaki pants and many-pocketed safari shirt was torn down one side and stained with traces of old blood. A bandage showed beneath the opening. He carried, surprisingly, a pair of guns slung under both armpits in shoulder holsters and a large knife that might as well be a short sword along one hip.

The pistols—semi-automatic types, as far as Arthur could tell—were a surprise to see in the Tower. They worked quite well, but the problem of having sufficient ammunition was a major problem even in countries like the United States with their gun-crazed culture. Since bullet supplies were only available via individuals entering the Tower, it was mostly only Guilds that could keep a supply chain, allowing their people to use these modern weapons all the way up a Tower.

In Advanced Towers, certain cultivation techniques were powerful and fast enough to supplant guns. But those techniques were also locked behind guild memberships, never mind the energy costs of using such techniques.

And, of course, there were also significant legal constraints about owning a licensed firearm in Malaysia. Realistically, only the army, the police, security guards, and criminals owned them, and of those, the last three barely even knew how to fire their weapons. He'd heard of more than one security guard company handing a shotgun to their employees with empty shells, just so that they'd look intimidating while they sat outside jewelry stores.

Which is why the presence of those two guns were a real surprise. Assuming they were real.

"They're real," the man said, his voice surprisingly deep. Arthur jerked, surprised to hear his own thoughts echoed. "Everyone always wonders."

It took a moment for Arthur to realise that the man's accent was not a Malaysian one but American. Deep South American, that is, the kind of places that if you believed Hollywood had rednecks and cowboys and horses galore. Also, racism, Christianity and hatred of anyone not falling into their narrow definition of 'normal'.

"Unusual, here."

"Not where I grew up. You can call me Rick." A hand was shoved forward, the smile widening a little. The name, the guns in shoulder holsters, the khaki and the floppy hairstyle. It all came together, into an image of an old school movie about a mummy and a sexy librarian.

Arthur shook the man's hand, letting his spear prop against his shoulder as he did so. If the man wanted to cosplay, that was his problem. It didn't suggest the most sensible of mentalities, but then again, they were pitting their lives against an alien artifact in vague hopes of power. Sanity was in short supply in the Tower, really.

"Arthur." Releasing the man's hand, Arthur cocked an eyebrow. "What are you doing here, then?"

"My parents came back a few years ago for work. I chose to tag along," Rick said, smiling. "I heard the Tower here is easier, and since it's geared towards people who don't have guns…" He shrugged.

"Cheating your way up?"

"You're not trying if you're not cheating, eh?"

"Some people might take offense at such views."

"And do you?" Rick searched Arthur's face as he asked, eyes narrowed a little. That same easy smile still on his lips.

"Who am I? Your father?" Arthur snorted. "Climb the Tower however you need. Just, you know, don't shoot me by accident."

"Good. Then I'm part of your Clan?" Rick said.

"That wasn't an invitation," Arthur replied, letting his gaze roam over the man. "I don't know you. And while I can boot you out later, I'm not sure why I'd add you just because you said so."

Rick grinned, put his thumbs into his belt, and puffed his chest out a little. "I can think of two good reasons." Arthur's gaze dropped to the guns, and the man continued, "One, I've got guns. And that's a big advantage in this Tower, I'll tell you."

"Noisy. Brings even more trouble *lah*," Jan muttered, who had overheard their conversation and dragged Su Mei over with her. The girl had shouldered her backpack on and was looking curiously between the two men.

"Killing fields. Great for core collection!" Rick replied. "And secondly, I can pay you. Over and above whatever taxes you might have."

"Really." Arthur perked up. "Now that does sound interesting."

"I thought so."

A quick understanding of the man before him was growing. Rich kid, probably someone connected enough to have the license to carry not just one but two guns. Having someone like that in their clan could be really useful. Assuming he could be trusted and wasn't an ass who threw his weight around just because he was richer than the rest of them.

"Alright. Let's talk." Arthur scanned the surroundings, but none of the other Tower climbers were looking to talk to him. The others merely went about their own business. "Elsewhere though."

"Of course." Rick took a step back, leaving Arthur to look at Jan and Su Mei.

"Done. You can now do it anytime," Jan whispered to Su Mei, keeping her voice lower so as not to attract any attention.

A single raised eyebrow and a nod from Su Mei confirmed her agreement, making him wonder what had been said between the two. Still, he could ask or he could just get it done, and he knew which way he leaned towards. Micro-managing was never his style.

Now that he thought about it, he wasn't sure he had a style. Su Mei brightened up as details of clan acknowledgement flickered through her interface, and Arthur mused about his past and managing people.

Planning to be a Tower climber, working as an odd-jobs person, running errands—mostly deliveries—and the occasional cage fight were not the kind of resume one built to become a manager or clan leader. He had never really worked with others before, never had to train or deal with them. Sure, he'd been "managed" but mostly by AI apps that tracked his various metrics from delivery times to customer satisfaction levels. In fact, even those few people who found themselves with better jobs were mostly managed in that way, their actual managers too busy doing their own work, trying to hit their own quotas so as not to get fired by an impersonal HR AI.

Funny to think that perhaps the people who might have the best skills at dealing with people on a daily basis were those in the underworld. Most of them refused to use AI tech, refused to download or make use of a variety of apps that made everyday life easier. Too easy to track, too easy to tap into. So they did things the old-fashioned way.

All of which meant that when he pushed a clan invitation via the internal Tower system to Su Mei, he had a little bit of a concern about how the hell he was going to manage the organization he was technically in charge of.

Chapter 16

When the girl accepted his clan invitation, Arthur felt a little shiver pass through him, a connection forming. Weird how he felt this one more closely than he had the Tower connections on the first floor. While Su Mei read over the clan notification, lips moving wordlessly, Arthur abandoned her to Jan and made his way over to the quest board. Let her figure out what she had gotten herself into and the advantages of his clan. They were numerous after all.

In the meantime, as much as he wanted to take a break, the idea of trekking all the way back here in the morning just to grab some quests was less than happy-making. Which was why he was perusing the quest board now.

Best to get it over with.

Quests. Lots of them. In fact, there were more posted here than on the first floor. The entire cork board was covered with little slips, pinned on top of one another. Few kill quests, of course, since it only made sense to have those with particularly dangerous monsters. Not so many of those named monsters on this floor.

More interestingly for Arthur were a half-dozen quests nearby that were a mixture of mapping quests and eradication quests. The former were not Tower-made quests but posted by human individuals and organizations, asking for maps of specific locations and directions. The latter, of which there were four, were Tower-made and focused on four villages of monsters called *orang minyak*.

In any case, eyes moving along, Arthur noted the next batch of quests. He rolled his eyes at them, remembering his own experience with these quests and couldn't help but ask, out-loud. "Does anyone actually like gathering quests?"

"I do!" Su Mei piped up from a short distance away. She was back to smiling and looking happy, regarding at Arthur with newfound, dare he say it, respect. "You get to earn credits, you know!"

"More for you then," Arthur said. He flicked his gaze over the list. He didn't bother taking any gathering quests himself, since he didn't really know the difference between the items requested. Also, he would likely be working with his team so it didn't make sense to take a gathering quest—they were geared towards an individual working alone.

On that note...

"You want to take some of these then?" Arthur asked his newest recruit.

"Sure!" she said brightly. She pushed past Arthur without another word, pulled a pen and notepad out and jotted down quest notes.

In the meantime, Arthur was checking out the "miscellaneous quests" section. The quests here were mostly posted by fellow cultivators. There were quite a few escort or party-up requests. Basically the weak looking to group together or be carried along till they could grow in strength. A bunch were just asking for direct purchases of credits or cores. Then, of course, you had the ones asking for cultivation manuals and techniques, training in techniques, or sparring partners, and even alchemical pills.

All in all, a big smorgasbord of requests, none of which Arthur needed right now. He did mark down a few that he felt were interesting, nothing that was single-recipient though, and made his way over to speak with the attendants. Jan did the same. At that point, they confirmed what the mandatory quest was for the second floor.

Mandatory Quest

Clearance of the currently designated village locations of threats to the settlement.
Current designation: Orang Minyak Villages
Max Party: 8

"Can I register for it now, and form the party later?" Arthur asked.

"All members of your party must register together," the attendant replied politely.

"Figures. Thank you!" Arthur said quietly. "Help me out here, Jan?"

"What?"

"What's an orang minyak again?"

"Ooooh, that one? You don't know. How can?"

"Hey, you try remembering everything there is to know about a Tower."

Jan let out a tired huff but still answered. "Orang minyak. Literally, oil person. Monsters covered in black... grease, I guess. Like one of the movies, the one with the monkeys."

"Apes," Rick cut in. "They look like the apes from the third remake of *Planet of the Apes*. Or maybe, the original. Not the second, those were too, uh..."

"Apey," Arthur said, nodding. "I remember now. Someone uploaded a picture of them. Was a meme for a bit."

"Exactly!" Rick snapped his fingers. "Who got the monkey."

"Which, again, makes no sense," Arthur said. Then again, memes never made sense. There was a period when everyone was into a gorilla from the past. It still cropped up once in a while in those "can you name the meme" quizzes.

"Four villages. 'Twenty or so orang minyak'? Waaah, so many." Jan muttered, finger running down one of the quest notices. She moved to the next quest and read it over. "Same-same." Another one, and then the final one before she winced. "Forty?!"

"Forty orang minyak?" Arthur's eyes widened, elbowing her aside to read it. "Oh, wow. That's like nearly two hundred credits, though. And we get to keep whatever we find and their cores."

"Forty's a lot, especially for four of us," Rick said. "Explains why it takes everyone so long to clear."

"There aren't just four of us," Arthur muttered. He noted how Rick had added himself to the total but chose to ignore that point. He'd deal with the man later.

Once he had registered for all the other quests he wanted, Arthur moved to grab a seat as they had to wait for Su Mei, who had the longest list by far. Of course, those gathering quests were particularly long and detailed, requiring the attendant to provide details of how to gather each of the herbs or other items.

Eventually though, while Arthur was half-asleep and Rick stood to the side, spinning gun in hand again and again, the newest Benevolent Durian was done. Arthur jerked upright when Jan placed a hand on his shoulder, lips pursed in annoyance.

"I'm awake, I'm awake." Arthur popped up on his feet, grabbed his backpack and slung it over his shoulders. "Shall we find a proper place to rest?"

"Clan building?" Jan said.

"Clan building."

The grin she offered was a little too vicious for him to consider as happy. He looked around once more, still not spotting any of the other teammates who should have arrived already. It was a little concerning, especially since the young lady who was supposedly his sponsor hadn't shown up. But there was nothing he could do.

Yet.

Chapter 17

Stepping outside of the Tower office building, Arthur almost expected to find Raahim waiting for him. Or perhaps a half dozen thugs, ready and willing to beat them into the ground for whatever goods they might have purchased or credit tokens they had gathered. Finding nothing of the sort was both a relief and a disappointment for Arthur—guess his life wasn't as trope-ridden as he thought.

Perhaps he would soon find a young master who needed to be smacked down. After all, wasn't that the most common trope in stories about cultivators? In the West, of course, it was trust-fund kids and corporate toadies, but in the East it was the sons of clan heads and the like.

Instead, his life in the Tower seemed to revolve around thugs and the underworld. Which, really, was a somewhat Malaysian thing. At least at his level. He was sure he'd have to deal with money-grubbing politicians that needed bribing at some point and... well, more underworld figures. Corruption was, after all, rife in the political and business scenes.

Perhaps, in the end, what he was experiencing was the Malaysian equivalent of the young master story. At least his young mistress interaction had worked in his favour so far. If she hadn't gotten herself killed trying to do a speedrun.

Travel through the brighter portions of town was much faster. For one thing, the major thoroughfares were not just better lit but also wider and generally built in straight lines. Guided by the tug in his mind towards where his clan building was, and by a general sense of direction, Arthur trudged through town, eyes flicking back and forth.

The second floor was an interesting mish-mash of people. There were a few food stalls around but nowhere near as many as on the first floor. No real surprise there, since the higher up you went, the more logistical support you needed to keep a stall running. On top of that, the Tower climbers' lack of need for actual food made eating more a luxury and a habit than a necessity, though that last part could be argued against vigorously by most Malaysians, being raised in a foodie culture.

Still, in replacement of these stalls were shops of other kinds. Small speciality shops, especially, opened onto the streets. They were busy at night as climbers prepped for another hard day. While the few large stores sold more mundane but still useful equipment—like camping items—the speciality stores focused on armour and weapons. Occasionally, Arthur noted the presence of books and scrolls, documents that he assumed were about cultivation techniques, and these were often less trafficked.

Mostly, everyone checked out the weapons—almost all melee, though a few bows and crossbows were present. Slingshots and javelins, too, plus what Arthur assumed was an atlatl. In a busy jungle, it was difficult to get a good sightline, never mind the necessary training to use these weapons.

There was, after all, a reason why guns had taken over in the history of weapons.

The big three storey building for the TG Inc. dominated the skyline, occasionally glimpsed through gaps in the surroundings as he moved through the town.

The second-floor residents were just as worthy of notice in Arthur's view, many of them sporting cuts and scars that spoke of a hard ascent. Many were on the more athletic side, ranging from broad and beefy to thin and gangly. Yet most moved with a degree of grace that was missing among many of the first-floor residents. Most of all, it was the look in their eyes—a hardness in the majority—that made the biggest difference.

No real surprise. While the final trial to get through the first floor varied, many of those trials required violence. Defeating a boss monster and facing a physical trial like Arthur had been forced to do, or even hunting down a specific monster type was common. Sometimes the trials were simpler, but since "simple" could never be assumed, only the confident were likely to make a try of the second floor.

Or the desperate.

"There's an edge to the people out here, isn't there?" Arthur muttered to Rick who was strolling along without a care in the world. It seemed the gunslinger was well known, for more than a few offered a friendly nod to Rick. However, Arthur was not oblivious to the glares that also got shot at Rick—and at himself and his group in turn.

"Second floor. I hear it gets worse. As you climb, you begin to realise the extent of your strength and will," Rick said. "I hear that on the seventh floor, there's a full city of people who have given up."

"Yeah, the so-called Tempat Rehat that has become a little more than a rest stop," Arthur said. "The place where dreams come to die."

"They're smart, really." At Arthur's look, Rick shrugged. "The Tower creators, I mean. Creating a place of rest, so that those without the will would stop and give up. If it was just death and destruction, all kinds of trials again and again, then even the weak would push on. Now, though, the temptation to stop is too much…"

"You don't consider yourself one of the weak, I suppose?" Arthur said.

"No." Rick lifted his chin a little, the square jaw and dark skin jutting out, before he flashed Arthur a grin. "Not at all. I'm a real climber. I'm going to climb them all and find out the truth."

Arthur looked Rick over. When he didn't see what he expected, he opened his mouth to enquire, only for Rick to pre-empt him, saying, "You can't join the Climbers Association till you've cleared at least one Tower. And even then, only as an associate member."

"They don't have a branch here in KL, right?" Arthur said, trying to recall.

"No. The Malaysian government didn't want them there," Rick said. "So there's no government funding for them like in other, more civilized, countries."

Jan hissed a little at those last few words, and even Arthur found himself narrowing his eyes. That arrogant attitude of a Westerner was grating, especially when it was lobbed into the middle of a conversation without any preamble.

Then again, if Rick was from the US, it made perfect sense.

"*Ham ka chan*," Jan cursed. "They only want to register all the powerful climbers, *lah*. Keep track of people."

"They're a premier organization. Their information and auction house is the way to advance if you're not in a guild. Or even if you are," Rick said defensively.

"Clans," Jan said. "We don't call them guilds here. If your Association so good, why join us?"

"Every advantage should be taken," Rick said. "And a new clan, in this Tower, starting from floor one? My parents would kill me if I didn't try to invest in you immediately."

"Invest," Arthur said, his voice flat. "Do you think I'm selling shares or something?"

"Not right now. But when you're out..." Rick opened his hand. "You never know the kind of support you'll need. For now, we can just talk about me joining and the payment I'll make for being part of your guild."

"Clan," Jan insisted.

"Sure, sure." Rick waved her insistence away blithely.

"You've mentioned investing and family, twice. Who, exactly, are you?" Arthur said, cocking his head to the side. He noticed that his group had drawn together a little, now that they were turning off the heavily lit main throughfares to get to the clan building.

"My father is no one special, but my mother is Jordan MacKenzie." When no one reacted, he shrugged. "That's why I didn't mention it. Unless you follow venture investing, my family—the MacKenzie Trust, really—would not be something you'd recognize."

Arthur gritted his teeth, reminding himself not to strike this idiot. Even the way he said the last couple of sentences was off-putting. But he knew better than to say anything. After all, the young man had mentioned two rather important things: trust and venture funds. If he wasn't just lying—and the guns made it unlikely—he had some pull. Potentially quite a lot.

The question, of course, was whether Arthur even wanted to be tied to these Americans and their venture funds. He'd watched and heard enough horror stories of people being knocked out of their own companies or forced to work against their own interest in guilds. So he wasn't giving Rick an automatic yes. Even if these venture funds were the most profligate with their spending.

Problems and opportunities, all around.

Chapter 18

"It took you long enough."

The voice surprised Arthur. Reflexively he turned to level his spear at the speaker. His group moved quickly too, including Rick whose hands dropped to his guns. The only one not going for a weapon was Su Mei, who actually started edging towards an alleyway, ready to bolt. Not that he blamed her. Sometimes, running was the smartest choice.

"Ms. Chin." Arthur relaxed when he saw who it was. Eyeing the woman and then glancing over to her bodyguard, he said, "I didn't realise you were waiting for me."

"When the notification came that a new clan building was formed, I assumed you were in town. It didn't take long to find it," Casey said, rapping a wall of the alleyway she had walked out from. She would have been hard to make out, what with the alleyway cast in shadow. Even the looming bulk of her bodyguard was hard to make out, though a quick verification showed that both were missing backpacks and other gear like he and Jan were carrying. Likely they'd been in town for at least a day.

"I was picking up some quests," Arthur said, then jerked his head sideways. "And some new and potential allies."

"Really." Now Casey's voice grew chillier. She stepped closer, dark eyes glittering, the long hair that she'd tied off in a tight pigtail swaying. Once more Arthur was struck by how pretty she was. Also clean. That reminded him that he really did need a bath. "You're taking on allies without my approval?"

"My clan, my choice," Arthur said, bristling a little.

"Still, as *current* allies, I assumed you'd speak with me before making any serious decisions," Casey said, stepping closer. Her gaze rested on Rick, who had taken his hands off his guns and stuck them in his belt. He was wearing a grin that Arthur assumed was meant to be charming. "Especially when dealing with sharks."

"Sharks?" Rick said, shaking his head. "Nothing that dire. Nice to see you too, Casey."

"You know him?" Arthur said curiously as he stepped aside.

"His parents mostly. His parents bought up a few manufacturing plants in Shah Alam, fired all the locals, retooled some of the machines, and then rehired people at half the number and cost," Casey said coolly.

"That was my parents," Rick said, mostly to Casey though he looked to Arthur as he said so, indicating who he was really interested in. "I don't have much to do with that."

"Makes me doubt you have access to any money then," Arthur pointed out.

"I'm more with the Tower side of our investments," Rick replied hurriedly.

Casey snorted. "Did he mention it's a trust? And he only has an allowance? He's not even on the board."

"I didn't want to be," Rick snapped. "I'm a Tower climber. A real one." He huffed, then faced Arthur fully. "If you'll let me explain, I think you'll find I can offer a lot. We can offer a lot. And yes, I can make certain promises." He growled at Casey before she could reply. "Just... let's talk somewhere more private?"

Arthur looked around automatically as his words, scanning the surroundings. Like most non-main thoroughfares, the road they walked on was neither paved nor lit well, with a number of quiet lurkers who were watching—and listening—to them. Not to mention, the makeshift housing all around them likely housed other cultivators, some of whom might have an Enhanced Hearing trait.

"Fair enough," Arthur said. "Later."

Casey's lips pursed but he ignored the young woman, walking up to the main door of his new clan building. He placed a hand on it and waited a second. Not getting any notification from the Tower, he tried the door handle. That swung open easily enough.

He got in about a foot before he had to stop, with a blade resting against his throat.

"Urk." Frozen Arthur stared down the blade and at the hovering, faceless figure that held it. The Tower guard retracted the blade after a moment, and now notifications bloomed.

Clan Head Confirmed

Control of Benevolent Durians Clan Building (Second Floor, Tower 2895) Confirmed

Type: Residence

Building Bonus Chosen: Security (Town Guard assigned)

Total Number of Floors: 1

Total Number of Residents: 0

Total Number of Rooms: 18

Would you like to review the layout?

Arthur pushed the notification down for a moment without answering it, peering at the Tower guard before him. He could not help but ask as the silent faceless guard stood before him. "Why aren't you named?"

No answer from the guard itself. In fact, after a moment, the Tower guard shifted away to stand by the side as Jan wandered in. Rick hovered near the door, not daring to enter while Casey looked on, annoyed as her bodyguard held her back with an overabundance of caution.

"Am I allowed in?" Casey said.

"And I?" Rick muttered.

"One second," Arthur said. He flicked on the details of the layout, scanned through it for the rooms, noting it was rather a simplistic design. Main hallway they were within stretching on all the way down, with the room on the right designated as a dining hall and living room. The ones further down were all residences, storage closets, and shared bathrooms. The last four towards the end were larger, by a small amount, than the ones towards the front. Nothing much to hide or designate, not that the layout or options offered to him gave him much choice.

"Dining hall," Arthur pointed. "Washroom right next to the dining hall. You're now allowed to enter and use those for the moment, Rick, on a temporary basis." He made sure to stress those words as he eyed the Tower guard. "Let's call it a night."

"Much appreciated," Rick said, stepping in and making a motion like the tipping of a hat. He still made sure to keep a distance from the Tower guard that eyed him as he stepped in.

"And you're good to go, Casey. You and your bodyguard," Arthur said after a moment, designating them as long-term guests. "Rooms are down the hall, feel free to take any one you want that isn't already filled." He shrugged. "There's enough right now for everyone, though I'm sure once the rest of the team get moving on finding members of the Thorned Lotuses, we'll be filling up fast."

"Good." Casey stepped in and then turned to the bodyguard. "Get our gear. Check if Ah Kit has arrived. If not, leave a note for him to come meet us. And make sure they know to send what they owe us here as soon as they can."

The bodyguard hesitated, then nodded. He left quickly. Casey closed the door after he was gone, then smiled grimly.

"Alright then, let's see what Rick MacKenzie wants." She strode towards the dining hall door immediately, throwing it open and leaving Arthur to watch, shaking his head.

"Ten seconds in my clan building and she's ordering me around like she owns it." He rolled his eyes, while Jan smirked at him. She mouthed something he found hard to read, though he assumed it was something along the lines of "I told you so."

Really, she had. Still...

"Rank hath its privileges. Put this away for me?" Arthur unclipped his backpack and tossed it underhand towards Jan. The woman growled, refusing to grab it, but Su Mei smoothly stepped in and caught it for her.

"Where?" she asked.

"Last room at the end of the hall. Take the one on the right," Arthur said, recalling the layout. Then he turned away before she could acknowledge him.

After all, Casey was not wrong. It was about time to deal with Rick.

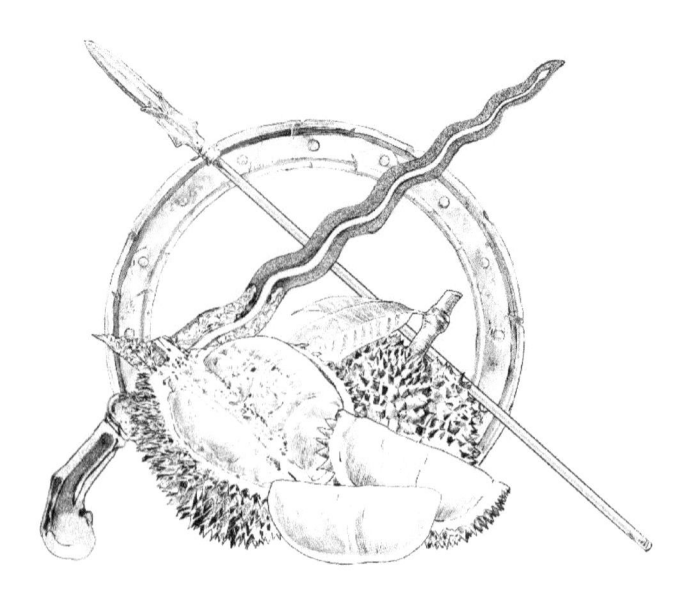

Chapter 19

Dining hall was pretty empty outside of a few tables. Arthur was not surprised. Mostly, he was grateful they even had provided him that much. As they ascended, the number of Tower buildings available for him to take control of would decrease. On the second floor, it was a given that he would have something to choose from. The third floor was a maybe. Then, he might be better off just pouring in resources, acquired from the Chin family, to just get a new one built or acquired.

Higher up, it was pretty much either build or have buildings transferred over to him. None of the other floors would have pre-built Tower buildings for him to take over. Which was why her support was so important. Even the Chin family did not have buildings on the last few floors of this Tower, what with the state of those floors and the requirements of passing through.

For now, though, they had a place to stay where energy was concentrated. And that was a big plus, along with the degree of safety that having something like the Tower guard on hand offered them all.

"Thanks for the water," Rick said, waving the cup. "Poured you one too."

"Thanks." Arthur grabbed the cup, eyed it, and then shrugged and finished it in one gulp. He then grabbed at the pitcher that had been put out, pouring himself more. He idly wondered where it had come from before dismissing the thought.

"Not scared he poisoned it?" Casey said, disapprovingly.

"We're in my clan holding. The Tower guard is right outside. If he did poison it, he's the dumbest assassin in the world," Arthur replied, taking a seat. "And if he wanted me dead, he could have pulled those guns and shot me in the head on the way here."

"Still risky. You should only drink or eat what you know is safe," Casey said. "I do not want my investment to waste itself so quickly."

Arthur waved her words away as being all too paranoid, instead fixing a flat gaze on Rick, who had been watching all this with a small smile. "So. Spill. What do you offer, why should I even consider adding you to the clan?"

"Firstly, let me be clear. I understand that clan setups are different from our guilds Stateside. As such, there is no such thing as replacing you as the leader. No matter what some people might think," Rick smirked at Casey, who sniffed but said nothing. "You will always be the Clan Head till you die. If you do not designate an heir, the entire clan will disappear upon your demise. For this reason, of course, my family considers clans a more risky investment than guilds.

"Nor do we, normally, invest in early-stage startups like this. Especially in North America, where guilds are quite common. Too high risk, unless there's an appreciable USP."

"USP?" Arthur said.

"Unique Selling Proposition," Casey said. "Business speak for cheat."

"Oh! I get that."

"That's not—" Rick started to protest, then shook his head. "Never mind. My point is, we—my family's trust—don't normally invest in clans this early. As such, what I offer is more personal. My support, my funds, my aid."

"Worthless," Casey sniffed. "What do you have? A couple million maybe?"

Arthur goggled at Casey's mention of a mere couple million. Sure, things had inflated a bit since the early part of the century, when a million still meant something; but for most people a million was still something they could only hope to dream about.

Well, outside of Tower climbers who had done a couple of Towers. Which was, of course, why it was such a popular profession. All you had to do was risk your life and limb.

"I haven't checked lately, but last I saw, I had about 1.4 million." Rick replied. "US dollars."

Casey grunted, looking unhappy. Arthur understood that with the current exchange rate the way it stood, that was a significant amount in Malaysia, even for Casey herself. He made sure not to let his jaw drop too much.

"I had a few good investments early on," Rick said with an expansive shrug, as though he dismissed the casual display of wealth. "Of course, not all of it is liquid. She's right, only a few million dollars are easily accessible." That brightened Casey up, but Rick continued, "On the other hand, because I've done well investing in individuals and guilds, it means my family listens. If you start showing you're a winner—having you emerge from the Tower by my side is going to be a damn good indicator—there's a lot more."

"Promises, promises, promises," Casey said bitingly. "And it's just as easy to break one's word when one exits. Not as though he could do much to you, if you chose to break your word. Not after you've made full use of his resources here."

Rick opened his mouth to protest then shut it, shrugging after a moment. "I guess that's a risk he has to take, isn't it, Arthur?"

"Nice that someone remembered I was here," Arthur said. "But no, you guys keep arguing. I'm just here to watch."

"Sarcasm?" Casey snorted. "Really?"

"Sort of?" Arthur replied truthfully. "Seriously, you keep interrupting him and he hasn't even told me what he's here to offer. But the interruptions are useful, so..." He shrugged. "You guys keep arguing and I'll keep my mouth shut till there's a decision to be made."

"As I was saying," Rick raised his voice, cutting Casey off before she could reply to Arthur, "I can offer financial support from myself on a guaranteed basis once you're out of this Tower. I figure, a monthly rental agreement for a room would be about right. Say, five thousand?"

"Hah! Five thousand a month? Why don't you try to cheat someone else," Casey spat.

Arthur had to admit, quietly, that she was right. Even if Rick did not know they were going for a speedrun, a monthly rental agreement was not in his best interest. Among other things, keeping track of exact time within the Tower was a struggle, with each floor having varying daylight hours and no central timekeeping. Electronic watches were fine, but the delicate instrumentation in most meant that they were subtly altered and many ran a little fast or slow, such that it was often hard to tell whose clock was right. In most cases, the difference was only by a few minutes a day, but such things built up over time.

"If not time-based, then floor-based?" Rick offered. "This is, of course, on top of the usual clan tax. How much is it, anyway?"

Arthur was about to answer when Casey waved him quiet. She leaned forward, fixing Rick with a look. "That's clan business."

"And you're clan?" Rick smirked. "I'm pretty sure you're just a hanger-on like me."

"Ally. A real one, paying real resources. Not make-believe money," Casey said. "Arthur, you really should just kick him out. He can promise the world out there, but he can't be trusted to come through with it. His family has shown that."

"I already said, my parents aren't me," Rick said heatedly.

"Wait one second," Arthur raised a hand. "Explain this, will you?"

"This, look." Now the young man looked uncomfortable. "My parents, they—"

"They broke their word and their contracts."

"Let me explain it!" Rick shouted at Casey, pounding the table and glaring at her. Not that he managed to intimidate the woman, whose smile grew even wider. When he saw she wasn't going to interrupt, nor was Arthur, he continued, "When they bought those manufacturing facilities, they were contracted not to make any major changes in personnel for a number of years. My dad said there were material aspects to the business that were hidden from them, and that they had to fire everyone to keep the business profitable." Rick paused, then breathed out slowly. "I don't know if they are telling the truth. I don't have the details, but it's not as simple as she thinks it is, nor are we bad people. And I'm certainly not my parents."

"Right, but that could just be an excuse, couldn't it?" Arthur said simply.

"And you think they aren't likely to stab you in the back?" Rick pointed at Casey. "No organization or family gets that big without getting their hands dirty."

"That's why all the payments are happening now. You know, so he can verify it," Casey sniffed. "Whereas all you've promised are promises."

"I don't have anything else to offer!" Rick snapped.

"Then go away!"

"Enough!" Arthur said. He had to repeat himself again at a louder volume as the pair continued to squabble. "I get it, I get it. He can't be trusted, you say. You insist you can, and can offer money when we're out. But that's about it."

Rubbing his temples, Arthur pushed himself to his feet. "I've heard enough for now." A finger rose and pointed at Rick. "You. Go home. I'll talk to you tomorrow." Another finger tracked over to Casey. "You, go to sleep or something. He's right, you know, I still haven't seen what you promised for this floor. So. Rest now, talk tomorrow. Both of you."

Rather than deal with them further, he turned and walked off. His head hurt, having to listen to them argue. And the worst part was, Arthur knew, this was just going to be the start of it. Once word got out that there was a clan building on this floor, everyone and their dog was going to want in, if nothing more than to make use of the higher concentration of Tower energy within.

Chapter 20

"Morning, sleepy head."

"About time you got here," Arthur grumped as he finished washing his face. One of the nice aspects of the four larger bedrooms at the back of his new clan building was the integrated washing room. The negative part was that there wasn't a lock on his bedroom door—something he intended to get fixed—which was why Mel was leaning against the doorjamb of his washroom, appraising him.

He didn't even bother trying to cover up. Not that there was much to hide; he was fully dressed anyway, even if the clothing was rather rumpled. Sleeping nude was all well and good in theory, but when one was in a hostile environment, that just meant you'd end up fighting floppy.

Add in swinging, sharp weapons and that was just a recipe for disaster.

Not that his *sifu* hadn't had him and his fellow students try that a few times. That happened about once a year or so, when new students arrived and everyone had to be reminded that clothing was not optional. Nor were ballcups for men or padding for women.

"Snuck in late last night with Uswah," Mel replied, hiding a light yawn. "We got the notification you had the clan building up, so figured it was time to make an appearance."

"Nice. So we're just waiting for Yao Jing?" Arthur asked.

"Nah, he's already here. He's... visiting... with Jan." Mel said delicately. Arthur cocked an eye at her, a little amused to see that the young Malay woman might even be blushing. She didn't meet his eyes as she continued, "And Uswah and I weren't exactly hiding. We were speaking with the local branch of the Lotuses."

"Oh, good. We got a lot of people to come in?" Arthur said brightly as he finished strapping on his weapon belt. He checked the pull on the kris, then went to grab his spear.

"About that..."

"Shit. No one starts a good conversation with that line."

Mel shrugged when Arthur looked at her. "There's some hesitation. Amah Si has pull, but each floor..." She shrugged. "Let's just say that things get a little tougher the higher we go. And you know there are fewer of us as we head up."

"Just like every other group. Yeah," Arthur said. The Thorned Lotuses, not being an official clan or organization, had that harder too, of course. They were more of a sorority, a self-help group to keep the predators away than anything that was strongly built up, and the Lotuses were concentrated on the first floor because so many of them found it difficult to progress upwards. They were, in many ways, dregs—people that the corporations, big gangs, and powerful families didn't see worth investing in.

Kind of meant that he was working with the weakest for his recruits, but at least he had recruits. Which, considering he was starting from nothing, was a decent start. And heck, there were a lot of things a clan needed that didn't require strength.

Like simple conveniences such as washing and mending.

Was that sexist? It wasn't as though he were choosing the Thorned Lotuses to do it because they were women; they just happened to be a majority-women group. He'd be perfectly fine with a guy washing his clothes. Hell, he washed his own for a long time, but now he did have better things to do, supposedly.

Eyeing the pile of dirty clothes discarded in the corner, he pushed mundane thoughts aside for now. Recruiting first. Housework later.

"So who am I talking to?" Arthur asked, waving her out of his room and closing the door. He strode down the hallway, ignored the noises coming from a closed door he passed and headed for the dining hall cum meeting room.

"Jaswinder Singh." Mel said smoothly. "She's been the leader of the Lotuses on the second floor for the last five or so years."

"Oooh, a Sikh." Arthur said. He liked the Sikhs. The warrior caste had mostly jumped into the Tower with gusto. Partly it was their upbringing and traditions, but mostly it was their close network of support that had helped them achieve quite a few accolades early on. He was a little surprised that she wasn't already part of any of their own organizations or temple groups, and he was rather certain there was some story there. Only question was if it was worth digging into.

"Yeah, just don't mention her arm."

"Her arm?" Arthur muttered, just as he was turning the corner into the dining room, only to realise why. And why Jaswinder was still on the second floor, even if she might have been a decent fighter. Hard to climb when you only had a single hand.

"It was cut off early on this floor," Jaswinder said icily. "If you had to ask."

Mel sighed, while Arthur offered Jaswinder a half-smile as he took a seat across from the woman, propping his spear against the table casually. Even if she was injured and nearing forty, the woman was still battle fit. There was a hardness to her eyes and a rather long polearm with a spike and spear configuration over her shoulder.

"Apologies," Arthur said. "She was the one who brought it up." He jerked a finger at Mel, who huffed at him, but he continued blithely, a smile on his lips, "If she hadn't handed it to me like that, I would never have dared arm myself with such a subject."

"You—" Her left hand slammed down on the table, and she stood abruptly. Her chair went skittering backwards, and the pair of Thorned Lotuses standing beside her both gripped at their weapons. "You mock me!"

"Yes," Arthur said, looking unfazed. "Now, let's see if you can learn to cool your temper and talk like adults. Or we can move on, and I'll have Mel make the offer to your people anyway, but without you being in charge."

Jaswinder leaned over, glaring at Arthur. "I'll never let a bully like you have my people."

"And I'm never letting someone who can be so easily goaded run my clan on this floor," Arthur said just as smoothly. He stood up, grabbed his spear and departed from the table, leaving Jaswinder staring at his back as he strode for the door. Mel, stunned by the interaction, was looking back and forth between the two, before she finally tore herself away to hurry after him.

Well, that was a good start. Now, what else was on his list for today?

Chapter 21

"What are you doing?" Mel whispered frantically to Arthur as they walked back down the hallway, leaving the second-floor Lotuses still standing in the dining hall, stunned by Arthur's abrupt departure.

"Testing her," Arthur replied, keeping his voice low too. "And Jaswinder failed." He shrugged. "So far. We'll see if she recovers."

"But we need her."

"No, we need her people. We don't need her," Arthur said. "If I have to, we'll leave this building empty till Amah Si sends more up. It's not the end of the world." By that point, they'd made it most of the way back down the corridor and he started knocking on the doors of the larger bedrooms.

"What are you doing?"

"Looking for Casey. I'm still owed a cultivation manual, along with some cores," he replied. "After that, we all need to spend some time cultivating to get up to speed." He gestured back the way they had come. "In the meantime, we can spread word to the rest of the Lotuses and let them all stew on it."

Mel stared at Arthur as he poked his head into each room after not receiving any reply to his knocks, before moving on. Just as he was about to rap on the final door, it swung open, revealing a sweaty and annoyed-looking heiress.

"What?" she said.

Arthur could not help but notice the sword in Casey's hand. A real sword, not the single-edged, guard-less parang many Malaysians used. The parang was the Malaysian equivalent of the machete, a little longer and thinner than its Western counterpart, but similar in function. It was easy to acquire, plus cheap and effective as a weapon, on top of being a worthy tool.

Swords, on the other hand, while less restricted than firearms, still required a degree of skill to wield and were looked at more askance. While local police forces saw the necessity of weapons training, they much preferred that any training was conducted in private, not in public places. As such, anyone seen carrying swords or other melee weapons in public could expect to be harassed.

On top of the necessary skill and a suitable place to train, there was also a certain image that came with sword wielders. The parang was a weapon of the everyman, of thugs and the desperate. Sword wielders were either trained combatants and rich Tower climbers or, more likely, wannabes more intent on image than practicality.

All of which meant that, for people like Arthur, the spear was always going to be more commonplace.

"Just checking if you have my cultivation method?" Arthur said. After his initial automatic sweep of her body, he found his gaze wanting to drift lower. It wasn't that he wanted to be rude, but the fact that she was wearing no more than a sports top that bared her midriff and shoulders and tight yoga pants was making it really hard, even with the cool Yin chi that poured through him.

He could almost hear Jan cackling, making jokes about his manhood, as he stared into Casey's eyes. Which were, in their own way, just as dangerous.

"No. Once we have it, you'll hear from me. Probably later today. I'm sure it'll arrive soon," Casey said firmly. "And before you ask, no, I haven't heard anything more from Rick. He left right after you did." She paused as a droplet of sweat ran down the side of her face, making her swipe at it. "Good job at handling him, by the way. He's a little too arrogant."

You all are. Arthur chose not to mention that thought, his gaze tracking the hand that she'd used to wipe herself. He yanked his gaze right back up, only to catch Casey looking back at him, her own eyes narrowed. "Right," he said. "In that case, I'm going to cultivate."

"Whatever." She slammed the door shut, leaving Arthur shaking his head.

How rude.

Turning away, he found Mel staring at him, arms crossed.

"What?" he asked.

"Don't flirt with that Chin girl," she said. "She's the golden goose that you do not want to fuck."

"I wasn't thinking that!" Arthur protested.

"Mm-hmmm..." Arms crossed, she continued, "Who is this Rick?"

"Oh, that's a good question." Waving her to follow him, he walked towards his own door, explaining as he went. By the time he was done, he was inside his room, having propped his spear against the bed and rolled out a meditation mat on the floor

"So you want me to deal with him when he arrives?" Mel said, guessing at Arthur's objective after he was done speaking.

"Yup!" Arthur gave her a thumbs up. "Delay him a bit, have Uswah work out who he is. Get some information on him, what he's been doing. We'll probably want payment on a per-floor basis, either way. Don't think we need a time limit if he's actually good with those guns, I'm sure he's on a limit himself." He paused, then added, "Oh yeah, and you probably should check out the new recruit."

"Already?"

"Blame Jan." Pointing over Mel's shoulder through the open doorway, he watched as Jan froze at the sound of her name. She turned around to catch Mel glaring at her. Jan offered a weak wave, making Mel roll her eyes. Yao Jing, who had stepped out right after Jan, looked between the two women and slowly slunk backwards into the room.

"And what the hell are you going to do while *I* do everything *you're* supposed to do, Clan Head?" Mel bit the last two words off, making Arthur wince a little.

"Cultivate, of course." He fished out the pouch he kept his cores in and waved it at her. "I got to get stronger, and you've got a little more time to do that yourself." He hesitated, then tilted his head to the side. "I assume you are coming? Up?"

"About time you asked." She sighed. "What exactly were you going to do if I said no?"

"What I've been doing since the start. Making it up as I go along." He shrugged. "But I figured you and Amah Si had a plan, for when you found the clan seal."

"If you could call it that," Mel said. "It's not as though we were sure we could get one. And we certainly weren't thinking we would have the opportunities you've gotten. Or the need to move so fast. But..."

"But?"

"We'll spread the Durians." Her lips twisted at the name, and Arthur couldn't help but chuckle quietly. "So long as you keep your word and help the Lotuses, we'll integrate them in. Make a clan that's for everyone, not just for the rich." There was a fervour in her eyes now, though she spoke softly. "We'll make sure no one takes advantage of others again. We'll build a company that benefits everyone, not just the rich. Not if we can help it."

"But we'll take them for all they're worth before, right?" Arthur said carefully as he eyed Mel.

"Well, yes." Mel blinked, shuttering her emotions again after a moment. "So I'll do your work, but I do need to train too."

"Promise I won't be adding that much more to your plate. We'll eventually have a proper setup."

"Good. Now, go. Cultivate," she said. "You are right, you do need to get stronger."

With that she turned and walked out, pausing at the door before closing it. Arthur frowned. Well, that was enlightening. If a little scary. He'd have to keep in mind that his allies also had objectives of their own, some of which might one day conflict with his.

But that was a consideration for another time. For now, he had cores to cultivate and a cultivation manual to read. Whenever it finally arrived.

Chapter 22

Brushing off the dissipating fragments of a monster core from his pants, Arthur wandered over to his door and opened it. On the other side, a much more presentable young heiress stood, hand raised to knock again. In her other hand, she held a heavy pouch and a rolled-up scroll.

"About time—hey!" she cried, as Arthur interrupted by snatching the scroll and pouch from her.

"Thanks!" Arthur began to close the door, only for Casey to jam her foot in the way.

"I told you your supplies would come. Just as we gave you that other cultivation technique on the first floor. But these cores aren't just for you, they're also for all of your people who came along," Casey said. "First delivery. We'll have more tomorrow."

"Gotcha. Send them to me, will you?" He tried to nudged her foot away with his own, but she refused to move it. Arthur could have pushed harder, but then he'd move from being rude to outright hostile, and that was a line he wasn't willing to cross.

Even if he was in a hurry to get back to cultivating.

"Three days," Casey said, firmly.

"What?"

"You have three days to sort out your clan and cultivate. And then we're going to work on the mandatory quest."

He met her challenging gaze with a nod of his own, before she finally got her foot out of the door. He shut it swiftly, dropping down to his mat and slipping his own pouch of cores back onto his belt before he began the process of checking the contents of Casey's pouch. As much as he'd like to read the scroll, verifying how many cores had been provided was more important.

"I need a scale," Arthur muttered after a few minutes. Of course, a scale wouldn't actually help since the cores weren't all the same size or shape. They varied in every possible dimension including colour. Still, individually counting cores that were each the size of a marble was painful. By the time he was done, he sighed and leaned back.

Sixty cores, broken into groups of twelve each. Enough for five people to cultivate for twelve hours. With these second-floor cores, he'd be able to cultivate for most of the day, setting them on the path to finishing the climb. A fifth of the way to getting a full point, really. And that assumed he didn't spend more cores on himself.

One of the most dangerous times for a cultivator was when they first arrived on a new floor. They would struggle to match the strength of upgraded monsters.

Arthur had experienced a little of that problem himself in recent days.

"Cores?" Yao Jing said, swinging the door open without asking. The brawler and self-appointed bodyguard to Arthur looked around the room, spotted the piles of cores beside Arthur and walked over to squat down beside his boss. He waited for Arthur to nod before he grabbed one pile, stuffing it into a breast pocket. "You want me to wait outside?"

"Might be a good idea," Arthur said as he reached for the scroll. "Got to get reading."

"Okay, boss," Yao Jing said. "I'll cultivate outside your door and keep watch."

"Don't think that's a concern," Arthur said. "We've got the Tower guard."

"Creepy fella." The big man shuddered. "Why can't he have a face like the one downstairs."

Arthur had no answer for the man after some futile searching. Yao Jing offered Arthur a nod before he left, though Arthur was barely paying attention by that point since he had the cultivation scroll open.

Finally, he had a proper Yin technique. It was a pity he couldn't share this scroll with Uswah, but whatever insights he gathered, he'd do his best to pass it on to her. Arthur had to admit he felt a little guilty for making this demand, considering there were only two of them in this clan with Yin Bodies. Even if it was imperative for him as clan head to grow stronger.

"Now, let's see," Arthur muttered as he unrolled the scroll and made a face. "Why, oh why, does every single technique have to be so damn pretentious? Night Emperor's Cultivation Technique. As if it's that great, being a two-star technique. Might as well just call it Yin Technique 2.12 or something."

Another long sigh, but then he focused. After all, the Night Emperor's Cultivation Technique was better than the pretty much unnamed technique that Uswah had offered him long ago. Which she had studied because she'd known beforehand that she would gain a Yin Body, unlike him.

"Oh, look. A treatise on Yin-Yang bodies…" Arthur sighed as he read the initial portion, figuring he knew that much. Then, after a moment, he discarded his own assumptions. Better to start with the assumption that he really did know nothing, rather than end up making a mistake because he was too arrogant to read a page of words.

Well, it looked like it was just a page of words, and if one were to copy the words down, it really would just be a page. However, the difference between a Tower-generated cultivation method and a plain pen-and-paper one was the magical ability of Tower documents to pass on intent and meaning directly.

Which was why anyone who could buy or find a cultivation technique from the Tower would do so over reading a mere handwritten copy. Even if there were limitations of transfer and movement of such techniques, it was still the best way to learn and could shave days and weeks off learning.

"Blah, blah, blah, balanced Yin-Yang bodies are the natural state." Arthur read quickly, skimming over the words to focus on the intentions being poured into him. The first few paragraphs were about the nature of cultivator bodies, how individuals were mostly balanced. Part of the process of early cultivation was the complete balancing of the body, since most individuals had some degree of variance. This generally happened during the period of transition towards the second transformation.

Reaching ten points in all three attributes was the actual triggering point of the second transformation. That was when the body was able to take in additional Tower energy and achieve complete Yin-Yang balance. During this period of transformation, the cultivator would receive a significant increase in strength.

For most Towers, that timing could happen between floors two and four. What made a Tower easier or harder was partly the layout of the Tower's lower floors, whether they allowed an individual the leisure to actually reach that second transformation in peace.

In that sense, the Malaysian Tower was considered quite easy. There was no time limit on the first or second floors. You could, theoretically, achieve second transformation on those floors, which of course put a much higher pressure on the cultivator to keep climbing to deal with the increasing rate of energy drain. But, once you had those upgrades, it was much easier to forge ahead too.

Since a balanced body of Yin-Yang energies was the norm, it was considered deviant to possess a "specialized" Yin Body or Yang Body—or even more esoteric body types which required specialized body alteration techniques.

At this point of the scroll, Arthur was imparted information he had not expected.

"That's going to suck, like getting a tummy tuck," Arthur muttered, pinching the bridge of his nose. "When the transformation comes, it won't be once and done."

No, each transformation that occurred would once again attempt to forcibly push Arthur back into the "normal" state of balanced Yin-Yang energies. If he wanted, he could return to a balanced body in the second transformation; he would just need to purchase a certain cultivation method and some herbs to prep himself for that forcible change. If he resisted or didn't prep himself, he would experience incredible pain fighting against the Tower's efforts to balance his energies.

It could even damage him, such that progress and cultivation in the future were more difficult. Not impossible, or at least that was the impression Arthur got, but more difficult. In the end, without a good cultivation technique, at a certain point the demands of his body to support itself would balance out against his cultivation techniques, pulling him to a stop.

Before that, he would need to prime himself.

"And that's what this technique does..." Arthur said, shutting his eyes briefly. This was important. This was really important and something he'd need to pass on to Uswah. And any in his Clan for that matter, if they chose to take a non-standard body.

"Of course, there's advantages..." A properly set up Yin Body was stronger than another Tower climber's body of equivalent investment. There was a lot of theoretical talk about why, much of which Arthur found himself unable to understand without a non-existent dictionary, but it boiled down to one simple fact. Yin Bodies were refined bodies ahead of the transformation curve. Because of that, they had physical advantages, plus some mental or spiritual advantages, that outweighed their negatives.

All of which was a long way of saying to Arthur that it would be a bad idea for him to give up on the Yin Body now. It was, after all, even possible to revert to a normal body much later on. It just took a lot more resources and prep time.

In the meantime, he was better off studying the document before him, reinforcing his body and prepping himself for the second transformation.

There were other, more detailed notes about the various stages of Yin Body cultivation, all with flowery names but Arthur dismissed them soon after reading. No point in worrying about the many stages, not until he had at least completed the second transformation.

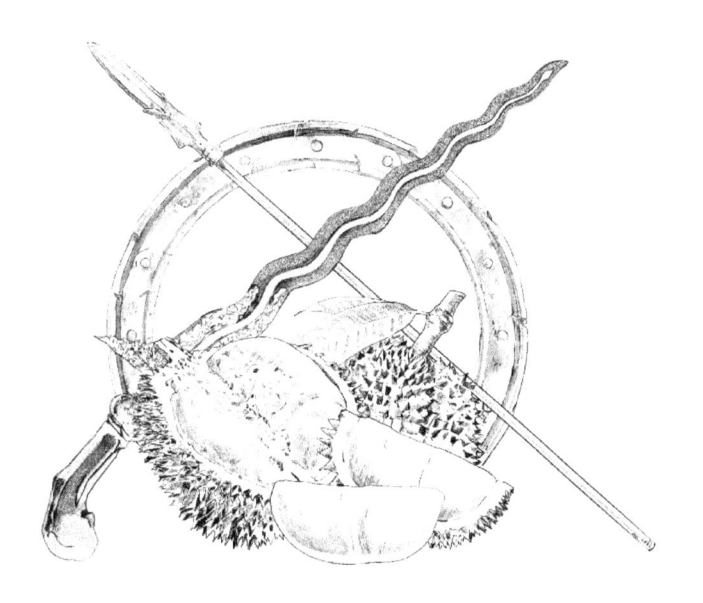

Chapter 23

"Cultivation manuals suck," Arthur said, letting his head flop onto the floor. He watched as frost puffed from his mouth and had to contain the shivers that kept running through him. The entire room was cold, frost riming the wall. The bedroom door was propped open, and there was quite the crowd outside, enjoying the accidental air conditioning created by Arthur and Uswah's attempt at the Night Emperor cultivation technique.

"This does seem more complicated than normal," Uswah said, her voice soft. He could hear the hint of an Australian accent from her time overseas as she came out of her own attempt at cultivating. She was, as usual, clad in *tudung*—the headscarf that was an expression of faith and modesty among Malay women. "Do you want to return to refining cores?"

Arthur absently tapped the pouch by his side where he kept cores. Nearly a day after he had started reading the manual, he had to admit that his progress was definitely sub-par. While he understood cultivation in general, the whorls and loops and mindset required for this particular cultivation technique were rather complicated. The actual processing of energy to make it Yin was the easy part. If anything, Arthur could tell it was more efficient and faster than the technique he usually employed—which was, of course, part of the problem. Being faster and more efficient meant that he had to handle the transformation of Yang into Yin at two to three times the speed that he was used to.

But that was just the processing section. The utilization section was even worse and entirely new. Part of the reason why it was so complicated was that the cultivation exercise was making use of waste Yin energy, the portion that was not going into his dantian for storage, by pouring it through his body. That helped refine his body further into a proper Yin Body, permeating cells with cold, death energy. It was what had created the cooling effect in his room.

"What time is it?" Arthur asked, continuing to stare at the ceiling.

"Eleven p.m.," Jan said, legs propped across the doorway. Along with Yao Jing, Jan was his other self-appointed bodyguard. It still itched him, deep in his soul, the idea that he needed one. But discomfort was not sufficient reason to add risk to his life and the new organisation and all those it supported.

"Christ. Day two." He closed his eyes, then called on his status.

Cultivation Speed: 1.412 Yin
Energy Pool: 14/17 (Yin) (Yang – unusable 0.4)
Refinement Speed: 0.0387
Refined Energy: 0.151 (6) (Yang – unusable 0.102)

Attributes and Traits
Mind: 5 (Multi-Tasking)

Body: 8 (Enhanced Eyesight, Yin Body)
Spirit: 5 (Sticky Energy)

Techniques
Yin Body – Cultivation Technique
Focused Strike
Accelerated Healing – Refined Energy (Grade III)
Heavenly Sage's Mischief
Refined Energy Dart

Partial Techniques
Simultaneous Flow (17.1%)
Night Emperor Cultivation Technique (18%)
Yin-Yang Energy Exchange (28.4%)
Bark Skin (0.02%)

He grunted, eyeing the percentage progress of his Yin-Yang Energy Exchange technique, which had decreased. One of the negatives of studying the Night Emperor was that it seemed to conflict with the Yin-Yang Energy Exchange.

He assumed it was because part of the goal of the Night Emperor technique was to prepare the body for the second transformation and rebalance the flow of chi, and the more Yang energy there was, the greater the difficulty in adjusting the body. Still, watching numbers go down was never as fun as watching them go up, so he focused his attention instead on the much larger amount of basic energy and refined energy he now had.

"I actually need to refine the rest of this energy," Arthur said eventually as he opened his eyes. He considered clambering to sit up, but he could refine just as well on his back as he could sitting up. And it was, frankly, more comfortable. After sitting upright for hours on end, his butt was beginning to hurt.

"Very well. I'll continue to try to puzzle out section four," Uswah said, picking up the scroll he had rewritten the technique onto. Unfortunately, she could not read the original cultivation scroll gifted to him, what with it being keyed by the Tower to his aura. Rewriting the technique was the best he could do. "Are you sure you copied this exactly?"

"For the hundredth time, yes," Arthur said with a huff. "There's just... stuff too, you know? Impressions and visions and that 3D scope of the body that goes in and out of meridians..."

"I do." Placing the paper down, she shifted her only remaining hand onto her lap in preparation for cultivating once more. Like Jaswinder, Uswah had lost part of a limb.

"Finally. Some of us are trying to sleep," Mel's voice drifted over from her room. Of course, she had left her door propped open, what with the nice cooling effect they were offering.

Arthur turned his head sideways, eyeing a trio of newcomers who were either snoring just outside his door or cultivating and ignoring the byplay with studied casualness. These new Durians were second-floor Thorned Lotuses and hadn't been willing to wait for Jaswinder to make up her mind whether she was going to swallow Arthur's insults or not.

Though from everything that Mel had said, the answer was likely yes. Jaswinder was just looking for a way to do so without losing too much face. At some point, he'd send Mel to deal with them. As for Rick... to his surprise, the gunslinger hadn't returned the next day. He'd disappeared, and Mel hadn't been able to figure out where he had gone and Arthur did not have time to deal with it.

His disappearance did make collecting information on Rick easier, in theory. Except for the fact that his main spymaster was here, cultivating beside him.

Personnel problems. What a pain.

Snorting to himself, Arthur rolled his head back in line with his body. He reached within himself, gripping the cold Yin energy within and began compressing it, running it through his meridians as he refined it once more.

After all, if he was going to practice this new technique more, he needed space in his core for all that energy. And there was only a day and a bit left before Casey would demand their presence.

Chapter 24

Arthur sighed as he walked out of his clan building for the first time in three days. Behind him, the rest of the team were gathered, ready to start the process of completing the second-floor mandatory quest. Everyone was accounted for—except Casey's second bodyguard, whom Arthur had yet to see on this floor. That left them with a group of seven, one below the maximum allowed for the quest. But Prime Group and the Chin family had no one else to spare for her to move up with. At least, no one that Casey was willing to work with.

"What do you want?" Arthur asked as he found Rick lounging on the stairs, waiting for someone to exit the building. Arthur wondered if he'd slept there, considering how early in the day it was.

"Ah!" Rick jumped up, grinning widely. "Showing I'm more than talk." He reached into a pocket, pulled out a pouch and tossed it to Arthur, who caught it easily, feeling the cores within moving. "Eighteen cores. Payment for this floor, in advance. And I'm still willing to pay cash."

Arthur opened the pouch, frowning at the cores within. He stayed silent for a time even as the rest of the team streamed out, looking between the two.

"Eighteen?" Mel said, eyebrows rising. "That's... a lot for two days."

"It was," Rick said. Arthur looked up at last, eyeing the man and noting how disheveled he looked and the bags under his eyes. "And cost me a bit to get this many." He gestured to the bullets on his belt in indication of what he meant.

Mel nodded slowly, then could not help but ask, "Are you going to be able to keep up when you run out?"

"If I run out, we've got more problems than my guns," Rick said. "I've brought three times the number of bullets than my most pessimistic estimate." Then he frowned. "And what do you mean 'keep up'?"

"Yes, what do you mean by keep up?" Arthur muttered, looking over to his second-in-command. Meanwhile, Casey drifted closer, her bodyguard following behind.

"We could use him." Mel nodded towards Rick. "Ranged attacks, money and support from outside…" She shrugged. "He's also carried himself well enough."

"Well enough?" Arthur asked.

Rick coughed. "If it's about the brawl…"

"Brawls," Mel interjected.

"They started it," Rick insisted. "I don't like being called a coconut. Or *gweilo*. Or mutt. And if that's a problem, I'll take my cores back."

Arthur snorted. "Nope. I'm keeping them." He grinned. "We share cores equally when we run, minus the clan's take." He jerked his thumb at Mel. "Mel's second in charge after me." Then he pointed to Uswah who had drifted up behind Rick, causing the man to jump in surprise at the woman's silent appearance behind him. "Uswah's next."

Casey frowned. "I do not like this."

"Yeah, well, your Uncle Willis agreed to my rules. So suck it up. You're next after Uswah anyway." Arthur then pointed to himself. "Finally, main rule. We keep me alive. There's no clan, no deal, nothing if the Clan Head dies."

"More like *kepala besar*," Jan said derisively.

"Uh..." Rick looked at Jan, confused. Arthur guessed Malay hadn't been part of Rick's language education.I

"Means 'big head,' *lah*," Jan said, rolling her eyes.

Arthur rolled his eyes too. He didn't correct Jan though, even if he wasn't the one who had created that rule. Amah Si had insisted on Arthur's right to decisions in the initial discussion with Willis Chin when the agreement between the Chins and the Durians had formed.

"I hope you're able to keep up." Arthur descended the rest of the steps and turned down the alleyway, heading for the center of town. "Because we're headed out to hunt right now."

"Watch me," Rick replied. A moment later, he stumbled, distracted by the sudden appearance of a notification before him. Moments later, he shuddered when the Tower bestowed clan member advantages on him. It took him a half dozen steps to catch up and he was grinning even wider by then. "Damn. That's better than a good cup of coffee."

"Quiet!" Jan snapped, slapping Rick on the top of his head. "Don't talk about clan things in public."

"You didn't have to hit me," Rick said, glaring. "In fact, do that again and we're going to have problems."

"Problems? What kind, ah?" Yao Jing suddenly loomed over Rick, arms crossed and biceps flexing. Rick's hands crept to his gun handles.

Alerted by the increasing noise, Arthur turned around and glared at the group. "*Oi*! Same team. Jan, don't hit him. Rick, listen." Then he pointed at Yao Jing. "And you, aren't you supposed to be guarding me?"

"Yes, boss. Sorry," Yao Jing ducked his head and hurried over, ignoring the smirk Rick sent his way.

Arthur could just see those two clashing again, but he really did not have time for this. Looking to Mel and then Uswah, he flicked his hand between the two. It was Uswah who nodded, drifting over to Rick and bumping Jan out of the way as the group started walking again.

It took another block before Casey came over, a small smile on her lips. Somehow, she had a way of saying things without saying anything, enough so that in the end Arthur sighed.

"If he doesn't work out, we'll send him to work with others." Arthur didn't bother lowering his voice. "But Mel's right. Hard to turn down help like those guns."

"Sometimes, it's not just about firepower," Casey said.

"I know. As I said, if it doesn't work out—"

"Mm-hmm."

Arthur contained his next sigh. Best not to let her know she had gotten to him either.

It wasn't as though he were unaware of potential problems. Like Rick choosing to shoot him in the back. Accidentally or on purpose.

Truth was, sooner or later, people who really did want him dead were going to arrive. And he'd rather have Rick on his side, wielding those guns. Much better than turning Rick away, who might feed information about the clan to others. Or even bear a grudge against Arthur. He was rich enough to hire killers.

With those rather morose thoughts, Arthur led the group onward to register the whole party for the mandatory quest. The best way to safeguard himself from machinations was to get moving, get stronger, hopefully faster than those machinations were contrived.

Chapter 25

Registration for the group—a full team of eight now—was a simple enough matter, though they had to wait nearly half an hour in the early morning queue. Then, of course, was the process of exiting town for the nearest hunting grounds. By common agreement, the plan for the first day was to test themselves against a few orang minyak and other second-floor monsters. If they were able to handle them, they'd take on their first orang minyak village soon after.

The first thing they had to do once they actually entered the forest was sort out their line of movement.

"Uswah in front, we're all agreed on that, right?" Arthur said, exasperated by the argument they'd all just had. He glared at everyone until he got a series of nods. "Then Rick second because he's got the guns. We good with that?" In fact, he'd wanted to be second but had been shouted down.

"So long as he promises not to shoot me," Uswah said grumpily.

"Rule two and four," Rick said. "Relax."

"Not helping," Uswah replied.

"Stop. Shut up," Arthur snapped at Uswah and then Rick, respectively. "Otherwise, we're going to be here the rest of the day." The two glared at him, but eventually nodded. Casey, standing by the side, nodded in approval too. "Now, who's next?"

"Me," Mel said, raising the halberd she was holding. "Need someone who can stop the rush."

"Then me," Jan added. "Got my parangs and spear."

"That puts me next, right?" Arthur said, scratching his nose. "And Yao Jing after. That means: Casey, you're behind him."

"No." For the first time, her bodyguard spoke up. "She is behind *you*."

"I don't need to be babied," Casey snapped, glaring at her guard. But after a moment, she inclined her head to the older man, acknowledging his concern. "However, I'm not against being safe either. I'll be behind you, Arthur."

Yao Jing looked unhappy but nodded. That left him in the rear. It was the second most important position, due to the need to watch for creatures that had a tendency to sneak up on them. Or stalkers.

"Finally!" Arthur muttered, turning to tell Uswah it was time to go. Only to realise that she had already disappeared, swaying branches nearby the only indication of her departure. As he searched for her, a little whistle caught his attention, drawing his gaze to where she was standing and waving him on.

Grumpily, Arthur waited for the group to move out, then took his place in line. It didn't take long for Arthur to realise they had another problem and call the team to a halt over a pair of smoking corpses: two kuching.

"If you're going to be shooting those things all the time, we need earplugs," Arthur said, rubbing at his ears. A chorus of agreements rang out.

"Sorry," Rick said. "I have a few spares…"

"More importantly, all that noise is going to make sneaking up on anything impossible," Casey said.

"Ya *lah*! So loud even a *hantu* get scared," Jan muttered. She looked spooked herself.

"Well, I can't do anything about that," Rick said defensively. "They're guns."

"*Jangan guna, lah*," Uswah said, drifting back from where she had gone scouting.

"What did she say?" Rick asked.

"Maybe you shouldn't use them, not yet," Arthur translated. He added, "And maybe you shouldn't be in the front."

"I can take his place. Put him with you," Mel offered. "All the rich kids and precious cargo in the center."

"Hey!" both Rick and Arthur protested at the same time while Casey kept her mouth shut, looking impatient. A minute more of discussion and the group finally started off again, only to come to a stop as Rick's new restrictions on using his guns were put to a test.

The herd of babi that rushed them from behind came at an angle, forcing both Yao Jing and Casey's bodyguard to act first. Yao Jing took to the challenge in his usual manner, throwing himself forward to grab hold of a boar, hitting it at a slight angle so that he could put his hands under its belly. A twist and heave had him tossing it aside, even as Casey's bodyguard took a more sensible method of planting his spear while standing next to a tree and bracing. Unlike their lower-floor cousins though, these boars chose to stream around the bodyguard to attack the rest of the team. Maybe they weren't as stupid, after all.

Alerted by the shouts of the rearguard, Arthur formed a Refined Energy Dart in one hand, leveling the attack to fire at the first pig to skirt around

Yao Jing and the bodyguard as it attempted to shift direction to continue its charge. The bolt of energy tore through the side of the creature, releasing a spurt of blood. Unfortunately the attack was insufficient to stop the pig, forcing Arthur to pour energy into his Heavenly Sage's Mischief technique to increase his strength as he thrust his spear at the monster.

At the same time, Casey's sword left her sheath. The sword draw was followed by a flash as she sent a slash of energy, catching another babi on the opposite flank. This attack bowled the monster over as one of its legs was parted entirely, creating a giant pileup as more of the herd crashed into it.

Rick stood between Casey and Arthur, guns drawn but fingers off the trigger. He kept darting glances back and forth, unable to do anything without attracting further attention. Arthur managed to spear one of the monsters, his feet sliding backwards and only stopping as Rick's greater bulk was added to the spear.

More pigs were arriving on his side of the group. Out of the corner of his eye, Arthur noticed that a pig that had tried to sideswipe him with its head was on its way to crash into Rick. He tumbled, his spear ripping out of a dying target, at which point the battle became pure chaos.

Pigs squealed, Tower climbers shouted, and the meaty thunk of weapons on flesh and tusks piercing bodies filled the air. The smell of feces and musky, unwashed pigs. The tinge of sweat and exertion.

The team fought for their lives.

Chaos.

Utter chaos.

Chapter 26

"That was a mess," Arthur complained, leaning against a tree as he finished winding the bandage around his leg. The tusk that had hit him had torn his pants, piercing halfway through his leg before it was yanked out. Keeping a tight pressure on the wound helped slow the bleeding down, though it was not perfect. If not for the fact that his sped-up healing technique would patch him together soon enough, he would have packed it with gauze. As it stood, he'd just have to suck up the pain for now.

"Bad luck, to draw two dozen down," Uswah said. Of them all, the shadow user was the least injured, having taken to the trees and then wielded her techniques to trip up monsters while everyone else was fighting below.

"What bad luck? More like stupid guns. Too noisy!" Jan screeched. A moment later, she let out another loud shout as Yao Jing popped her shoulder back into place. The brawler offered her a sympathetic smile, letting her hit his arm before she wiped away the tears that had gathered around her eyes.

"I didn't fire them this time!" Rick protested. He too was winding a bandage, though it was a compression bandage around his ankle where he had twisted it after being battered and thrown around by the monsters.

Fascinating that, considering he'd been tossed about and gored, he seemed to be lacking any other major wounds. Arthur could have sworn he'd noticed a glow around the man, subtle but persistent during the fight; but he was not willing to bet on it.

Not yet.

"You did not," Casey said, surprising Arthur at her coming to Rick's defence. "But you weren't very useful otherwise. You have a knife, use that!"

Ah, there it was.

"Oh, and your bodyguard bundling you away so you didn't fight was useful," Rick snapped.

Casey and her bodyguard had almost ended up fighting, getting in each other's way.

"Let me handle my own people." She lifted her chin as she said that, while the bodyguard glared, shoulders hunching a little in anticipation of an argument.

"He's right," Arthur said softly. "You're either going to be fighting with us, or you're not. We can't have you and your bodyguard not contributing. We might make it through the next few levels that way, but it'll bite us sooner or later." He stared at the older man flatly, trying to make him understand. "You got to let her fight. She's got the training."

"It's not that easy," the bodyguard rumbled. "I'm the only one left!"

"No." Arthur shook his head. "There's all of us. We'll help protect her, but you got to work with us, man." Arthur waited until he got a nod, then asked, "What's your name, anyway? We can't be calling you 'the bodyguard' all the time."

The man looked a little uncomfortable but he offered, "Call me Lam."

Arthur acknowledged him before returning to the subject of teamwork. "Going back to the fight... So that was painful. I know some of us have worked together before and others haven't, but we're going to have to learn to fight as a team if we want to survive. The monsters here are stronger, faster, and yes, smarter. What we did before isn't working, so... adapt."

He waited for the reluctant chorus of agreements before he continued, "Alright, in that case, let's talk about what we did wrong. And what we can do to fix it." He then added, waving at the corpses, "And let's get those cores out while we talk. Each of us suggests one thing, and one thing only, to improve. Then we do it again, till we figure it out."

Rick and Casey both looked doubtful, but his team acknowledged his words, spreading out to begin digging into bodies. He knew they understood his reasoning at the least. With as many fights as he expected them all to face, spending time going over every single mistake would just drag on too long.

Better to focus on one problem at a time, make that better, and then move on. Especially since they had a lot of ground still to cover. Flexing his leg a little, Arthur winced. That is, even if they didn't all get injured further.

***

Two thirds of the day on, a couple of hours before sunset, Arthur waved the team to a halt in the clearing Uswah had located for them at his request. The slope of land was against a small cliff, one that could have been leapt off if needed but that would impede entrance by non-goat creatures. And monkeys. Which, frankly, were becoming the most hated group as far as Arthur was concerned.

The golden monkeys that swung through the trees wielded a series of hit-and-run tactics against the team on the regular, pelting the group with rocks, coconuts, and dung in equal measure. Since the majority of the team had no ranged attacks, it left them vulnerable especially since their slings, throwing knives, javelins, and Refined Energy Darts were easily dodged or lost. Or just were not sufficiently intimidating to keep the creatures from returning after they'd lost a few members.

It was in the last hour that Arthur had finally given in and allowed Rick to unleash himself. The bark of his weapons had taken a half dozen of the monkeys before they had managed to escape. Since then, no sight of the group was to be found, the creatures having left for easier prey, Arthur hoped.

Of course, all that noise had brought more monsters to them, including another herd of babi and a kuching that had lurked to attack them in the middle of their fight. Luckily, Uswah had counter-ambushed the cat, stabbing it through the side as it pounced on Mel and leaving it hanging from strings of shadow.

Sadly, the monsters were not the only creatures that had been drawn by the explosive noise. A small team of cultivators had arrived not long after their last fight and a tense standoff had ensued. It was only their own greater numbers and Rick quite pointedly tapping on his holstered guns that had seen the other cultivators back off.

After that, Arthur had the group on a forced march, barely pausing even when they ran into a couple more monsters and looted their bodies. He had pushed them hard, and now the exhausted and annoyed team flopped down in a clearing, resting gratefully while Uswah and Jan took up their flanks to watch for anyone who might have followed them.

"What do you think?" Mel said as she wandered over to sit next to Arthur.

He could not help but sigh as he rolled over to look at her, propping his head on his arm. "Couldn't let me have at least five minutes to catch my breath?"

"It's been ten."

"I mean metaphorically, not literally."

An arched eyebrow was all that she had to offer him in answer.

"I'm conflicted. Those guns attract a lot of attention. But we really do need ranged weaponry." Arthur shook his head. "I don't think any of us are up to learning how to shoot bows, or to carry them, or anything else. Surprised more of you didn't study the exploding slingshot stone technique."

"Specialization," Mel said, opening her hands sideways. "And you're the one who chose us."

Arthur could not help but grunt. He knew Jan and Mel and, yes, Yao Jing weren't really geared for long-range fighting. He just hadn't realised they were that bad at it. His allies who had fallen on the first floor were the ones who had studied the few ranged techniques the Thorned Lotuses had, leaving their present party a little bereft.

Which was, of course, why Rick had been a blessing in a way. Except for how noisy his weapons were...

"I don't know," Arthur said, eventually. "He's a glass-half-filled case, eh?"

Mel nodded a little. "Maybe wait till we see the orang minyak?"

"About what I'm thinking."

"And her?" A slight nod to where Casey lounged, her guard having already strung a tarp to shade her from the sun and potential rain.

"She's staying, of course."

"But what do you think?"

"She's competent, alone. Not very good at integrating with the rest of us, but she can learn." Of course, not very good was a little bit of a lie. Casey was, in fact, horrendous at working with the team. In the end, Arthur had to leave the two to fight alone in a small satellite formation next to the other six of them, so that they'd stopped running into, swinging their weapons at, and clipping people by accident.

The fact that Casey didn't even notice the difference spoke to how oblivious the heiress was to her own actions. For all her training— and she was very well trained, probably the most deadly fighter on an individual basis even—she had no sense of the rest of the team, instead charging forward or retreating as she felt fit. Leaving poor Lam to rush after her, doing his best to patch gaps in her defence.

"Think we can keep her alive?"

"We'll see, won't we?" Arthur said tiredly.

And the gods help them if they failed, because having Prime Group after them would be... interesting.

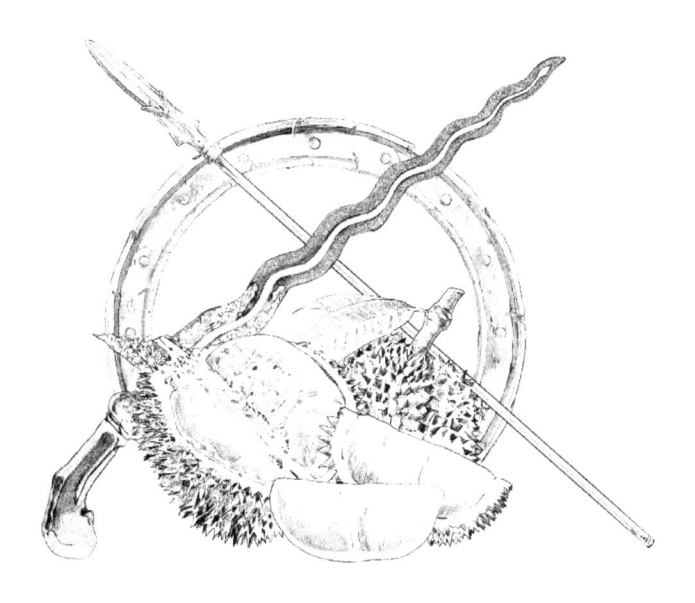

Chapter 27

The first orang minyak that Arthur saw truly lived up to its name. A weird mix of bigfoot or sasquatch and greasy, oiled porn actor, the creature loomed out of the gloom of the forest suddenly, the shimmering aura around it indicating a magical camouflage technique being broken. It swiped at Yao Jing, catching the big brawler in the side and throwing him a half-dozen feet away and leaving blood spiralling through the air. Its clawed fingers glistened with ruby droplets.

Directly behind his friend, Arthur lowered his spear and thrust, the weapon on a direct trajectory to pierce the monster's throat, Focused Strike flowing through his arms to empower the attack. To his surprise, the orang minyak managed to slide away, avoiding the attack and battering his weapon aside a moment later. Only quick feet let Arthur get out of the way of a return kick, the butt of his spear sweeping up to pull the oily foot higher.

Momentarily thrown off-balance, the humanoid creature was unable to dodge the sweeping blast of energy from Casey's sword draw. After having seen her sword technique in action, bisecting golden monkeys and babi ngepet alike, Arthur was surprised to see the orang minyak only mildly injured, a mere bleeding wound that parted greasy but tough black fur.

Then, he was too busy to worry about such minor concerns as the creature started swinging its claws. Joined by Casey, Arthur was forced to pay full attention not just to his attacker but also the heiress who waded into the fight without care for Arthur's spear, forcing him to restrict his own motions and dance out of her way or risk hitting her. Or being hit.

"Oi!" He shouted, more than once. Or words to the same idea, though it mattered little to his companion as sword or arm swung, dark eyes glinting with fierce concentration.

A series of quick exchanges later and another presence joined them, Lam slipping into the space on Casey's right. He paid less attention to striking, instead wielding his metal polearm in defence, blocking and swinging the spear to defend his charge from strikes. It offered Casey the opening she required and she began to make her opponent bleed. Sword cut, skittering across and tearing glossy fur.

Arthur pushed forward, though he kept a distance from Casey. He noticed Jan hurrying past the fighting trio, her focus on something beyond them. He was grateful for her attention, knowing that there might be additional attackers coming. Now, he could truly pay attention to his battle.

Together, the three pressured the monster, forcing the humanoid into a corner. It backed up against a tree, unable to escape further. Rather than give up, it grew more agitated, preferring to take additional wounds in exchange for the chance to strike against its attackers. More than once, a wild swing nearly tore Arthur's spear from his hand, the creature's greater strength causing him to stumble about and widen his stance.

"MINE!" Casey shouted suddenly. She threw herself forward into a full lunge, her sword glowing. A moment later, the blade sunk through ribs into the center of the monster's chest where its heart might have been.

However, the creature did not fall or pause in its motions, instead joining its hands and interlacing its fingers to swing the hammer of its fists down upon Casey. Oblivious, the woman snarled and twisted her blade, widening the wound and sending another pulse of energy. Light flowed from her shoulders down the sword, pulling the light into a single ball of energy that entered the chest.

Having understood the woman by now, Arthur and the bodyguard both acted at the same time as the heiress, thrusting their spears at the descending hammer of fists. Spear tips pierced the creature's arms at crossed angles, the pair bracing against the greater weight and failing.

Hands partially pinned by spears came crashing down on the woman's head and shoulders. Yet, what would have been a life-ender was slowed, the blow dispersed a little by the spears that were in the way and drained strength.

Sword yanked out of body, and the energy that was sent into the orang minyak exploded. Light shone from the wound briefly, illuminating the insides. Arthur was surprised to note the colours, lighter where Casey's weapon had entered and darker where lungs and a heart were—lower in the orang minyak's body than a human's.

Then, finally, the creature slumped over, its will to fight finally destroyed. Arthur managed to shove the hands off Casey, pulling his weapon back and checking for additional dangers even as the bodyguard pulled her free, checking over the woman.

"Owww... that hurt," she complained, rubbing her head and chest.

Arthur frowned, looking down at the woman. He noticed a trace of blood on her fingers, where the edge of one of their spears had grazed her scalp, but more concerning was the way her eyes failed to focus on him.

"You okay?" he asked.

"No. You didn't block it."

"Not my job." Arthur huffed. "You need to guard yourself better, woman."

"That *is* your job." She rolled her head a little to the side, accepting the pill offered to her and swallowing it, letting the healing energy roll into her before she went on to scold her bodyguard. "And yours too, Ah Lam."

"My apologies, mistress," Lam said. "I told you, it's hard to guard you adequately with only one of us. Without Ah Kit—"

"Do better," Casey snapped.

Arthur frowned, then looked at Lam, watching the older man bow his head a little as he was rebuked by someone nearly a decade his junior. Like Arthur, Casey was barely over twenty. Lam fussed over Casey a little more before she dismissed him, allowing her to prop herself up against a tree as he went to extract a core from the body. For a moment, he debated if he was going to say anything.

"Lam Kor," Arthur said respectfully, using the Cantonese title for an older brother, "Please open the corpse up a little, will you? I want to take a closer look at its vital organs."

Lam froze for a second before he nodded. "Good idea."

"Thanks."

Then, now that the man was sufficiently distracted butchering the body, Arthur walked over to squat next to Casey. She was holding a compress to her scalp wound. He waited for her attention to turn to him before he spoke, his voice low but intense.

"I'm not going to tell you how to speak to your employees. I do think it's foolish, but you do you. I am going to say this and I want you hear me." He watched as she rankled, but at least she wasn't speaking. Not yet at least. "You need to stow that attitude and start guarding yourself."

"I'm more effective this way," Casey snapped.

"And you're making the rest of us worse off," Arthur said. "You're the one who wanted to do a speedrun. If you haven't realised it, that means working with us, not against us. That means joining together and figuring out how to work as a team, not acting as though you're the shit."

"You dare to speak to me like this?"

"Yes. Because I can," Arthur said, still keeping his voice low. "And obviously, no one has told you otherwise. You're not horrible, but you're a little too self-centered. Wake up, figure out how to work with us, or we're going to fail your speedrun. Quite possibly someone's going to die—if so, trust me, it isn't going to be me or my people."

"Are you threatening me?" Now her voice rose, causing her bodyguard to look over to her.

"We're just chatting, Lam Kor. Good work on finding the core, by the way," Arthur said, giving the man a thumbs up. He waited till the bodyguard turned away, grateful that Casey did not choose to interrupt them. Grateful that the rest of the team was carefully giving them the privacy to have this conversation. "No threats. Just observations and statement of intent. I'll pull my people out of a fight long before you cause real damage. Then we'll train till we're ready to do it your way, however long it takes."

"That's not what we agreed."

"Plans change. Deal with it."

Having said his piece, Arthur stood up. Casey still looked half-dazed, though the healing pill seemed to have gotten rid of the confusion a bit. It was a little naughty to tackle the subject while she was semi-concussed, but on the other hand, it might just leave her open to suggestions.

And if not, well, he wasn't lying. Not at all.

Chapter 28

The group got moving a half hour later, travelling deeper into the nearby woods towards the first of the orang minyak villages. Once the group had gone over the lone orang minyak's body, verified where some of the larger vital organs were positioned, and dealt with their own wounds, they had begun the trek again.

Three times, they were attacked by orang minyak. Even Arthur's Enhanced Sight trait was insufficient to pick them out from the undergrowth, the monsters' camouflage technique keeping them entirely hidden from their senses till they chose to move. Only once was Arthur able to spot a monster before it shifted and that was due to a leaf dropping from above by pure coincidence, knocking the creature's camouflage through a swift alteration before the stick itself blended into the fur again.

As the evening came to an end, the group gathered in a small depression and semi-cave near an overhang. Arthur chose to call a quick meeting to review what they had learned. As the team took seats, pulling out weapons and gear to conduct simple maintenance on their weapons and clothing, Arthur went over a mental list of information.

Over the remnant of the day, the group had slowly ironed their fighting strategies out. Rick now carried a parang along with his bowie knife, pulling both out to wield whenever they were forced to do battle. Of course, he still hung back for the most part, allowing the more experienced melee fighters to do battle unless there was an overwhelming number of monsters.

In addition, the team had gotten used to wielding their javelins and slingshots to take out smaller groups of monsters, whether it was a monkey swarm or a clutch of mutated, overly large spiders waiting to drop upon them.

Casey, after initial hesitation, had begun to fight with more care. She was, if anything, stiffer than before, her effectiveness having dropped significantly. Still, she no longer swung her weapon as wide and did her best to stick to formation, allowing logic to overcome her instincts. If anything, Arthur assumed, he'd have to speak with her about loosening up eventually; but for now, he'd take it.

As for the rest of the team, most were handling themselves as well as they usually did. It was only Uswah that Arthur was concerned for, her lack of a hand throwing off both her balance and her lethality at times. For the most part, though, she wielded her shadow strings and traps to slow down and disrupt attacks, allowing the rest of the team to take advantage of attackers.

All in all, for the second day working together they were doing well. There were few deep wounds and nothing that crippled their effectiveness.

"Alright, so today wasn't bad. No one's been injured, at least not too badly," Arthur said, nodding to Yao Jing and Casey who both sported the worst of the day. "And we should be back up and running to nearly full effectiveness by tomorrow. Not bad for day two, not bad at all."

"Yay," Jan said, sarcastically.

"Funny," Arthur replied. "But I wanted to talk about the orang minyak. Everyone saw the first corpse?"

"Yes. A bit disturbing, cutting it up like that," Rick said.

"It works, doesn't it?" Arthur said. He then pointed to his own body as he spoke. "Heart's here, roughly. Lungs are wider apart, four instead of just two. So piercing the lungs won't likely drown them in blood or anything like that." He traced a hand down his side. "What looks like a liver here. And what seems like a single kidney, though I wouldn't bet on it." Then he tapped the throat. "Throat is good. There's no soft palate under the jaw, though, so no piercing upwards. Temple seems quite prominent though, so side blows are good. Got it?"

"Ya, ya," Jan said impatiently.

"Good, then you can write it all up for the clan records later." Arthur grinned, making the woman grimace.

"Actually, I already started on that," Mel said softly. "And no offense, but Jan's handwriting is—"

"Oi!" the woman protested.

"It really is," Uswah contradicted. "I can write better with my left hand." Then she raised her stump and waved it back and forth. "And that's a problem because I don't have it anymore."

Silence greeted her words, an uncomfortable one as no one knew whether to laugh at the poor attempt at humour or offer consolation. When no one laughed, Uswah sighed and Arthur pushed ahead.

"The worst thing is their camouflage. We're only fighting one at a time right now, but it's taking three of us to take one down."

"Two," Yao Jing said, chin lifting. "If it's me and Jan."

"Yeah, you took one down together," Arthur acknowledged. "But that still means if we meet, say, three of them at a time, we might be hard pressed."

"What are you suggesting?" Casey asked softly. There was an edge to her voice that Arthur noted.

"That we should attack the village. But not on this trip."

"Scared?" she taunted.

"Yeah. Also, cautious." He waved at the group. "We're not strong enough. We all need to hit our second transformation first." He stared at Casey as he repeated, "All of us." Then, he continued, "We can try fighting two or three, which is why we're still heading that way. But twenty?"

"We have my guns," Rick offered. "It's not useful in small groups, but for the village…"

"Yeah, and I considered that," Arthur said. "And we'll want to try your shooting at some point. But one step at a time. If we find those bullets don't do as much damage as we think…"

Casey shook her head. "We promised to supply you a starting amount of cores to increase your strength. But the amount my family can supply at short notice, it's not enough to get all of you to the next level."

Arthur grimaced. "I know. It's why we're hunting. But attacking that village and just relying on Rick is putting the cart before the horse."

"Except if we use the cowboy just for this," Mel said, interrupting. "It could work then."

"What?" Arthur said, surprised to see her on Casey's side.

"We use the guns to kill the *orang minyak* in the village. Gather all the stones and the scouts after we killed them all. We'll have what? Twenty? More? Then we go back while collecting more. At the end, we'll have what? Another fifty? Add what Casey's supplying us and what the rest of the Clan can provide…" Mel shrugged. "Might be enough to get at least a few others to the second stage. And then they can hunt and farm the stones to us."

"While the rest of us cultivate?" Arthur said, slowly. It made sense, even if it was riskier than he'd liked.

Casey was smiling at Mel, having nodded along to every single suggestion.

"She's not wrong," Rick said, tapping his guns. "I can't finish off twenty by myself, but if you cover me, I can take many down."

"You're sure?"

"Of course I am." Rick sniffed. "Do you think I've been wasting my time here?"

Arthur hesitated but, as he looked around, realized he might be the only one concerned. Even Lam seemed less concerned. Perhaps he was underestimating Rick and the power of the pistols.

Letting out a long, thready exhale, he nodded at last.

"Fine. But the first sign of trouble, we run." When he extracted an acknowledgment from everyone else, he added, "Then get some rest. Tomorrow is going to be busy."

Chapter 29

Arthur swept his spear end up, catching the descending claw and pushing it off-line. He took a short step to the right to avoid a fast-descending attack. Then, reversing the spear, he swept the point up to tear another cut along the orang minyak's lower torso, parting oily flesh with ease. Once more, Arthur gave thanks to the team for gifting him this black spear on the first floor—so beautifully carved with a wavy design and still sharp like a razor without losing its toughness.

Then he was moving again. Weave under the return strike, step in to the left, and lunge forward. Plunge the weapon into the creature's lower torso, jamming it into where the hip and leg joint met, tear sideways. The attack was meant to cripple rather than kill, and even as the orang minyak roared, Arthur danced back.

Too slow to get away entirely unscathed, but his spear held sideways took the blow for him. He skidded backwards a couple of feet and then had to reset footing as a root threatened to trip him over. For a few precious moments, he was unbalanced and vulnerable, the creature pushing past the pain to come for him.

Only for tendrils of shadow to reach out from the ground and grip its torso and one leg, forcing the monster to put more weight on the injured hip. Blood spurted and a noise like velcro tearing echoed through the forest as its leg gave way.

Jan, sweeping in close, struck in quick succession. Her hands blurred, one parang to the arm that was in the way, another to the vulnerable side of the head, splitting it apart like an overboiled egg. The creature started slumping, but the woman was unwilling to let up, her parang yanked out and returning. Meaty thunks rang and blood flew through the air.

Arthur turned aside, scanning the surroundings. The other two orang minyak were down too, or close to it. The team had handled this attack with aplomb, and Rick had yet to unleash his weapons. If anything, he had been forced to help with the fight, though he now cradled his side.

"What happened?" Arthur said, striding over to the man.

"Caught a blow to the ribs," Rick said heavily. "Hurts like the bitches. I think I broke something."

"Let me see," Arthur said. He pulled the man's hands away and then lifted the shirt, prodding at the side. To his surprise, it was not a wide bruise but small and tight, twice the size of a large coin perhaps. Not at all what he would expect from being struck by the orang minyak.

"What happened?" he asked, puzzled.

"He stepped into my pommel when I was pulling back," Casey said.

"Really?" Arthur said.

"Yes!" Casey hissed.

"I actually did," Rick admitted. "I thought she was going forward so I went right... didn't realise she was just setting up."

"See! I told you."

Arthur ignored Casey, prodding Rick again and making the man hiss. "Yeah, it's either badly bruised or broken. Good news, though."

"What good news?" Rick said.

"It'll probably heal pretty fast. And we don't wrap broken bones, so you just got to make sure you don't walk into other people anymore," Arthur said, stepping back and clapping Rick on the shoulder. "Now, if everyone's ready?"

He got nods from those around, including Lam, who had just finished pulling his hand out of the creature's stomach, hand bloody as he clutched its core.

"Let's go. We got more to find."

Walking off, Arthur could not help but hear Rick complaining behind him. He had to smile a little, even if he had been utterly serious. The boy had no sense of how to fight in a group either, while Casey was trying her best.

Still, as they kept fighting through the day, making their way towards their first orang minyak village, Arthur could not help but note that they were actually doing pretty well. Even if the creatures were still managing to escape notice by Uswah for the most part, the team at least knew what to look out for, prodding suspicious bushes and lingering shadows in trees before moving closer. More than once, these simple precautions revealed the hiding creatures, allowing them to deal with the orang minyak pre-emptively.

And more importantly, they'd begun to suss out the rhythm of the fights. Surprisingly, or perhaps not, there were not many variations to the attacks employed by these monsters. Unlike humans and their endless variations and weird techniques—who could imagine a Superman punch to be effective till it was tried on them?—the monsters kept to a small but effective routine of attacks.

All of which meant that the fighters were fast gaining an understanding of how to do battle with orang minyak. And while they were still needing two fighters per oily man, Yao Jing, Mel, and even Arthur could briefly hold their own one-on-one if necessary. They might not win a fight alone—the disparity in strength being a little too one-sided still—but they could delay long enough for the rest of the team to arrive.

With those optimistic thoughts, Arthur was happy for the team to press ahead.

Unfortunately, as though he'd raised a flag signaling their own doom, his hope for the future was soon shattered in their next battle, where not just three or four but five orang minyak turned up. Almost immediately, the team was put on the backfoot, Arthur and Mel forced to take on one monster each, while Yao Jing and Jan paired against the third. But left that two unaccounted for.

Casey and her bodyguard then took on one of those, while Uswah was on her way back to help. The last monster, having battered Rick backwards little, now chased after the gunslinger, forcing him to pull a pistol out. He was now his back, one hand bracing the other.

The crack of multiple gunshots rang out, one after the other. The orang minyak staggered a little, surprise making it twist and clutch at its body as each bullet tore into it. Four, then five shots rang out, before the monster stumbled to a stop and crashed down by Rick's feet a moment later.

After that, it barely took any time to wipe out the rest of the orang minyak as Rick fired whenever he had a clear shot. He took his time, careful to watch his back. And so the monsters fell. One after the other.

Leaving Rick reloading with a new magazine and the rest of the team rubbing at their ears.

"Shit. Well, that's torn it," Arthur said, yawning loud as he tried to get his hearing back. Thankfully, his healing technique should be fine fixing it. Or so he hoped. "We're close to the village, right?" A nod from Uswah, who'd scouted ahead. "Then let's get moving. Fast as we can."

The team worked quickly, hands coming out bloody from cavities as they extracted cores. They regrouped and Uswah led the way once more. Hoping against hope that the monsters would not have heard them coming, and knowing that was utterly unlikely.

Chapter 30

"Move, move, move," Arthur chanted as he ran, drawing the others to him. "We're hitting the village and wiping them all out. We'll deal with the ones on the periphery later."

"What if they gather?" Mel asked as they ran in a double line.

"That's why we move fast." Arthur jerked his head towards Rick, saying, "He takes out the ones in the village first, then we deal with the stragglers."

A cry from ahead had Arthur tensing. His eyes swept over the bobbing figures of Jan and Yao Jing. The big man had leapt forward, one hand glowing as the knuckles of his fist glowed. A moment later, he crashed down onto his target, the attack flashing forward and blasting the orang minyak back. On the opposite side, Jan ducked under a sweeping attack, her parang catching the monster in the torso to score a light attack as she ran right past it.

Right behind her, Mel used the creature's distraction to slice it across the eyes with her spear tip, refusing to slow down. Another pair of orang minyak were shifting out of the brush, their camouflage broken. Before Arthur could react, the bark of pistols rang out. One bullet took one of the humanoid monsters in the temple, throwing its head back. Uncertain if it was alive, Arthur hit it with his shoulder to send the body sprawling back.

Then, he was past, unsure of what had happened to the other orang minyak. His heart thudded in his chest with each breath and the cultivator had to force himself to calm his breathing. They were running right into danger and if he tensed up now, he'd be too tired to actually fight when they reached the village.

Once more, they encountered another group—scouts or guards—on the periphery. But only two this time, the creatures battered aside with ease. Arthur wasn't sure if they survived the combined attacks as his group ran past. His own Refined Energy Dart shot through a raised elbow as he skidded past, the attack tearing into exposed flesh.

As suddenly as it began, they broke out of the forest into a clearing, in which ramshackle huts made of woven branches jutted out of the rolling earth. Orang minyak were waiting for them, dozens it seemed, screaming their readiness. No smaller creatures, no children, no women. Not that female orang minyak were to be expected—after all, the legends spoke of orang minyak as male, always looking for female prey to copulate with.

Uswah, in the forefront as always, adjusted the direction of her run, hurtling herself to the side even as she wove tendrils of shadow to slow the creatures' attack. Not fast enough, but Jan and Mel were next, the pair having shifted position in line.

Mel cast her spear forward, the weapon glowing as it took the first monster in its chest, combining a Focused Strike and another elemental technique to blow the monster back. It left her without a weapon briefly, but it created a gap. One that Jan made use of. She sped up, pouring energy into her own version of the Heavenly Sage's Mischief, making her faster than ever. Her blades cut deep, slicing into the group as she plowed in and danced between the monsters.

Arthur and Yao Jing were next up, the pair splitting to the sides as they sought to deal with monsters that were trying to surround them. It also, coincidentally, allowed Rick to open fire without worrying about hitting them. His guns barked away deafeningly. Only Jan was in the line of fire, and she was crouched low, spinning beneath the bigger monsters.

From Casey's hand, a series of small stars flew. None of the attacks themselves seemed to do much damage, but they were distracting. Blood blossomed around them as Arthur and the rest of the team plowed in. Only Lam chose not to attack, focused on the backline as he was.

Spear spinning constantly, Arthur struck and struck again. Heavenly Sage's Mischief roared through his body. His sweeping attacks pounded opponents away. Each movement, each strike and kick, was combined with Focused Strike—no need to conserve energy at this moment.

After all, their goal was not to win but to create chaos for a short period. Uswah, hunched behind him, was contributing to that as best she could, her fingers weaving and tugging, pulling monsters off-balance with strings of shadow even as the continued flurry of bullets took monster after monster down.

Then... silence.

"Reloading!" Rick cried out.

"Oh hell," Arthur cursed, blocking an attack. He staggered back as he blocked an overhand sweep, the shaft of his spear bending before rebounding. He kicked out, his foot staggering his opponent back, before the monster swept him aside with a powerful knock of its fist.

He tugged the kris out of its sheath and plunged it into the lunging monster. The orang minyak staggered back, clutching at its new wound and letting out a burbling hiss. Arthur blinked, his balanced regained as he grounded his back foot.

"Hey, that's mine!" Arthur cried.

Mel, clutching his kris stabbed again, pinning an arm and tearing downward. Then, she danced to the right next, swinging the kris still. "Borrowing."

"Gah! Give it back," Arthur grumbled, backing her up with his spear.

Out of the corner of his eye, he spotted the rest of the team fighting. They had fallen into a defensive formation, holding off the roaring monsters rather than going for the kill as Rick finished reloading. A dozen, maybe, creatures left, and another ten or so already on the ground, messing up their footing with blood, guts, and corpses.

Together, the team held the monsters back. For a second, then two, then a dozen. But inadvertently, the monsters' greater weight and numbers began to push the team in retreat, their feet sliding on blood- and oil-slicked ground.

"Reloaded." To punctuate his words, the roar of Rick's pistols began once more.

All in all, things were going swimmingly. Which was when the scouts finally arrived, of course.

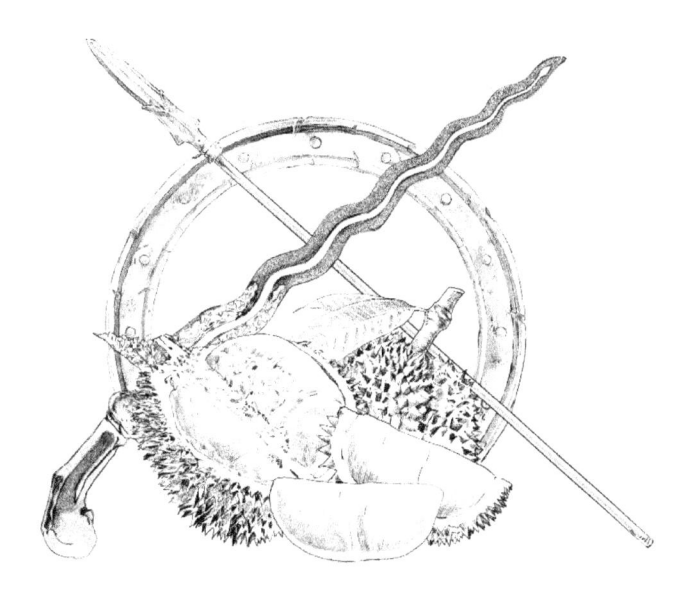

Chapter 31

"Reloaded, they folded; but now we aren't uploaded," Arthur said as he blocked an attack, slammed the back of his spear into a face, then retreated as inhuman screams from behind him arose. He watched as a bullet burst through the throat of his opponent, forcing the monster to stagger back, clutching the ruined neck.

Then, silence.

Arthur spun around, crying out as he moved, "Take over, keep them busy." There were five orang minyak left up front, but now behind... Behind there were another four monsters. Casey was fighting back against one; Lam was on the ground, attempting to block the attacks of the creature that was punching at him.

Leaving two more, one chasing after Rick who had been struck aside and was sprawled on the ground, cradling an arm which had been broken. The last one was coming for the team holding the monsters in front.

"Shit!" Arthur shouted, spinning both the spear and his body. The spear flew forward, only for it to be blocked and struck aside by the orang minyak. No surprise there; it was only meant to buy Arthur time.

Time for the Refined Energy Dart he had formed where his third eye would have been. He watched as the monster staggered back, surprised at the sudden dart attack that burrowed through its flesh, and then again as Arthur kicked his spear upwards, causing the tip to tear through gonads and flesh. Using a passing step, Arthur grabbed at the spear as it began to fall again, thrusting once more to drive the monster back with Focused Strike.

No time to conserve energy at all, he poured refined energy into techniques, his mind splitting across multiple avenues. The energy that flowed through his meridians formed easily as he pushed at it, another Refined Energy Dart forming even as he watched his spear tip pierce another body.

Arthur kept pushing forward, his spear spinning and striking from all angles. The orang minyak was bleeding from its numerous wounds, but initial surprise was giving way. In a few moments, Arthur knew, he was going to lose that momentum so he turned his head to where Rick was kicking futilely against the monster's leg.

The second Refined Energy Dart flashed forward, catching the monster in its lower back. It shrieked, surprised, and clapped a hand to its wound. Rick, freed for a second, managed to raise the other pistol he had held onto, opening fire once more.

Unfortunately, all that meant was that Arthur was distracted, such that the kick that came for him caught him in the side. It threw Arthur aside, his body bending around the big hairy leg. He crashed to the ground, turning and tucking into a roll without thought, hours of training pulling his body into a reflexive roll.

Even so, his head struck an upturned root, sending stars shooting through his vision. He groaned, pushing himself up only to catch another kick across his stomach. He was lifted feet off the ground, and a claw came down to strike him as he fell.

Pain, again and again, Arthur rolling over sideways as he was struck. He brought his spear up, blocking an attack that swung down. Fingers and knuckles bled as the skin was torn by the claw that struck at him.

Again and again, the monster kept attacking him, pounding at Arthur with arms and legs. Muscles strained, blood flowing, his world narrowed down to each second as he blocked the attacks. Fist, claw, feet, it blurred together into a red haze of pain.

And then, it was gone, though Arthur flailed for a few moments longer. His brain caught up, and he stopped moving, the injuries flaring in warning of incoming agony. Yet, his nerves had yet to catch up fully and so Arthur managed to get himself to stand, taking the proffered spear from Casey who was looking just as bad.

"How... ?" Arthur said, or tried to. His jaw wasn't working right. He flexed it, or tried to, and had the disturbing sensation—followed soon after by blinding pain—of bone snapping back into place. He clutched his face, barely recognising her words as they came.

"Dead. Most of them are."

Now Arthur realised what was quiet. The roar of firearms was absent, the sound of battle muted. He forced himself to look around, realized that most of the team had collapsed where they stood among corpses. A lot of corpses, many of them with bullet wounds.

"That... was close. Anyone dead?" Arthur winced, hating to speak but forced himself to ask. Even if he slurred a little still.

Casey winced as she pushed bloody hair away from her face, a deep wound down one side still fresh and bleeding. "No," she croaked. "A lot of injuries though."

"Told. You." Even muttering those two words hurt. Then, realising there were no more monsters to fight, he let himself slump, using the spear shaft to help him to sit. He groaned, hanging his head a little as he did so. Something inside his chest was shifting, his insides hurt in ways that made breathing or even flexing his stomach muscles a pain, and his vision kept wanting to narrow to pinpoints.

"Healing. Watch out... for me."

Then, rather than wait for an answer, he delved into his body, tugging at the refined energy within his system to form the strands of energy needed to accelerate his healing process. He needed to fix himself and fix himself fast, because from the looks of it, the majority of his team was out of commission. If there were more stragglers coming in, they were in a lot of danger.

It would be nice if they could leave, but not only had they not looted the bodies yet, he was also pretty sure they wouldn't manage to stumble more than a few hundred feet anyway before people collapsed. Better to deal with the shakes here.

And hope he could pull enough energy into fixing himself before they got moving.

Still, he could not help but curse them all. He told them they were too raw to be trying this. It was sheer luck, and a lot of firepower, that had saved them from losing anyone. Next time, they might not be as lucky.

Next time, they'd be better prepared.

Chapter 32

A day spent resting in the village allowed the team to heal up the majority of their injuries. A day was long enough to finish off two more scouting parties and to push all the bodies outside but not too long before the monsters would eventually respawn. Arthur was relatively liberal with his use of the accelerated portion of his healing technique, not content to be injured badly while behind enemy lines, so to speak.

Or was it "in the field"? He had no idea. It wasn't as though he had ever been in the army—not that joining the Malaysian army was something he'd ever consider. For one thing, it was blatantly unfair and rather disheartening to be fighting wars in-person when the enemy likely used drones.

"Don't die for your country, make their drones die for theirs" just didn't have the same ring to it. Some people thought, without even the slightest fig of shame over real personnel injured, that some of the richer countries were about to wage wars of conquest again before the coming of the Towers. Now, Tower climbers made the mathematics of violence a little different.

An angry, high-level Tower climber could do more damage than an army if needed—and was, in their own way, harder to stop.

And even harder to predict.

Israel had learned that lesson the hard way early on, when an angry Palestinian Tower climber had snuck into the middle of Jerusalem and proceeded to require nearly half a day before he was pinned down and killed. Even now the concern was ever present, even as some countries eased up on human rights violations.

Didn't stop the corporations much though, but those *kai dai* were another kind of sociopathic, narcissistic set of fools.

All of which was to say, wars and civil wars and violence were not a thing of the past, but just very, very different. They were less likely to be utilized by governments that had any sense, but also more prevalent in everyday life as Tower climbers became living weapons in the real world and everyone else hoped they never blew up.

Or armed themselves when they did.

"You can't sulk the entire walk back," Casey muttered, walking alongside Arthur with just the slightest limp.

"I'm not sulking," Arthur said as they slogged their way back. With the majority of the orang minyak dealt with in this region, the group had relaxed a little on the way back. The other monsters were dangerous, of course, but less immediately fatal.

Mostly.

"I said you were right already, didn't I?" Casey said. "Did you want me to apologise too?"

"I'm not the one you should be apologising to," Arthur replied. "I'm not the one still sporting broken bones and torn tendons and muscles. Or have half my face swollen and an ear ripped off."

Casey could not help but look back and nod apologetically to Lam at his last sentence, wincing a little at the swath of bandages that covered the bodyguard's face. The man had been half-dead when they finally got to him and even now he limped behind slowly.

Most of the group moved at a glacial pace. Healing technique or not, the amount of injuries they sported was significant. It was why Arthur had pushed for his own healing early on. And why Rick now had a secondary set of responsibilities. If they did run into major trouble, conservation of ammo and auditory levels were his last concern.

"Don't tell me how to manage my employees," Casey snapped at Arthur. "I know what I'm doing."

"Like you knew how fast to push?" Arthur shook his head. "I've burned a ton of energy, which means now I'm behind on growing. We should have waited a few weeks, trained, and at least gotten our second transformation."

"You said that already," she growled.

Arthur opened his mouth to continue arguing, then snapped his teeth shut. He knew better. He'd made his point. He was just grumpy because everything still hurt, and he was forced to focus and watch what was going on. And he worried, just a little, that returning as injured as they were, they were asking for additional trouble.

Casey stared at him for a time before she realized he was done arguing. She let out a long sniff but turned away rather than prod him further.

Later that evening, Arthur found himself propped up against a tree once more, having volunteered to take the majority of the night shift, what with having healed the most. As the night drifted on, he spent his time watching the surroundings and reviewing details about the Night Emperor's Cultivation Technique, making use of the time to slowly pull at Yin chi from the surroundings. It was a half-asleep attempt, never truly focusing or drawing too intensely, and yet still continuing the effort.

It was wildly inefficient, but taking the time to take tiny sips of energy rather than breath deeply as he should while properly cultivating meant he could watch the flow of energy more closely, attempt to perfect the flow and control and increase his efficiency.

Most importantly, it kept him from boredom. If one had ever done watch before, the realization that keeping one's mind active and watchful was all too necessary.

Still, Arthur missed it entirely when Uswah drifted over to join him, nearly startling himself awake and hurting himself when he finally sensed her presence looming over his shoulder.

"What?" Arthur snarled, then held a hand up. "Sorry. But what's up?"

"I'm sorry," Uswah said, ducking her head a little.

"About what?"

"Being useless." She raised her arm, the one half-missing, and waved it. "I couldn't, I didn't, do much. When things went bad."

Arthur breathed deep, forcing the Yin energy he had been gathering to disperse before it made itself all the way through him. He could have continued to try to work on the small sips of energy, but she deserved his full attention. It also allowed him to take his time considering what he should say to her. The truth? Partial truth? Mollify her concerns? In the end, he was uncertain what to do, but he chose to go with the only examples he ever had.

"You weren't able to help much, it's true," Arthur said. "But, and I can see you already dismissing my words, so don't do that and listen." A finger pointed at her arm, he said, "That is just an excuse. You're not as deadly as you were before, but that doesn't have to be true forever. We're in an alien Tower that gives us magic powers. If you can't figure out how to make that work for you, with or without an arm, then I'll take your resignation from the team and wish you the best of luck."

Uswah glared at him, but Arthur was unrepentant. "I don't recall why you wanted to be here," he continued. "I don't know if we ever talked about it. But it might be time to reconsider whether you need to finish the climb or not."

"I have to," Uswah said. "I have family. I can't just..." She waved downward, though Arthur couldn't figure out what she meant. "I'll get better. I just, I'm sorry."

"For getting injured?" Arthur shook his head. "Don't be. For not being stronger already?" He shrugged. "You weren't the only one to mess up." He sighed. "I should have stopped us from going on. But all we can do is learn and get better. And since no one died, this is the perfect time to do that, eh?"

"Ya." Uswah smiled a little. "You know... you aren't bad at this."

"What? Kicking people into getting better?" Arthur shrugged. "I had to do that with my master."

"You kicked your master?"

"No, no. I meant in my school. I had to help teach," Arthur said. "Not that he ever forced people to, but you often had to push those who did come to better themselves. Mostly, people would sit around and whine about how they weren't good enough yet. As though just coming to class was how they got to be great, rather than the hours spent sweating in class."

"True." Uswah gestured at his seat. "Anyway, it's my turn. For watch."

Arthur hesitated, sweeping a gaze over the woman once more. For all she had said about not being helpful, she also had managed to avoid getting injured. Which was just as important, what with their need to get home.

He considered mentioning that as he stood up and Uswah replaced him at his spot, but chose to keep silent for now. Whatever dark cloud she'd been carrying was driven away for now. Let that be enough, for the moment.

After all, he needed some ammunition for the future. Because sure as the clouds would turn, she'd get depressed again. Kind of the name of the game, being human and wounded.

Chapter 33

For all the painful slog that it was to get back and the mild concerns that Arthur carried about potential trouble, they actually managed to make it back most of the way before running into another party that wanted a word with them. Thankfully, it was just the local floor boss of the Double Sixes gang. After an explanation of the current state of the team and their desire for rest, they were escorted back to their clan hall.

An hour later, after washing both the grime and blood from his body, Arthur joined the patient man and his friends in the dining hall. The room had undergone minor changes, the addition of even more tables and chairs, though it was a rather mixed collection of furniture, more akin to a junkyard dive than a unified redesign.

"Clan Head Chua." Standing up, the gang boss offered his hand. "Dev Patel." He noticed Arthur's raised eyebrow and shook his head. "My father was a fan. And well, Patels are…"

"There are a lot of you," Arthur finished for him. He wasn't sure of how many but he did know that they were quite a number of them. Not as many in Malaysia as in the States, but still not an entirely uncommon surname here. "Trust me, I get it."

Patel chuckled, taking a seat. Whether he had decided to go in the opposite direction of his namesake or just because he liked the style, Dev wore his hair long in a ponytail but had kept his chin smooth. "Mohammad Osman sent word up, but at the time he simply said you were newly formed and he wasn't certain how long you'd be working together." A gesture down to the outside hallway. "And now, you're part of Prime Group."

"Just an alliance with the Chins," Arthur said. "And the deal is with them, not Prime."

"Even better, isn't it?"

Arthur shrugged.

"Well, Raahim said you were nice enough, if a little ruthless with the bargaining," Dev said. "What can the 66 do for you?"

"I think it's the other way around, isn't it?" Arthur said, smoothly. "I have room here, for more people. If you want it."

"And will pay for it?"

"That goes without saying."

Dev hesitated, raising his head a little. He visibly drew a deep breath, cycling the energy that was contained in the room through his body, testing the energy concentration here. It amused Arthur a little that while the energy concentration in the monster cores was significantly higher, the concentration in the air itself was much the same. It was the same for all levels of the Tower, such that on higher floors refining via cores was significantly more advantageous than transferring from the environment.

It did make one wonder why cultivation methods were at all useful, until one realised that the environment in each Tower was different and Advanced Towers had greater concentrations of energy than Beginner Towers.

As such, cultivating on the lower floor of an Advanced Tower was still significantly more advantageous than on a higher floor of a Beginner Tower. Not taking into account rest places like Arthur's clan hall, cultivation nexuses, and cultivation oases that cropped up, where the ambient energy levels might increase even further of course. Then, the 'usual' numbers got weird.

On top of all that, of course, was the fact that once mastered, cultivation techniques actually helped refinement techniques too. It took mastering the main form first, before one could really benefit from the progress in refinement speed, but it was a considerable improvement.

Unfortunately, that advantage and boost in refinement speed mostly dealt with cultivated energy from the Tower surroundings. Since monster core energy was technically already refined, drawing such energy into the body was actually an entirely different process and subject to other limitations.

This was where specific traits helped. Arthur's own Sticky Energy trait was more focused on energy already stored within the body, but other Spirit traits could help build the suction power of a Tower climber, making it easier to draw from monster cores.

Of course, the only people who chose to go down that route heavily were the rich and connected. After all, for most people, a reliable and constant supply of cores was not guaranteed. Though, Arthur had to admit, he might one day be considered a rich and wealthy layabout too, being a clan head.

All that flashed through Arthur's mind while waiting for Dev to make up his mind. In the meantime, Arthur was also eyeing the trio of individuals who made up his entourage. It amused him, a little, to watch them and try to figure out if they had a tell. Unlike in the world outside the Tower, where thugs and gangsters might dress or move in a certain way to show how much of a badass they were, or felt they had something to prove, these three had little to mark themselves as gang members beyond a strip of red and black cloth tied around the left arm.

Then again, it wasn't that surprising. After all, most Tower climbers—on the second floor more than the first—had an air of danger to them that outside civilians lacked. A hard-won confidence, a way of looking around constantly to detect danger. And, of course, a rather horrible dress sense, what with the amount of clothing they dirtied and destroyed.

"It might be worth it," Dev said finally. "But how many rooms are you offering?"

"How many are you looking to get?" Arthur temporized.

"Five."

"I can let go of three, max," Arthur said after a moment. "And that will house a max of..." He frowned, running dimensions in his head. "Twelve people."

"I don't think that's fair," Dev said. "Putting limits on how many people we can place in a room."

"Right, right. Two rooms then, and six people," Arthur said.

"Are you an idiot?" Dev snapped. "That's not how you negotiate."

Arthur nodded seriously. "I am. I really am." He continued, "I also realised you might just be looking for a way to sell space in the rooms, which is why I'm limiting both." He opened his hands. "But look at it this way. If we get to an agreement now, at least the people on the next floor won't be pissed with you."

"What?" Now Dev looked confused.

"Well, right now, I'm making deals with the 66 and the Chins. This floor, pretty sure that's all we can handle." He turned his hand sideways. "Eventually, getting actual buildings is going to be a real pain. And what we can offer, whether it's three rooms or two or one will reduce. But I'll still be approaching the 66 first, if I have extra space. If you make a deal now."

"And if I don't, you'll blame me when you go to the next floor." Dev's eyes narrowed in anger. "You're blackmailing me."

"No, no. Blackmail is..." Arthur trailed off. "You know, I might be. I actually don't know the real definition of it."

"And?" Dev said impatiently after Arthur fell silent.

"Hmm?"

"Aren't you increasing the number of rooms available? Or apologizing for blackmailing me?"

"Oh, yeah, no." Arthur shook his head. "I'm okay being a dick." He smiled. "Now, are we going to talk price or are you still pissed? Because if you are, I can just go and sleep for a bit. I did just come back from being stabbed, clawed, and kicked around. And I really, really, want a night's sleep."

"You could have been nicer," Mel said later, after the door had closed and Dev and his people had been shown out. He needed to verify numbers and collect the first week's payment before the 66 floor leader could come back and take advantage of his new rooms.

Arthur sighed and started walking down the hallway, waving her to follow. He idly nodded to a group of second-floor newcomers, pausing only to promise to come and enact joining rituals later in the day after he had gotten some sleep.

Only when he was inside his room, away from the crowd, did he finally answer Mel. "Nice or not, doesn't matter. He could have come back later too." Arthur shrugged. "They chose to talk when I'm tired, hoping I give them what they want easy. Now, he knows. I just get grumpier and more stubborn."

"Noted," Mel said. "Treat you like a child. Feed and rest you appropriately."

"Exactly. Also, I like shiny things," he replied.

She could not help but chuckle. "You don't think he'll cause problems?"

"And do what? He's already supposed to help guard us," Arthur said. "Killing me or our people just makes him look bad."

"We could use more security." She chewed on her lower lip for a second before adding, "Recruitment is low. Jaswinder still hasn't changed her mind and the Lotuses are following her lead."

"Then we wait. We don't build Durians in a day. Or a week. If she can't control her temper, she isn't of any use to me. Especially if she can't work with people like Dev later on."

"Says the person who was all kinds of rude."

Arthur was about to reply when he broke out into a long yawn. Forced to hide his mouth from her, he struggled to get his body under control, his eyes squinting as the yawn just kept going.

"I get it, I get it," Mel said, opening the door. "I'm leaving. See you at the induction ceremony."

By the time he finished dealing with the multiple yawns, she was gone, leaving him alone. Muttering to himself about bad timing, he flopped back onto his bed and closed his eyes. Whatever was to come—and most of that, he knew, was a lot of admin work—he still needed his rest.

Especially since they'd need to try the next orang minyak village soon enough.

Chapter 34

Weeks flew past, Arthur rarely finding the time to leave his clan building. Speedrun or not—and the fact stood that speed was a bit of a misnomer when it came to climbing a Tower—there were still some important administrative and cultivating work that needed completing.

In theory, one could gain a new point within fifty hours by just refining monster cores constantly. That, unfortunately, depended on having an unending source of such cores. Granted, the Chins were generous as per their deal. Also, the clan was now earning cores from renting out rooms to the 66 as well as gaining cores through hunting. But Arthur did have a full team to upgrade, and that wouldn't be easy.

And as usual, he needed more cores than other people because, other than Casey, he was the most junior member—in terms of how long he'd been in the Tower—and also the least progressed. The other team members were close to, or even already at, their second transformation. And because of that, more often than not, he was stuck cultivating indoors while the rest of the team had fun outdoors.

His world narrowed to a series of meetings, whether to bring in new clan members or to deal with petty issues that others could not handle, and then back to his room where he cultivated most hours of the day or slept when he was not cultivating. Outside of necessary breaks, Arthur was stuck in a training routine, almost no different than his time before entering the Tower.

Except with a few important differences.

"You cannot let them do this, boss," Yao Jing said, arms crossed.

"I have to agree," Rick said, nodding along.

"Really not right," Yao Jing added.

"Oh cry us a river," Mel huffed. "There's only a few of you men. Giving you all an exclusive bathroom is a waste of resources."

"A man needs his privacy," Rick protested.

"For what? *That?*" Jan rolled her eyes and gestured with her hand to indicate what she meant.

Rick spluttered, "I do not—"

"No, ah? Can't get it up, is it?" Jan said.

"You—!"

Arthur groaned, burying his face in his hands. He half-listened to the two bickering, Jan slipping out of Manglish—the local variety of English—into Malay and even Cantonese just to frustrate Rick. Yao Jing was dragged into all that, forced to translate.

"How many clan members do we have here now?" Arthur asked Mel, refusing to referee those children right this moment.

"Just over forty. And only five men," Mel said.

"Including me?"

"Excluding you. So, six."

"Not sure he is a man, anyway," Jan couldn't help but interject, alluding to his Yin Body.

"Don't start that again," Arthur said dangerously. To his surprise, Jan immediately bobbed her head, mouthing an apology. It seemed she knew when to shut up after all.

He had imagined handling many things as clan head, but refereeing bathroom usage had not been on his list, and he was fed up of it.

"You need to learn some manners, girl!" Rick snapped.

"Girl? I'm more woman than you can handle."

"Oh yeah, want to see me try?" Now the man was grabbing at his crotch, which was the point when Arthur had enough. His hand came slamming down on the table, palm flat so that it echoed through the dining room. Without a proper meeting room, it was either meeting here or in his bedroom. And considering how often these meetings grew in size, Arthur had learned his lesson about using the bedroom. Among other things, it also meant that people stopped trying to barge in to have conversations with him while he was cultivating.

"Quiet now, yes?" Arthur said dangerously when Yao Jing made to speak. "We're making all the public washrooms co-ed."

"What?" Jan and the boys shouted at the same time.

Mel knew better, just looking at Arthur as he made his pronouncement. There might have been a small shake of her head, but Arthur kept talking.

"I'm serious. Make it known. Everything's co-ed for now. Or intersex or non-gendered or whatever you want to call it. Also, make it known that anyone trying to take advantage of that for stupidity gets one warning, after which I will, personally, cut off the offending part." Arthur shook his head. "Consent in everything, and that means consent of everyone in that bathroom. Everyone has bedrooms, use them." This time, he was looking directly at Yao Jing and Jan, causing the pair to cough in embarrassment. Yes, he had heard those rumors too.

"Now, go away and leave me alone. I have…" He trailed off, looking at Mel for a clue. "Something more to do, I'm sure."

The trio left, heading off to report the news to everyone else who had shoved them the dirty job of dealing with Arthur. Leaving him alone with Mel, who waited for the others to get out of earshot before she lowered her voice and spoke as they exited the room themselves.

"You're making that a habit."

"What?"

"Annoying people as a management technique."

"I don't know what you mean," Arthur replied.

"It's not always true that a good compromise is when everyone is left unhappy. Sometimes, it just means you're not trying hard enough," Mel said.

Arthur opened his mouth to object when he sensed movement. Head turning, he saw the Tower guard leveling a blade at a familiar face who was leaning dangerously close to the blade at the building entrance. Eyes searching, the visitor spotted Arthur and her face relaxed a little.

Even before she spoke, Arthur's sense of foreboding grew. It was never a good thing when someone stressed looked happy to see you. In his past life, that either meant a beating or extra work.

Sometimes both.

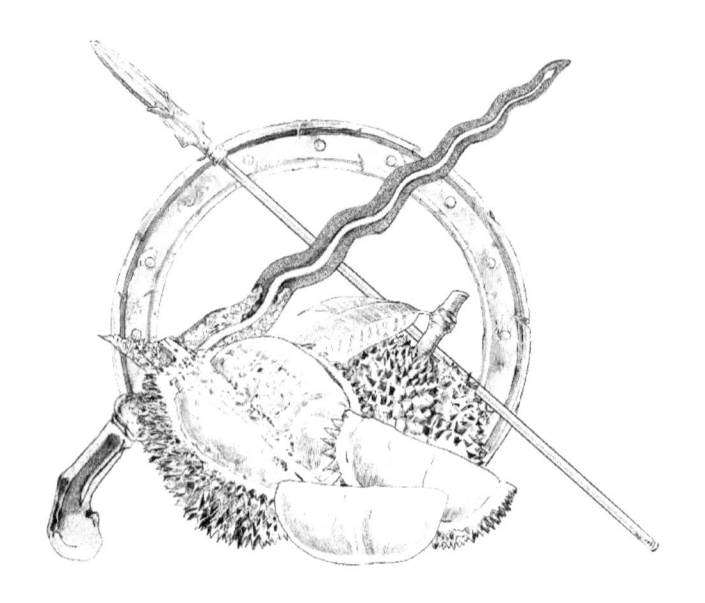

Chapter 35

"What's wrong?" Arthur said. He gestured to the Tower guard and, when it failed to understand him, verbally commanded it to let Jaswinder in. "Why are you looking like someone made you eat a cactus and a bag of limes?"

"I need your help," Jaswinder said immediately. "Please."

Arthur crossed his arms. "Why should I?"

"Because it's the right thing to do?" she replied, glaring at him. Then, seeing his coming refusal, she added. "Please?"

A slight clearing of a throat behind him made Arthur look at Mel. He noted her patient expression and eventually sighed. "Fine. I'm listening."

"I..." Jaswinder gulped and then went on. "One of my people. She's been taken. I need you to get her back."

"And by your people, you mean the Lotuses still part of your group?"

"Yes."

"Okay. Next question, for a thousand dollars. Who?"

Again, the woman frowned. She was, obviously, not a fan of his tone or idiosyncratic way of speaking, but at least she did answer. "It's Harley Lee. You don't know—"

A raised hand cut her off. "I meant, who are we getting her back from."

"Oh." Now she looked nervous, chin jutting up as she found a modicum of courage. "Promise me you'll get her back."

"No."

"You have to."

"Pretty sure I don't have to do anything," Arthur said, crossing his arms. "You, all of you, had the chance to join us. Weeks ago now! And you chose not to. But the moment you run into problems too big for you to handle, you run to me."

"Only because you've stolen half my people!"

Arthur refused to feel guilty about that. Sure, she was right, but that was also characterizing his actions as stealing, when all he was doing was recruiting as best he could. And really, the sheer volume of people who wanted to join was now rather overwhelming. If they hadn't needed to be careful about who they let in, he could have filled the clan building easily.

"Tell me who." Arthur let a little steel enter his voice. But he wasn't going to commit himself to a fight just because she wanted him to, no matter what his conscience might insist on. Or, at least, he told himself that.

Who really knew how good a man they were, till they were tested?

"The Ghee Hin." Jaswinder said softly. Her shoulders slumped.

Arthur frowned. "I don't understand. They're not actually here, right? I know they have some presence on the upper floors, but mostly they're not here?"

"Just one of their members. A nephew of one of the higher ups. Nicholas," one of Jaswinder's hangers-on spoke up. When Arthur looked at the woman, she continued, "Harley and I, we were coming back from harvesting. Nicholas saw us, wanted to talk to Harley again."

"Again?" Arthur asked.

"They'd been dating for a bit. But she didn't want to talk, they struggled, she fell and hurt herself. Then, Nicholas took her. To the Suey Ying headquarters."

"Of course it's the Suey Ying. Always has to be, right?" Mel said, exhaustion in her voice. She had, herself, been abducted by the Suey Ying tong on the first floor.

"Ixnay on the flag-ay," Arthur said. "Otherwise, we'll have a bad day."

"Not the time!" Mel growled.

"It never is." Arthur ran the numbers through his head, the political considerations. Then, he had no choice but to ask, "And you're sure she went unwillingly?"

"Yes. I saw it myself," Harley's companion said, arms crossing. "She was still angry with him, because she saw him with someone else."

This time, Arthur did groan audibly. Love problems. Who said being a clan leader was fun?

He sighed. "Get Rick and Yao Jing and whoever else in the A-team. Have them arm for bear. Looks like we're going on a tear."

At his words, Jaswinder looked both happy at his acceptance and a little wary. Which Arthur couldn't blame her for.

If a rhyming fool wanted to help him, he'd be wary too. But since he was the fool in question, all she could do was...

"Say thank you," he said, winking at Jaswinder. He waved her to stay and went off to get dressed for battle. After all, if he was inviting himself to a party, he should at least dress appropriately. Maybe even bring a few gifts.

"Sometime, someplace, I'd love to actually surprise someone," Arthur commented to Mel, who was hurrying alongside him. The majority of his team was with him, along with a number of clan members that they'd managed to round up. Of course, such a large armed group moving through town was enough to get people following or running ahead in an attempt to figure out what was happening. So any chance of a quiet entrance was shot to death, much in the same way Rick had dealt with orang minyak.

Even worse, unlike on the first floor, he was now missing help from the 66. So it was going to be just his team against the entirety of the Suey Ying tong if it came down to blows. Not the kind of numbers that he looked forward to having.

Which was why, even without Mel haranguing him to consider something other than kicking the door down, he was thinking through other options. Negotiations, perhaps. Maybe bribes. Hell, he'd even pay a ransom if it wasn't too absurd, though only if he thought he could push them back long enough for his clan to grow in peace.

The last thing he needed was to start a war with the Suey Ying and Ghee Hin at the same time. The Suey Ying were just a tong with a strong presence on the first few floors, but at the end of the day they were a small fry. They had not much more than local strength to contend with and if you managed to destroy that, they were done for.

The Ghee Hin, though, were an actual triad in the outside world. They had people not just in KL or all of Malaysia, but all across Southeast Asia. If you believed some of the more outlandish stories, they were a global underworld organization.

They could drown Arthur and his people in bodies, just by putting up a big enough bounty, and there would be nothing he could do about it. So, negotiation was definitely the first option. On the other hand...

"I can't just leave her, right?" Arthur said softly to Mel. He kept his voice low, though between the hubbub of the audience and his companions and the clank of armour and weapons, it wasn't easy to hear.

"No. She's a Lotus, so she's part of us. You leave her, you show you aren't any better than the people we banded together to protect ourselves from." Mel shook her head. "If you did that, what's the point of joining the Durians?" Then a flicker of a smile. "Anyway, we're not Benevolent otherwise, right?"

"I knew that name was going to bite me in the ass."

She laughed, though the humour had an edge to it. He wouldn't dare call it a hysterical laugh, but he certainly felt a little on the verge of mania himself. For all of their desire not to start a fight, if the Suey Ying and this Nicholas boy refused, they would have to fight. If nothing else, to protect their growing reputation.

All those thoughts pinballed through Arthur's head as they made their way through town, only to be brought to a stop a short distance from the Suey Ying headquarters. A dozen men, armed and armoured as they were, stood in his way, blocking the entrance.

Immediately upon spotting Arthur, one of them—a muscular, tattooed man—shouted, "What you want? You *nak mati, ke?*" This did indeed feel suicidal.

Well, this was going to go great. Just great.

Chapter 36

"I'd prefer not to die, thanks. Or for anyone to die at all," Arthur said smoothly to the Suey Ying thug. Tattooed, muscular, and with a torn T-shirt, the man could have stepped out of the set of an Indonesian gangster movie. "Violence is really the last choice here."

"Then why so many, ah?" Parang rose, pointing to Arthur and then swept sideways to take in Arthur's entourage.

"Last choice. Didn't say it wasn't an option." Arthur took a step closer, holding a hand up to stop the others from following. He used the spear he carried as a walking staff, grounding it as the parang shifted back to point at him. "I just want to talk."

"We talking already."

"Yes. And that's good. Better than fighting, eh?" Arthur said, smiling. "But I'd actually like to talk to, uh..." He paused, looking back to his group. No answer, until Jan hissed from behind, "What's his name again?" to Jaswinder and her group.

"Nicholas Lim," Jaswinder hissed back.

"Right. What she said," Arthur said. "Nicholas Lim. Just want to have a word with him, and the girl he brought back. Then after that, she'll come home with us, and we'll all be gone from here." When the other man began to speak, Arthur raised his free hand and beckoned Mel.

The woman came forward with a package wrapped in cloth in her hands. "Oh, and we brought gifts too," he said. "A 'we're here and friendly' gift."

"What?" The man stared at the gift, frowning suspiciously. "How I know it's not a bomb?"

Arthur shook his head. "Nothing that crude. You can look it over, while you call for Nicholas, right?"

Thrown for a loop, the thug just stared at Arthur and the wrapped box, obviously uncertain of what to do. He kept hesitating, and Arthur almost spoke up when a voice called from inside the building.

"Invite him in. With his gift."

"Boss?" The thug hesitated again before he shook his head, not daring to contradict the other in public. He gestured for Arthur to come, and Mel followed them. The doorkeeper looked like he wanted to object to Mel coming, but when the voice didn't, he chose to keep quiet too.

As they neared the entrance, Mel lowered her voice so she could whisper at Arthur, "This is a bad idea."

"Yeah. But better this than fighting, right?" Arthur said. "We can't be throwing fists to solve all our problems."

Mel had no answer, at least none that she found worth offering. Inside, the building—what looked like a converted warehouse—was a single large open space with a wall partitioning a small area in the back. Within the open space, numerous cots and tables were spread out. Sadly, while the building had a few windows, the entire area smelled like the third day of a geek convention, unwashed humanity all too prevalent as the odour du jour.

Guided by the doorkeeper, the pair were brought over to a table that sat near the center of the warehouse. A little too far from the doors, but Arthur made sure to not think about that. At least they hadn't taken their weapons away, allowing Arthur to prop his spear against the table as Mel offered the box to one of the men. During all this, a glowering older man with a scar running down one side of his face that bisected a milky eye watched them all.

"You're Arthur Chua, eh? Leader of the Benevolent Durians. You're older than I expected." The man's voice came out rough and raspy. One of his hands brushed at stringy, unwashed hair a little so that that blind eye could be more easily seen.

Arthur smiled, meeting the other's gaze easily. He even went as far as to offer his hand while he spoke. "I don't hear that often. But I must admit I don't know your name."

"You come without learning my name?" He shook his head at Arthur's foolhardiness. A long look at Arthur's hand before he grabbed it, giving it a tight squeeze and shake. "Kong Hua."

Arthur kept his face serene even as the other crushed his hand. Pain was something he was used to after all. Eventually, the Suey Ying floor leader released Arthur's hand and sat down, turning to stare at the box that was being unwrapped.

"What did you bring me?"

"A gift." Arthur sat at the offered chair, slipping his hand under the table and flexing it surreptitiously to get blood back into his fingers.

"What kind?"

"The best." A slight pause as he waited for the box to be brought over. Uncovered, it revealed glistening slabs of barbecued sweet pork jerky with a hint of honey. "*Bakkwa.*"

Now Kong Hua looked surprised. He sat up, stared at the meat hungrily, licking his lips.

"Wasn't easy, getting this. You know how it is, getting food in here. But one of our clan members, they couldn't meet their core quota and offered this instead," Arthur said lightly.

"And this is a gift?" Kong Hua said carefully. Of course, it was not just a gift. You didn't just take gifts, without the expectation that you would, at the least, begin a relationship with the giftee. Accepting a gift came with unspoken obligations of courtesy and manners. Gifts could be as dangerous, if not more, than straight transactions. "To us?"

"Yes."

"Even after what happened on the first floor?"

"I never had a problem with your organization," Arthur said, firmly. "It was just Boss Choi."

"I've heard of him," Kong Hua said, again, carefully. "He was after my time, though."

Arthur nodded. He could understand why Kong Hua was here. Better to be boss on the second floor than try for more, especially missing an eye as he was. He was likely a significant force in himself, while Arthur and his people lacked in such personnel.

One day, perhaps.

Kong Hua fell silent, then turned to meet his doorkeeper's gaze. "They asked to speak with Nicholas?"

"And his girl."

Kong Hua let out a long sigh and pushed the box back to Arthur. "I cannot. If you start a fight—"

"We're just gonna talk. That's what I hope anyway. I need to make sure she's good, you know? You understand how it is. Got to make sure my people are good." Arthur nodded at their surroundings, to the few women he spotted in the vicinity, to the couple of injured in the far corner.

"I do. But *they* are our sponsors."

"Then let me just talk to him. And we'll see what happens." Arthur offered as winning a smile as he could. "What's the worst that could happen, eh?"

Chapter 37

"How dare you!" A hand slammed on the table, cracking it. The cups of water that had been placed on the table spilled, and the box of bakkwa tumbled off. Thankfully, that had been shut firmly, leaving the glistening, tasty meat unspoiled by an impetuous child. If not, Arthur was sure he'd have to kill the boy for ruining it. He could only think of Nicholas as a boy, even if the lad was his age and pretty tall.

Arthur bent down, picking up his spear where it had fallen and propped it against his shoulder. He did so slowly, not just because everyone was jumpy after the boy had shouted and struck the table, but also because he wanted to irritate him further.

Seated properly, Arthur continued, "I didn't dare anything. All I'm asking is if Harley is okay."

"She's fine. She's always fine with me," Nicholas snapped. "I'm her boyfriend. Of course she's fine."

"Sure, sure." Arthur nodded along. "But I hear she got hurt, talking to you. And you brought her back, against the protests of her friends?"

"She fell and hit her head," Nicholas said. "I didn't hurt her. I would never!"

"Okay, but you did take her without her agreement."

"I'm her boyfriend!"

"According to my people, that's not true."

Now Nicholas looked a little unsure. He hesitated for a moment, before adding, "We're having a fight. She saw me talking to someone else and overreacted." Cutting his gaze over to Mel, who was standing behind Arthur's chair, he added, "You know how women are."

Arthur was definitely not dumb enough to answer that. Among other reasons, there was no lock on his bedroom door. Instead, he pivoted the conversation. "Well, can we see her?"

"Why?"

"Because she's my people, and I have to check on her condition. If she wants to stay, she can. If she's injured, we've got some things we can try to help her heal faster." For that matter, a small knock on her head was something that the healing technique would fix soon enough, Arthur was sure.

"And if I say no?" Nicholas glared.

"Why would you?" Arthur said, refusing to rise to the bait. "She's your girlfriend, right?"

"Uh, yeah. But she's still resting."

"I can wait," Arthur said. "Maybe Mel can check on her while she's sleeping." He gestured at Mel. "She learned a little about how to fix people from Amah Si. You know Amah Si from the first floor?"

"No," Nicholas said.

"Well, if it's not a problem. It should be fine, right, Kong Hua? For Mel to see Nicholas's girlfriend? Let the girls talk it out?" Arthur smiled at the gang leader who had been watching the entire interaction with strained patience, biting his lip while the kid paced around.

Arthur could guess at the undercurrents here, since it was an all-too-familiar thing. Nicholas was a nepo baby, a nephew of someone important. So he was being babied all the way up the Tower by the Suey Ying tong, till their numbers decreased as the floors went higher and the Ghee Hin situated above took over. Till then, he was a precious jade that couldn't be dropped, or their entire tong would be in trouble.

Didn't make it any easier to have a kid like this strutting around, causing trouble.

"He doesn't get a say in this. That's my girlfriend," Nicholas growled.

"But this is my organization," Kong Hua said, finally fed up with the blatant disrespect.

Nicholas looked surprised to be contradicted, but Kong Hua continued, his voice growing gentler as he tried to mollify the young man. "And it's just this girl, right?"

Nicholas looked unsure, before he nodded. "Fine. Just the girl, though."

"Great." Arthur gestured to Mel who stepped forward. Kong Hua sent her off to see Harley with the thug who had brought them into the Suey Ying headquarters before Nicholas could say anything else. In the meantime, Arthur took a casual step forward, picking up the box of bakkwa. Before straightening, his spear dipped dangerously close to Nicholas. "Why don't we sit at a new table," he suggested. "Have a drink or two. You can tell me about what you're doing out here while we wait."

"Give me a gift and then you want to drink my alcohol..." Kong Hua grumbled, but he had stood up too and walked with Arthur, forcing Nicholas to hurry after them.

"Eh, I'll settle for a good *kopi ping* if you have one."

"Kopi ping? Got, got." Kong Hua looked surprised. "You don't?"

"*Takde.*" Arthur shook his head in negation. "We're still setting up. Luxuries come after, you know?"

"Understood. Same also," the older man said, lounging back in a chair. He waved for his people to serve cups of coffee, though not iced as Arthur had requested, as that would be a bit much. A little too eagerly, Arthur picked up the cup and breathed in deep the smell of Malaysian coffee, the aroma of cheap coffee beans and evaporated milk filling his lungs. "Maybe we can help one another, eh?" Kong Hua said genially.

"Long time before I can deliver more things regularly," Arthur said. "Communication, you know?" After all, the only way to get information to the floors below was to actually get out of the Tower and tell someone who was going in and let them handle things.

It was why the floor lords were mini-bosses. The people who actually stayed on a floor were either too weak to progress or the ones lording it over the weak. Being a floor leader wasn't as good as getting out of the Tower, of course, because one was basically trapped. But if you didn't mind that, it wasn't a bad life either.

"I can wait. Not going anywhere," Kong Hua replied.

"Are you... trying to cut a deal with him?" Nicholas said, having finally caught enough of his bearings to cut in. He looked between the gang boss and Arthur in disbelief. "Why?"

"If he survives, his clan is going to be big, you know?" Kong Hua said. "Better to make deal now than later."

Arthur had to smile at those words, though their weight was slightly undercut by the way Kong Hua's gaze kept drifting to the box of bakkwa, which had been brought to their new table. Then again, Arthur could understand it. If you were stuck here forever, then life wasn't just about monster cores and getting stronger; it was the little luxuries, the things one missed from the real world.

And Kong Hua wasn't wrong. If Arthur managed to get out, the Durians were going to be massive. A clan building on the first floor of the Malaysian Tower? Anyone with any brains on them would definitely try to exploit that. With size also came stability, which meant a good and semi-consistent flow of goods. Which, of course, meant luxuries.

"Whatever," Nicholas said. "Boring shit. I'll make my own group, when I get out."

Kong Hua managed to not roll his remaining eye, but Arthur could swear it was a close thing. He chose not to continue their conversation though, not with Nicholas here. They could follow up on deals later, when the boy wasn't there. So instead, they sipped at the coffee, waiting. Neither of them missed the way Nicholas would glance backwards to the private rooms once in a while.

Which was why, when Mel came out with Harley and Nicholas reacted badly, neither were at all surprised.

Chapter 38

"You're not going," Nicholas insisted as he stood before Harley, arms crossed. But he was quite a few steps away. Mostly because Mel had, rather pointedly, lowered her spear in his direction when he looked like he was going to move closer.

"I want to go back with them," Harley said.

Arthur and Kong Hua were watching the entire interaction a short distance away with studied patience. Personally, Arthur would have gotten up to deal with it, but Kong Hua had given him a look. Figuring the older man had a reason for his reticence, Arthur had chosen to keep seated. That gave him more than enough time to watch the two.

He had to admit: Harley was pretty. In a Korean pop princess kind of way, with almost-too-perfect, long, lustrous hair and a manufactured sort of pretty that some people liked. She even dressed in a shirt that showed off her midriff and shorts that were short but not scandalously so. Just tight. Overall, he understood why Nicholas might be into her.

"I told you, we have to talk first," Nicholas insisted.

"There's nothing to talk about," Harley said.

"I didn't *do* anything!"

"Except kiss her!"

"*She* kissed *me*!"

"And your tongue just slipped out into her mouth, ah?"

"*Ikan bilis*?" Kong Hua's question startled Arthur, and he turned to see the older man offering a bowl of, well, ikan bilis. The dried anchovies that he thrust at Arthur was a popular Malaysian ingredient, side dish, and snack. The bowl had a small scattering of peanuts as well.

"No popcorn?" Arthur said with a smile.

"Don't have," Kong Hua said.

"I didn't kiss her back! She lied," Nicholas was insisting again.

"And why'd she lie for?"

"Because your friend hates me!"

"I wonder why!"

Mel was looking over at Arthur beseechingly, even as the pair continued their lovers' tiff. Stuck refereeing the two, her weapon about the only thing stopping the guy from coming closer, she looked entirely uncomfortable. On the other hand, to give Nicholas his due, he didn't try to push the spear away, though Arthur wondered if that was because he was focused on the argument and had forgotten about the weapon.

"Children." Kong Hua shook his head. "Their love is always so… heated."

"Yeah, tell me about it." Arthur rolled his eyes. "I don't want to start a gang war over a lovers' quarrel."

"Same here," Kong Hua agreed.

The two leaders shared a knowing look, before they broke off eye contact self-consciously.

"So. You want me to bring up goods for you guys?" Arthur said, changing subject a little awkwardly. "Not take any rooms in my building?"

"66 already there, right?"

Arthur nodded in reply.

"Then, rooms don't work," Kong Hua said. "But I bet they haven't asked you for goods yet. Right?"

"No, not really." Arthur leaned back, considering Kong Hua. "I can't guarantee anything till I'm out. Don't even know the quantities I can get. And we're not moving anything dangerous to begin with."

"Ya *lah*. Understood. But you can bring luxuries, right? Kaya. Bakkwa. Kuih. Maybe rice and soya sauce. *Kopi*." He raised his cup.

"Sure," Arthur said.

"Why won't you give me another chance!" Nicholas wailed, his voice rising. Kong Hua and Arthur looked over to see Harley retreating further from him, tears falling from her face. Mel stepped in the way, though she was using her body rather than the spear and a change in demeanour that told Arthur a lot.

"Talk later?" Arthur said, then downed the last of his coffee. The older man sighed and nodded. It didn't take Arthur long to arrive on scene. All the while, Nicholas was almost begging his girlfriend to change her mind. He dropped a hand on the boy's shoulder, gently, and watched him spin around in anger. "Easy there..."

"What?!" He shrugged the placating hand off, then stepped up into Arthur's personal space, looming over him.

Gods, the kid was predictable. Keeping a smile off his face, Arthur stepped back, the kid immediately eating up the space he had surrendered.

"Look, I was just going to say..."

"Stay out of it." The kid was now trying to intimidate Arthur by looming over him. It was all in the old playbook, one that Arthur had himself enacted all too often. Tall people always thought their height made them scarier.

And if you stepped back, they always followed. Because the hind part of their brain was telling them their intimidation tactics were working. For most people, that'd be true.

Hand low, Arthur waved Mel and Harley out, even as Kong Hua judiciously did not pay attention as the two hustled out of the building. "Alright, I will."

"Good." Nicholas relaxed a little, pulling back from Arthur as he felt he had won.

Another half-step back, so that the boy could not see what was happening. "Just one thing…"

"What now?!" Nicholas went back to his attempt at looming over Arthur.

"I figured you might want some advice," Arthur offered his most harmless smile.

"Don't need it!" Nicholas growled. "Who do you think you are?"

"Arthur Chua. Clan leader of the Benevolent Durians. I told you already, you know."

A hand shoved him back. "I don't care."

Arthur let him, stepping back with the shove and retreating out of range. His eyes flicked behind the boy to track movement before Arthur continued, "Sure, sure."

Again, Nicholas started to turn.

"So about that thing—"

"I said, enough!"

This time, Arthur didn't stop talking. "They're like deer," he said.

"What?" Since Arthur wasn't within easy punching range anymore, Nicholas hesitated, adrenaline and pride warring with confusion.

"Women. Deer. Skittish, both of them. You make a lot of loud noise, you scare them off. You can chase, but they'll keep running." Holding his fingers up, Arthur mimed a deer running and bouncing along the flat of his palm. "You got to wait, give them space till they calm down."

"Are you stupid?" Nicholas asked.

"A little." Arthur smiled, then stepped back again. "One last thing."

"I'm going to kill you..."

"Yeah, sure. But also, she's gone."

Nicholas whipped around, fast as a snake, and Arthur took the opportunity to start running. He felt a little bad leaving the clean-up to Kong Hua, but he figured the older man knew how to handle the kid now that Arthur and the girl weren't in his building anymore.

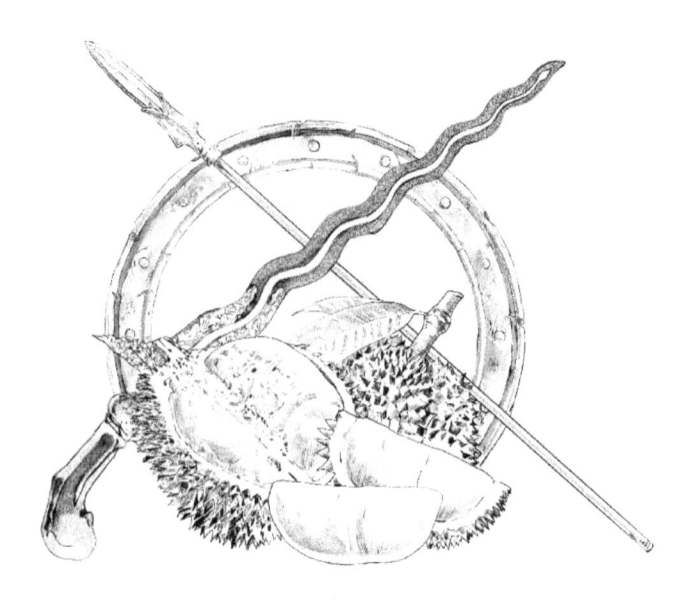

Chapter 39

Back in their clan headquarters, Arthur was quick to induct Harley and a few other Thorned Lotuses into the clan. He flopped down into a seat in the dining room while leaving Mel to deal with the arrangements—most importantly, sleeping arrangements. Building bunk beds and, more often, stringing newly woven hammocks between walls in rooms helped them maximize space, but it was not comfortable by any means.

Still, it would have to do until they hit the next inflection point of clan growth. At which point, Arthur could only hope they'd get a building upgrade option.

"That was not the solution I expected from you," Jaswinder said, arms crossed as she watched her people disappear towards their new rooms. She looked highly conflicted as she watched her people leave, before she looked at Arthur. "But... thank you."

"You're welcome." Arthur sniffed. "I prefer not to fight." Sobered, he added. "Especially people. Killing people is... different."

"It is."

For a time, the pair fell silent as they struggled with their own demons. Then, Arthur shook his head, discarding dark thoughts aside. He would deal with his own misgivings about killing people—and his rather scary lack of morals about it—for later.

"So. You owe me."

"I do."

"You know what I want."

"My people."

Arthur nodded.

"I'll... I'll tell them." Then, Jaswinder added, "I was going to do it anyway. You got her out, without anyone dying. I promised myself: If you did it, if you actually were good for us, I'd tell the rest to join you."

"And you?" Arthur raised an eyebrow.

"I thought you didn't want me."

"Uswah's told me a little about you." Arthur propped his chin on a hand, staring up at Jaswinder from his seat in the dining room. "I think we need you." He watched her brighten, before adding, "As a spear."

"Not as a leader?"

"Nope. You have the wrong temperament for it. For being a big boss, at least. Maybe head of security or something, but not the floor leader," Arthur said.

"Oh, thank Vishnu." Jaswinder said, taking a seat with a sigh.

"You're not angry?"

"Do you think I wanted to be their boss?"

Arthur frowned, then nodded. That... actually tracked with what Uswah had learned about her. An overbearing sense of protectiveness and duty, probably one of the best fighters on the second floor, and... someone who had not progressed for nearly five years.

"So, what are you going to do?" Arthur asked curiously.

"Well, you mentioned head of security, right?" Jaswinder said slowly.

"For now. Until things stabilize." He paused, then shrugged. "If you can find a replacement, or the floor boss decides it, then no more than that."

"Good." She smiled, looking younger now. Less stressed and angry. "Then, maybe..."

"Maybe?"

"I can leave."

"We'll do our best," Arthur said, looking around the building. "That's the point, after all, of all this. Making it viable for everyone to actually climb the Tower. Not have people stuck, for no good reason."

"Some of us..." She grimaced. "Have injuries."

"I'll find a solution," Arthur her cut off. "There's always a solution, if you try hard enough." He laughed softly and a little wryly. "Isn't that the promise of the Towers? A solution to our problems."

"I never believed that. Did you?"

Arthur shrugged in response and Jaswinder's grin widened. "You really did!"

"It's not a perfect solution. But what kind of world did we live in before? AI and automation and corporations owning everything. Us given a small allowance, just so we wouldn't starve. And any kind of attempt to fix that or protest crushed by the police or army or by others of our own kind," Arthur said. "The media makes it seem like we all hate each other, and of course, we end up doing so."

"Are the Towers any better?"

"It shook things up, at least," Arthur said. "But we're getting off track. We were talking about your place."

"Decided already, no?"

"I guess. Though... any suggestions for who should be the floor boss?"

Jaswinder snorted. "If I knew, I wouldn't be the boss, would I?"

"Were the boss."

"*Chui!*"

Arthur chuckled and waved his hand. "Whatever. Glad we sorted this out. Go tell the rest of your people, and we'll start adding them in." He sighed, rubbing his face. "It's going to be a pain figuring out how to fit them all in."

"Can you?" Jaswinder said, looking back out the door.

"Not really, at least not without stuffing people into rooms and piling them on top of each other. But... " Arthur shrugged. "It comes with the benefits, right?"

"What if they didn't want to stay?" Jaswinder said.

"Who wouldn't? You can cultivate in here much better. And it's safe."

"Some of us aren't looking to go up and aren't in a rush. And many of us have our own residences already," she said.

"Ah, right. I didn't think about that." Arthur frowned, then brightened. "I'll just have Mel sort it out."

"Do you make her do everything?"

"Only the boring parts," Arthur said.

Jaswinder looked like she was about to say something but, after a moment, turned around and walked out. Arthur watched her leave, humming to himself. So. She could learn.

Now, it was time to find Mel and dump more work on her. Whistling to himself as he exited the building, Arthur went searching for the lady.

This was, in spite of all expectations, a good day.

Chapter 40

Arthur stared at his pack, mentally reviewing everything within. Snacks, change of clothing, bandages—a lot of them—and a first aid kit. Whetstones. Replacement spear head and knives. Twine, cooking implements, and utensils. String. Water bottles—two, just in case one got pierced. And more, whatever he needed for a multi-day trip through the wilderness.

They were going to hit their second orang minyak village. This time around, if things went well, they might even hit a third village soon after. Location-wise, it made sense to finish off both villages on the same trip. They were roughly the same size, though the fourth and final one was larger.

All in all, nearly seven weeks after arriving on the second floor, the team was ready. Everyone, including Casey and Arthur, had managed to achieve their second transformation. More than that, he'd managed to absorb the full details of the Night Emperor cultivation method, with Uswah managing to learn it just the day before. Even without the magical aid of the original Tower scroll, she had figured it out eventually.

Drawing a deep breath, Arthur pulled up his status screen again.

Cultivation Speed: 2.371 Yin
Energy Pool: 19/19 (Yin)
Refinement Speed: 0.0921
Refined Energy: 0.31 (18)

Attributes and Traits
Mind: 10 (Multi-Tasking, Quick Learner)
Body: 10 (Enhanced Eyesight, Yin Body, Swiftness)
Spirit: 10 (Sticky Energy, From the Dregs)

Techniques
Night Emperor Cultivation Technique
Focused Strike
Accelerated Healing – Refined Energy (Grade III)
Heavenly Sage's Mischief
Refined Energy Dart

Partial Techniques
Simultaneous Flow (37.8%)
Yin-Yang Energy Exchange (31.8%)
Bark Skin (4.02%)

Along with the increase in his attributes, Arthur had also managed to gain three new Traits, one in each attribute. It had taken him quite a while to decide which traits to pick. First, he'd increased his Body to ten points, which had triggered a painful rush of energy as his body rebuilt itself upon hitting that second threshold.

Choosing the Body trait from there had been easy though, since he had realised a while ago what he lacked. And while he still had no time to practice the Bark Skin technique to increase his physical robustness, he could at least try not to get hit. The Swiftness trait was just a general increase to his reflexes and speed, but it had the advantage of also boosting future upgrades.

He would not be as quick at running as someone who specialized in that, or have the snakelike reflexes of the same named trait, or even have a twitch muscle response to duck a sudden attack. But the overall increase in speed would allow him to edge out anyone else in each of those areas. Add his spear use to it and he could potentially save himself from getting injured by just not being there when a hit came.

After he finished with his Body upgrade, he focused on Mind. He would have done Mind first, if not for the fact that he had still been a little wary about Casey pushing to continue their advancement and needing to have the ability to deal with the calamities her insistent and continuous momentum would cause. In other words, increasing his ability to fight.

Increasing the Mind attribute sped up refinement speed of the energy in his body and from monster cores. He had debated what he should choose as a trait, whether it was to boost his Multi-Tasking ability as he had planned or instead choose more a socially-oriented technique. There were a lot of ways to approach problems in the Tower, but in the end he resolved to keep to his initial plan.

That meant finding a trait that worked with Multi-Tasking. The obvious ones, like Parallel Processing or Disparate Thoughts or Second Mind were interesting, though urban legends of individuals going down that route and fracturing into multiple personalities had pushed him away from that.

Instead, he chose to go with a more broad-based option called Quick Learner. It allowed a small increase in analysis speed, understanding, and learning; but it was a low-grade support for Multi-Tasking. In fact, the moment he had taken the trait—and dealt with the resulting headache—he found his ability to process and consider multiple sources of information easier. He started reading over various documents and then letting his subconscious deal with it while he focused on more important aspects like cultivation.

Lastly, of course, came the upgrade to his Spirit. Those were always the weirdest. Instead of physical changes, Spirit upgrades elicited a cold shiver through the body like getting dumped into an ice bath and then warmed up again.

Or at least, that's what Arthur assumed an ice bath felt like. He had not actually taken an ice bath—that was way too expensive to do in Malaysia—and there weren't exactly glacial lakes to jump into.

Upgrading his Spirit with a trait had required a little bit of thinking. The last time, he'd gone with Sticky Energy to add a little to the speed he could refine at. This time around, building upon the idea of sticky energy and in consideration of his lack of time, Arthur leaned into making the most of the energy he did have. From the Dregs was a weird trait he recalled reading about before.

It allowed him to keep a small portion of the energy he refined in his body rather than in his dantian. It was a tiny percentage to begin with, but as his Spirit attribute increased, that tiny percentage would add up, ensuring that he would need to refine less in the future.

Between the three new traits and full-body transformation—which, not surprisingly, was an agony and a half that had left him crippled and bleeding sweat for half a day—Arthur was now feeling like a whole new person. Not only was he stronger and faster than ever but he could also process information better and he had a significant store of both basic Tower energy and refined energy.

All in all, he was as ready as he could be for their next expedition. This time around, Arthur was sure, things were going to be different.

Chapter 41

Arthur stepped back, twisted his hips and heaved, throwing the spear directly at his opponent. The forest troll took the spear right in its chest, even as Mel chopped at a limb reaching for her and Jan ducked low beneath Arthur's flying spear to chop at hairy, warty legs with her parang.

The creature staggered back, green blood blossoming around its chest wound where the spear pierced it. Arthur took off running and leapt high to grab at the spear shaft. He levered the staff upwards with his trajectory, forcing the massive creature to crash to the ground as damaged limb and greater weight took its toll.

The smell of moss and spilled green blood filled the air. The aroma had a salty, musky tinge, more reminiscent of breaking mushrooms away from the earth than bleeding a living creature. Not iron in its blood but something else.

Arthur was not, of course, staying still long enough to figure out exactly what. Instead, foot planted on the body, he twisted his body sideways as he yanked the spear out, only to find it caught between hardened bone. He lost a precious few seconds, long enough for a swinging hand to nearly catch him unawares.

Nearly, because shadow tendrils rose up on one side, gripping the troll's limb and pulling it back to the ground while Mel's swinging halberd took the other arm off, finally. In the meantime, Jan scurried around to the creature's head and started swinging a parang. It rose and fell in rhythmic *thocks*, like a gruesome drummer.

"Ah-hah!" Arthur cried in triumph, managing to yank the spear free.

He backed away then, choosing not to attack the creature's torso. Like the mushrooms it smelled of, it had no internal organs that were necessary for its survival. No heart, no liver, no kidney. The only way to truly kill these things was to behead or delimb the creature entirely, or burn it.

And since Jan had the beheading part well in hand, he surveyed their surroundings. The other forest trolls were being dealt with, the mushroom-scented monsters each taking a group of three at least to manage. Luckily, Casey and Lam with the help of Yao Jing were more than competent at managing their creature. They were herding it back for Yao Jing to release concussive fist strikes into its body. The empowered concussive blows shook up the creature's internals—whatever they really were—pulping them such that it moved like it was punch drunk more often than not.

Noting that no one was in any danger, Arthur ambled over to Rick, nodding to the man as he stood guard, crossbow in hand. The mounted crossbow bolt was a broadhead, its tip nearly the size of Arthur's palm.

"How are you liking your new toy?" Arthur asked.

"It's not a Benelli Super Black Eagle, but it'll do," Rick replied. "It's a lot quieter and most things aren't going to get up again after I shoot them with this."

"Isn't there another term? 'Loose' rather than 'shoot'?" Arthur said.

"How would I know?" Rick asked. "I'm not an archer." He hefted the crossbow. "I'm using this because it's the best option otherwise." He shook his head. "I can't believe you people didn't have something more modern."

Once more, Arthur eyed the contraption Rick was carrying. He had to admit the man was right. Instead of a modern steel-and-plastic body, this thing was all metal and wood and more closely resembled something he'd see in a medieval movie.

Then again...

"They're illegal mostly. Or at least, I think they're illegal." Arthur shrugged, not really caring. "I'm surprised Kong Hua was willing to sell us one."

"He's still trying to get in good graces with you," Rick said. "After you managed to keep Nicholas from getting skewered by the Tower guard, I think he's trying to mend fences."

"Don't remind me," Arthur said with a roll of his eyes.

The lovesick boy had actually attempted to climb through an open window of the Durians' clan hall to meet his lady love. Of course, what Arthur hadn't told Kong Hua was that Harley had left the window open for the boy on purpose, thinking it would be a rather romantic final act by him to showcase his love and devotion. Mel had managed to extract that crying confession while Arthur was handling the Tower guard and then patching the injured young man together.

There was a reason Arthur was enjoying their current trip through the woods, even with the forest trolls, babi ngepet, kuching hitam, massive spiders, and the rest. massive spiders, and the rest. So were the rest of his team. They didn't fancy Nicholas and Harley's antics, which smacked of too much Bollywood and anime

"You know, I have gotten better," Rick said, leadingly.

"We need someone to be on watch when we're in a fight," Arthur replied.

"Isn't that Uswah's job?"

"She doesn't have the stopping power your toy has."

"Still..." Rick began to say.

Arthur cocked his head as he studied the other man, frowning. "Are you seriously trying to suggest you get in close and dirty with that knife? You don't have anything to prove any more, you know."

"I know." Rick shifted on his feet before he added, "I just like fighting, you know?"

Arthur hesitated before he nodded. "Fine. Next time we run into something, you can switch with Uswah."

"Good. I prefer watching."

Arthur managed to stifle his yelp as Uswah made her presence known right by his elbow. Rick swung his crossbow towards her before he caught himself halfway, glaring at the tanned, *tudung*-clad woman. Her face wrinkled a little as she laughed silently at their reactions.

It didn't, of course, help her creepiness factor that she had managed to acquire a further understanding and expansion of her shadow techniques. Now, wherever she stood, it seemed like she was partly shaded, even under the bright sunlight of day. During periods of twilight or the evening, she had a tendency to fade into the background.

And as always, there was her missing limb. Still missing, but a new, flickering darkness sat in its place. Shifting with the sunlight, fading away as Arthur paid attention to it, and then reappearing as he looked aside. Uswah refused to speak about what was happening there, only saying that it was a work in progress.

All kinds of reassuring really.

"How much further?" Arthur said, refusing to let her see how much she'd rattled him. "Until we get to eat some burgers?"

"We just ate," Casey said as she joined them.

"I could eat more," Yao Jing said.

"Look, it was a bad rhyme." Arthur sighed. "I ended with 'further'. And then the only other word I could think of was... not great."

"So you went with 'burger'?" Casey said.

"Better than being insensitive."

"Now I'm curious what you were thinking of."

"Stay curious." Arthur nodded firmly and a little patronizingly before looking at Uswah. "Seriously. How much further?"

"Another day. This infestation of trolls is slowing us down," she replied.

"They'll hibernate in a few days," Mel replied. "They cycle through every six weeks. We're just unlucky."

"We could wait?" Jan said.

"No," Casey replied firmly. "We push ahead. It's not that bad. And at least there are fewer patrols."

Arthur had to admit she was right. The forest trolls had a tendency to attack everything, even other monsters on the floor, so the orang minyak "scouts" had pulled back as they seemed to be aware of the trolls' pattern of behavior. Still, reading about how the forest trolls presence affected the cultivator city and dealing with them in-person were two different things.

"Let's go then." Arthur waved the team on. "If we're not stopping, then we've got ground to cover. A lot of it."

The group started off, with Casey falling in step with Arthur as usual. It took them half a dozen steps before she said, "So, really. What were you rhyming it with?"

Chapter 42

Coming up to the second orang minyak village while forest trolls were awake was very different from their expedition to the first village. Rather than running into numerous scouting parties of orang minyak, Arthur's team had to deal with these mushroom-trolls. Yet, the time invested beforehand to get everyone to their second transformation had proven its worth; each troll group was dealt with in quick order.

When they got within a few hundred feet of the village, the team ran into the remnant of a battle between a bolstered orang minyak scouting party and a group of trolls. The oily humanoid creatures were in the midst of feasting on the bodies of the fallen—of both species—when Arthur's party launched their attack, Rick's massive crossbow bolt tearing through and nearly beheading its first target. Smaller slingstones caught creatures as they stood and thrown javelins nearly finished off half the group.

After that, the team's melee fighters closed in and mopped up the last few monsters. Rather than wait and potentially be found out, the team stripped the monsters of their cores quickly before forging ahead to the low-slung, less protected village.

This time around, the group chose to split their forces. Not too far apart, and with a wide enough distance between the parties such that they could offer mutual aid if necessary. The reason for that change of tactics was one simple factor: the majority of the creatures were hiding within their ramshackle huts from the rain, staying out of sight rather than keeping watch for invaders.

In this way, the team intended to ghost through the village and strike at the huts, tearing into the monsters in small numbers before they could group together and react. That, hopefully, would mean that the larger-than-normal numbers in the village would be less of a factor, since the scouts were pulled in.

"Ready?" Arthur looked around, checking on his team. Following him were Casey, Lam, and Yao Jing. The other small strike team with Jan, Mel, Uswah, and Rick were already moving to the nearest hut. He waited a second, noting that Rick had raised and loosed a crossbow bolt into the village. Arthur's breath caught as he waited for shouts or screams, but nothing arose.

Whoever Rick had taken out, their dying had not breached the thunder and constant patter of rain. Exhaling, he waved his own team on. He chose to stay outside as they swept in. The cry of surprised orang minyak and the clash of blades barely escaped the hut.

But it was not entirely quiet. From a nearby hut, a head poked out. Arthur sent a Refined Energy Dart at the creature, catching it on the forehead. But unlike Rick's massive crossbow bolt, his attack was insufficient to kill the other immediately. The orang minyak staggered back, clutching its face and keening loudly.

"Shit! On me," Arthur cried, sprinting forward and thrusting his spear. This time, his attack was fatal, Focused Strike piercing chest and heart with ease, and the monster slumped over, dead. Arthur's spear was battered down a moment later by another creature who had emerged from the hut, already shouting.

"No good, no good." He cursed, letting the spear fall to the ground from numbed fingers. Instead, he snatched the cursed kris from his belt and swiped it across throat, ducking under and back as he backpedaled. His opponent clutched a bloodied throat, the curse of poison working its way deeper and freezing vocal chords.

Then another lunge, followed by a series of quick thrusts and cuts. Arthur felt the Heavenly Sage's Mischief surge through his body at his beckoning as he held the ground against the orang minyak that kept trying to exit the hut. His strength now matched the monster, who was wounded and poisoned.

He held the line, even as the clatter and clamour from within the hut grew. Just as the rest of his team arrived, one of the monsters from within gave up on the door. It crashed through the side of the makeshift hut, causing the rest of it to begin collapsing, only to face the weapons of his team.

Surprise distracted Arthur's opponent, allowing him to step in and shove his kris deep into the creature's heart. Leaving the weapon in it, he ducked low and grabbed his spear from the ground, retreating only after he retrieved both weapons.

Then Arthur scanned the surroundings. Unsurprisingly, nearby huts had orang minyak exiting. They were slow in coming out, surprise slowing their reactions down. Even if the struggle with his opponent felt like it had taken forever, he knew that was just the distorted sense of time that happened during a fight. In reality, not even a minute had passed.

Rather than wait for the creatures to regain their footing, Arthur took the fight to the nearest. He took off at a run, spinning his spear to clip an emerging head in the temple before he leapt into the sky, thrusting as he did so with the weapon to extend his reach.

Surprise caught his next opponent, spearhead punching through the monster's futile defence. Then, landing easily and only stumbling a little as his feet skidded in the mud, Arthur was beset on both sides. Behind, his team hurried to catch up and strike while the creatures were yet to rally. Monster after monster fell, but soon, even amidst the panting of monster and human, the constant drumbeat of falling rain and the rumble of thunder, cries of surprise took hold, echoing.

That, of course, was when Rick's weapons of choice were unleashed.

A new thunder filled the surroundings, the hammer of bullets falling on furred, oiled bodies and dropping them one after the other. Flashes of light filled the night sky, strobing as flashes of light exploded from muzzles in the twilight of heavy rain.

Before, as suddenly as it began, the battle was over.

Perhaps it did not go entirely as they had planned, but it was easier—so much easier—than the first village. Soon enough, they regrouped, pouches bulging from extracted cores.

"Next?" Casey said.

"Yes. One more village, then the real test," Arthur confirmed.

Perhaps, just perhaps, this idea of a speedrun was not entirely insane.

Chapter 43

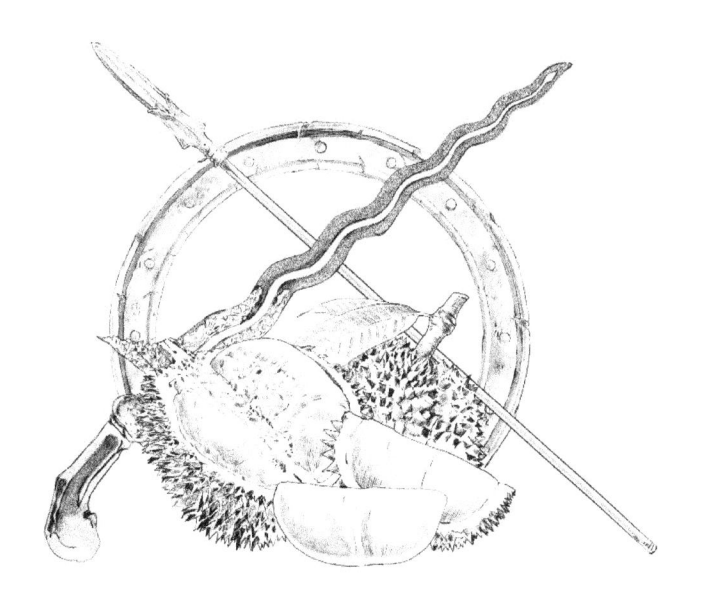

"You're insane," Arthur snarled.

"I'm not," Jan said. "We can do this *lah*!"

"She's right. We can do this," Casey insisted, leaning forward over the dining hall table and encroaching on Arthur's space. He refused to budge, instead raising two fingers and using them to push her head back rather rudely.

"Firstly, personal space. Learn it, live it, love it." Arthur cocked his head to the side. "Unless, of course, you intended to kiss me. Then, you know, feel free to come that close again. But otherwise, please don't get into my personal space unless you're a lover or..." He considered it briefly. "Well, a sparring partner. But when we're sparring, kissing is not allowed."

"No?" Mel said with amusement. "Why not then? I'd think it was quite distracting to the opponent."

"It is. Except, you know, what do you do if they kiss you back? It's rude to really get it on in the middle of class. And if they don't, you might end up with a broken arm. So here's another rule: Don't break your partners."

"You sound like you're talking from experience," Mel said.

Arthur shook his head.

"What? So shy now?" Jan tried to tease it out of him.

"While Arthur's love life in all its variety and forms is fascinating, we were talking about finishing the final village," Casey said impatiently.

Behind, Arthur noted that Lam was looking a little tired. He'd mention that, but he doubted Casey cared. For that matter... "We just got back three hours ago," he said. "My hair is barely dry. And you want to go out again? We've been out for seven days already. People need a break."

"But you saw how well we took the last two villages. Barely any injuries!" Casey waved her hands around excitedly. "We can do this."

"Sure, because we're in a max-sized group and cheating with guns." Arthur shrugged. "So what? We still have to worry about finishing the next floor."

"Exactly!" Casey snapped her fingers. "If we finish fast on the second floor, we can churn and burn on the third and finish there faster."

"Churn and burn?" Mel asked.

"Churn through monsters and burn through cores," Casey explained. "There's no specific quest there, just a guardian."

"Which we have to pass, individually," Arthur pointed out. "So rushing here doesn't help."

"But we'll be able to use more powerful cores on the third floor," Casey said.

"No clan building there though," Arthur countered.

"We have a building we'll turn over to you," Casey said.

"Assuming we don't lose too much time finding one another, finding the third-floor town, and getting that building transferred."

"All the more reason to get it done now!"

"Except most of us will be underpowered for the third-floor monsters," Arthur said. "We haven't pushed into the deep wilds at all. We're still vulnerable, even as a group, if we're up against third-floor monsters. Or a gang of climbers."

"They wouldn't dare challenge us." Casey glowered. "Just tell them you're under Chin family protection."

"That assumes they let us talk. I don't think monsters will." Arthur still remembered the mangled body he'd left behind on his first few days here and the token he had looted off the corpse but had yet to utilize. Something to deal with, soon enough. "We need to strengthen up *here*."

"Fine, then we stay here for a bit after we take out the fourth village," Casey relented. Arthur noted that Lam, her bodyguard, looked relieved when she gave in. He didn't blame him, since Lam likely would have been blamed if Casey got killed, even if he had no way of protecting her during that vulnerable period right after being transported to the next floor. Only later would getting tether enchantments be viable.

Or perhaps they had some already? Arthur had never asked, but it would make sense to provide some to someone like Casey and her bodyguards.

"Well, what do you think?" Casey said.

Arthur hesitated a little, glancing to the side. Jan gave him a thumbs up, while Mel—who was the only other individual to have turned up to this impromptu meeting—looked hesitant.

"We still need to rest here. Decompress a little. Restore some of our energy reserves," Arthur temporized. "Going out under strength is a bad idea."

"Fine," Casey offered, crossing her arms. "One day."

"Three."

"Two."

"Deal," Arthur stuck his hand out, offering it the other woman. She took it reluctantly, shaking his hand before releasing it with a little smile and leaving the room. That smile made him wonder if he had been conned by her. Hopefully she was gone to train and refill much-needed reserves.

That was what he was headed to do anyway, once he checked in with the rest of the team and left orders to let everyone else know about their shortened timeline. He wasn't entirely happy about it, but they had previously promised Casey to do a speedrun.

"I'll inform the others," Mel offered.

"Me too," Jan chimed in, standing up.

"You guys sure this is the right thing to do?" Arthur said as he surveyed the hall. It had gotten busy again, word of his presence spreading as hopeful recruits streamed in. Most were, of course, previous members of the Thorned Lotuses, but he was sure there'd be a small scattering of other hopefuls hanging on. As though his thoughts had made Jaswinder appear, the dark-skinned woman ducked through the doors, smiling at Arthur in a predatory way.

"It's what we agreed," Mel echoed his earlier thoughts. "Just trust that Jaswinder will find someone good. And that we'll be able to find someone good too on the next level. Or at least have someone good assigned from this floor."

Arthur could only grimace at that thought. Rushing to get buildings built up was all well and good, but if he couldn't assign floor leaders, it was just going to be a mess.

Heck, assigning floor leaders who weren't of any use was going to be a mess too. But for now, he could only hope to muddle his way through and figure out how the other clans managed to deal with these issues. He had a speedrun to complete in the meantime.

Chapter 44

The next few hours passed in restoring his basic cultivation pool. In between, he had to give orders, interview prospectives, and confirm them as new members—all done quickly before he closed his eyes to cultivate again.

Aiding Jaswinder in recruitment was Su Mei, his very first recruit on this floor. She had fallen into the role of administrative aide with practised ease. The pair had grown close over the last few weeks. Having skipped first-floor growth, the young lady had also taken to cultivating and strengthening her attributes, on top of taking on small tasks for the clan.

As it would have been pretty risky to go monster-hunting, the young lady instead became the impetus for the formation of their clan library and quest board, through which members traded requests and aided one another. Working with Mel and borrowing from their library on the first-floor clan building, she had built a fast-growing library on the second.

Of course, the paranoid portion of Arthur worried that she might run off, stealing manuals and other information, leaving the clan bereft and exposed. Then again, there was little he could do about it.

At least, with the current controls offered to him. There were hints, discussions with Mel and Amah and others who had read about Clans that indicated there might be additional security options available once he actually upgraded the Clan itself and exited the Tower.

But they were just that. Hints. Till then, he could only hope for the best.

Finishing up with the latest batch of applicants, Arthur waved Jaswinder over. He pointed to Su Mei, who was speaking in one corner of the dining room by the bookcase she'd started. It was half-filled, mostly with paperbacks from the real world donated to the cause, but some hand-penned manuals and guides took center stage.

"Whatcha think?" Arthur asked.

"She'll do," Jaswinder said.

"Yeah, I think so too. Keep her on as librarian. But make sure to train someone else too."

"Librarian?" Jaswinder said, surprised. "I was thinking floor boss."

"Are you insane?" Arthur said, cocking his head to the side. "She's too new."

"So am I."

"Yeah, but these people know you." He shook his head. "I don't know anything about her. Including whether she's going to stick around. We need people like you and Amah Si if possible, to just keep recruiting."

"And what if you can't find someone, in the future?"

Arthur shrugged. "Then the clan doesn't recruit on that floor."

"Sounds like a missed opportunity."

"It's all very makeshift," he admitted. "But we make do, eh?" Then he added, "You're quick to trust. Any particular reason?"

Jaswinder shrugged. "She's committed. At least a dozen of the new applicants were thanks to her. She's friendly. Has a good head for organizing things."

"And that's all it took?"

"She's a cute one but tough. Saw her tell off a young man who tried to bribe her to put in a good word, then she broke his fingers when he grabbed her. Has some skills." Jaswinder chuckled. "Though not the strength."

"Oh?"

"Mmm... he and his friends were beating her rather badly when we finally stepped in." At the look he shot her, she grinned, "I'm not completely innocent either, boy."

"Fair enough." Arthur stood up, rolling his shoulders. "I've done all I can. Tomorrow at nine in the morning, I'll start again. As for now, I need to refine a little, study a little more, and then get some actual sleep."

Dark eyes ran over him, searching, before she offered him a grim smile. "Don't let her run you all ragged. Won't be much of a clan if you die of exhaustion."

"That's the plan." Offering her one last wave, Arthur slipped back into his room.

Except that, rather than refining energy immediately, he let himself flop onto the bed. In the silence of his room—broken only by the noise of the clan creeping in through the door, though being at the end of the hall helped somewhat with that—he managed to get a moment to think.

He certainly needed stronger attributes, but more importantly, he felt the need to start studying some of the cultivation techniques he'd been pecking away at too slowly. The Bark Skin technique in particular would increase his chances at survival, and it was certainly something he intended to make better use of. He'd only been practicing it on and off, so a period of intense study was required.

But more than that, Arthur could not help but consider what he needed for the next level. His spear was strong, but it was not enchanted. Finding someone to enchant it was nearly impossible on these lower floors. That left him only with the option of asking the Tower itself to do so, which meant he could do it on either this floor or the seventh. Or much later. An enchantment would, almost immediately, give him a boost in lethalness.

That wasn't the only way to make himself more dangerous, though. Cultivation techniques were, of course, the bread and butter. He had Focused Strike, which was the most basic of techniques but useful. He also had Heavenly Sage's Mischief. Both already gave him a close-combat boost, though he was tempted to pick up a third. After all, while having a ranged attack like Refined Energy Dart was important, he was in the end a melee fighter.

He still remembered information on the Heavenly Sage's Heaven Beating Stick technique. From what he gathered, he should be fine using it with his spear, and since the spear was something he intended to use for a while—and this one was unlikely to break too easily—it seemed the perfect technique to add to his arsenal.

If not for the fact that it required refined energy.

Heavenly Sage's Heaven Beating Stick

Staff technique that infuses weapon with energy. Initial stages reinforce the staff, increasing durability and damage done, allowing it to strike ephemeral and spirit creatures. Higher stages of the technique will allow the projection of energy-infused extensions of the staff.

Cost: 1 Refined Energy per minute. Must attune to weapon beforehand.
Credits: 12

Costly. But better to get that now than later. Of course, first defence, then offense. Then, after that, maybe he should consider something a little more tricky, a utility skill that had a wider degree of options rather than "Arthur hits them very hard."

But that was later.

Struggling out of bed, Arthur pulled cores from his pouch. He had work to do, and he didn't have the credits for a new technique just yet. In the meantime, refining energy from within and from the cores was the way forward.

Chapter 45

Arthur felt the core in his hand crumble, the last dregs of energy removed from it. He opened his hand and reached for another core, only to find the pouch empty. He searched within before picking the pouch up and turning it over, failing to find anything.

"I guess that's it..." Arthur muttered. Twenty cores. Generated from the tithe given to him as clan head and from the monsters they'd killed, all used up that quickly. Not even enough for a whole point, which was amazing to him.

But it was what it was. In between sleeping, cultivating, and training, time had passed quickly. He'd even managed to get that token sorted out, only to find that it had only had a handful of contribution points that he could use. Not much of a bunch, but better than nothing.

Finally, it was time to get going—to the final orang minyak village.

A few minutes later, after he finished repacking his bag and checking on the time, he wandered back to his seat. He had overshot his timing by a little, with another four hours left before it was time to leave. The clan building was quiet. In the dead of the night, everyone was either asleep or cultivating. Arthur would have caught a few more hours of rest, but he knew himself. Sleeping now would mean he'd wake grumpy.

Besides, the first day out of town was unlikely to bring any real dangers. Better to suffer from a little lethargy now and make use of the free time to work on the Bark Skin technique.

He extracted the Bark Skin manual, flipping through the document's well-thumbed pages and read through it once more as was his wont. It helped him memorise the instructions. Occasionally he highlighted areas that he had missed. Most importantly, the re-read ensured he didn't make a mistake when enacting the technique.

The Bark Skin technique was interesting because, unlike most other cultivation techniques that required energy to activate, Bark Skin had both active and passive components. The passive portion primed the body to be physically reinforced. Over time, passive use of the technique would harden the skin against damage.

However, it was the active use of the skill that provided the greatest degree of protection, hardening the skin against significant cuts and stabs. It was not, of course, anywhere as effective as actual armour. But since there were large portions of the body not covered by armour anyway, additional security was nothing to be scoffed at.

After confirming the flow of power and the necessary mental landscape required to use Bark Skin properly, Arthur began the process of pulling cultivated energy from his body. He directed it through the meridians as per the guide, then started infusing this altered energy across his body.

Triggering the process was both a physical and mental workout. The former involved energy flow and the latter required you to hold the right form and guide nebulous energy. Cultivation techniques were in many ways like teaching yourself to sketch or dance. You might know how to move or draw, but you might not know a particular dance or sketch. Only practice of that particular form could make one better.

Of course, the more similar the routines one used, the more practice you had. Like practicing or getting good at certain styles of dance, or drawing individuals rather than landscapes. Over time, one just got better overall too.

Which was why, in some ways, Arthur's disparate series of cultivation techniques was not the most optimal. On the other hand, like a beginner who had just started dancing, gaining a broad base of knowledge and practice could pay long-term dividends.

Or it could just slow down his overall progress.

Like most things, there were arguments both ways. Considering that he had lacked the funds until recently, Arthur had planned for a generalist approach anyway. He had not seriously considered a multi-Tower specialization. Now, he might have to reconsider that assumption. Though, he still did not think that further generalization was going to hurt him.

Idle thoughts as he worked the energy through him. One downside that came from being able to multi-task was that idle thoughts would invade his mind while cultivating. It didn't pose a danger; it just told him that he was bored. Maybe he could find some audiobooks to listen to?

Skin prickled, and occasionally muscles twitched and clenched as he continued to cultivate. Arthur felt the hair on his skin stand and then lay flat, ripples of power hardening and softening his flesh in turn as he practiced the Bark Skin technique.

Too much energy on the left hand. Not enough on the right. Pull back on the amount entering the flesh there, infuse more here. Watch as the energy in his core slowly squeeze itself out as he ran it through the paces, guiding the amount of energy he was wasting.

Hours of practice passed seemingly in moments before Arthur opened his eyes. He had poured nearly eight full points of energy through the cycle, a significant portion of his reserves before he had stopped and began cultivating to restore himself.

Now, finally, as the noise from outside his door grew, he knew it was time to go. A flick of his hand brought up his status.

Partial Cultivation Techniques
Bark Skin (37.1%)

Not bad for a few days of focused practice. All these additions to Mind and Spirit and energy pools were finally paying off.

Time to take on the last village. Then more cultivation, more fighting, and another floor.

Where new challenges awaited.

But... one step a time.

Chapter 46

"We have a problem," Uswah said two nights later as the group sat around their campfire.

"*Eh!* I already moved my bed away, what," Yao Jing complained. "Come on, the beans aren't that bad…"

"No, they really are," Arthur said. "But I don't think that's what Uswah was talking about."

"I was not," Uswah said, frowning. "And what is this about beans?"

"*Bodoh* ate canned beans," Jan said, then waved a hand in front of her nose to explain Yao Jing's issue.

"Problem?" Mel queried before they got distracted again.

"We're being followed," Uswah said.

"Kuching?" Arthur asked, though he doubted it. She would not have bothered raising the issue with the whole group. They'd been stalked by the solitary black cats often enough, but those were more an annoyance than a danger. But if they ever chose to attack in groups like the babi, then he'd start worrying. In fact, now that he thought of it, Arthur couldn't help but worry about that.

"No. People," Uswah said. "From town. At first I thought it was just people moving along, but... yeah. Definitely following us."

"Shit," Arthur said.

"Damn it!" Casey swore, crossing her arms.

"They going to rob us?" Rick asked, frowning. He touched his guns, looking uncomfortable. Arthur did not blame him. It was one thing to kill monsters, another to kill a human. For one thing, the monsters didn't have children or parents. They also didn't look at you as they died, their hopes and dreams fading, hand clutching at yours and leaving bloody prints, betrayal deep in their eyes, taking with them a portion of your life as they departed.

Uswah shrugged. "Maybe scavengers."

"Scavengers?" Arthur said.

"That's what we call people who pick over bodies after a battle. They might be trouble," Mel said, but there was amusement in her eyes.

Arthur narrowed his gaze as he stared at Mel, recalling their very first meeting. Mel and her friends had demanded he justify his presence in the woods on the first floor. Even as those memories and others returned, he saw Mel's humour fade. Recollection of the near past clouded with memory of even nearer pain. It had only been a few months, really, since the death of her closest friends. She had suffered a near-total loss of her team. Shar, who had been both brave and human in the end. Rani, who'd sacrificed herself. So many others.

Though she seemed to have managed well enough, as well as one could, some scars did not fade easily.

"You never know what trouble, indeed," Arthur said softly as he kept his gaze locked with Mel's. Trying his best to share the pain she experienced. He knew not her friends, what they had done or shared before his arrival. But he did know Mel and he did know loss, and sometimes, all you could do was offer to be there.

"Yes, it really was," Mel said quietly.

"What—oof!" Yao Jing began to comment, but he let out a pained expulsion of air as Jan put her elbow into his side. He looked over at his lover. Hurt but seeing the seriousness of her expression, he shut his mouth.

Neither Mel nor Arthur missed the interplay, and Mel smiled a little, the darkness fading slightly. It was not gone, could not go so easily, but for the moment it had lifted. Memories of loss and pain could fade, if handled gently—with care—by others who could or would share some of that burden.

"So. Scavengers," Mel said clearly into the silence. "What do we do about them?"

Rick looked between the two, then over at Casey who was frowning darkly. He caught Arthur's gaze, but Arthur refused to acknowledge the byplay. Definitely not the time.

"Can we lose them?" Arthur asked. "If we move fast enough, is there a chance to hide from them?"

Uswah frowned, looking over the group. She pondered the question deeply before she eventually shrugged. "I would need to see them to know."

"That's..." Arthur hesitated before he sighed. "That's reasonable." Then, biting his lip, he added, "How far away are they? How many?"

"Ten." She hesitated a little. "Or at least ten. I might have missed a few."

"When did you spot them?" Rick asked.

"Around lunch and a little after. When I had Jan scout in my place," she explained.

"Let's not do that again," Lam said. "She led us right into a mudslide."

"It was the most efficient way!" Jan protested.

"Filled with leeches."

"Ei, come on *lah*. You so tough, you worried about a few leeches?" she scoffed.

"I do when I'm wearing loose underwear," muttered Lam, whose remark startled a few of them into looking at him.

"Ah!" Yao Jing shouted, grabbing everyone's attention. "Did I ever tell you about the leech lake?"

"No," Rick said, eyes narrowing. "I'm not sure I want to know."

"Same," Casey said firmly.

"*Wei*, it's really funny."

Arthur shook his head, cutting off the subject. Considering Uswah's report, their surroundings, and the hour of the evening, he sighed, realizing what they had to do. He did not like it, but he knew they had to do it.

"Arthur?" Mel said softly, catching his attention.

"You all stay here," Arthur said. "Get ready to come and help, but otherwise, try to rest."

"Help how?" she said, carefully.

"Help Uswah and myself, when we go on a little walk to see the sights."

Chapter 47

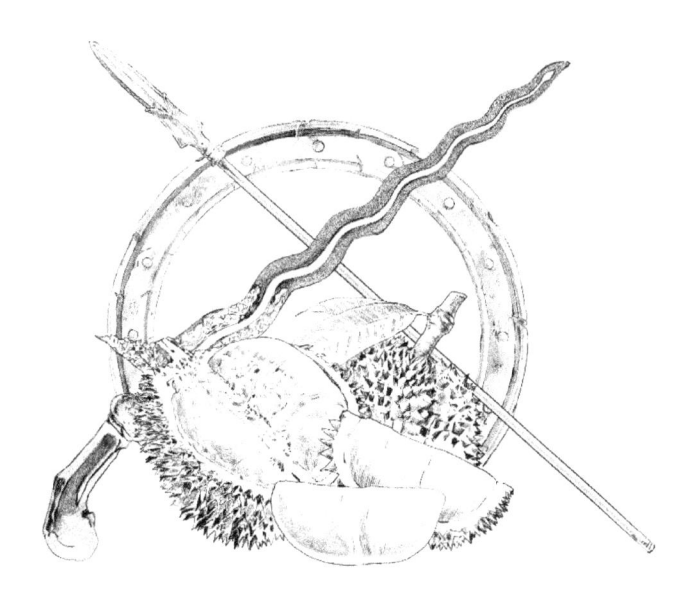

It made a lot of sense, at least at first, to Arthur. Especially a few hours ago, before he had to trek through the darkness in search of those assholes. Traveling through the night was the worst, because all the markers that he was used to looking out for faded in the darkness and a whole new host of monsters awoke.

"Quieter!" Uswah hissed for the umpteenth time that hour. She turned around and glared at Arthur.

"I'm trying! I can't see anything," Arthur groused. Even with his Enhanced Eyesight trait, between the current lack of moonlight, the heavy foliage above, and his unfamiliarity with the area, he was short on his usual grace and stealthiness. Unlike Uswah who seemed to wrap herself in shadows and managed to just be as quiet, if not more, than during the day. It was really, really annoying.

"Then you shouldn't have come," Uswah said, exasperated. They were both speaking softly, though not to the point of whispering. They knew better than to whisper for whispering sent words further than just speaking softly. A weird trick of harmonics, that. But the fact they were even talking was probably a break in good sense. "They're close. Now, please. Softly."

Arthur grunted in agreement. Together, the pair slowly drifted forward, heading for the clearing that glowed with flickering light. Finding it had taken them about an hour, Uswah's initial estimate of where their followers had gone to ground incorrect. Whether they had worried about being found out or had just located a better campground, the pair had only found the group upon spotting their fire, after Arthur had climbed a taller-than-normal tree on a rise.

Now, the fire had dimmed significantly, only flickering light from faded coals. The pair crouched low as they snuck forward, Uswah taking the lead and scanning the surroundings for watchers. Yet, neither party saw the actual guard until they were within a few feet.

Arthur's heart thudded in his chest, so loud that he could have sworn the other person heard him. Palms wet, breath coming all too slowly, he continued to stare as he waited for some sign that the other man had noticed. In doing so, he had more time than ever to watch him.

Pudgy, slumped over with a stained, dark shirt and black jeans. A rather robust beard on dark skin. Northern Indian, or perhaps Bangladeshi. Probably that, actually, considering the sheer volume of illegal immigrants who had arrived in Malaysia, looking for work. Most had worked in the construction industry until the jobs disappeared and then found themselves without any way back.

Uswah froze as well, a little ahead but nearly as far away from the other as Arthur himself. She'd gone left when Arthur had gone right around a bushy obstruction. For long minutes, the pair stared at the figure that just lay there in shadows, unmoving.

Muscles began to cramp as Arthur stayed frozen and crouched, trying not to blink. Trying not to breathe. Every second stretched on, and on. Sweat began to drip down his nose, an itch near the side of his torso begged him to scratch at it.

And then, the head shifted. A snort, a huff, and then a low, startling noise arose from the guard. One that sent a rush of adrenaline through Arthur as he straightened, hand falling to the hilt of his knife.

But the guard was asleep. Asleep!

Caught between relief and readiness to attack, Arthur stared at the inert body before he stalked away. One of his footsteps came down on a branch, cracking it open, and Arthur froze. He turned, only to see that the sleeping watcher hadn't even shifted.

Uswah was by his side by the time he turned back, glaring at Arthur. For a second, he struggled with his own feelings before Arthur inclined his head and dropped down again into a crouch. Silent chastisement finished, she led the way once more, the pair crouched at the edge of the clearing moments later.

Silently, the pair counted the number of figures. Nine that they could see. Including the guard, that would be ten. They waited for another long, interminable period where not a single figure stirred, the entire group either deep in cultivation—three figures, eyes closed—or asleep.

And then, Uswah gestured for them to back off. It took them a while to move away from both the guard and the rest of the group, before the woman was willing to speak again.

"So?"

"Definitely following us, I'd say," Arthur said. He could not think of a reason for such a group to be coming out this way, not so close to where they were. It was not as though they were taking the most direct route to the orang minyak village.

"And?"

Frowning, Arthur didn't not answer immediately. Could he justify acting against them, on just a base suspicion? If he could, how far was he willing to go? On the other hand, could he refuse to act, knowing that they might attempt to attack his team later?

At which point did self-defence become offense? Did such concepts and morality even exist in the Tower, where survival of the fittest was the prevailing wisdom? Then again, was not the idea of the Benevolent Durians the antithesis of such self-interest? And if he attacked now, would he be betraying his clan's ideals?

Yet...

"If we let them attack, I'm putting our people at risk," Arthur said softly.

"Right."

"But we can't just kill them," Arthur said, firmly.

"Okay."

"Leaving them alone, though... that doesn't sit well with me."

"Ya."

"You're being very helpful."

"Not my place."

Arthur grunted and nodded. She was not wrong. He had chosen to come here because he was the one in charge, after all. At the end of the day, he was here because he wanted, no, needed to be the one to make this call.

So he best make it.

Chapter 48

It was only a few hours before dawn by the time Arthur and Uswah rejoined the rest of the team. Casey popped right up when the pair finally made their presence known, making a small cacophony with the clatter of weapons and goods they were carrying. Most of the other team members woke, only Rick and Jan managing to sleep through the noise.

"What is all that?" Casey said, eyes bulging. "And what took you so long?"

"Their stuff," Arthur said, tossing a bundle of spears into the center of the group where they bounced off the ground. Grunting, he unslung the heavy backpack he was wearing.

"You killed them," Casey said, awed. There was something else in her voice, something Arthur could not place immediately.

"Of course not," Arthur said.

"Oh." Was that disappointment in Casey's voice?

"Eh? Then?" Definitely disappointment in Jan's as she helped Uswah with the bundle that was strapped around her back. She frowned as she dug into the pack, swearing a little as she cut herself on a badly packed parang.

"We stole their weapons and cores," Arthur said. "Not all their weapons, just most of them." He grinned, pulling open his backpack to showcase the three crossbows he had picked up and the bundle of bolts within. "They've got some parangs and swords left."

"Took all their spears, though. And ranged weapons," Uswah said, unable to keep herself from smiling.

"Really. So you thought stealing from them was the answer?" Casey said.

"Yes," Arthur replied, waving the others over to grab the weapons. He then walked over to Rick and kicked at his feet, nearly jumping when the first thing Rick did upon waking was to grab and point his pistol, only stopping when he saw he had the weapon pointed at Arthur.

"Shit, man. Don't wake a man like that."

"Fine. How should we wake you?"

"Call my name?"

"Right, sweetie pie. Got it," Arthur said sarcastically as he backed away and Rick holstered his weapon. He was not going to let Rick know he might have peed on himself a little when that all-too-big pistol was pointed at him.

Gods, he hated guns.

"Why'd you wake me?" Rick complained.

"More crossbows. Smaller than the one you have. Figured you'd want one?" Arthur said with a shrug. He had considered grabbing one himself, but he just did not know how to shoot one well. Problems for the future. Anyway, he had his sling and Focused Strike, which worked well enough with some modifications and experience using it.

"Oooh, I could, maybe…" Rick clambered to his feet, grabbing his own crossbow and the belt with bolts, buckling it on before wandering over. That was the point that Arthur realised the young man had literally slept with guns under his arms, which was…

"Uncomfortable, no?" Arthur muttered to himself. But since he didn't get a reply, he left everyone else to divvy up the gear. Which, sadly, still left them with extras.

"What do you want to do with these?" Mel said, gesturing to the pair of extra spears and trio of parangs that no one had taken.

"We keep the parang," Arthur said. "The clan could always use more." The spears were a problem, since they were unwieldly to carry around. "Let's chop off the spearheads. We can always make shafts, but the metal is harder to find."

Jan and Yao Jing happily got to destroying things while Casey looked on disapprovingly. Deciding he should deal with that matter early, Arthur wandered over to the woman and raised an eyebrow. "What?"

"Why not just kill them?" Casey said.

"Do you want to be partnered with a psychopath?" Arthur asked.

"No, but it's more efficient. My uncle would have wanted them dead."

"I'm not your uncle. Or your family," Arthur said, though he made note of what she'd said. Not that it was particularly surprising. There was a reason the big players were, well, big players. A certain level of ruthlessness was required. "I'm not going to kill people just for following us. They might not actually have intended to hurt us but just pick up whatever they can. Or, you know, pick from our corpses."

"And if they intended to attack us?"

"That's why we stole their stuff."

"What happens if they follow us?"

"Without weapons?" Arthur snorted. "If they're still on our tail by tomorrow morning, we'll deal with them." He let his voice harden. "Permanently."

Lam, standing behind Casey as usual, nodded a little, looking satisfied by Arthur's answer. Casey on the other hand seemed less enthused, but she did reluctantly nod in the end. Arthur wondered if she was upset because he didn't want them dead right now. Or for some other, unknowable reason.

People were complex and the rich and powerful even more so.

"Now what, ah?" Yao Jing said, holding aloft the broken shafts. He wielded one idly, as though he intended to use it as a walking stick now. Which made no sense to Arthur since he might as well as have used a whole spear, but that was not a point worth arguing. "Sleep? Or we're leaving now?"

Arthur hesitated, then shook his head, recollecting how hard it was to travel in the dark. Never mind the few nocturnal animals he had to kill. A large group like theirs would be even more vulnerable for the noise they'd make. "No. We cultivate for a few hours and then once light arrives, we leave."

Then he grinned, finding a comfortable spot and flopping down. "Or you guys will. I'm sleeping." Then, closing his eyes resolutely, he caught finally some rest.

After all, they had a long set of days left before they reached the final village and their next trial.

Chapter 49

The first sign that things were going to be messy arrived in the form of larger-than-normal scouting parties. Instead of the small parties of one to three orang minyak that they had come to expect near a village, the groups they encountered here had three to five oily men. In and of itself, the additional scouts were a non-issue for the team.

Dealing with them were fast and efficient. In fact, Arthur started utilizing the skirmishes as an attempt to expand upon his fighting techniques, attempting difficult and often flashy techniques against his opponents while also circulating the Bark Skin technique through his body. The additional pressure over the last few days and the occasional, painful backlashes helped Arthur improve his understanding of Bark Skin significantly.

Nothing like adrenaline and fear for one's life to improve one's abilities.

But the increased number of scouts was a concern, never mind how illogical it was that these scouts grew in number when bad weather approached but never entered a village unless it was attacked.

And what greeted them upon arrival at the fourth village was over and above Arthur's pessimistic considerations.

"A wall." He sighed, rubbing his face. "Did someone drop the ball? Because I'm sure, this is not a lure, and no one mentioned, a big damn wall."

"That wasn't a rhyme at the end," Mel noted.

"Wall!" Arthur stressed, gesturing through the treeline towards the impediment.

"Looks weak," Jan said.

"It's eight feet tall. It's good enough to stop us from looking in," Arthur said. "Who knows what else is in there?"

"Dunno," Jan said plainly. "Must look first, *lah*."

"Great." Arthur made a face, eyeing the big gate they'd made their way over to look at. "Are there more ways in? Multiple gates?" Already, after complaining, his mind was wheeling. Perhaps the wall could be of use. The creatures never seemed to have much in terms of ranged weapons. With the addition of the crossbows they'd "acquired," the team had some decent ranged firepower now. Could they perhaps block up the exits and wage war from the outside?

"I'll find out," Uswah said, rising to her feet. Within moments she was gone, leaving Arthur contemplating how damn useful she was, despite whatever she said about being useless.

"We could bottleneck them," Casey said, echoing his unspoken thoughts. "Kill them as they try to exit."

"Maybe pincer," Rick said, looking excited. "We send a strike force in, attack them from behind."

"And get overwhelmed inside and outside?" Casey replied, snorting. "Splitting and getting defeated in detail is a horrible idea."

"Not if I'm in the strike force," Rick said, raising his chin.

"Only takes one lucky hit..."

Arthur tuned out that argument, letting them discuss matters. Instead, he was eyeing the walls, imagining the orang minyak and their hands, their size and the way they clambered around. Perhaps he was wrong, perhaps they would try to crowd out of the gates. But for creatures that could climb and leap pretty high, and who were used to living in the jungle, would an eight-foot wall prove impossible?

And if not, would gates matter?

He now regretted sending Uswah off. Then as his thoughts turned over the options, he pushed those regrets aside. They still needed information, especially since their initial plan was not going to work.

"I don't think fighting them directly is a good idea," Arthur said softly. "I think we should try to at least do this smart."

"That's why we should block them from coming out," Casey said. "Fight them in smaller numbers."

"No, more than that. We should try luring them out. Defeat in detail, was that what you said?" Arthur said.

"We discussed that before. The answer was no."

"Before we knew about the wall. And whatever else is in there."

"Why do you keep saying that?" Casey said.

Arthur opened his mouth to answer and then frowned. It was not as though they hadn't learned what they could about the villages, though the villages themselves did vary—from composition to layout to the exact number of monsters within. Never major variations, but just enough to keep things interesting. So the wall was within expectations. But why did he keep thinking there was going to be more?

"No reason, right?" Casey said. "So let's just hit them and finish this."

"You're too impatient," Arthur said eventually. "And maybe I'm too paranoid. But we can slow down, play this safer. It won't hurt us." He gestured backwards. "We saw a few places that might work. Make some basic traps, fallback points. It'll cost us, what? A half-day? A day?"

"Exactly!" She leaned forward. "Time we don't have."

"I know we're behind your schedule," Arthur said softly. "But that'll change as we climb. When the buildings give us an edge when the cores aren't as common, when we don't have people feeding us resources."

Casey looked mulish but stopped objecting. Arthur sent some of the team back the way they came to start laying out some traps. Nothing too elaborate, of course. Just trip wires, a few pongee sticks that would snap back and impale enemies, and a few stacks of wood shifted to cut off entry and allow people to fight from a guarded position.

By the time Uswah came back to report on the compound, the group was halfway ready, with their current space rebuilt such that they could fall back if needed.

"Now remember, they marked the way back," Arthur said, eyeing the group as they congregated. Jan was wiping her blade clean, the trio of Jan, Yao Jing, and Mel having swept the surroundings to finish off any nearby scouts. "Keep to the path. Don't stray or else... traps."

"We know," Mel said firmly. "We doing this?"

Arthur looked around, waited for confirmation, then nodded. It looked like they really were.

Chapter 50

The group marched forward, Arthur and Yao Jing leading the way. Casey, Rick, Lam and, surprisingly, even Jan were the ones wielding the crossbows this time, with Mel adding to the fusillade with her spinning sling. Arthur had kept his packed away, instead opting to form a Refined Energy Dart over his third eye for use later. As for Uswah, their scout was hanging back in the treeline, able to use the majority of her skills from there and, also, spot orang minyak reinforcements coming from outside the village.

Prepped as best they could, the group strode towards the open gate. No guards there, but an unlucky orang minyak was caught crossing in front of it. A bolt sprouted from its head, nearly shearing the majority of it off as it punched through.

Arthur slowed and stopped, waiting as Rick reloaded the weapon. It did not matter if he took his time, since he preferred not to go in. Even if the huts within looked similar to the other villages they had hit with the same shanty town appearance—though larger and more numerous, of course—he knew that the irregular placement would put them in danger of being flanked if they stepped within.

Better to stay outside, better to wait. Better to draw them out.

"Come on," Casey grumbled. "Why did you pick something so damn big?"

"Stopping power," Rick said, grunting as his arms strained. He managed to haul the arm back finally, and he lifted the entire contraption to load another bolt. "This is the way."

"It's how you use it." To punctuate her point, Casey fired, sending the bolt through the head of an oily man that had hauled itself up the wall to look over before its unfortunate demise. "See?"

Arthur snorted, but since the other crossbows were actually smaller and easier to reload on the fly, he started forward again. Thirty feet, twenty...

Then, a racket of shouts and screams, unintelligible to his ears, rose from within the village. He could see the humanoid monsters gathering near the gate, though the crowd fell pretty fast as bolts flew now, loosing as soon as they had a target. Jan missed, but Lam winged his target. A fast-moving slingstone cracked against a body and made its target howl before another crossbow bolt from Casey took the monster in the stomach, dropping it to the ground to clutch and scrabble at its wounds.

Ten feet before the gate, Arthur called a halt. They could not see around the corners, but urgent whispers from Yao Jing had him glancing at the sides of the walls. He watched as one orang minyak managed to clamber over a wall before tendrils of shadow grabbed it and pulled it over, headfirst onto the ground behind the wall. The sickening crunch of its fall and snap of bone spoke of its demise.

"I hate being right," Arthur muttered, for rather than face direct fire at the gate, the monsters were scrambling up the walls. "Fire on the climbers. Rick, hold off for the center."

"I could pick them off with my pistols," the gunslinger offered.

"Wait." Still Arthur wondered what it was that was making him hesitant.

The click of crossbow bolts leaving their seating, the twang of string releasing and metal unbending, filled the air briefly. This time, all shots hit, some more fatally than others. Arthur noted the hesitation, the retreat of fingers over the ledge as the creatures paused to assess their options.

Then, movement. A large group hurrying down the street and carrying... "Is that a door?" Arthur said, jaw dropping a little. He had expected an adaptive response, but a door? "Rick..."

He might as well not have bothered. The gunslinger had already raised his overly large crossbow, seated it snugly onto his shoulder, then fired. The large broadhead of the crossbow bolt not only punched through the door but also punctured a creature behind it, causing the impromptu defence to fall.

Not that it mattered, for now the gathered monsters charged. Releasing howls and yips, as though understanding that taking their time would prove fatal, they came running through the gate and clambering over the wall.

"Fire!" Arthur commanded, picking the closest fool on the wall to loose his own Refined Energy Dart at. It punched through hand and upraised arm. His opponent fell and hurt itself on the wall's spikey edge.

Crossbow bolts released and the cultivators reloaded as quickly as they could. The deep thump and bark of Rick's pistol consumed the silence. Semi-automatic weapons that had twenty-one bullets in each magazine—not clip, though Arthur didn't give a shit about correct terminology—meant that he could fire forty-two times before reloading.

Of course, it took anywhere from two to five bullets to end a monster's life, depending on accuracy, placement, and sheer luck. You could hit a heart, but they had two. Plus the monsters were hyped up on adrenaline, or whatever monster equivalent. Crack sternums, shatter ribs, and fill lungs—yet they would keep coming.

At least for a while.

Ten seconds, twenty. Monsters rushed forward and were met with bullets and crossbow bolts. And when they finally reached the team's frontline, they met fist and spear.

Arthur ducked left, mindful not to step right at all and thrust. The blade of his spear entered an arm, was ripped out, and then slashed downward. Cutting into tendon and muscle near the kneecap before he twisted and cracked the backend across a face. He spun on the tip of his toes, kicked, and dropped the monster back further.

But as good as Arthur's team was now—practised and efficient—creatures kept coming in numbers. Somehow, forty suddenly seemed like too many for their team to handle. Though shadow tendrils rose up from the ground and gripped at bodies, even as bullets tore holes in furred bodies and crossbow bolts injured and killed at range, the orang minyak were too many.

"Retreat!" Arthur called. He could sense it: the fear, the desperation, the determination. The shift in battle as one side was about to crumble. "Back off, Yao Jing!"

The brawler's answer was to surge forward, grapple an opponent, then—lifting it off the ground—throw the oiled monster into the incoming group. It bowled over several orang minyak. Yao Jing skipped back and sideways, eliciting a curse from Rick who had jerked his hand up at the last second, his shot spoiled.

But now that they had space, even as Arthur loosed another Refined Energy Dart to create his own gap, the team retreated. No turning and running, but a careful and controlled backing away. Ranged weapons were discarded and melee weapons drawn. They retreated.

Slowly.

Even as more orang minyak swarmed out of the village like a flood of ants.

Chapter 51

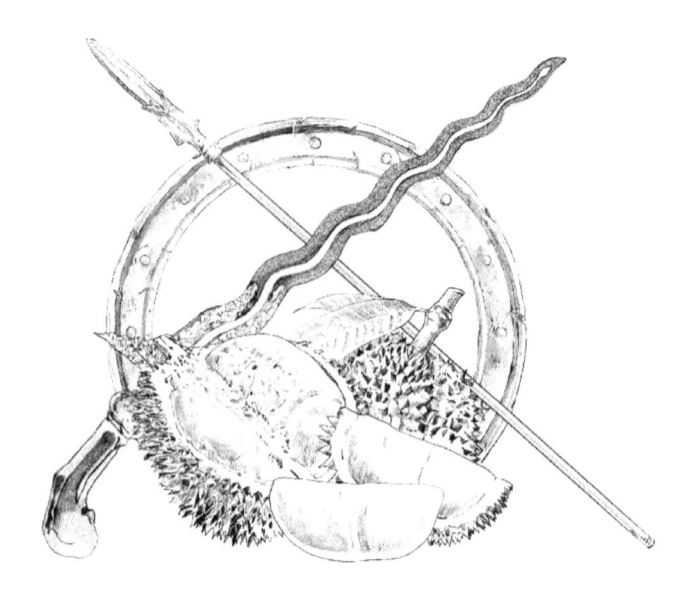

Arthur stabbed and cut amidst the press of fur and claws and even weapons. The orang minyak swung simple tools and weapons that, rudimentary as they were, could deal significant damage if he missed a dodge or block.

Then he had to fall back, and now he realised why armies used the same weapons, fought the same way all the time. His greater reach with a spear meant he could ward off more blows, retreat more slowly.

Yao Jing was a grappler; he fought with fists and arms. His legs, too, when needed. In a scrum, he was tough, stronger than any individual Arthur had met, and well trained. On the other hand, when they were being swarmed by orang minyak here and his job was to hold them back while retreating slowly?

He failed. Against a group, he could do little but duck and weave and punch whatever came close enough. His projected chi fist exploded into the fray once in a while, but he could only use the technique so many times.

For the first dozen feet, they were on the backfoot, almost backpedalling constantly. More than once, having to retreat so fast, Arthur and Yao Jing nearly tripped and fell. Only the sudden intervention of Rick's bullet or Uswah's grasping shadow tentacle managed to keep their line from collapsing entirely.

Teetering on failure, sweat flying, breath exploding with each exhale.

Chaos reigned, until—like a breath of fresh air—the rest of the team arrived. Yao Jing fell back, allowed to take a backline effort. He kept in check monsters that tried to flank them. Jan did the same on the other side of the team as the others took to the front line.

Only Rick stayed behind, his weapons barking. Until they stopped.

"Reloading!"

Arthur nearly froze before he pushed the surprise aside. Additional energy from his core flooded into his body, Heavenly Sage's Mischief taking full effect to empower his strikes. He swung hard and fast, battering monsters back with each swing of the spear, its tip glistening with blood.

The rest of the team unleashed their own techniques. Mel's halberd grew in size and sharpness, the weapon still light as a feather as it struck monsters with greater lethality. Lam's technique was only a little less showy, causing him to speed up until he was a blur. Casey empowered the crescent blades of energy she projected from her sword, cutting into monsters one after the other.

Yao Jing's body gained a sheen, like it was covered by energy as hard as stone, and the man waded deeper into the fight, caring less about getting struck now. He punched monsters with attacks empowered by a small explosion of chi and sound, blasting them back.

Jan's technique was similar to Lam's; speed-based cultivation techniques were, after all, quite popular. Arthur had one too, though his focused on whole-body improvement rather than pure speed like Jan's and Lam's. Still, when you had enchanted weapons in play, strength was often less important than speed. The curved, guardless blades of Jan's twin parangs sliced easily into the monsters.

But the team could not keep such a pace forever. If nothing else, their stamina and energy would bottom out soon enough. But for a short period, whilst their companion reloaded, it was a non-issue. In an explosion of gore, they even managed to push all the monsters back, and the orang minyak seemed surprised by the burst of ferocity.

"Loaded!"

The roar of bullets punctuated the words moments later. The pistols fired slow, though, Rick taking care to pick his shots with the team being so close to their enemies. He took care to attack only when he had a clear shot.

With the added weight of Rick's firepower, the tide of the battle shifted in their favour finally. The seemingly never-ending numbers decreased, and it looked like the last of the creatures had come out of the village now. Some ran around Arthur's team, hoping to catch them on the sides. But with many orang minyak still on the front line, it was a secondary concern. Uswah picked them off anyway, grabbing them with shadowy tendrils, and a bullet would inevitably find them.

To Arthur's surprise, their planned fallback position was not required. They had been pushed nearly to the edge of the clearing they had prepared, but they'd been able to hold their current position. The creatures could split up, but none of them wanted to stay out of the fight too long. Whether it was instinct or base aggression, they chose to come in close as fast as they could rather than take their time. It was perhaps the right choice, for if they traveled too far, Rick and his bullets would find them.

As energy ran out of Arthur's empowered body, he began retreating again. He was the first to do so, and the others followed soon after. All but Yao Jing, who was gripping one of the creatures by the head and dragging it along as he retreated, throwing uppercuts one after the other as he did so. His slow retreat allowed him to be assailed by a small mob of orang minyak. But he refused to let go, and was blood streaming down his side.

"Idiot!" Arthur snarled. Of course, he was too far away to do anything about it, so he had no choice but to wait, stabbing listlessly with his spear to keep monsters off him.

Then, just as things were stabilizing, a roar rose from the compound. Eyes swivelled and even the monsters fell back a little.

An orang minyak twice the size of these ones stalked out of the village, a massive sledgehammer in hand.

"Oh hell," Arthur swore. "Of course I was right."

Good thing they had a backup plan.

Chapter 52

"You shot it," Arthur said a half hour later, hands bloody and plunged midway through an orang minyak's body.

"Well, yes. Did you expect me to fight it hand-to-hand?" Rick said, puzzled.

"No, but you shot it."

"He wanted to fight it himself," Mel said, working a short distance away on the same task—extracting cores.

"No, but he shot it!"

"You said that already," Casey said. "Though, I actually wouldn't have minded trying my blade against it."

Arthur saw Lam wince at that.

"You're nuts," Arthur said firmly to Casey. "We're only slightly better than one-on-one right now, and taking that thing on would definitely have been a loss."

"Then, what's the point?" Casey said.

"Oh!" Uswah said. She had been silently on watch rather than digging into corpses. Looking at Arthur, she said, "It's that vidmeme!"

"What?" everyone else said.

"The vidmeme. The one with the Middle Eastern swordsman waving his blade around and then he gets shot. Arthur's trying to be, umm..." Uswah frowned. "Dated?"

"It's not that dated!" Arthur protested. "And it's a golden oldies classic!"

"Ooooh, that was popular for a bit, wasn't it? Sometime in the 20th century?" Mel shook her head. "And there was a push by the Hollywood studios to make it a thing again, what, ten years ago?"

"Twelve," Yao Jing said. "It was when they had *King Kong* playing."

"Oh, with Godzilla!" Casey said brightly.

"Oooh, where Kong and Godzilla fight?" Rick said.

"Freddy and Jason versus Godzilla better, *lah*," Jan said.

"There was such a show?" Rick's eyes grew wide.

Excitedly, Uswah added, "*Monster Mash 4!*"

". . . 4?" Rick said, his voice filled with dawning horror.

Arthur groaned, burying his face in his hands and then immediately regretting the action since he hadn't washed his hands yet. Making a face, he pulled gore-filled hands away and walked off to the next monster. With nearly everyone involved in harvesting, the process went by relatively fast.

Once they were done, the group quietly gathered the cores together and checked the count. Including the extra large one from the final boss—Hah! Not much of a boss when one could simply shoot it repeatedly in the head from a distance—the battle had gained them over sixty cores.

"A lot more than the quest said. And I read what it 'cause I was afraid," Arthur muttered. "Even with the scouts thrown in, it shouldn't have been that many."

"We did have to deal with the adds after Rick dropped the boss," Casey said.

"Still..." Arthur frowned. "The quest said forty."

"Approximately," Casey replied. "You know these things change."

"Yeah." He fell silent for a moment. "Could it be an evolution? A revolution?"

The words sent a shiver through the group. Everyone knew what he meant, though no one liked it. One of the greatest concerns about Tower climbing were floor evolutions. To a smaller extent, there was also concern over a whole Tower evolution, though those were even rarer.

The terms were self-explanatory: a process of change in the Tower. As more and more individuals passed a floor, the Tower seemed to adapt. Sometimes, that adaptation was as simple as introducing new monsters or changing the kind of monsters that showed up at any one time. Other times, those evolutions could be more wide-ranging. In most cases, the evolutions were always to make the floors harder and nearly always because a higher percentage of individuals were passing through floors than before.

And no surprise, each evolution always preceded a spike in climber deaths. It was one thing climbing a Tower knowing what to expect. Another to do it in the dark. It took a special kind of individual to be willing to do that.

"The last floor, that trial, it was different too, wasn't it?" Arthur said, softly.

"It was," Mel confirmed.

More confirmations, from those who recalled reading up Tower information. Even those who had little interest in climbing would at least read up on the first few floors. If nothing else, it became part of the popular lexicon.

"Once is chance, twice is coincidence," Arthur said.

"How about three?" Yao Jing said, confused.

"Oh you himbo," Jan said sweetly and smiled at Yao Jing when he looked over, clueless as to her meaning.

"Three means we're likely seeing an evolution. Whether it's just the first set of floors or the whole Tower itself. We won't know till we push ahead," Mel said. "But it's something to keep in mind. Especially if we're going to try cutting it close…"

"Are you looking at me?" Casey said angrily. "I feel like you're looking at me when you say that."

"It's your speedrun."

"You agreed to it!"

"Before we knew there was an evolution."

"We don't know if there's an evolution yet!"

"Enough," Arthur cut the two women off before the argument could spiral. He clapped his still-sticky hands together. "We don't know. We won't know. And we'll worry about it later. We're safe for this floor, and we have better things to do than sit around arguing." He waved a hand about. "Especially in a hostile environment. Let's get clean, packed and moving. We can argue, if you have to argue, when we're back."

Arthur watched as everyone acknowledged his words and got moving. He smiled a little grimly before he relaxed, grateful to have cut that disturbing conversation off. Now, all he had to do was convince himself that there was nothing to worry about.

Easier thought than done.

Chapter 53

Cultivation was never actually fun. Arthur knew some people found tranquility and peace in it, and he had done enough meditation that he could achieve those states of serenity for a time. But for the most part, the mind had to be active enough during the process that one couldn't actually consider it meditating. Outside of a few cultivation fanatics, most people just found the task tediously repetitive.

Like going to the gym, but even more boring.

Arthur never found the actual act of cultivating fun. Long years of discipline helped him keep going longer than others, and he knew how to break up his routine sufficiently so that he never actually grew too bored. But there was, he had to admit, something extra boring about cultivating while sitting in a room. Compared to his early months in the Tower, when he had nothing to his name and no abilities, the safe but all-too-quiet sessions of cultivation and study in the clan building were practically torture.

In between he had administrative meetings, of course. Ones he was forced to join, being clan head and all. But while he did not care for these meetings, at least there he could find some amusement.

"And eleven tins of *kueh kapit* a month," Arthur said firmly. "And we're talking big Milo tins here, not canned-food size."

His pronouncement had much the effect he expected, causing the group to start. The young man sitting across from Arthur stared at him, jaw shutting before he spluttered, "What?"

"You heard me. Once you exit with our help, you supply us eleven tins a month. We'll handle the delivery, but you have to supply it," Arthur said adamantly.

"Eleven?"

"Yes. And that's not negotiable."

"Why me?" the young man said.

"Su Mei said you're Nyonya?" Arthur said. A slight nod from the young man of mixed-race heritage. "Then you'll know where to get the good stuff. And eleven tins should be nothing once you're out."

"I could just give you more money."

"Eleven tins." Arms crossed, Arthur waited for the man to nod in assent before he drifted out.

Only then did Su Mei looked at Arthur, perplexed. "Really?"

"Ehh, I'm sure he could do it. And the additional clause and weirdness will keep him on his toes. If he starts forgetting what he owes us, that'll likely be the first to go," Arthur replied. "My green M&Ms."

"What?"

"Never mind. I might be misremembering it."

"But why eleven?" Siao Mei said. "It's oddly specific."

"A man's got to eat, you know?"

***

"This technique manual is around eighty percent accurate," boasted the balding man on the other side of the table. "We've got two out of ten people studying Harvesting Rain. With this technique you can tap into ambient humidity. Perfect if you ever run into a desert environment."

"Which is not present on the first few floors of the Tower," Jaswinder said, bored. "We don't—"

"Four copies. You create four copies of the manual and we'll pay you," Arthur cut in.

"Four copies?" The man frowned. "We are looking to sell a single copy."

"One copy or four, it's just a question of who spends the ink." Arthur pointed a finger at him. "That's you. Or the deal is off."

"The deal is already off," Jaswinder complained. "We have a budget, boss."

Eyes darting between the two, the man grunted. "Eleven cores."

"Four."

"Daylight robbery!"

"I'm not the one trying to sell snow to Eskimos," Arthur said. "Three cores."

The man opened his mouth to object, then seeing the glint in Arthur's eyes chose to give a single, jerky nod.

"Perfect. Payment on delivery." When the man left, looking annoyed, Arthur gave Jaswinder a thumbs up. "You were great playing the part of the customer who doesn't want the goods."

"That's because we don't! What's the point of having that technique?"

Arthur smiled. "None. But there's always the future."

"So you want to join the Durians?" Arthur said.

The young woman was barely over eighteen at most, if Arthur was being generous. Frankly, she looked fourteen, but some women had baby faces. He had one too, till he reached his early twenties. Still, being shy was not helping her case right now.

"Okay," he continued. "Then, the most important question: Durians, bitter or not?" He stared at her seriously, while the young woman looked surprised. She started to turn towards Jaswinder when Arthur added, "Don't look at her. Just answer the question."

"Uhhh. Not bitter. I like it a little sweet," she said.

"Hmmm." Arthur nodded and sat back. For the rest of the meeting, the poor girl kept looking at him nervously as she answered the remainder of questions, which came from Jaswinder. In the end, she was dismissed.

"And what was that for?" Jaswinder said. "Bitter or sweet?"

Arthur grinned. "Just having a little fun." He stood up, stretching. "Let her in."

"So sweet's the right answer?"

"Oh, hell no. Not my problem what she likes to eat. But the rest of her answers were good, even when she was nervous. She's truthful, even when she's not sure if it'll get her kicked out." He smiled grimly. "We'll need people like that."

He left her with that to think about, while he went back to refining cores. The plan was to use up the cores they had acquired and whatever the Chin family could provide. Soon enough, it would be time for the next floor.

Chapter 54

Arthur watched the parang flash by his eyes, just inches from taking his nose off. He waited a blink, just far enough for the hand that gripped the parang to swing by his chest before he beat it with the knuckles of his right hand. He struck hard, slamming into the small bones of her hand and causing a shock through the tendons in her fingers, forcing them to spasm open.

Weapon clattering to the ground, Jan shifted her front foot back and pulled her injured hand away. At the same time, her opposite hand came upward, rotating over so that she could swing a knife hand strike at his throat. Arthur dodged the attack, lashing out with a cut kick to her new lead leg. She growled, pulling her leg back and moving away from his attack.

Arthur kept pushing, the pair flowing through forms. Occasionally he moved too slow, and the parang blade cut into upraised arms, bare torso, or his thigh. The weapon was blunted by the Bark Skin technique he had activated, but even so, it was not Iron Body or Steel Body or one of the higher-grade defensive systems. As such, with sufficient force, cuts bloomed along his body.

Blood and sweat ran down both their bodies. Rough exhalations and the occasional grunt of pain rose from around them as well. The pair were not the only ones fighting this morning along the land they'd fenced off near the clan building. The remnants of the neighboring building they'd purchased still showed, mostly in the wood of the fences they'd repurposed from the building.

When the bell rang finally, the pair sprang away from one another, creating enough space that a surprise attack was no longer possible. Then, and only then, did they relax. Arthur bowed a little to Jan automatically, a time-honored tradition ground into him over the years. Jan just grunted as she grabbed her parang from the ground and wandered over to where they'd left their water bottles.

Arthur joined her a moment later, grabbing a towel and wiping himself down. He saw the blood and sweat streaked across him, surface wounds beneath already half-closed. "Thanks for the fight."

"You put more into Body, ah?" Jan said.

"I did," Arthur said. "I'm up another two so I'm now cool."

A snort from the sidelines which Arthur ignored. Everyone was a critic.

"Ei, don't forget the rest, okay? If you forget, more problems," Jan said. "You the boss, not Yao Jing. Even he got put points there."

"I know," Arthur said, firmly. "But we've got another trial coming up on the third floor, I've got to pass it."

"Ya *lah*," Jan said. "Just, remember."

Watching her head over to speak with someone else, Arthur let out a long breath. They were coming to their final day. Casey had exited cultivating yesterday and she was the one with the most resources to burn. Truth was, he and the others were just passing time, training and fighting and cultivating while waiting for her. And, of course, setting up the clan further on this floor.

Given the spare moment, and while his breathing was still calming—though that was happening fast—he called up his stats to review the changes.

Cultivation Speed: 2.371 Yin
Energy Pool: 16/21 (Yin)
Refinement Speed: 0.1421
Refined Energy: 0.823 (25)

Attributes and Traits
Mind: 15 (Multi-Tasking, Quick Learner, Perfect Recall)
Body: 12 (Enhanced Eyesight, Yin Body, Swiftness)
Spirit: 10 (Sticky Energy, From the Dregs)

Techniques
Night Emperor Cultivation Technique
Focused Strike
Accelerated Healing – Refined Energy (Grade III)
Heavenly Sage's Mischief
Refined Energy Dart
Bark Skin

Partial Techniques
Simultaneous Flow (41.2%)
Yin-Yang Energy Exchange (32.56%)
Heavenly Sage's Heaven Beating Stick (31.8%)

He had poured more points and cores into his body than ever, refining the energy over and over again and empowering himself. He'd gone with increasing his Mind stat first, pouring as many attribute points into it as he could afford. Perfect Recall was the trait that he'd picked up this time, but the name was not exactly accurate. The trait improved memory for sure, but it was based off the Mind stat. The higher that went, the better his recall. And like the rest of his Mind traits, it synchronized well, such that he could feel his mind thinking and recalling and processing things faster than ever.

It was kind of scary, in fact, how much better he could think now. There were certain limitations in terms of what the improvement in Mind could do. You couldn't turn someone of below average intelligence into Einstein. Certain fundamental aspects of an individual—or perhaps, of how they used their mind—just couldn't be changed by the Tower.

On the other hand, a number of neurological or neurodivergent symptoms could be dealt with. Have trouble concentrating? Well, certain traits could help fix that. Not entirely, but often better than the drugs that were prescribed.

Arthur knew there were arguments about it on both sides. Some were all for jumping on the fixes, anything to help them live their lives easier or simpler. A fringe element considered the Tower and the way it altered the neurodivergent a genocidal act prescribed upon them. Of course, the them was undefined or just plain crazy – well, as crazy as calling the Tower creators green skinned aliens or shape-changers or floating jelly fishes, which since no one knew anything might not be that crazy – but it was a recurring theme of doubt and mistrust aimed at the Tower.

In either case, improving his Mind helped him study and gain the Bark Skin technique at last, which increased his overall ability to survive—perhaps even more than upping his Body attribute, though he'd taken the time to do that too. His Spirit required the least amount of improvement since he had a cultivation technique.

While he was not, in any way, feeling confident about their upcoming ascension, he figured that Bark Skin and an upgraded Body would help him at least survive initially. If Casey was willing to wait another week, he might even finish learning the Heavenly Sage's Heaven Beating Stick technique, but that was as futile as expecting a politician not to take a bribe.

No.

They were headed up, and whether the clan would hold or not in his absence on this level, he could only hope.

Anyway, the third floor couldn't be that bad, right?

Chapter 55

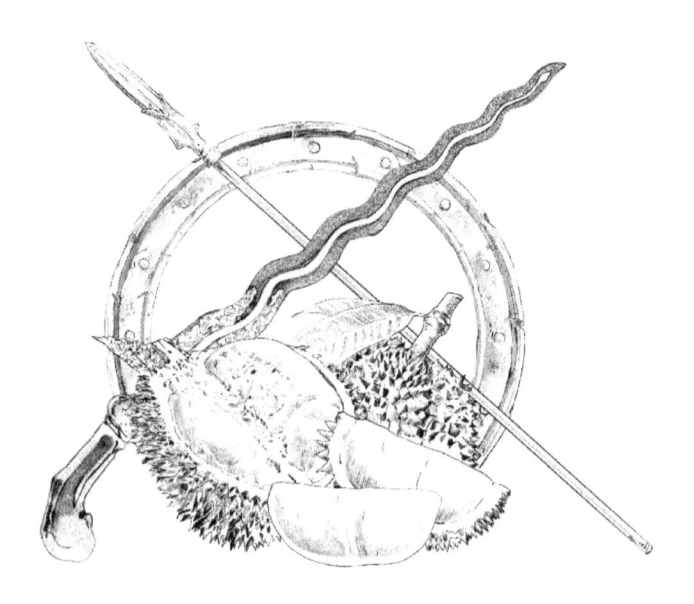

It wasn't that bad. It was worse.

Worst?

He could never tell which was the right word. In either case, the damn third floor was a pain in Arthur's ass. First, of course, was the teleportation which dumped him away from his friends and in a random location. They landed even further apart from each other than on the previous floor. Normally not as much of a problem, because there was a mountain that people used as a landmark. In the shadow of the mountain, everyone had gathered. A village of climbers had been established there.

He was in a mangrove swamp, a nasty, boot-sucking, mud-covered marsh that threatened to drag him down if he fell in rather than traverse the roots of the mangrove trees or the occasional raised spots.

It helped, of course, that the boots he wore were literally meant for this. He'd suffer the slightly too large sizing for the enchantment laid on the boots themselves.

Water Skimming Boots of the Insect
Enchantments: Increases surface area of the standee, allowing dispersal of weight across a wider surface area. Water-wicking effects of the boots keep feet dry whilst traversing puddles and shallow streams.

Of course, the degree of help the water-wicking effects had were negligible if you spent the whole day wading through swamp water, which was what Arthur found himself doing more often than not. After the second time he'd slipped and managed to put half the valley's water into his boots, he'd taken his socks off and went barefoot, just because he—occasionally—managed to get his feet entirely dry thanks to the spell effects.

Even so, the mud-sucking ground, a humidity level well over a hundred percent on the regular, and omnipresent heat that bathed the surroundings and created heat mirages were all annoyances but expected ones. After all, he'd read enough about the third floor to expect this.

No, what he knew about but was not ready to experience were the leeches.

They came in three forms, each more aggravating—and dangerous—than the first.

The tiny leeches crawled all up your legs and down into boots or other, warmer areas. The leeches were all searching for nooks and crannies that were warm, which meant wearing tight underwear was ultra important. There were just certain spaces you never wanted to find a tiny leech hanging from.

Compared to the other two forms of leeches, these tiny ones—most no more than an inch long and a millimeter wide before they were fed—might be numerous but were just annoying. More often than not, they'd crawl into boots and hang out in the gaps between toes, drinking their fill before moving on. Other than leaving small puckers of flesh that bled freely for a while before the toxins they introduced were washed out and you clotted again, they were just disgusting, wiggling annoyances.

But still annoyances.

Next up were the medium-sized leeches, the ones the size of a slug, a couple of inches long and nearly an inch thick. These were found inside the marsh waters, most likely to stick to a body when one fell in. No surprise that his legs were their most common attack points, though the occasional leech that fell from a hanging branch onto his head or arms were a pain and a half too.

Again, their bites were neither painful or singularly debilitating. As a cultivator, he just needed to cycle a little more chi, increase the consumed among of chi within him to actually provide the blood that they fed upon so eagerly. It did leave his clothing streaked with blood like he had exited a bad slasher film, one who was about knee high, but that was, again, an inconvenience but not a danger.

No, the biggest problem with the leeches was the third type. And big was the answer. Going from idly opportunistic feeders to full-on predators, having consumed a sufficient amount of Tower-enriched blood, these leeches ranged from the size of a flat palm to arm-length.

When they fell or attacked, they did so in swarms. While the attacks in themselves were not dangerous immediately, once properly latched on with their pharynx attached to the body, they began to consume blood and Tower energy in equal measure.

That was the greatest danger, for if a cultivator ran out of Tower energy entirely, they were forced to cultivate to make their body move. Of course, in that case, even more leeches would arrive to consume them. Only luck and sufficient stamina might allow the cultivator to survive such a fate, as they drew in enough energy and produced enough blood to survive the consumption by multiple bodies.

Much better then, to kill the creatures before they landed their attacks.

Arthur was battling his first swarm, standing precariously along the roots of reaching mangrove trees and swinging his spear with speed and alacrity. Burning energy to enhance his Bark Skin technique meant that only a well-placed strike could pierce his body and allow the monsters to latch on.

Which was a good thing, for the seven leeches coming for him were not taking turns. A swing with the butt end of his spear sent a leech flopping backwards on its muscular, segmented body, even as its rear sucker kept it attached to the root it had hung upon.

Then, a thrust caught a lunging leech in the body, black spear scraping along bottom suckers before biting into flesh and tearing the monster apart. Blood, consumed from another victim, rained down in a sickly mess, filling the surroundings with the smell of half-consumed and rotted blood, viscera, and old marshy water.

No time to be disgusted, though, for he had to keep the shaft spinning to bat away another strike, jerk his head to the side to keep his eye on another, and then step backwards right onto a body and grind his feet into another, just to reduce the number of attacks.

Of course, moving around and fighting on top of a squirming body was tough; but the greater grip and surface area provided by the boots helped. It let him grind downwards and still have grip on the roots, even as he spun and ducked, both ends of the spear tearing into bodies even as the creatures bounced off armour, his Bark Skin technique, and the spear shaft.

A hectic minute of fighting later and the last of the bodies were laid out around him. He'd managed to dodge or block the majority of attacks, leaving only a single monster attached to his lower hip on the bottom left.

Twisting around, Arthur's lips tightened. He extracted his kris and sliced with it, over and over again, quickly applying the enchanted effects on the monster. He could try to pry it off directly, but that left the chance of leaving the head and the pharynx lodged within him. And while he could burn it off, or even use salt—he had a couple of bags—he'd found that Yin poisoning worked just as well, if not better, than both those other methods.

Soon enough, the creature curled up, detaching itself from Arthur's side. Blood dripped from his open wound even as Arthur finished the kill, cutting open the leech to check within. No full monster cores—or beast stones, as they were sometimes called—not in this or any of the other bodies.

But there were monster core shards, which could be used for alchemical techniques. Which was good enough for now. Storing them away, Arthur scanned the surroundings, listening as much as he was looking.

The biggest problem about this floor and the leeches?

The constant bleeding put the scent of blood in the air, which drew other Tower monsters to him. With as much blood dropping into the water, he might as well have lit a bonfire, put out a bunch of refreshments and a notice that it was an open bar for the creatures.

Time to go. And go fast.

Chapter 56

"Celaka!"

Swearing under his breath, but only on the exhale, Arthur limped away. He was doing his best to get away before the creatures found him, but one of the biggest issues with the spear was that it just didn't have a good way to be stored. Not when you were in a jungle or a mangrove swamp with branches hanging everywhere, ready to catch the edge if you slipped it into a back holster. If you held it in hand, though, you couldn't use that hand to wrap a bandage around your body to help stem the constant bleed.

After a dozen meters, Arthur gave up and propped the spear against a nearby tree, making sure it was resting properly before gripping the bandage with both hands. He spun it around his body in swift but practiced motions, keeping a constant tension on the bandage as it went around his torso so that it wound tight without being too tight.

Even as he wrapped himself, the cream bandage soaked through with bright-red blood, dripping down his side. He grimaced as his flesh shifted with each breath, the sting of the open wound and sweat reminding him of the damage. Contrary to common belief, leeches did not inject an anaesthetic into wounds, a fact that he rather wished was wrong.

Tying off the bandage and securing it with a bobby pin, Arthur stretched a little and shifted, looking around for trouble. Not spotting anything, he exhaled and grabbed his spear before moving on. Just because he saw nothing right now didn't mean he was safe.

Nearly forty minutes later, a creeping sense of wrongness had Arthur putting his back against a tree, feet planted on relatively solid footing. He lifted his gaze, searching the branches above and the shimmering green leaves, before looking around. The shadows all around him shifted as the wind blew, hiding movement.

Movement there was, he was certain. Not just the never-ending leeches and mosquitos and other buzzing insects but also of things more dangerous. For while the kuching hitam had stalked the first and second floors, a different breed lived here. Upgraded by the Tower, the *harimau hitam* was more dangerous than its Earth-cousin.

It didn't need to be bigger, though Arthur had heard that some of the harimau hitam were twelve feet long. No, the common beast was "only" between seven and nine feet long and weighed just over a ton. Only. Also, in the gloom, they changed colour, fading the black-and-yellow-striped figure into almost pure black and void-dark black, to allow the creatures to lurk in the dark.

Add on an ability to alter their weight, so that they could stalk across the mangrove swamp and roots without leaving a disturbance or, just as often, take to the branches of the interlocking trees above. They were the apex predators of this location.

Unlike real tigers in Malaysia, though, who'd rather eat a good durian than a human; the harimau hitam were all for snacking on Tower climbers. Though, if they ate him, they were returning to their roots a little and snacking on a Benevolent Durian.

Something shifted in the dark and instinct had Arthur pulling his feet up to his butt, dropping faster than any muscle-driven explosion could pull him down. It still wasn't fast enough as the explosive leap from the harimau a short distance away from the hiding branches nearly decapitated him, leaving a long line of burning pain along his throat where a claw had scraped in passing.

Behind the creature, the branch shattered, thrown backwards and away as leaves rained down upon the marshy land. He fell sideways, his spear entangled and twisted even as the spearhead, raised in defense, tore into the creature's back legs as they tried to claw him open.

Arthur did not get away without being cut, but with his back to the wall, the massive tiger had aimed itself at an angle when it launched its attack. That meant that when it landed, oh so gracefully, on the tree roots further past the tree, the monster was ready for it and leapt away immediately, long before Arthur had managed to turn and form his Refined Energy Dart.

Up into the branches the harimau bounced, once and then again. Eyes narrowing, a hand clutching at his throat, the other holding the formed Energy Dart, he watched for it, hoping for a proper attack. However, rather than lurking on the branches to come back to attack him, the monster kept fleeing, heading deeper into the woods, its journey visible by the unnatural swaying of branches and the falling leaves.

Long moments, Arthur held himself on guard. His healing technique worked overtime, clotting his wound, beginning the process of stitching him together. Hand holding the loose hanging flaps of his skin together, he exhaled and breathed in quickly, wincing at the sudden pain. Surprised that he had stopped breathing entirely, long hours of training driven out by pain and surprise and adrenaline.

Sucking in breaths, forcing himself to calm down, even as he felt the muscles in his throat, in his neck shift with each moment. Pain radiating from his side, from his neck, from a foot that had caught wrong as he fell and twisted an ankle.

And worry, because the damn tiger likely was waiting for him to bleed out. Lurking, somewhere in the darkness, prowling.

Damn ambush predators.

The harimau hitam never came back, which was for the best. For a short while, he had not been in any position to defend himself. Having reabsorbed the chi for the Refined Energy Dart, he'd propped his spear up at an angle so that it would be harder for the creature to jump at him, before he squatted back down and got to work stitching his wound close.

That had required extracting a mirror, propping it up against a branch, and then extracting needle and thread. He did not need to do a proper job, but he needed to close enough of the muscles and flesh that his healing technique could do the job. As it was, it was already focused on closing up and restitching blood vessels and deeper damage, but any help he could offer would speed things up.

Of course, what they didn't say about speeded-up healing was the very real problem of having to yank out thread that had been healed around, fixing splints and bandages that had become embedded in the body, even watching as the body eventually pushed out splinters and other pieces.

Rumors were, some of the older climbers had found themselves in a lot of pain when metal pins, donated organs, pacemakers, and other artificial aids were pulled out. Of course, those rumors were always for someone who knew someone.

All those thoughts and more drifted through his head as Arthur stitched himself together. He'd practiced. On leather, on cloth. He hadn't had much chance to do it on flesh—there was always a line back in the dojo when someone got hurt bad enough that a stitching was required—and definitely never on his own before ascending the Tower.

There was something morbid, something different about cutting into or piercing your own flesh. It required a degree of willpower, an overcoming of inherent instincts to do so. It felt different from throwing a punch into a wooden block, even knowing that one action would cause pain.

Pushing through the flesh, feeling it tug, that initial piercing motion causing him to hiss through his breath, the tugging sensation as it tried to bypass defenses and then metal sliding through flesh as he pulled the curved needle through skin before it had to twist and pop out of the flesh the next spot...

He might have cried a little.

He might have cried a lot.

But that was what they tried to tell you when you climbed. It was what they tried to warn you about. But there was no way to describe that feeling, no way to train without doing.

No surprise that some climbers stopped. No surprise that some climbers died.

To do it once? Most could find it within them.

To knowingly go out, understanding one might have to do it again? And again? And more? Pushing through pain, through discomfort, through that instinctual flinch within.

Well.

Sometimes, you failed.

Luck held, long enough that he was able to finish the stitching. Resting against the tree, eyes half-closed, mind drifting in and out of self-induced shock, Arthur could feel as his body continued to heal him. Drawing in Tower energy, pulling muscles and skin back into place. Tired and exhausted, he thought at least he had enough awareness to notice if someone snuck up on him.

Which is why, when Uswah stepped up next to him and blocked his instinctive chop, he was surprised.

"Can't even leave you alone, boss." She shook her head, releasing his hand as he let it fall back. Eyes drifted over the blood-soaked leather armour, the ragged stitching and the flickering mirror above and the slight tremble in his hands. "I see you met the harimau hitam, eh?"

"Yeah..."

"Don't worry. I scared it away a little further," she said, grinning. "It wasn't happy being snuck up on, while it was sneaking up on its own prey." Then, tilting her head, she added her thanks in Malay: *"Terima kasih."*

"Sama-sama," Arthur muttered reflexively, before he let himself relax fully as she leaned over, taking hold of the needle and thread to finish the job properly.

The third floor really did suck.

Chapter 57

Healed and sorted, Arthur found himself standing up and testing his range of motion. In a few hours, they would have to remove the stitches again, but for now, it would do. In the meantime, it was best for them to get moving, especially since they had already had to deal with a swarm of leeches once before.

"Which way?" Arthur asked.

"Came that way." Uswah gestured in one direction, then waved towards the mountain. "We headed there, right?"

Arthur nodded. No point in spending time outside. They were better off trying to get through the third floor as quickly as possible. No one liked hanging out here, what with the mosquitos, leeches, and larger predators.

Stepping forward, Arthur was not surprised to see Uswah fade away. Her own techniques were well suited to this floor, being able to hide and travel through shadows. Using them as stepping stones. He really wanted a *qinggong* technique, a movement technique, of his own.

Of course, part of the reason he'd held off was time. But another was because this was the floor most people acquired theirs. Not only did the Tower Administrators have a larger number and variety of movement techniques on this floor, but it had been unnecessary till now.

Trudging through the mangrove swamp the rest of the day was a pain. More than once, the pair caught sight of movement in the distance. Birds taking to the air, the ripple of water, and the sudden churning of mud before the sudden dearth of silence coming from a distance.

Each time, they angled a little towards the disturbance. Hoping to find others, hoping to locate their friends. They were unsuccessful at doing so, never coming across another member before the night fell and the pair had to decide upon a method to sleep the night away.

Climbing the trees was the obvious solution, though it came with its own dangers. Ascended monkeys of one kind or another lived in these trees, though most were uninterested in disturbing the climbers. No pack of monkeys was nearby now, but more pressing concerns lay in the presence of snakes and the harimau that prowled the branches.

After clearing their chosen residence of a lurking snake and watching its body disperse in the night after its core was extracted, the pair took turns resting. Strapped to the tree trunk as they were, it was an uncomfortable night, made more so by the constant stinging and buzzing of insects.

"Sleeping at night, while the insects bite, a pair of strangers abide," Arthur said, then smiled. Not bad, if he might say so himself.

Yet, watchfulness kept the pair safe till dawn the next morning, at which point they continued their journey to the mountain. Kilometers away, the entire process of reaching it would have been a quick few hours' jaunt if they had covered the same distance in the tropical forests of the floors below.

In the mangrove swamp here, however, trudging through mud when they were unable to find drier ground, it would be the work of days. Yet, as they grew closer, the presence of more climbers was easy to discern. Occasionally, the pair glimpsed other cultivator groups far off; but by unspoken agreement both parties kept their distance.

It was the raised voices after noon that had the pair pausing and staring at one another. Uswah raised a single suggestive eyebrow, then gestured sideways from her position crouched under a tree. Arthur hesitated, but there was a tone to those voices that set the hair at the back of his neck on edge.

He knew those voices. He'd heard them often enough, running deliveries in Kuala Lumpur to some of the seedier parts of the city. Taunting voices, almost jackal-like. Scavengers finding prey and running it down, knowing they had something, someone, weaker than them to pick on.

Without conscious thought, he found himself moving in that direction. He caught a slight smile on Uswah's lips before she faded away, leaving him to wade and then jog forwards, pushing himself to hurry as best he could. When he found a patch of clear-ish ground, he pulled himself up and threw himself into that loping, jumping run, though he risked slipping and falling on hidden moss and wet roots for additional speed.

"You come here first! I'll cut you up properly." There was a trace of fear mixed in the rather fierce declaration from the male voice.

"You can, *meh*?" the other voice answered mockingly. Female, this one, though higher and shriller than average.

"You try, *lah*!"

A loud smack, then a cry and splash soon after. More laughter, even as the spluttering sound of someone trying to get muddy water out of their mouth arose. More threats, more imprecations and curses filtered out.

Arthur kept focused, moving as quickly as he could across the marsh. The voices were close now, close enough that they were dampened by the heavy foliage.

Rather than tromp into the middle of the circle like a charging bull, Arthur slowed. He crept forward, waving one hand to the right before he headed left, figuring Uswah was keeping an eye on him for her orders. He trusted that she knew what to do, if things went to hell. Certainly, now that she only had one arm, she was going to avoid a direct confrontation.

He should probably try avoiding a direct confrontation too. Or a confrontation at all.

Of course, just jumping people from behind and leaving them as corpses was probably a bad idea. That was how you started feuds, especially since there was going to be at least one witness he had no direct control over. Because that man's voice, the one being threatened, was definitely not one he recognized.

Peeking around the corner of a spiky tree, one he was sure not to get too close to—and gods, did the tropical rainforest here have a ton of spiky plants, as though at least a good third of the plants had decided that the only good defense was a good offense—Arthur took in the scene before him.

Minor surprise. Four figures, not just three from the muted conversations he had heard before. Three assailants and a fourth member, stuck in the center of the triangle. Even more of a surprise, Arthur realized the three bullies were women.

"*Hah?*" Surprised, he spoke out loud. Maybe he shouldn't have been surprised. After all, he ran a guild that was mostly filled with women. But he'd also caught sight of white armbands, around the arms of all three women.

Immediately, the closest two looked at Arthur. The third kept an eye on their victim faithfully, though, so when the man tried to run, she swept his feet out from under him with the backend of her spear. Sent him sprawling again into the water. Coughing, the man struggled to get up.

"Who are you, ah?" Belligerent and loud, the first woman turned to Arthur as she gestured for her friend to watch over the other man. Not that the third needed it, what with the foot she had put on the middle of the man's back, pushing him into the water to splutter and thrash around.

"Arthur Chua. What the hell are you people doing?" Arthur said, stepping out of the trees to wade forwards a little. He lowered the tip of his spear towards the women as he continued. "You're going to kill him."

"Nah, we know what we're doing, right?" The second woman said, laughing a little as she kicked a hand that had managed to grab a tree root and gain leverage. He crashed back into the water, spluttering. "Just teaching a lesson."

"*Ya lah*. Asshole thought he could cheat us," the erstwhile leader said, eyes narrowing. Idly, Arthur noted that the older woman—she was at least in her 40s—had curlier hair than you'd expect for your average Chinese and a prominent jawline. Maybe mixed ancestry somewhere in the bloodline? Certainly, she tanned rather well for a Chinese. "You don't interfere, ah!"

"And who is this us?" Arthur said, mildly.

She twitched her arm, on which the band was tied off. A band of white with, well, a thorned lotus stitched in. Or at least, Arthur assumed it was a lotus. It wasn't exactly the best piece of art. "You blind?"

"Thorned Lotus."

She smirked. Behind, to Arthur's relief—and the man's obviously—they let him up again. He panted and spat, doing that half-vomit, half-cough thing that those who'd gotten water into their lungs had a tendency to do. Still, they weren't pushing him down anymore, though he noted that the dagger the man had been holding was now in the second woman's hand.

"What did he do?" Arthur said, eyes narrowing as he readjusted his evaluation again. He'd never heard of them bullying others, but the group could be different on each floor. Maybe the Thorned Lotuses here were the bad guys. Or maybe, they were just enacting some street justice.

Eyes narrowed, the leader looked him over before she answered. "You new, ah?"

"Yes."

"This is Ah Lok. He's a real work, but he got together with one of our girls – Emilia. She loved him, so we kept him in line, made sure he didn't hit on the girls… but then, he got her to help him. Help him steal from us." Now the woman looked disgusted.

"What did he steal?" Arthur asked.

"Our training manuals. And movement techniques, all three that we put together."

"You had three!" Arthur said, surprised.

"Had."

"Shit." Now Arthur wanted to kick the shit out of him.

Before he could speak, he was interrupted by the man. "Lies! Boss, they all lying, *wan*. You know ladies. They all like this."

"Like what?" the second woman asked. Meanwhile, the foot that had been removed from him now shoved him down back into the water with a savage twist that ground the heel into his back.

"What he'd do with them?" Arthur asked, moving forwards only to find the leader had raised her hand, telling him to stop moving closer. "Right, sorry. I'm Arthur Chua."

"Said that already."

"Yeah, I've started a Guild, the—"

"Benevolent Durians." The first woman nodded. "I heard. But I don' know if you're him or not."

Arthur grunted. Fair point. "What you going to with him?"

"Beat him. Then find out where he put the techniques. Then beat him some more."

Released for air, the man heaved once again. He let out a series of mewling cries while Arthur frowned. "That's..." He shook his head, then had to ask the obvious question. "Why not kill him?"

"Because if he lies, then we can find him and beat him again till he tells the truth," the woman replied grimly. Then she jerked her head in the direction of the mountain. "Now go, *lah*. Not your business."

"It will be," Arthur said.

"Not yet."

He hesitated again, but for the moment, Arthur really could not find a reason to stay. He didn't have enough information, and waltzing in and making decisions like a storied hero was only going to cause resentment. Better to just let it go as she said.

It sat ill with him, the torture. But the Tower was its own domicile, its own kingdom. The laws of Malaysia and pure justice were far away and theoretical. Here, might made right and you did what you had to do to climb.

You just had to make sure you could live with it, after you left the Tower.

Chapter 58

A couple dozen meters away from the altercation, Arthur slowed and stopped. He waited long minutes before Uswah appeared beside him.

"Ya?"

"You okay with keeping an eye on them?" Arthur said.

"Watch, can." Uswah smiled grimly. "Hard but possible. I can't stop them though."

"Yeah..." Arthur drew that word out before he exhaled, heavily. "Yeah. I didn't think you could. Just watch. Let me know, will you." He paused, then added, "If they really do just get his information, keep an eye on him. Figure out where he goes." A raised eyebrow and Arthur added, "And if he did lie..."

"He'll go right to the techniques."

"Or the person he sold it to." He shrugged. "Or so we hope."

"Can."

That was all the answer he got before she faded back into the shadows, headed back to watch. Alone once again, Arthur set off for the village. He needed to establish the clan here, fast. If nothing else, he had no legitimacy among the powers that were here, not until he had some leverage of his own.

Never mind the fact that his friends and allies were likely in the village already. Or would be soon enough.

Head down—just metaphorically, since doing it literally was a good way to get his head torn off by a sneaky, evil harimau hitam—Arthur made his way through the marshland. Twice more, he had encounters. More leeches in both cases, which sucked—literally—but this time around, he didn't have an ultra-predator after him.

It probably had something to do with the volume of climbers. Even if he didn't see most of them, Arthur could sense or note their presence. Broken branches here, scuff marks on roots there. Bark torn or pulled off or a fire started. Even the droppings from food wrappers, leaves that were used to wrap packages, or bandages and ripped cloth were markings all about.

Never mind the more ephemeral senses, of Tower energy expanded and the destructive attacks that some of the more advanced might unleash. They were all still in the beginning stages, so few had attacks that could destroy entire groves. But the occasional pockmarked tree, the burnt area where a flame technique was unleashed, or floating blobs of ice fast melting in the oppressive heat were all signs of climbers having been by.

And then, of course, were the actual run-ins. Third-floor climbers were a different lot. For one thing, armour was much more uncommon. Not that they didn't have any, but full sets were just too cumbersome and hot in the swamp. Not as many spears, most opting for something easier to carry and wield—and less troublesome to maneuver amongst the trees. But also, that same air of hardness that second-floor residents carried with them was more pronounced.

They'd had to kill and kill a lot to get so far. Even if it was just Tower creatures, the act of killing itself—the determination to strike, to push ahead even when a creature screamed, shouted, cried and groaned—grew calluses on the soul that few would ever understand. Some let those calluses numb them from simple concerns. Others tore open the scabs continually, wanting to suffer, wanting the action to ache and hurt, believing somehow that in their suffering they were more noble.

Most found a balance like his own sifu had tried to teach them to find. Tried to force them to come to terms with, by bringing them to slaughter houses, by having them slaughter their own chickens and fish—and once, a pig—for their meals. To accept their actions and separate it with their empathy, to see the humanity in others but also their own right to defend themselves and to progress.

Grieve, but move on. Life was too precious for anything less.

Here, among those who were now only beginning to learn that lesson—or trying to grapple their way to their own answer—Arthur realized how deep his sifu's wisdom had been. Perhaps it would not, did not, work for everyone. Certainly, not all the disciples had followed his master all the way. Some left, upset at the focus on things outside of violence, outside of practical skills. Others were never accepted, unable to pass his sifu's own vigorous selection methods.

Those that survived, though... most had accepted his teachings. To one degree or another. But these people, so many of the survivors, they had come into the Tower out of desperation or need, without training, without mentally girding themselves.

Now, the scars were everywhere.

The way one man flinched at every movement, glaring at Arthur as he strode past him. Even though there was a good ten plus meters of space between the two.

There, three climbers screaming at another trio, their voices rising as neither party knew how to back down their egos. Faces flushed, weapons clutched, discerning insult where none might have been offered on purpose. Somehow believing that strength meant hardness.

A man, stabbing at a leech, watching it squirm aside, bleeding to death slowly from dozens of cuts. Easily dodging attacks, chuckling to himself as he tortured the Tower monster. Uncaring about Arthur's presence.

And there, a mixed group, laughing and joking as they moved on. Relaxed and easy, except for the last one who carried their burdens. Their porter, their slave, their beast of burden.

Arthur briefly considered stepping in to talk to them. But he pushed that thought aside. What was he going to do? Offer a place of safety? Pay for their survival?

Perhaps one day, but his clan was still building itself up. For now, he could only focus forward. Focus on building his clan so that it could provide aid and shelter for others. Maybe even training, like his master had once given him.

He could do those things, if he was strong, if he was powerful. If the clan he built became something powerful, rather than a footnote. Till then, he could only slog onwards. Pushing on to the third-floor village.

Village it was, because the numbers of survivors kept dropping. Add in the lack of desire to stay on this floor longer than necessary and so the third-floor settlement was barebones. Barely larger than the Tower-engraved buildings: the simple hut for an administrative center, the shop and auction house, and the inn.

No guards.

Beyond the circle of those buildings, another two dozen or so ramshackle constructions on stilts, swaying bridges of rope and wood connecting everything together and from there, poled barges and a few more permanent wooden bridges led into the swamp proper.

The entire settlement was situated on the edges of a clear-ish lake, lily pads clogging the ground beneath the swaying bridges along with the mangrove and coconut trees, monsters lurking in the waters waiting for those foolish enough to try to swim their way through.

Arthur shuddered, his mind's eye recalling the list.

Giant catfish, poisoned frogs, overgrown blood leeches, and nippy eels.

No surprise few chose to swim, and most took the bridges.

And no surprise, again, that a group had posted up on the main bridge, taking a cut from those coming in. Arthur's footsteps slowed as he took in the sight, counting off the four doing the shakedown and the quiet half-dozen coming in. He stopped near the edges of the swamp, keeping to the shadows to watch.

Wondering what his next step would be. And how much of a ruckus he wanted to create.

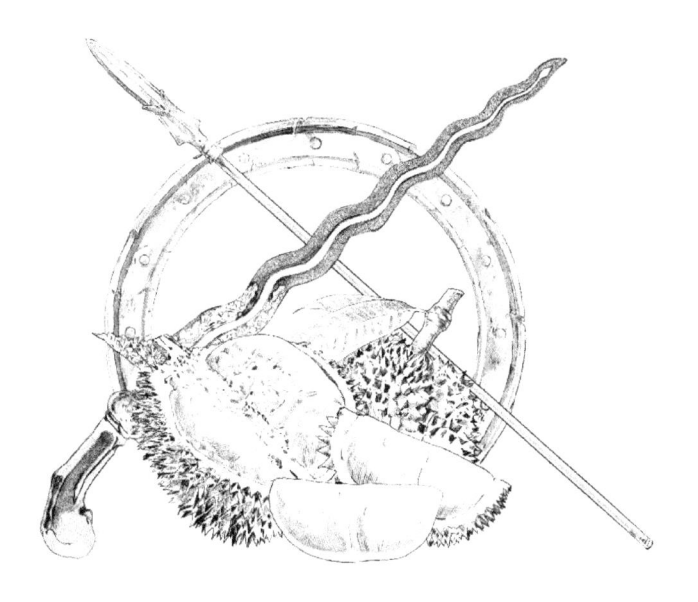

Chapter 59

Arthur hung at the edges, watching from the shadows. He was not the only one, for he spotted a couple of unfamiliar faces. Some were a little more blatant than him, one he had not even noticed till they had chosen to move and head for the boats, choosing to pay for a private ferry than whatever amount was being taken from those at the bridge.

He did not blame the man who slunk away. There was no discernible rhyme or reason for how much the group took from each individual beyond the appearance of strength or lack of it—and wealth, or lack of it. Add in the ability to ingratiate oneself and the occasional times when they ignored others who strode right past the shakedown crew and it read as a recipe for confusion.

"So much trouble, for a handful of glittering stones. Better to have double, rather than take out loans. But to steal, is not a fair deal."

Something to look at changing perhaps, if he had time. If he had the resources. Probably not this run, not when he was trying to get out and up.

He started to stand, heading for the boats himself when he spotted a commotion and a familiar pair of figures striding right up to the bridge.

He nearly smacked himself on the forehead as a foretelling of the future arrived.

Arthur began moving but knew he'd be all too late.

Bold as brass, Rick sauntered forward. Beside him was Yao Jing, shield unslung on one hand, sword still in the sheath. Of course, everyone was looking at Rick, the floppy-haired, khaki-wearing idiot with his pair of guns in holsters under his shoulders and a large backpack. He had a tendency to elicit that reaction. Arthur had to admit that he wondered how someone as vain as Yao Jing managed to handle Rick's ability to draw attention, but the pair seemed to get along well enough.

Maybe inflated egos became stronger when shared?

"What do you mean I have to pay a dozen stones to cross?" Rick said, eyes narrowing. He had stopped far enough away that a simple extension of a hand would not reach him. But way too close if he wanted to clear the pistols and not get stabbed. "Do you own the bridge?"

"For you? Ya," said the speaker, a wiry short man, as he glared up at Rick, swaying from side to side as he spoke. "So. *Cepat bagi*!" He threw out an open palm and waggled his fingers.

"I don't know what you're saying," Rick said. "But I'm guessing my answer is still going to be 'no'."

"Yeah. No!" Yao Jing said, shifting a little to put himself between Rick and the thugs. His shield was leading the confrontation, hiding the way he'd freed his sword a little from the scabbard to make it easier to draw. "Just let us go. No one needs to get hurt."

"You think you can, ah?" Another gymbro, this one only two thirds the size of the muscular Yao Jing. He flexed his pecs, making them dance.

Yao Jing narrowed his eyes and responded with a little flexing of his own. Rather than be challenged, the other man nodded in appreciation.

"I swear, if they start screaming 'muscle brothers unite,' I'm going to cry," Arthur muttered to himself as he stalked over. While the flexing seemed to have calmed the gymbro, Rick's own confrontation with the short man was heating up.

"Stop speaking Malay. I can't understand you, damn it!"

"You in Malaysia, can't speak Bahasa? What kind of Malaysian are you?" sneered the man.

"I'm not," Rick snarled.

"Oh..." The shortie nodded as if in understanding, then added, "Then pay double, 'kay."

"I'll show you double," Rick snarled, reaching for his guns.

Faster than he could react, a hand flashed upwards and lay against Rick's neck. It glowed with an unnatural purple light, a flickering edge of energy running alongside it that sliced into the man's neck gently and left a trickle of blood. Rick, thankfully, froze as did the others.

"Now, you pay triple."

"You... Urk!" Rick shut up as the blade hand pressed upwards, forcing him to expose his throat further.

"Ei, boss," Arthur called out, finally close enough to intervene. "I know he's an idiot, but three times is a lot." A slight pause. "What is three times?"

"For him? Nine stones." Shortie stared at Arthur, shifting a little without letting up the pressure on Rick. Not that the kid was looking that confident anymore, with his hands up and a blade against his throat.

"This floor?"

"Huh?"

"Third-floor stones? Nine of them?" Arthur clarified.

"Ya, *lah*."

"Yeah... no." Arthur shook his head. "Go ahead and kill him. Yao Jing, let's go."

"What?!" Shortie's jaw dropped.

"Okay," Yao Jing said as he turned around casually.

"Urk!"

The blade was shoved even further up Rick's neck, drawing more blood. One hand had twitched down towards his weapon, only for it to be blocked by another thug with his truncheon. However, they hadn't actually killed Rick as yet, which meant Arthur's gamble was correct.

"You know him, ah?" Shortie called out, as Yao Jing stepped towards Arthur.

"I do. He was following my group, but he's not part of it, you know?"

"What's your group?"

"The Benevolent Durians." Arthur shrugged his shoulders. "We're a new—"

"Clan." Shortie frowned even more, glancing to the side. "You work with the Thorned Lotuses, right?"

"Yup. Absorbing those who are willing."

"Celaka," Shortie cursed. "But this one, he's not with you?" he asked hopefully.

"Yeah. But he's rather important." Arthur shrugged. "Outside at least."

Shortie looked at Rick's guns then. Rick had stopped moving since everyone was talking and even started looking hopeful.

"Celaka." A violent shake of his head, one that did not shift his hand at all, much to Rick's gratitude. "Fine. One stone. Each." He paused, then added, "Later."

"Done," Arthur said, walking to the man. "Shake on it?"

Climbing the Ranks 2

Shortie snorted, lowered the blade hand and dispersed the energy. Arthur noted that with interest. Obviously, the technique was the blade hand itself, and so the energy could not be reabsorbed. Good to know for the future.

Sticking his hand out, he shook Shortie's hand. "Arthur Chua."

"Leon Wang," the man grunted. "I give you one week to pay. Good?"

"Good enough."

With that, the group parted, allowing the trio to enter the village. Arthur shook his head a little, as Rick pressed a sodden handkerchief to his neck and glared backwards in disgust.

Now, the question was, how would the boy handle this? Would he suck up the bruising of his ego and move on, or would he carry a grudge? Times like these defined a person, if not within themselves, to others around.

Did Rick know that?

Chapter 60

It took them two thirds of the journey across swaying walkways to the Tower administrative center before Rick chose to break the silence. Over wood and rope suspended between stilted logs, over darkened water reflecting the fast-falling light of the evening.

"Why did you tell them to kill me?" he asked.

"Because I knew they wouldn't."

"How?" Rick asked, forcefully. He raised his hands before dropping them, choosing not to touch Arthur who strode ahead of him on the narrow bridges. Probably a good thing too, for right behind him, Yao Jing had narrowed his eyes. After all, for all their friendliness, Arthur was Yao Jing's boss and the man he was meant to safeguard. "How could you know for certain?"

"Not for certain, but there's a rhythm and tradition to such things," Arthur said, glancing back over his shoulder at Rick as he spoke. "You don't shakedown entire groups by killing those who annoy you, not unless you need to prove a point. They also weren't asking for too much, which is why most people just paid them and moved on."

"I don't understand," Rick said.

"I know." Arthur sighed, rubbing his face. How did you explain the intricacies of the street, the give and take, and the quiet, unspoken rules that everyone lived by? You absorbed such information as you grew up, knowing where to walk, how to walk, how to speak and not give offense, and when one needed to accept minor transgressions. And when it was time to be firm with one's own boundaries.

"Look, it's relatively simple. There were only four of them. They weren't part of any larger groups, because they were letting anyone who was particularly hard or connected through. That also meant they had been around long enough to figure out who was who." Arthur kept walking, his head on the pivot as he took in the surroundings. Clocking information as he took in the flow of climbers here too, slotting it into his mind.

"When you came up, they did a simple assessment. Unknown face, so that means you're new. Your guns mark you as a Richie Rich. So that's dangerous, because there's no guarantee you aren't backed by someone else. If they killed you, in public, there was no guarantee they wouldn't end up dead later." Arthur shook his head. "Troublesome rich kids are better off killed in alleyways and in their beds, when there are no witnesses than out in public."

"Why do you sound so confident about such things?" Rick said.

"We all have our pasts," Arthur replied, turning a little as he replied.

That made Rick blanch and Yao Jing raise an eyebrow in amusement. Of course, the truth was that Arthur had never taken part in such things as extortion or murder outside the Tower, but it was easy enough to fool a rich *gweilo* like Rick.

"Anyway. Killing you wasn't in their best interest. If nothing else, that would make more people willing to pay for the boats. Even if boats cost more and take longer to arrive, no one likes dealing with the bloodthirsty."

"Why didn't they stop the boats?"

"Not enough people. They're just small-time thugs," Yao Jing said, from behind.

"Exactly." Then, stopping at the end of the platform and stepping aside to wait as another pair crossed the bridge ahead of them, he added to Yao Jing, "Don't think I forgot you were part of that idiocy. I expected better from you."

"Sorry, boss. I thought we could go. Didn't think they would stop the two of us." Then, Yao Jing sniffed. "I had my side covered."

"No, you really didn't." Arthur sighed. "We're new to the floor, remember? Everyone's tougher than we are."

Yao Jing opened his mouth, then shut it with a snap. He offered a sheepishly mouthed "sorry," forcing Arthur to shake his head.

"So, Rick. You weren't in danger of dying. Not unless you really pushed them to it. And the fact that killing you would leave a witness, one who had some contact with you and had been, at least, willing to get paid..." Arthur shrugged.

"But what if they figured I wasn't that important if you were willing to let me die?" Rick asked.

"Then... ooops?" Arthur said. That got him a glare. "What do you want? You're not a Durian, right. And you started that fight. I don't have any obligation to pull your idiot ass out of the fire."

"I don't like bullies."

"Neither do I. But you don't go challenging them unless you can win."

"That's not how Captain America does it."

"He's not real. And he has plot armour." Arthur tapped his own breastplate. "This is all the armour I've got."

Silence now. Which was for the best, because the trio were finally nearly the administrative center. A part of Arthur knew he had been reckless with Rick's life there. He had reasonable assumptions and guesses, drawn from his experience dealing with thugs and watching the way they interacted, but it'd all been a guess at the end.

There had been no guarantee.

And yet, a brief flicker of annoyance, a reckless choice to keep upping stakes had him play with the other man's life. He hadn't even gotten nervous doing it. Perhaps he had grown a touch more callous than he had thought.

Something to consider.

Later.

"About time." Arms crossed in front of her, Casey Chin regarded them. Ah Lam was with her, the faithful bodyguard managing to arrive beside her once again. He really did wish they had more of those tethers which he suspected Casey and Lam used when they ascended floors. Then again, considering how expensive those things were, Arthur wasn't surprised he had not been offered one, if even the Chin family had another to spare. "What took you so long?"

"It was a bit of a slog." Arthur glanced past her at the administrative building, his hand unconsciously rising to touch his neck where a cut was mostly healed. "And I ran into a kitty that was rather irritated with me."

"A harimau?" Casey blinked. "And you're alive?"

"Thanks for the vote of confidence," Arthur muttered, waving bye to her as he kept walking. "I'll just be a moment."

She opened her mouth to speak further but closed it. After all, she was the one pushing for them to speed up. As he walked by, she joined him, ready to do her part in setting up the clan hall.

Now, he just had to see what this floor had to offer.

Chapter 61

The inside of the administrative center was both smaller and sparser than before. There was the quest board and a rather sullen older woman sitting behind the only desk. She was still finishing up on preparing an individual's quest marker as they came in, forcing Arthur and Casey to wait.

While they waited, Arthur could not help but look around curiously. The scribbling on the quest board was terrible, but rather than having only a few markers like he'd expected, the board was overflowing with notes, pinned upon one another without rhyme or reason as far as he could tell. There was no organization involved, just a mess of documentation.

Arthur did his best to read them over.

Raw tobacco (5 packs). Urgent!

Leech shards: 11 shards to 1 core

Gingko biloba (Tower-modified), 3 bunches: 1 point.
Repeatable.

5 buckets of rubber sap: 1 point.
Repeatable.

Leech shards: 12 shards to 1 core

Heart of the mangrove tree: 3 points
Repeatable.

Leech shards: 12 shards to 1 core.
Bonus loyalty program 1 point every 3 sets!

"Loyalty program?" Arthur muttered, with slight amusement.

"Lots of competition," Casey said. "No surprise."

"No." Arthur scratched the back of his neck where some particularly ambitious insect had taken a nip out of the skin. His fingers came away bloody, and he grimaced. His damn healing system was overworked right now, dealing with his neck. "We could do it like them, you know."

"Just sit in the hall, pay for cores?" Casey said. "My family isn't rich enough to pay for all of you. Nor would we."

"Nor is Rick."

"Yes. If you're willing to leave some of your people behind..." Casey trailed off.

He just snorted, and she shrugged. They both knew that was not happening, for a variety of reasons. Her goal was to get out as fast as possible. His was to establish clan halls on different floors and the clan itself. If he didn't at least set up the beginnings of a decent organization, he would be leaving behind a mess that would be even more difficult to manage.

Never mind the kind of leverage he'd leave himself open to, weakened as he would be alone.

"Still..." Arthur rubbed his chin, considering. There were two kinds to those quests on the board, as far as he could see. The ones trying, desperately, to collect enough monster cores to exit the floor and those who were asking for materials that could be more easily found here. The first kind came from the tourists, the climbers who were just trying to leave.

The second were from the residents. He couldn't understand it himself. There were a lot of nicer levels after all, but some chose to stay here. For a few months, a few years even. Sometimes their entire lives. It made for a good place for those, he guessed, for those who disliked others. Or had reasons to avoid large crowds.

The tricky part was getting enough of such individuals to join, or somehow making contact so that his nascent clan hall wasn't left entirely empty either. Or at least, finding a few who might want to stick around long enough for his hall to function.

Unless he left it as an empty waystation. Accessible only to clan members...

"Oi! Coming or not?" The glare the older administrator leveled at him made Arthur blink. He shook his head clear of the thoughts flashing through his mind and stepped up.

"Sorry."

"What you want?" the administrator asked in a clipped tone.

Arthur extracted and handed over his personal token, the woman continuing to glare at him as he did so. She swiped it over her board after his prompting, though not without letting out a long huff of irritation. A moment later, notifications flooded down the Tower connection.

A slight prod by Casey had him moving to the side so she could hand the woman her own token. The administrator took a few moments to pull her gaze from Arthur, her lip curling up a little in a sneer as she took and swiped Casey's token.

"So?" said the older woman to her.

"I'd like to offer one of the three buildings my people have built to the new Clan Head to use as his Hall."

"So?"

Casey blinked, then rallied at the unresponsive customer service. "I was hoping you'd tell me how to do that."

A shrug was her answer, as the token was shoved forwards.

"What do you mean?" Casey said, her voice growing a little more strident.

"Not my area."

"But I was told he could do that. That clan halls can take over residences." All that she could get was a shrug. Then, to her growing fury, a hand waved her away from the desk as the older woman returned to filing her fingernails.

"You—"

Arthur, not looking, grabbed hold of her arm and dragged her away from the table. Since they were the only ones present, he saw no issue with touching her at the moment. As Casey turned on him, he shook his head.

"I know how."

"What? Why didn't you say so before?"

"Because I just learnt it. And you won't like it," he said.

Chapter 62

Standing beside him in the small administrative building, the disinterested and surly administrator working her nails, Arthur hesitated to speak. He wasn't sure he could trust this administrator to keep her mouth shut. They were, after all, still human. Then again, he dared not leave the building. Who knew what might happen if he didn't finish what the Tower asked of him while in here.

"*Faai sau di laa!*" Casey snapped.

"So." Arthur gestured, knowing that she could not see what he saw: the grid overlay of the surroundings and all the buildings that appeared there. *All* the buildings. Not just the clan administrative buildings, but all other buildings in the little village. "It looks like, without any other clans in play or taking over the place and no one actually having bought any buildings or arranged for anything with the Tower..."

"In a Beginner Tower? That'd be insanely expensive and not at all worth the cost," she scoffed.

"Yes, yes. Did you want an answer or not?"

He just got silence, so he continued. "Without any of those impediments, what we have is the entire village on offer."

"What?"

"Right. That's what I was thinking too." Arthur shook his head. He wondered if that was always available at upper levels, in more advanced floors and Towers. Was it possible to just swoop in, purchase a building out from another person if they weren't a clan and just... laugh? If so, why hadn't he heard of such things happening?

Well, beyond the fact that the entire area of retail and office purchasing and lease agreements and how clans worked were not something he'd researched because, well, that would have been insane to do. What right had he to even think about such things.

The gods really did like their jokes.

"*Ham ka chan.* Don't."

"I'm not that stupid. And wash your mouth out." Shaking his head, Arthur added, "Now, describe where the places are. Use the walkway we came in as pointing north."

"Wait, *lah.*" Casey hurried out, even as Arthur raised his hands, shifting the wireframe around as he peered at the buildings. Not a lot to choose from, but the two dozen or so buildings were still enough that he wasn't looking forward to just grabbing one and getting into trouble. Many were circular-shaped, big enough for a large family with a single room and simple, thatched roofs that sloped to keep the water out. Easy to build, easy to care for.

However, there were a few that were shaped like longhouses, rectangular with sloping roofs and simple, high joists that kept the planked and thrushed roof aloft, with spacing between the roof itself and the walls to encourage air flow. It didn't do much for the insects, of course, but the constant burning of lemongrass and other natural vegetation in braziers all across the village helped with that.

Mostly.

"Ready?" he asked as Casey walked back in. "Got yourself oriented?"

"I think so." The woman looked a little uncertain. "It'd be easier if we just walked to it."

"Sure... but there's no guarantee this isn't going to disappear. Not risking it, right?"

"I guess." She quickly described the three locations they had. Two small, circular buildings, the third a longhouse towards the southwest—as oriented on the mountain and the way they had arrived. As Arthur grinned and began to choose it, she held a hand up. "What?"

"The longhouse isn't yours. You know that, right?" Casey said.

"We agreed on a building." The look she offered made him let out a huff. "Fine. It's probably a bad idea to take the whole place. But these other houses. They don't look that big."

"Can't be helped. The longhouse is where my family stores the goods and hosts anyone who moves through. You're lucky we even have three buildings on this floor."

"Yeah, I guess." Arthur made a face, before asking the obvious question. "Why do you have three?"

"Originally, we only had one built out, one of the smaller houses. Then, as we grew, we added the longhouse. The last house, one of my cousins' won in a gambling match. Took a few months to register and get it all sorted, though."

"So no one in there?"

"We rent it out when we can. And any of the main family who wants to use it can take it, if they don't want to sleep in the other places or they're full. Otherwise, yeah, it's empty."

Arthur shook his head a little. It boggled the mind that the Chins were big enough to just leave a residence empty, but they were one of the major players. He was sure some of the others, like the Ghee Hin and the like, had their own residences set aside. On that note...

"Eh, do we know exactly which one has the *bumiputra* and crony space?" Arthur said.

Casey frowned. "Why do you care?"

"I don't want to accidentally take it. So let's check that, eh?"

She hesitated, but then nodded and headed out. There were a lot of ways to screw up, but screwing with the government and their buildings were one of the major ones. For the most part, they left climbers alone and even the actual climbing, only making sure they had buildings and infrastructure so that their cronies and their sponsored climbers had a way to ascend easily. Outside of that, there were just too many competing interests for them to mess with others in the Tower, including the Tower itself at times. Not that Malaysia had managed to screw up to that level, but no one wanted the Tower messing with floors or people as retaliation.

It took a few whispered words, a quick check, and a few shouted questions at nearby climbers before they verified what they needed and returned. After that, with almost 90% certainty, they knew where everything was.

Not the best numbers, but at this point, the insistent pinging in his head and the open connection to the Tower was giving Arthur a headache. So taking the second circular house—inconveniently on the opposite end of the tiny village to the Chins' longhouse—was a matter of selection and will.

At which point, the usual notifications arrived.

Third floor Clan Building Selected
Building Type: Residential
Residential Bonus: Security – One Tower Guard assigned

Easy peasy. He almost wished he could choose a different residential bonus, though. Maybe something like air-conditioning for this floor. Or insect repellent?

Update: The Benevolent Durians Clan Status
Organizational Ranking: 182,762
Number of Towers Occupied: 1
Number of Clan Buildings: 3
Number of Clan Members: 146
Overall Credit Rating: F-
Aspect: Guardianship
Sigil: The Flame Phoenix

Not much change there. Still, he'd pushed up on the rankings again, with more clan buildings. A quick review of the details on the clan members showed that he'd increased in numbers a little more on the first floor, though the increase had slowed down somewhat. Most of the gain was on the second floor. He figured he'd see an overall decrease in numbers soon enough, as each floor he'd have trouble gaining members.

After all, the Thorned Lotuses weren't very populous on the higher floors. If anything, he was surprised by the presence he'd seen here.

"Done?" Casey said, impatiently.

"What's the rush?" He waved his hand, dismissing the message and heading for the exit. She fell in with him.

"We're on a timer, aren't we?" she groused.

"I guess," he said. "But a few seconds won't make a difference."

"But having a proper bath might," she groused again, looking down at the mud that caked her legs and shoes. "And maybe it'd be a little away from the damn insects."

Arthur just chuckled, but he nodded. Might as well get on it. Not as though they needed to do anything about the floor quest to proceed to the next level. That was well known and had never changed, as though even the Tower creators had taken pity on the climbers.

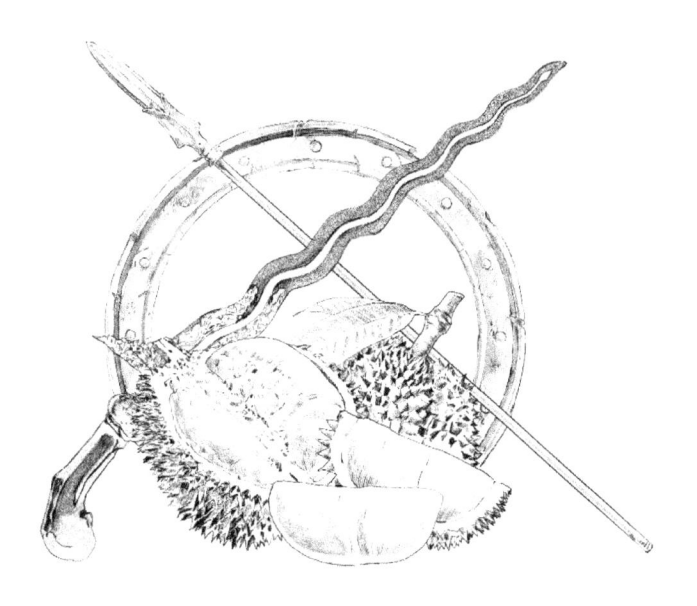

Chapter 63

Settling in was simple enough. Thankfully, this time around, the Tower guard that had appeared for his clan hall had chosen to wait outside and let Arthur confirm ownership of the building before it tried to chop him in half. Of course, the presence of the Tower guard—not seen on this floor's settlement—had attracted the attention of other climbers, which was why Yao Jing was outside, explaining what was going on. Lam Kor, once he was certain that Casey was safely ensconced in the clan hall, had disappeared to check on the rest of their holdings.

In the meantime, while Casey took a shower using the time-tested method of bucket and pail, Arthur reviewed the last of the clan information updates he'd received.

Clan Head Confirmed

Control of Benevolent Durians Clan Building (Third Floor, Tower 2895) Confirmed
Type: Residence

Building Bonus Chosen: Security (Town Guard assigned)

Total Number of Floors: 1

Total Number of Residents: 0

Total Number of Rooms: 0

Would you like to review the layout?

Arthur snorted at the last question. He didn't need to review it. He could literally walk it in less than five minutes, and that was only because the residence included an outdoor kitchen, a couple of storage rooms partitioned off, and washrooms plus one shower room connected via hanging branches and a simple covered walkway off the small hillock to hang over the water. Made for easy cleaning, in all senses of the word, when things just... dropped away.

"We're going to need some more bunk beds in here," Rick said, eyeing the large, circular main room where they'd have to live. "And cultivation is going to be a chore."

"You can leave, if you want?" Arthur waved his hand to the exit.

Rick shook his head, dropping his bag and other equipment next to one of the few beds. Once he was done, the man pulled out his pistols and laid them against the bed, beginning the process of stripping one of his guns down and cleaning it.

There were six, each of them single beds, all set along the circumference of the walls, leaving the space in the middle open. Arthur knew they'd have to build out soon enough, though the amount of space available on the little hillock they'd taken was rather limited. They'd have to sink piles into the ground or something to get themselves more space.

"Why are you frowning?" Mel said, slurring a little as she spoke and startling Arthur. The Malay woman who'd once led the party hunting for a clan seal and, now, one of his most trusted lieutenants stood before him, utterly drenched in mud with a bandage wrapped around one side of her face.

"What happened to you?"

"Leech. You?"

"I don't know how to build buildings." He gestured downwards and then around. "Or furniture."

Mel looked around, then shook her head. She stepped aside, dropping her own pack to the ground before asking. "Bathroom?"

"That way. But Casey's in there!" he shouted, only to shake his head as Mel just walked right past him, ignoring his comment. Left alone, he sighed and rubbed the back of his neck, going over the numbers. Only one missing now was Jan.

He shook his head, knowing there was little he could do. On impulse, he checked the number of clan members on the third floor and confirmed she was still alive. Having that option was useful for now, though once they started recruiting that'd be a pain.

Which reminded him.

Standing up, he wandered outside and looked over as Yao Jing continued to speak with curious onlookers. He waved to the man, and after a few words, his erstwhile bulky bodyguard sauntered over to Arthur. Interestingly enough, it was obvious that what was going on—and the silently hovering Tower guard nearby—was enough to keep the onlookers back.

"Yes, boss?"

"How you feeling?"

"Good!" Yao Jing confirmed, loudly. "Ready to go."

"Great. Then find whatever Thorned Lotuses there are. We should get moving on the recruiting." He hesitated, then raised his voice as he looked at the lookie-loos. "We're also in the market for bunk beds or anyone who knows how to build them." A slight hesitation, then he added, "Cupboards or shelving too."

Surprise registered on their faces, but it was wiped away after a moment. While an unexpected request, it wasn't unusual after all. They had just taken over an entire building and were in the process of getting it outfitted.

"This one really a clan hall?" one of the braver bystanders called. Arthur turned his attention to him, noting the way the man held himself slightly apart from everyone else, the soft leather armour he wore that covered his body and the hardened strips of leather over his form along with the bracers. A kris and a curving blade, almost like a scythe but a little less pronounced, sat on his hips, both no longer than a large knife in length. Malay from his features, with a much larger-than-normal nose for his kind. It didn't help that he had a scar that ran across the tip of it—that sure drew a lot of the attention.

"Yes," Arthur said. "I'm also the Clan Head. Arthur Chua."

"You *nak* recruits, *ke?*" the man asked, eyes narrowing as he regarded Arthur with suspicion. No surprise. The man was at least half a decade older than Arthur.

"We will. Not just yet," Arthur said. "We're getting settled."

"*Saya* Mohammad Aziz." A slight pause, then looking at Arthur a little closer, added, "I'm interested."

"We'll let people know." Arthur shrugged. "In a week or so."

"Others can go in? Use your Clan Hall?" Another man, Indian of some form. Lighter-skinned, so maybe a Punjabi or Bangladeshi originally? Or a descendent. Malaysia had received quite the number of them in the later part of the last century and early parts of this one, when it had still been growing and accepting migrant workers to do the necessary hard work. Now, they made up a sizable portion of Malaysia, whether they were here legally or not.

Some—many, actually—tried to get into the Tower to better their lives. Stolen identity cards, or fake ones, or even a few careful bribes to the guards all meant that there was a constant trickle of the illegal residents into the Tower. The better-off just bribed to get their children or themselves officially registered in Malaysia, rather than risk being caught. Most who did never got past the second floor. Not unless they got lucky and the challenges changed. Here, on the third floor, anyone could pass if they were careful and willing to work for it.

"No," Arthur replied. "It's Clan-only."

"Rent?" The man touched the side of his pants where a rather thin pouch hung, an obvious indicator of what he was thinking. On second thought, he might be Pakistani.

"Maybe." Arthur shook his head. "Later. All of this, later. Furniture, my allies, then recruitment."

"Okay." The Pakistani-looking man spun around and headed away, his head down. A moment later, two of his friends hurried after him. Arthur blinked at the sudden departure while Mohammad Aziz looked between the remaining group and Arthur before he shrugged and walked away, headed for the woods instead.

Just like that, the group dispersed. Probably to spread rumors, though one enterprising youngster had crouched down, eyeing the crowd coming from farther away. Possibly to answer questions when Arthur and Yao Jing.

On that note...

"Why are you still here?" Arthur said to his bodyguard.

"Was going to ask them," said Yao Jing and jerked his chin at the departing crowd.

"Well, nothing stopping you now."

A grunt was his only reply before Yao Jing dropped his backpack, with a muttered "keep that for me" and then hurried after the others.

Bemused, Arthur grabbed the pack and retreated before he had to do any more public speaking. Not that the crowd was that large, but he'd noted a sudden surge in his heartbeat at having to do so. Only after he'd started speaking, though.

Sometimes, acting without thinking had its advantages.

Sometimes.

Chapter 64

He had to admit, he was rather surprised that there was no screaming when Mel had disappeared to the shower room. Even more surprised to find both Mel and Casey returning together, chattering away. When they caught sight of the boys, they fell silent, towels wrapped around their hair. They were in new, slightly damp clothing.

"Me next," Rick said, jumping up and heading for the shower room. He grabbed the gun he hadn't stripped down, pausing only long enough at the doorway to turn and look at everyone. "Don't touch my stuff, okay?"

"As if," Casey said.

Arthur just nodded, having chosen to follow the man's example and take out his own weapons to clean. Not that the enchanted kris or the black spear needed much work, but it never hurt. Especially after trudging through the moisture-laden and swampy marshland outside. The occasional spot where rust was beginning to show was buffed out before he began the process of sharpening the edges.

Very carefully in the case of the kris. He'd nicked himself a few times on the weapon and it had been less than pleasant when the Yin poison had kicked in.

With Rick gone, Mel wandered over to his bed to look down at the pieces of the gun that he'd been cleaning. She frowned at the surprising amount of springs and metal pieces on full display. The cloth he'd so casually discarded was dark and stained, the gun oil he'd been using capped.

"So complicated," Mel said.

"And only useful in a Beginner Tower at most," Casey said. "Unless you're lucky enough and with the right kind of build." She shook her head. "Wasteful."

"Our techniques aren't that much different, though," Arthur mused. "Also complicated in their use. Push through this meridian, shove it down that pathway, turn it around and pour it here. Only use this much energy, or else..." He shrugged. "It's just that it all happens inside us. And the guns are outside."

"I guess," Mel said.

"Our way's better. The Tower and its techniques are better," Casey said, heatedly. "You can't take away a man's cultivation, not easily. Not like a gun. And what power you create within you, it's yours forever. It can't be stolen."

"But it can be controlled," Arthur said, a wry smile crossing his face. When Casey noted his look, she snorted.

"We've got a deal. That's not manipulation."

"Well, actually..." Arthur began and then dropped the tone, though he didn't drop the point. "That's almost exactly what a deal is. Manipulation. Though it's nicer, I'll admit."

Casey shook her head but chose not to get into that argument. Instead, she sat down on her own bed and extracted her own weapons to do a cursory check. Most were well kept, only needing a minor polishing before she put them away. As she did that, she asked, oh so casually, "Now what?"

"Same thing, isn't it?" Arthur said. "We need to cultivate. Grow stronger. Pick up some qinggong or other movement techniques. Then, we've got to get collecting."

"Cores."

"Exactly," Arthur said. With a slight pull, he extracted the floor quest.

Mandatory Quest

Collect twenty-four (24) full third-floor monster cores
Type: Individual

"With most leeches giving only shards, and us needing full cores for our own use, this might take a while," Arthur said, out loud. "Even if the Chins are able to provide the necessary funds for some of us."

"We will," Casey said, rolling her eyes at his words. "But you're not wrong. We need to spend more time hunting than I'd like if we were to use the cores to empower ourselves. Unless…"

"Not happening," Mel interrupted, firmly.

"You don't know what I was going to suggest."

"Going up the floor as fast as possible and forget about increasing our strength here."

"Fine, you did know," Casey said. "I mean, do you want to be here?" She waved a hand around and then snatched a bug out of the air, crushing it and tossing the carcass away before grimacing at the mess in her hand. She extracted a rather damp cloth and wiped her hand off, before putting it away back in her pouch.

"No. But I'm not going to get jumped by the Ghee Hin or anyone else waiting up there," Mel said. "Nor is Arthur."

"He can make up his own mind."

The pair turned to look at him.

"Two ladies, staring at me. Loving me? No, for they aren't my babies..." Arthur offered before he pointed at Mel. "But that one is right, we are doing this right."

"You just used the same two words to rhyme."

Arthur shrugged. They weren't all going to be winners.

"Then we should get cultivating," Mel said, extracting one of the second-floor cores she'd kept from her pack. After a moment, she added, "How many shards to a full core anyway?"

"Varies, depending on the size of the shards, but anywhere from eight to twelve is common," Arthur replied, citing from memory. "Occasionally a lot fewer. We'll need to use some of those cores to pay for the furniture I ordered too."

Casey didn't answer him, instead focusing on a monster core of her own. Her breathing deepened as she began the process of extracting energy from it into her body's core, threading the pull inwards.

Mel, having returned to her own side of the room and making use of one of the few dressers, began to lay out the contents of her bag. She made a face as she noticed some of it had gotten wet, though plastic Ziploc bags kept most of the material dry. Anything not, she began to hang out to dry.

"We got to wait for Uswah and Jan. I hope they're fine," Mel said, softly.

"Just Jan. I met Uswah on the way in. She's on a job for me."

"A job?" Mel said, looking up.

"Ran into a spot of trouble," Arthur said, putting on a faux British accent before dropping it and explaining. Mel frowned in turn, before she shook her head in surprise.

"What?"

"Didn't realise we had that many people up here," Mel said, waving a hand around her. "I mean, sure, the organization was mostly focused on the first floor, and we certainly had people who managed to go upwards. But the numbers were always small. I don't get why we'd be so strong here?"

"Neither do I," Arthur said. "Maybe it's an easy point to stop off at and slowly gain power? While the fourth floor…"

"*Tempat mati.*"

"Yeah." While the first floor still killed the most people—by sheer volume since the largest number of people appeared there—it was the fourth floor where relatively more people were winnowed out. It was deadly to the extreme, and as a percentage, more died on that floor than anywhere but the top floor of this Tower.

Or at least, that were the numbers people had pieced together. As always, much of this information was second-hand, put together by the curious or the analytical or, on occasion, as a sponsored study.

Which was partly why Arthur had turned down Casey's suggestion they push ahead without further training. If not for the fact that the challenges were stepped – quite literally – and thus just appearing wasn't a guaranteed death sentence, he would have thought she'd have an ulterior motive beyond haste.

As it was, he still didn't like the fact that she kept pushing them to go fast.

Finished with cleaning and oiling his weapons, he sheathed and propped them next to him before standing up to retrieve a towel and a change of clothing. Moments later, Rick, singing *She Bangs!* under his breath appeared, offering the group a grin before turning back to his bag.

"New rule," Arthur declared, as he headed for the showers. "Everyone stays dressed."

"Oh come on!" Rick complained. "I have a towel!" Gesturing down his ripped and toned body covered only by the towel, he continued. "I like to air dry!"

"Air dry in the shower then. Or shower somewhere else. But, we all stay dressed."

"Prude!"

"Agreed," Mel said, nodding firmly as she continued to stare at Rick. "I think we should let him, umm, everyone... wear what they want. So long as they cover themselves."

Arthur rolled his eyes, ignoring her obvious lust as he left.

Some people.

He did, however, poke at his own abs when he stepped into the shower and stripped down. Entirely unfair that the Tower seemed to give some people a more "cut" body than others.

Chapter 65

"Oh, you're here," Arthur said, coming back from the shower. He was toweling his hair with one hand, and in the other hand were washed and wrung-dry pieces of clothing. His kris was already belted on one side, his everyday carry on his hips, though the spear stayed by his bed. Not exactly the kind of thing one brought to the bath.

"Yup," Jan said from where she'd leaned against the propped-open door, letting the little wind that had entered run over her body. It also, coincidentally, brought the stink that surrounded her, which had Rick holding his nose and Mel sighing. Loudly.

"Out of the door and get washed up, will you?" Rolling his eyes at having to play parent, he spotted the top of the doorsill. Remembering a few movies, he made a note to potentially add some hooks to hang a weapon or two there.

Be kind of cool and useful, or so he'd assume from a million movies. Give or take.

"Just waiting for you, boss." Grinning, Jan wandered right past Arthur, forcing him to skip away rather than get dirty. How she managed to reek so bad and still not look like she had rolled around in sewage, he had no idea.

Dismissing the thought for now, Arthur returned to his bed, hanging up his clothing on the way before beginning the process of cultivating. After all, he had nothing better to do for the moment.

"It was millipedes, *lah*," Jan answered their questions later, when she had returned. Smelling rather better, thankfully, though her hair seemed to have undergone some degree of savagery beneath the uncaring swipes of a knife wielded by a blind man. Or a woman with no mirror on-hand.

"Millipedes caused your hair to smell?" Mel said, surprised.

"Dropped on me from the branches. Splat, splat, splat." Jan made the motion to mimic the actions. "I used my hand... and then *ah*, the live ones, they started smelling bad. Made my hair bad also." A haunted look reached her eyes as she added, "It smelled worse before."

"Why stand in the door?" Mel asked, curiously.

"Then I don't smell it."

"And not outside?" Rick grumbled.

Jan just grinned at him. "Looking for Yao Jing also."

"He's doing something for me. As is Uswah," Arthur explained. When prompted, he went into a little more detail, though before he had to explain it further, a commotion outside drew him outside. To his surprise, Yao Jing led a trio of familiar faces towards him.

"So. You're really the Clan Head, huh," said the woman he'd last seen abusing a poor man in the swamp.

"I am," Arthur said, inclining his head. "Surprised to see you back so fast."

"He gave up, soon after you left." She grinned at Arthur. "So thanks. I didn't actually want to torture him."

"You're welcome?" Arthur replied, dubiously. "So. What are your names?"

"I'm Michelle Teo. This is Aisha and Kavita," Michelle said, gesturing to herself and then to her friends. Aisha was the silent one who glowered at them, mouth pressed tight, while Kavita offered them a smile. Of course, her friendliness was a little off-set by his memories of her helping drown a man.

"So, where's the rest of the Thorned Lotuses?" Arthur said, peering behind the group. Yao Jing grinned, looked between them, and took position behind and off to the side but within easy reach of Arthur as he watched. Not that anyone was likely to start anything with the floating Tower guard near them but... you never knew. They'd gathered an audience again, after all.

"Just because the others joined you doesn't mean we will do the same," Michelle said, crossing her arms. The movement drew Arthur's gaze down but he yanked it up after a moment. Not that she had much to showcase, and she was definitely not doing it to seduce him. This was more of arms crossed in grumpiness, not the push-up kind.

Anime really did have a lot to explain about the sheer volume of incidents of the second kind in one's life. Why, he'd only ever experienced someone trying to seduce him twice. Once for free food and another, to distract him while someone was trying to run off with his bike. Which was why he was even more wary now and defensive.

"And why not?" Arthur waved behind him. "You can sense the energy going to the building and it's not even finished yet. Safety, faster cultivation speed. Resources even, eventually."

"Oh? Maybe *we* have more to offer you."

"You found your techniques?" Arthur said, curiously. "How'd you have some written down anyway? Amah Si never mentioned you having any."

"She doesn't know anything."

That was a non-answer if he'd ever heard one. "Fine. Well, the offer is open. That's the deal I made with her. Everyone currently part of the Thorned Lotuses can join. If you don't want in, that's fine too." Giving an elaborate shrug, Arthur turned away.

He managed to make it nearly to the entrance when a new voice cut him off. "RUDE! We're not done here." Turning around, Arthur noted that the speaker was Kavita, the woman having a rather more typical Indian accent. She did a little head bobble as she continued, "You think we're your slaves?"

"Not slaves. Partners. Willing partners, hopefully," Arthur said. "Or, more to the point, clan members. But I'm not here to force you." Eyes narrowing, he looked at Michelle and added, "I'm also not here to negotiate. You come, you bring what you can. If what you bring is good, you get promoted and what not. If not..." He shrugged.

"Why you think we should believe you?" Michelle asked.

"Now that's a good question," Arthur said. "Didn't you get word of us?"

"Got. Heard about you," Michelle said. "Some said not so good words."

"Those part of the Ghee Hin or the Suey Ying?" Tough fighters they might be, but they were horrendous poker players. Then again, poker was not as common a game as mahjong or Big Two around here, especially in the lower classes. It was more a game for the pretentious, especially when most people just didn't have the money to waste on gambling. "We had a few run-ins with them." He paused, then added, "Mostly on the first floor."

Then, curiously, he turned to look at Yao Jing. "Are they around here?"

Yao Jing shook his head. "Didn't see any. Maybe, but..." He shrugged. "Didn't hear of any."

"Most moved on," Kavitha said. "Not much money to be made here."

"Fair enough." Another breath, then he sighed. "So. You can wait, watch, talk to your own people." He waved towards the hut where Mel was within. "I have some of your own members from the first floor here. They can talk to you."

"Why not now?" Michelle challenged.

Arhtur opened his mouth, then shut it. He turned around again, called for Mel. A short while later, Mel wandered out, looking a little annoyed at having her nap interrupted. A quick explanation later and his second-in-command turned right around, walked back into the hut.

"Uhh..." Arthur looked confused, glancing back to Michelle. Kavitha looked highly amused, while Michelle was frowning. Aisha just continued to look surly.

Moments later, all of that was wiped away as Mel walked back out, her knife strapped to her side and spear in hand. She nodded to Arthur as she passed him, eyes on the trio of women. Who, Arthur had to admit with a small smile, were a little on guard at the suddenly armed woman approaching them.

Thankfully, no one was exactly reaching for a weapon either. Going around armed—even in the village—was not uncommon after all, even if a little paranoid. Soft words were passed between the women before Mel and the three women left, leaving Arthur and Yao Jing alone once more.

It was just as he was stepping back into his new home that another voice called out to him and interrupted his return.

Chapter 66

"Is that going to hold?" Arthur said, eyeing the newly constructed bunk bed. The Pakistani gentleman had come back with a bunch of his friends and after a quick discussion, an agreement had been made. A half-dozen shards as prepayment and the group had tromped off into the woods before returning with freshly cut branches that they began to lash together to produce the bunk bed.

Yao Jing reached out and gave the entire thing a shake. Surprisingly the bunk bed barely moved, the multiple legs having been leveled and then a border added at the bottom to help stabilize the thing. Not content, the muscular man shoved harder, only for the structure to flex under his hand, shifting as the springy wood moved.

"I'd be more worried about the sap," Rick said, arms crossed. "Not sure sleeping on newly cut wood is a good idea."

Arthur shrugged. "They put some tar around the edges or something. It seems to have stopped it from leaking." He had to admit, he was more city boy than intrepid wildlife adventurer, so what they were doing or constructing was entirely out of his experience. "But it seems to work, no?"

"Oi. You all, so fussy." Jan shook her head from where she lounged on her own top bunk. The men were still working, putting together the third bunk bed while another was outside, building a series of simple shelves with wood and vines. "This is fine, *lah*. And they promised to come back with proper wood later or fix these ones."

"If they're still here," Rick said.

Yao Jing could not help but nod.

"If we're still here," Arthur pointed out quietly. "Not like we intend to stick around, eh?"

"How long you think?" Yao Jing asked, curiously.

"Isn't it like two or three months to finish the floor?" Rick said.

Arthur was shaking his head already as the man spoke. That made Rick frown, and he gestured over to Casey as he continued. "Only if you wanted to do a stupid speedrun through the floor. Ms. Chin and I have agreed: we're not doing that."

Rick frowned. "Why?"

"No time to grow, what," Jan said, scorn filling her voice. "We need time cultivate, *lah*. Otherwise, you go fourth floor, *habis lah* you."

"You know I don't speak Malay," Rick said, annoyed.

Jan snorted, but Yao Jing translated, "You're dead. You will be, if you don't prepare. Fourth floor is very dangerous." He glanced at Rick's guns, both of which the man had finished cleaning and returned to their holsters under his arms before he added, "For most of us."

Arthur tilted his head to the side, considering. That was a good point. With Rick, they'd picked up time by—literally—blowing away the competition. While his guns might not provide a huge advantage here, the leeches being mostly a matter of volume rather than difficulty, the fourth floor was almost perfectly suited for Rick.

But there was no guarantee that Rick would be with them through all the trials, and because of the way the trials were set up, he wouldn't be able to help them all. Still, it was an advantage that Arthur would be foolish to ignore.

"End of the day, there are techniques we need to learn here. At the minimum, a good movement technique and a combat one," Arthur said. "Or one that works as a distraction. Either or."

The others were nodding along, all but Rick who studied the faces of the Durians one after the other before he relented. "Fine. But I don't like spending more than I need to."

"You can go ahead," Arthur said, gesturing upwards. "Not as though we're holding you back. You're just a paying guest."

"Not much to pay for, if I go before you."

Arthur could only shrug at that comment. He was not wrong, but it wasn't as though he could change it. More importantly, he was rather curious about something else.

"You don't need a movement skill?"

"I have one," Rick said.

"Really?" Arthur said, surprised. "You haven't really been..."

"Moving much?" Rick chuckled. "Hard to do so when your front line isn't moving either." He shrugged. "Anyway, not much cover around. Lots of concealment, but not much cover."

"Difference?"

"One I can shoot through," Rick said, miming the motion. "You want cover if possible, concealment if you can't. Move and shoot is great, but moving in the jungle means I might hit you all, because you bounce around. Anyway, I always try to make sure I've got some easy cover if necessary. Close enough I can duck into."

Arthur considered, then nodded. Rick wasn't wrong, and most times he was right. Sticking the man directly behind the firing line—or at an angle or above—gave him opportunity to open fire. But it did mean that when they clashed, he couldn't afford to move much; at least not when they were dealing with the jenglot.

He also never did ask the man what might work better. Which was, perhaps, a failing on his part. Making a mental note to get back to that conversation another time, he forced himself to focus on his initial question.

"So, you have one? What's it called?"

"The Gunfighter's Walk," Rick said, completely unembarrassed. Not even when Jan and Yao Jing laughed, and even Arthur had to smile a little. "I didn't come up with the name. But it works."

"How?" Jan said, blunt as always.

"I can move without affecting my aim when using it. It's not meant for long runs, but for quick bursts. It's very energy intensive, though," Rick said, making a face. "Really meant for those with a higher cultivation base. But when I grow into it, I can strafe without messing my aim at all." He raised both hands, floating them one above the other parallel to the floor. "Don't even have to worry about terrain much either."

"You fly?" Yao Jing said, excited.

"Sort of?" Rick shrugged. "I don't actually leave the ground, but it sort of levels out for me as I move. Or I move like it levels out."

"How does that even work," Arthur muttered, trying to picture it and the physics involved. It made little sense, especially on a root- and hole-filled terrain like a jungle. But then again, it wouldn't be a true technique if it didn't mess with, well, causality and physics, now would it?

Echoing his unspoken thoughts, Rick simply answered, "It's the Tower."

Dismissing the thought, Arthur also cast aside any hope of getting something useful from Rick. Something that cost a lot of energy was not what he was looking for in a movement technique. He wanted—needed—something efficient.

"So, Boss, what you thinking of?" Jan said curiously as she cocked her head to the side.

"Not sure."

"Really? You didn't check before coming, meh?"

"I did. There's options. Wind Steps is, of course, an option—"

"Boring!" Yao Jing complained.

"It's efficient," Arthur said, before he continued. "But like Yao Jing says, it's boring and commonplace. Which is great because it's easy to get access to and everyone knows it. But it's also a little restricted."

"No progression." Jan nodded. "Well, not to say 'no progression,' but…"

"Progression is expensive. Yeah," Arthur replied. "Fixing or improving it yourself is extremely expensive." Then he held up his own hand, staring at the pale skin, before smiling slightly. He lowered his voice and cast a glance around at the men building furniture. "There's also Uswah's…"

"*Aiyoh!*" Jan complained, not lowering her voice.

"What?"

"Boss, you get that, if you end up passing it along…" She sighed. "*Banyak susah, lah.*"

"I know." He sighed. "Also, it's a little restricted and a little theme-y. Don't want people to think, umm…" He looked over at their hired help and shrugged. He wasn't too worried about Rick; nothing he'd said so far was exactly a clan secret from the man who'd actually worked with Uswah. "Well, you know. Makes us look real sketchy."

Jan grinned. "Exactly!"

"So? What else did you research?" Rick said, curiously. "I did a bit of a study myself too."

"You did?" Jan said.

"No need to sound so surprised. I'm not a complete idiot."

"You are."

Rick pursed his lips, but Arthur held a hand up.

"There were a few. Flash Step is useful, but no endurance. The technique is also more common in Japan than here, though I'm sure we could find it if we had to. Or purchase it from the Tower." He ticked his fingers off. "There's Gecko Sprint, which does some nice things for balance and grip, but..."

Arthur continued, happy to talk techniques he'd researched. Talking it out might trigger additional memories, memories that he had forgotten. After all, as Jan had pointed out, he was not just focused on building up himself anymore.

Eventually, whatever he learnt might be passed on as bonuses for the clan, or as embedded techniques in the clan library. If so, he had to concern himself not just with this Tower but all the other Towers he would have to climb.

And that, if nothing else, required a completely different build.

If only he had the chance to put an ideal into play. But, as usual, he'd just have to scrounge and grasp, hoping that whatever he could get his hands on would fit.

Typical.

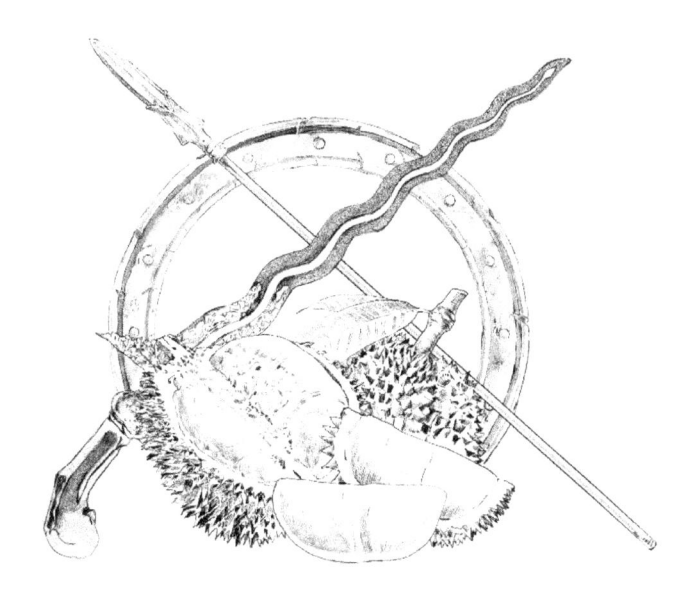

Chapter 67

Mel made it back later that day. By that point, they all had beds. Or, at least, a Tower equivalent of beds. The mattresses had been stitched together from discarded clothing and rush leaves dried and packed together. Apart from the beds, they also had free-standing shelves. All in all, the place was much homier, even if Arthur was a lot poorer.

"They'll join you," Mel said. "Eventually."

Arthur grunted, "Eventually?"

"No point now." She gestured around the now-crowded clan building. "Nothing to give them, and this way they can make sure you're actually, you know…"

"Who and what I say I am?" He snorted and nodded. "Damn."

"Why so worried?"

"Just hoping we could get some taxes coming in, like the floor below," Arthur said. "Make it easier to ascend."

Mel frowned at his words but chose not to say anything. Curiously, Arthur asked, "What?"

"Nothing. Just a thought."

"Spit it out."

"Don't tax people here."

"What?" he said, surprised.

"Don't tax people here."

"Yeah, I heard that. But why?"

"Makes people angry, *lah*." She waved a hand around, catching a mosquito and squishing it with that motion. She shifted her hand, turning it over to show the splotch of blood and darkness where the mosquito, having fed well, was now smeared across. "Who wants to stay here for long, anyway?"

"So, what? We offer this place to let people get through faster? What do we get?" he said.

"Loyalty. Gratitude." At his grimace, she added, "Later, tax them more. To make up for it."

"The fourth floor?" Arthur hesitated, considering. It was the death floor, but the deaths often happened during the trial to ascend to the fifth floor, rather than immediately. Which meant that there was a good opportunity for the Durians to establish a decent beachhead, keep their people safe-ish as they came up, and help them train and empower themselves further before attempting the trial.

Increase their chances of survival, and add to his own tax base.

"So we make *this floor* easier for people to pass through, by giving them everything they need," Arthur said, slowly. "No taxes. A place to cultivate and rest in safety. Techniques?"

"If we can." She hesitated, then added, "That's what they were trying to do."

"They?"

"Michelle and the Lotuses here."

"Oh." Arthur frowned. "Whose idea was it?"

"Kavitha's."

"Huh. Didn't strike me as the thinker of the group." He glanced over to where the rest of the team were quietly cultivating on their beds, pulling in energy. The only person not doing that was Yao Jing, and he was deeply engrossed in a second-floor technique book of his own.

Without anyone to bounce the idea off, Arthur could only add, "I'll take it under advisement."

Mel nodded, moving away from his bed to her own. Like the rest, she needed to cultivate.

After all, the first step was to grow stronger.

No matter what.

***

Two days later and the team had run out of monster cores, even with the return of Lam with their payment from the Chins. There just weren't a lot of cores being held back on the third floor because of the general desire to leave the place, meaning that few enough were gathered. Overall, there just wasn't a good reason enough to store up cores here.

That viewpoint kind of pushed Arthur towards considering Mel's suggestion even further. It made sense that such a benefit would attract even more clan members, from prospects already on this floor and others below.

Of course, letting those on the lower floors know what he was doing was going to have to take a bit of time since there was no real method to communicate downwards without sending a new climber into the Tower.

Ah well, at least it'd be a nice surprise for those arriving.

Without cores to cultivate, the team had a discussion about whether to continue normal cultivation or take to the marsh to find the necessary stones. It was, of course, rather dangerous. But traveling in a group, it was likely they would be fine.

The negative to that, of course, was the division of stones. Eventually, they decided to split into groups of two to balance safety with speed. After choosing a three-day period for the exploration and return, the team was just about to leave when Uswah stepped into the clan hall and threw things off course once more.

"And you managed to steal it all from them?" Arthur said, holding three documents in hand and turning them over and over, a little incredulous.

"Yes. They weren't watching for me," she said, just a little proudly.

"So no one knows you have this?"

"Exactly. He ran off to meet with those he stole it for. And led them to where he stashed it."

Arthur was not surprised that the man had lied to Michelle. That was, after all, one of the problems with torture. Verification of information was always tricky, especially if you weren't very good at the interrogation. "So when they slept that night, I led a bunch of leeches over and, while they were fighting, stole it."

"Good work."

"Thanks." Then, she pointed to the shower room. "I'm going to wash up and sleep a day now."

"Yeah, you do that." Arthur watched Uswah leave, the woman almost sauntering off. He was glad she was feeling better. After losing half an arm, she'd mostly recovered, but he still caught moments of self-reflection and doubt. This was a win she had needed.

Of course, it did leave him with a whole new problem.

"Now what?" Arthur asked Mel. She looked at his documents, frowning.

Casey, looking over the group and seeing them settle down for another long discussion, let out a long sigh. "I'm going out."

"Me too," Rick said. "I don't need to be here for this." He hesitated, looking at Yao Jing, who glanced back at Arthur. Offering the man a nod, Yao Jing grinned and the two men headed out as well, following after Casey and her bodyguard.

Leaving the remaining three to decide what to do about their windfall.

"It's stealing, right?" Jan said, slowly.

"Possession is nine-tenths of the law, no?" Mel said, frowning. "After all, can you steal from a thief?"

"I don't know. I'm not sure I want to take ethics classes from the British Museum, you know?" Arthur said.

Mel snorted at his comment.

Jan laughed a little. "Okay. So how, boss?"

Arthur shrugged. "I'm not sure. But I think we should let the ladies know."

"Don't know if Uswah will like that," Mel said. "She gets nothing for all her trouble."

"Other than whatever else she stole," Arthur said. "Also, the gratitude of the other Lotuses can't be discounted." Then he smiled a little as he eyed the documents. "Anyway, these aren't Tower-locked, right?"

"No..." Mel said. "Are you suggesting what I think you are?"

Arthur smirked. "I'm nice. Not an idiot."

"So what we have, ah?" Jan asked.

Rather than directly answer her, he handed out a document each and then opened his own, scanning the contents. Most cultivation techniques had a quick summary at the start, giving an idea about what the technique did and, also, the kind of energy usage and the meridian flows. While most wouldn't register till they were actually trained, it was still a non-Tower magic way of understanding what one had.

In this case, he had a simple cultivation technique. It was not particularly better than the previous generic technique he had used upon entering the Tower. It was, at best, a half star. Which, considering everyone was basically using a 1-star technique, unlike his own 2-star one, meant that it was useless.

Sighing, he explained it to the others and set the scroll aside. No point even making a copy.

"This one is better," Mel said, handing over her document.

"Oh?" Arthur asked and got to reading immediately. It took him all of two lines to start nodding his head and about three minutes to make his way down the document before he had to push himself to stop reading.

"Water Walking. The insect kind." You'd think, with the full range of the various human languages available, names would get more creative. But the sheer number that defaulted to the basic varieties was rather staggering. There were, at last count, something like eleven Sprints and twelve Strikes. And over forty-seven varieties of Heavy Strike.

"Yes. Very useful here," Mel said. "Lightens the body and spreads the weight out, so you can run across the water. Doesn't make you any faster but..." She shrugged. "I bet, if you can figure a combo, you might even do tree walking."

"Ah yes, the goal of every weeb." Arthur hesitated, then frowned. "What's the term for the Chinese-obsessed?"

"Egg?" Jan offered.

"Does that work for us? We're not exactly white on the outside." Arthur gestured at the group, which made Jan snort. "Sinophile? Too nice, right?"

"*Yu xia ren*," Mel supplied, though she might have bungled up the tones.

Arthur's face scrunched up as he tried to translate the words. "Useless... heroic... person?" At her nod, he snorted. Well, that was one option. Certainly, ever since the export of a bunch of bad Chinese web-novels and some much better TV shows, the obsession by certain groups had grown significantly. Helped along even further by the Tower's ability to make such things viable.

"Okay. So, Water Walking is a win," Arthur said, pulling the conversation back. "What's the last one?"

"Movement technique also, but body-boost type," Jan said, handing it over.

"Accelerated Metabolism," Arthur said, reading the heading of the document as he opened it. No surprise with that kind of lead-in that it was the kind that accelerated the entire body. Very similar to his own Heavenly Sage's Mischief but with a few minor differences.

The Heavenly Sage's Mischief was meant to be a combat bonus, so it scaled in the boost that it offered to an individual. In that sense, it could be built upon with more refined techniques in the future so that the total Body stat boost was higher. The amount it boosted the body by, even in its base form, could be increased. After all, a stat increase in Body at the lower levels was entirely different when you added to your Body at a higher attribute base. The requirements and energy forms and what it increased varied.

On the other hand, the Accelerated Metabolism technique was a persistent boost that focused mostly on increasing an individual's overall speed. That meant a minor increase in strength, but it also granted an equivalent increase in balance and twitch muscles, so that the user could—literally—react and move faster. It wasn't, however, a significant increase in the Body attribute and would likely fall out of use after a while. In other words...

"Not that great, eh?" Arthur said, frowning at the document.

"Good for training?" Jan said, while Mel made gimme motions. He handed the document over, sitting back as he waited for her to finish reading.

"Yeah," she replied. "It's not much use for most of us. We'll want an actual movement technique, even if it's a boosted one," she said. "High speed movement, Flash Step, anything like that. This just makes you move faster, which..." She shrugged, looking around.

He had to concur. Well, at least he wouldn't feel bad returning these documents since they wouldn't make a major difference to his clan.

"I wonder why they bought them, then," Arthur mused.

Chapter 68

"We traded for these," Michelle said with a shrug as she looked over the documents, checking them over for damage the next day. "The original buyer thought it was something else. Then realized it was crap." She chuckled a little. "We bought it for cheap."

"Oh, that makes sense..." Arthur said.

She shrugged in answer, not wanting to provide further detail. She'd been annoyed when she realized that Arthur and his team had read over the documents, but only marginally so. Mostly, she'd been appropriately thankful. After she'd grumbled and muttered quite a series of threats at the poor thief.

"So, this might not be the best time but..." Arthur waved at the documents she held. "Where do you intend to keep them?"

"Why you ask?" she snapped.

"Because now that we know people know you have techniques, and are trying to steal them, wherever you put them might not be that secure."

Arthur gestured back towards the clan hall a short distance from where they were meeting, on an open gondola under a tree. "Whereas I've got the most secure location on this floor."

"Till you die."

"Till I die."

"I'll think about it," Michelle said.

"Okay." Arthur waved the rest of his people on, many of them impatient to get moving. After all, they'd been waiting since yesterday, copying down the various techniques in the meantime. Now, they were a day behind the others and still in need of monster cores if they wanted to empower themselves.

The only major advantage with there being only three documents was that Arthur had a chance to cultivate himself, pulling Tower energy in the middle of the night until Uswah had woken up and taken over the shift. He'd been able to add more energy into his core and even refine a little, though no major breakthroughs had occurred.

Still, having taken the Accelerated Metabolism technique to read over and then copy, he had a few ideas now of how it might work with his own Heavenly Sage's Mischief. If nothing else, he thought he had a better understanding of it and what it did. Some careful testing might see greater efficiency.

"We'll be back in a bit. Be ready then, eh?" Arthur reiterated.

Michelle frowned but nodded. She had no right to gainsay his movement, even if she wanted to. Waving her friends to her, she departed down one swaying suspended bridge, Arthur and his team heading down another.

Arthur's group would split up, once they had moved some distance away from the village. For now, there were too many eyes on them. Even if, he assumed, this floor was going to be relatively conflict-free.

No one wanted to hold a fight whilst being eaten alive by mosquitos and other, nastier insects.

One of the most annoying aspects of fighting to collect monster cores and shards in general, Arthur realized, was that you had to be careful about the kind of techniques you used. Couldn't shoot Refined Energy Darts willy-nilly. After all, each Dart was basically ten minutes of dragging energy through a core. Which worked out to be at least a half hour of hunting—that being the amount of time before they found another cluster of creatures to kill.

There were, technically, more creatures. But Arthur neither had a trident nor a net, or a desire to go fishing. The giant catfish that lurked below waters might have full cores ready for plunder, but first you had to get them to rise. While your normal catfish might not bite, Tower-mutated ones did and could take a chunk off any climber's body. Never mind the venoms that were all too common in the barbs located on the creatures' fins, which they used to attack. Since most of the time they were in the water, the muddy water, you couldn't even see them before they brushed up against you, dropping a ton of venom and leaving you incapacitated.

No surprise that few people, other than the dedicated anglers, were interested in hunting them. The mutated leeches and the occasional giant beetles were all simple enough to handle, along with the occasional Tower snake.

And the harimau hitam. Which, thus far, they'd not seen.

No one wanted to meet that creature. It was, overall, considered overpowered for this floor. It could be killed, and a few had reported doing so. But since its monster core was not much more powerful than a giant leech's, and the higher mobility and deadliness of the harimau meant it was much more dangerous to hunt, most just avoided it.

There was, beyond the ability to boast about it, nothing to be gained from hunting the black tiger. Not that it stopped certain groups, but it was as much an exercise in frustration as anything. As Arthur had noted, the creature was prone to running away if its surprise attack failed.

All that really meant was that Arthur and his teammate, Mel in this case, were stuck with poking and stabbing with their spears, relying on their base abilities to deal with swarms of leeches. Of course, this being the eight hour in the swamp, it was neither normal or routine.

"I told you this was a bad site for sleeping!" Arthur snapped, ducking a leech that somehow had managed to get up onto a higher branch than the one he was fighting on, swung his spear and knocked another off, and then stabbed a third that felt that flinging its head at him beneath the trunk was the way to win.

Mel, fighting on a nearby branch with her legs splayed across two thinner limbs of the tree was dual-wielding, her spear held mid-haft to knock things around and occasionally slice something open with the tip, but mostly, it was her parang that was doing the work of killing leeches.

"How was I supposed to know they'd swarm here at the end of the day?" Mel said.

"The pile of bones!" Arthur said.

"They weren't in full pieces. And looked old. And were in the water!"

"I told you what they were."

"You're a city boy!" A twist of her wrist decapitated a leech, but then one managed to sneak up her unmoving legs. Unlike him, she couldn't exactly dance back and forth—not that he had that much space to move himself—with the branches they'd chosen to sleep on a touch too thin.

They were constantly swaying and bobbing as they fought.

"Who's seen bones." He slid backwards, letting his feet slide across the bark as he did so to get the angle he needed. A quick stab caught the leech that had snaked upwards, lancing through the upper half of its body before he twitched his hands, tearing his blade outwards. He used that same motion to sweep another pair of leeches off the tree and leave a long score across another, causing it almost to deflate.

Then, he had to focus on his defense again. A leech dropped from above, letting its upper body un-attach from the branch that was nearly entirely covered with moving leeches rather than leaves by now and he caught its attack on his bracer. It snarled as it attached itself to him, and Arthur proceeded to swing his arm side-to-side, using the fatter body to cushion the blows as he bludgeoned others.

If nothing else about the leech swarm, they were definitely going to get their share of monster shards when this was over.

If they survived.

Chapter 69

Way too early in the morning the next day, Arthur was below, slicing open another leech to get at its body. The intervening hours and the slow dispersal of the bodies meant that they should, if they worked hard, get most of the shards. And they got shards only, for the most part, though the occasional full core was found.

As he sliced downwards, his hand slipped and the knife that had been in its grip sliced a chunk of flesh off the fleshy part of his thumb. Wincing as the skin flapped open, he was grateful he was utilizing a skinning knife rather than the kris, having switched out due to the sheer slickness of working with so much gore.

He watched as the blood poured from his wound, joining the sticky gore that covered the rest of his hands, the viscera and blood of multiple beasts, the sap that many had managed to pick up as they fell, and slime from the water itself. As for the smell... best not to even consider it.

"Your turn," Arthur said after a moment and straightened to walk over to the only piece of land that wasn't ridden with blood and corpses. He handed the skinning knife with a casual flip that nearly sent the blade flying again as his slick hand fumbled the motion.

"You cut yourself," said Mel. "Again."

"I haven't had any kopi yet," Arthur replied.

"You haven't had any since you came to the Tower. Why's today any different?" she said. "Anyway, I'm sure I've got a pack of Old Town 3-in-1 somewhere."

"Instant." Arthur made a face.

"You know, almost everyone else drinks it."

"Almost everyone else never had my grandfather's," Arthur said, smiling a little at the cherished memory. Not that he had much of it in his inventory, but proper coffee—bought from a coffee roaster, ground down, stored in Milo tins, and then brewed at home before an unhealthy amount of sugar was added and the whole thing stored away in the refrigerator for the next day—was one of his foundational beliefs.

He wouldn't dirty himself with instant coffee.

Rather than answer him, Mel took the knife and glanced down at his wounded hand at the same time. She cleaned the blade by bending down and washing it in the water. "You should at least put some pressure on that."

"I'll heal it in a bit," Arthur said, shrugging.

"You're over-relying on that technique of yours."

"Maybe. But I can also work on learning what it's doing by giving it different kinds of circumstances to work on." It was really weird how the technique managed to pull his body together. Or perhaps it was the Tower.

You would assume, with an open wound that wasn't stitched together, that new flesh would grow over. He might even end up with a divot in his hand. He'd seen that often enough in some of the industry workers, those who worked in industries that hadn't bothered to modernize because the work was too dangerous or too finnicky for robots. People were cheaper, especially if you paid them under the table.

But here, in the Tower, that flap of flesh would slowly pull itself upwards. It'd stick itself back towards him, in some way that he had not managed to fully understand. Almost like a guiding hand took hold of the flesh and pulled it back, knowing where it should be.

Mostly.

It didn't always happen. If the cut was too much, or if there wasn't enough skin left to cover the wound. If the flap was jolted around too much or was reinjured. Or if that portion of skin just didn't matter, like along his calves where it was half as much bunions.

Pulsing his intention and focus through his body, Arthur could feel the Tower energy coursing through his limbs, pulling from the environment and down his meridians, breaking off from the major ones into smaller and smaller branches till it merged with his very body and worked its magic on him.

One portion of his attention was focused on the feel of the energy; another he kept on their surroundings. After dealing with so, so many leeches, the creatures had chosen to back off. Now, the concern was that there were bigger predators seeking them out.

Which was why he had his spear in hand and his gaze flicking from side to side. Enhanced Eyesight as a trait was powerful in this regard, allowing him to pierce the shadows, to pick out camouflaged monsters like snakes or geckos that hid, waiting. Or even, to notice the ripple in the water, when something a little larger was coming along.

"Water." His voice was calm, almost absent-minded as he watched. No reason to panic.

Mel didn't, of course. By this point, hours after they had begun processing the bodies, they were bone-weary and used to these attacks. She picked the spear she'd left behind, turned and thrust behind almost without looking.

Aimed Strike was not fancy. It wasn't even a proper technique, as far as Arthur was concerned. It was almost useless outside of the Tower, because it relied upon the Tower to aid its use so greatly. It was also extremely costly. All reasons why Arthur had never even considered learning it.

But it did have some major advantages.

Including allowing Mel to attack the swimming eel and strike it without seeing it properly. She skewered the creature and then pulled, lifting the six-foot, purple-skinned, yellow-spotted creature out by its neck. She slammed it a couple of times into a tree, dodging the flailing tail before it stopped moving, and then finished gutting it and tossing it back into the water before continuing her skinning.

An hour, and the patch of skin had stopped bleeding. It was not reattached, though it was well on its way. Mel was walking back over, the last of the monster shards being stuffed into her pocket as she returned. "Time to go."

"Give me a moment," Arthur said. He didn't move though, till she was on proper ground and ready to take over the watch. Then he began to bandage his hand, pushing the flesh back into place. He wasn't entirely certain he'd gained a lot from his contemplations of the healing process, but he had gained... something.

All he could do was push ahead. There was a woman who was counting on him to progress their healing technique and he would not let her down.

Perhaps, more than anything, that was what it meant to be a leader. To do the best for your people, no matter your own doubts.

Or at least, the leader that he wanted to be.

"Damn *monyet*!" Arthur snarled, dodging behind a tree as a clump of rotting food sailed past where he had been. He glared upwards at the monkeys that were hooting and hollering, daring him to stick his head out. Switching hands and grabbing his sling, Arthur dropped a stone in it and began to whirl it around without looking. Sufficient momentum needed to be built before he could loose it, after all.

Behind him, a short distance away, Mel was hiding and doing the same, though her fumbling was a little more clumsy. As the former leader of her own team, one that had been balanced with actual ranged attackers, she had obviously not grown as used to wielding the sling as he had.

"I thought they didn't like marshlands," Arthur said. Not that he was actually trained in the lives and ecosystems of Tower creatures, but he was sure he remembered them being an unusual add on this floor.

"You're lucky."

"Damn my luck!" Stepping out and then jerking back, letting the monkeys waste their ammunition, he waited a beat before stepping out again and releasing the stone. He watched it arc through the air and miss by a good foot, receiving in return the splatter of fruit as he ducked back. "I need more practice."

"You're going to get it," Mel said, amused. She could afford to be, since the monkeys were mostly targeting him. Putting her own words to action, she sent a stone through the air and struck one of the monkeys in the shoulder. It screamed and cradled the injured arm, wobbling away, its affliction unnoticed by the others.

Cursing, Arthur began spinning his sling once more, gaze darting from side to side in search of other ways around. He spotted a quartet of the creatures attempting to flank him. Stepping away to give himself more space, he sent his stone winging over. It caught one of the monkeys mid-leap, bowling it over and sending it crashing down.

More screeching, more screaming, and even greater fury as they realized what he had done. Arthur smiled grimly, dropping another stone in his sling and spinning it up again even as the horde rushed forwards. This was going to suck.

"Why do they hate me so much?" Arthur grumbled, splashing more water on himself. Once the monkeys had run out of easily accessible projectiles, they'd switched to bio-generated ones. Much less deadly, especially since the Tower didn't bother with things like bacterial plagues or infections.

The battle—if you could call being pelted by a bunch of unmentionables a battle with few enough opportunities to return fire—had ended with a draw. After knocking off about four of his hairy assailants permanently, the rest of the injured and angry monkeys had left.

Leaving the pair to collect their winnings and then for Arthur to find a swifter flow of water to wash up. Thankfully, soap was not hard to come across. Not just from the Tower itself but from the creation of the smart and enthusiastic.

Swiping himself down once more, he dunked his clothing once again and then proceeded to wring it all out. Mel glanced over one last time, watching as he draped the still wet article over his body before he began to buckle on his armour.

"Didn't think you were the kind to know how to wash your own clothes," Mel said.

"Heh. I'm no rich kid."

"Really? Because most training camps for the Tower are meant for the rich."

"Not my sifu's." Arthur shook his head a little. "He's old school." He paused, and added, "Real old school. If I didn't know better, I'd swear he was squatting there. Place was made of corrugated metal and salvaged wood. No fans, you cooked with coal fireplaces and you liked it."

Mel blinked, looking at him, and Arthur shrugged. "I think he figured those of us old enough to be there full-time between our other jobs needed to learn to rough it."

She grunted. "Unlike Rick. Or the princess."

"Casey?" he said, surprised. He'd not heard that nickname. "She hasn't done that bad. Doesn't complain."

"Doesn't do much unless she remembers." Mel sniffed. "Her man does it mostly for her."

"Well, I'm sure I'd be lazy too if I had a helper."

"There's a difference between having a servant and... well... what she does. You can tell she's grown up with them," Mel said.

"How?"

"How what?"

"How can you tell?" Arthur clarified.

"It's just the way she moves, the way she reacts. It's a thing," Mel said, waving her hands around as she struggled to answer his question.

"A thing."

"You'll know it when you see it."

"Except, I've seen her and I've not seen it."

Mel just shook her head, refusing to get dragged further into that conversation. Arthur finished buckling, then hefted the backpack he slung over his shoulder. It was rather heavy, what with the various necessities for camping and living outdoors including multiple sets of clothing and the rope they'd used to secure themselves to tree branches while sleeping above-ground.

No tent, though, and no gear for cooking food. Not necessary in this case, though they did bring water filters to at least make sure they could wet their whistle. One advantage of Tower bodies: not needing to eat.

Though most climbers still did—if nothing else, because the habit was hard to break. And they could still taste.

"So. One more day?" Arthur said.

"One more day. Good haul so far, though."

Arthur could not help but nod. So far, the third floor was a slog and a pain, but not too dangerous.

Chapter 70

"You guys again," Arthur said, shaking his head as the quartet came to the bridge. They'd run into Casey and Lam as they were coming back towards the late afternoon and, rather than split up again, had chosen to stick together. From the heavy packs the pair were carrying and their own packs, they'd all been quite successful. Now, though, they were standing before the bridge shakedown quartet who'd clustered together upon seeing Arthur and his group.

"Mr. Chua... How are you? Your trip, successful?" the leader said, grinning widely. Shorter than Arthur though he might be, he did have a good smile as he stepped forward. Not too far from his friends, though. The thugs who'd tried to shake down Rick and Yao Jing.

Arthur eyed the man's hands, remembering how fast he'd moved. Crossing the short distance to Rick, drawing that curved knife he used—what was it called again? The one held underhand and liked by Filipinos and wannabe gangsters in the West. He remembered how the little man had held the blade to Rick's throat.

"My trip was pleasant enough," Arthur said. He glanced to the side, noted how there was a clear path for him and his friends. How even one of the thugs, the gymbro, gave a respectful nod. "You boys have a good day too, eh?"

"Thank you, Mr. Chua." A hesitation that Arthur took to be a pause. Arthur had started moving, hoping to keep a good distance from the man when the other said, "Clan Head Chua?"

Foot half-raised, Arthur let it drop and turned. He was a lot closer than he would have liked. Couldn't actually move far enough away without looking weak. And something in the way the other man stood, the way they clustered, the use of his surname told him that this was a much less antagonistic start. "Yes?"

"What happen last time… we don' wanna trouble you, okay?" Then, looking over to a bemused Casey, the guy nodded to her too. "No offence, ya, Ms. Chin."

"What's your name?" Casey spoke up, piercing brown eyes fixing on the man. Arthur, stepping aside—and coincidentally giving himself more space just in case—idly noted that the pair were almost of the same height. It made Casey decently tall for a woman. Well, a Malaysian woman.

"Leon Wang, Ms Chin." Leon ducked his head low.

"Your idea to hold people up for shards?" Casey said.

He hesitated, then nodded. "We just need a few more, then we cultivate and go. Could go now, but…"

"You don't want to go into the grinder that easy?" Arthur said. "What makes you think they do?" He jerked his head to the others.

"They don't have to go."

"Nor do you," Arthur replied.

"I…" Now Leon hesitated, looking back to his group. When he spoke, his voice was a little less firm. "We got to be faster, *lah*."

"Really. How interesting." He kept his voice cool, but noted how Casey was looking the four over. He could see her turning it over in her mind. Could see her putting things together and making decisions. He was tempted to butt in. They had talked to him. But on the other hand, he was in a more precarious political position than she was.

"Lam. Talk to them," she said. "Test them."

"Yes, Miss."

She didn't even bother to ask what Arthur thought about having his rest interrupted. Instead she strode on back to the clan hall. Arthur sighed and started walking too, so that they matched pace soon after, with Mel trailing along bemused. He waited until she was nearly gone before he added, idly.

"You know, I think they were angling to join us," he said.

"You were slow," Casey said without any remorse.

"Didn't say I was going to take them."

"No? Why not? They're strong-looking climbers who want to leave," Casey said. "And yours aren't as strong, not yet."

"It's not just about strength," Arthur replied.

"It's always about strength."

He shook his head but then considered her words. Maybe she wasn't exactly wrong, but she was looking at it too narrowly in his view. Then again, she never had to worry about the overall strength of the Chins, at least not yet. Adding a couple of strong fighters made them stronger overall. And the ding to their morale was minor; same with the politics.

On the other hand, the Durians were just starting. Adding people who resorted to bullying: it sent a message. It might piss off other climbers on this floor. He might be sacrificing potential new recruits here for this quartet who were, at best, only slightly stronger

To the Chins, they were just a bunch of low-level henchmen, really.

For him, for the Durians ought to be adding people who represented what they stood for.

"There's different types of strength," he said eventually, as they traversed the swaying rope bridges. Neither of them felt like visiting the administration center right away. While Arthur himself had a few items asked for on the quest board—various herbs, gills, and other wanted items—a few hours would make little difference to the quests themselves.

It would, however, make a world of difference in the way he smelled.

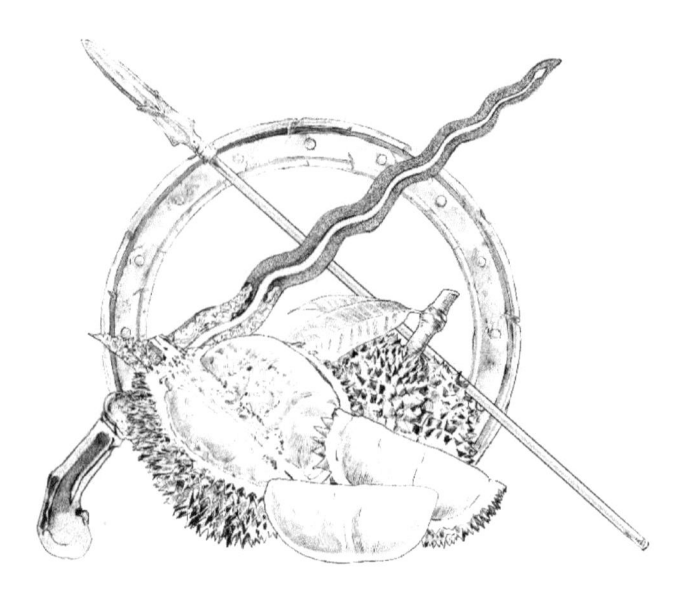

Chapter 71

The clan wasn't ready to upgrade yet. He would not be able to insert another boon for everyone into the clan crest at this time, so whilst speed at getting appropriate cultivation techniques would benefit his peace of mind and his soggy feet, it would do little for the overall clan. Haste, in this case, could lead to significant waste.

That was what Arthur told himself, when he refused to train the movement exercise they'd copied down. Sure, Water Walking wasn't a bad technique. He'd certainly seen worse. But it just wasn't that great. It took a lot of energy to utilize. Sure, it spread the weight-bearing load over a wide area. Great for water walking, but it mattered less when one was climbing around on trees.

Something like Wind Steps—which was, as he'd mentioned, quite popular—actually lightened the body through the use of Tower energy. It was, however, quite intensive on the energy cost, especially as the amount of energy used kept increasing according to the amount of "lightness" needed.

Supposedly, with the right amount of energy, one could fly.

"Come on. You've got to have something," Arthur said, leaning on the counter as he spoke to the floor administrator. "I'm not asking for that much. Low energy use and upgradeable in the future."

"I do not have any such technique for purchase," the attendant repeated for the third time, patiently.

"Look, Wind Steps just isn't cutting it. Or any of these others—Walking Water, Air Skimming, Shadow Jumping. And this one you showed me, a fire-jumping one?" Arthur sighed. "In this place? What's the point of a fire jumping technique?"

"I would not know."

"Exactly. You're the Tower shop, you have to have *something*."

"I do not have any such technique for purchase."

"You said that already." Arthur paused amidst complaining and repeated his words again, slower. "You've said that already."

He saw the smirk, the relief flicker on the attendant's face. Too fast to register normally if you weren't watching for it, but he was. He was. Which meant...

"You have something I can get. Just not by purchase." Silence greeted his words, as he stared at the other. Then he added, slowly, "Or you can't say that."

He turned and glanced at Mel who'd accompanied him over. The rest of the team were back in the clan hall, meditating or just resting after their recent excursion. He'd gathered taxes from his people and brought along his and Mel's share to see what they could acquire.

"Not many options if he can't talk about it," Mel said. "Could it be a hidden quest?"

"Is it?" Arthur asked.

Of course, there was no answer. Wouldn't be much of a hidden quest if the man just said so outright. On the other hand, the thought that it might be a quest had Arthur's mind churning as he recalled the initial period when he'd acquired the clan.

"Wasn't there something about getting access to new quests and reputations because we are a clan?" Arthur said.

"Oh! I remember now. Yes," Mel said. "Is that it? Is there a clan quest for us?"

"Finally!" The attendant threw his hands up. "So slow."

"Hey!" Arthur said, insulted. But rather than follow that useless line of discussion—especially since he couldn't exactly smack the guy over the top of his head, not with the Tower guard so close—he prodded, "What is it?"

"Here!" Reaching under the table, the man extracted a document and slapped it down. "Formed itself and deposited in my inbox the moment you guys arrived."

Mel was impatiently staring at Arthur while he was looking at the document, a dawning horror arriving within him. "Wait. When we arrived, it came?"

"Yes."

"Shit, shit, shit." Arthur stared down at his feet, then stomped off, waving his hand around theatrically in frustration. After a moment, he was back at the table and looking at the puzzled Mel. "The second floor."

Realisation dawned, and she cursed too.

Too late for that option. If there was a clan quest on the previous floor, there was no way they'd ever know. Assuming it was something that Arthur only could trigger. Maybe any one of the Durians could do so? If that was the case, they'd have to send word as fast as they could.

Making a mental note to do that, Arthur turned to the document and pulled it open, eagerly reading what the Tower had in plan for them.

The Heart of the Lost City

Locate the rumored lost city of D'mai and retrieve its heart. Return the heart to the floor administrator for your reward.

Reward: Seven Cloud Stepping Technique (Original), 3 * Seven Cloud Stepping Technique (one use per applicant), Clan Reputation

Along with the document, to Arthur's surprise, was a map. It was not the most detailed of maps—certainly a far cry from the satellite images or driving maps one was used to. But it gave rough coordinates and a few landmarks, including a rather twisted tree with a hole in the center that would be quite distinctive. Good enough, if one was willing to put in the work, to locate the lost city.

"Ever heard of this?" Arthur said, offering the document to Mel.

"The hidden quest? Of course not."

"The city. D'mai. Da-mai. D'may." Arthur tested the word out, going through various pronunciations. After all, it wasn't a word he had come across before.

"Wouldn't be a lost city if I had, would it?"

"Might be lost, lost. Like no one knows where it is. Like El Dorado."

"It wasn't a bad cartoon."

"What?"

"Just an old cartoon. From Disney," Mel said. "El Dorado. Lost city."

"Oh. I was thinking of the actual legend." He paused, then pushed that aside. No point in that discussion, the quest itself was good enough. Though... "What's the heart look like? What *is* it?"

"You'll know it when you see it," the attendant answered.

"Or you could tell me and then I'll definitely know it."

All he got was a shake of the head in answer, making Arthur sigh. Damn rules. Then again, he didn't know how strongly the Tower bound attendants. No one did, since they didn't really discuss their service. Or how they'd ended up serving the Tower.

It was known, though, that once you joined the Tower's service, you didn't ever go back to the real world. Though, there were always persistent rumors that attendants could be promoted, even transfer Towers. So perhaps the life itself wasn't so bad.

Smacking a buzzing mosquito and looking at the smear on his hand, Arthur corrected himself. Unless one was stuck on a hellhole floor like this.

Chapter 72

Days later, the group were on their way out again. They had kept a small portion of the farmed monster cores with them, rather than use them all. After all, the map was vague enough that the question of how long it'd take them to find the lost city was a major unknown.

Of course, they hadn't left the village without issues.

"Seriously, you're leaving for a quest now?" Casey snarled, when Arthur came back from the administrative center and explained things.

"Sure?" he said, shrugging. "It's a good technique that will be important for my clan."

"And what about our deal?" She waved a hand at the building they were in. "What about this, then?"

Arthur's lips pressed tight before he shook his head. "I won't miss out. You need a few months to grow stronger anyway, right?"

"How are you going to grow stronger, tramping through the woods?" Casey said. "If you die, it's useless."

"Well, it'll get you further up, and faster, no?" Arthur said.

She shook her head. "My gains have been marginal so far. If anything, I could have used all the stones for myself and been faster."

"But you couldn't have passed the last floor without us. Not that fast," Arthur pointed out. "And you'll need a group on the sixth too at the very least."

"You think I can't hire people?" she sniffed. "You think me and Lam can't do the rest ourselves?" She gestured over to Rick who was in his corner, cultivating. Not that Arthur expected he wasn't listening as well. "There are always people who could be useful."

"Then you won't miss out much by staying here," Arthur said. "If we don't get back by the time of our deadline, we'll—I'll—still come up."

Again Casey shook her head. "Don't bother if you aren't strong enough either. If you die, then my family will be even more angry. At least, if you come out slow, we still have a clan."

He could see she was severely unhappy with him, but the fact stood that they were allies, not subordinates to one another. He had something she wanted, and she the same. So long as they moved towards the same goal, they'd stick together.

Of course, if he didn't manage to make it back in time, it'd be a problem.

Which was why he pushed them as hard as he dared, his team tromping through the woods as best as they could. Uswah ranged out front, the only one with a working movement technique in the clan. Of course, it wasn't the only movement technique Arthur's present team had.

"Teach me, *lah*. It sounds cool…" Yao Jing continued to pester Rick, chatting away happily.

"No," Rick replied, for the tenth time.

"I'll teach you *my* technique." Yao Jing flexed his biceps not so subtly. "Makes sure you don't lose your physique at all."

So that was how the man had kept his muscles. Without having a set of weights to train against, he had wondered how Yao Jing continued to bulk up. If anything, each time he increased his Body stat, he seemed to look even stronger.

"I don't need a technique to look good," Rick said, running a hand through his floppy hair and flashing a pearly white grin. "I already am."

The snort by Yao Jing said a lot of what he thought, but Arthur could not help but acknowledge Rick's point. The man was good-looking. More than one woman had literally stopped to look him over while they'd wandered around on the second, and now third, floor.

It'd hurt a lesser man's ego.

"Just remember not to use those guns. They're not a lot of fun," Arthur said, reminding Rick. "We don't need to draw in more problems."

"I know!"

"Even if there are concerns." Arthur hesitated. "Problems. Concerns. Blem. Drum. Dumb. Even if it seems dumb."

"*Tak boleh lah*, boss." Jan, behind, shook her head.

"Yeah..." Head bent, Arthur reworked that rhyme in his head as he picked his way across the roots. They were in a "good" part of the marsh right now, where the trees were all close together enough that it took only a little hop to cross open water.

So far, they'd been leaning towards speed and ease of travel rather than moving in a straight line, though eventually, they'd have to curve further east to meet their objective. There had been a brief discussion about borrowing or purchasing boats, but not knowing the terrain in between and when—or how soon—they'd need to discard the flat-bottomed rafts, they'd chosen against it.

By the time nighttime and enough shadows had arrived that the group was forced to wait, they'd covered another good fifteen kilometers or so. A very good distance, considering they were wading through marshlands. It was even in the right direction, mostly.

Of course, the team was mostly dirty and sore by that point. However, the handfuls of core shards from the two swarms of leeches and a flock of nasty birds they'd had to deal with had filled their pouches, which meant that once they had relocated themselves to higher branches where they were marginally safer, it was time for cultivation.

"Remember: minimum six hours sleep, people." Except for him. He and Uswah, thanks to their Yin Bodies could likely run on fewer hours of sleep; but she was their scout. Asking her to not rest fully and be half-functional seemed like a bad idea to him.

He, on the other hand, only needed to plod along and fight. So cutting down to four hours of sleep would be fine enough.

Or at least, that was the plan over the next few days—or weeks—to get to the lost city of D'mai. So long as tromping through the marshes required little complex thought, he'd power on and try to catch up in the few hours in between he had to pull energy into him and upgrade his cultivation.

That way, when they finally got the right technique, he would be ready.

Chapter 73

A week later to the day, they finally arrived at the site of the lost city of D'mai. The trek to the city had grown increasingly perilous, the introduction of non-native fauna to the marshlands adding to the difficulty. The first time a crocodile appeared to pull one of their group into the water, only Rick's deployment of his pistols had ended things without human fatalities.

While Yao Jing spent the day healing, the group took to building makeshift rafts from cut wood and rough-woven vines. Strapping them together and then caulking the gaps with boiled rubber sap and various wood and tree debris kept the rafts mostly waterproof at the bottom and their bottoms dry. The addition of simple benches in the low-walled vessels allowed them to push onward faster. Arthur made note to consider supplying paddle boards in the future.

Inflatable paddle boards, probably.

Once they'd committed to the use of the rafts, travel had grown somewhat less arduous. Not easier, of course, but Uswah was able to pick waterways that allowed them to pass through the marshes with minimal trouble. Where that was not possible, the light rafts could be schlepped over roots till they came to more open areas once again.

It made Arthur regret not doing this from the start, but traversing unknown terrain was always a gamble. That time was simply lost.

"Not much to look at, is it?" Rick said, arms crossed and hands buried in his armpits. Bobbing in the water next to Arthur, he was at the front where his guns were most useful for meeting incoming threats. Not that they'd had to use Rick's guns too often, though glimpses of something large and white in the water had them all on edge.

"No, but I guess that's why it's called a lost city." Arthur had to admit, the man might have been selling the ruins a little hard. Beyond a few crumbling stone walls that peeked out of the water, the lost city of D'mai was truly lost, sunken beneath the water. If not for the walls and the sudden change in vegetation, they might never have realized they'd stumbled upon it.

"Rectangle," Jan said, calling down from where she'd climbed a nearby tree. Yao Jing and Mel traded cores behind Arthur, almost making him roll his eyes at the betting. "This lake is definitely not natural."

"Not sure you can call it a lake, what with trees inside," Arthur said. Of course, the trees in the rectangular expanse of water were mostly young, significantly smaller than the ones all around. The occasional large trees were few and far between, most likely from someone's precious garden.

Most interesting was the massive tree in the center. Not a marshland tree with its wiry, crawling roots but something from the western hemisphere. An oak or something like that, with silver bark on its wide trunk, broad leaves, and massive branches that sheltered any beneath its shade.

"Then, what do you call it?" Jan said with a snort. She dropped low, adding, "Saw fish. Water's very clear."

"No lotuses," Arthur said, idly. "Not muddy enough for leeches."

"Thank God," Rick muttered.

They weren't moving now, just waiting for Uswah to scout their surroundings. It would be hours before she was back as she was jumping from shadow to shadow on the perimeter of the lake, intent on ensuring there were no traps. Or any obvious clues they might be missing for the quest.

"Any ideas what the Heart of the Lost City might be?" Arthur asked the group.

"The tree," Mel said, immediately.

"*Aiyo! Ngo yao gong go dit!*" Yao Jing complained.

"I'm not carrying a tree back," Arthur said, flatly.

"Maybe its heart? Heart of the tree," Rick ventured.

"What heart of tree?" Jan scoffed.

"Sap, maybe?" Rick said.

"The inner core?" Mel offered.

"I'm not cutting that tree down just for a quest." Arthur jerked his chin towards the immense tree in the distance. "Never mind the sheer destruction of a natural beauty, I didn't bring an axe. Did you?"

"Then what?" Jan asked.

Arthur could only shrug, feeling his low-berth raft bob as he did so. He had no idea, but there was another, bigger problem. Thus far, to move, they'd been using poles. The marshlands always offered something to push off; if not the ground, then nearby trees and the like.

However, the rest of the lake—the submerged city—looked a lot deeper. He could see, reflected in the nearly clear water ahead, portions of the ground below. Their makeshift poles might not reach, and the worst thing they could do was float out to the middle and end up stuck.

"We need oars," Arthur pronounced.

"One, two?" Mel said.

"Double-headed?" When everyone stared at Rick, he mimed the motion of dipping one side and then another. "Like kayaks."

"Maybe?" Arthur considered. He wasn't sure that oars like that would make sense, not with the way their skiffs were made.

"Single oar and rudder," Yao Jing said, gesturing to the back of his own craft. The group stared at it, the way there was a cradle of sorts to allow placement of a spear, or perhaps an oar that was sloped and twisted a little. Arthur leaned back a little, staring at the whole thing as his imagination put two and two together.

"Was this drawn from something?" Arthur said.

"Traditional." Yao Jing gestured to the side where the trees were. "I can make. Not good but will work."

"Yeah, I guess that makes sense." Arthur gestured for the others to get to work, knowing that Uswah was going to be focused on keeping them safe when she got back. "Rick, you're on guard duty."

"Why me?" Rick said, affronted.

"You good at carving?"

"Actually, yeah. Shop was one of my favorite classes."

"Shop?" Arthur said, confused. Before the man could explain, he held a hand up. "Fine, you carve. I'll watch." He was not ashamed to admit, woodwork was not a skillset he had. Now, all they had to do was wait for Uswah.

She slipped in next to him. Uswah had nearly caught him by surprise again, if he had not seen the flicker of movement out of the corner of his eye as she emerged from a nearby tree and then jumped again, slipping between whatever realm there might be in the shadows to reach him. Her ability to step between shadows was powerful but short-ranged. At least for now.

"What did you learn?" Arthur said.

"No one else around. Lake's rectangular. Very long. No creatures that seemed different, no settlements or other boats." Uswah replied, only a trace of disappointment registering on her face at not being able to scare him. Even when she wasn't hiding in the shadows, she blended in pretty well with the trees. Unlike some of the bright colors favored by Malay women, Uswah's tudung—her headscarf—was an olive green that made for decent camouflage.

"So, nothing," Arthur said to tease her. He received a flat stare in return which made him smile before he gestured at the boats and the work being done. "Any good at carving?"

"No."

"Neither am I." Arthur stared outwards, into the water, and shook his head again after a moment. "I don't like it. It's too easy."

"Probably."

"Suggestions?"

"Up there."

"What?" Arthur looked upwards, crouching down a little at the same time while his spear head came vertical. Instinctively, just in case something was jumping at him. Not that there was anything, but he was looking up anyway. After a moment, he got it. "You want to look from up there."

"Yes," Uswah said. "Maybe I'll see something more."

"Good as any suggestion I have." He hesitated, looking at the distance into the lake, the lack of shadows and tree branches for her to use. She might be able to make it… or probably not. "Who are you joining for the trip?"

No answer. When Arthur looked over, she was gone, already faded into a shadow. He'd figure it out, later. It was not the biggest concern after all.

Right now, working out what the trick was, was.

Chapter 74

Poling their way with their makeshift oar-and-rudder combination across the water, Yao Jing's craft in the lead by sheer dint of skill, the group traveled the unnatural lake with bated breath. Weird to think that a marshland had a lake, but the clear water beneath them, the fish that darted in and out of sight at the edges of their vision told the truth of the lake beneath.

Why build a settlement on a flood plain? Why was a flood plain even possible, when the marshland all around should have drawn in the water? Perhaps the land beneath had washed away? Perhaps the marshland had appeared afterwards? Perhaps the Tower builders had failed geography and landscaping class?

Questions, questions, questions.

As usual, few enough answers.

"Buildings are remnants," Uswah muttered, crouched beside Arthur as she peered below. Her eyes were narrowed in thought. They caught an occasional glimpse of a particularly sturdy piece of construction beneath the waters. "Must be old."

"Or the way the water came in and washed it away did a lot of damage quickly," Arthur said. "Anyway, you're supposed to be watching for monsters."

"I am." Uswah looked up and scanned the surface of the lake before shaking her head and turning back to stare underwater. "But there's nothing above. So it's going to come from below."

"Yeah..." He sighed and turned to look backwards. Most of the team members had a boat to themselves, though the makeshift boats they were using could fit two comfortably, three possibly. Which meant that having everyone having their own boats left them with spares if trouble began.

However, Uswah was better off watching than poling, given her disability, and Rick's handguns were still their most powerful short-range weapons. Of course, unlike in movies, creatures didn't drop immediately after getting shot once or winged, so it was foolish to put him to work poling when they might need his support soon.

On the other hand, having him team up with Jan might have been a bad idea.

"What you mean I'm splashing," Jan growled. "You try oaring."

"Rowing. No such thing as oaring."

"Why not?" Jan said. "Pole. Poling. Sail. Sailing. Oar. Oaring!"

"That's not how it works!" Rick said, exasperated. He ran a hand through his flopping hair, his tanned skin and bulging arm muscle showing for a second. Arthur turned away, idly wondering if he was flexing on purpose while doing that or because he'd been hanging out with Yao Jing too much.

"This is Malaysia. It can work." She smirked.

"You don't change a language just because you want to!"

"Why not?"

"Because that's not how it works!"

Arthur tuned out their arguments, shaking his head a little. He knew their voices were likely carrying, but that was for the best. If they were going to be attacked, they might as well get it over now, rather than wait when they were in the middle of the lake.

Sadly, that idea had yet to bear fruit. Beyond some flying fish that had struck at them initially and been killed with ease, they had yet to be attacked.

"What do you think? Mythical or mutation?" Arthur asked, curiously.

"Myth," Uswah replied immediately.

"Like?"

"*Hantu air.*" Water spirits. She touched her lips and chest then, warding against bad luck as she looked around. "*Dah banyak orang mati di sini.*" It was said that the spirits inhabited places like these where people had drowned.

"Water spirits don't really tell me much, you know," Arthur said. "And that's mostly malaria and dengue and dysentery from before. Nothing too worrying..."

"We are in the Tower." Uswah's lips thinned. "They made our beliefs into mockeries." Then, a slight tilt of her head. "At least, the legends. Not Allah."

Arthur grunted. True enough. They might mock or pervert the older mythologies, even some of the current ones, but so far, he'd not heard of any creatures calling themselves gods appearing in the Tower. Not Hindu or Muslim or Christian or Norse. Angels, Valkyries, servants, surely. Including about half a dozen variants of them, in one form or another. But no gods.

Which was probably for the best. The kind of shitstorm that would create, Arthur had no desire to see. There were enough crazies trying, and failing, to blow up the Towers as it was. So much so that the UN had given up and even designated a Tower in the middle of a desert to allow the most enthusiastic zealots a chance to try their best at taking one down.

Last he heard, the waitlist to try whatever explosive they meant to wield was half a year long.

"So. Hantu air," Arthur said as he strained to push the boat onwards, shifting the oar from side to side and trying not to overshoot. Easier said than done, of course. "What exactly does that mean?"

"Depends. Lots of types," Uswah said. "Mostly, spirits you cannot see. Just must be appeased." She raised a hand and waved it around. "But we're not in an Advanced Tower yet, so no need to worry about the immaterial."

Arthur's lip twitched, grateful that at least one other person had a vocabulary. Well, Rick did, though he might not admit to it. The man was strange. "Good. Because I haven't learnt how to coat my weapons with chi just yet." He took his hand off the oar for a moment to waggle it around. "Only got my dart and those are..."

"Not good."

"Exactly. So what else?"

"Snakes, water skimmers. Fish and eel. Twisted humans."

Behind them, a voice called out, "Zombies."

"Nah, we don't really have that tradition," Arthur said, confidently.

"No. Zombies!" Mel's voice grew more strident. "On the right."

The pair turned, eyes widening to see nothing that disturbed the serene water. There were ripples, of course—a low breeze blowing through the lake could create that—but nothing else. Except... Arthur looked down, trying to stare through the refracting walls beneath the surface.

"Now this is just insulting," Arthur hissed, reaching for his spear that he'd propped up beside him. "We don't do zombies."

"Now you know how we feel," Uswah said, half-amused. "As bad as the *gerak lu* for changing things."

Then, there was no time to talk, as their assailants reached them.

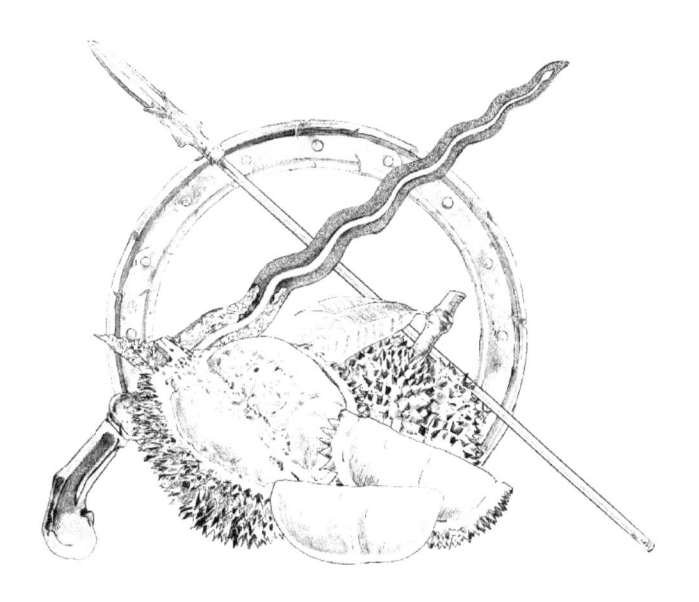

Chapter 75

The water was shallow enough at points for the zombies to rise. At other points, they swam upwards, buoyed unnaturally to the surface by withered flesh and stringy muscles to reach for the boats, tearing at string and ivy and at the edges. Faces, familiar in the bioprop way of being in the background of every movie, stared up at them, faces melted, eyeballs missing or falling apart, bone beneath.

They were dressed in torn t-shirts and worn jeans, in underwear or nothing at all, so rotted through that they might have just been skeletons. They glowed in Arthur's cultivation sense, seeming to pull energy from the Tower towards them to power their movements.

Myth and movies failed them. No one needed to be told to aim for the head, to crush skulls and pierce brain cells, to destroy what was meant to empower them. But these weren't really zombies, these were hantu air in possession of human corpses, and because of that, they weren't powered by a twitching mass of brain cells but something more, something darker.

Something that much preferred its space.

A spear shot forwards from Arthur's hand, piercing an eye socket. He twisted and lifted, pulling the head off the body to bring the entire weapon down in a swirling loop onto another water spirit that had managed to get half of its body on the boat.

His spear crushed both skulls. But the first body had not stopped scrambling, moving a little more mindlessly now, unseeing of the world around it. It continued to attempt to rise, even as a curved scythe sliced at its fingers and dropped the clambering monster back in the water.

"They're not dying," Arthur swore over the racket.

People were shouting and grunting and crying as they fought, between the crack of bullets striking bodies as Rick unloaded his weapon. He fired swiftly and constantly, the retort of bullets piercing enemies continuing to fill the air.

Of little use.

"Body, body, body!" Uswah said, eyes almost seeming to glow. "The Yin energy, it's collected in the chest. Strike the chest!"

"What?" Arthur said, surprised. But he was too trained to stop just because he was surprised, too experienced to let himself freeze. One of the creatures was nearly over the stern, fuller and more put together than the others. His spear shot outwards, crashing into the body, piercing all the way through. He yanked the weapon backwards, felt it catch, and swore as he booted the now unmoving thing off his spear.

Feeling fingers grasped at his leg, pulling at his stability. He stumbled sideways, using the edge of his spear to trail along the water, across bodies as he raked through flesh. A darting figure took the fingers off, giving him a little reprieve to steady himself.

"Body shot. Body shot!" Uswah kept calling, taking a swipe when she could.

He had a few moments to handle himself and focus. Balance set, he struck. His spear pierced bodies, its shaft crushed ribs, and the occasional boot took a monster in the sternum to send it off his boat. Where they had been nearly overwhelmed, they regained space.

Enough for him to look up and assess the damage.

It was bad.

Rick and Jan were doing fine. Though now that he had a moment, he realized he'd not heard the retort of the loud—yeesh, guns were loud—pistols going off for a bit now. One was holstered, he could see. He wasn't certain where the second one was, as Rick fought with a parang and a bowie knife in either hand. Strong as he was, he took off limbs and punched through fragile rib cages with overhand crushing moves of the parang, or stabbed and sliced with the bowie knife.

Jan was doing fine on her end as well, spinning her spear and battering monsters aside with casual ease each moment. Together, the pair had mostly dealt with their attackers.

The problem was Mel and Yao Jing. Mel was nearly overwhelmed, fighting by herself on her boat. Only thing that kept her in the game was the pulse of power she sent rippling along the edge of her spear to empower attacks. But all too soon, she'd run out, Arthur knew. And then, the monsters still clambering onboard would overwhelm her by sheer volume of numbers.

As for Yao Jing...

"Where's Yao Jing?" Arthur cried, eyes widening. The man in front was gone from his boat, and the zombies that had clambered onto it were milling around, puzzled.

That was all the time he had to think, before he had to get back to stabbing. The creatures kept coming, forcing him to strike out again and again whilst quietly cursing their lack of mobility. With ten or so feet between each boat, providing direct aid was impossible.

But he had to do something.

As he fought, he pulled energy into his hand, pouring it into a Refined Energy Dart. Inspiration and madness ran through him, as he saw Mel slowly get overwhelmed. Her spear attacks were shortened and then the weapon was dropped, traded for knives and elbows.

Energy built up, each moment. Rather than releasing it, he kept the energy contained. He took the precaution at least of pushing it to the outside of his hand, within his own aura but not within his skin. It was harder than ever, and he felt energy drain at an exponential rate.

Control began to slip aside, and he turned to the bow. He released it, just overhead, just as a zombie was clambering up.

The explosion of bones and flesh threw the corpse away along with other bodies it pushed aside. He grinned triumphantly, almost getting clobbered by a swinging hand as he reveled in his victory.

"Oi! Move," Uswah snapped.

"Right! Jump to her. I got this," Arthur said. "Give me... five!"

Uswah booted another figure away, saw his left hand begin to glow, and nodded.

He just hoped that her jumping to help Mel was not sending her to her death.

Like Yao Jing's.

Chapter 76

"Ready!" Arthur roared as he dropped the spear and elbowed the zombie attempting to grab him. He shoved, pushing it further back and then swept his hand down and outwards, twisting at the hips to complete the throw as the creature chose to grip him rather than just tumble over like the good little possessing spirit it should have been.

Left hand glowing with energy that cackled, fingers burning and hurting, Arthur pointed at Mel's boat and released the ball of power. He watched it streak off, crossing the space at the speed of a fastball. Moments later, just as the energy was about to impact, he shouted:

"Go!"

Energy released, exploding outwards and sending rib cages and other portions of zombie aside. Piled as they were all around the boat, piled on top of Mel herself, the boat rocked and parts of the raised lip tore apart. Vines that held the whole craft together began to come apart even as the creatures were cast aside.

In the gap that formed, in the shadow of moving bodies, a figure wielding a knife and shadowy tendrils rose, throwing and upsetting zombies and chopping with swift strikes, over and over again. Arthur spotted her olive-green tudung. Long sleeves whipped around her as she struck, over and over again, to free a friend.

For a moment, Mel stood clear, bleeding from wounds on her scalp, on her arms. Knives kept moving, threading their way through the bodies pressing against her, punching and pushing.

For a moment, it looked like it might work.

Then the boat rocked, balance was thrown and Uswah stumbled. Mel moved to back her up, and in that moment, the space cleared was filled again with hantu air. As the concussive blast faded and the surprise ended, the creatures rose again and the pair were forced to fight back-to-back.

Arthur himself was hard pressed. No longer aided by Uswah, he was forced to focus on his footing, on swinging and striking and pushing the hantu air away. The smack of the heavy spear and the black spearhead rang through the surroundings; Heavenly Sage's Mischief surged through him, giving the strength to push on.

And on, and on. Moments dragged on, and the group was forced to hold without sight of aid or a potential rescue. How many had he killed? How many had he dispersed or cast back into the water? Arthur could not count. Each shattered chest, each ball of Yin energy held deep within the corpse's chest that was disrupted was another spirit chased away.

But they kept coming.

Breathing grew hard, his motions jerky. He shook another monster off, even as his limbs burnt. Eyes stung from sweat, and he swore. Something shifted and the boat rocked.

And then, a roar as a body was picked up and spun around. Slamming into other figures, into one another. Yao Jing swung another body, crushing a pair of hantu.

"Into the water!" the soaking-wet man cried.

"What?" Arthur said, surprised.

"Into the water! Dive. NOW!"

Arthur froze. The thought of jumping in, where the monsters lurked. He could not, would not... There was no reason for this. It was insane. It was dangerous and likely to end them all. Others hesitated too, the precarious balance between zombies and Tower climbers broken.

Before he could make up his mind, his choice was taken away. Arthur was bull-rushed and shoved into the water by Yao Jing, taken over the edge as his knees clipped another. Together, they fell into the water, tumbling past bodies. The watery embrace took him.

Under, where the corpses lay.

And moments later, the rest of the team joined him.

***

Arthur went in holding his spear. He dared not let it go, even if it was probably not the most appropriate weapon for wielding in the water. Contrary to Greek mythology and numerous movies, including *Aquaman*, long weapons meant to sweep and twist were not exactly the easiest weapons to wield underwater. Tridents were used above water, after all, to stab at fish swimming below while you stood on rocks or the shore or river's edge. Not for swimming in the water and trying to impale things or sweep them up, like any good polearm wielder knew to do.

Despite the impracticality, Arthur wasn't about to let his spear go. It was his first weapon he had been gifted. Back braced, he had hit the water hard and was driven below the surface by Yao Jing who kicked and kicked till they were fully submerged. Then, the man broke away after shoving Arthur deeper.

Water pressure around his ears, some of it going up his nose. He fought the instinctive need to breathe and spit and exhale, kicking hard now that he was free, twisting around as he instinctively sought to go deeper and away from the writhing mass of rotting flesh and enchanted limbs above.

He figured he had about a few seconds before the hantu clocked onto his presence and came after him. Until then, he needed space. Maybe with a bit of distance he might last. Even outswim them...

The silence of the water was startling, after all those wheezing gasps, thump of weapons, tearing of flesh, and panting humans and droning insects. The drone and lap of water against his ears, the muffled movements and noises from above might as well be whispers.

Peering about through squinting eyes that had begun to burn just a little, Arthur was faced with the sight of even more zombies rising from the depths. He disassociated for a moment, his mind picturing the scene like a movie poster, creatures of horror and fear and death rising from below.

He saw them swarming up in singles and doubles, breaking through the surface and clustering around the boats. Emerging dripping, pieces of flesh pulled free as long-rotted bodies came apart. Others emerged from the earth, struggling upwards as twitching limbs sought to reach the boats.

Feet kicking in rapid motions, he angled away. One of the zombies came near and he swiped to the left, cutting with his kris that he'd drawn. Poison rushed into the body, the monster twitching a little but not shifting course as it kept ascending.

Leaving him alone.

All of them were leaving him alone.

Surprised, Arthur floated in the water, holding his weapons aloft. He stared as zombie after zombie headed for the boats. Further above, Yao Jing was bobbing in the water, paddling away from the boats with big sweeps of his hands.

Well, he'd be damned.

Or not.

Chapter 77

By unspoken agreement and a bit of waving, the group had retreated and regrouped around the tree. No zombies around the tree itself, not even under the massive shade it cast. The creatures kept clambering around the skiffs, taking tents and bags to the water, crushing and separating their goods, though somehow Rick had managed to snag his own bag when he went down, and so had Yao Jing.

Dripping wet and grumpy, Arthur rested against a massive tree root, watching the slowly subsiding swarm, the occasional zombie still clambering around or trying to tear down the water. But his team was here, wet and injured and miserable, but alive.

"What the hell?" Rick said, dragging himself upwards along the root along with his bag. "What was that?"

"Hantu air," Uswah replied, swiping at her face with her free hand. It did little for the blood that dripped from a ragged cut along the edges of her tudung, the wet headscarf pressed against her head such that it had molded itself to her. She grimaced at the sight of the blood, pressing with her hand against the cut in a vain attempt to stop the bleeding.

Arthur looked around, taking in the damage. He was grateful everyone had, for the most part, left their armour behind. The humidity, the sweat, the moss that grew on armour, and the constant threat of falling into the marshlands was enough to have driven them to discard the greater protection. It meant no one had drowned trying to swim over.

That, of course, meant that everyone was more exposed to getting cut and stabbed and otherwise injured. Thankfully, one of the aspects of the hantu air was their lack of focused attacks. Human fingers just weren't very good at clawing. Sure, you could rip surface skin easily enough if you didn't cut your nails, but to get a good grab? And not tear off your own nails, especially when the same flesh that held those nails in place were rotting? Much more difficult.

And teeth... well, there were much the same problems. Never mind the fact that unlike real zombies, the possessed corpses had been less likely to try for a bite or two. So the damage from each monster that had gotten into grappling range had been minimal: bruises and torn flesh and surface cuts.

But there had been a lot of them.

And there was, of course, the mental damage to be weighed too.

"So disgusting," Mel complained, running fingers through her hair again. She managed to find another finger that had been pulled off a corpse. She yanked it off her dark hair, tossing it into the water where it sank without a trace.

She was one of the worst off, multiple cuts across her face, upper arms, along her neck and down her torso. Her clothing had been torn quite a bit, though the sports bra beneath ensured she had a decent amount of modesty preserved. The worst was along her left collarbone where a ragged flap of flesh hung loose, shifting and bleeding with each movement. Her other hand pushed against that flap as she tried to staunch the bleeding.

"I want to know why they stopped attacking us!" Rick said, looking around at the recovering group. "Is no one else concerned that might just, you know, change?"

"Of course we're worried," Arthur said. "And I'd like to know that too. But we're tired. And we have injuries to care for."

"You got that healing technique, right? Just heal them," Rick said dismissively.

Arthur shook his head, choosing not to answer the question. He should know by now it didn't work that way. And if he didn't, Arthur saw no point in discussing it. More importantly, he was curious how the man managed to escape with barely a scratch.

When Arthur voiced his question, Rick shrugged. "I'm just that good." A glance at Jan had her shrugging. She mouthed something, but Arthur had a hard time reading her lips. "How'd *you* manage to stay in one piece?" Rick asked.

Arthur smiled back, mockingly. "I'm just that good."

Rick snorted, looking back to where the horde was slowly dissipating. "We got a lot of cores lost in there."

"Not all of us," Yao Jing said, tapping his bag with his knee where he sat. He was busy tearing up some of his shirts to offer them as makeshift bandages to the others. Not that most were bothering with bandages, the bleeding having already slowed. It would have been a waste anyway, what with their lack of supplies.

"Enough complaining already," Mel said, when Rick opened his mouth. "We got hurt, but no one's dead. Now we just have to heal and get ready."

Rick frowned, and Arthur pointed to the man's chest. "Don't you have to clean your guns?"

"Gun." Reflexively, Rick touched the hilt of his remaining weapon and grimaced. "Shit. We got to get my pistol back."

Arthur waved his hand to the water. "Go ahead."

"I can't... I don't have a full replacement!" Rick said, frustrated.

"I'm not getting into that water again, not anytime soon. And neither are my people."

"What is your problem with me?" Rick exploded, stepping over to where Arthur lay, fists clenching by his side. "You've been riding me hard. I offered to join your clan. I offered to pay you. I AM paying you. And even on this shitshow, where your precious Chin girl isn't around, I came along when she didn't. But you won't give me a break."

Silently, Arthur returned the look, then glanced at the clenched fists. He waited a beat before he spoke, slowly. "You're a spoilt rich kid who has been throwing his weight around." Arthur raised a hand, cutting Rick off before he could speak. "I don't care if you brought guns to a Tower where most don't. But did you ever consider what happens if you die and those weapons get stolen? What having you in my clan might mean if you do die?"

"I can't help the advantages I have. And I won't tie a hand behind my back just because you don't like it."

"No one's asking you to. I'll even take advantage of it. But you don't know what you don't know, and you won't admit it." Arthur's jaw jutted out, indicating Yao Jing. "Then you drag my people into trouble and try to pull us deeper into your shit.

"You want to compare with Casey? Fine. She's a spoilt rich kid too, but she knows it. And she's not trying to join my group or act like she's one of us. We've got a business relationship, and that's just the way it'll stay. Better than an ally that drags you into trouble." Arthur pointed to the water, continuing. "You lost something important. But rather than asking for our help, you demanded it. So yeah, I have a problem with you."

"No manners, this guy!" Jan muttered.

Arthur shot her a look, not needing her to contribute. Rick looked taken aback at the vitriol spewed at him, then shock turned to rage. His fists trembled and his face turned red, suffusing the darker complexion as he almost snarled. Then, turning on his heel, he stalked off.

Silence filled the clearing for a while, a strained one, as they all stared at Arthur. He turned away, not wanting to deal with them and stripped his shirt off, wringing it out. He really wanted to deal with his boots and socks, but that was later. He needed to be able to run if the zombies did come back after all.

Chapter 78

It was a short while later, when the rest of the team had slumped over to cultivate or just grab a few moments of peace—and sleep, in the loudly-snoring Yao Jing's case—that Mel made her way to sit beside Arthur. She offered no commentary, watching as he scanned the water obsessively and worked on wringing out his damp socks, the pair of boots propped up beside him slowly dripping dry.

"Well?" Arthur snapped after a moment.

"Why do you think the hantu air didn't follow us, after we dove into the water?" she said.

Having expected a different question, Arthur answered without thinking. "I don't know."

"But you've been thinking about it, right?" she said.

"I..." He hadn't, of course. He'd been mulling over the confrontation with Rick, thinking about what they had both said. Wondering if the other man would return, if he would try for his pistol in the water. Wondering if he'd been too harsh on Rick.

Or just harsh enough.

"You should be thinking," she said. Nodding at the spearhead that he had cleaned off and was resting against him, she continued. "Your job isn't *that*."

"I have to be strong."

"You have to be smart," she said. "Yao Jing saved us out there."

He grunted in reply.

"It should have been you," she added.

"How was I supposed to know they wouldn't attack us in the water!" Arthur protested.

"I don't know. But you should have."

"That's not fair."

She arched an eyebrow. When he still looked stubborn, she added, "Didn't you just tell someone else off about their own background, about holding on too tight to it? It's not fair. But it is what you have."

He winced, bending his head. Unspoken between the two of them was the knowledge that he held what she had wanted, what she had sought. What she had sacrificed friends for. Sharmila, Rani, Daiyu. Friends who had followed her, only for her to lose out on the final prize at the end: a clan seal, the one he had used to establish the Benevolent Durians and now marked him as clan head.

"Why don't you hate me?" Arthur said, softly. "The clan..."

"It's too late for that," Mel said, a twisted smile on her lips. "Killing you won't change it. Beating you won't make you a better clan head." She tilted her head to the side, regarding him. "Well... maybe."

He snorted at the attempt at levity, but it was strained. This was not a topic that either could find funny. Not for a long time, at least.

"There's a small part of me glad that I am not you." Mel shook her head. "It's not like I was trained to be a businesswoman either, like Casey." She tilted her hand sideways. "My mother makes *kuih*. My father cooks *goreng pisang*."

"Oh, which one?" Arthur said, curiously.

"It's in SS2."

"Wait, the one in the corner? Across the durian stall?" When she nodded, he laughed a little. "I used to have a regular pickup there. For a customer."

"Small world."

"I guess." He paused, humming in thought. "Your father, eh?" When she nodded, he frowned. "Saw your sister too, then." Unsaid was the other side of that comment. That Mel had never been there.

"I didn't want it." She waved a hand around. "I couldn't, wouldn't, slave over hot oil or steaming pans. I wanted something more. They let me go... even if they hated it. Let me train with my sifu, let me study how to make it through."

"Like me."

She nodded.

"But then I came in and it wasn't anything I dreamed of. But Amah Si needed me. So I helped her." She made a face, as she added, "Maybe longer than I should have. But we had a chance at something. Something more."

"And I took it from you."

Now, she smiled a little. "We still have a chance."

"If I don't mess it up."

"Yes. Start thinking." She nodded to the water that had grown peaceful, lapping gently at the roots, the drifting pieces of their rafts floating aside.

"And start doing it fast. Before we really do lose anyone else." Quieter now, she added, "Don't fail like me. The regrets..." She wiped at her tears then and Arthur reached over to give her a side hug. She stiffened at the contact at first, but eventually she just leaned into him, their conversation over for now.

Long minutes later, Arthur spoke up, softly.

"I can think of three reasons for why the hantu air didn't chase us in the water." He paused, and when Mel made an agreeable sound, he continued. "The first is the most obvious. It's just what the Tower programmed them to do." He frowned before adding, "Not that they're actual programs; they're too... alive for that. But they also sometimes have weird rules. And maybe those rules make coming to this tree or going into the water safe."

"How do you tell?"

Arthur could only shrug to her question. Someone smarter than him might be able to figure it out, but he certainly hadn't come into the Tower to get a PhD on monster dynamics.

"Second possibility. They can't sense something that's all the way wet, or is mostly wet. Or, they are trying to make us wet." He grunted. "That'd explain why the rafts took so long to attract them. And why, when we were in the water, they stopped caring." Then he added, slowly, "But it doesn't explain why, when I attacked one in the water, it didn't divert to me. But maybe they just don't react to attacks, to pain, like we do." He shrugged. "They are just possessing the bodies, right?"

A nod greeted his assertion before he sighed. "The third idea is, well, sort of the same. But subtly different, maybe. They're spirits of the water, right? Maybe what they want, or need, is for the living to become part of the water, to join with them. So when we went into the water and swam through it, we basically did what they wanted. If that's the case, they're not necessarily hostile at all. And that means it'd be safe to get our gear."

Mel nodded along quietly to his words as he spoke, eventually pushing away to stare back at Arthur. "But why won't they come here?" She gestured to the tree they sat upon. "Why aren't we being attacked?"

Arthur let out a long huff. "In scenario one, stupid Tower rules. In scenario two, they don't know we're here yet. And for scenario three..." He trailed off, then shrugged. "No idea. Maybe the tree itself has a spirit which pushes them away?"

"You don't sound very confident about that."

"That's because I'm not."

She nodded. "Now what?"

"A few things. We need to test whether we can get into the water." He grimaced, then gestured outwards. "If we can get Rick to help us, and if we work out that they don't really care about us at all, he can get his gun back. And us, our stuff. Also, rather importantly, a way back."

"That's one thing."

"The other is finding the Heart of the City." He looked around, grimacing. "Maybe Rick's spotted something, but so far, all I've got is a big tree."

"So, we split into two groups? Or three."

"Two for now." He tapped the tree, continuing. "I need to be on this one. Can you... ?"

"Placate Rick and apologise for you?" At his slight nod, she snorted. "Yes. And no. In that order."

"Fine, I'll apologise myself."

"Good boy."

Eyes narrowing, he shooed her off so he could cultivate. What was it with the women in his clan giving him sass?

Chapter 79

Hours. It took him hours to pull energy from the Tower into his body, to refill his stores of cultivated energy and to ready himself for the next fight. He had not progressed much since their leaving the clan hall, only adding a few more refined energy points that he was storing away for a fight or eventual use. With only a few cores in the pouch he'd attached to his belt, he would need to be careful about his energy use. At least until they managed to retrieve their stores from the lake.

Or found more monsters that dropped their cores.

Cultivation Speed: 2.371 Yin
Energy Pool: 22/22 (Yin)
Refinement Speed: 0.1421
Refined Energy: 0.412 (26)

Attributes and Traits

Mind: 15 (Multi-Tasking, Quick Learner, Perfect Recall)
Body: 13 (Enhanced Eyesight, Yin Body, Swiftness)
Spirit: 10 (Sticky Energy, From the Dregs)

Techniques
Night Emperor Cultivation Technique
Focused Strike
Accelerated Healing – Refined Energy (Grade III)
Heavenly Sage's Mischief
Refined Energy Dart
Bark Skin

Partial Techniques
Simultaneous Flow (54.7%)
Yin-Yang Energy Exchange (34.6%)
Heavenly Sage's Heaven Beating Stick (33.8%)
Refined Exploding Energy Dart (54.3%)

Two fairly new entries among his techniques, one of which made him smile a little. The Bark Skin technique kept him in one piece, though he had been careful in its use. After all, it drained energy, even if it was just Tower energy.

Bark Skin
Toughen the cultivator's skin to make it like hard bark, offering greater protection from cuts, scrapes and crushing techniques. May be upgraded in the future.
Cost: 1 Energy per minute

In a fight, a full point for a minute wasn't that much, but he'd been lucky enough not to get swarmed and thus had not needed it. Not that it had helped Mel that much. Then again, there was a reason it was a beginner technique.

More interesting was the other new technique that had popped up. For something he'd put together out of desperation, it had worked out quite well. While the Tower hadn't provided him a full description of the technique, he knew enough to know what the final result should look like.

Refined Exploding Energy Dart

Project a dart of compressed and refined energy, to strike an opponent at range. Will explode upon impact.

Cost: 0.3 Refined Energy

It was one of the reasons he'd even dared try for it. There were other options that he'd browsed, including producing multiple energy darts, piercing energy darts, and the like. Yet, making things go boom had an appeal. Especially when it was something that formed from one's own hand, rather than via an external instrument. Like a gun.

Lips compressed, Arthur pushed away the thought. Whatever his prejudices about the weapon, about Rick, it was his own problem. The man had been, for the most part, fair with them.

Sticking the most recent point into his Body stat had been almost a no-brainer. While he did want to increase his other attributes, Body was always going to be his most important one. After all, he had to keep himself alive.

And frankly, looking at people like Ferdinand of the Reborn North and any of the members of the Valorant Guild, there was something to be said about just being so tough that no one dared mess with your guild. Strength was strength, no matter how you cut it. Especially when the world bent the rules for Tower climbers, once they got back outside.

His Tower energy was now fully topped up and his injuries mostly healed. But damn it, he really needed to find time to figure out how to upgrade that healing technique. The fact that not even a single line had appeared showed that whatever he was doing was refining the speed and his technique as it stood now, but it wasn't transformative enough to be a new technique or even an upgrade on the current one.

But there was a lot to see and do now, including figuring out what the heck the Heart of the City was. So Arthur was the first back up on his feet.

Grabbing his spear, Arthur took to walking the circumference of the tree. Moving in a slowly closing circle, peering down into the water, poking at roots, and clambering up and down, he searched.

Quite quickly, he noted a few things. Firstly, outside of the occasional tree leaf or weed, the water itself was extremely clear. He could look down into the water with ease, spotting everything from darting fish to a slowly swimming turtle. The surroundings smelled similar too, full of clear, fresh air and the slight humidity of the lake itself. The breeze that ruffled the leaves above constantly brushed against his skin, the entire tree bringing with it a sense of overall serenity.

He'd idly noted that cultivating beneath the tree had been marginally better too. Not as good as the clan residence, of course, but the energy around the tree was definitely more concentrated. Of course, coming from the tree itself, much of the surroundings was flavored with Yang energy, but the sheer density was sufficient that he had no issues speeding up his overall cultivation.

For those who weren't Yin-based and took a more regular cultivation path, it would benefit them even more.

All of these factors were why it took him nearly the entire circumference before he realized that he had been missing a rather obvious fact. Unlike beneath the waters they had crossed, there were no other ruins—even broken and shattered and worn away as they might be—to be sighted.

Crouched on top of one particularly low-dipping root that had a broad footing area, Arthur stared at the waters below, frowning. The earth below the roots, what little he could see of it, was bare. Sandy and water-clogged, with pebbles and the occasional floating plant. But there were no large paving stones, no shattered walls, or any other indicator of civilization.

"A heart is a center. A center is a core. The core is what is important. In some cases, temples. Others, palaces. Or city hall." Biting his lip, Arthur puzzled this through slowly. "But what we have here... we have a garden? A tree?"

Standing up, he peered up and down the lake, taking in the shade cast by the tree. The rough shape of the lake itself. Then, he looked up, to the leaves that shimmered in their myriad greens, twisting and fluttering. He stared, hard from branch to branch, sudden suspicion burning.

Nothing.

Maybe he was wrong?

Maybe he wasn't.

Rather than give up immediately, he began to pick his way along the roots again, moving under the shade further. Peering upwards, always upwards. Searching and yet failing to find what he sought. Once, twice, and again he made his way around.

His companions peered at him, between moments of cultivation or when they surfaced from the water. Mel and Rick, soaked through to their skin, cotton clinging to muscular bodies and highlighting curves. Each taking turns to dive as they slowly made their way farther and farther from the safety of the tree. Testing the reactions of their enemies.

And all the while, he walked.

He was about to give up, when he spotted a glimpse of it. Another might have missed it. One who hadn't possessed his Enhanced Eyesight trait. Another might have given up. But he had not, and in doing so, he found what he sought, high in the branches of the massive tree.

If a civilization valued its plants and made a singular tree the center of its city... then what was a heart that could be brought back to fulfill the Tower quest? Not the broken and chopped remnants of the tree itself.

But a fruit.

A fruit, glittering green and yellow and shining with potential, high above.

Chapter 80

"You sure, ah?" Yao Jing was saying doubtfully for the fourth time as he peered upward, the waning light of the falling evening making it hard to pick out even individual leaves, never mind the fruit.

"Yes." Arthur's tone of voice was a lot shorter than before. Especially after the first three times he'd said the same thing. He gestured for Yao Jing to return to his seat, as he continued. "The fruit is up there."

"But the heart?" Jan said, doubtfully. "Not very… center."

"It's not, except in a metaphorical sense." He slapped the side of the tree he was leaning against, its huge diameter easily reaching forty or fifty meters. "But I didn't see an opening. Unless it's under the water, between the roots, but this doesn't seem like the hollow kind either."

"Can't be, *lah*," Jan said. "Not the right kind."

"That's what I thought too." Arthur shrugged. "Which means that we're looking at either cutting it down, or searching the waters for another building…" He waved towards the pair of climbers who were still in the water, diving over and over again. They'd made it quite far by now without any indication of problems from the hantu air, which meant they could focus on finding Rick's gun and the rest of their items. Already, one soaked bag and its contents lay drying on a series of roots. "And they're doing that. Sort of."

"Maybe something else up there?" Yao Jing offered, gesturing upwards.

"Or magic door? Press a knob and it opens?" Jan said, miming the motion.

Arthur snorted. "You're welcome to press on the tree knobs till you find it, but I think that might take a bit."

Jan eyed the bark, the way it warped and twisted. The hard bark that slowly peeled away and the numerous whorls and knobs within easy reaching distance. And then she looked up and up, staring at the hundreds of feet along the bark that might contain a magical doorway that she theorized existed. And winced.

"Maybe just climb up and look first."

"That's what I thought too," Arthur said. "We climb up, check out what might be out there and move on from there." He hesitated, glancing at Uswah who would find the climb a little difficult. It was not as though they had bought a hook attachment or anything else for her missing hand yet.

Something to look into in the future perhaps, if they had a moment.

"I'll stay and watch," Uswah said, gesturing at the diving pair. "Someone needs to."

"Thank you."

She shrugged in answer.

"So, if everyone is properly topped up, I recommend climb tomorrow morning. I'll bring the bag," he said, nodding to the emptied-out bag that they had left drying, "and we'll stick to shorter weapons otherwise. If we're not back by nightfall..." He grinned. "Come and rescue us!"

There was a little laughter at that, but the team nodded in agreement. There was little enough for them to do but finish cultivating, sleep and rest, and then get ready. Climbing the massive tree was something to do in daylight, after all.

Amusingly, for Arthur, the night did not end with rest but with cultivation. He'd poured the first hour into refining Tower energy rather than sleeping, then proceeded to refill his stores to full once again in the deep of the night. He repeated the process a couple of times as the night went on, making full use of the increased Yin energy to benefit his cultivation before he finally crashed for a few hours of sleep until dawn fully broke.

Washing his face and then brushing his teeth down with a cloth was all he could do for ablutions in the morning. Thankfully, with the Tower having rebuilt their body entirely during the process of transporting them in from the outside world, the problem of bad morning breath was entirely missing. The very bacteria that were the cause of such things were not replicated, leaving the Tower blessedly stink-free in that regard.

Not that he'd ever admit that or fail to use the insult. After all, that was an insult that was still politically acceptable. Weight, penis size, body proportions, and height—those came and went in terms of insults. Race, of course, was always tricky—and quite inflammatory. If for no reason other than the fact that some of the stereotypes reached for were all too common.

But bad breath? That was something anyone with a little care and a toothbrush could handle. That was a choice, unlike so many other things.

"Let's go," Arthur said simply to Jan and Yao Jing when they were ready. He chose not to bid goodbye to the others staying behind. After all, this was just a simple climb, without any concerns at all.

Or so he forced himself to believe.

Climbing the massive tree was indeed tricky. No way to tie oneself to the circumference, allowing the body to lean against and use the friction of a belt to help take the weight off. And for the first fifty or so feet, there were no branches to utilize to pull oneself up. Such things had grown upwards with the tree, leaving the lower trunk bare of simple handholds.

Bark was tough and grainy. To climb, the team had to search for minor protrusions, knots, and gaps in the bark and wedge fingers and toes within or upon. And then, utilizing these minor edges, they would pull themselves up.

"I'm a lousy boy scout. Who never thought. To pack a spike, for a hike." Cursing quietly, he kept hauling himself upwards. There were bear claws that ninjas utilized, that he was missing now. It would have made climbing simpler, if he had them.

Instead, at best, they had knives that sunk into the hardened bark and into the even harder wood beneath. It required some effort to do so and the group was careful not to do it too often. After all, once the last member, Yao Jing, had passed the knife, they had to pry it free carefully and pass it upwards so that Arthur was never entirely bereft of their improvised handholds.

No, for the most part, they free-climbed their way up. They didn't even tie themselves off to one another, what with the rope they had brought along now sunken at the bottom of the lake and lost, for the moment.

It probably was for the best anyway. Without pitons or other levers to brace against, a falling body would likely just drag the rest of them down if they were joined by rope.

"Remember, three-point holds if you can," Arthur called out again as he levered himself upwards and caught sight of Jan pulling her whole body up using just her hands. He shook his head a little at her before returning to his own climb.

Truth be told, he could understand her impatience. For all their lack of preparation and the overall lack of experience showcased by his companions, they were making good time and distance. A climb that would have been challenging, if not outright impossible, for most people in the outside world was relatively trivial for the Tower climbers. Multiple points in Body had increased not just their strength and stamina but coordination as well.

Hold yourself up with two fingers wedged in a sliver of space where bark had cracked and separated? Easy. Painful, admittedly, but easy. And while mortal climbers had to concern themselves with stamina and exhaustion, the trio were empowered by the Tower and the cultivation energy within them, as well as the persistent healing side effects of their clan technique.

This increase in their overall endurance was not a factor Arthur had ever considered, but it was obvious that it had provided them with significant benefits. How much faster and further had they hiked because of the technique? Hard to tell, in the end, but something worth noting.

And further worth considering that Rick, who did not have the technique, had kept up with them during this trek without complaint.

Rough bark beneath fingertips, wind pressing against skin and clothing. The smell of fresh sap, dried wood and clean water arising all around him. Though his mind wandered, the motion of climbing, of searching for a new handhold or place to wedge a foot was familiar. He took his time, making sure Jan could watch his motions behind him, and Yao Jing hers.

Took his time to look around, take in the world below. The marshes that surrounded the lake of a destroyed city, the tree that dominated the surroundings, the hills in the distance, and the smoke rising in the distance from the Tower village.

This was an adventure, and for all the watchful eye he kept, Arthur could not help but marvel at that thought.

A far cry from sleeping on a dojo floor and running mundane errands for portions of the dollar.

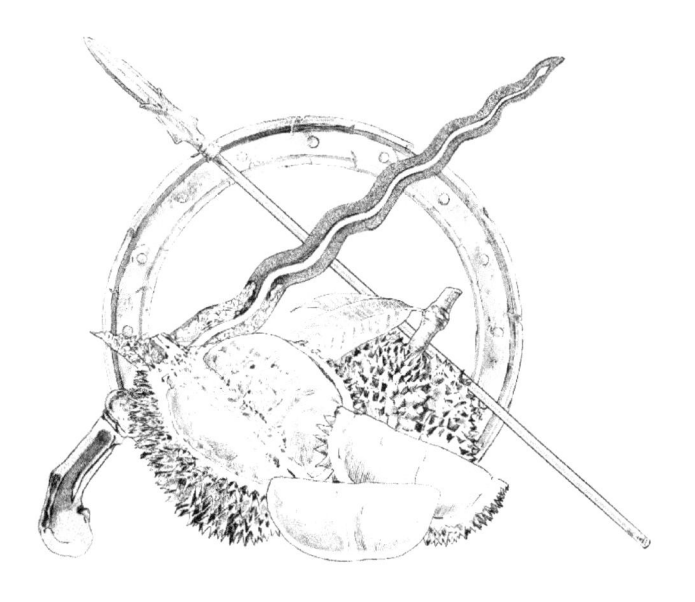

Chapter 81

Climbing the tree was a process. The first step was crossing the threshold between clear bark to the first of the branches. That had seen a major change in geography, since they no longer had to hold tight to gaps in the bark but could instead lever themselves upwards on massive branches. There were still gaps between, large amounts of space as massive branches shaded the world around them and forced the group to leap, grab, and shimmy over.

But it was easier. Much easier. Which was why, of course, when the monsters came, the trio were entirely unsurprised. After all, this was the Tower. If something looked easy, it was almost definitely a trap. On the other hand, the nature of their new enemy had been a surprise.

Dual-wielding his kris and his rather abused knife, Arthur fought and shuffled along the branches carefully, deflecting the leaping wood ticks that sought to latch their spindly legs and their snapping thoraxes on him.

Dark brown in the majority with streaks of lighter colour, the insects had hard shells that made strikes from knives futile.

Luckily, their attackers had a habit of leaping at them just as often as they shambled along the branches to clamber upwards. In those leaps, it offered the group the opportunity to plunge a knife into the softer chitin beneath.

Of course, doing so required exquisite timing. A factor that was made more difficult when multiple such creatures were attacking at once, whether leaping for one's face or crawling along branches—and eventually, legs.

"Why are they all horde creatures?" Arthur complained, shaking the impaled body of one wood tick off his kris while deflecting another. He tried not to do that too often, for deflected monsters tumbled far off below them, either to fetch against new branches and begin their ascent once more, or all the way down where they might rain splattered shells on his friends.

"Oy, don't! You're losing the cores," Jan complained, watching the body fall away.

Also, that.

Jan had more time to complain, being perched on a branch above his own. Sometimes, it was hard to tell which was the best way forward, and so leaping between each as they explored was required, shuffling the order of ascent randomly.

"You want to take over?" Arthur challenged as he backed off another few steps in the hope that some of the mites might try the leap to bother Jan instead of him. He bobbed a little as he did so, the branch he was on thinning dangerously.

"*Tak mau.*"

"I thought so," Arthur said. "Then stop complaining."

"Give. Me. One. Second!" Each word was punctuated by a crunch as Yao Jing fought gleefully closer to the opening in the trunk that the mites had crawled out of. Wielding his favorite brass knuckles on each hand, the brawler was finding the battle more to his taste. Each punch crushed chitin or cracked legs, leaving the insects to squirm in pain.

Of course, the wood mites weren't leaving them alone. At least three of them were clambering over Yao Jing's body, one hanging off a thickly thewed arm as its mandibles closed in attempt to bite his limb in two. But a sheen of dark energy surrounded Yao Jing as the man triggered Bark Skin. Even so, blood fell from his torn sleeve and ripped skin, which the man ignored with great aplomb.

"This isn't going to work," Arthur snarled, as a mandible clamped around his ankle. He collapsed a little, using the pommel of his knife to strike at the creature rapidly, shattering eyes and feelers before freeing himself. "Jan, take over."

"I already said no!" But for all her complaints, she leapt forward to put herself between Arthur and the oncoming horde, kicking and stamping and booting the monsters aside. Her single knife cut with speed, Focused Strikes slicing monsters apart with ease.

"Always complaining about me!" Arthur muttered, finishing off the remaining few with a series of stabs and stomps. Leaning sideways and favoring his leg, he focused on his left hand, slipping the kris back into its sheath as he did so.

Pull energy through the lung and kidney meridians, turn it through the gall bladder meridian and then collect at heart 3 and lung 6 before moving on, always flowing through him. When it was ready, push it to the outer edges of his aura where he contained it by sheer force of will.

Build up the power, forming it not into a single dart but a swirling cone of a missile. Taking inspiration from a fan-favorite anime, he adjusted the energy to keep it swirling as he knitted the Explosive Energy Dart together.

He laced tendrils of energy and spun them to compact more and more energy into the dart.

When he could no longer hold it together, Arthur pointed his hand at the crack the mites had emerged from and let loose. The Explosive Energy Dart flashed forwards in a screaming shriek, dark blue and white energy tinting the attack as it entered the shadowed recess.

Moments later, light flashed and wind roared as the attack exploded within the trunk. Along with the wind came sap and portions of wood mites, the insects shredded by the power of the attack in a tightly contained environment. A deluge of sticky innards and sap rained upon them, the majority coating Yao Jing, who nearly fell off. The man grasped on with a single hand and furiously wiped sap away with the other.

"Aiyoh!" Jan exclaimed.

"Careful, ah!" Yao Jing cried, more concerned with nearly falling than the sap. Or at least, he said so, though he still wiped and scrubbed as he hauled himself up one-handed, massive arms flexing.

"Show-off…" Arthur grumbled, but he did make sure to deal with the remaining wood mites while his friend got himself situated. After all, jealousy was not sufficient reason to let someone die.

Anyway, all that bulging muscle was unnecessary for Arthur as a climber. Entirely unnecessary.

Chapter 82

Oblong, green, and purple, weighing just over a few pounds, flesh firm. Reminiscent of a large mango, though the curling shape around both ends and a slight spike from the hanging end was a little different. Holding the object in his hands after hours of climbing, Arthur pursed his lips.

"That's it?" Yao Jing said. "We can go now?" Every once in a while, the man cast a glance down, licking his lips as he stared at the plunge far below. Even if he had not chosen to say anything, it was clear Yao Jing was still a little nervous at the height they had reached.

"Spotted any others?" Arthur asked instead.

Jan, who had been peering upwards and all around, shook her head. "You got the eyes, right?"

"I do." He slipped the fruit into the bag and then slung it over his shoulders, tightening the straps. He looked up, scanning the foliage. There. One… two… three. All of them similar to the one in his bag. So, either this one was already ripe, or they were all not.

When he related the sights and his thoughts, Jan shrugged. "Up? More better, right?"

"Or one is enough." Yao Jing touched the injuries he'd accumulated, scratching a little at the edges where flesh was beginning to reknit. "Dangerous, *lah*."

"It is always dangerous, though. And Jan's right. We should get at least one more." He pointed to the closest one. "Not that far to go. Maybe twenty minutes?"

"*Haiya*... Okay, *lah*." Jan stood up, heading for the next branch without further prompting.

Grunting, Yao Jing took to his feet too, following after. Leaving Arthur to lead from the back, keeping an eye for further threats. The wood ticks were one thing, but the snakes were another. And finally, that giant spider...

Entirely unnecessary.

While the creatures were dangerous, they were certainly not sufficient a defense to protect the fruits. They were just speedbumps in the quest, a struggle to make it feel worthwhile. No, the real danger lay below, in the hantu air that had come for them when they first arrived at the lake.

He shook his head, dismissed the thought. It was time to focus, to get this job done and get another fruit. Then, back down, swim back to shore, rebuild their rafts and float home through the marshlands. After which, they'd have to start training again.

Simple enough.

So long as there were no further complications.

"That's it?" Arthur said, eyeing the packs Rick and Mel had fished up. A short distance away, Rick had his guns spread out, dried and oiled and rubbed clean. Weird that he felt the need to dry them out that much, since the bodies were mostly plastic. But, he assumed, things like the firing pin and springs were still a concern.

"All we found," Mel confirmed.

"That's almost everything," Uswah said.

"Or close enough to not matter. So how are we getting across the lake?" Arthur gestured. "I assume you tested that out too?"

"We did," Mel said. "Nothing attacked us."

"So we swim?" Yao Jing said, shaking his head. "That easy?"

"Easy for you," Uswah said. "I don't swim."

Yao Jing grunted, then looked at the others. "Pull her along?"

"On what? A boat?" Arthur shook his head. "Might trigger an attack. Remember, they don't like us on boats."

"No, just behind me." Yao Jing made a motion as though he was cupping something close to his face and then waving his other hand behind. "I can pull her along."

"You swim well enough for that?" Mel said, surprised.

"Can, *lah*."

"Then that's what we'll do." Arthur shrugged. "I can switch out with him if necessary." He glanced at the spears they all carried and sighed. "Bundle those, someone will have to drag them along. It won't be fun, but we should be able to do it. Now get some rest. We'll get moving tomorrow morning."

Once he got confirmations from his team, he moved to put his back against the tree's massive base. He'd have to take his turn on watch soon enough, but for now, he had a pouch full of cores and a lot of cultivating time to catch up on.

Tense, swimming in water where they had nearly died. Discomfort and pain, from wounds he'd accumulated. Compared to the others in his team, he healed fast, though. And spending a short time pouring actual cultivated energy into the healing process allowed him to speed that even further. He'd done so a little, just to deal with some of the biggest injuries; but mostly he had worked on increasing his energy stores.

Now, in the water, his wounds stinging and his lungs and muscles burning as he swam, he cursed himself out. He should have brought himself up to his full fighting potential. Though, if he had to deal with the possessed corpses in the water, he wasn't sure how much he could do.

Pull, frog kick, pull, frog kick. Step by step, he swam forward. Beneath, he could see the mud and seaweed below along with the corpses that had previously risen and then returned to the bottom of the lake below. They lay still, unmoving, dead as they should have been.

Unmoving bodies. So many of them.

Where did they come from? Were they climbers? Or just corpses created by the Tower, just like it created other monsters? And if it could create human corpses, could it create living people too? The attendants, the Tower guards—they were not exactly normal. At least some of them. And how that happened, who knew. After all, they weren't saying. At most, they'd mention an oath tying them to secrecy.

So many damn questions. And there was no way for them to get answers, not until they...

Well, who knew.

"Trade?" Jan breathed. Amusingly, unlike him, she was doing the backstroke. Mel, swimming next to her, occasionally had to make Jan adjust her course since otherwise she'd go in the wrong direction. When asked about her choice of stroke, she explained that she had never learnt another. At least, not well. And well was what she needed to drag the bundle of spears along.

Treading water, Arthur glanced to the side. Uswah was being dragged along, Yao Jing occasionally cursing her out to stop kicking or moving. Rick swam along beside them all, bringing up the rear. He switched between breaststroke and crawl as necessary, towing along a couple of bags as well.

"I got my own," Arthur replied. "We all do."

"It's... tiring," she panted.

He snorted. Looking back down, his breath caught for a moment as he noted movement in one of the corpses below, but after a second he realized that it was just an underwater current pushing the body along.

Painful as it might be, exhausting as it was dragging all their gear, tense as it might be... so far, everything was going fine.

Which made him wonder when the next boot would fall.

Chapter 83

That boot did not drop, not for a while. Not even when the team made their way across the lake in one piece. Not a single ripple of the damn hantu air had appeared, the water demons choosing to leave them alone so long as they stayed in the water. In the end, picking up the Heart of D'mai was just a slog. Outside of the one rather scary incident.

Rebuilding the rafts took longer, with the group forced to range a little deeper into the marshlands before they could acquire more building materials. After that, rather than waste time, Arthur took to cultivating while the others built the rafts. It was a choice he made reluctantly, knowing the entire team needed to strengthen themselves but he most of all.

Sometimes, being the boss was a benefit, but it still weighed heavily on him.

He cultivated with the monster cores they'd garnered on their way to D'mai and while climbing the great tree that had held the object of their quest. Long hours processing energy through his body, over and over again so that he gathered it within his dantian, building upwards. Cores were the most efficient way to cultivate, but soon enough he ran low on his share of cores.

Rather than ask for more, and while they were still in the vicinity of the large tree, he turned to cultivating Tower energy. By the time they were ready to go, Arthur had gotten bored and had switched over to training, trying to hold and enhance his ability to form Refined Exploding Energy Darts and channel energy through Focused Strike.

Splitting his focus was hard work, and working on two different, untrained techniques was even worse. But the process of study to improve his ability to split his focus and use multiple battle techniques was necessary. It would significantly increase his effectiveness in combat and in general.

By the time a day had come and gone, Arthur felt he had made a decent degree of improvement and the Tower seemed to agree.

Simultaneous Flow (57.9%)
Refined Exploding Energy Dart (61.1 %)

For Arthur, the Refined Exploding Energy Dart came naturally. It made sense to him in a way that the Simultaneous Flow technique did not. If not for his traits giving him a leg up, he would have required significantly more time to improve it.

"Time to move, O great lord," Jan called out, breaking Arthur from his contemplations. He pushed away the notification of his progress and grabbed his spear, grateful they had managed to fish it out of the lake.

"You know, speaking in Manglish and saying 'great lord' just doesn't sit well," Arthur said.

"Who want to sit?" Yao Jing asked, using the pole he'd buried in a nearby root system to shift the raft back.

"No one." Arthur stepped over carefully to the raft, noting it was a little more slipshod than the previous one he'd built. Then again, it only had to hold together till they got back. "Time to go."

He looked around, waving Yao Jing to lead the way. He followed soon after, trusting that Mel would take the rearguard once again, with Rick close by. Maybe he would look at having people carry some paddle boards along into the Tower—when he got out. There could be some decent income to be made here, renting them out.

Plans for the future swirled through his head and he could not help but touch the bag he'd stored one of the tree fruits in. They had chosen to take two fruits, and the second was with Rick, since the man was the least likely to get engaged in direct combat. One way or the other, they would get the Heart of D'mai back.

※

Exploding from the water, eyes stinging and hacking with water having entered his nose, Arthur swam for land. His spear was lodged in the creature's side—a massive green-brown snake that had dropped from a tree.

He dodged to the side as it lunged for him, less worried about getting bitten than getting caught. The creature's body splashed against the surface of the water with quite the explosive violence before it pulled back, retreating upwards to the thick branch it had lain upon.

"Celaka!" Arthur backpedalled in the water as furiously as he could, trying to put some distance between him and the creature. He had no time to attack it, trusting instead to his friends. The first to engage was Jan, her spearhead plunging into the body and ripping sideways. The wound itself was bloody but thin.

The snake hissed, pulling back further. It swayed to the side, dodging the next spear strike and struck at Jan, battering the shaft of the spear aside and striking her with its body. It pushed her back, nearly knocking her off her raft.

His grasping hand found a root. He scrambled backwards, trying to stand and get into the fight. Moments later, the roar of a pistol firing. Again and again, the bullets struck the creature along its body. It twisted and hissed, trying to get away from the attacks and launch itself at the others. Moving downwards, it landed on the raft, nearly sinking the craft with its weight as it did so.

Realising he couldn't move closer, he raised his own hand and focused. The Refined Energy Dart formed there, even as the snake managed to wind the top of its body around the base of Jan's feet. Then, twisting, it kept rising, attempting to wend its way up her.

"Off, off!" Jan said, pushing at the body, trying to get away.

Rick's guns had fallen silent, no longer having a clear line of sight. On the other hand, Arthur could see the back of its body clearly and he fired at it, watching his dart enter the flesh from behind. It struck and drilled through; the creature twisted and thrashed but kept climbing.

Realising that ranged attacks weren't going to be enough, not while the monster kept crawling along Jan's body, he waded into the water again, moving towards them. Rick had done the same, holstering his pistols and then pushing with the pole he retrieved.

Even so, the snake was nearly two thirds of the way up Jan's body, tightening its grip with each moment and causing her to scream. Arthur made his way there first, and his kris slipped through scales into the creature's body after a second strike.

Immediately, he dragged the snake towards him, using it to help haul him up the raft. The entire thing tipped precariously, almost depositing Jan into the water before Rick reached over and jammed his foot on the other end. Planks splintered under the rough handling and the raft bent, but the ivy holding it all together did its job.

Gripping the creature with one hand, Arthur used Focused Strike to plunge his weapon along the body again. The kris entered the flesh with ease, the wavy blade edges slicing through and helping him flense his target with ease. At the same time, the enchantment kicked in, sending waves of poisonous Yin chi through the creature.

Single-minded as it was, the snake kept its attention on Jan, tightening its body as Arthur kept striking it and pulling himself upwards till he got to the head. Finally, he plunged the kris into the monster's head, even as it hissed and thrashed in death throes, crushing Jan.

Panting, the pair pulled the monster off her.

"You okay?" Rick asked.

"NO!" she shouted. Then, she hissed and feebly clutched at her sides. "Ribs. Broken. Hips..."

"Shit." Arthur looked her over, winced and helped straighten her out. She let out little moans, and he gestured for Rick to drag his boat closer. They'd have to transfer her over to Rick's boat, since hers was about to fall apart. Never mind the fact that she wouldn't be able to do anything for a bit, much less row.

This was going to slow them down again. But at least, for now, they'd survived.

Chapter 84

Days later, the team were finally back. Delays had pushed them further behind schedule, everything from more frequent monster attacks to having to ward off that damn harimau hitam that nearly took Yao Jing's head off. It would have, if not for Uswah reappearing on its back and throwing it off course. As it stood, she had been knocked into the water before the black tiger had been forced away.

The only advantage, if you could call it that, of the various attacks were the number of monster cores they had managed to accumulate. The one from the massive snake that had crushed Jan's hips and chest was particularly large and was stored in a pouch all by itself by her side as she lay beside Rick.

"You could have just healed yourself," Rick was complaining for the umpteenth time. "Instead of making me do all the work."

"Cannot, *lah*. I wanna save my energy," Jan rebutted.

"And avoid any fighting!"

"I killed that spider that tied you up!" She mimed thrusting with the spear that she had laid beside her.

"I could have gotten free myself!"

"Okay, whatever."

Tuning out the arguing behind him, Arthur stared at the Tower village with a smile. As he floated by the main bridge, he noted the absence of shakedown artists. Had they given up or been pushed away? Or finally ascended?

He shook his head, making note to look into it later. Not that he could do much about it either way, but knowledge was power. He also needed to check on the Thorned Lotuses on this floor and verify if they'd finally decided to join them.

But first...

"Let's go," Arthur said, grounding his boat against the edge of a tree, watching as his raft slid up one marshy root. He let his pole fall to the side, grabbed his spear and jumped up, bounding on roots as he ascended, leaving the raft behind.

The team came after him at first, though they split off soon to head for the clan building. All but Yao Jing, who followed Arthur as a good bodyguard was supposed to do.

Voices faded behind him as Arthur headed for the administrative building, a small smile pulling across his face as he listened.

"I can't believe you have been faking being injured for so long!" Rick said.

"You so bodoh!" Jan taunted, as she bounded along happily beside him.

"I know what that means!" Rick shouted after her.

Tuning them out, Arthur slowed down as he neared the administrative building, where a pair of familiar faces appeared. He watched as the women came up to him, arms crossed.

"Where you went?" Michelle asked, frowning at him.

"Out. Doing a quest," Arthur looked the pair of Thorned Lotuses over, noting that Kavitha looked a little worse for wear at the moment. "What's it to you?"

"You said you want us to join, then you disappear," Michelle replied.

"You said you wanted to wait and watch," Arthur shrugged. "And I don't owe you information of what I'm doing, not yet."

Kavitha made a little growling noise in her throat while Michelle narrowed her eyes. Then she sighed. "Fine."

"Anyway, it's good you're here. Let's talk tomorrow. I need to turn this quest in and then we can discuss whatever you want."

"Why tomorrow?"

"Because I want to make sure we get what we're owed," Arthur said.

Michelle hesitated, but at Kavitha's nod, she stepped aside. Taking her movement for acquiescence, Arthur kept moving, choosing to let them follow him. If they succeeded, they would learn about this soon enough. And if not...

Well, he'd been embarrassed before. He'd survive.

To his entire lack of surprise, the administrative building was empty when he arrived. Middle of the afternoon was rarely the time that the building was crowded, since most would spend the day out of the village making the most of their trip.

"You're back," the attendant said, looking expectant.

Arthur grinned in reply, unslinging his backpack and dropping it with a thump on the table. He opened the ties and reached within, pulling the fruit out and handing the first to the attendant.

"What's this?" the attendant said, surprised.

Arthur's breath caught, his hand trembling at the man's words.

Even as he spoke though, the attendant was reaching out to take the fruit from Arthur, pulling it into his own hands. He frowned, turning it over. "This a fruit?"

"It's the heart. As per the quest." Arthur replied, trying not to let the panic escape from beneath his cool exterior as the man turned the fruit around and around. He was going to scream if they had really missed the point or had to cut down that tree. There was no way they could go back, cut the tree down, and return by Casey's deadline.

"Is it?" The attendant shrugged after a moment. "I guess we'll find out."

"Don't you know?"

"Why would I? I just work here."

Arthur stared at the attendant, who was purposely ignoring him as he took the fruit and placed it behind the counter on a simple stone tablet. Leaving it on the tablet, he started drumming his fingers on the table. Each tap was like a nail pounded into Arthur's ears as he waited, until he felt a familiar and insistent push from the Tower.

Of course, he allowed it to form.

Quest Completed: The Heart of the Lost City
Locate the rumored lost city of D'mai and retrieve its heart. Return the heart to the floor administrator for your reward.
Rewards: Seven Cloud Stepping Technique (Original), 3 * Seven Cloud Stepping Technique (one use per applicant), Clan Reputation increased by 7.

Arthur grinned and did a fist pump, the motion making Yao Jing holler too and then slap Arthur on the back. It made the smaller man stagger, wincing a little at the hard strike before he turned around and offered his fist for a bump. Michelle and Kavitha frowned, watching the celebration in confusion.

"Yes, boss!"

"Ahem." The attendant spoke the words out loud, drawing their attention.

Arthur turned and noted the scrolls he was holding out. Snatching it from the man's hands and mumbling a quick thanks, he flipped the first open to glance through the details and verify that the Seven Cloud Stepping technique was inscribed on it.

"What is that?" Kavitha could not help but ask.

Shaking his head, Arthur put the scrolls in his backpack and waved Yao Jing to come with him. When the woman shifted as though she intended to block his way, he added, "Tomorrow."

Kavitha hesitated but Michelle pulled her back. Arthur nodded to her firmly, then pushed past her, tightening his grip on his spear. They weren't likely to have a problem with these women, but you never know.

He wouldn't feel safe till he got the scrolls back to the safety of the clan building before someone stole them.

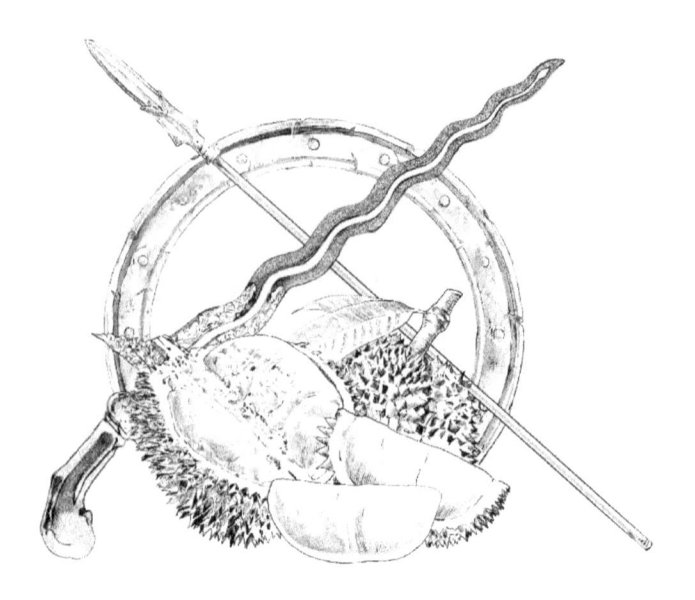

Chapter 85

The group were split apart, all staring at the original technique scroll sprawled across the top of the table. Rick was relegated back to his bed while the group excitedly pored over the document, staring at the details within. Yao Jing was quietly mouthing the words as he read, while the rest scanned the document silently, Arthur using a finger to trace his way down.

In short order, Arthur was done with the initial readthrough and did a second scan. He was halfway through the document before the rest of the group had finished and pulled away a little to give him some space.

"So?" Arthur said, placing his hands on top of the document and table as he waited.

"It's good," Mel said immediately. She tried to suppress the grin that was slowly spreading across her face before she gave up. "At least a two-star, maybe even three."

"Damn cheapskates," Arthur grumbled. You would think that they would at least indicate the quality of the technique since he got it from the

Tower direct, but did they bother? No. Not at all. "What's Wind Steps these days? One?"

"Ya," Jan confirmed. "So, I can learn?" Yao Jing frowned, grabbing her hand before she went for the document. She tugged her hand away, pouting at Yao Jing and almost making Arthur gag. He waved her away from the documents—one original and three copies—which made Jan pout further.

"We only have three copies," Arthur said. "We should think about this before we use them up."

"You want one or more of us to study from the main technique scroll," Mel said frankly.

"Yes."

"*Tak mau.*" Jan was shaking her head in negation.

"You should take one," Mel said, tapping the table. "I'll study from the main scroll."

Jan frowned at Mel, then looked over to Yao Jing who was scratching the side of his head in thought.

"Thank you." Arthur hesitated, feeling absurdly guilty. But studying from the main scroll would only provide a minor boost in learning the technique, unlike the Tower invested scrolls. Considering he was still behind the curve of everyone else, he needed all the time savings he could find.

"I also don't want," Yao Jing said, arms crossed. Then he added, after a beat, "But I can do the main scroll."

"You?" Jan said, frowning.

"I'm pretty good, you know." Yao Jing lifted his chin, as though daring her to argue with him about that. Something in his eyes, the way he said it, had Jan hesitate and she ducked her head after a moment, nodding at last.

"I'm also good, what," she muttered.

"Then, what do we do with the other two?" Arthur frowned, turning them over.

"Bring one along. Keep the other here," Mel said, firmly. "Gift for someone who comes up and does well. Later."

Arthur grunted. Considering they could, theoretically, with ownership of the master scroll continue to produce such gifted scrolls in the future if they were willing to pay the administration center, it made sense. They didn't have the contribution points or the time to build up enough credits with the center for this to happen now, but in the future... well, it was possible. Of course, that was so long as they still had the main scroll.

"Do we have to bring the main scroll for them to copy it from?" Arthur said, curiously. He knew from his reading that producing working Tower-empowered technique scrolls could be done by the Administrators and also via certain techniques. Of course, the individuals who bothered to study such techniques were incredibly rare. Something that only large clans and guilds could even hope of supporting.

A round of shrugs and negatives came from his people. Such details were not what they had studied. Or, for that matter, perhaps this information was not even available in the widely touted forums. After all, it was not as though the clans or other major corporations wanted to bandy about any weaknesses they might have.

"Can you look into it?" Arthur said. If they had to cart the scroll around each time, it would raise the danger significantly. "Also, if not, do we have to leave it on this floor? If I take it up to the seventh floor or something and leave it in a secure location in our clan building there, is it then available for everyone?"

Mel was nodding at his words, before she asked the obvious question: "Guild treasury?"

"I don't know," Arthur said. "I'd heard of it before, but..." He sighs. Low as they were on the totem pole, it was possible such abilities were locked out from the clan for now.

"What if we can? Outside the Tower?" Mel asked the next obvious question.

Again, Arthur could only shrug. He drummed his fingers on the table, glanced outside, and then looked over at Rick. He raised an eyebrow in question. When no one answered, he got up and walked over, waiting for Rick to exit his cultivation before he spoke. In the meantime, the quiet discussion by the trio reading over the original technique manuscript behind him filled the air.

"What?" Rick said.

"I have a question. Questions." Arthur hesitated, then added, "I thought you might be able to help."

"Oh, I'm useful now, eh? So how long more before you decide to just discard me again?" Rick said.

Arthur glared at the man but swallowed his ire. Rick was right; Arthur had been making use of him with little thought. He was in his rights to be angry. The question was, what Arthur should do about it, if anything.

He pondered the question for a few moments before he nodded firmly to himself. Rick had sat patiently during the period, choosing not to say anything.

"You really want in?" Arthur said.

"Yes," Rick confirmed. Then, lifting his chin, he added, "But I stop paying."

"Usual clan dues are still owed," Arthur said, firmly.

"That's nothing here, right?"

"Right," Arthur confirmed. "But out of this floor, it can add up."

"Whatever." Rick shook his head. "Not as though I'm hurting."

"You'll be under the same restrictions and rules of the clan, and that means no discussing what we do with outsiders and there's likely going to be a penalty if you leave us after exiting each Tower."

"Each Tower?" Rick said, amused. "Assuming much, are we?"

"I'm not stopping with one. Are you?" Arthur said. Not that the likelihood of them being able to do so was high. After all, the Tower really didn't like it when people quit, and the cost of acquiring the cores needed to keep one strong outside a Tower was prohibitive. The rich could afford it, but he certainly wasn't one of them.

Never mind the quiet promise he'd made by taking on so many hopefuls to build a proper clan.

"Seven. I need seven Towers."

That made Arthur blink. The numbers dropped off drastically after four Towers. One was easy enough, and you could often buy yourself a few years if you stocked up properly and worked hard when you got out. The second Tower was harder, but not impossible to clear. Most bought themselves another decade of real-world time by going through and powering up. Enough to establish their families and provide for those they loved before they inevitably disappeared into a Tower again.

The third Tower was where nearly fifty percent of the survivors never came out. Some just chose to spend the rest of their lives there, collecting cores and sending a small portion upwards via clans or families like the Chins who had regular messengers in. The fewer levels one had to pass, the cheaper it was; but by the time one was in the third Tower, those stones were worth quite a bit. Even a small trickle, going to a family outside, made a big difference.

Those that exited the third Tower varied deeply. Many were strong enough and in-demand enough that they could, if they were willing, work for others and extend their real-world existence for many years. Some even brought out a large enough fortune in monster cores that they could become real world powers if they wished, often marrying into established families.

By the time one exited the fifth Tower, if one did, those individuals were all powers in their own rights. If they were not already tied to an existing power structure, they could establish their own guilds or clans or businesses without an issue.

Of course, the major issue by that point was how few years they had. Unless they stocked up themselves, time outside of the Tower was extremely short. Their very existence bled power into the surroundings constantly and with so few exiting, and most keeping their cores to themselves, it was rare for such individuals to stay in the real world for long.

Even rarer for individuals to exit a sixth or seventh Tower.

"Ambitious," Arthur said finally. "Then, we'll see you through it all." He hesitated, then added, "Though we'll probably need to take our time."

Rick shrugged, as though it mattered little to him. That level of disregard was why Arthur hesitated so much with the boy. Yet, when he spoke those words earlier, there was a fire within him that he had not seen before. This wasn't a game, even if he acted like it was at times.

"Then, welcome to the clan." Sticking his hand out, Arthur watched Rick shake it and a notification bloomed, adding another one to their clan. "Now, let's talk about our most recent acquisition. We have questions and I'm hoping you have answers."

"I'll try," Rick said, following Arthur as he led him back.

"All we can ask." Of him or anyone else.

Chapter 86

Arthur was grateful, once again, that he was using the Tower-enabled scroll, rather than a copy. It still required him to read it over and comprehend the techniques, but between the 3D projections, the almost mythical way it entered his mind and the clarity of the words, he was learning how to use the Seven Cloud Stepping technique faster than the rest of the team.

Of course, he'd also taken to sitting on the top of their building to train and study, since the inside of their building was a complete mess. The quartet below—Rick having joined them to at least understand the technique if not learn it fully—were constantly attempting to test various aspects, providing one another insights as they ran around trying to climb on beds, step-stools, and pots and pans in a racket that was doing his own quieter, study little good.

Occasionally, they'd come up to share their latest understanding and borrow his own insights. In this way, what should have taken a week or two to understand at the least was compressed significantly. Arthur figured he'd be done in a day or two more, which was why he'd kicked the can of the Thorned Lotuses even further down the road.

Best to have something to show them, not just words.

Breathing out, Arthur forced Tower energy to suffuse his meridians. Energy coursed through the various whorls, meridian points, and the meridians themselves to alter the form and format of the energy, bleeding normal Tower energy into various elemental alignments.

In this case, the Seven Cloud Stepping technique at the first level was mostly wind and water, with just a touch of gravity. It lightened the body but also connected the user with water and wind that suffused the environment, allowing one to basically step on tiny cloud projections beneath the feet.

This had the advantage of creating the very stepping stones one needed to traverse the air, meaning that one did not need to find a landing spot. Of course, the negative of this was that it was quite exhausting to create the clouds themselves, the amount of Tower energy used being quite intensive. As such, initially, one would only form a single step or cloud to use. Each cloud was a level in the technique, allowing one to bound further and lighten oneself even more, such that you could, in theory, walk across seven clouds.

At the penultimate level, theoretically, each of those clouds would form again allowing the user to continually stride across the air. At least, that was what Arthur thought it meant, though specific details were hidden from him till he finished understanding the technique.

It might be that there was an entirely different technique to use.

Unlike other qinggong techniques, the Seven Cloud Stepping technique had certain disadvantages too. Rick's own technique pulled him along straight lines with great speed, which the Seven Cloud Stepping technique did not. While an individual was mildly faster when suffusing the body with the technique due to the lighter weight, it did not, by itself, make the climber faster.

Nor was it a teleportation technique like Uswah's. And because it only made the individual mildly lighter, one could not stride across water like the water-stepping technique the Thorned Lotuses had. Branches had to be picked carefully too, if one used it.

But having so many steps to learn, the Seven Cloud technique had more variability and more uses. Arthur had a feeling that if he could learn this technique and then study the Water Walking technique's ability to diffuse his weight over a larger area, he might be able to truly develop a powerful qinggong technique.

Then all he needed was a movement technique that sped up his actual movement and he was golden.

Right now, though, he had to figure out how to make this work. Focusing within, he pushed the Tower energy that was ready into his flesh. Technically, you were supposed to start with your feet, but he was looking to short-circuit the training a little.

After all, you eventually needed to infuse the entire body with the elementally infused Tower energy. Better to do it from the start. In addition, the Heavenly Sage's Mischief was built upon the idea of suffusing the body with energy anyway, such that the methodology of such things was much simpler and easier for him.

There were only so many techniques out there, and once you studied a few, adopting the next one was easier. It was one reason why more powerful or more experienced Tower climbers were able to study and make use of early beginner techniques quickly—because they already knew the infusion and diffusion methodologies in play. Or even knew better ones.

Energy suffused his body, and for a few moments, he felt himself lighten. He pushed a little with his crossed legs, testing the change. The moment he did so, his concentration broke and he found himself falling back down with a thump.

Over the course of many attempts, the pain was like getting pummeled all over by a padded bat. All at once at the same time. Painful, but not particularly dangerous. He did, however, let himself slump onto his back, lying down till his breathing recovered.

"Still nothing?" Casey asked. Like him, she had taken to sitting on the rooftop to avoid the chaos while benefiting from the clan building's denser energy.

"I'm getting there." Arthur sat up, forcing himself to circulate his breathing slowly. "I just need to split attention and make it, well, normal."

"Always hardest, making it second nature," Casey commiserated. "Once you get it, though, the Tower will help."

"For definitions of help."

Lam over in his own seat smiled, though he did not shift. His pull of energy from a monster core in one hand never stopped. He kept pulling the energy to his core as he did so, head turning to watch for potential trouble.

Not that there was likely to be. Not only was the building set apart from the trees, but the only ways in were via a couple of suspended bridges. Add the Tower guard and they were pretty safe, unless someone decided to fire on them.

"It's not a bad technique at least," Casey said.

"Not as good as yours," Arthur replied. "What was it called again?"

She smiled in reply instead, forcing Arthur to give up on that line of questioning. Casey and Lam Kor had trained in and mastered a technique the Chin family supplied while Arthur and his group were looking for the

Heart of D'mai. It sped up their movements and lightened their body, making it an almost perfect qinggong method, from what Arthur had seen. If there were disadvantages, it likely would be apparent in the name or under closer observation.

For now, though, with the pair choosing to cultivate instead of practice that technique, he had little chance of discerning it. All he could do was practice his own technique and get it ready to showcase to the Thorned Lotuses. And, hopefully, finally get their buy-in.

Chapter 87

"No."

Arthur sighed as Kavitha replied immediately. Mel was nodding along just as fast behind her, and the other handful of members that made up the Thorned Lotuses on this floor look ready to rebel.

"Not long, just long enough for the others to appear and fill up the clan ranks. Then, you let them get ready, show them the way, and move on," Arthur said.

"No way." Michelle crossed her arms, looking mulish, the prominent jaw jutting out further as she raised her chin. "Have you actually stayed here?"

As though to punctuate a point, a mosquito buzzed by Arthur's ear, forcing him to snap it out of the air with one hand and kill it lest its incessant buzzing distracted him. He opened his hand to see the red splotch of blood. He grimaced and wiped it away on his pants.

Pristine cleanliness in the jungle was just not something that happened. Germophobes would either go insane or learn to deal with it. Dirt and grime from sand and soil and trees rubbed all over clothing and bare skin. The constant humidity and heat would force sweat from pores. And the ants and beetles that made up the surroundings had no sense of personal space, much like a toddler who'd recently learnt to walk.

"I have. And it's a lot to ask," Arthur said. "But it's necessary. We need someone here for the newcomers and you are the best choices."

"No way, I said," Michelle repeated.

"You'll have a lot of chance to study the qinggong methods available here. And the new cultivation methods. You'll need at least a few weeks to learn all those," Arthur said.

"We can learn it on the next floor."

"The one where people start dropping like flies?" Arthur said, raising an eyebrow.

"Not straightaway. At the beginning there are safe parts."

"But they aren't as safe as this clan building. And you would be much more prepared if you spent more time here." He could see them shaking their heads again and he glanced between Michelle and Kavitha; after some time he could see that Kavitha was as much a leader here as Michelle was. After a moment, he made up his mind and added, "I'll also leave word that you don't have to pay clan taxes next floor."

"Just next floor?"

"Don't push it," Arthur said, crossing his arms. "I can just leave one of my people behind if I have to."

"No, you need them," Kavitha said.

"No, I need to get up fast. For the good of the clan. Not waste time arguing with you." He gestured at them, continuing. "You said you're Thorned Lotuses and want to help others. But now you're inconvenienced a little and you refuse? Maybe you aren't who I think you are."

"What is this, reverse psychology?" Michelle said, sniffing. "Doesn't work on me."

At the same time, Kavitha growled. "Don't tell me what I believe, boy."

"Or what?"

"I don't need you. You need me."

Arthur opened his mouth to reply and then shut it.

"What? Nothing to say?"

He breathed in and out, forcing his temper down. He shook his head, refusing to acknowledge her provocation and forced himself to calm, counting off in his head till he hit seven. He should have done ten, but well...

"I have a lot to say. But none of it is useful. You don't want to help, fine. I get it. So let me talk to the others," Arthur said. "You can't say this isn't good enough, that the clan isn't good enough to join anymore. So you guys go. I'll talk to whoever else wants to stay." He shrugged. "They can just hide in the building if they have to, to be careful."

Kavitha frowned. Behind her and Michelle were three other Thorned Lotuses all looking uncertain, none of them much older than in their early twenties. The youngest looked to be no older than fifteen, though he knew that was deceptive. No way they'd let anyone younger than eighteen through the doors.

"I don't think they want to do it." Michelle smirked as she said it.

"So what? What do you want to do?" Arthur said. "Leave the clan building empty while you go gallivanting around?" He received no answer, so he continued. "You know there's no clan building, nothing, above us without me, right? If you don't wait long enough for me to set it all up, there's no real point in coming after."

"No real point anyway. How many more buildings can you build?" Kavitha shot back. "The Chins might have a few, but not next floor. That's just stage running. No place to set up." Arthur had to admit, she was right. Even with the initial, safer start points, the entire fourth floor really didn't do much for people to rest before they had to tackle the trial. There was a finishing and resting spot at the end of the floor, but most people passed on to the fifth floor afterwards unless they had wounds to care for. Among other things, the fifth floor started much easier, in a localized area that allowed for rest and resale of goods to an administrative building. Something the fourth floor didn't have. "So you got what? One more building before the seventh floor? And then what?"

Arthur shrugged. "Ninth at least."

"So no use, *lah*." Kavitha sniffed.

"And outside?" Arthur crossed his arms. "We're going to be building out in the real world. Organisations, companies, buildings. We'll be able to help your family." He watched as Kavitha ignored the obvious bait but Michelle and the youngest member stiffened at that mention. "Even if you can't do much yourself. There will be jobs for them."

"Nepotism," Michelle grated out.

"Big word," Arthur said. "And what are you? Some white-collar elite from America? Of course it's nepotism. That's how we exist. That's why we're a clan, not a damn guild."

Social and familial pressure kept people in line when you hired within the family. It made sure that workers put their all in and strengthened bindings of loyalty. And it didn't matter, sometimes, if it was the idiot cousin you hired to mop the floors or play office assistant or gave a big but meaningless title to, when you then had the services of someone who was truly good.

It was the trade-off that cronyism, favoritism, nepotism, familial ties—whatever you wanted to call it—

played out. Sure, it could introduce inefficiencies, but it also introduced bonds of loyalty that transcended the individual. Maybe they did fire you because you screwed up. But they were still hiring two thirds of your family, so that dishonour could be swallowed for the greater good.

Or they asked you to work a few extra hours? Well, maybe you owed it to them, because your foolish niece who got an Arts degree needed a job and she was still learning. So what if you burned the midnight oil a little? When the time came to call in a favour, you had tokens to offer.

It all worked out, give or take a little, so long as everyone was on board and played by the same rulebook.

"I'll do it." The youngest girl, the one who looked like she shouldn't even be in here, spoke up. "I'll wait around."

"Liv!" Michelle hissed. "We talked about this!"

Arthur's eyes narrowed, suspicion given evidence. But he ignored it as he stepped past Michelle and Kavitha, using his hand to push Kavitha aside a little when she tried to stop him. Yao Jing, standing behind, had stepped the rest of the way into her space, forcing her back by his sheer bulk.

"Liv? Interesting name." Arthur said, conversationally. He noted how the others had moved back to give them space.

"It's short for Olivia." The young girl grimaced. "I hate that name."

"Family name?"

"Li."

"Liv Li." Arthur smiled at the mild alliteration, then nodded. "Done. You stick around, hand off information and the scrolls to the ones after, make sure they'll stick around, and then you can go. Or you can stay here, longer. Your call." He offered her his hand. "Deal?"

There was a brief hesitation, but she refused to look back to where Michelle and Kavitha were as she took it. "Deal."

"Great." A notification that she had been enlisted in the Durians scrolled past, and he added, "Let's talk." A slight beat, then looking back to the others, he said, "Offer to join is still open. But no special privileges for you lot." He raised a hand when they moved to speak with him. "After we're done talking."

He ignored the angry looks that Michelle and gang were shooting at Liv and him as he led her back over the rope bridge and into the clan hall.

Teach them a lesson for trying to have him over a barrel.

Chapter 88

They took a seat on the roof. Arthur, Yao Jing, and Liv sat on the opposite side of where Casey and Lam were practicing, away from sight of the remaining Thorned Lotuses. Liv looked bemused to be forced to come up here, though she stayed silent all the way up.

"So, why'd you break ranks?" Arthur asked, curiously.

She looked at him askance, sudden doubt flitting across her face. He had to suppress a smile at how easy it was to read her face. Some people—mostly Mat Sallehs, white folks—might think Asians were hard to read, but it was simple if you grew up watching for it.

"Relax. I'm not kicking you out. I just need to know why." Besides, if she didn't have a good reason, he'd have to start rethinking his decision to trust her with clan property. Damn Tower didn't make it easy to keep things safe. At least he could carry the original Seven Cloud scroll with him, since the Tower considered anything in his possession owned by the clan. Later on, when they had more clan officers, a Treasurer could do the same job. For now, though, that meant that Floor Bosses could purchase one-off scrolls easier. In addition, of course, to the physical copy they'd leave behind.

"I didn't want to do it in the first place," Liv said, looking down and refusing to meet his eyes. Her voice had grown softer, younger, as she spoke. "It wasn't nice. But they said you needed us. That we could get more from you. Maybe become an officer or something."

Arthur snorted, and when she looked at him, he explained, "I don't have any officer slots. Just floor boss slots. Which, you know, I was already offering."

"Oh."

When the silence between them stretched too long, Arthur prodded. "Was that it?"

"No." Not looking up, a hand had drifted down to the reeds that made up the roof. She played with loose reeds, tugging on them idly and wrapping them around her finger as she refused to meet his eyes. "I'm scared."

"Of the next floor?" he guessed.

"Yes." Softer, almost so he couldn't hear. "I don't want to die."

Arthur exhaled in understanding. The next floor was brutal, and if she wasn't confident... "Then stay." He gestured around them to take in the floor. "It won't ever be the nicest place to live, but there's nothing stopping you from staying here a little longer. Train, strengthen yourself till you are confident."

The look she gave him said he was stupid and of course that's what she was doing. He chuckled and reached over to ruffle her hair, forcing her to squirm away and glare at him.

"I'm not your kid sister."

"No, you're not." Arthur said, sadly.

She wasn't, but she reminded him of others at the training hall, youngsters with whom he had felt that same kind of kinship and sense of protectiveness. None of them were coming up, luckily. And shouldn't. But if he got out fast enough, maybe he'd be able to get them to join his clan if they ever went in, giving them an easier way up.

It also reminded him that he hadn't seen any of his seniors either. That was a little worrying, though he'd sweat it on the next floor—or on the fifth—when they didn't show up. After all, they were his seniors. They surely weren't going to die.

And if he told himself that loudly and firmly and often enough, he might believe it.

"Did they die?" Liv asked.

"What? Who?"

"Your little sister."

"No!" Arthur said, shocked. Then, realizing what she probably guessed, he shook his head even more vigorously. "Nothing like that."

"Oh! You're a lolicon!"

"I am not."

"There's nothing wrong with it. I have a friend who is." She narrowed her eyes, looking Arthur up and down. "You might be a little old, but I guess that's okay. Older men are part of the scene."

"I'm not old! How old do you think I am?"

"Thirty."

Touching his face, Arthur said. "I'm not thirty!"

"Really?" She pursed her lips, doubtfully. "Okay."

"I'm not!"

"I said okay."

"I'm not."

"Uh huh."

Letting out a huff, Arthur waved his hands to the side, dismissing the topic. There were not getting anywhere and they definitely had more important things to discuss than his age. Like her responsibilities, what she had to do when a new Thorned Lotus came, how long she figured she'd be here and, rather importantly, handling her disgruntled friends.

Which was a thing.

Watching the group depart with Liv in the lead to have a conversation with the other Thorned Lotuses and Mel accompanying to help placate them, Arthur found himself chewing on his lip. None of this was perfect, none of this was ideal. There were too many cracks, too many risks being taken to build this organization, and it was happening all too fast.

He could almost sense the cracks he was creating in the foundation of his clan by moving this fast, by taking on individuals without proper vetting, by flashing benefits and making promises but building them upon visions of the future only and not benefits in the present.

Unable to help it, he found himself going over his options, thinking once more about what he could do, what he should do. Worrying about the decisions he had made, forecasting future issues. So deep into his thoughts did he dive that he startled when a hand touched his shoulder, forcing him to jump.

"What?" Arthur said, one hand falling to his kris only to still when he realized it was Casey.

"You should be cultivating, not worrying."

"I wasn't worrying."

"So you chew on your lower lip for fun?" she snorted.

"Whatever. I just..." He sighed. "It's moving fast."

"And you're worried it'll come crashing down." Casey said.

"How...?"

Casey smiled. "You don't think we thought about that? That we discussed the possibility? I'm tying my family, my own future to you. Of course I thought about it."

Arthur grunted. "You can always run back to your family, if it fails."

"I could," she acknowledged. "But just because I have a safety net doesn't mean I'm not taking a risk either."

Arthur nodded. "*Maaf.*"

She waved aside his apology. "But if you're worried about moving too fast, also consider that you might be moving too slow."

"I know, we have a speedrun." He hesitated, then added, "You have a speedrun."

"Not that," Casey said. "Though, it's good you remember. I'm talking about you."

"How could I be too slow?" Arthur said.

"How many clans and guilds do you think have formed recently?" she asked.

"I don't know."

"Very few. Thirteen in the last three years, worldwide," she said. "That number is dropping, every year too."

"Why would the Tower give out fewer seals?" He frowned, considering. "We're hitting the cap? Or..."

"Or someone's killing those who are trying to make new clans and guilds," she said flatly.

"What? Why?" Arthur said. "No way. I'd have heard about that."

"Are you sure?" she said archly. "Anyway, it's just a guess. That some don't want the competition. A conspiracy of clans and guilds, of the powerful."

"And you think they might come after me."

She shrugged. "Or others might come after you anyway, to make you serve their purpose. The longer you stay in here, the more time they have to prepare out there." She grunted. "Our influence can only go so far."

Arthur lips pursed. There were no instantaneous transmissions of information in and out of the Tower. Knowledge was passed on by climbers as they ascended. New climbers brought in messages. Bigger organisations and networks with the money could push more people in to pass on these messages. He knew Casey's family had done the same.

It was possible that news of his clan's establishment had not even reached the outside world. Possible, if unlikely.

"So get cultivating. Because there's nothing you can do about that out there," Casey said forcefully before she stood up to return to her own seat.

Arthur watched her go for a second, then sighed. She was right. New technique or not, he still needed to strengthen himself. They all did.

And now, he had more worries than ever before. Because having strength was great, but he would still have only climbed a single Tower. In the greater world, that meant little enough.

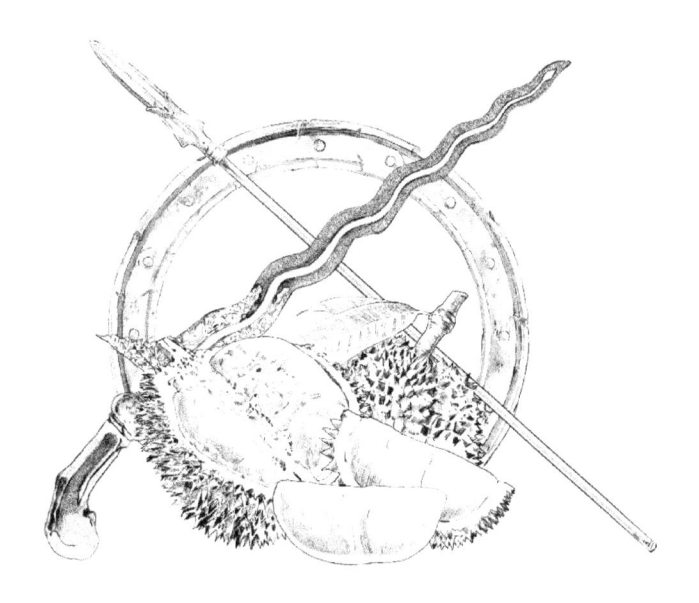

Chapter 89

Arthur took to the marshlands by himself, no Yao Jing, none of his other teammates. They were still working on learning the Seven Cloud Stepping technique and couldn't be bothered. As for Casey and Lam Kor, they were busy cultivating. So, alone, in the middle of the night, Arthur journeyed into the surrounding areas to hunt for monsters and gather their cores. A rather necessary requirement of pushing ahead.

Now he was ahead, the energy of the Seven Cloud Stepping technique infusing his body as he jumped from one location to another, spear in hand and searching for monsters to kill. As he did so, he learnt about his technique, understanding it better and better with each moment.

The first part of it, the lightening, allowed him to cross wider stretches of water without even having to utilize the cloud-stepping. He flew across tens of feet with ease, bouncing off root after root, footing firm on the slippery ground. Occasionally, he'd land and pivot, push down on a cloud that he formed and strike.

Upwards, sideways, downwards.

It varied, depending on where the monsters were. Monsters abounded, leeches, snakes, even a large catfish or two that he found as he jumped all around. He struck, injuring or killing with ease, before he'd reposition himself, allowing himself to stop long enough to pluck the monster core from their body. And then, he'd move on.

A single cloud was all he could form, and not very long. A second or so, sometimes a little briefer, sometimes a little longer. Enough time to stand and strike, but not long enough to stand still upon anything. Not just yet, though he felt that at some point, he'd reach that.

A lot of information that he was learning, and little of it included in the actual description.

Seven Cloud Stepping Technique
This movement technique lightens the body, reducing the user's weight and allowing them to form clouds which may be stepped upon for leverage and footholds. As user strengthens their knowledge of the technique, additional clouds may be formed up to a maximum of seven.
Cost: 1 Energy per Minute. Cost increases if clouds are formed.

He finished pulling a monster shard from the latest leech corpse and sighed. One of the worst parts of this floor was the lack of full stones. The creatures themselves were easy enough to kill, so long as you didn't let them swarm you. And being able to literally leap into the air, kick off a cloud, and keep moving helped with that a lot.

On the other hand, it did make collecting a little less efficient. Having to travel to his prey rather than have them come to him was always going to be slower. Especially if, for example, a monkey tribe or leech swarm chose to attack him.

"About time to stop?" Arthur muttered to himself. He hopped up and down a few times, looked around him and nodded. Not here, though. Over there was a bigger tree with some actual earth gathered around its trunks such that he would have more space to fight on his feet.

He took a leap over, marveling at the distance he could make now, and landed smoothly, killing the Seven Cloud Stepping technique the moment he had his balance. Even knowing it was about to happen, he tottered for a moment as his balance came to rest more firmly on a root.

Then, squatting smoothly, using his spear as a third leg, he breathed in and focused within. If he was going to be in a real fight, it was time to pull some energy to him. He could wait for the monsters to arrive while he cultivated and refilled the tank.

One day, perhaps, he'd actually have a proper tank. But not yet.

Arthur lashed out with the kris, never moving from the squatting position he was in. The fifth leech that had come up to him died, its body deflating as the liquids rushed out of it and the poison within the enchanted kris entered its body. It twitched and squirmed, the slimy, wet feel of its body making Arthur shudder a little, the grossness added to by the coldness of its body.

"Leeches all want to suck, but they're just made of yuck."

Stopping his cultivation, Arthur swung his freed kris a few times to get rid of the blood before he sheathed it. In the periphery, he spotted the growing leech swarm coming for him. He had managed to get a good twenty minutes of peace and quiet, only having to kill a single leech in the first six minutes.

But time for relaxation was over. These creatures were swarming and it was time to get to work.

Arthur debated his options, eyeing the numbers coming. Best to start with what he knew. He would only use the Seven Cloud Stepping technique when he needed it. He was going for endurance here, and that meant being careful about how much energy he was using.

On that note, he stood and rotated his feet and ankles a bit, swaying his hips as he loosened up. Then, a single step and thrust, sending the haft of his spear skittering along the hollow of his lead hand as he guided the attack to strike. It plunged in with little issue, slicing through bulbous flesh and erupting out the other side before Arthur yanked upwards, flipping the body backwards.

As though this most recent attack was the trigger, the leeches started moving faster, attempting to swarm him. His spear never stopped moving, slicing along bodies to tear long lines of injury, thrusting forwards or battering aside with equal fervor.

He chose to walk, carefully, steps crossing root and soil in a circular fashion as he traversed the land around the tree by which he had chosen to take his stand. Uncountable numbers of leeches kept coming, filling the night with their dark, squirming shapes. Only reflected moonlight and the twinkling of skies highlighted them.

If not for his Enhanced Eyesight, if not for his Yin Body, they might have been hidden to him. If not for their unnatural persistence, they might have fled. Or just slept. But instead, they came for him, and Arthur answered their unwanted interest with the sharp end of his spear.

Blood splashed, bodies deflated, and guts spilled. Bodies piled in the water, sinking into their depths, or covered the branches and mud near his location, staining the water. Feeding frenzies below the water, glimmering darkly and observable by the increased ripples, spoke of battles held even deeper underwater.

Arthur ignored it all, his weapon striking and spinning, twisting and battering. A leech, somehow managing to make it to the treetop branches, dropped from above and met a headbutt before it could latch on. Another climbed up his pants, wrapping itself around his leg, teeth burrowing into the side of his thigh and eliciting a hiss. He struck it three times, battering it with the back of his hand before it was crushed. Its body deflated and blood mingled—his own and the leeches'.

They kept coming, filling the surroundings, and finally, Arthur chose to flee. The flow of the Seven Cloud Stepping technique energy gave him strength, lightened his body. Flagging limbs and exhaustion that threatened to pull him down washed away for a brief moment as he leapt sideways and away, staff battering one falling leech aside as he jumped.

A cloud formed ahead of him, firming moments before he landed, the creation simpler in this humid environment. He landed, and with his foot on the spongy mixture, Arthur leapt again to a less crowded tree.

He dared not flee too far or lose out on his corpses, on his loot. But repositioning to strike, to attack and kill more of the creatures, that was viable. Necessary even.

There had to be an end to these monsters, and he would find it.

Or run away.

Because he certainly wasn't going to die trying.

Chapter 90

Spitting to the side, Arthur groaned. Tired muscles ached as he cut open the next leech. The problem with being successful at killing a horde of these creatures was that you had clean up afterwards. Unlike video games where you just had to click once and all the gold would fly through the air into your pockets, in real life, in the Tower, you had to do the hard work yourself. No helpful loading bars, but hands dripping with gore.

He sighed, slipping the shard into the pouch hanging open by his side. It was pretty filled and Arthur hesitated as he wiped his hand against a root. After a moment, he sighed and shut the pouch, pulling the drawstrings closed. He slipped the pouch further in, making sure it was tightened and then pulled a second one, intent on putting on his belt.

"Will you look at this!" High and bright, a female voice.

The voice caught Arthur by surprise, forcing him to turn and stare. He scooped up his spear at the same time, angling it in the direction of the noise.

"Wah! So many, ah!" Deeper voice. This time, Arthur saw them, an unfamiliar group skimming across the ground from the direction of the Tower village.

"Watch for the harimau!" An older man, wary and tired. Big and muscular but not ripped like a bodyguard.

Arthur could not help but scan the surroundings again. He'd been watching but hadn't caught sight of any harimau. No surprise, at least to him. They were more daylight creatures than nocturnal ones, though they slept so often you would never know.

"What's that?" A slight pause, then carefully. "Who is it?"

Arthur's mind spun and his answer came without much thought, especially since one of them was raising what looked like a bow in his direction. Hard to tell in the dark and with the camouflage paint on them. "The person who killed all these leeches."

"Shiiiit," the first voice said. Arthur saw the girl gesturing to her friends. She shifted to the side, allowing the biggest of them to lead the way as she and her other companion moved to flank him. "Impressive."

"Yes. It was," Arthur said, eyeing the way they were moving. The bowman was skimming over the water, literally gliding along like it was a plane of glass. The girl who first spoke was using something more traditional, a Wind Step variant where she kicked off the water as she stepped forward. And the third, the well-built older man, waded forwards and the water itself seeming to part before him without care. "And who are you?"

"Just climbers. Out hunting, like you."

Arthur eyes narrowed in surprise. Her voice, so high and bright, came from a direction he didn't expect. In the gloom most people might not have noticed. But he did, and he was curious if it was just plain ventriloquism or a technique.

"Okay, well, hunt somewhere else." Arthur gestured to the side as he kept his gaze fixed on the man in front, allowing his peripheral vision to take in the others. The bow man had stopped, content with the angle he had on him.

That was the most dangerous.

The thought triggered his own preparations as he began to form a Refined Exploding Energy Dart in his hand. It was a little overkill if he managed to hit, but the noise and surprise might be sufficient to throw the others off.

"Eh, don't be so rude, *lah*. We just want to talk!"

"I don't. So move on. Or I'll consider you hostile."

Arthur bent lower, splitting his attention a little as he began the process of channeling the Seven Cloud Step technique. Splitting his attention would be difficult, and he wasn't ready to do it properly, but the Refined Exploding Energy Dart was ready in his hand, held just under his skin, the energy pulsing within. Of course, it wouldn't help if his opponent shot at him first.

They didn't heed his warning, the girl and the older man still moving towards him. He figured that they were able to see him in the early dawn light, just about enough to pick him out, but not enough to get details. A good thing in this case, since the Dart was beginning to glow a little.

"Last warning."

Perhaps his words were the signal. Or perhaps the archer was always going to start the dance. He would never know. The loosed arrow hissed through the air, aimed at his chest. Arthur leapt forwards, turning as he did so to point his hand at the archer.

Even anticipating the attack, he was too slow, the arrow tearing a line of pain along his side as it narrowly missed pinning him. Hand raised, he released his own attack, the white-blue glow of the spinning energy dart lighting up the surroundings as it flew towards his opponents.

"Celaka!"

The archer dodged too, having anticipated an attack. What he didn't expect was for the explosion as the Energy Dart struck the tree behind, sending shards of wood and water to pelt him from behind. Surprised, he fumbled the arrow he had drawn, dropping it, and spilling some of the other arrows in his quiver.

In the meantime, Arthur poured his full attention into his movement technique and played another trick. He bounded aside mid-air, away from the large man in the lead. Instead, he went after the archer.

He cursed as the archer skated backwards, pushing away as he reached for another arrow, forcing Arthur to splash into water, missing with his outthrust spear.

Behind, he could hear the other two rushing after him, but he had no attention to spare them. Instead, he swung his spear upwards, trying to catch the arrow as it was being fitted and loosed, his opponent only conducting a half-draw.

Arthur poured his energy into Bark Skin. It saved him, somewhat, as the attack pierced his side but failed to pass all the way through. Forced to wade through water when his opponent tried to run, Arthur cursed.

He couldn't keep trying to switch techniques or use them simultaneously, especially the ones he hadn't mastered. He had to do something and do it fast. Ducking to the side and seeing his opponent smirk, Arthur made up his mind.

He leaned back and lunged forward, allowing himself to splash into the water moments after he hurled his spear at the archer. He could see the man duck the attack, the spear parting his hair.

A waste of an attack, but it was a good distraction.

Rather than follow up again, Arthur forced himself to swim sideways, heading for a marshy piece of water. If he couldn't catch the slippery ass, he'd have to deal with the other two first.

Chapter 91

He swam for a few strokes, pulled himself along some roots, and dragged himself out of sight. It wouldn't do much to truly hide him, but it helped that the group was shouting at one another. Arthur cursed himself a little for coming out by himself without backup. But he had been certain he could handle anything out here, forgetting, once again, that monsters were the least of his concerns.

Leaning against the tree trunk, trying to breathe and pushing himself out of the water quietly, he listened, trying to gauge where everyone was. A lot of splashing in the direction of the archer, and for a moment, he worried that the man might have taken his spear. Or, at least, was trying to find it in the water.

He heard another of his attackers wading through the water—the big older man, probably. And the girl... unknown. He couldn't pick out where she was, not over his harsh breathing and the thunder of his heart. If he went for the obvious option, he was going to expose himself to attacks from the archer and the girl, while the tank likely had some technique to make himself invulnerable for a bit.

Speaking of that...

Arthur pushed a hand to his wounds, touching the scored line across his side. Somewhere along the way, he'd worked the arrow out, and now the wound pulsed a little, dripping blood. Thankfully not too painful, except when he moved or breathed. Then, it was like getting a coal shoved into his stomach again and again. One reason he was breathing so shallowly, now that he was focused on that. No good.

He forced himself to slow down, to breathe as his mind spun across options, head tilting back to get rid of water threatening to drip down his eyes.

Up.

A smile crossed his face, as he realized how he was going to turn this around.

***

Arthur breathed slowly, carefully. Crouched in a tree above, he waited to see if they took the bait, moving through the darkened marshlands in search of him. A short distance away, the glitter of spilled monster cores and his shirt lay, stuffed full of leech bodies and propped against a tree. A flick of one of his sling stones to knock against the wood had brought attention to the location, and now he waited.

Wading through the waters, coming in slowly and carefully around the edges, the group's muscular tank edged over. He was careful in his movements, barely creating ripples or splashes as he arrived, even as early morning light began to brighten the sky.

Forced to breathe slowly and deeply, Arthur mentally urged the man to speed up. He needed them to speed up, or else his minor advantage in the darkness would end. As it was, he had smeared his shirtless body with mud and gone high in hopes of hiding from their view.

He could tell when his opponent caught sight of the bait, the way he tensed and then slowed even more. Stop, and then move, ever so gently. A hand came up, waving a little to the side, making some form of gestures with the fingers.

Arthur looked to the side, figuring out line of sight for the others and caught sight of her. The girl was angling sideways, coming to flank by hopping along. She was, smartly, scanning the tree above where Arthur was supposed to be, but finding nothing.

That was why he hadn't crouched there. In fact, he wasn't in any of the immediate trees surrounding that group, trusting his eyes and other senses to give him enough perception. There was, also, some minor hope that the damn archer would have come by this way, but he was nearly on the opposite side, sweeping out wide of the bait.

Mentally charting the likely course the girl would take as she jumped along, intent on approaching and following her friend, Arthur made a decision.

That tree.

Exhale. Wait. He wiped his hands on his pants, carefully balancing the kris for a moment as he did so before snatching it back. Cloud Step to Focused Strike, that was what he'd need to do. He wanted, needed, to release his Energy Dart at that damn archer; but he was too far away.

Just have to deal with him later.

Or let him run.

She jumped, leaping lightly from side to side. Her ability to move swiftly, to land and push off with barely a ripple of sound was impressive. In any other scenario, Arthur might have asked her about it. As it was, he waited, timing.

He leapt when she leapt, knowing it would take time for him to arrive. Kris extended, he adjusted course and pushed off even harder midway, knowing he had to cross the twelve or so feet between them quickly. The noise he made was sufficient that an arrow came winging its way towards him on reflex, but it buzzed by without striking him.

She turned too, a heavy stick barbed with nails leading the way defensively. Rather than deal with it, Arthur sacrificed his arm, pushing it aside and feeling nails dig into his flesh even as he crashed down on her, kris sliding through collarbone and downwards as he struck, Focused Strike bypassing whatever technique she was using for defense.

The pair of them crashed, tumbling over roots as she lost her grip. Using the weapon as his handhold, yanking her along with it and his other arm grabbing at her, he winced as they landed and his breath exploded out of him.

She wasn't better off, as they scrambled across uneven roots and into the water. Ripping his kris out of her body, he struck again and again, wielding the short sword like an ice pick. Wounded fatally on her neck, yet she thrashed in frenzy... till she finally stilled in the water.

Then he was up and away, only to be nearly skewered by an arrow that came winging in now that Arthur and the girl were no longer entangled.

One down.

One there.

The third... there!

Hands grabbed hold of him and pulled him out of the water. He was yanked up by large hands, fingers which dug into his mud-covered limbs. Arthur struggled, kicking outwards. He caught his opponent in the stomach, then levered himself sideways.

His kris hand thrust forward, cutting into the body of the muscular man. The first attack slid along the skin, not even puncturing it. Arthur snarled, thrusting again. Again, he barely pierced the other. But even as his opponent grabbed his face to smash into him directly, Arthur did not stop striking like a sewing needle that failed to pierce hardened leather.

Just a half-inch at most, enough to draw blood—he could dig deeper if he struck properly.

Then another headbutt. Arthur angled his head a little, trying to make his opponent smash into the crown of his head rather than his nose. He failed, feeling the nose break, eyes tearing up immediately as pain overwhelmed him.

Focused Strike.

He plunged it deep into the man's body, punching through the outer layers of skin, into the muscle and flesh beneath. Something twisted beneath his blade as he did so, almost feeling like it was squirming. Over bloody nose and teary eyes, Arthur grinned.

In disgust, his opponent tossed him to the side, sending him flying through the air to impact against a tree. Even as he slid down, an arrow came, slamming into his left shoulder and pinning him in place. As he pulled at the arrow, he felt it connecting itself to the tree behind, holding him in place through a technique.

"You... I'll kill you," the big man snarled, clutching his side.

"Big man don't like little needle?" Arthur taunted, letting the kris he'd held fall to the ground. He gripped the arrow, pulling at it as he focused within himself and pulled Bark Skin to the fore. Not a moment too soon before another arrow slammed into his reaching arm, punching halfway through it and causing him to gasp.

Even so, his hands reflexively tightened on the first arrow he gripped and broke the tip off. The arrow end broken, he threw himself forward and slid off the damn thing. He screamed as he did so, tumbling forward to the ground.

By the time he got back to his feet, the tank was looming over him, one hand raised and filled with energy. Ready to end it.

Chapter 92

Unable to dodge the attack, Arthur managed to roll with it as the big man's fist came crashing down. He shifted his injured left shoulder and hunched.

The blow cracked bones and burst muscles, throwing him to the ground and bruising him against the roots that stuck up around them.

Scrambling to the side, Arthur kicked out with his foot, striking his opponent in the leg. It barely shifted his opponent, who merely drew another fist to slam down on Arthur again. No enhanced attack this time, though, yet Arthur felt his Bark Skin technique dissipate; he couldn't sustain it.

Instead, he could only weather the sudden flurry of punches that came his way. Blocking it with his left arm, feeling the punches sink into his body, into his shoulders and his face, reeling from the attacks that kept coming, Arthur was battered senseless.

But killing a man with punches took a lot more work than most people realized. And after the flurry of a dozen blows, maybe two dozen, Arthur could sense the slowdown. Exhaustion and the Yin poison finally working its way all through the man's body.

Attacks slowed, then stopped.

His opponent tottered, swayed backwards and forwards, attempting to focus on him. Arthur wanted to move away, but everything hurt. He couldn't find the energy to do so, even when the large bodybuilder finally crashed backwards, falling with an almighty crash.

"Got you," Arthur whispered.

He grinned, even as a niggling sense of incompleteness tugged at him. In his concussed, injured, and punch-addled brain, he couldn't figure out what it was.

Whatever. Probably wasn't that important.

He flopped backwards, sinking into the water, barely keeping his face above it as he leaned against the roots beneath the water. For a time, he just floated in the pulses of pain and agony that ran through him, fighting it back with every breath.

Then, movement.

Feet. Elegantly turned out.

Oh, the archer.

Arthur knew he should have been surprised, worried, scared. Instead, all he could feel was an empty numbness. He could not move, could not even make himself care through the fog.

The only thought he had was that he never noticed the archer had so small and delicate ankles.

"*Bodoh!*" Uswah said, leaning over and gripping him by the arm.

Arthur blinked.

She used her single hand to pull him out of the water and drag him out, rather roughly.

"You're here," he said, dumbly.

"You think what?" Uswah snorted. "You think we leave you unwatched?"

"But... training..."

"I already have a movement skill. Idiot."

"Oh... right." Arthur winced, remembering. He found himself trying to understand why, why he needed to leave. Why didn't he think of that earlier. Why didn't he ask? Then again, he sort of knew why. He had been enjoying his time alone, doing what he had thought would be his life. Hunting, fighting, killing. Training.

Not being a politician, not building a clan or being in charge of others.

"Go heal," Uswah said, firmly.

"Uhh... yes," Arthur said after a moment, closing his eyes and focusing on his Accelerated Healing technique. He struggled to do it, struggled to pull the energy needed and, in the end, gave up. It was always working passively, after all, so rather than triggering it in active form, he tried to push the energy into his mind instead, to regain focus.

After all, till he fixed his concussion, everything else was going to be a problem.

Unknown mindless hours later—or probably just minutes—Arthur coughed and spat to the side, clearing clots of blood from his throat and broken nose. He moved to wipe at his face, only to wince as he realized his right arm was still shot through with an arrow.

"Uhh... Uswah..." he called out, coughed, and winced at how weak even his voice was.

Luckily, she did hear him. She came over, frowned, and yanked out the arrow. With a quick slap of a bandage around his arm, she kept it in place until it clotted again, all rather rough and shoddy nursing.

Arthur sighed and leaned back. He needed to fix more: his arm, his shoulder, his stomach. The cracked and broken cheekbones...

He had so many injuries and not a lot of time to work on them all. More importantly, now that his head was clear, he gestured to the body of the big man with his right hand, wincing at the movement.

"He's still alive," Arthur said, calling to her.

"He's not," Uswah said, as she came back with his spear. "He drowned."

"Shit…"

Uswah shrugged, propping Arthur's spear next to him. "Where's your kris?"

"I lost it." Arthur waved in the direction that he had dropped it. "Near that tree."

"Idiot." Tromping back over, she went to look, leaving Arthur alone.

He sighed, closed his eyes again, and tried to focus on his healing technique now. The only advantage of being so beaten up was that he had a good opportunity to test his technique. In particular, with so many crushed bones, he had a chance to see what he could do about healing bones and perhaps even reinforcing them.

Eyes closed, he let his focus fall within. It took his mind off the pain. More importantly, he could sense there were refinements to be made, the way the body pulled and tugged at the shards of bones, the way it stitched itself together.

He had a lot of healing to do, and some learning.

And after that, he had a real test. Dealing with the rest of his clan and apologizing.

For all his desire to not be stupid and reckless, he had done it again.

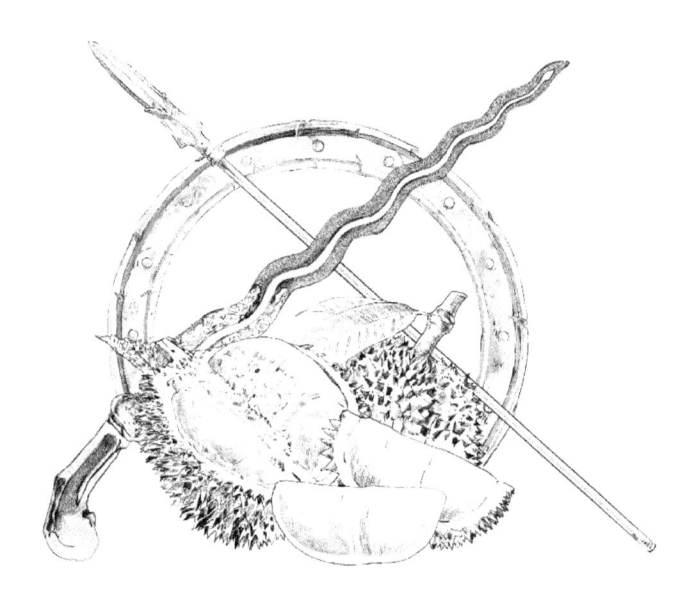

Chapter 93

Early morning dawn had come and gone with its soft light and gentle waking. They were left with the harsh light of mid-morning and the reminder that they had things to do. In this case, after finally finishing the healing process and pulling a small amount of energy from a monster core to refill his reserves, Arthur and Uswah were making their way back.

Silence had fallen between the two, a recriminating and disapproving silence for the most part. Eventually, though, Arthur could stand it no more and spoke up.

"How long were you following me?" he asked.

"Since the start." Uswah hesitated, then added, "You left me behind quite soon though." She grimaced. "It costs me more to push through."

Which probably explained why she was jumping between or hopping between locations rather than just disappearing and reappearing. When he enquired, she added, "It costs me a fraction of Refined Energy to pull myself through each time. I can do it if I have enough reserves, but I'm trying not to..." she trailed off, shaking her head. "I didn't think you'd run away that far." A hesitation, then she added, "Or at all."

"Yeah... sorry."

She sniffed and Arthur ducked his head again. He was getting tired of apologizing, so he wouldn't again. At least not to her. "Is that why you took so long to arrive?"

"Yes." She grimaced. "You all fighting quiet didn't help either. If not for that first explosion..."

It hadn't seemed that quiet, at least to him, in the middle of it all. But he guessed that, outside of the explosive dart he'd released, they'd mostly been quiet. He certainly had kept stealthy once he had set up his trap, hoping to surprise them.

That thought somehow brought a flash of memory: surprised, long-lashed and pretty eyes, wide open as panic reached them, bringing pain and fatalism... after Arthur had stabbed her again and again. He remembered her face, in parts, but it was her eyes that he recalled the most, the way they looked as she realized it was over.

His stomach rebelled, and he wobbled as he landed. Hand extended, pushing into a prickly outer trunk as he steadied himself, grimacing a little as blood was drawn, Arthur tried to find balance. In all ways.

"You okay?"

"Just... recovering."

Silence, and Arthur removed his hand, pulling it away from the prickly tree and flexing it, grimacing as he realized there were a few thorns embedded. Using his teeth, he pulled them out while regarding Uswah who had a look of pity and understanding. Spitting to the side, he broke eye contact rather than see those eyes. He didn't need pity, not over something like that.

The understanding was worse, because it reminded him that they all were killers. Murderers. Enders of lives and hopes, of dreams and sons and daughters. The tragedy of death was not simply loss of potential, the threads snipped even as new cords were pulled tight and others frayed.

Who was she? Did she have family outside? Friends? Parents? Maybe even children. The desperate made up the majority of those who came here, people who could not, would not, settle for a life outside. When most of the ladders to climb higher had been chopped short, when the ones standing at the top hired others to shove everyone else down, a chance like this in the Towers to make life better, however slim, became tempting.

Not everyone would take it. But a run, a period of being someone's mule and climbing higher and higher, that was better than nothing. Never mind the fact that you could stop on the first floor. Build a new life there, even if it was not all that comfortable.

So many reasons to come in, and he would never know hers.

Theirs.

"The archer..." Arthur said, glancing at the bow Uswah had slung over her shoulder. It was still strung. No way to unstring it and carry it easily, so she'd kept it strung even if it was not best for the weapon. The quiver knocking against her hip had a half dozen arrows left, not that many at all.

"Yes?" Uswah asked, softly.

He shook his head. He did not need to ask. He knew what happened to the man, even if he did not have the exact details. A part of him wanted to scream at the stupidity of it all, that they could have just moved on and not forced his hand.

Another part of him, the rational part, noted that they had attacked him first, without provocation. Not the actions of upstanding citizens but of bandits. Of thugs and gangsters and assholes. There had been nothing he could have done to stop them.

Except, maybe, not go out alone.

"You did well, you know," Uswah said as the pair walked over the main bridge that led into the village. Traffic was mostly headed the opposite direction, light though it might be. No sign of the shakedown quartet still. Arthur debated looking into it further and then dismissed the idea. He had no reason to spend time and energy on something like that. They'd show up or they wouldn't.

"Well?"

"They were all strong. Must have been close to leaving," Uswah said. "You took out two yourself. If there had been only one, you'd have been fine." She smiled a little, amused. "Other than the archer."

"Other than him." Arthur agreed, though he wondered about that. He had no methods to stop someone from running away, not yet. But he could have perhaps surprised the other with a burst of speed, or something. "Thank you."

"Keep training. You'll get there," Uswah said, somewhat approvingly.

They fell silent as they made their way back to the clan hall. There were climber tokens that they'd gathered to verify in the administrative center, but Arthur was not feeling it right now. Later on, perhaps, he'd do it. But for now, there was clothing and armour and other goods to sort and deal with, loot from their attackers. That gauntlet that banged against his leg might be something Yao Jing wanted, if it fit. The girl's spiked club had been discarded, the weapon of no use to them, but her belt and the bandolier she had worn had been of good quality. As were all their shoes.

Tools and clothing and, of course, more beast stones. All to be cleaned and distributed within the clan, or left behind for others who would ascend to this floor. He needed to clean himself too, his clothing now stained and torn. And while the weather was warm enough that he wasn't particularly fussed about being shirtless, it didn't stop the mosquitos from sucking his blood or the other insects from crawling on his bare skin.

"Where were you?" Mel snarled, the moment they stepped into the room. She almost bounced right in into him, so he came to an abrupt halt at the doorway.

Uswah, stuck behind, grunted and squirmed through. Before Arthur could say anything, Uswah answered Mel: "Hunting."

Her gaze locked onto the diminutive Malay woman. Mel softened her tone a little as she spoke to her. "You were with him."

"Yes."

Mel frowned, stepping back and looking Arthur over. "What happened?"

Glancing over to Uswah, surprised she had partly covered for him, he chose his words carefully. "We got attacked. Got stuck with some arrows and caught by a grappler." He touched his nose where he remembered the crack and smush. "It took me a bit to heal up and rebuild my energy stores."

"And collect the stones." Uswah held up a heavy bag of monster cores, swinging it back and forth. "Took from our 'friends.'"

Arthur unhooked the gauntlet from his belt, waving it towards Yao Jing. The man was still meditating, eyes closed, so Arthur shrugged and walked past Mel, dropping everything on the ground.

"I'm fine, and outside of losing some energy, nothing bad happened. I needed to test my techniques out anyway," he said.

Mel shook her head, obviously wanting to continue to berate him but forcing herself to not do so. She glanced at Uswah who nodded a little, and in the end, Mel just let out a huffy breath. "Just, leave a note, will you?"

"I will. Figured I'd be back earlier, but things happened." He made a face. "I guess I need to learn to play better. Now, if that's it, I'm going to bathe and put some new clothing on."

He dropped the last of his gear, keeping the kris with him. As he wandered towards the showers, he mentally thanked Uswah. And resolved not to make the same mistake again.

Whatever he thought, he had new responsibilities. Running away from them, even to practice, was a bad idea. He just needed to make sure he wasn't so hard-headed that he needed to learn this lesson again.

Chapter 94

Arthur opened his eyes as he felt the monster core crumble beneath his fingers. A light drizzle had started, coating him and the others seated up here in water, but it was easy enough to ignore since it was lukewarm. Between his increased Body stat and the ambient heat, it was almost nice to be rained upon as he cultivated.

Rather than reach for another beast stone, Arthur stood up and stretched, wriggling his body around to ensure he didn't stiffen up. It was about time anyway, and squeezing a little more energy into his practice wasn't going to make that much of a difference. Just over a week had passed since his ill-fated expedition, and while the team had gone out without him to return with even more stones, the period had been quiet enough.

Of course, the reason he was up here rather than downstairs was that the Thorned Lotuses, now Benevolent Durians, were down below practicing. Under the leadership of new floor boss Liv they were increasing in strength at a decent clip and mastering the Seven Cloud Stepping technique.

But Arthur had delayed as long as possible, and Casey was leaving tomorrow. So it was time to move on, even if he didn't feel entirely ready.

Mentally, he pushed in a direction that was not a direction, and the Tower filled his view with a status report even as he continued his stretches.

Cultivation Speed: 2.473 Yin
Energy Pool: 23/23 (Yin)
Refinement Speed: 0.1421
Refined Energy: 1.381 (28)

Attributes and Traits
Mind: 15 (Multi-Tasking, Quick Learner, Perfect Recall)
Body: 14 (Enhanced Eyesight, Yin Body, Swiftness)
Spirit: 11 (Sticky Energy, From the Dregs)

Techniques
Night Emperor Cultivation Technique
Focused Strike
Accelerated Healing – Refined Energy (Grade III)
Heavenly Sage's Mischief
Refined Energy Dart
Bark Skin
Seven Cloud Stepping

Partial Techniques
Simultaneous Flow (89.7%)
Yin-Yang Energy Exchange (44.6%)
Heavenly Sage's Heaven Beating Stick (34.2%)

Refined Exploding Energy Dart (59.3%)
Water Walking (5%)

He hadn't had much time to practice much on the other techniques he was working on; even the Refined Exploding Energy Dart hadn't seen much use. More importantly, after his recent fight, he had realized how he restricted he was by a lack of ability to split his mind and cultivation flows.

If he had his way, he'd have spent more time learning Simultaneous Flow, but between just cultivating and refining energy from the stones, he hadn't had time to properly extend his training and understand Simultaneous Flow properly.

For all that, he had enough power right now to pour into a new attribute point. As much as he wanted a higher Spirit attribute to increase his cultivation speed, he was riding the rich man train. Which meant increasing his Mind and refinement speed was the way to go. But if he was going into a tough trial on the fourth floor, a stronger Body was more important. And he was only one attribute point away from getting a new Body trait. So sinking that last point into Body was the way to do it.

Pushing the energy through him, letting the Tower guide the process, Arthur felt his body twist and change, filling out and strengthening. At the same time, it was held in abeyance as a prompt came to him, asking what Trait he'd like to add to his body.

Physical traits were always both the simplest and hardest to work with. While it was easy to understand what one got from each trait, they were also both minute and broad too, depending on what you wanted. As usual, Arthur ignored any of the traits that pushed for appearance like Appealing or Refined Skin. While some would consider making themselves more good-looking as useful for a clan leader, it was only viable if he had more time to build himself up.

For now, it was better to focus on traits that would help him survive.

Enhanced Endurance, Thick Blood, Anaerobic Enhancement—all of those would increase his stamina both in general and in battle. Thick Blood had a bonus of also enhancing his platelet levels, allowing him to clot faster, something that the Platelet Factory trait enhanced even further.

Useful, considering how often he got stabbed or otherwise had a hole punched in him.

On the other hand, some might think that *not* getting stabbed or otherwise holed was the way to go. He'd already taken Swiftness the last time, and adding something like Fast Twitch Faster would actually synchronize with his other trait, boosting his overall speed even further.

He knew the speedster build was quite common; mobility was so important. It was why it was so common, and with the addition of weapons, it made pure strength less appealing to Arthur. If nothing else, being fast meant he could, well, run away faster.

Which kind of made up his mind. It wasn't as good as an actual technique that would speed him up, but if he ever learnt one of those, he'd be blazing fast. Even faster than anyone who had such a technique and didn't have the traits to back it up.

Though, what he meant to use was the question. The first, most basic option would be upping Swiftness further. It increased his overall ability to move, strengthening twitch muscles, reflexes, perception, the whole shebang.

On the other hand, specialization might help. Explosive strength via Fast Twitch Faster would allow him to change course, to move and attack more swiftly. It would also make him hit harder, by virtue of the kind of muscles it used. The negative, of course, was that he would tire himself out faster too.

Then there were other things like Catlike Reflexes, Snake Snap, Lightning Reflexes, Instinctive Twitch, and the like, which basically increased his ability to react to things. That could be rather important, especially as he grew stronger. There was a set speed at which humans could react to things, dictated by genetics for the most part. At 250 milliseconds, it was a fraction of a moment and for most, it didn't matter. But then, in close combat where bodies were pressed against one another and blades were flying and everyone else was moving at superhuman speeds, that might seem like forever.

Of course, the negative of taking such an ability too soon was the same as enhancing the mind to process information too quickly. Just because you could perceive it and tell your body to react faster, it didn't mean your body could do so. That was dictated by other factors, which was why it was often recommended that such traits be taken later rather than sooner.

Better to build up the other side effects—or just go generic for a bit—and then add to it. By then, an upgraded Swiftness would help bear the base explosion of movement.

Muttering to himself, Arthur went over his options again. "Strength, speed, stamina, toughness. Co-ordination." He hesitated, trying to dredge up any other major categories.

At last, he shrugged. Good enough for now. Speed was the way to go; it was just a question of whether he wanted to specialize or not.

"In for a penny, in for a pound, just so long as you aren't a hound."

He sorted out traits that the Tower presented and examined the constellation that floated around the Fast Twitch Faster options. He scanned the names, trying to recall what he knew of each.

ATP Reserves increased the amount of adenosine triphosphate, which was the fuel for anaerobic-using twitch muscles. It would allow him to use them more, generate explosive force faster and longer. Eventually, of course, the body naturally replenished reserves of ATP, but if he wanted a quick burst of constant burn to allow him to accelerate to top speed faster and even have a higher top speed, this was the way to go. Less useful in combat, though, since the amount of distance he had to cover was often much shorter than his reserves.

Fast Twitch Faster was just an overall increase in density and volume of his fast twitch muscles. It also increased the ATP reserves to keep a basic baseline speed, if Arthur remembered correctly, which was for the best. Like Swiftness, this was a generic increase, but a specialized sort of generic.

If that even made sense.

Chimpanzee Strength was basically the same thing, though it actually changed the ratio of muscle fibers. Arthur vaguely remembered that being not as good, something to do with faster exhaustion levels for those using it due to the lack of slow twitch muscles. Great if you were constantly fighting, not so good if you had to hike a full day.

A lot of other mentions of different animals followed that, all of which Arthur dismissed from consideration. While there were a few that might have been useful, he liked the current configuration he had, especially since he knew he could train to improve if he needed more of one or another. Though with a trait influencing how his muscles grew, that option would disappear.

Then there were the marked improvements in type a and b twitch muscles. Unfortunately, Arthur couldn't remember which was which. He knew one type was aerobic and the other anaerobic, but it had been a while since he had read the wiki. He'd also seen constant arguments going on about which to mess with or not, with proponents on both sides being entirely too confident they were right. Arthur had decided to abandon the idea of taking either. When two parties were absolutely sure they were right, you could almost always be certain they were both wrong.

No, in the end, Arthur came back to the various generic enhancement options. Fast Twitch Faster was idiotic in its name, but was slightly more broad-based than Twitch Density Increase.

Tired of trying to cudgel his mind for knowledge, Arthur made his choice and felt the energy flood through him, changing him fully.

By the time he opened his eyes again, which had closed involuntarily as he changed, he noticed that Casey was waiting beside him.

"Ready?" she said, impatiently.

"Ready." He stretched his neck out, bounced up and down once more, and then nodded.

Time to go. They had another floor to clear.

And new trials to face.

Chapter 95

With passing the third floor a matter of just handing over the beast stones, it had taken the group little enough effort to cross over into the portal that snapped open within the administrative center. No boss to finish off, no trial to clear. Simple.

As Arthur landed in the next floor, lurching a little as the teleportation dumped him out, he scanned the surroundings. No surprise, there was no one around. Part and parcel of the fourth floor. At least, no one on his particular platform. It was, in fact, a series of linked platforms, floating mid-air. He was on the bottommost landing, which meant there was only one way forward: up the series of landings.

From this starting position, he could see the vegetation that awaited him on these landings. No creatures, but that was the trick of this first portion of the floor. The monsters here were the plants themselves: the snapping ivy, the moving vines, and spitting flowers.

Upon their first revelation years ago, it had even revived interest in an old mobile game involving living plants fighting off undead enemies. Thankfully, for now, the plants would ignore him till he attempted to ascend to the next level.

Scanning the surroundings once more, Arthur verified he truly was alone before walking to the edge of the floating level he was upon. The entire platform was no bigger than twenty feet across by forty. Large enough that you did not feel like you'd roll off if you went to sleep. Almost too generous a size, if not for the fact that the entire thing was just there… floating.

At the edge, Arthur stared down at the ground hundreds of feet below. He felt a moment of vertigo push at him, whispering for him to take just another step before he pulled back, and he ignored that intrusive thought. Instead, he raised his head and looked around, noting the presence of other such floating, linked platforms.

Hundreds of them. Each set of platforms floating independently, somehow managing to avoid one another even as they drifted through the skies. Some, he knew, would grow close enough that enterprising climbers would attempt a jump.

Mostly at higher levels, of course. It was rare for the bottom levels to get close enough that such leaps were viable. And not a single time was the leap clearly safe. Of course, stories abounded of climbers who had found their way stymied and leapt to other climbers' platforms; but such successes were also drowned out by the volume of those who failed and plummeted to their deaths.

As he was thinking that, a chirp drew Arthur's attention. The flicker of motion, moving almost too fast for him to perceive, crossed his vision as one of the floor guardians made itself known. The Battering Birds weren't part of any normal biome, their elongated and curved heads allowing them to ram climbers as they tried to leap between platforms.

The fact that they left those who stayed on their original platforms alone made it clear that the floor designers did not intend for much transition. On the other hand, the fact that platforms could be jumped gave some climbers hope, hope that was often dashed as they were struck by the birds and plummeted to the ground below.

For the average Tower climber, it was enough to complete the floor on the platforms they started upon. While the trials themselves were difficult, they were not technically impossible unless one was extremely unlucky. Or unprepared.

Staring at the floating platforms, Arthur watched for others that he might recognize. Even with Enhanced Eyesight boosting his ability to pick out details at a distance, he soon gave up. Other climbers, he spotted. But his companions, he found none. An unsurprising result. Most of those close by were being ascended at this moment, climbers appearing on the second, third, or, in one case, sixth platform.

Each climber's platforms were different, each configuration different. From his own location, as Arthur stepped back to the center of the first landing, he could only catch minor glimpses of the next biome. Mounds of sand, piled high against an invisible barrier.

"Garden then desert, but at least it's not a dessert." Arthur sighed. "That doesn't rhyme, which is a crime."

Another breath, as he debated waiting. But there was no point, he'd already refreshed himself before coming.

"Now, what was the rhyme?" Face scrunched up, Arthur slowly ran through his mind, finally coming across the details as he stared at one swaying pod-filled vine. "Peas lack bees, for they shoot when you loot.

Cactus for tractors, make sure you're not a detractor. Audrey likes melee, so flee easily."

He confirmed his knowledge by eyeing the pea pods that swayed around, the cacti that lurked as mines, and the weird, monster-alien-like creature that was seeking to bite him if he got too close.

"Right, magical hopscotch it is." Arthur pulled energy from his core to infuse all over his body as he triggered the Seven Cloud Stepping ability. Hopping a little, he checked the energy rushing through him and the lightness in his body before he tugged on the straps of his backpack.

Another deep breath and then he charged forward, angling not for the center where a bump in the ground spoke of a low-lying cactus waiting for him to step onto it. He could not veer to the right, because an Audrey was waiting, so he'd have to go left.

Nearing the sheer cliff that broke up each level, he leapt, extending his left hand to leverage himself higher as he reached the next landing. Between the increased physicality of his climber body and the Seven Cloud movement technique, it was a simple matter to ascend to the top.

Immediately, he struck to the left and blocked the pea that fired itself at him, slicing the green sphere apart. He did not wait for the pea pod to recharge, instead rushing onward. Further to the left, he ducked the Audrey that tried to bite him as he triggered his first cloud step and leapt forward, jumping on the cloud rather than land near the clear space where a group of cacti awaited.

The leap took him high and he tucked his legs in close, going into a front flip to dodge a pair of peas. Then, as he untucked himself, he struck to the right and speared an Audrey as it began to pull itself upward, using the momentum of his earlier movement and the spear to push himself onward.

Magical hopscotch and dodge ball, all joined together. Arthur bounced, ducked, and slid his way through the level, rushing forward with each moment. His spear kept moving, slicing at Audreys and blocking peas fired at him.

The second platform was nearly thrice the length of the first platform, but even so, Arthur found himself nearly at the end within a few minutes. Rather than wait, knowing that the pea pods would continue to fire on him so long as he stayed on this level, Arthur grabbed at the cliff and leapt.

Flipping himself upwards again to land on the third platform with a little flourish.

One down. A lot more to go.

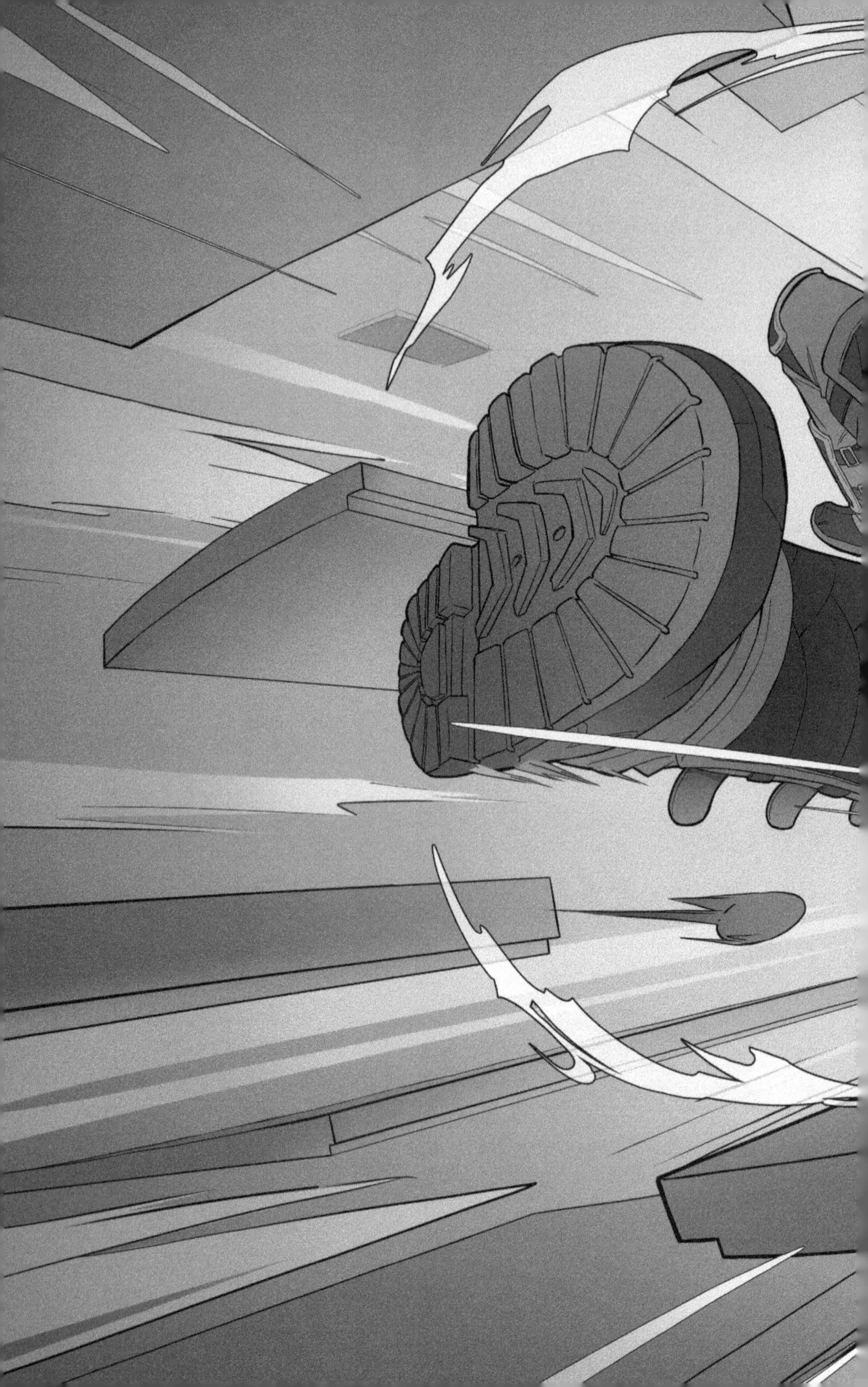

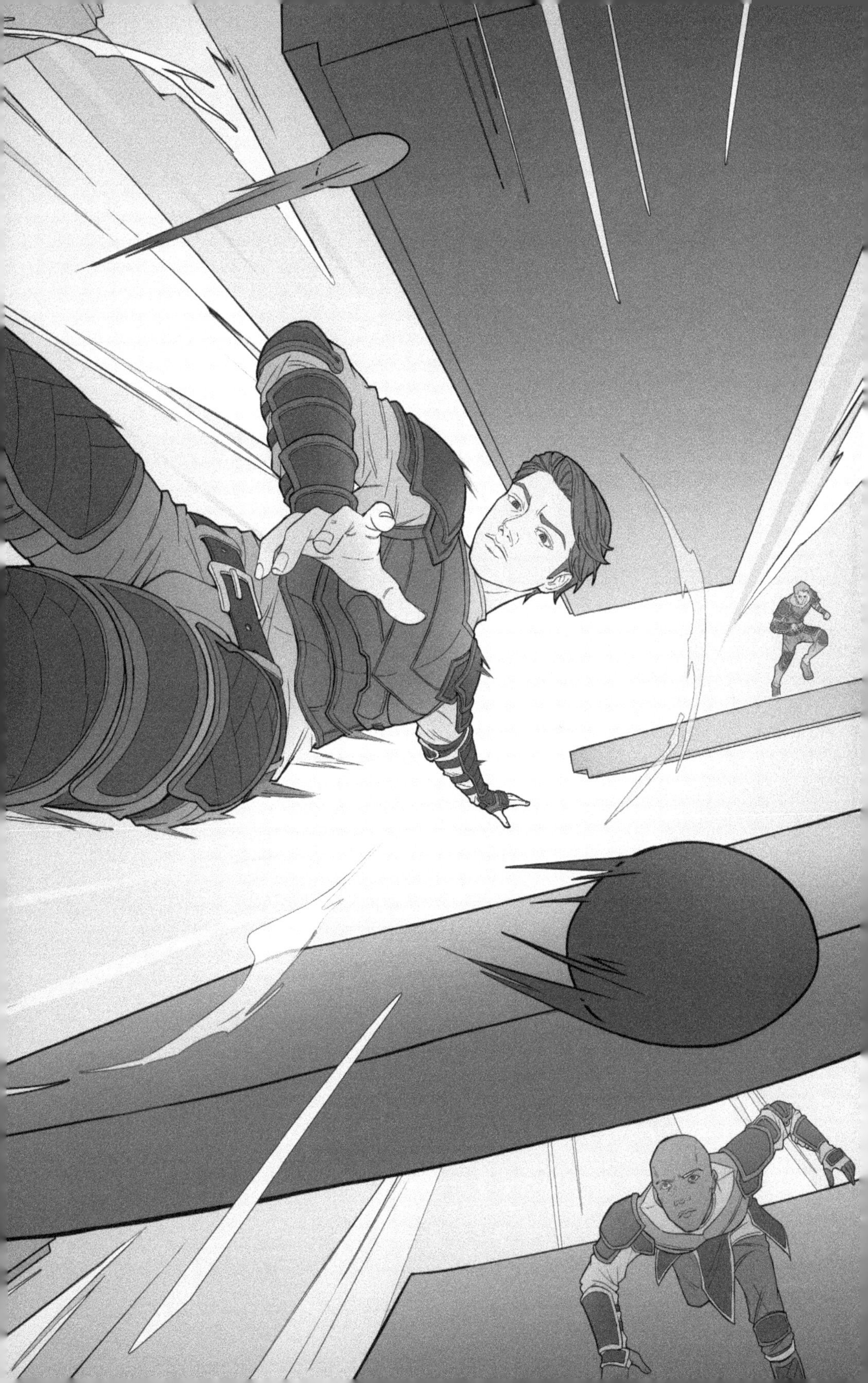

Chapter 96

Arthur grimaced as he walked along the sand dunes, his spear stabbing into the ground as he walked to provide stability. Each step he took had his balance shifting, boot sinking deep into granular sand, forcing him to pay attention to his balance.

At the same time, he scanned the surroundings and wiped at his face occasionally where sweat had been squeezed as from a rather damp sponge. Worst was the dampness beneath his armour that stained his undershirt, underwear, and pants. Each moment of movement made the shifting fabric and the straps across his body and along his armour chafe.

"Damn but it's hot. And not a shady spot." Well, not every rhyme was going to be a winner. But the idea was the same, what with the sheer heat of this platform. It made little sense, what with the lower platforms nowhere as hot, but that was the Tower for you.

Sometimes, logic just had to take a vacation. Especially considering the entire floor was floating through the sky.

Not that any of this was unexpected. The desert platform was quite common, though there were a number of variations in the type and, more importantly, variety of monsters there were around. Right now, Arthur was looking around trying to figure out what exactly he was dealing with.

Rolling sand dunes, as far as the eye could see. No cacti, no oasis, nothing at all. Just sand. This entire platform was huge, comparatively; but it should not take him more than an hour, even with the shifting sands, to get to the end. It would have taken less, but again, space itself had warped so that he had quite the distance to walk.

End of the day, once he reached the end, all he'd have to do was climb a much higher wall.

So far, though, he couldn't see a single monster. No lurking scorpions, no underground cacti with deep roots, no camouflaged snakes with rattling tails. Nothing at all that worried him.

"Perhaps it's too hot?" Arthur muttered to himself. Or, you know, it could be that he was lucky and it was one of the rare empty platforms. They happened, of course. And while he wouldn't say no to a rest—as much as sweltering in the heat might be a rest—the fact that this was only his second biome meant that he really wasn't ready to stop.

Best to get at least another one done, especially while he was still fresh.

Out of the corner of his eyes, Arthur noticed a shifting in the sands. He turned to the motion as he stepped forward, lifting his spear entirely out of the sand and shifting the angle. He took hold of it with both hands as he waited.

Might just be shifting sand. The breeze that blew sometimes toppled over tiny mounds, the addition of one too many grains sent a chain reaction off. But…

No.

Movement, undulating movement. Barely a dozen feet away from him.

Thinking fast, Arthur shifted course rather than meet it straight on, trying to move away. He took his gaze off it for a second to check for additional threats in the direction he was moving, and by the time he glanced back, it was gone.

"*Hun dan!*" Arthur cursed. He took another step away, hoping to draw out whatever it was, but if it was moving, he couldn't see it now. Perhaps it had stopped moving. Perhaps it had gone away. Perhaps it was his imagination.

He snorted. Not a chance. Instinct buzzed and he channeled the energy he'd kept at the ready, humming at a low level through his body. He lightened up immediately as the Seven Cloud Step took effect, making his next step easier, his feet not sinking in as deep.

But he wasn't done.

Instinct made him trigger the cloud formation as he took his next big step, rearing up over the ground and pulling himself out of the sand. He pushed hard on the cloud moments before it dispersed, casting himself into a long leap away from his original position.

He tried to form a second cloud and failed, the slight wisps of smoke disappearing as he crashed through the location his foot impacted, feet sinking in deep into the sand. He barely noticed as he reflexively surged forward, head turned back the way he had come from, such that he caught the next motion fully.

It exploded out of the sand, nearly a foot long. Its back was curved a little, a half-dozen spindly legs propelling it forward as the bristly edge of its carapaced body twitched. More worrying were the giant pair of pincers in the front of the body, which opened wide atop its thinner head, the "shaft" portion of the arrowhead-like body.

The name of the creature, sketches of it, and pictures of the real thing it was based on flashed through Arthur's mind as he watched it try to catch him where he had been. If not for his surge of motion, it would have caught up.

As it was, Arthur stumbled up a dune and watched it burrow into the sand and scuttle forward, legs digging in deep and allowing it to rush after him faster and more lightly than he could move.

Making a snap decision, Arthur spun around, letting his spear extend above his head before crashing down in the direction he thought the half-buried creature was. A hard snap and a bounce as it impacted the ground and threw up sand told him he hit something.

Moments later, as he retracted his weapon, he watched the insect crawl out, half its body shattered. He struck again, crushing the monster, forgetting one rather important part.

Like their namesakes, the damn creatures worked in packs.

Feet grounded, he felt a sharp pain along his legs as another antlion bit into his feet, pincers biting into the flesh of his leg. Letting out a hiss, Arthur forced himself to engage the cloud again and leapt upwards, dragging the light insect with him as he bounced away to a safer spot moments before more of the insects arrived to attack his former location.

Cursing as he landed, he shortened his grip on the staff and used the metal-tipped end to smash into the monster's body a few times. The soft, yielding sand absorbed his attacks enough that he needed multiple thrusts to break it free.

The moment he was done, he was scrambling away, scanning the ground for telltale waves as he hunted for the next attacker. He could not outrun the creatures, but he definitely could not stay still. This was going to be a drawn-out battle of maneuvering and camouflage.

With him already crippled.

Chapter 97

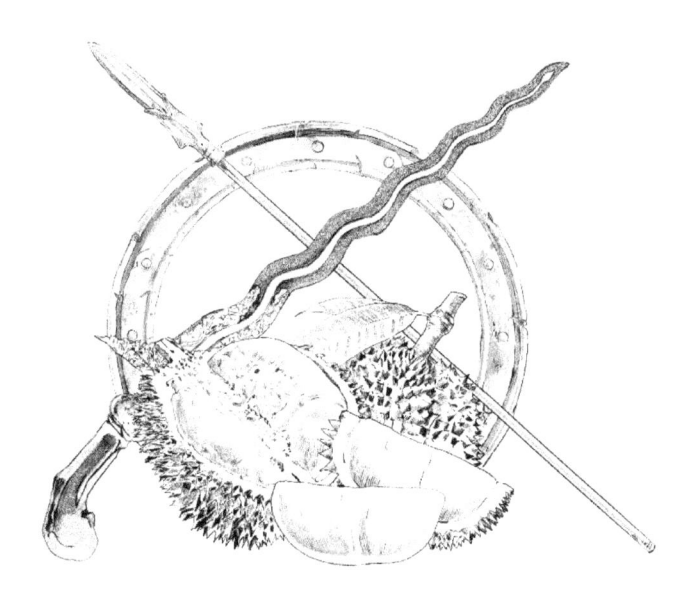

Arthur twisted his body, felt his leg give way, and found himself collapsing over the injured ankle. It didn't stop him, though. He adjusted the angle of his thrust, catching the mutated antlion in the underbelly as it leapt and tearing through the softer chitin within. Speared through its body but still moving, it tore itself off the spear as it fell, twitching to the ground.

Panting, Arthur twisted and caught the next antlion that went for his neck with his forearm. He felt the pincers close on his arm, crushing the bracers and hand at the same time. Pulling his hand towards him and then surging sideways, he slammed the trapped creature into the sand, watching as the curved body imprinted on the ground.

Once. Twice. He kept slamming it into the soft ground, feeling the body give way beneath his thrashing motions until it pulped and stopped moving. Rolling over, the insect still gripping him tight, Arthur scrambled to his knees and scanned for additional threats.

As he'd counted before, this was the last one. Eighteen corpses lay on the ground around him, the last antlion still hanging from his arm and occasionally twitching. Grimacing, he ground the spear deeper into the ground to ensure it wouldn't slide off before gripping the antlion pincers and attempted to work his arm free. It took him a minute or so, angling the body for leverage and even putting it between his legs before he managed to work it free, having to stop at times as the pincers dug deeper.

Released at last, he untied his bracer and stared at the depressed flesh underneath it, watching as the entire arm began to mottle and turn purple. He pressed against his arm a little, wincing in pain at the tenderness before forcing himself to continue tracing the edges of the injury.

"Not broken, I think. Maybe cracked?" Arthur muttered to himself. "And, I'm cracked for talking to myself, of course."

Not that it would stop him.

Shifting again after he re-tied his bracer, gingerly, over his wound, he checked his ankle that had given way. That initial antlion had come off during the skirmish, but his leg throbbed, the area around his boot ballooning to comic proportions and pushing against the laces.

"Oh, that's not good." Arthur pressed against it, shaking his head. The first attack had been bad, and the subsequent monsters seemed to sense his injury and had continued their assault, managing to inflict another scraping bite and a couple of ramming attempts on his ankle during the battle. All of which had resulted in this, his final indignity. "Can't tell if it's broken, but it's definitely not right."

Not much he could do about it. Leaving it strapped in was incredibly uncomfortable and painful, but he was certain that it was the best option from what he recalled. Releasing his ankle now would likely mean he wouldn't even be able to fit his foot back in the boot later. And he wasn't losing these enchanted boots if he had any say in the matter.

Though, Arthur thought as he fingered the ragged edges where the sharp insides of the pincers had punched holes in the boot's outer layer, he might have to give the boots up if they kept getting damaged like this.

Pushing aside that thought, he turned his attention to the corpses around him, pulling out his skinning knife. He reached for the nearest corpse, using the edge of his knife to peel the body apart and search for the monster core.

The monster core within was an inch in circumference, a rough-edged sphere that glowed from within with flickering blue, yellow, and green lights. He raised it to his eyes, staring at the lights that glinted and then smiled. Definitely larger and pulsing with a greater store of refined energy than on the previous floors.

He grinned, slipping open the laces of his pouch to store the core. You'd think that with all the technology of the modern world, they would have come up with something more than reinforced leather pouches, secured by cords. And, of course, there were other storage options in richer countries. But the problem with things like plastic ziplocs or velcro was that they had a tendency to break and were hard to replace in a Tower. A string was simple enough to replace, and pouches were cheap and effective.

Idle thoughts while he did the gross job of pulling monster cores out from the insect bodies around him. No matter how often he did this, Arthur could not shake the instinctive disgust at putting his hand into slimy flesh each time he dissected the monsters.

By the time he was done and had secured the pouch again, his arm was throbbing a lot less. Background healing from Accelerated Healing was probably his most overpowered technique, Arthur had to admit. If he could just figure out how to upgrade it further, he had a feeling he would definitely be a real threat.

Still, for all that, a single step was enough to make Arthur hiss in pain and sink back onto his knees. "Can't walk with this leg."

Problem was, the longer he stayed put, the higher the chance another swarm of antlions would find him. On the other hand…

"Maybe that's for the best?" Arthur said, patting the pouch. He reached into his backpack, unslinging it long enough to drink from the water bottle he had attached to it before nodding to himself. He would wait and fight, because if he was going to get the most out of this floor, he might as well do so on the platforms that made sense.

Squatting carefully and placing his backpack aside, Arthur focused within. Best get to healing, though. He didn't want to do battle with an ankle that couldn't hold his weight at all.

Two rounds of monster killing and looting later, Arthur limped parallel to the wall of sand, his backpack once again slung over his shoulders. He used his spear to aid his movements as he scanned for trouble, watching the sand dunes for the faint tracks the antlions had left behind.

It took him just over fifteen minutes before he found the nest. Rather than walking straight at it, he scurried higher up on the sand dune, grimacing as his ankle and body protested at the movements. Even forced healing had barely brought his leg back to working order, especially after the damn insects had kept coming after it.

Anyway, he wasn't going to attack them directly, not if he had any choice. Even though he had resolved that, the antlions were already swarming out of the hole in the ground and coming directly for him. It wouldn't take long for them to reach him, forcing him into battle again.

Which was why he was forming the Refined Exploding Energy Dart in his left hand already, pulling the energy into his hand so that when he reached a position where he could look down into the nest, he could release it.

Targeting the opening, he released his attack. Immediately, he began pulling even more energy into his arm as the shrieking, swirling ball of energy flew through the air. A little twisting of the energy flows had it drop down a little as it arrived, so that it managed to fall even deeper into the nest itself.

The ensuing explosion shook the sand all around while sending solidified sand and clay into the sky. Arthur grunted, his ears ringing from the painful thump that he felt deep inside his chest. The attack agitated the antlions even further, making them scramble after him.

He lowered his spear towards the first to reach him, thrusting at its clacking pincers. He scored against its chitin, cracking the edge of its head and slicing off one of its antennae. Pulling his hand back, Arthur noted the nest inhabitants were already beginning to swarm out of the thrashed hole in the ground. However, the sand and stone that made up the nest was still surging, the creatures only able to squeeze out in smaller numbers.

Rather than release his attack immediately, he swung and thrust his spear at the crawling insects. A half dozen attacks later, he finally managed to kill the first monster and bat the other two back down before he pointed his hand at the nest again.

The ensuing explosion made him wince, even as bits and pieces of the insect bodies crashed all around. He could see he had managed to damage a few of the insects and killed even more, but rather than release another dart attack, he gripped his spear again.

Time to get to work cleaning up the ones near him before they grabbed and tore him apart.

Chapter 98

Spinning his spear, he brought it down on the side of the antlion, crushing its body into the sand. Arthur kept moving, shifting position so that the lunging other antlion missed him, spinning a little to boot it back down the hill. As he did so, he found himself slipping a little and he forced his toes deeper into the sand as he finished pulling more energy into his hand.

Another unleashed Refined Explosive Energy Dart tore through the air, impacting the hole that had been gouged from the land after numerous attacks. Bits and pieces of antlions and the hardened sand of the nest were scattered all around, the smell of burnt flesh and the stink of open insect wounds filling the air.

By this point, seven Explosive Darts in, the roar of the explosion and the thump that reverberated through the air was old hand. Ignoring the explosion and shower of sand and monster bits, Arthur returned to the monsters that were trying to swarm him.

Not that many left, thankfully. After all, he had already dealt with three different swarms that had crawled out of this very nest, such that the creatures he was dealing with were the nest guards and the half-sized juveniles.

Switching tactics, Arthur kept shifting and swinging his spear, striking some of the insects down onto the sand or shattering carapaces and legs. He aimed to cripple more than kill, focused as he was on keeping himself safe.

Sliding the spear along his hands, Arthur kept moving and attacking till he finished dealing with all of the insects. The battle itself, with the majority of the antlions dead, was a lot simpler than he expected. Of course, it helped that he had not held back on using his techniques while doing so.

Grounding his spear in the sand, Arthur leaned against the shaft and panted, taking deep breaths as he tried to slow down his breathing. A minute later, Arthur straightened up fully and began the slow process of plucking the beast stones out of the monsters.

By the time he was done and seated on the dune floor, he could not help but roll his shoulders and ankle, grateful the pain had reduced. He'd picked up few injuries along the way and with the corpses all stripped, he was looking forward to grabbing his real goal.

Putting the spear aside, Arthur drew the kris with his main hand and slowly sifted the sand and rocks and corpses aside. Twice, he had to strike at a still-living body, killing the insects and pulling out their cores before he managed to make his way to the eggs below.

Those were useless for his purposes. They would break if he tried to bring them with him, and other than some weird gourmets who would pay good money for the eggs, they had little value otherwise. Now, if he had a storage device...

Pushing the thought aside, Arthur kept digging. A flicker of movement and instinct had him yanking his hand back moments before the antlion queen clamped down on it with her oversized claws. Then, having located the creature, Arthur grabbed at his spear.

Taking his time, he aimed and struck at the creature, driving his spear all the way through its bulbous body. He twisted and turned the spear a little, making sure the queen had stopped struggling before he pulled it out, finally extracting the oversized, fat insect.

Pulling the large stone from its body, about the size of his fist, Arthur grinned.

"Score one for reading the forums," Arthur said. He could, of course, use the queen's monster core to refine the energy; but it had a much better use. Storing it away, he stood up and rotated his ankle to test it again, heading to grab his backpack from where he'd dropped it off.

He needed a good drink of water. More importantly, somewhere along the way in these last two fights, he'd felt something click. The Tower had pushed down even more information when it had clicked in his mind, and now he reviewed it:

Simultaneous Flow

The ability to easily control multiple flows of energy through the body at the same time. Mastering this skill allows the user to activate two techniques at the same time. Further mastery of this technique will allow additional techniques to be used concurrently.

Cost: N/A

Arthur read it over once and then again and then snorted. It really wasn't a technique per se, in the sense that it needed energy to be used. It was a technique in the same way that his cultivation method was a technique, like a way of thinking and his martial arts were techniques. A way of moving the body and controlling his energy overall.

Still, Arthur knew, it was a necessary next step. While he couldn't cultivate while using the technique—it wasn't meant for that—his effectiveness as a fighter was, without doubt, increased significantly. Now, he just needed to continue utilizing it and become proficient at the next level so he could work three flows at a time.

"Been a good platform, but you're way too hot," Arthur muttered as he reached his backpack. He bent down and grabbed at the water bottle, draining it dry before placing it back in the backpack. The moment the water entered his body and began to permeate the lining of his throat and stomach, he could sense the drain on his healing ability lessen.

"Huh. Didn't even notice that…" Arthur glanced upward at the blazing sun and then shook his head. It was obvious that the monsters were the least important aspect of this platform. If anything, they were the bait that drew climbers to stay too long, at which point they would dehydrate and fall over dead. Or become easy prey for the monsters.

In either case, he knew better than to stick around any longer. He had two more bottles of water left in his backpack, but that meant little if he found himself unable to refill them. Focusing on moving forward, Arthur directed his energy into the Seven Cloud Stepping technique to speed his movements along.

It was time to get out of this platform and onto the next.

Chapter 99

"Forest, desert, and now, rolling plains? We really are going for a theme with this platform, aren't we?" Arthur grumbled to himself as he sat at the edge of the platform he'd just ascended. He wasn't hanging his feet over but, rather, facing inwards as he cycled his breath and pulled at the energy surrounding him, cultivating the energy to restore his stores while he cooled down.

The plains were significantly cooler than the desert he had most recently traversed, though without shade he knew he would dehydrate eventually. One of the first courses of action then, while he was relaxing, was figuring out if there was a stream here.

Plains generally meant water, though whether the platform bothered with such simple logic, he had no idea. Thus far, he had yet to pick anything out. The waving long strands of grass and the gently rolling hills probably hid a lot.

At the same time, while waiting, he kept an eye out for trouble. The first few platforms rarely had aerial attackers. In fact, overall, the floor had few enough of those creatures that he, for the most part, ignored scanning the sky. More importantly, he had to try to recall what kind of monsters were in the plains. No helpful rhyme this time, but there were at least a dozen creatures that Arthur could recall off the top of his head. There were minor variations, the plains' and savannahs' fauna being close enough that he often got them mixed up.

"Deer maybe?" Arthur shrugged. How dangerous could a bunch of herbivores be? Sure, there might be some concern with the number involved; but so long as they didn't attack him, he would leave them alone. From what he recalled, the various deer and deer-like animals were considered relatively safe, just requiring the Tower climber to go around them.

Not an issue.

Feeling another slice of energy bubble upwards, Arthur called up the first part of his status screen just to check. He could, of course, just feel the level of energy within him; but it was a lot simpler to use the screen. It also helped him get a more accurate picture, rather than just relying on his senses.

Cultivation Speed: 2.474 Yin
Energy Pool: 14/24 (Yin)
Refinement Speed: 0.1421
Refined Energy: 0.181 (29)

Problem with all these brightly lit areas: he was having trouble pulling in enough energy to get new points. The fifteen minutes he'd been seated, getting his breathing back under control and cooling down while cultivating, had only seen a single point being added to his energy pool.

Of course, he also had a much larger pool than he had started with, but it did mean that he'd need a break in between refilling. Hopefully, when the biome changed next, he'd find a place with a little more Yin energy—which would come with darker or more shaded terrain.

Discarding the thoughts for now and corking the half-empty water bottle, he struck out for the nearest hill. It was foolish to outline himself on the top, especially against intelligent enemies, but the higher vantage point would give him a chance to spot a water source.

Anyway, it was really unlikely he'd meet anything too intelligent. Not just yet at least.

It took him three hills and nearly an hour of walking before he spotted what he had expected. He was, at a rough guess, about another three hours away from the edge of the platform; an easy walk which would put him into early evening. A small concern, especially as he was tired already; but at least he could see in the dark, unlike the average Tower climber without Enhanced Eyesight.

In the meantime, the pool of water running to the east—assuming forward was north—was exactly what he needed. He probably wouldn't use the pool itself for his water bottle, but it had to have a source and that would work well enough.

It was when he had managed to make his way down into the bottom of the rolling gully when they attacked. Of course, the numerous holes throughout the ground was clue enough about the kind of monsters he could expect in these lower areas, and so when they came dashing out—all tiny fur bodies edged with metal—he was ready.

The clash of his spear head with metal fur sent a shock through Arthur's hands, his spear point skidding a good inch before it finally caught in a fold of skin and muscle. The blade slid within with ease after that, passing through gaps in the metallic fur, leaving the groundhog squealing and dying.

"Cute and evil." Arthur snorted and flicked the blade sideways to knock another creature off course as he hopped forward, careful of his footing to dodge a couple. He hated these swarm attackers, though at least after he dispatched another four with only minor lacerations on his leg—but much more damage to his trousers—the rest fled.

Recalling warnings from the past, Arthur made sure to grab the bodies and head up the hill, depositing them there first before he attempted to skin the creatures. The largest mistake newbies made was skinning near the holes, where the groundhogs would wait till the climber was distracted before launching their attacks again.

Not particularly nice, but effective.

Pocketing the stones, Arthur returned to making his way to the water, edging around the warrens when he could and dealing with the monsters when necessary. Dispatching the metal-furred groundhogs grew harder as his weapon was blunted with each clash.

"Going to have to sharpen this," he grunted, testing the edge with his thumb as he finished the ascent for the last hill before reaching the water source.

Of course, as any hunter could tell you, water sources are a great place for animals to gather. Both a boon and a problem, since predators have a tendency to hang out near such sources.

In this case, he didn't see any—unless they lurked in the water itself—but Arthur did spot another problem.

Chapter 100

"Remind me not to talk shit about herbivores," Arthur muttered, staring at the massive… moose? Was that the right term? He really was not up to date on such creatures, even if there were pictures included in the wikis. Holding a hand up to frame the creature and its antlers, he muttered to himself. "Scoop-a-doop, makes for a moose on the loose."

Yup. That was a moose. With antlers that looked like it could pick up and toss him aside if he got too near—plus flames flicking to life every couple of seconds—it was a rather intimidating sight. Also, the damn thing looked, even from this distance, the size of a Perodua subcompact. They always came out with one of the small car lines for the poor. Considering that it looked like a supermini car at a good couple hundred feet away, that thing was massive.

And hanging out at the pond, glaring at everything that looked askance at it.

"You know, those flaming antlers really aren't practical." At least not in the real world. After all, with the volume of forest fires that were happening these days, the existence of a creature—any creature—that set its surroundings on fire on the regular would be a natural Darwin Award.

Then again, he couldn't see a single spark actually falling to the ground. And the area around the moose, even as it dipped its head towards the bush, was unburnt. Even brushing against the branches didn't do much but sear the branches aside.

"Magic."

Good enough explanation. Content that the creature was just guarding the pond, Arthur searched for the water source. Ponds meant streams, right? Except, without rain, there was no new water entering the surroundings and no easy flow of liquid to spot or acquire from.

Which left him with the choice of either hopefully finding another water source—and he'd yet to see anything, and the edge of the platform wasn't that far—or, giving up on refilling his water bottles for now.

Decisions, decisions, decisions.

***

Arthur walked, carefully, towards the water source. He had skirted around a little on the plains and the hill before making his way towards the pond itself, such that he was two thirds of the way across the pond from the giant moose. He would have chosen to go directly opposite if he had thought it would help, but that would also put him even further out of his way. And if the creature was aggressive enough that over thirty-plus feet of distance was enough to anger it, he wasn't sure another ten or so feet would matter.

He walked with confidence but slowly, not varying his speed, not hesitant about his actions. He kept a close eye on the fire moose, though he made sure to watch for additional threats as he moved along. After all, Arthur knew well enough that there were usually ambush predators around.

When he got within about sixty feet, the fire moose that had been busy stripping the nearby tree of its branches had stopped, turning its head to focus on the human interloper. Arthur felt a slight hitch in his steps occur at that point, fear coursing through his body before he pushed it aside. He could not, would not, show the nervousness that thrummed through him.

After all, the mutated moose that had looked like the size of a small car at first was now looking more like the size of an SUV. Not the massive ones that still graced certain parts of America as status symbols, spurting out underburnt diesel fuel with dangling testicles on the back, as though the ability to pay $20 a liter was something to be proud of.

No, the moose was more the size of a working SUV, a truck used to take immigrant workers into plantations or to trawl their way through tough and underserved roads. Even with all the automation and push in technology, the cost of laying and keeping good roads along with significant environmental protections meant that there were many roadways still unpaved, untarred.

Weird thoughts, to consider the use of large motor vehicles when a monster with flaming red eyes stared at you, daring you to come closer. And Arthur, had to admit, he almost backed off.

But a parched throat, the sight of water, the knowledge of the monster core within and, frankly, a stubbornness and idiocy that had seen him taunt his attackers rose up. Even if the fight—if it came down to that—was tough, he was sure he would win. It was a single monster, and avoiding battles entirely was as detrimental to his progression as throwing himself into every battle there was.

More importantly, he had the Seven Cloud Stepping method. He could quickly flee into the water, and even if he did become wet, the fire-based creature was unlikely to follow him in. After all, wading into the middle of the water was foolish.

Comforting himself with that knowledge, Arthur took another step forward. He managed to make his way to the water, slowly detaching the first empty water bottle from his belt with one hand. Still with the spear held in the other and one eye on the moose that had not stopped looking at him, he bent down to put the bottle's head to the pond.

The moment the water bottle touched the water and liquid began to pour in, the moose charged.

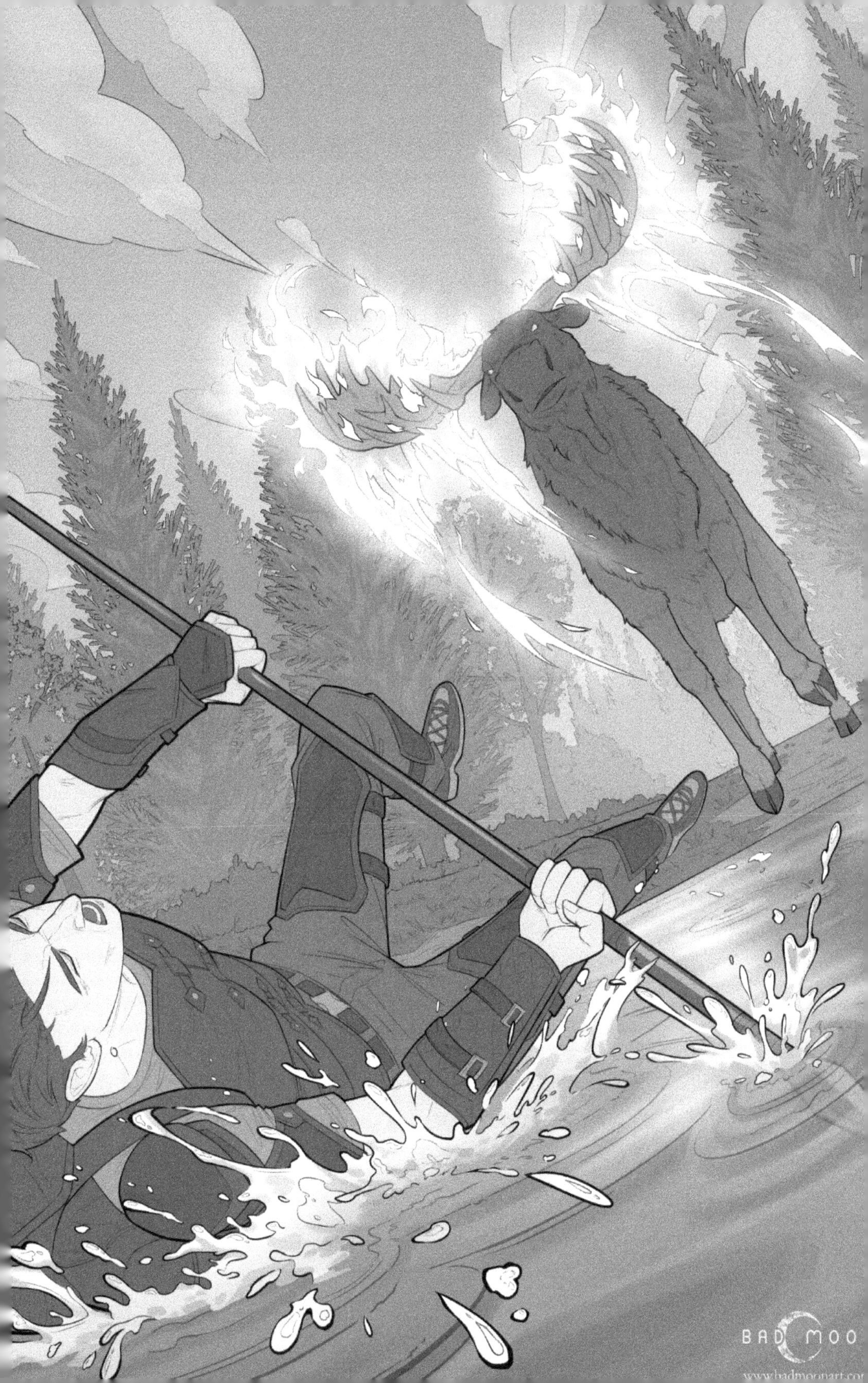

Chapter 101

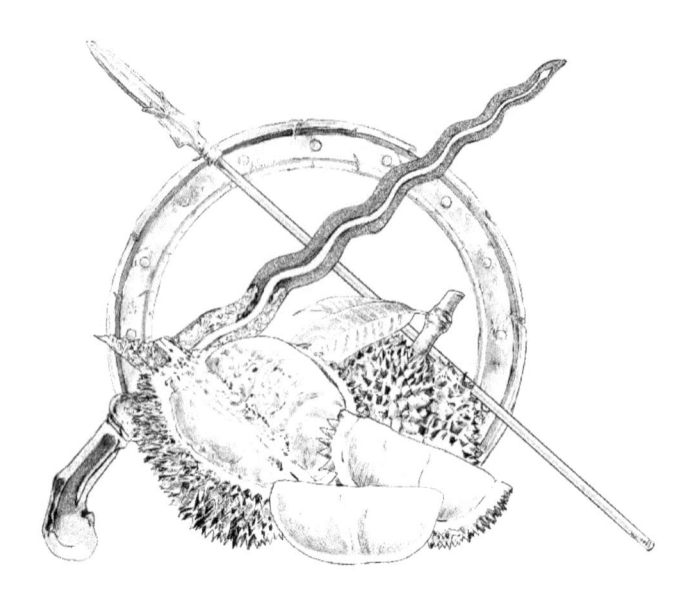

"Of course it's coming now," Arthur sighed, pushing the bottle in deeper before releasing it. Hopefully the bottle wouldn't float away, but he had a more immediate problem.

Options flickered through his mind. He mentally kicked himself for not prepping a Refined Energy Dart, or even pulling out his sling. Then again, he had only two hands. Holding the sling, the water bottle, and the spear would have been difficult. No, he was better off just trying to deal with the flame moose up close, now that he had lost the opportunity to kill it at range.

Not that a single Refined Energy Dart would have done that. He doubted the creature would let him one-shot it, not with a pitiful basic attack like his dart. Punch a hole and annoy it, sure, but kill it? He'd have to figure out a different spell technique. Maybe a refinement—hah!—on the Refined Exploding Energy Dart. Make it pierce and then explode.

Something to look at later.

Thoughts firing like a machine gun, Arthur moved slightly away from the muddy ground near the water. Once he was on rockier shore, Arthur considered his next steps. The problem with crouching low and "setting" the spear was the size of his opponent and his own spear. The six-foot spear was great for close fighting, but it lacked the proper length to ward off charging monsters like the fire moose, especially when the creature was longer and wider, and the distance from vital spot in the chest to the end of its antlers were a good three feet.

He could bend down, crouch low, and hope that he got the numbers right; but if he was wrong he'd be scooped up or impaled by the antlers before he sunk in his own attack. Also, to get the attack properly attached, it'd need a good foot at least to pierce within.

That meant no setting himself, butt of the spear against his backfoot. Which meant he was better off fighting mobile rather than just stopping.

He could try tossing his spear, but then he'd be fighting the damn thing with a kris if he missed. Or if the spear toss didn't kill it. And somehow, Arthur knew, the single toss would be vastly insufficient to end the moose.

By the time he had made up his mind, the creature was nearly on him. Barely ten feet away and Arthur crouched low, his mind doing the math of how far, how quickly the moose was arriving. He would have to time this perfectly, and with that thought he flooded his body with the Bark Skin technique. It would protect him, a little. At the same time, he had already been weaving Focused Strike into his spear, intending to use it to help punch through the creature's thick hide.

Straight charge, not much deception. One nice thing about dumb animals: they weren't particularly wily. Which was why all Arthur had to do was time it perfectly and leap aside. Pounding earth, the ground feeling like it was shaking a little from the size and weight of the creature before him.

Heat ratcheting up each second as the monster grew closer, the flames licking across those large antlers blazing through bright reds into deeper oranges and sometimes even blue. His breathing forced slow, brushing against his sweating lips, hands damp against the wood of the spear.

Three.

Two.

One.

Arthur did not jump, knowing better than to put himself in the air. You couldn't move in the air—at least, he couldn't, not without an active qinggong technique—and that just left you vulnerable. Instead, he lunged to the side, letting his front leg hit the ground and bend and bend and bend till he was parallel and at an angle, his body shifting so that he could thrust with his spear. He couldn't get the rest of his body into it, just arm and shoulders and hip, but it was enough even as he recovered his other leg back, knowing that leaving it behind would see it crushed.

The moose turned as he lunged forwards, shifting along the line of his movement. Body moving forward, the spear tip with focused chi bursting through it pushed aside hardened fur and thick muscle to punch through. Fur, skin, muscle. Then, bouncing off the side of a moving bone at the front of the leg, it pushed deeper and nicked another rib as it went in. Arthur could feel the minor jostles as the spear sunk in, pushed forward by his own strike and the creature's momentum, the pressure on his own grip nearly tearing the weapon out of his hand even with additional strength of a climber's body.

It sunk all the way in, the spear twisting and turning as the moose thundered past. But its head had kept turning, and those antlers, glowing and red, had their own surprise for Arthur. Energy exploded forth in a wave, catching him before he could recover, his own balance thrown off by holding onto his spear and attempting to extract it.

The best defense Arthur had, moments before the flame arrived, was to close his eyes and shove his head down, so that he caught it at an angle rather than directly in his face.

Breath held, even as flames washed over him and any open skin. His leather armour heated up immediately, the straps for his backpack burning, metal buckles warming. But it was his skin, his exposed hair, the flesh on his ears and body that caught the heat most of all. Flames washed over him, burning his body and causing him to flinch and release his weapon, to roll away.

Surprisingly, the heat was not painful, at first. His movements were the reactive flinch and fear of a mortal towards fire. It was only afterwards that the pain arrived, as flames licked at exposed skin and burnt away hair. Ears, nose, eyelids, thin flesh all along his upper body where the creature had targeted.

His bracers...

Choking back screams, Arthur rolled, twisting and turning. Bark Skin offered some protection, made the flames harder to burn, but it was not enough. Not enough at all.

He rolled and rolled, trying to get away from the fire that refused to die, hands gripping and tearing. So distracted was he that he never noticed when the damn moose arrived again. When it picked him up with a scoop of flaming antlers and tossed him, twisting through the air, third degree burns upon contact, seared flesh tearing free as he was tossed.

Luck was with him though, as he crashed into the water.

And enchanted flames or not, they were still fire.

Water beats fire.

Flames extinguished finally, Arthur spluttered to his feet. Thankfully the pond was not too deep. Throat and mouth and lungs hurt, for flames—or heat or smoke or something—having gotten in as he had tried to clear himself. Not only that, of course, but the water from the pond.

Worst, he was blind. The world was darkness, flashes of colour only. Atavistic fear brought hands scrambling for his eyes, searching for them. Pain coursed through his body, all the various burns lit on fire as water lapped at them and movement worsened the tug and tear of open wounds.

Fingers, scrabbling at eyes, found eyelids in one piece. Eyelids closed shut, sealed shut. Panic and knowledge that he needed to see forced him to tear them open, wounds weeping and eyes tearing up. Sight, though, was restored.

Splashing from behind had him turning sideways, feet shifting on muddy ground. To see a completely incongruous sight. The moose, spear dug deep into the side of its body, flames dancing across its antlers, red blood pouring down and foam flecking nostrils the size of a dinner plate... that fire moose was wading into the water.

Into the water.

It made little sense to Arthur, but that was the truth. And worse, he realised what the colours on its antlers meant. The red turned orange, turned blue. Arthur backed off further.

When the flames came the second time, he was ready.

Chapter 102

Down, under the water. Hands scrabbling against his belt, feeling reddened skin and even more injuries stinging as he searched for his kris. At the same time, Arthur dropped the Bark Skin technique, picking up the Seven Cloud Stepping technique in its place. The movement of his chi felt twisted, pained as he tried to drive energy through him. Pouring energy through his body, he pulled at a second technique, his Refined Exploding Energy Dart.

He should have done it the first time.

Kicking sideways, angling away from where the flame burnt, Arthur popped back up while his lungs were still burning. The flame attack by the fire moose was, at least, thankfully quite brief. That meant that when he did come up, there wasn't fire all around him, ready to set his hair and eyes and skin ablaze.

Instead, all he had to contend with was an angry, angry moose that stared at him and was ready to turn him into so much paste.

Instinct drove his block, kris angled so that he could catch the heavy clobbering motion of the antlers as they came sweeping through, an explosion of steam arriving first as the antlers dipped into the water and heated it all. Once again, skin burnt from steam and proximity to the damn antlers as they struck his weapon, pushing him off his feet and back-first into the pond.

He backpedalled and tried to get away, and surprisingly, managed to do so. Eyes wide with surprise, Arthur scrambled backwards, nearly losing his kris as he did so till he managed to make it to shallower water and pop back up.

Only to see the fire moose standing where it was, shaking its oblong head, the flames on its antlers dimmed. It tried to take a step as it caught sight of Arthur, but then shuddered and stopped. Something in its eyes had grown dim, the fiery anger and aggression faded. Now, instinct pulled it back. It retreated, moving towards the deeper end of the water, slowly, trailing blood behind from the open, torn wound that gushed with each beat of its massive heart.

Oh…

Arthur scanned the surroundings, unable to see his lost spear. Carefully, he backed away, releasing the weave for the Refined Energy Dart. Instead, he pulled that energy into him, across his body and all around as he triggered another full-body technique. All the while ready to flee using the Seven Cloud Stepping technique if he had to.

A small gibbering part of him noted that it was entirely insane for a creature to wander into the water. What kind of prey animal chose to go there, when crocodiles, alligators, giant catfish, and water snakes lurked? It wasn't just unsafe, it was actively courting new danger.

But as the moose waded into the center, taking station there, Arthur had to admit that was what he was seeing.

Content that the monster was not going to attack him right now, he stumbled back to where he had arrived, using the sight of spreading blood in the water to gauge where his spear would likely have fallen. He found it, of course, by kicking it by accident. The only good news was that he hadn't kicked the pointy end.

Bending low, Arthur scooped up the spear, struggling a little to lift it out of the water. He had to shift his grip a bit as he came out, resetting it, the flush of adrenaline pulling aside and the pain of his myriad injuries coming to life in full. He grimaced, staring at the creature before him, the one that just stared and stared and refused to die.

Just standing there, in the water.

"You know, you could have just gone in first time..." Arthur muttered in frustration. Or thought he muttered. It was hard to tell what he said, what with his mouth not wanting to open properly, the damage to his throat and lungs and general exhaustion.

No answer, of course.

Leaning against the grounded spear, the pair of them just stared at one another. At one point, Arthur was sure, he faded out. Not exactly unconscious, but his conscious mind checking out for some spicy *mi goreng* and sweet *cendol* to chase the salt down. The good kind of cendol, from Malacca, with proper *gula malacca* made from the sap of coconut palms.

By the time he came back, the fire moose was still staring at him. Just... blankly.

"You dead?"

Of course it didn't answer. Arthur considered shooting it, but decided against wasting his chi. He'd need it. Eventually, he bent low and scrabbled in the water till he found a rock. Tossing it overhand, he had to try twice before he managed to land a rock on the unmoving monster.

Even then, it didn't twitch. Not even a bit.

"I guess so..." Arthur said. "Now, we have to sew... a jerkin?"

Delirious, he couldn't figure out a rhyme or an ending that would work. Instead, realising he hadn't checked, Arthur looked for additional trouble. Finding none, he hurled his spear back onto shore and waded closer to the moose corpse.

Normally he'd use his rope or something to drag it over, but unusually, the antlers were glowing still and releasing heat. Nowhere near what it had been when it had caught him in his leg and hip—and he was not even going to look down there till his damn healing had taken care of it, because just from the radiating pain that made his steps hitch and the way the weaves of energy worked through him, he knew it was bad—but the antlers were still hot.

On the other hand, he'd never been burnt before. Never had to replace so much skin and flesh and muscle. A part of him, the part that had released the Seven Stepping Cloud technique, was cataloguing the way the technique was working. Learning from it. Split mind was damn efficient in that sense.

Mostly, though, he was focused on trying not to whimper and cry as he moved. Not that it stopped the snot or tears leaking from his eyes, but those were physiological reactions to outstanding pain and the post-adrenaline dump crash. Arthur could not help but recall the number of times his master had smacked around newcomers for trying to tease the women and the occasional man who had teared up or cried after a particularly intense training session.

The entire shaming of individuals, for things that their bodies could not help but do—at least till the body, conditioned after repeated trauma had normalised it all—was foolish. It was one of the reasons he'd liked his sifu. Well, that and he was cheap and willing to let Arthur stay with him.

Especially after his parents and...

Mind reared backwards as he touched on that topic. He pulled away, his soul reacting to those incidents like his hands did at the thought of touching those antlers again. No, and no, and never.

Someday, he'd have to deal with that, but that someday was not now and that was good enough for him.

At the body now, almost up to his chest, Arthur debated how to get the core out of it. He could gut the creature, pull out the entrails, but he wasn't entirely certain exactly how balanced it was, what with the damn thing's legs locked out. If he unbalanced it, and then had to scramble to gut and skin it in the middle of the water, it would be even worse.

Better to see what he could do about dragging it out of the water. Of course, carrying it might be a problem. It was easily a ton or two. Probably two. Maybe three. Really, how heavy was a ton? Did humans really know? It was not as though he had a weighing scale and the ability to play with a bunch of weights to figure out how strong he was.

But at Body 15, he was at least twice as strong as he had been. Not exactly five times, but somewhere in the range of three to four times if he had to guess. Body increases were not a direct linear increase in strength, what with him focusing on speed and reflexes. None of which would help him here.

"Where's Yao Jing when you need him?" Arthur muttered to himself, even as he got underneath.

No point in complaining.

Underneath, at the back rather than the front where those damn antlers were still radiating heat, he submerged himself till he was directly under the creature. Then, slipping one shoulder over and bracing himself, he tried to lift. Thankfully, between the water and his increased strength, it worked.

For about three dragging steps before the entire thing became a problem and he stumbled, the body crashing into the water, the antlers bubbling and hissing as steam ran around.

Grunting in pain, Arthur could not help but shift tactics. Feet digging into the ground, hands on the antlered hooves at the back, ignoring the shit and blood and other things coming out and the bubbling steam, he pulled. Dragging the submerged body along, stumbling and fighting his way back.

One way or the other, he intended to pull the body out of the water.

Chapter 103

The problem with chopping up and skinning a beast like a moose was that it was large. The process of butchering was never easy, and when you lacked the proper tools and had to make do with a kris and a gutting knife, it made things even worse. However, Arthur knew he had to work fast, and luckily, he wasn't exactly looking to get to the meat.

Oh, he chopped off one large leg, tearing through flesh and then carving in between bone to get to what he needed before tossing it away. Then, afterwards, he went for the monster core. That meant gutting the creature, pulling out the entrail sack and then yanking it all away before he moved on.

In through the stomach and guts, into the heart and lungs, searching around the chest till he finally found the beast stone. There, he had to cut entirely by feel till he pulled it free, slicing into his fingers a couple of times due to the angle and size of the creature. Then, tossing the stone aside with the hunk of leg he'd sliced apart, he began the next process.

Kris slicing, he began to tear into the creature's neck. He would have to do something about stripping the moose antlers from the head itself at some point, and if his guess was right, he might not even need to do that. But he would rather be safer than sorry, and that meant beheading the dead monster.

Of course, wiping away blood and skin as it kept flooding the water was not simple. The kris was not a butcher's cleaver, meant more for cutting in simple sweeps and slices rather than chopping up a body. In the end, he had to pull and cut with long sweeps of his blade, watching muscle part before he hit spine. Then, he had to wiggle the kris around to part the spine.

Head detached, Arthur booted the creature away and watched it roll along the ground till it began to smoke and smoulder against the grass where the antlers touched the ground. Frowning, Arthur hoped that it was not going to start a problem before he turned to the next step.

Skinning.

Grab flesh, pull against the fur and use skinning knife to slice upwards where the fat and flesh and fur joined together. He kept tearing and sweeping his blade against the parts that came out, slicing along the skin of the legs downwards and circling the hooves so that he could tear it outwards.

Arthur had some skill with this, but he'd never done such a large body. Still, without the danger of getting burnt by the moose antlers, the entire job was simpler. Falling into the routine of parting flesh and fur, Arthur ignored the pain from healing his burnt body, only stumbling to an end when he rolled the furless body once again.

Woozy and exhausted, Arthur stared at the fur partly soaked in the water and gave up. He knew he should pull it out, let it dry and... something. But exhausted, he just stumbled further up to the monster core and just crashed, staring up at the sky and relaxing.

When he next opened his eyes, he blinked blearily around him, taking a long moment to realise where he was and what he was doing. It took him a few minutes to realise that, and even more to locate his spear in the dark.

"Shit... that was a bad idea." Arthur gripped the spear tight to him, as though its presence could protect him against the danger of being burnt to death if grass had caught fire or a monster had found him while he was asleep. But, of course, it was not possible. He really had been worse off than he had realised, to have crashed that badly.

On the other hand, looking around, Arthur grinned.

His guess—educated, from the wiki in this case—had been right. The damn creature was unique. While the meat had not been left behind, the fur and the monster core were still there. As were the antlers, now lying quietly by themselves, glowing in the dark but no longer smoking and heating the earth.

Sneaking over carefully, Arthur reached out and touched the antlers, grinning as he confirmed they were hot but not scorching.

"Score crafting materials."

Now, he just needed to figure out how to carry them with him.

Dirty, disheveled, and smelly, just like a homeless beggar. "I'm looking like a damn *pengemis*," Arthur muttered to himself, resettling the rope around his shoulders. Thankfully, his guess had been right, and after rolling up the antlers in the fur, the massive thing longer than a human body, he was mostly ready to go. He'd strapped the entire thing to his backpack after spending some time sewing some basic patches and replacing the straps with rope, so that he could still carry the entire thing.

The ropes themselves were set up so that he could release the entire contraption with a single tug, because if he had to do anything like fight with it on, he was going to fall on his face. There was absolutely no way he was going to be at all effective or balanced with the fur-wrapped antlers hanging off him.

Arthur was also, quite firmly, not thinking about the various burns and injuries he'd found on himself after he had stripped down. Aloe vera had, at least, been part of his first aid bag along with rolls of bandages, all of which he'd utilised. Of course, he had not enough aloe vera to cover all the burns, so he'd focused mostly on the deeper burns before packing them with gauze and bandaging the entire thing and putting on a new pair of pants.

As for the previous pair, those were shorts and rags now.

Bag refilled with water at last and the antlers on his backpack and a snack consumed—if nothing more, for the restorative properties of tastiness—Arthur was ready to finish with this platform.

Turning over the antlers and the Tower information, he began the trek to the next level.

Fire Moose Antlers (Crafting Material)

Dropped from a fire moose fought on the fourth floor of the Malaysian Tower, this semi-boss creature has a powerful flame element imbued into the antlers. These antlers may be used to craft weapons and utility equipment by a climber or passed on to Tower administrators as the basis of an enchanted item.

Thankfully, outside of dealing with some large groundhogs, Arthur's trip to the edge of this platform was simple enough. And, amusingly, there was even a slope to ascend.

Which, of course, screamed of a trap to Arthur.

Chapter 104

Rather than jumping straight up, Arthur chose to split the difference. He moved halfway up the slope first, then jumped upwards to see what he could expect. Upon sighting the next area, he was suddenly incredibly grateful he hadn't chosen to just jump straight up.

"Seriously, who goes from desert to plains to lava fields?" Arthur said as he dropped to the ground.

Since he'd had an involuntary nap, he was not feeling particularly tired. Layering Bark Skin but not turning it on and then the Seven Cloud Stepping technique—which was ready to activate—Arthur made his way up the slope. It led onto rolling pools of lava and clear, open trails in between.

He could not help but shake his head.

"Shake-a-leg, start-a-break. We got lava on the left, and magma on the right," half-singing to himself, he carefully edged along.

Whoever the designers of this platform were, they had to be sadistic. There was no other reason to set a fire moose on him the level below, burn him to a nice crispy bit, and then put him in a lava field next. Especially when, the moment he had stepped in, the temperature had shot up.

The only good news was, as far as he could see, there were no monsters. Or perhaps that was bad news. Definitely bad news.

It was this paranoia and the ensuing constant scanning from side to side that allowed Arthur to catch the salamander rising out of the pool of lava, moments before it spat a glob of fire at him.

Jerking backwards, Arthur felt the heat of the ball of magma pass him by, inches away from impact. With the creature a good dozen feet away, it was too far to kill with a spear strike. And worse, even if he did kill it, the damn body was likely to fall inside the magma. Since there was no real gain to be had, Arthur made a decision.

"Time to run, for the sun!"

Starting out at a jog, Arthur hurried his way through, the spear held upwards and ready to deflect the globs of magma if necessary. Of course, breaking apart those fast-moving spheres were the very last thing he wanted to do, what with the likelihood of them just exploding on impact. Dodging and outrunning the salamanders—there were now more than one—seemed the best option, and it helped that they required a bit of time to refill their attacks.

Moving fast, head on the swivel and the Seven Cloud qinggong technique active; Arthur tore through the level. Sizzling globs of magma would fly through the air on occasion. Juking left, right, and sometimes even directly upward, Arthur dodged as best he could.

The first time one of the globs of fire impacted him, it was on his back. If not for the sudden shove and change of energy, he might not even have known it. And, of course, unable to check on the damage, he could only keep running and hope that it hadn't frayed the ropes holding his burden together. Or burnt away the rest of his clothes or opened a gap in his backpack to tumble out all his beast stones.

That thought almost had him run right into a ball of flame, an instinctive block and twist of his spear deflecting it just enough to have it skip over his shoulder rather than impact him. It still burst apart slightly, leaking magma onto his arm and shoulder and causing Arthur to hiss and his grip to spasm tight and almost drop his spear.

Rather than stop, though, he kept running. Nothing good would come of stopping.

Seeing a trio of salamanders get ready to fire on him as he neared a particularly narrow portion of the trail, a trail that Arthur could swear was set up to ensure someone would get burnt, he waited. Waited until he saw the first one spit and the second follow before he jumped to the right.

Right into the middle of the lava pit, forming a cloud beneath his feet.

What he had not expected was how hard it would be to do so. The cloud struggled and fought him as he attempted to pull moisture underneath his feet. He almost failed, and only a last-minute surge of energy managed to form the unstable footing. Even then, he felt the entire chi construction give way beneath his foot as he pushed off, landing back on the thin trail and nearly stumbling face-first onto the other side and the lava pool there.

Cursing, Arthur let himself fall and scrape the ground, ducking low to dodge another magma ball before he pushed himself upward and began running again. He was sweating, desperately, over the near-miss and cursing himself out for not realising how dangerous it was. Of course the Seven Cloud Stepping technique would struggle here. It needed moisture after all.

And the one thing lava fields lacked was moisture itself.

Yet, even as he cursed himself and dodged, Arthur could not help but turn over the thought. Sure, he could not use water, but the technique itself was based off Tower energy. It was pulling together insubstantial items together, binding them all so that he could step on them in ways that would be impossible otherwise.

So why did it have to be water?

There was, after all, a lot of smoke here.

Breathing harshly, his body working overtime to heal him as he drew in poison from the air, Arthur could not help but turn the idea over in his mind as he ran and dodged. A part of him realised, for the first time, why this floor in particular was put here. It was a way of pushing the climbers, to make them think about their techniques. To make them better, stronger.

And reward them, of course.

He grinned as he felt the fur on his back jostle, the pack pulling at him as he ran. A part of him wanted to lean into the test, to try utilising the smoke as a foothold. Another, more sensible portion noted that doing so could see him dead.

So he compromised.

Running, dodging, and wielding the technique while letting the Bark Skin method drop aside, Arthur focused on pulling at the smoke. Trying to build it around him, near his feet and where he would land as he ran. He focused on a spot a good distance away, so that when he stepped out—still on the trail, just a few inches higher—he should have been fine.

Failure.

Failure.

Magma ball.

Failure.

Missed dodge. Hissing smoke and another ruined shirt...

Failure.

Caught up in his tests, Arthur almost didn't realise he was near the end of the platform. Rather than a simple ascent, Arthur leapt, forming the smoky foothold. Kicking off the cloud of dust and soot to grab the edge of the cliff and haul himself upwards, so that he could see the next challenge in this hellhole of a level.

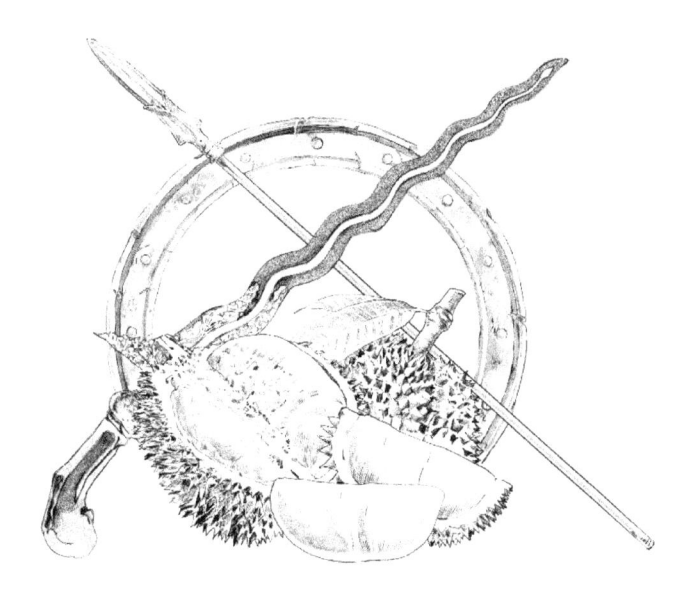

Chapter 105

Three more. Arthur only had to survive three more platforms if he pushed onwards now. Yet, staring at what awaited him on these platforms, he could find no energy to continue onwards.

"At least, this is safe. Ish," Arthur said. Then, compelled by his own idiocy, he added, "Don't you think, bish?"

Of course there was no answer. Never was. He struggled over to a corner, a nice little overhang and slipped the pack off. He took a moment to check over the bindings, winced as he realised one set of ropes had nearly burnt entirely through and fought against his fatigue to retie the moose hide and its antlers properly.

Funny, even though he'd collapsed barely a few hours ago, he was exhausted again. Perhaps, falling unconscious did not count as actual rest. The other reason might have to do with the poisons that his body was even now combating. Breathing in the stink of the lava fields had not been good for him. He remembered warnings of poison in those fields in a documentary he'd caught once, the TV blaring its dutiful noise while they drank and played Big Two on a card table.

Good times.

Arthur blinked, realising he'd curled up against his bag somewhere along the way. He tried to keep his eyes open, to set up some safeguards and traps, but he found himself unable to do so. Exhaustion pulled him down, the lack of danger washing away the desperate energy. His eyes drifted close and he slept.

Only to awaken with a gasp and jerk, leveling his spear at an unseen enemy.

Empty air.

He sucked in a breath, coughed a little, spat to the side at the taste in his mouth. Finding a water bottle and washing soot and other unnamable products out, Arthur checked around once more before relieving himself off the edge of the platform. Far below, his gift sprinkled across multiple platforms and a little mischievous smile had him attempting to hit the X below.

Then, tucking away his package, Arthur drank again and scrubbed at his face, cleaning it off with water and letting the rest air-dry. He grimaced at the dark rivulets that ran from his face and hands as he did so, wiping them clear a few times before slumping beside his pack. One last scan for trouble before he called forth the rather insistent notice from the Tower.

Toxin Cleansed!

Toxin Resistance in Accelerated Healing - Refined Energy (Grade III) increased due to repeated exposure.

"That bad, ah?" Arthur muttered to himself. He wondered how your average ascender would have dealt with that. Or if they would have. After further consideration, he figured if they weren't too damaged, they'd probably do the same as him and collapse and let the Tower's passive healing fix it. Also, they would likely have been out for much longer and be even more susceptible to the poison. "At least, I got something from that place..."

He wondered if this upgrade translated for the rest of his people. He hoped so. He couldn't see that particular platform working well for others otherwise. These platforms were what he would consider lethal, the kind of place that most Tower climbers would die if they faced it.

It was possible some might even have backed off and waited, tried to jump to another series of platforms.

Either way, he was through. Which meant it was time to deal with the next level.

"I really am not Tarzan," Arthur said. The lonely lost white boy with gorilla friends came to mind due to the hanging vines that seemed to appear from nowhere and were the only way to go from one platform to the next. Of course, none of them were close enough for him to reach out and grab, so he'd have to take a running leap, jump and swing over to the next platform.

And repeat the process.

"What do I do about my spear?" Arthur muttered to himself. He could strap it to his backpack horizontally, but it might smack into a branch and throw his balance off. Angling it might work, but he'd used a lot of the rope up already and the antlers were bulky. Still, it seemed his best option unless he wanted to leave it behind.

That wasn't happening.

Which meant repacking his backpack and the rest of his gear. While he did, he could also keep an eye out for potential trouble. He really doubted he'd be so lucky not to have anything bothering him, but thus far, he'd not spotted anything flying or swinging through the area.

Maybe on the next biome after this jungle one? That would be fairer, and simpler. He even hoped that was the case because, if so, he could deal with them without having to worry about how he was going to fight monsters while gripping the vines. He definitely was not like Lord Greystoke with buns of steel.

Nope, nope, nope.

Pack re-strapped and unable to think of any other options, Arthur made sure to loop his pack over tighter, made sure his kris was strapped in and the safety clip flipped over. Then, taking a breath and activating the Seven Stepping Cloud movement technique and the Refined Energy Dart, he ran for it.

The first grab and swing was easy. Only a single swing, no harder than playing at monkey bars. There was even a space for his legs to land on, though he barely needed it before he released and dropped onto the platform. The platform gave way a little, compressing a touch when he landed, which surprised him.

What surprised him more was that it kept sinking.

"Oh shit." Arthur's eyes widened when he realised what kind of test this was. No monsters on this one. They didn't need monsters to kill him. This was a timed test. Every moment he lingered, the platform would keep sinking. Eventually, at some unknown distance below, it would just... fall. Taking him with it. Well, before that though, the next set of vines would be out of reach quickly.

Climbing the Ranks 2

Even as he was taking in all this information, he was running. Eyes flicked forward, taking in the platforms and the vines before him. There were two platforms, one closer than the other. But the closer one was a trap, because it had fewer vines, longer jumps between and a double swing. So he went for the longer jump and swing, using all the contained power of his Tower-ascended body to push him forward.

He grunted, smacking into the next vine with his face, sliding down it a little before he grabbed it securely. Momentum and timing lost, but he managed to land on the other side, nearly tipping over as the next level sank down. A kick backwards to form a cloud behind him gave him balance and allowed him to push off, to run faster.

Eyes were fixed ahead as he ran, taking in the platforms, plotting his course. He saw the dangers, the little tricks. Empty platforms with no ivy, or ivy that was a little slicker. No more footholds halfway through, so you'd have to grip with all your strength and hope you didn't slide off into the abyss.

Arthur suddenly wished he had gloves, cursed at not carrying any. Ignored the fact that if he did, they'd probably have been too hot, or been burnt off or destroyed in the preceding levels. The Tower was many things but kind to clothing was not one of them.

He ran and jumped, bouncing between platform to platform. And if he laughed a little as he did so, who could blame him. After all, this biome might have been dangerous for anyone else. But he had a safety net in the Seven Cloud Stepping technique, his ability to split his attention and focus with Multi-Tasking and Quick Learner, and the ability to spot trouble with Enhanced Eyesight long before it became a problem.

This level might as well have been called easy mode as far as he was concerned.

Chapter 106

Swinging vines and dropping platforms were one thing, but whoever decided floating platforms that shifted silently in different patterns was the way to go was just sadistic. Furthermore, the platforms varied in biome. The issue was figuring out how they moved, if it was indeed not random.

The open plains or carved stone squares were about twenty feet across. Those generally contained a couple of monsters, none of them too difficult to defeat. Annoying, though, since some were bouncing slimes or earth elementals that required you to pound or pierce them just right. Even so, those were the nicest ones to be on.

However, that was not the only variety that Arthur faced. There were the magma, the lava-filled walkways that would choke and kill those who clambered within, spitting salamanders always waiting. The sand-laden rolling hills of a desert where scorpions and beetles lay in wait were just as bad, especially since they occasionally swapped those creatures out for even more dangerous snakes.

He'd already been bitten once, and Arthur's head was woozy from the poison pumping through his body, each thud harder than the next and bringing a roaring to his ears.

It was why he was seated here, on one of those rolling hills, watching the world go by as he struggled to get his body under control; actively utilising the Accelerated Healing technique and borrowing some of the precious energy in his core. He couldn't refine any of the monster cores he was acquiring right now, but there was another thing his mind was doing anyway, beyond watching for more trouble.

He was trying to piece together the puzzle that was the sliding platforms. They came together and parted in a pattern that tickled the back of his brain, taunting him that there was a way that it all came together such that you could cross them to the final, unmoving finish line.

However, he hadn't explored it all yet, and after reaching two dead-ends, characterised by platforms that just refused to connect further and forcing him to backtrack till he grabbed another one that would move him ahead, Arthur was intent on figuring this out. His initial attempts at just winging it weren't succeeding, only adding to his injuries—but also to his pile of monster cores—as he traversed the land.

Five different platform types were here: desert, plains, lava, night, and forest. Two maps he'd found so far showed a third of the pattern of movement for one kind of biome. In this case, the lava and the plains movement. It would have been simple if everything moved in a single horizontal pattern. After all, just like those children's games where you slid tiles around, there was an eventual solution if you just kept moving.

Unfortunately, these platforms added vertical movement too. Going up or down at set intervals. With three different layers, there were dozens of platforms in play at any one time. Trying to actually understand where each platform linked up and moved ahead seemed to be a matter of luck rather than strategy.

Unless you had some insanely mathematical mind. Or grabbed enough clues. And the slight yellow glow on a half-dozen tiles or more showed where such clues might be found. All he had to do was make his way to one glowing tile, beat the monster that guarded it, and take the clue from the pedestal.

Once joined with the map he had stuffed into his pocket, the clues blended and added to the map.

Easy. If he wasn't already poisoned, tired, and rather grumpy.

"Why isn't this easier?" Arthur growled, forcing himself to his feet. Two options from here, both with a potential for a clue coming up. He just needed to decide if he went forward or back. The one ahead might mean a single platform traversal, the one behind two. That assumed they didn't rise or drop. Or that he didn't.

He figured he needed to move soon though, or else his current platform was going to move on him. Cursing under his breath, he moved forward. Always forward, because you never knew what might be behind.

With a grind and thump, the two platforms glided across one another. He snorted a little at the sight and stepped across, dropping to a knee immediately even as his Enhanced Eyesight struggled to deal with the sudden danger the loss of light resulted in. Going from bright daylight to pitch-black night had a tendency to do that.

It wasn't, of course, actually pitch-black. It just felt like it, what with his eyes taking a bit of time to adapt. In the meantime, he listened. Good thing too, as the ribbit that preceded the creature's jump was signal enough for Arthur to lash out. He missed the silhouette that threw itself at him for the most part, clipping only the creature's leg as it tried to land on him. Good enough that it dropped to the earth not far away, at which point he slammed the haft of the spear down on its body a few more times till it stopped moving.

Peeling the body apart and wishing he had gloves as the poisoned skin took effect on him, Arthur was nearly able to see by the time he was done. Nearly.

Night-time swamp area. All kinds of joy. At least, the ground here was marshy and swampy, but it didn't require him to wade through the water. A good thing too, though staying on the path meant he was easier to attack. Keeping his spear moving and clipping off overhanging branches and the occasional spiderweb—and dealing with said web owners—kept Arthur busy, long enough to make his way to the center of the platform.

To spot the giant frog that guarded it. Half the size of a human, it opened its mouth to release its sticky, nasty tongue which Arthur dodged by stepping behind a tree. He released a Refined Exploding Energy Dart, and the timing was perfect, leading to the muffled thump as mouth closed in on the attack and the resulting explosion stayed concentrated within the creature.

The only negative was the cumulative effect of wading through and touching even more poisoned skin, this one blistering his hands and fingers even as he used strips of cloth to provide some protection. It wasn't great, but at least the beast stone was of a decent size and quality and the next clue filled in more of his map.

Just a half-dozen more platforms like this and he would be able to saunter across them to the end.

Right?

If you believed that, Arthur had a great piece of plantation land, filled with ripe durian and mango trees he wanted to sell you. Land that the government really, really, wasn't going to take back. Pinky promise.

Chapter 107

One last monster, standing before him and the exit of this biome. It had taken him nearly three hours and forty seven minutes to get this far and he was tired, injured, very, very grumpy and not at all in the mood to deal with the latest problem. On the other hand, he could not help but shake his head a little at what he saw.

"What exactly am I supposed to do about those?" Arthur growled, eyeing the boss—or the bosses—as they came apart and then joined together. He wasn't sure if that was good or bad, that these glowing stone creatures were the equivalent of Transformers, or was that Voltron or... his retro cartoon knowledge was, he had to admit, rather a touch out of date.

"Kill them individually or...?" Arthur considered out loud even as he pulled energy, feeling it sizzle along the meridians of his hand, collecting it like he was holding lightning.

Power.

On the other hand, he wasn't the only one who was pulling power. That rock creature with flames or lightning dancing across it had power pulling into the center of its body. He could see that amassed energy growing stronger and stronger with each second.

Nope. He was not going to stand around for that. Hands raised, he released the Energy Dart, watching it wing its way towards the creature's head. At the same time, he crouched low, tracking the build-up in energy, tracking the way it would shift.

Funny thing about energy, about light. It moves faster than you can. Much, much faster. Same reason you can't dodge a bullet once it leaves the barrel of a gun—well, not unless you were one very powerful climber—so there was no way to dodge the flare of energy that struck him.

Arthur found himself burnt directly. He had bent his head low and squeezed his eyes shut so that he wouldn't be blinded entirely. Lightning dancing down his body, locking up his muscles and causing Arthur to fall over. He twitched and whimpered, tears springing from his eyes. Not enough to hide the fact that the Refined Exploding Energy Dart slammed into the top of the monster's neck and exploded across the body, tearing the head off and breaking it apart into multiple rock creatures.

By the time Arthur managed to get his feet under him, the four were nearly on him. Spear thrust forward caught the monster on the right, causing it to jump back with nary but a nick. Then, a spin across the top of his hand to strike with the shaft and he hit the one on the left that was jumping high, intent on tearing his throat out.

He went low, struck to the right on the rebound. Got his feet under him and backed off, retreating a little but remembering that there was not much space at all, not with the platform behind having moved away. Kept the spear spinning and attacking, never ending as he then pushed forward as managed to smack one hard enough across the head to give the earth elemental equivalent of a concussion.

Kept pushing, kept pushing till he had them all down, shattered across the platform. Never mind the lightning that danced across skin and caused muscles to seize, that caused jaw to clench and teeth to grind. He fought on, till he managed to stab the last one across the body, pinning it to the earth and slumping beside it.

Having forgotten to drop his damn backpack and giant pack of moose antlers behind him.

"I need a better defense," Arthur groaned. "One that deals with poison and lightning and things burning me. Can't be all offense."

Then, he pushed himself up and began to collect the monster stones left behind.

Limped over to the end, stared at the next level. No climbing this time; it was just a straight walk to the next biome. Easy peasy. One more of these idiotic game-like platform levels and he was done. Even if it was harder than he had expected, he could do it.

A moment, to breathe and then check his stats.

Cultivation Speed: 2.474 Yin
Energy Pool: 3/24 (Yin)
Refinement Speed: 0.1421
Refined Energy: 0.03 (29)

Another breath, another look at the numbers. He shook his head, reached for the rope that served as his straps and dropped them aside. Fingers scrambled in his pouch, found the stones that he needed and collapsed with his legs crossed on the ground. He drew a deep breath, forced his exhaustion aside, and began the long, long process of pulling energy to him, into his meridians and finally into his dantian.

He would need to process a half-dozen stones to refill his core. Then even more Tower energy so that he wasn't entirely out of power. Running on the dregs of energy was not a good idea, and this platform at least seemed safe enough.

Hours passed, energy drawn through him, stones he had picked up and used crumbling in his hands as he poured power through him. He kept going till he had refilled a large portion of the energy he needed. And then, finally, he was ready. To finish this damn level. How bad could it be, this last stage?

It was just another Tower platform after all.

"Oh, that's why it was level," Arthur said, stepping forward to look upwards and upwards and upwards. It made sense, of course. Moving platforms, disappearing platforms, and now, vertical platforms that he had to deal with by jumping up and up.

He eyed the heights, unable to spot the ending due to the various shifting platforms in the way. It reminded him, from this vantage point, of a series of very narrow walkways—without the necessary safety railings—in an abandoned factory. Abandoned, mostly, because so few of the current factories had such walkways. Much easier to send robots and drone cranes to extract portions and enact repairs than worry about humans and their clumsy movements. Worst case scenario, there were drones and 3D movement packs that aided repair workers to get to such places, though the increase in danger was significant.

Not that anyone cared anymore, not when the chances of finding a job kept dropping every day and the basic income provided was insufficient.

More importantly, staring at the platforms, noting how certain portions dropped low or rose up later, Arthur understood that he would have to do his best to climb towards the next level. Shimmering vines that occasionally disappeared, falling platforms and, of course, monsters to complicate things.

Of course, why the monsters were a mixture of rolling ball-like feathered creatures, hopping mushroom-like attackers, and the occasional goblin with a throwing spear, Arthur had no idea. Especially that last one.

"Guess I'll have another monster to add to the wiki," Arthur said, watching as the goblin hauled and tossed its spear at him. He didn't even flinch, watching it arc through the air before getting knocked off course by the moving platforms that made up the distance between them. Not dangerous, at least in the short-term.

Once he got closer though... "And I'll name the goblin spear chucker... Dicky!"

Yeah, it was a stretch. But better get it out before he felt the need to come up with a rhyme while clambering upwards.

"Time to go, put on a show. "

One last tug on his straps to ensure everything was secure, then Arthur leapt to the right. Right where the thrown spear had fallen.

Waste not, want not.

Chapter 108

Snatching up the spear, he eyed the make and feel of it. Rough build, stone spearhead. Probably quite blunt too, though he neither had the hands free nor the inclination to test it out with his fingers. Keeping the Seven Cloud Stepping technique running beneath his skin but not active, Arthur took another jump, angling sideways to land on the next walkway. Seven feet, straight up and at an angle, was a little on the harder side for most people. Before the Tower, he would have struggled to do that, even when they had trained for plyometrics.

Now, it was an easy hop. Sometimes, he wondered what was the point of all that training, all that time pushing himself outside the Tower. All the blood and sweat and tears, the torn muscles and the hobbling around when after a few days in the Tower and some cultivation and you could just increase your base stats.

Then, of course, he kicked himself. Arthur knew the truth. The base of an individual, that they started from was important. Just as important, surviving the first few levels to increase their base stats. It was hard enough surviving the start of the Tower if you weren't trained or fit, and unless you were some preening crony's son, you'd be dead.

Or stuck. Which was just a slow death in the Tower. Without modern conveniences like indoor plumbing.

Thinking idle thoughts helped keep his mind active as he ran up the minor slope of a walkway, eyes flicking sideways as he searched for more trouble. He timed it, waiting for that rolling ball of fluff on the higher walkway on his right to bounce down and across before he leapt, crossing the distance before the mushroom monster landed on the walkway he just left.

He could fight them, but the longer he was stuck in battle, the more likely he'd get hit by a random spear chucked from above. Stripping monsters of their stones while potentially getting stabbed from above was not his idea of fun. Nor, for that matter, was he particularly in need of monster stones, what with the numbers he had accumulated.

Just as bad, the fact that some of these platforms had a tendency to shift meant that he might find himself moving backwards or rolling down, rather than progressing upwards. Better to keep moving, dodging and stabbing when necessary but only when necessary.

Two more platforms, including one rotating sideways as it rose, had him stepping across to an unmoving one that shuddered and nearly threw him off as it came into contact with his previous ride. Arthur grunted, realising that one of the feather-balls was coming at him, having dropped from above.

He bent low, fitting his new goblin spear to the ground and propping it up while keeping his black spear slightly angled and away. No need to mess up both his spears. Braced for the impact, what Arthur was not expecting was the explosion as the spear pierced the bouncing, feather-filled monster.

No fire or shrapnel, thankfully. It was more of forced air and explosive decompression which threw him off balance enough to knock him off the platform, what with the impact and weight forcing itself on him at the same time. Arthur flailed, dropping the new spear shaft as he fell, twisting around and trying to get his bearings.

Too slow. Too close. The platform that he struck, turning as it was beside him, caught him hard across one arm. Another bounce, another spin through the air. But this time around, he poured energy through the Seven Cloud Stepping technique to offer him purchase moments before slamming into the next platform. He pushed up and sideways, hopping a little to land against another platform that was swinging upwards.

Slamming his spear into the ground, Arthur fought for balance, inner ear still thrown off by the explosion and spinning through the air. He struggled to focus, the scream coming from the creature that just leapt over snapping attention to the forefront. He spun his spear to focus on the hopping mushroom, thrusting forward only to feel an impact on his backpack that forced him to his knees and miss the hopping mushroom.

Another impact, a spear falling off-course and hitting his leg. Blood welled up, the attack coming in sideways and not lodging within but leaving him disoriented further as his face filled with frills and scrabbling, clawed hands and bouncy feet that tried to pound him into the ground. Behind, on his backpack, his balance constantly thrown off.

Panic welled up. Arthur drew on the Heavenly Sage's Mischief, pouring energy into his body to give him strength, stability, speed.

Explosive movement, one hand grabbing the monster in front of him, hauling it away. Body turning sideways, as a glimpse of something falling caught his attention. Another falling feather-ball, coming for him. The monster jumping in the air fell, its perch knocked away even as Arthur hauled and threw off the mushroom-hopper.

Explosion of air. Blood and musk and anise filled his nostrils.

A foot, booting away the damn hopping mushroom, and he skipped back, moments before a spear embedded itself in the ground. Energy poured through him as Arthur scanned the surroundings, realising the quiet, routine movement of the monsters had sped up. They were all aiming for him now.

Mind spinning through options, Arthur took off. His eyes flicked across the platforms, assessing dangers, movement options. He jumped onto the next platform, wobbled for a moment as it swept sideways, nearly knocking him off as he failed to account for momentum. Forced himself to keep moving.

Ran sideways, nearer to the center where the spin was less pronounced. Wait...

Jumped to a falling platform as it rotated down, running straight up. He blocked a spear with his own, smacking it aside. Saw the feather-ball come ricocheting down the steadily rising platform, picking up speed and bouncing. He ducked low, dodging the monster before it hit him, using the creature's momentum to let it bounce away.

Watched as a mushroom-hopper landed on the platform and then fell, unable to keep its balance. He was finding it hard to do so himself, the damn platform nearly at a seventy-degree angle and still rising.

No platforms on hand to jump to, not easily. Not in a single bound.

He steadied himself then leapt, conjuring a cloud to land upon. Step and push, going higher. Landed next to a goblin readying another spear, surprising it. He grabbed the spear just behind the head, hauling the monster close as he stabbed upward. Caught it in the heart, yanking up with his spear to gut the monster before he turned and flipped the body off the platform. A quick flip of the other spear got him into throwing position and he hauled off, tossing it at a feather-ball further upwards.

Explosion, one that he followed, jumping upwards to reach the platform. The decompression knocked off the feather-ball, setting off another explosion further below. Ears ringing, the tube-like structure he moved within amplifying the noise, mixing with the shriek of goblins, the squishy sound of falling mushroom-hoppers and the squealing grinds of the platforms moving.

"Going to get ear damage, from all this slammage," Arthur ranted, even as he took off running. Surprisingly, there was a ladder to the next level, which was good because he needed a moment and the unmoving platform underneath the ladder and above it worked for him. He dodged another mushroom-hopper as it tried to get to him, outpaced it and skidded to a stop, squinting upwards.

Jerked his head back, seconds before a spear pierced the air, tearing skin and fraying one of his ropes for his backpack. Arthur snarled, jumped up and headbutted the goblin that was grabbing for another spear. A hand on the edge of the ladder was all that stopped Arthur from falling back.

Blood dripping down his forehead, head ringing and filled with the roar of pain, Arthur stabbed at the flickering movement. Once, and again and then once more just to be sure. As his vision cleared up, the goblin wasn't moving anymore, and Arthur scrambled the rest of the way up the platform. Moments later, a mushroom-hopper jumped up, only to get speared.

Breathing heavy, Arthur spotted the monster core in the goblin's chest, torn open in his frenzy. He grabbed it, slipped it into a pocket, and then looked up.

A third of the way there, and the monsters were not stopping.

Getting up was going to be a pain.

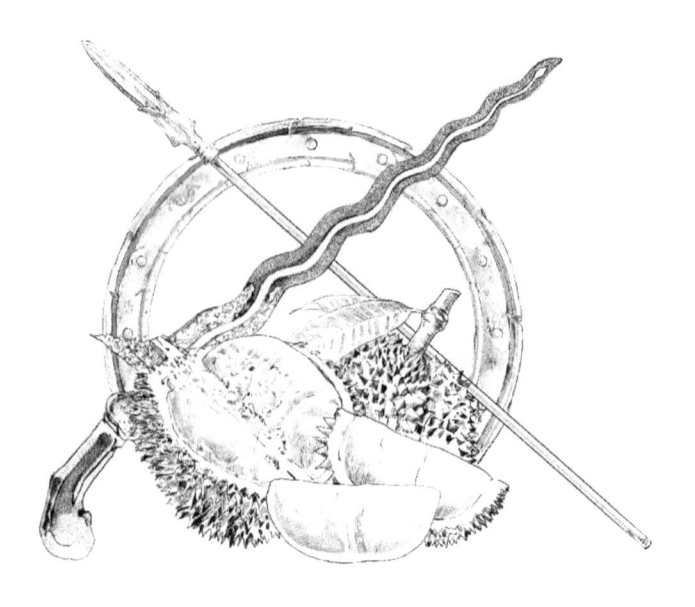

Chapter 109

Energy Pool: 4/24

Arthur dismissed the notification with a flick of his mind, pushing it away. He could feel the lack of energy, the dire dregs of how little he had left. Getting up, fast, had required liberal use of the Seven Cloud Stepping method. Going slow might have been fine, if the damn Tower wasn't literally spawning new goblins and mushroom-hoppers and feather-balls in the middle of the fight.

Damn cheaters.

So he'd gone fast, as fast as he could. That meant taking wounds and running himself ragged, bouncing across open air and trusting in his technique to give him footholds where there were none. Not the end of the world if he had to stop and kill his way upwards a few times when the route before him now was just giant pathways and ladders and monsters in the way.

Then, he'd had to use his Refined Exploding Energy Darts just to clear the walkways of the feather-balls. That had worked well for him, since their presence actually caused as much trouble for the other enemies as him. At least, so long as he had them on the backfoot and they didn't get near him.

Once they did, then it was all just havoc and explosions and concussions and ear damage.

But now, he was here. Last platform, just a straight shot to the glowing portal at the end which he knew marked the end of this particular level and entry to the fifth floor.

All he had to do was kill the Goblin King standing right in front of him. Well, Goblin King and two bodyguards.

Unlike your usual green-skinned, scrawny goblins that made up the lower levels, the Goblin King was almost as large as a human but on the shorter end; to compensate for height, it was bulky. And instead of utilising a spear, it held a sword and shield and wore actual armour. It was also, unlike its compatriots, silent as it waited for Arthur to cross over.

Not that he was intending to get started with that right away. Among other things, he needed to catch his breath. With a force of will, Arthur pushed aside the Seven Cloud Stepping method, replacing it with Bark Skin. He considered trying to blast the damn Goblin King from range with his Energy Dart and would have if it was a spear user. That shield, though... he figured that creature knew how to use it.

He had his slings, of course, but the goblins were pretty fast, and the bodyguards looked to be bigger and stronger than the common ones below. And they weren't dumb monsters either, which meant that if he tried pulling out his sling, they'd likely charge him. Maybe he'd get one or two swings in, but then he'd be scrambling to get his spear in hand.

Not impossible, but it wasn't exactly perfect. This wasn't a game where he could just click over and be ready immediately, and if he fumbled the switch at any time, he would be down a weapon.

So...

Breathing slowing a little, Arthur shrugged off his backpack. He didn't need that. Bark Skin ready to be utilised, he moved forward smoothly as he poured energy into an Exploding Energy Dart. He wished he had learnt how to make more of them at once, but utilising this as a secondary, surprise attack was his best option.

Other than Focused Strike. But he didn't have enough energy to use both Focused Strike and Bark Skin.

Closing in on the pair, moving slowly with a relaxed gait. That was the thing most newbies missed, those who hadn't actually ever fought before. Or those who had but hadn't received the training, the wisdom to help them survive better. There was no point in being tense, in being "hard" for no reason. A relaxed body used less energy, required less oxygen. Relaxed muscles reacted faster; relaxed eyes that weren't focused on a specific spot saw things easier.

Calm, collected, easy. You went into a fight that way, because tension was a killer. Made you miss things.

Like the way the goblin bodyguard on the right was angling outwards faster than the one on the left. Hoping to stay on the outside of his spear. If he stepped towards the left, where he had more flexibility, he would open himself to attacks from behind and from the monster on the right.

If he turned with the monster on the right, he'd pull his gaze off the other two, especially as it kept trying to edge to the side. Giving him worse options each moment.

Rather than wait, Arthur charged, intent on covering the distance between him and the smarter bodyguard on the right. They used clubs instead of spears, weirdly enough. Not what Arthur would have chosen, what with their lack of lethality. But no one was asking him, and if the Tower creators actually did ask, he'd probably not have made a good suggestion anyway.

Two steps closer, he thrust at full extension. He let the spearhead dip at the last second, knowing his opponent was going to bat it away and hoping to slip under. Damn goblin was good enough to wait till he was almost fully committed and had started the dip so that it could block properly, leaving his own strike knocked off course.

Not an issue.

Arthur spun the spearhead around, using the momentum of the attack to come back up in a semi-circle. The attack went high, forcing the goblin to duck low, the spear tip tearing a line across its scalp as it moved too slow. He let the momentum carry over, pulling it down even as he swung his back leg behind him, spinning his body and spear along to threaten the other goblin bodyguard and the king as they neared.

Kept it spinning, raising the whole thing above his head so that he could continue with the built-up momentum. He took a step forward then, swinging it low and around to threaten feet that jumped or hopped back, before he brought the weapon in close for a lunge. A short lunge, using body rather than arm and spear.

The attack came up short, the left bodyguard raising its weapon to block an attack that never made its way there. Then, a moment later, Arthur thrust forward with the full strength of his arms, shoving the spear point into the monster's chest. He could have targeted the head or neck, go for a guaranteed kill; but the way the goblin twitched its body, attempting to dodge was reason enough not to. Too easy to miss such attacks.

Whereas the unguarded chest, with only soft leather armour over its heart, was easy enough to pierce. He shoved, pushing through ribs and skin and flesh, twisted and yanked back even as the Goblin King rushed him. He took his left hand off the spear shaft, turned his head to the side and released the Refined Exploding Energy Dart at the smarter bodyguard, moments before it arrived to swing its club.

A little too late, the creature having moved faster than he had expected. It caught him with the edge of the club, jagged edges tearing and ripping across his shoulder pauldrons and skipping off. His own attack caused more damage, the explosion too close and hurting his ears, punching him across his body with the softball impact of released energy and expanding air.

Arthur recovered, only to find another weapon coming at him. He caught the attack with his spear, but with only one hand on the shaft, it did little other than divert an attack meant to chop his head open into merely glancing off and slamming into his chest. Arthur retreated, grabbing at his spear with his other hand, swinging it low and trying to dodge the return backhand swing, taking it across the elbow guards and feeling his fingers go numb.

Then, he had hold of his spear and a threat to the feet forced the Goblin King to stop its forward momentum. It hunkered down, protecting its legs with the shield and allowed Arthur to reset.

Unfortunately, so too did the other two bodyguards. Both grievously injured, one with its face half-torn off, eye blinded and ear missing. The other clutching a seeping chest wound. They flanked their king now, letting it take the threat and forcing Arthur back. He tried to circle sideways and attack the bodyguards, but each time, the other two rushed him.

"Shit. I hate smart enemies," Arthur muttered.

A few more steps, and he realised they were herding him. Back, to the start, off the platform. Every time he tried to circle, they pushed him back. He began forming another Energy Dart but knew it was not going to be enough. They knew that trick now. Still...

He passed his backpack far to the right, and then he knew what to do. Arthur thrust hard, let the bodyguard on the left beat his spear down. Took his hand off the spear, releasing the Energy Dart at the monster on the right. The Goblin King was waiting, darting forward to catch the Energy Dart on its shield, ready for the explosion.

It never came, the attack drilling into the shield but not exploding.

In the meantime, Arthur jumped forward, spear left behind as he scrambled for the kris. He let the monster hit his upraised arm, Bark Skin activated to help diminish the club's crushing impact as he absorbed the hit. Kris came up, sweeping across the neck and cutting deep. He spun the bodyguard by the club arm, bent low and flipped it over him to where the others were coming.

Came around, hand seeking the spear. He grabbed it close to the tip, pulled it close and grinned.

One down. Two to go.

And now he knew. He was smarter than them.

Chapter 110

Smarter did not mean better.

Slammed backwards by a shield bash, Arthur found himself in a flip, barely able to complete the simple procedure before he landed on his feet woozily. He managed to keep hold of his spear the entire time, bringing his weapon back in line with his opponent, forcing the Goblin King to bat the weapon tip aside before it could close on him.

Arthur stumbled back a few more steps, resetting himself fully while spinning his weapon, intent on keeping his opponent away from him. That was the point, after all, of having a spear. Longer reach, more flexibility in attacks. The chance to actually give himself time so he could pull off something interesting.

Unfortunately, his opponent had learnt its lessons well. Lessons that had come at the cost of his remaining bodyguard. Now, the Goblin King took hold of the spinning staff and pressed forward. It knew if it let Arthur reset, it would be worn down, tricked. Better to keep the pressure up, especially since it was better armoured than Arthur.

Of course, that assumed Arthur was going to let it. And the goblin wasn't the only one who had learnt. A slight switch of stance and the spear went shooting forward, a direct attack that the Goblin King used its shield to block. The spear struck and bounced off, but this time around, Arthur followed up not with a spinning attack but with his foot.

Focused Strike flowed through him, all but one other point of Tower energy gone as Arthur poured his attack into a front stomp kick. He hit with the heel of his foot, striking hard at the exact center of the shield. The shield had been hammered and struck repeatedly by Arthur, a crude wooden construction lacking an outer banding of metal to hold it in place. As such, a crack had already begun to appear in the center and with the application of foot to shield, all driven forward by the Tower technique, it shattered along with the arm behind it.

The goblin staggered back, though not without twisting its body at the last second, cutting at Arthur's retreating foot. It caught the edge of his foot as he pulled back, lopping off the bottom of the boot and part of his heel at the same time. The blade was jagged and ragged, tugging through and sending jolts of electric pain through Arthur as his foot came down.

The pair collapsed in unison, staring at one another. Arthur had fallen from the pain; the Goblin King from momentum and force. Together, they stared at one another across the span of space for a brief moment, eyes locked in impromptu standoff. The first to flinch and move was Arthur, hands sliding up the haft of his shaft before he thrust.

The spear shot forward, only to be deflected by his opponent's block. It still slammed into the Goblin King's chest, skittering off hardened leather armour before falling aside. Then, the goblin was scrambling on its hands and knees, sword aiming for Arthur's throat.

An upwards block with the flat of his arm saw more blood drawn. More cuts, but the awkward scrambling attack went over his shoulder. Rather than try for the spear again, Arthur grabbed the arm, pulling the weapon and wielder close as he utilised his forehead on its nose. And then, forehead on forehead and body, slamming over and over again to force his opponent into defense, before it stopped twitching under his arms.

Finally done, Arthur collapsed on top of the creature, exhaustion and blood loss robbing him of energy in a great wave. He lay still for long minutes, his breathing slowly evening out as his techniques finished clotting his wounds and began the arduous process of healing him.

Stripping the damn goblin of its armour to get to its monster core was a pain. Then, limping over with the aid of his spear was even more so, as he repeated the grisly process of carving into the bodyguards' bodies. There was a disgusting intimacy to doing this to a humanoid being, one that looked significantly closer to his own species than the *jenglot* had. Even so, Arthur pushed on, rolling the freed beast stones on the ground to clean them before dropping the contents into his pack. While they would, eventually, dry out and the blood magically disperse, it was still disgusting and had a tendency to stain the pouches if he didn't at least try to clean them somewhat.

Funny, really, how the physics of what disappeared and what didn't, what ratio and rates, did not exactly follow any specific rules. In general, bodies disappeared, but blood that interacted directly with a Tower climber and their equipment didn't. Stuff in packs were a bit more iffy, though the general belief was that the climber's aura helped contain Tower energy, preventing the dispersal of Tower-constructed blood and viscera.

Of course, it didn't work out entirely. For example, the sword and broken shield that Arthur was now checking over would likely disappear, and almost certainly the armour. Didn't matter if you put them on, or wielded them, unless the Tower was being generous and decided it was loot. They were good as gone.

It was one reason people were hesitant about putting on and using newly acquired items. The last thing you wanted was to have your armor or weapon disappear on you in the middle of a fight. Of course, it mostly happened within the first hour or so, but there were stories of weapons disappearing hours later when said Tower climber was in the middle of a boss fight. Which was another reason most Tower climbers didn't use such weapons till the next floor. Or at least, had the gear checked out by Tower personnel.

"I'm being greedy, wanting a big sword that is stabby, but that's all I got, the love of... rot? got? No, used got... got, rot, bot, fought...?" Arthur muttered to himself, one leg splayed out. He was using his Multi-tasking trait, forcing himself to think about silly rhymes to ignore the pain and the aching loss of damaged footwear. Maybe he'd be able to find a cobbler, but even if he did, he was not certain they could do much about the lost enchantment.

More importantly, watching bits and pieces of his body grow back was a disturbing sight. He didn't want to focus on it too much, though in another way, he was ultra-focused on the progression. He could feel how his technique was pulling energy towards his foot, the way it had stemmed the flow of blood, how it was even now layering new tissue over it. He could direct the energy, but for the first time, he was beginning to sense the blockages. A part of him knew what was supposed to be there. The curve of the heel, the nub of the skeleton. The soul, the body, knew what was missing. Fleshy pad that was meant to take impact was gone, and the body, in its haste to recover, was just papering over the cracks.

But another portion—the technique, his soul, his DNA—wanted to fix it properly. It was trying but was being held back by the speed of the healing process, the overlay of new flesh and bone. It was fascinating, to watch two competing healing processes fighting one another, each with their own objectives.

All he had to do, Arthur realized, was put his own weight down one way or the other.

Easier said than done, of course. He could feel the competing directives, feel how they intended to move; but figuring out which particular directive came from what flow of power and how those directives balanced against one another was infinitely more complex. Pushing down on one side, slowing down energy flow through one meridian point or speeding it up in another, altering the mix, had cascading effects throughout the entire technique.

A failure could result in multiple issues. Growths that ran rampant, the creation of cancer within his own blood. Too high blood pressure, cracking the seal around his wound and causing it to weep. Inflammation as more white blood cells flooded the region, turning to attack the stem cells. Stem cells, given no real direction, rebuilding on the core but years too far behind.

One problem after the other, Arthur could feel it coming on. Sometimes, he relaxed on his techniques, letting the normal and perfected method take over to remove the issues. Other times, he pushed on, knowing he would suffer later as he sought the fix. Arthur lost track of time until, suddenly, there was nothing else to heal.

Eyeing the scarred and misshapen heel, Arthur winced. "Club foot isn't really a weapon of choice..."

Then again, allowing the Tower to push the notification through, he could not help but grin.

Accelerated Healing – Refined Energy (Grade IV) - 11.2%

He was on the right track, finally. After so long with his trusty technique's progress in abeyance, getting poisoned, stabbed and cut seemed to have kickstarted things at last.

Now, all he had to do was lose another body part and figure out how to heal it fully.

Dismissing those thoughts, Arthur looked at where the bodies and weapons had been. He sighed. Of course the Goblin King had left nothing behind, no weapons, no broken shield, no armour. Nothing but a necklace of teeth that he hadn't even noticed it wearing. Grimacing, Arthur could not help but pick it up, eyeing the weird fetish before pocketing it. He'd get it identified later. He certainly didn't recall reading about it as a drop, which either meant it was so bad it wasn't worth noting in the wiki, or he'd forgotten it because it was so bland his mind had never retained that information. Or… it was so good that whoever chanced on it didn't tell the world they had acquired it.

Probably the first of the two.

Whistling to himself and limping onward, Arthur went to grab his backpack. He was, finally, done with the damn fourth floor. And not a moment too soon as far as he was concerned. Once he rested, refilled his Tower energy pool, and added a few more points to his refined energy pool, he was gone.

Chapter 111

Arthur slipped as he appeared on the teleportation platform, the slickness of the stone causing him to slide forwards. Only a last-moment shift of his weight and the grounding of his spear as he fell kept him on his feet. Raucous chuckles and a few groans met Arthur's ears at his performance, a reminder of another teleportation platform mere months ago.

"What the hell, *lah*?" Arthur cursed, stabilising himself just before a shift of the air behind him and a yelp had him automatically jumping away. More groans, as he turned around to spot another climber tumble right out.

A moment later, he recalled the note, that minor comment in a forum thread about this floor. Something about needing to keep throughflow, and then others telling the poster to shut up and not spoil the surprise. As he cleared the way, he watched Yao Jing fall to the ground, going into a roll that was only mildly fouled by his backpack. He still ended up on his feet, though at an angle from where he had meant to be.

"Damn. Didn't think there was that much traffic," Arthur muttered, keeping an eye on the surroundings and the teleportation platform. He offered his hand to his friend as he took in the benches that had been hastily built for the watchers, though none of them made a move to bother the newcomers.

Unlike the first floor where peace was enforced by the Tower itself, here, the lack of battle was entirely manmade. There had been periods when newcomers were attacked, to a point where few individuals even tried to cross the fifth floor. At that point, the government had stepped in, placing their own people to watch over this floor.

Most Towers had places like this—chokepoints where climbers were forced into direct conflict. Most Towers ended up finding a similar solution. After all, if no one ever managed to make it out of a Tower, then eventually the number of desperate climbers would fall to zero.

Much better for business all around if the flow of ascenders continued. Of course, that always made Arthur wonder why the Towers even bothered, but like so many other Tower-related mysteries, there were no answers. Just rife speculation.

"No fair *lah* boss, how come you arrive first?" Yao Jing said, standing up and brushing himself off. He looked at the group watching them, his hands dropping low into guard. "Shit..."

"Relax. They're just watching. And betting." A nod to where a bookie was moving around, collecting payment and making it. He gestured with his spear towards the exit where two men lounged. "Remember? *Polis Bangunan Ghaib*."

Yao Jing blinked slowly and then eventually answered, rather unconvincingly, "Ya *lah*. Of course I remember."

Arthur rolled his eyes, settled his bags a little better and waved his friend on. "Come on. We might as well get going before we end up getting caught."

Almost as soon as he finished speaking, he noticed the change in attention in the watchers. Looking backwards, he saw Uswah skim down the oiled platform, flipping it over once her toes touched the edge so that she didn't land in the uncertain sand. Her backpack, unlike most of theirs, was much slimmer and compact, meant to carry the most minimal of items to suit her role as scout.

"Or, we could wait to see if anyone else arrives?" Arthur muttered, rather incredulously. After all, they had all entered the fourth-floor trials at the same time but the amount of time each of them took should have varied to some degree. "Welcome, Uswah."

She offered him a nod in greeting and strolled over to them, the empty sleeve pinned up tight along her arm. She glanced around, taking in the crowd and self-consciously adjusting her *tudung* as she did so, making sure the head covering was well placed.

"Gambling? Really? So *haram*. The *polis* should just stop it..." Nose wrinkled, Uswah at least made sure to keep her voice low. After all, as much as her religion denounced it, complaining about gambling was not likely to make her any friends. Not in this place.

A flicker of light and a shift in the portal allowed Arthur to watch as someone else was deposited. This one came stumbling out, back facing the wrong way. He slipped as his foot touched the oiled platform. Sliding backwards, he tumbled over and hit his head, lying stunned and smoking all across his body even as raucous laughter broke out.

"That's not one of ours," Arthur muttered, crouching a little to stare at the other man.

"*Oi! Jangan sentuh!*" From behind, the policemen shouted at Arthur as he bent to examine the newcomer.

As Arthur straightened automatically, he caught a whiff of a familiar brimstone and sulfur smell and could not help but wrinkle his nose. Add in the smoking skin and clothing and the way the man wheezed, and he could guess what the poor fellow had to do to survive most recently.

"He's poisoned," Arthur said, though he made sure to step back as a policeman advanced on the trio. "Not by me, obviously."

The short Malay man in his police uniform that strode over snorted, the truncheon in his hand smacking into his palm as he walked over. A little on the hefty side, he moved with the swaggering confidence of one who knew he had authority on his side and wasn't afraid to wield it.

"*Jangan dekat dia. Cepat pergi!*" He waved his truncheon at the exit to punctuate his words, warning the group away and telling them to leave.

Arthur frowned as he watched the policeman grab the man by the scruff of his neck and yank him out of the platform none too gently. Yao Jing, more careful about matters, grabbed Arthur's arm and led him to the exit, muttering softly under his breath, "Don't, *lah*. It's not worth it, boss."

Exhaling hard, Arthur nodded. He understood, it wasn't his problem. And as much as he might want to help the man, if he had survived so far, chances were he'd be okay. It was quite possible the policeman might even have some antidotes on them, what with the government's avowed goal of having more climbers on this floor.

Of course, the poor guy probably would get charged an arm and a leg. And that also assumed that supply runs had arrived on time for the antidotes or that they hadn't been purloined for other nefarious purposes. Or just to line the guards' pockets.

If you weren't cynical about the government, you hadn't lived in Malaysia long enough.

"Eh..." Arthur frowned as they came to a stop, the remaining policeman standing in their way. He wasn't exactly blocking the exit, but he'd moved so that it was clear he expected them to stop, which Uswah—in the lead—had.

"You people came through pretty good, eh? Which group? Suey Tong? Prime Group? TG?" the Indian man asked, dark skin glistening with sweat under the green-grey uniform he wore.

"*Bukan*," Uswah answered in negation, then glanced back at Arthur. He gave her a small shake of his head, and she smiled. "We're just going to the admin center now."

"Ooooh, going to try to sell those horns, eh? Good luck always good. Better to share it, right?" The avaricious gleam in the man's eyes almost made Arthur roll his own eyes, but he managed to stop it.

It still smarted when Uswah dipped into her pocket and pulled out three beast stones and dropped them in the man's hand. Arthur frowned down at the monster cores in the man's hand, obviously unhappy, but when none of them made to offer the policeman more he reluctantly stepped aside. Annoyed as he might be at the size of the bribe, it wasn't enough to make a big deal of it. Or if he intended to do so, Arthur figured he'd change his mind soon enough.

More importantly...

"The watchers are leaving," Arthur muttered, jerking his head to the exits that emerged from the back of the stands that had been built up. Those spilled out direct into the surroundings, rather than forcing them to join the exit. He noticed a few of the watchers were eyeing the trio as they looked around, searching for wayposts.

One particularly enterprising young lady swaggered over, a rolled-up piece of paper in her hand. She waved it as she closed on them, smiling a little as she spoke. "Map?"

"This place isn't that big, is it?" Arthur said, even as Yao Jing started reaching for his own pouch.

"No, but there are places you want might want to avoid," the young lady said. "And my map includes places of interest and the surroundings, including the latest monsters along the platforms."

"I read the wiki," Arthur said, even as Yao Jing continued to scramble in his pouch before finally pulling forth a small stone from the second floor.

That made the girl open her mouth to protest, then, glancing at Arthur, she shrugged. "Whatever. Your friend wants it." She offered the map, which Yao Jing grabbed and unrolled quickly to verify it was actually a map before he dropped the stone in her hand. That she didn't make a break for it or protest was a sign at least that she was not anxious about what might appear. Once she had the stone, though, she turned to leave.

"Hey, why is everyone leaving? Aren't appearances... well, random?" Arthur said.

She looked back at him, her gaze almost pitying as though she was surprised he was even talking to her. Yao Jing cleared his throat, waving the map he had rolled back. One last glance at the big bodybuilder and she answered. "No point betting on the normal returnees, you know. Everyone remembers, so the regulars aren't as interesting. As for newcomers, you all only ever appear at dawn and dusk now."

"When did that happen?" Arthur said, but this time around, she didn't turn around or answer.

"That's why you pay, boss," Yao Jing said, looking satisfied with himself as he reopened the map to peer within.

Arthur shook his head, glancing at the map and using it to calibrate himself with his own memories of the place. After confirming their heading, he started walking.

Seems like even in the eternal Tower, things changed.

Chapter 112

The fifth-floor village was, like so many of the other beginner villagers in the Tower, a mixture of Tower-built buildings and slipshod structures thrown together. Due to the lack of urban planning, the pathways between buildings and across the entire village had grown somewhat haphazardly, with a couple of pre-built Tower pathways becoming narrow alleys where lazy ascenders had thrown their own structures up against the walls of the Tower buildings.

Unlike lower floors where such structures might be torn down by a Tower guard, there was not one in sight here. Here, more than anywhere else, the anarchic nature of the insides of the Tower held true. If not for the presence of the government police and the various Tower-enabled powers, it likely would have been even more chaotic.

It reminded Arthur of bad pirate movies, of places like Tortuga and other cities that came together and were held in place by the barest modicums of civilisation and pressing needs. It made the hair on the back of his neck stand on end, even as he crossed the grounds, eyes drifting over the ramshackle buildings and the occasional two-story in search of trouble.

Not much wood on this floor, so most of the buildings were thrown together with planks, canvas, plastic tarps, and mud. What wood there was had a familiar look of the trees from the floors below, though that in itself was rare enough. Over the years, enterprising climbers had made their way up, bringing new material from the outside world—or in some cases, just purchasing said material from the Tower itself.

As the trio made their way through the village, the hum of conversation and the presence and stink of humanity living in close quarters filled the surroundings. Arthur walked carefully, though the fact that ascenders did not need to eat ensured that refuse was kept to the minimum. It didn't, however, stop things like discarded and broken material from accumulating. Stubbing one's toe on a shattered bottle or broken chair was just as painful, even with a Tower body. Never mind the occasional plastic bag.

"Troublesome..." Arthur muttered, forcing his shoulders and neck muscles to relax once again. The narrow alleyways they were forced to traverse and the surprising crowds they had to push through were bordered by both solid makeshift walls or the occasional gap in a darkened tarp. It kept his gaze on the swivel, while the feeling of being watched had him clutching his spear tighter.

"Crowded," Uswah said. "Lots of people stopped here."

"Yeah, that's..." Unusual. In a sense. Arthur knew that the fifth floor was a common place for people to consolidate their gains and take their time finishing up the goals of the floor before testing themselves against the sixth. Thus, it was normally busy, but this felt even more crowded than they had expected.

"Change in layout?" Uswah offered.

"Maybe." Arthur looked upward, trying to spot something but the closed-in alleyway and the open skies only now lightening right above him gave barely any information. Annoying. "How much further, you think?"

"Soon..." Uswah muttered, slowing as they came to a split in the road. She glanced sideways, wagging her hand by her side as she tried to remember how many times they'd turned or drifted. Arthur lowered his spear, pointing to the right and she followed his directions. Arthur had to point his spear tip away from an annoyed passerby, and he flushed a little guiltily.

Maybe he should be a little more careful.

"You good back there?" Arthur called out, glancing back to see Yao Jing somehow having found a piece of jerky to chew on. He raised an eyebrow and Yao Jing offered the dark brown matter. On closer inspection, Arthur realised it wasn't jerky so much as... "A root?"

"Yes. Tasty," Yao Jing said. "A little spicy, you know."

Shrugging, Arthur took the piece offered and bit into it. His mouth flooded with saliva almost immediately even as a tingling numbness crept through his mouth. Offering the remainder of the root back, Arthur winced. Spicy. Hah! It felt more like it was poisonous, though it did leave a nice buzz in his mouth.

"Here," Uswah said, drawing his attention back to the front.

The administrative building was clearly a Tower construct, what with its smooth walls and actual windows with glass. The presence of a Tower guard—the first that they had seen—just on the inside of the open doors was also clearly an indicator of its official nature. And, whether through coincidence or the orneriness of individuals not wanting to be constantly squeezed, the administrative building even had a small square of free space in front of it.

Of course, that square was also filled with people, which made going through it a chore.

"So...." Arthur said. "In?"

"Of course," Yao Jing said, proudly. He stepped past Arthur, nodding to him as he said, "I'll make a path." Throwing his shoulders back, he plowed into the crowd, not at all being shy to make use of his elbows to make his way through. More than a few glared at the newcomer, but Yao Jing ignored the curses that he received as he shoved his way through, calling out constantly, "Coming through. Move. *Hang ah!*"

Following behind, Uswah slipped between the crowd in his wake with much less trouble. She did, however, occasionally utilise her shadows to tug people away, causing them to stumble and look around with surprise. Arthur had to hide a smile, only recognising what she was doing because he knew of her techniques.

As for him, he just stayed behind, happy to wade through and scanning the crowd. He was in particular looking out for gang tattoos, groups clustered into familiar signs of the underworld. He picked out the Ghee Hin pretty fast, facing off a short distance from the Double Sixes. Then, smaller gangs that he wasn't too familiar with all scattered around. Over there, in nicer clothing was the TG Inc. group, the men and women chatting together as they waited about and, in the corner, the Bumikasih clustered around a policeman in his uniform—the closest thing they had to someone who would help them out, what with being indentured to work their way up and out.

For all his looking, Arthur found himself assaulted by a hand on his shoulder before he spotted who it was. He almost punched the grabber, stilling his motions, though he did shrug the hand off.

"Is she with you?" Lam said, the bodyguard's eyes filled with worry. Behind him, he was followed by what looked like other members of the Chin family, pushing the crowd aside by sheer presence.

"No, sorry." Arthur said. "Surprised you weren't waiting and watching..."

Lam opened his mouth to comment, then glanced around and shook his head. An eyebrow rose in surprise, but Arthur chose not to comment. He did, however, add. "Hey, since you're here... can you—?"

"He cannot." Voice cold and cutting, another man stepped forward, pushing Lam away rudely. Surprisingly the older man did not protest, just slipping aside as the man in his mid-twenties stepped in. Even at a glance, Arthur could tell he was a member of the Chin family, the man having inherited the nose, chin, and thin lips. "Nor should my cousin have made such a suggestion."

"Sorry," Arthur said, inclining his head a little. "I'm a little lost here. I'm Arthur Chua. You?"

"Damian Chin. The manager of the fifth floor," Damian said, coldly. "And Lam has told me about your deal."

"Right," Arthur hesitated, glancing around as he noted the slight drop in volume all around as people tried to listen in. He shook his head after a moment, continuing: "Well, look. I have a deal, but obviously, you need to talk to Casey. So why don't we ignore that for now, and I'll go do my thing and when Casey arrives, you guys can chat, eh?"

Damian blinked, looking surprised at Arthur's quick and reasonable pivot. Before he could protest further, Arthur grinned and clapped him on the shoulder. "Great. Thanks. I really need a shower anyway. And then a nap. Maybe we'll do lunch after? Tea?" Arthur gave a nod, as though Damian had agreed, and added a quick squeeze on Damian's shoulder before he stepped away. "See you for tea then!"

With that, he hurried away, head down and utterly ignoring the hesitant "Wait!" that resounded behind him. Arthur might not have wanted to get involved in politics, but he knew when a scene was about to start. And drawing on his old delivery service experience meant that being nice and talking fast and then getting the hell out of there before he got blamed was the way to go. Whatever problem Damian had, it wasn't with him.

Not really.

Even if his attitude was going to complicate things for Arthur and the Benevolent Durians on this floor.

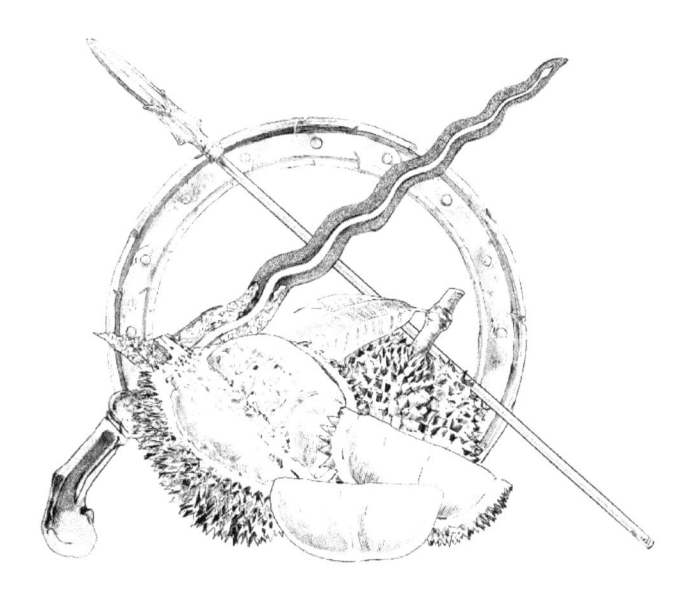

Chapter 113

Establishing the clan once he actually got into the administrative building was a simple matter. Just a bunch of conversations with the floor manager, an allowance for the Tower to send its notifications to him. The fact that he lacked a proper building to designate as a clan residence was a pain, but thankfully, the Tower wasn't going to force him to pick a place.

At the end of the flickering images and the usual floor-level notification, Arthur pulled up the clan detail page once more.

The Benevolent Durians Clan Status

Organizational Ranking: 182,748

Number of Towers Occupied: 1

Number of Clan Buildings: 3

Number of Clan Members: 198

Overall Credit Rating: F-

Aspect: Guardianship

Sigil: The Flame Phoenix

Arthur grimaced, noting the lack of change in the organisational ranking. Not a huge surprise, what with them not adding new buildings since the third floor, which he assumed was one of the major factors. And while the number of clan members was probably a factor, it likely had more to do with the type and progress of the clan members than any actual direct relationship to numbers. He also figured that the number of Towers they were within made a big difference. The only thing he didn't know how to affect was the credit rating. Or heck, what it really meant thus far.

"Sufficient, Clan Head?" the Administrative Manager's voice cut in, causing Arthur to blink. He stared at the lizard man that made up the Tower manager on this floor before he ended up nodding. "Yeah, I guess. Where's the inn, by the way?"

"Why do you require such lowly accommodation? Surely you can provide better for yourself?" The Administrator said, coldly.

"Eh, it's complicated," Arthur said. "I'll be back, but the inn now would be good."

"And is that all?" The Manager's gaze shifted to Arthur's backpack, making the man blink and remember what he was carrying. He'd been wearing it so long that he'd forgotten he was even carrying it around.

"Oh, shit. Need some new boots. Unless you can fix this one." He raised his foot where he had barely managed to stitch his boots together so that it could last the trip to town. "And, I need an assessment of this. And maybe... an enchantment? Have it rebuilt?"

"Was that a question of our ability to do so?"

"No, sorry." Arthur slung the backpack off, shaking his head as he tried to get his brain back into the game. Something about the Administrator, glaring down at him with his older face reminded him of way too many disapproving bosses and teachers. It was throwing him off his game. "I want to know what you can do with this."

Hefting his biggest package, he dropped it on the table beside the Manager, all the while ignoring the crowd that had formed within the building. He'd have preferred to do this alone, but it was not as though he could kick these people out, and the manager wasn't making any move to do so.

By this time, the manager had pulled apart the ropes, snapping them with casual strength and leaving the edges frayed. He flipped the leather and fur open, running a finger along the ragged edges of where Arthur had cut the fur off, as well as the occasional spots where he'd accidentally cut through. The sneer on his face grew with each moment, though thankfully the entire thing had somewhat cured itself during the magical disappearing process, leaving the fur at least not stinking and rotting.

Finished with his critique of the fur, the manager barely even glanced at the antlers, picking them up and turning them over before dropping the entire thing onto the table.

"There are things we can do, yes." A slight beat, before the man continued. "The fur is of poor to middling quality. We can strip the fur entirely, soak the skin and create some leather. There is enough here to make a full suit of armour or breastplates and pauldrons for two individuals." Eyes flicking over Arthur's own worn and damaged armor, he continued. "It will carry some of the same properties over. Or we can make a cloak and gloves and mittens. It'll be very warm."

Arthur figured that last bit was a joke. While there were Towers with colder climates, the Malaysian one was definitely not that. A warm cloak or mittens was just about the last thing he'd want to wear. Even with a body that could handle a wider range of extremes, overheating was just not fun.

"Armour." He hesitated, then pushed aside the flash of guilt at what he was about to say. He had to remember that keeping himself alive was still the number one priority—for practical and Clan reasons. "For me only. If there's extra, maybe a breastplate or pauldrons or greaves."

The manager glanced at the material, frowned, and then spoke. "We can either produce extra perhaps, make full use of it. We'll charge you for all of the production." A slight beat, then he added, "Or we can take the remainder and discount your work."

"Oh... that's... uhh...." Arthur hesitated now, tempted. He had money—beast stones—of course, but the chances were he'd have to cover some of this via contribution points. Which meant running quests, which would take more time. Which was time not spent cultivating. On the other hand, he could have the others help pay for it. But... "Exactly how much better will this armour be?"

A lip curled upwards, taking Arthur's present armour. "Significantly."

"Yeah, fine..." Arthur sighed and then tapped the antlers. "And this?"

"Now, this is an interesting drop," the Manager said, suddenly much more interested and less hostile. "Not common to get one in this condition. The Tower must really have liked you." Then he paused, eyes narrowing as he took in Arthur. "Or it felt your status needed additional help."

Arthur would complain about not needing help, but since this was working in his favour... He just grinned and waited.

"Now, the greatest issue is that you cannot truly afford to make full use of it." The Manager held a hand up before Arthur could protest. "It's not something that's viable on this level. The seventh floor maybe. The tenth for sure. Or another Tower entirely." At Arthur's frown, the man continued, blithely, "We can send it up for you, of course. It'd cost a little, but we can have the payment when you arrive."

"And you get to keep it, if I die."

"Of course."

Arthur snorted but nodded. That worked for him, since he was going to be paying off the armour as it stood. More time was good. "And the options?"

"The best use? We break it down and inscribe it onto your clan seal."

The silence that pronouncement created was so profound, you could have heard a bribe being passed. It took Arthur quite a few moments to shake himself free and ask the pertinent question.

"What would we get?" he said, slowly and carefully. Anything that improved the clan seal was an improvement, because the boost would transfer not just to himself but everyone involved. It was, obviously, the smartest play across the widest range of people, if one was selfless. Or looking to build up a powerful organisation.

"It is hard to say, though it always coincides with the creature's abilities and element." Tapping the antlers, the Manager flicked a gaze across the listeners before he continued. "I'm sure you can imagine what that might be."

"Yeah…" Arthur said. "But if I went with another option? What else?"

"The usual. A weapon or two." Eyeing the antlers, the Manager shrugged. "Utility tools. Make good spades I'm sure. Maybe we could split them apart—they're technically one drop right now and the magic uses both. And if so, we could get you two weapons. Which can be split apart or…" Frowning, he measured the pair with his hands. "A pair of short swords?"

"Bone swords?" Or, well, not technically bone but close enough. Still, rather savage, Arthur figured. But if they heated up to the same level, they'd be fearsome weapons.

"It would depend, of course, on the craftsman available. And what you can afford." Back to his stoic self now, the Manager asked, "So, what will it be?"

Chapter 114

Arthur flopped onto his bed, looking up at the ceiling in the tiny room that he had acquired for himself. After all, the inn did not have a lot of space, and certainly no luxury rooms. One of the aspects of the building was the almost dormlike rooms that were available, like the Tower was encouraging the development of clans and guilds.

Clad only in a towel, Arthur glanced over to his backpack and then the new set of clothing he'd picked up from the Tower before he'd arrived at the inn. It had been more expensive than purchasing it from your average stall around, what with the flow of normal clothing just one of the luxuries brought in by climbers. But that'd require him to look around, to go shopping, and right now… well, this was good enough.

Also, considering how much he owed them for his new armour—never mind the antlers—the minor cost of the clothing was a footnote.

"Two hundred and eighty-six contribution points," Arthur muttered. "And that's after taking away everything that I've earned so far. I'm going to be running a lot of quests, it seems."

A hand raised and traced along his chest for a moment, admiring the muscles he'd gained. Washboards flat and ribbed, a nice round number of eight. He'd heard that the number you had was all genetics, but mostly, it amused him that the best way to lose weight was just to have your body replaced by the Tower.

Then, he pushed the mild vanity aside. He ran through his options, then finally stood up, grabbing the pouch of monster stones from his belt and then the others in his backpack. He looked through the pouches briefly before he showered them on the table, sorting them quickly into levels and types and batches of ten.

"I could use this, give them a pouch or two," Arthur muttered. "With the income from the Chins I should be able to replace what I use. Except, of course, there's no guarantee I'll actually get any with the new complication." He sighed. "Casey, you really need to survive. Or else this will be a real pain."

No point in waiting or wondering. If there was going to be a choice to be made, it would be later. For the next few days or until she arrived, he'd train. That was the best he could do, increasing his own strength once again. After all, that was the entire point of climbing this Tower.

Even if, right now, all he wanted to do was rest. His body had healed for the most part, the Accelerated Healing technique constantly refreshing him, especially now that he wasn't pushing things. But his mind was another matter. He would need sleep eventually, but he'd rested enough on the previous floor.

Pulling the largest stone to him, Arthur took a seat on his bed and closed his eyes. He breathed slowly, forcing energy from the stone into his system, pulling it through his various meridians. The fourth-floor core, the boss core he held, was significantly stronger than the first-floor ones he'd utilised so many years ago. He could feel the energy raging, threatening to tear itself free of his control and damage him.

The initial pull from the stone was the worst, the untamed energy intent on escaping his grip. As it passed through his meridians though, he tamed it, mixing with the energy within him and giving him grips to wield and control it more easily. He knew that if he lost control even for a second, it would damage his meridians, escape into his bones and force him into a period of recuperation that would set him back.

Normally, you'd start by going up each floor, growing stronger gradually, and increasing the amount and density of the cores one used. With enough traits and experience, you would be able to manage the overflowing energy within each more powerful core. However, Arthur was already behind the curve with his speedrun antics and now he was utilising a boss core which was even more densely packed. If not for the superior cultivation method he was using and the traits he'd picked he would not dare try this.

However, with both, he could speed up his cultivation rate significantly. If he had to put a number to it—and not, of course, have the Tower do it later—he'd figure he was between half to two thirds of a full point coming from this single stone itself. It would take just over an hour plus, if he could control the energy.

Pulling it through his meridians, gaining millimeters of control with each passage, he finally managed to take full control of the energy and make it his own. Next step was pouring all this energy into his dantian, the storage area of his own refined energy. Problem was, the first gush started pushing at his core, causing him to ache and hurt.

He gritted his teeth, the pounding influx of energy pouring into him and pushing the bounds of his core to the maximum. Recalling the cultivation exercises, he began to compress that energy too, forcing it tighter and tighter into the center of him. Refined energy could be compressed, transformed, as he exerted the full strength of his will and stored it away. It was this very compression that would give it the necessary pathways to later on infuse him.

If he could control it.

Heart beating like a hundred horses going off in his chest, burning energy pouring through his form and leaking out of his dantian, Arthur struggled to breathe regularly. Once he started the energy pull, he knew there was no going back. He would have to utilise it entirely. Normally losing a stone wasn't a problem, and with the right kind of control, you could stop the process even.

However, control was a laughable concept right now. He had as much control over this energy as a road-raging BMW driver stuck in Monday morning traffic after waking up late for work.

Focus. Breathe. Not ignore the pain, because the pain was not something one could ignore. No, you just had to accept it and live with it, use it to sharpen your mind and focus.

Moment by moment, he pulled energy from the monster core into him, compressed it and made it his own. Only to do it all over again when the core was finished, so that he could pour the refined energy into his attributes and grow stronger.

Chapter 115

Arthur timed it nearly perfectly. He was only about twenty minutes too late. Pulling energy from the stones was never an exact science, though he had a rough idea of how much time was needed for each stone by now. But give or take a few minutes each stone and without even the option of a watch, he could not exactly schedule things to the second.

Which was why, after two days, he wandered out of his room to the bottom floor and waiting room of the inn to see a rather impatient and exhausted-looking Casey waiting for him. She looked up impatiently when he stepped within, shooting to her feet and wincing a little as the wounds around her stomach that had yet to close sprung open.

"What are you doing here? Are you that weak-willed that a little opposition is enough to push you back?" she said, glaring at Arthur.

"Don't get started on me," Arthur said, waving a hand in front of her face. "You're the one who's supposed to sort out your own Chin politics. I'm not getting involved in an internal fight."

"No fight. He's just being stubborn," Casey said, lips curled up. "I'll deal with him."

"Good, then go do that. Stop bothering me and come back tomorrow." Arthur then nodded to Lam. "Or just send him and I'll meet you at the administrative center."

"I'm not yours to command," she snapped.

"And I'm not yours to belittle," Arthur said with a roll of his eyes. "You want me to get involved in your internal politics? Please." He waggled his hand back and forth. "I'm not that dumb. And I'm not dumb enough to think that this, your delay, your injuries isn't all an act."

"An act?"

"Give it up." Arthur gestured to Lam. "I realised it when you messed up in sending Lam ahead to try to rile your cousin up. You wanted me to deal with him for you, didn't you?"

Casey growled. "Stop making conspiracy theories."

"Really? Then you're saying Lam is stronger than you?"

"I got unlucky. You know those platforms are all randomised right?"

Arthur snorted. "One day, I'd give you. Two?" He shook his head. "No. Not for you. I'm surprised you'd be willing to sacrifice your speedrun just to avoid dealing with your cousin. He that much of a problem?"

Silence, then eventually, she sighed. At the same time, she straightened, ignoring the bloody bandage on her side. "He's not the problem. It's his father. If I force him to do what I say, he'll complain to his father." She made a face. "Part of his punishment—and reward—was having full control of this floor. The fact that I'm making him do what I want..."

"It puts you in an awkward position. Or your dad, eh?" Arthur corrected himself. "Right, but if I forced the matter, you'd be free and clear."

"And I wasn't wasting my time..." Casey said. "You can cultivate just as well with stones at the end of the fifth floor as here." Then, she drew a breath. "Will you help me? I'll owe you one."

"No thanks." At she moved to protest, he held a finger up. "However, if your father owes me one..."

"I can't speak for him!"

"Pretty sure you have been." Another shrug as he turned away. "Tomorrow, then."

"I..." Casey hesitated, but Arthur wasn't waiting. He knew he was pushing her, but it really wasn't worth it for him without gaining a favor from her dad.

Still, he was a little surprised he managed to make his way back to his room without her protesting. He took a seat back on his bed, picking up a stone along the way. Moments before he started cultivating, he poked at the Tower information in his head to pull out his full status.

Cultivation Speed: 2.473 Yin
Energy Pool: 24/24 (Yin)
Refinement Speed: 0.1421
Refined Energy: 2.41 (29)

Attributes and Traits

Mind: 15 (Multi-Tasking, Quick Learner, Perfect Recall)
Body: 15 (Enhanced Eyesight, Yin Body, Swiftness, Fast Twitch Faster)
Spirit: 11 (Sticky Energy, From the Dregs)

Techniques

Night Emperor Cultivation Technique

Focused Strike

Accelerated Healing – Refined Energy (Grade III)

Heavenly Sage's Mischief

Refined Energy Dart

Bark Skin

Seven Cloud Stepping

Partial Techniques

Simultaneous Flow (113.8%)

Yin-Yang Energy Exchange (59.1%)

Heavenly Sage's Heaven Beating Stick (48.5%)

Refined Exploding Energy Dart (88.9%)

Water Walking (7.1%)

Two full points stored. He could feel the energy running through him, churning in his dantian. Intent on escaping even when he had yet to make use of it. He could, if he poured more power into his Spirit, probably finish learning the Refined Exploding Energy Dart soon, especially if he managed to get enough points to get another trait. He might even, finally, figure out the Yin-Yang Energy Exchange since Spirit was all about understanding the energy he manipulated.

On the other hand, Mind would let him learn techniques from scrolls, perfect the Heavenly Beating Stick technique and even integrate Water Walking to his own movement techniques. More importantly, the more Mind he had the faster he could learn new techniques, the easier it was to keep up in battle and even expand on things like the Simultaneous Energy Flow. As it stood, he needed to get at least four or five flows to be considered a top-level combatant.

On top of that, of course, he had to work towards the third transformation; but considering the minimum level he'd need in even one attribute was thirty—and quite likely a point total of around sixty or seventy—he was quite the distance away from that concern. But getting another Trait in Body couldn't hurt at all.

More importantly, he needed to start pushing through the energy. It was getting really crammed inside his own dantian, though there were a number of theories that discussed increasing the amount of unallocated energy; theorising that improvements could be made that way that were outside the norm.

If Arthur actually had concrete evidence of that, or techniques that could have helped, he would have leaned towards using it. But the truth was, all he had was theorising on the public forums. That wasn't good enough a reason to hold back, especially since it was now beginning to get difficult to control the amount of energy he was refining and storing away.

"When you don't know, best to go Body..." Arthur muttered. It hadn't failed him yet, and while he did want to at least get more Spirit traits, that was going to have to be in the future. For now, another Body trait and then more Spirit points was the plan. Or at least, until something else changed.

Which, he figured, was going to be about in a day or so.

Chapter 116

He was wrong. It took two days and the arrival of the rest of the team—all of them, thankfully, had survived—before things went to hell. In between, he'd received word from Lam and Casey that matters were proceeding apace, though slowly. Content to leave them to it, Arthur kept drawing on the extra stones he'd acquired, allowing Yao Jing and Uswah to handle the occasional query about their clan. In a way, without a clan headquarters to bring eye-catching attention, thus far the number of enquiries had been pretty low.

When chaos arrived, it wasn't in the shape or form that Arthur had expected. The incessant knocking on his door while he was cultivating had been annoying but ignorable till he was done with his current stone. But once he had finished, he found himself annoyed by the irregular knock.

Clambering off his bed, he grabbed his kris and flipped it over so that the blade rested against his forearm. Then, using his other arm, he threw the door open.

"Now, who the hell—urk!" Arthur snarled, his words stopped by the explosion of movement the door-opening threw. He saw the fist coming at his face and blocked it, twisting his hand to bring the side of the kris in to cut, only for the blade to skitter off the hard leather bracer. He shifted targets, aiming to slide it down and cut further, but the attacker was not done.

They stepped inside, knee coming in on the inside of his leg. Arthur shifted weight and raised his leg, taking the attack off-line a little so that, while it disrupted his balance a little, it didn't hit the nerve cluster. Not that that helped, as the arm was withdrawn, another hand smacking at his own arm that was slicing downwards, the kris being caught in a high grip even as the attacker's body kept moving in, checking him with their shoulder.

Arthur found himself sliding backwards, the grip on his kris slipping with each moment. Rather than fight it, he released the weapon and turned his own hand and body, pivoting to bring his other arm into play. Kept tight to his body, palm pulled back, he slammed a short and hard strike into the ribs of his attacker.

Hard enough to send his opponent back with a loud oof, grip on his arm relaxing a little. A snap kick from Arthur's front leg caught the side of a knee as it was withdrawing.

Then, finally, the kris clattered to the ground and the door, thrown wide open, slammed into the other side of the wall. Finally, Arthur caught sight of his attacker.

"*Tai Kor*! Really?" Arthur grumped, keeping his hands up on guard, but a portion of his mind relaxed a little.

His opponent grinned, standing at six-foot-one with a tight, fashionable buzz cut and the features that would have made him a movie star or model in a world without AI models and industry connections. "A little slow, eh, *Di Di*?"

"You've gotten faster. A lot more Body or what?" Arthur grumbled, shaking his arms out as he saw his "big brother" relax. "And harder. What the hell, it felt like hitting concrete." He should know. He'd punched enough walls in his time at the training hall alongside this senior of his. His toes were still smarting after that snap kick, the nerves along the ball of his foot tingling.

"Lightning Reflexes, Swift and Explosive Power," Arthur's Tai Kor said, proudly. A moment later, he winced as he got smacked over the back of his head. "What?"

"Don't just announce your traits, you idiot." Stepping in the rest of the way, Arthur's other visitor entered, looked around, and then closed the door firmly. "Good to see you, Arthur."

"Tai Chei." Arthur greeted her with the term of respect. "And you too." He frowned. "Surprised to see you two still on this floor."

"Blame this one," the pixie-cut beauty said with a roll of her eyes. "Broke his leg on the last floor and ended up taking nearly a month to get out because he kept having to backtrack."

"You could have kept going, Leia."

"As if. You think your mother would ever let me hear the end of it, Eric?" Leia replied. Or Aleia as her actual name was, but one only called her that if you were reading her government documents or wanted to really piss her off. She was looking around carefully, taking in Arthur's residence with trained eyes. They stopped on his armour, his kris that he had picked up and sheathed while the pair were arguing, and then the spear. "More surprising you're here this fast. I thought you were going to train longer."

"I did." Arthur hesitated, then admitted, "I'm kind of on a speedrun."

"With the Chins. So we heard." Eric sounded extremely disapproving, which was not surprising. Unlike many others, Eric had actually come from money. Or did, before his father had been fired and his job automated away when the Prime Group bought the manufacturing plant he'd been working in.

"Did you hear why?" Arthur said, straightening his shirt out and then glancing around. Realising there really wasn't a place to sit, he flopped down on his own bed, gesturing for them to do what they want. He knew they would. Formality was something you bothered with with strangers. These two were family. Or as close as you could get.

"Garbled rumors. Some rather unbelievable. Especially when it concerns a runt like you," Eric said. The last sentence and term should have been playful. Would have been, normally, but this time there was an edge to it that Arthur didn't like.

"I'm a Clan Head," Arthur said, simply. "Long story why, but I'm in the middle of putting together a clan. To do that, well, you need money."

"And so you went to the Chins." Eric sneered, then shifted when Leia shifted too, flinching away before she could strike him. "Fine, he can talk."

"It's not exactly how it happened. They came to me." Arthur hesitated, then shrugged. "But yeah, I'm allied with them. They have money and influence, and I need it." Leaning forward, fixing them with his gaze, he added. "We need it."

"We, eh?" Leia sighed. "You know sifu doesn't want anything to do with the Tower."

"Maybe. But he still trains us, and we all do, right?" Arthur gestured around. The answer was obvious. "And I think he'd be happier if more of us survived, no?"

"Fine. Why don't you tell us, about this long story," she said.

Arthur nodded, detailing his initial entrance, his troublemaking and the Suey Ying Tong, and then, later on, the events that led him to joining the Thorned Lotuses and finally ending up being the clan head. A couple of times, he could see the pair mentally facepalming themselves, but eventually, he ran down after detailing his most recent exploits.

"You weren't joking, were you? You really are a clan head." A slight pause, then Leia gestured. "Strip."

"WHAT?" Eric and Arthur shouted together.

"I want to see it."

"Tai Chei..."

"Stop playing stupid. The clan crest. Seal. Whatever. Show me *lah*!" Leia clapped her hands. "If I'm doing this, I want to make sure it's pretty."

"And if not? You going to give up joining us?" Arthur said, his last words muffled as he took off his shirt. Good thing he had chosen to keep it in a relatively easy to locate position, rather than somewhere a lot more private. Hiding his face in the shirt also let Eric take a moment to compose himself, what with the man's well-known jealousy about Leia. You'd think he'd learned to give up on her, what with her turning him down repeatedly, but he kept banging his head on that wall. Going so far as to introduce her to his family even.

"You really did call it the Benevolent Durians," Eric said, awe and surprise in his voice. "You really are an idiot, eh?"

"I like the name," Arthur said, crossing his arms defensively over his bare chest. "So you two in or not?"

"You have to ask?" Leia said, holding a hand up to his arm and then shifting the hand around on her body as though trying to figure out where to put it.

"Ya *lah*. You know someone has to watch over you with those *babi* about," Eric said. Then, he added. "So, there's just one thing..."

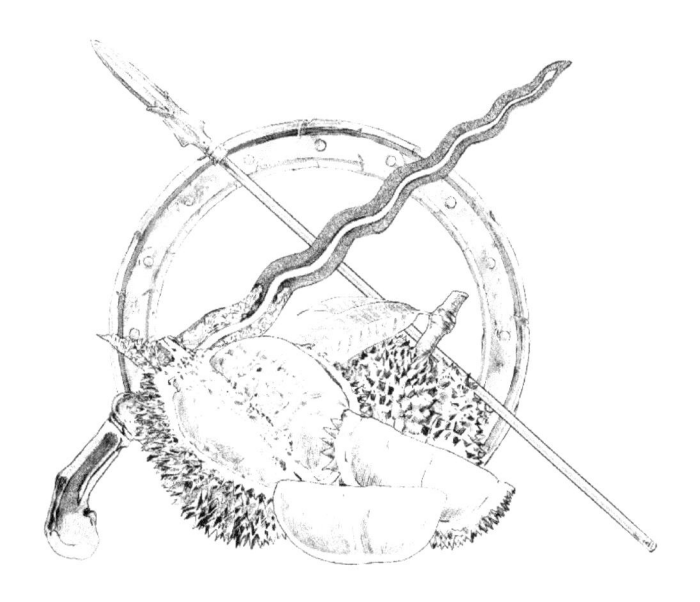

Chapter 117

The group drew more than a few looks as they traversed the cramped Tower village. If not for the unforgiving geography of the fifth floor, the village would have expanded a great deal more. But with the floor being made of distinct, geographically different platforms expanding outwards from the starting area in raised octagonal rings, it was impossible. They were just lucky that there were only three such rings, though traversing the ground from one location to the next was an expedition in itself.

If not for the teleportation pads that linked to the central portals, traversing the fifth floor would have been much more difficult. As it stood, it was just a pain.

One could mark and return to previous teleportation points. The Tower even made it possible to enact that pull to new places from various locations, rather than just the single return point.

All of which meant very little for Arthur's purpose, other than distracting him from his current goal. Which was important enough, overall, what with the news that his seniors had dropped on him. Or the questions that Mel kept peppering him with about his relationship to the two.

"Look, they're my seniors. I trust them." Arthur said, exasperated. "That's 'cause I'm their junior. And there's no way they'd spit phlegm."

"Still, to get so indebted to the Suey Tong..." Mel said, arms crossed. "You have to admit, it's one hell of a coincidence."

"According to them—"

"Exactly," Mel muttered.

"—they were already indebted before they heard any news of what we were doing." Arthur shot her a glare, stepping past a pair who were holding hands and squeezing at the edges of the crowd to get through. He wasn't going to try to throw his weight around or get angry, what with him still only being newly raised to this floor. One never knew how strong the other was after all. "And I don't like you throwing shade at them."

"Whatever. Just be careful about the kind of debts you take on."

"That's why I'm hoping they don't know who I am," Arthur said.

"Mmm-hmmm..." Mel glanced back, taking in the small procession following them. Eric was ahead, leading them through the streets to their destination. At the back, Rick and Leia were having a long conversation while Uswah flitted around, keeping a distant watch over the entire group. Jan and Yao Jing brought up the rear, trying—and failing—to appear like a pair of lovebirds.

Arthur shrugged. If not for the fact that they'd insisted on all coming, he would have chosen a smaller group for this discussion. He did have to agree that a show of force was necessary, but the sheer volume of people was rather foolish, it seemed to him. Then again, at least they'd mostly agreed to stay outside when they arrived.

Which they finally did.

The Suey Ying Tong's current residence was a rather intimidating-looking place, not because it was large or ornate but rather the opposite. If you looked up the definition of seedy underground bar, you might even find a picture of this place there. A sloping roof that looked like it might fall apart, dark shadows and minimal lighting, and trash strewn all around with a pair of lounging thugs on the outside, glaring at everyone who came close and interrogating them.

"Boss in?" Eric was saying, smiling at the one on the left. He was a big fella with ragged stitching crossing his forearms and a wicked-looked serrated knife being used to clean his nails.

"*Ya. Siapa ini?*"

"They're friends," Eric said. "We need to chat with the boss."

Scarry Boy glanced over at Rick and Mel, looking them up and down firmly. Rick was hanging off Leia's arm like he was just there for her. He was not carrying his guns openly, only a single one tucked into the back of his pants and covered by his shirt. After all, bringing in guns was a rather antagonising posture. A jerk of Scarry Boy's head sent the other thug inside, while Eric tried—and failed—to engage the bouncer in a discussion about recent goings-on.

"Thought they were in good..." Mel muttered, legs spread as she took in the group. Like Arthur, she was carrying her spear, since not being at least slightly armed would have been foolish.

The other thug came back, whispered to Scarry Boy, and the man glared at Mel and Arthur. "Weapons outside."

"Sure, sure..." Eric was saying while Arthur was already shaking his head.

"I'll leave my spears, but I'm not leaving my kris," Arthur said, firmly. "I'm not that dumb."

"Then *tak boleh masuk*." Scarry Boy stood up from his stool and crossed his arms, joining his other friend on the other side to bar them from entry.

"Fine with me, but you tell your boss we aren't coming back either," Arthur said, switching tactics. Looks like this wasn't going to be a negotiation after all. "And when these two stop working for you without recompense, that's your problem."

"What? You leaving?" Scarry Boy stared at Eric and Leia. "You still owe us."

"And we're here to pay it off," Arthur tapped the pouch by his side. "If you'll let us."

Scarry Boy pressed his lips together, while the other thug leaned over and whispered. After a moment the thug sighed and nodded. He then gestured. "Spears outside. The money, Boss will decide."

"Smart man," Arthur said, offering his spear. "Don't play with it. It's sharp."

It was the quieter of the two thugs who took both their weapons, seeming content to return to watching passersby as Scarry Boy headed in first. Eric and Mel were shooting Arthur a look, a mixture of exasperation and resigned amusement. After all, his ability to annoy people was well-known as was his stubbornness.

Inside, the bar was everything that you'd expect. Deep shadows covered the half-dozen round tables alongside a makeshift bar that seemed to serve cheap alcohol by the barrel-load. The smell of old vomit and piss mixed with spilled alcohol and fermented fruit caused Arthur's nose to wrinkle. It didn't slow him down as he walked in, picking out the half-dozen gang members within, including the one lounging near what Arthur assumed was the toilets in the back.

Down right at the back was their boss. Even having been informed, Arthur still found the sight a little incongruous. The young lady who sat there was maybe five feet tall in a pair of shoes that were slim and delicate. Not at all the image of a toughened tong boss. Her hair was cut short like most women here, all the better for upkeep, though she had taken the time to style it.

On the other hand, the cut that ran up one side of her face and bisected her lip and reached her ears was a clear sign that she'd seen some shit. As was the empty eye on the other side and the repeatedly broken nose. Add to that the very large mug of fermented fruit right in front of her and the entire thing was making Arthur's eyes tear up as he came to the seat before her.

"So, you Eric's guests?" she said. By this point, Scarry Boy had managed to lean over and begin whispering and a deadly presence filled the air. The tension that ratcheted up her body caused all the others to stare too, some reaching for their weapons. "They want to do what?"

"Buy out the debts for Eric and Leia," Arthur said. "We just need to figure out the price, Boss Kim."

"And who are you, eh? Demand we sell them?" Kim snapped.

"I'm their junior." Arthur smiled a little depreciatingly. "Just doing what a man can, for his seniors, you know?"

"Well, they're not for sale. Told them when they started. Deal is a deal. You work for us and earn it out."

"I'm sure exceptions can be made," Arthur said, offering a smile as he did so. "For the right price."

"No," Kim said. "No go. Especially not for my best enforcers."

Arthur blinked, then looked over at the pair who suddenly looked really uncomfortable. He thought they had been just making runs, collecting stones for the Suey Tong. Not playing enforcers and bringing back money for the Suey Ying.

"We had to…" Leia muttered. "We—I—needed the stones and a place to care for him. You don't know how badly hurt he was, when he arrived."

Arthur flicked a glance at Eric, noting he looked mostly fine. Then again, that could mean a lot of things. If he hadn't lost a limb or anything else, recovery via the Tower could hide a lot of sins.

"Whatever. That's between them and sifu," Arthur said firmly as he returned his gaze to Kim. "What's between you and me is how we're getting this sorted."

"You not listening, ah?" Kim said. "Best leave, now. Or you don't leave at all."

"Look…" Arthur offered her another smile, placing a hand on the back of his chair as he leaned in. "I've got stones, you've got my people, there's no need for this…"

He saw Scarry Boy move, coming in for him. The other two at her table were getting up, but as Sccary Boy reached for him, Mel acted. A flurry of motion happened out of the corner of his eyes, as Eric and Mel dealt with the three, even as Arthur channeled energy into his hand, pulling a Refined Exploding Energy Dart there, ready for use.

The violence was over in a blink of an eye, Eric holding a knife to one throat, his other opponent on the ground whimpering and clutching his balls while Mel had Scarry Boy pinned to the table, arm levered up behind his back. Behind, Arthur could sense Leia and Rick turning and staring at the others who had stood up, ready to take action.

And all the while, neither Arthur nor Kim had made a move, trusting in their subordinates. In one case, falsely.

"You people are good. But there's more of us," Kim said, conversationally and relaxed. She picked up her cup, a finger sticking out. A moment later, one of those not held down grabbed a whistle out and started blowing into it, the sound resounding and echoing in the bar and exiting it.

Noise, a lot of it, as passersby fled and but others started streaming in towards the bar. And even then, Arthur chose not to make a move, a small smile on his face. He could feel the tension ratcheting up even as he adjusted the flow of energy within him, layering a second technique.

"You done?" Arthur said, when the shrieking whistle had stopped. "Because we are good. And I guarantee you, if you start this, you'll end up with more corpses and no enforcers." He paused, then considered. "Or, well, someone will. Because you won't be around."

Cold eyes met his threat, the woman's cut lip and face freezing half of it so that there was no way to tell if she was smiling or not. But the dark, gleeful amusement in her eyes told Arthur she was.

"So, you ready to talk? Or are we going to have to kill to get my seniors free?"

Chapter 118

Silence filled the run-down bar, the slow breathing of the group and the pained grunts and whimpering of those still being held hostage the only sound. Arthur noted more shadows filtering in from the backdoor, his Enhanced Eyesight allowing him to pick them out without an issue. Uswah would have been even better in here, he thought idly, then dismissed it.

Not the time for shoulda, woulda, coulda.

"You've got guts," Kim, the tiny mob boss with the scarred and sneering face said. "But then, they said as much."

"They?" Arthur asked, though he had a guess.

"Suey Ying downstairs. You got a price on your head, you know. It's a rather pretty face too," Kim said, idly. She released the cup, tracing a line across her cheek where the scar was. "Shame to mess it up."

"That's not a problem, I heal well." Arthur inclined his head to where a tickle of blood was running down where Eric's blade pressed into a man's neck from underneath. "Can't say the same for the rest of your people."

"We heard." She smirked. "Clan seal, right?"

"Yes. One of the perks," Arthur said. A weird side-discussion, but he wasn't going to lead them away. She might be buying time to position more of her people, but at this point, he figured she'd have enough to drown them in bodies anyway. So better to see where they were going, especially since he really did just want to talk. "There's a few more too."

"Oh? More than healing?"

"Allies for one thing," Arthur said, smiling slightly. "People like the Chins. Or the 66. You might have heard."

"Or the Thorned Lotuses."

"Yes."

"You didn't mention," Kim said. "You ashamed working with girls?"

"Heh. You should see my party." He shrugged. "More they aren't that many here."

Silence then, as Kim stared at him. He met her gaze fearlessly, their standoff broken moments later as Scarry shifted a little and Mel shoved down hard to hold him in place, causing him to whimper. Kim looked at him, then at the other man standing on his tiptoes trying to get away from the knife pressed against his neck and, finally, towards Arthur's hand on the back of the chair. The one he'd concentrated the Refined Exploding Energy Dart on, though it should have been invisible. Unless she had a technique...

"Okay, *lah*. Let's talk." She gestured at the two being held captive. "Let them go. We talk."

"After you call off your others," Arthur said, immediately.

Eyes narrowed in thought, before she nodded to the whistle guy. He blew a series of short notes and once again there was a commotion. Arthur noted that the shadows in the backdoor didn't disappear, but he relaxed and nodded for the two captives to be released when Rick, returning from checking the front door, gave a thumbs up.

Some compromises had to be made after all.

"Sit," Kim said, when her people had been released. "Let's talk."

Arthur took his seat, pushing back a little so he had enough space to move if needed. Kim watched all this with bland interest before raising a hand and waving at the bartender. He brought over a mug of alcohol, that same fermented drink that made Arthur's eyes water just being close to it.

"So. How much?" Arthur said.

"You can't just waltz in, ask for them, and then act get away with it, you know," Kim said. "You're making trouble for me."

"Yeah, it's a problem," Arthur said. "I tried to make this easy."

"This is easy?"

"It is for me," Arthur said. He gestured backwards to his friends. "You might have realised, we weren't exactly being trained to be diplomats."

"Good fighters though."

"Yes." Arthur tapped the side of the mug before him. "So, what's it going to take?"

Kim leaned back and turned her head from side to side, taking in the rest of the Suey Ying members. More than a few looked upset at his group, a few ready to start the fight again. Arthur could not blame them; he felt it too, the agitation that came from the flood of adrenaline. It hit guys worse than women, at least at the start. Women adrenalized slower than men, took longer to dump out. It was why, partly at least, that Kim hadn't moved, being able to think rather than just act.

Also why she was keeping her hands on the mug now, as the excess adrenaline looked for a place to exit. Arthur was feeling it a little too, though only a trickle. Too many damn years fighting in the sparring rings, regulating his breathing, regulating his emotions and then, on top of all that, the Yin Body. He only really adrenalised and got on when things went bad.

And this was far from bad.

"Your healing technique," she said, eventually, surprising him.

"Pardon?" Arthur said.

"You give us a copy of your healing technique."

"Shiiiit." Arthur ended up inclining his head. "Good call." While it was a single technique, they could pass it on to their members if he handed it to them in a physical format like. Arthur paused; it was well worth giving up two good leg-breakers. Even ones trained by his sifu.

"Then, you'll give it to me?" Kim said.

"I can get you a copy, single use."

"No go. A physical copy, handed to me."

"We can..." Arthur said, then leaned forward. "However, do you know how the healing gets passed through my clan? How it works?"

"Spit it out."

"So, here's the thing. I have a technique that's available for me. That passes on to the clan. They get a lower-powered version," he summarised. "And my version? Not as great as you might think. Decent, but I can't replace missing limbs. Just heal things. Can't fix scars. Or eyes." Leaned forward and tapped his left foot which was still missing a portion of it, healed over and scabbed though it might be. It still messed with his movement a little, forced him to stuff a bit of padding into his new boots. Unenchanted boots, which sucked.

"So?" Kim said, eyes narrowed.

"I'm guessing you want a little more than just the basic version," Arthur said, glancing at her scars. "I'm not there yet, though. Not even for me." He turned his head a little, so that he could take in his group before he continued. "Not for them, for sure."

Kim's lips compressed. "You just don't want to share."

"I don't," Arthur said. "Because you might not be happy with what you get. So, I'll make you an offer. One of the healing techniques, at the level I have." He raised a finger. "Or the technique my people have. which is low grade, but still better than nothing. But in that case, I want one more thing."

"What?"

"You."

Kim frowned. " You want me join your clan?"

"Exactly." He gestured around the room. "And anyone who wants in."

"Why?"

"Because you're running this group without a problem." Arthur shook his head. "That can't be easy in any way. You're tough, smart, and you think well." A slight hesitation, then he added, "Also, I'm assuming you'll stick around, till I can get your eye healed."

Kim froze, then said, slowly, "Can you?"

"I believe so," Arthur replied. "Wouldn't have suggested it otherwise. I intend to keep pushing myself, advancing in this technique. And anything I learn, it goes back to my clan members." He hesitated, then added, truthfully. "Won't be fast, though. This might be years."

A hand touched her face, the scar rather than her eye. Arthur knew she was thinking about it. Passing the rest of the Tower without full vision was hard and likely half the reason she still stuck around here. As much as the Tower might help with the strength differentiation between men and women, there were still innate advantages to men being bigger or stronger. A hand came down, as she looked around, the naked longing having faded away as she remembered where she was. More than a few of her men were looking at her warily, though surprisingly Scarry Boy looked happy for her.

"So?"

"I bring some of my people," she said, firmly, glancing sideways at Scarry.

"No problem." Arthur paused, then added, "But you swear to play nice and for me. And I'll be picking your second in charge." She hesitated, then nodded. Arthur stood up, offering his hand to her. "Then we have a deal."

She stood up too, looking at him over the table and leaning forwards a little so that she could take his hand. He had to lean over too, what with the height difference. "When you deliver the technique," she said firmly.

"Of course." He released her hand, stepped back and then waved the team with him. They exited, carefully, picking up their weapons on the way out. It was only when they were a few streets down that Arthur found himself laughing, just a little. Mostly from giddy relief, because things could really have gone to hell there.

Sometimes, it was just better to be lucky than good.

Chapter 119

Arthur had to give it to Mel. She knew when to keep quiet, when to hold back. She did so, until they were back in the inn. Then she let loose.

"Are you insane?" she snapped, waving a finger at Arthur. "You just offered a technique and the leadership of this floor to someone you barely know!"

"I know. I was there," Arthur said, unable to stop himself from sassing her.

"Then why would you do that?" Mel said. "Without asking me?"

"Didn't have time," Arthur said. "You might have noticed they were willing to throw down. Also, could you pull your finger out of my face?"

Mel growled but she slowly lowered her finger. "And going in there! I told you it was a bad idea. That you couldn't just negotiate your friends out."

"Except, I did, didn't I?" Then, before she blew up, he added quickly, "It was a little rougher than I expected, but no worse than talking to a group of grumpy dock workers who've been waiting two hours for their food."

"And what were you going to do, if they did decide to fight? Watch us die?"

"Maybe." Arthur smiled grimly. "If that's what it took to get my seniors out. And to teach them we aren't to be fucked with."

"So we're not as important as your seniors, are we?" A flicker of hurt, of pain, as she stepped back. "I guess you're going to change one of them to be your second in command now? Replace your bodyguards?"

"No." Arthur stopped, noted how weak he had sounded and firmed his voice. "No. Nothing like that. I trust you guys too, but I can't leave them in the Suey Ying's hands." He shook his head. "Knowing they're my seniors, would Kim ever let them go? Make them a weapon against me, more like. We had to win. One way or the other."

"And Kim?" Mel said.

"She's smart. Strong. Able to keep cool. And we've got something she wants." Arthur said, noting her temper had cooled a little. He waved her to the bed, saw the glare she shot him, and shrugged as he went over and flopped down. Not as though they had much space to talk in here. Mel moved to the opposite side, to lean against the table. "And we'll have someone to watch over her."

"Someone?" Wry twist of the lips. "You mean, someone you want me to find."

"If there's a Thorned Lotus here, yeah." He rubbed his face. "Preferably not someone from the previous floors, eh?"

Mel grimaced, rubbing at her side absently. She'd only arrived a day before, limping from a bad fall. She'd taken a little longer than the other team members to arrive. At least she hadn't fallen to her death and, in the end, she'd been able to make it through with a lot more stones than Arthur. But she was still feeling the effects of her trip.

"You…" Mel shook her head. "If you're wrong…"

"I'm wrong." He opened his hands sideways. "What does she get? A movement technique in place of what she knows? Access to this floor perhaps?" He shrugged. "The Suey Ying are a gang, not a full triad. They break up and come together more, and leaving might have her with separate loyalties, but that can work in our favour too."

"Why?"

"Because we can't keep fighting them. And they're strong on this floor, if you hadn't realised it." He grimaced. "So long as we don't get too deep in with them, we could use them to help protect our interests. Maybe even make overtures to settle things better." He paused, then added, "It's a risk, but we're moving too fast to build anything for sure. Everything's a risk."

"And what if they decide to slip their people in? Try to take over that way?"

"Then, they do. Better than them attacking our clan on this floor, killing everyone and putting an end to our people before they can move ahead." He waved a hand around. "This is the perfect place to create a chokepoint."

"The *polis*…" Mel started, though even she sounded doubtful.

"Are useless. They'll stop them at the portal but elsewhere?" Arthur shook his head. "Better to see if we can get them to work for us."

"So you'll try to get Kim on our side?"

"So I try for the girl and get her on my side, fully."

"We'll need someone we can trust to watch her. Send messages up." She considered. "Create a code."

"Should have one already."

"Yeah…"

Silence, then. Mel stood after a moment, staring directly at Arthur. "I don't like it. You should have asked, checked in with me. But I'll do my best to find you someone worthwhile. Just..."

"Yeah, we work with what we have." Arthur watched as she turned and headed out, speaking out just before she left. "Hey." When she turned around, he added, "I do trust you guys. And I'm grateful. For everything. Really."

She didn't turn around as she pulled the door open, only stopping as she was about to exit to add, "Then show it."

Then the door closed, leaving Arthur to stare after she had gone.

When trouble came, it did so in droves. Later that night, Lam appeared, interrupting Arthur's latest cultivation session. Tired and grumpy and just wanting a few more hours alone, Arthur threw the door open forcefully.

"What?"

"Ms. Chin is waiting. We're ready," Lam Kor said. He stepped clear to allow Arthur to come out, only to blink as Arthur stepped back in. "Eh?"

"Tell the others. We might as well move in tonight," Arthur said as he started packing up.

"I..."

"Go on." Arthur said, stomping a little on the floor. "This place is expensive. No reason to pay more." He hesitated, then added, "Also, I've been reminded that this place is a little more dangerous than I expected. And bodyguards would be good."

Lam disappeared soon after, knocking on doors as he searched for the group, figuring they were all located near one another. A pretty good estimation, outside of Mel, whose room was one floor up, as was Rick's. Not his problem. He'd figure it out soon enough.

In the meantime, Arthur threw his stuff together. Being on the move all the time meant that he had little enough to put together. After all, other than buying replacement straps and finding some new clothing, he'd lost little enough at the last platform run. A couple of replacement items, the extra set of clothing, some emergency rations, water bottles, a new bar of soap, toothbrush, toothpaste, and he was good to go.

After that, he just had to help Lam find the rest of the group, ignore the grumbles for those woken up by the big man, and leave notes for Rick and Mel, neither of which were in their rooms. He assumed they'd know where to find them anyway, even if he didn't leave notes, but better to be certain.

Ten minutes and they were moving, and Arthur kept a close eye for trouble. His seniors were still stuck with the Suey Ying, staying in the ramshackle room they'd rented until they were released. It worked for Arthur, since it'd give them a chance to suss out further recruits or potential problems. At least, he hoped.

"Casey," Arthur greeted the woman as he arrived at the administrative building, the tiny square in front pretty empty. Considering it was close to evening, he was a little surprised by that, having expected a steady stream of returnees finishing up quests. Not really his problem, he guessed. Once she nodded back to him, he also turned to the side and nodded to her cousin. "Damian."

"You get one building. And not a good one," Damian said, not even bothering with formalities. "We talked, and there are two you can choose from."

"Two?" Arthur opened his mouth, then shut it with a click. He could tell the other man was trying to get a rise. "Show me and we'll get out of your hair."

"You won't because..."

"Damian." Casey cut him off with a warning voice, stepping forwards. "I'll deal with it."

"You better." Then, pulling out a folded map, he showed it to Arthur, pointing to two locations. One in the north, one in the east, judging from the central teleportation platform and the map's own guide.

After that, assigning the building was a simple matter. Thankfully, they were built up enough that the Tower considered them actual buildings, unlike many of the ramshackle additions around. At some point, Arthur swore, he'd get around to upgrading all these places.

Sometime. Maybe the next Tower.

When it was done, Damian stomped out and left Casey and Arthur alone—well, except for everyone else in the administrative center.

"So, I guess you guys got it sorted out?" Arthur said, though he had suspicions there was more to it than that.

"I did. But, well, there's something I have to talk to you about," Casey said.

"Talk to me on the way," he said, with a resigned sigh. Sometimes, Arthur really hated that he was right all the time.

It was a damn burden, being so handsome and good.

Chapter 120

Arthur swept his gaze over the interior of the building, grunting a little as he proceeded to pull himself up the ladder to the second floor. Rather than bother with a staircase, the Chins had constructed the second and third floors to be accessed only by a retractable ladder. It allowed for a greater amount of space to be used, especially on the first floor that had much higher ceilings due to its former role as a warehouse for the Chins. The second floor, on the other hand, Arthur quickly confirmed was a multifunctional space meant for offices and sleeping quarters, while the top floor entirely dedicated to sleeping quarters.

"Not much in terms of bathing or bathroom facilities," Arthur said, shaking his head. One bathroom per floor was not enough considering how many occupants there might be. And even if they needed to defecate and relieve themselves much less often in the Tower—between the changes the body had undergone and the lack of need to eat—it still happened. And obviously, hands and whole bodies still needed to be washed.

"There's a bathing space down the street," Casey said when Arthur dropped down to the second floor where she'd waited. "Makes more sense for us to use that."

"Why? Because your Prime Group owns it, ah?" Yao Jing opined.

"And that means none of the Durians have to pay to use it," she reminded him, patiently. Lam glanced at Yao Jing, who shrugged in reply.

Yao Jing was leaning against the side of a corridor, watching them speak and keeping an eye as was his job as Arthur's bodyguard. So was Mel who was just outside the room she'd chosen to take as hers.

"Now, you going to tell me what the problem is?" Arthur said. Depositing his gear in the room he'd taken had been simple enough, though he was not a fan of the lack of stairs. Dragging his spear up and down the ladder, even if he had a convenient sling for it, was annoying in the extreme.

"We have to set aside a room for Damian and his people. A few rooms, actually," Casey said to begin with.

Arthur's gaze narrowed, as he deliberately looked around the area and then down towards where the ladder hole was. "Be good to know that before. Along with the change in our deal."

"You're not saying no?" Casey said, hesitantly.

"We're changing what you're paying me, and will be paying on the regular, but I've rented rooms before." He shook his head. "Though if we had a proper bottom floor, that'd make more sense."

She shrugged. "Did you really want to stay in the other place?" Of the pair of buildings offered, this was certainly the larger. The other could have housed more people, what with it basically looking like a budget hotel or hostel—and was at one time filled with poor cultivators who rented the space out from the Chins. But it lacked the storage and training space that this warehouse had with its larger bottom floor.

"No, I guess not." Arthur said. Bigger footprint made for a better clan building overall, even if the warehouse was on the edge of the northern platform. Made for easy storage too, which was the reason it had been built in the first place. "What else?"

Casey hesitated and he mentally congratulated himself on waiting to negotiate the new income stream. For one thing, he was almost a hundred percent certain that whatever else she had to say, he was not going to like it.

"Two more things." She offered a half-smile, then dropped it when Arthur just stared. "The first is, for the next five years, you sell excess materials only to us." As Arthur crossed his arms, looking very unhappy, she rushed on. "And you also have to support our push against TG Group."

"Firstly, not going to happen. I need to get a lot of contribution points fast. And that means finishing up quests," he said, firmly. "So that's not going to work."

"Actually, umm, Damian also wants to buy one of the sets of armour you were building," Casey said.

"You're kidding right?" He shook his head. "You must be kidding."

"I'm not." She paused, then added, "You could mark it up? It'd help a bit. And if you do that, he'd probably be fine letting you do quests till your contribution points are sorted. I know he wanted the armour sooner than later."

"Because he wants to fight TG Group."

"Yes."

"Wah!" Yao Jing said. "You guys think we're just hired thugs, eh?" Then, looking at Arthur, he added doubtfully. "We're not, are we?"

"No, we normally aren't. I don't see a good reason for getting into this for you." Arthur lips curled. "And I'm not seeing what kind of leverage you have to make us do it."

"We haven't given you the stones yet..." Casey said, then shook her head a moment later. "No. No, you'll get them. I'm not holding it hostage, just because…" She exhaled. "We made a deal. But if you don't help, he's going to be angry. He's going to make it harder for us, for you, when you come out."

"Me? You're the one agreeing to things in our name."

"I know!" she snapped. "But he is the owner—the manager—of this floor. I didn't think he'd…" Casey looked uncertain, then straightened. "I'm willing to compensate you, outside." Turning, she glanced at the room that Rick and Jan had disappeared into, adding slowly, "I know you have options, but you can't have enough allies out there. The outside world…"

"Is not here," Arthur said. "On the other hand, if I do what you say, I'm making enemies. Not exactly what I was hoping for."

"You already have, helping me."

"Not the same thing."

A single arched eyebrow and Arthur couldn't help but repeat himself. It wasn't, it really wasn't. But she wasn't wrong either, that by allying and helping her, he was in the bad graces of TG Group to some extent. On the other hand, actually attacking the other group was a whole different story.

"What exactly do you need us to do?" Mel said, cutting through the bullshit. "What are you guys going to do?"

Casey looked relieved the next moment. Turning to Mel, she said, "We're going to take over some of their buildings."

"I got to admit, that sounds bad. What are you going to do, if they don't agree?" Arthur said. "Beat them up?"

She nodded. "No deaths. But, yes. Thrash a few of their buildings and take over the other two bath houses."

"And then fight them when they try to push back."

"Yes."

"No." Arthur crossed his arms. "And that's a no for a few reasons. Including the fact that we won't be around long enough for you guys to properly hold those buildings. Unless you intend to kill someone while we're gone, they'll just take it over again." Casey didn't say anything, but Arthur frowned as he stared at her face. "Oh, shit. You know that, don't you? You're counting on it."

Silence, while Mel snorted. "You want him to fail. You're maneuvering to have him fail when we're gone."

No answer from Casey. Arthur sighed out loud, seeing the play. He stepped closer to her, anger filling his voice. "I told you, stop trying to drag us into your damn internal politics. This is the second time. There isn't going to be a third warning." Casey hesitated while Lam shifted, glaring at Arthur. The two had a decent relationship, but Arthur knew that if it came down to it, Lam would have no problem putting a dagger in his lungs. "He can have three rooms, for a monthly stipend." Arthur glanced around, trying to recall how much he had charged Rick earlier. "The rest isn't my problem." A slight pause, then he shrugged. "He can have the armour too, for a markup for sure."

Yao Jing didn't look happy at that, but he kept his mouth shut. Mel, on the other hand, looked approving.

As for Casey, she just nodded.

Which worried Arthur more than if she had protested, really.

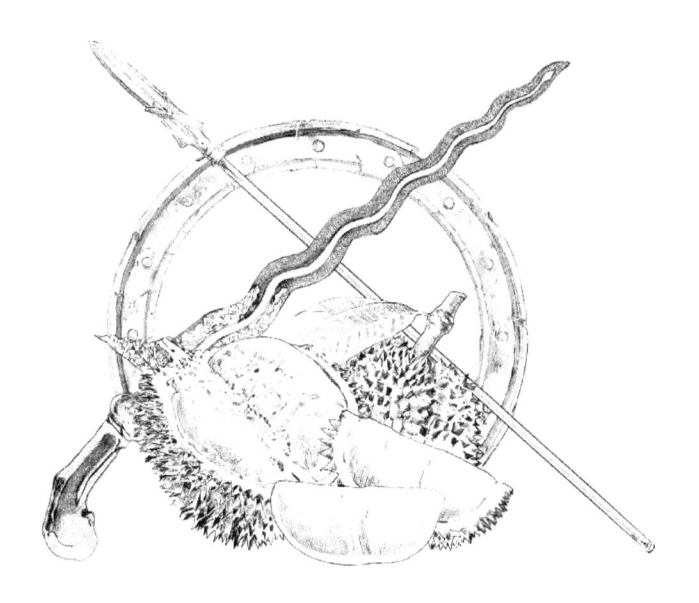

Chapter 121

Days later, Arthur and his team found themselves in the first stage of the platform they meant to explore. The goal, for today at least, was a moderate journey within, an exploration and testing of the murderous interior before they searched for the exit and the level's first teleportation platform. Of course, the team knew where it was—they had a map—but it was one thing to see an object marked on a map and another to find it while wading through deep jungle, pushing against ivy and vines and brambles. Only one who had never actually managed to make their way through a proper rainforest would mistake it for an easy task.

On the other hand, unlike most "normal" jungles, one of the major threats within was the wasp. It was a massive insect the length of Arthur's arm from head to tail. It was easier to hit than a swarm of its smaller counterparts, but it also meant, rather significantly, that it could—and did—sting much harder.

As Rick, stung in the arm and clutching the bleeding hole that was the entry point, was finding out at the moment. He was rolling about, mouth open in a rictus of pain but his voice and throat so strained that he could not even make a sound. Rather than scream, his entire body was locked in pain, and that was warning enough about the danger.

Standing right above him was Arthur, spear held carefully in guard as the buzzing wasp flew up and down, twisting and dodging the sweeping and cautious attacks the man swung at it. All around, in the dense undergrowth, the rest of the team fought their own attackers, with Mel and Jan ganging up on a single other wasp. Yao Jing was gripping his own attacker by the body, arching his body in a concave twist as he tried to avoid being stung by the twisted opponent. Uswah was missing, the scout either in a desperate battle of her own or unknowing of their trouble.

"Stop. Moving..." Arthur snarled, though softly. He was more worried about the thrashing man beneath him knocking him over. He was beginning to get a feel for the wasp's jerky movements and with a swing down, he watched the hornet duck sideways and up. With a cut again on the return, he caught it. Almost perfectly, slicing off a portion of the extra-large wings rather than the body, exactly as planned.

Spiralling, the hornet fell, angling itself almost to sting Arthur in the leg. Checking an automatic reflex to kick it away and potentially get stung Arthur pulled back and swept the butt of his spear upwards, striking the hornet away. It bounced off, its flight still erratic, falling into a nearby tree before it crashed.

Moving swiftly, Arthur struck once, plunging his spear into the creature's body and pinning it to the ground. A yank outwards and then another quick strike ended that threat, before he spun around to see who to help. Only to see his help was unnecessary, as Mel had finished her own attacker and Yao

Jing was pounding his wasp into the edge of the tree, repeatedly such that his fingers had managed to dig into the body of the creature. Then, with a twist and turn, he tore gobs of flesh out, wrecking body and wings. A few quick stomps afterwards ended the attack, even as Arthur turned to Rick.

"It hurts. It hurts…" Rick moaned, dark skin gleaming with sweat and arm clutched around the bleeding wound.

Trying to push the hand aside, Arthur cursed. "Let me look, damn it." He rocked backwards a bit on his ankles, then leaned forward and pinned Rick down with his knee against his stomach as he cursed. "Someone help me hold him down!"

Mel came over, helping Arthur hold Rick still as they worked to calm him. It took a while before they managed to pull his hand away and pin it down, allowing them to see the wound in its entirety. It continued to pulse blood, though slower now. More worrying were the black veins that spread along the wound, red and inflamed skin all around.

"Shit. Poison?" Arthur said, then shook his head. "Of course it is. Never mind… Is it lethal?"

"Yes! Please… I need… need… antidote," Rick blathered.

"No," Mel said, confirming what Arthur had remembered. "He'll be fine. Especially with our technique. He just has to heal it."

Arthur grunted, staring at the wound. "Should we try to suck it out?"

"What?" Mel said, confused.

"You know, in the movies. They always suck out the poison."

"Snake bites, not stings, and it doesn't work."

"Really?"

"Yes." She confirmed, shaking her head. "Don't accept everything from TV. Otherwise, you'd think Mexico is all yellow and all Muslims wear hijabs and kill non-believers, screaming about jihad every other sentence."

Arthur snorted at her description but had to agree. Malaysia itself was a Muslim-dominated nation, and while certain things were rather annoying—like the lack of porn which was one of the biggest underground markets, along with weed—it was, overall, relatively fine. They separated ruling for their people and for everyone else well enough, even if it did make certain deliveries tougher. If, somewhat more profitable.

"Alright, you heard the woman. Focus, Rick."

Instead, the East Indian just moaned and groaned, fighting against the pain that tore him apart. Arthur tried, for a few minutes, before he eventually gave up with a frustrated sigh and stood, looking around.

"We can't wait for him to get his act together. Volunteer to watch over him while the rest of us keep finding stones?" Arthur said.

No surprise that no one offered, and in the end, Arthur pointed at Yao Jing. "You're up."

"Eh, me?" Yao Jing said in surprise.

"Yes, you. You can carry him more easily," Arthur said. "If he doesn't get better."

The man frowned, but eventually nodded and with a wave to Uswah who'd just returned, the group moved on. It seemed at least their first encounter with the monsters on the fifth floor was less than stellar. Not surprising, of course, but the toxin in the sting seemed to be even more dangerous and painful than descriptions had led Arthur to believe. Or Rick was just a wimp. Either or.

Two more fights, including a close shave and save via a wrapping shadow tentacle by Uswah later, and the group ran into the next monster on the list. That was somewhat more amusing for Arthur, for the giant spider that dropped down led to a new realisation about one of his party members.

"Die, die, die!" Jan screamed, finishing with her stabbing at the spider that had dropped on its silk tendril onto her head. She'd battered it away, moments before it managed to inject her with a large trace of venom, and then proceeded to use her dagger to stab it to death while pinning it down with her other arm.

Effective, if noisy.

"Don't like spiders?" Arthur said, amused as he tore the monster core from his own dead spider before grabbing a flask. He milked the creature, pushing down on its fangs—the chelicerae—to extract the venom. It took a bit of work, though the extra large size of the creature helped in extracting a few decent drops.

"Don't like it near my mouth *lah*!" Jan snapped. "Especially surprised."

"Ah, that's probably for the best," Arthur said, keeping a straight face. "Also, try not to smash its head either, will you? You know we need the toxins for the quest."

"Sorry boss."

Arthur shrugged, handing the flask over to Mel who was waiting. He cleaned his hands on the ground, not daring to touch the various leaves around without a better idea of the plant types. Never know what might be poisonous. Mostly, it'd all be mild irritants, but even mild irritation could get very annoying very fast. So, the first rule of going through the jungle held. Don't touch anything you don't need to—and always watch what you grab.

"We good?" Arthur looked around, checking on the team before nodding. Time to move on. They had a lot more drops to grab before they were done.

Chapter 122

A day later, the group had returned to the warehouse-slash-headquarters. It was beginning to fill up, the earlier quiet broken up by new members. Unlike the previous few floors, acquiring the aid and buy-in of the Thorned Lotuses has been simple. It was only now that it was dawning upon Arthur why that might be.

"Those stings are a bastard and a half, aren't they?" Arthur said, staring at the still closing wound on his arm. Not only had it been painful, but the wound refused to close quickly. Only his growing resistance against poisons had kept him from curling up and crying like Rick. And even then, it had been a close thing.

"Looks like it," Mel said, trying to hide a smile. Only three of them had managed to get stung, Rick and Yao Jing making up the other two. Yao Jing had ended up literally walking into another nest, and only quick thinking had seen him survive by jumping into a nearby river. Rick was currently curled up in his room, downing pain killers and working through three stings. Yao Jing wasn't much better off with his two.

"So what can we do about it?" Arthur said.

"You could increase your resistance?" Uswah opined, a small smile on her lips.

"You mean get stung voluntarily and work through it." He could feel the way his technique was working on the poisons, flushing them out. Thanks to his recent experiences, he could sense the changes that happened and was working on weaving it through his body on an active level, trying to improve the technique's poison resistance and cleansing. Being able to split his conversation and wield the technique at the same time was making it harder, but he would have just been harvesting stones otherwise anyway.

"If it works..." Uswah said.

"No thank you," he chirped, brightly. He was pretty certain she was kidding, but in either case, no. "Other options?"

"There's an antidote that you can use. It's in a paste, you slap it on the wound." Mel mimed the motion. "I have a couple of applications."

"Then...?" Arthur said, trying not to resent the fact she only mentioned it now.

"It supposedly slows down healing," she said.

"Oh." Another frown, as he considered it. "So why use it?"

"Makes it less painful, which is what most people have issues with."

Arthur shook his head. "We'll keep it for backup, if necessary." Flexing his hand, he noted that the wound was finally closing, the black veins gone and the redness faded to just around the wound itself. "It isn't that bad, if you manage to flush the toxins out."

"That's at your level," Mel said, serious now. "It's taking Rick a while."

"He's not actively healing, though."

"Too painful."

"So we combine the two?" Arthur frowned, staring at the paste that Mel took out to let him stare at. Charcoal black, the paste looked like a mixture of plant and root matter and dirt, and it smelled worst. Arthur shifted away, trying to push away thoughts of rotting garbage as he waved for her to put it away. "Fine. I'll... try to get stung at least once a fight, or something. At the end..."

"Really?" Uswah said, surprised.

"Yeah..." Arthur sighed. He really did not want to do it. But, while painful, it wasn't worse than taking a liver shot or two or taking a proper kick to the gonads. In other words, bad and likely to drop him for a bit while he recalibrated to the agony, but he had done it before. Unlike Rick, he'd been hurt bad. Broken bones, crushed fingers, torn tendons. Being nearly gutted and gored and stabbed. But the Yin Body allowed him to regain control faster, and having experienced worst before, this was just... bad.

Each new high watermark of agony made everything else after it less. And whether that was a good thing or not just depended on your perspective.

"So. We headed out again tomorrow or...?" Mel said, tapping her small pouch. They'd all managed to get a half-dozen or so stones, which wasn't much. And the two injured were likely to be back to fighting fit, even if still injured, if they wanted to head out. A half-dozen stones wasn't enough other than for a day at best of cultivating.

"Give the stones to them—the injured—have them get cultivating tomorrow. We'll go out, keep sweeping the local area. Two more days, maybe three, get used to the place while we dig deeper and get more stones." Because even with the size of the perimeter, it was still true that there'd be monsters the deeper they went. "Then we cultivate and push in."

A slight hesitation from Mel made Arthur raise an eyebrow.

"I want to spend some time with the Thorned Lotuses," she said.

"Ex. But in a few days?" Arthur said.

"Cultivation time isn't time spent together." She frowned, then smiled. "I could go out with them?"

"Uhhh...." Arthur paused, then wanted to smack himself. That made a lot of sense. In fact, he almost wondered why he didn't do that before. No better way to get an idea of someone in a life or death situation.

Also a good way to get backstabbed. But...

"Can you send a few of them with me? We can split up: you go with them and we get two newbies. What do you think?"

Pursed lips, then Mel nodded. "Makes sense. They could probably give us some tips about this floor too."

"What I was thinking," Arthur said, then looked at Uswah. She shrugged, happy to accept the change and he nodded. "Then I guess we're a go." A pause, then he added. "Have them introduce themselves later today, eh?"

"Karen Raj," the woman who strode up to him stuck her hand out, forcing him to shake it. Arthur took it automatically, blinking at the direct and clear gaze in the older woman's face. At least forty years old, with a bob haircut parted in the middle, the Indian lady looked like she'd be better suited for a boardroom than wearing the scale and leather armour that clad her presently.

"Arthur Chua."

"I know." She stepped aside, nodding to the shorter woman behind her. "Devi. My daughter."

He didn't need that second descriptor, since the pair carried much the same bearing, nose, and eyes. The only difference being the daughter having a more fashionable hairstyle and red lipstick on.

"Good to meet you. How long have you guys been here?" He gestured around at the fifth floor, trying to gauge their strength. Hard to say, though the casual pressure of their grips told Arthur they had significant points in Body at the least.

"Just about a year and a half so far, I think." Karen smiled grimly. "We're taking it slow. Better to do it right, than rush, right?"

"Heh" was his reply. Uswah snorted behind while Arthur waved towards the exit. "Shall we just get going?"

"Of course." Karen straightened herself, tested the backpack she was carrying and then swept her gaze over the trio before giving a short, firm nod. "Let's go. We'll talk about what you're doing wrong once we're inside."

"Wrong?" Jan said, quiet till now. She had been looking up towards where she'd left Yao Jing but the casual insult had her paying attention bristling.

If Karen noticed, she did not seem to care. Striding out of the building, she left the group to rush after her. Arthur shook his head Well, he did ask for this. Better to learn now at least, rather than later, even if this was going to be *fun*.

Chapter 123

Arthur cursed, struggling to free himself from the spider net that had dropped over him, sticking to his body and holding him down. His movements only managed to get more of the sticky web to stick to him, the strength of the spider silk too great for even his enhanced body to break free, not without proper leverage. Cursing, Arthur could only drop his spear and try for his kris while watching the rest of his team fight.

He had gotten a little cocky, figuring the spiders were the easiest to handle. He should have known that none of the creatures of the fifth floor were actually easy. They had only run into the outlying scouts of the spider nests, dealing with the small groups that bordered the deeper layers of the jungle.

By themselves, a larger number would have been manageable. Expected even. What he had not realised was the combination of the acrid poisonous flowers that had acted upon them all, slowly poisoning the group. Not to damage them, or even cause injury, but to lower their inhibitions, to basically make him and the rest of the team feel drunk.

They'd lowered their guard then, and wandered right in.

And now...

"Fire is good, but a little painful," Karen was saying, holding a hand above her head. It caught against the strings of webs trying to fall across her, and a flash of fire rushed along the threads, burning them up and shriveling the air itself. She kept her head bent a little low, hiding from the flames before she took a fast step to the side and slammed the same, still-burning hand into the body of a spider as it dropped. The creature curled up reflexively, its plunge faltering, and bounced away from the fallen Jan. "You should consider getting Flaming Hand. Or Flaming Aura. Or Aura of Fire. Or something like that..."

Out of the corner of his eyes, Devi was ignoring her mother's prattlings as she ducked between falling nets, using a long stick that she'd been carrying around to smack them away before they struck. She reached the trapped Uswah, standing over the scout as she drew a pair of short swords—actual swords and not parangs—from her back and got ready to deal with a few scuttling spiders.

In the meantime, Arthur kept struggling, cutting at the web. It stuck to the blade, refusing to cut well, and he yelped when the same burning hand ran over him. She was not wrong that it was painful, for the silk burnt up fast, blistering his skin as it sparked and released him.

"You should keep some flame, or at the least, a Sparking Stick for when you get captured," Karen continued, casually grabbing hold of another spider that tried to swing itself at her. She held it by its body as it clamped its fangs on her arm, stopped by the metal bracers she wore on. She ignored struggling, dying spider. "Also, if you see the yellow flowers, you should watch out for the nest."

On his feet, spear still webbed, Arthur formed a Refined Exploding Energy Dart and launched it at the trio of spiders that were nearly on Jan. They were blasted aside even as the younger woman finally managed to tear herself free, her greater strength and boosted traits giving her the ability to do so, unlike Arthur.

Then, catching sight of a pair of scuttling spiders near his feet, he casually dodged them and struck with his kris as he bent down, slicing feet off with quick chops that left them writhing on the ground and unable to get to him. He spun around, took a quick step, and stabbed another spider attempting to escape and leaving it pinned with his kris. He almost pulled another Refined Energy Dart into being but realised that the team had things well in hand.

Especially as, he noted, Uswah was doing something to the webs. They kept darkening, twisting, and freezing before suddenly, they shattered as she pushed. Standing, the one-armed woman flicked her only hand outward, shadows reaching out of the ground from underneath the spiders and yanking them down. With a sickening crunch, two of the creatures lay writhing under the grip of the tightening shadow fists.

"Or you could do that...?" Karen for once seemed surprised. "That's... different."

"She's unique for sure," Arthur muttered, yanking his kris out. The burns on his body were slowly healing. Karen moved away to help Jan deal with the rest of the sticky webs on her, offering a flask of what smelled like strong alcohol to help dissolve the thread. The group fell silent, finishing the last of the spiders off before they raided the bodies.

When everyone was back together, Arthur could not help but ask, "Why didn't you warn us?"

"Would you have learned better that way?" Karen said.

"You're one of those," he said with a sigh.

"One of those?" An arched eyebrow met his accusation.

"Sadists."

"Hey!" Devi protested, but Karen just shook her head, silencing her daughter.

"Should we return? Should I stop?" Karen challenged Arthur, though her body language was not confrontational. Just firm. A fine line to tread, he noted.

"No..." Arthur laughed softly. "No, I'm good. I just like to know what I'm in for." He rubbed at his neck where red blisters were already beginning to form and shrugged. "Let's go. I'm curious to see what else you have to offer."

As it turned out, the answer was a lot. Not only did Karen and Devi have a great deal of experience and knowledge of the terrain, leading the group to fight and deal with multiple monsters in quick succession, but she also understood the biology and ecology of the jungle. She pointed out various herbs and plants that were often put up for quests, allowing the group to quickly collect them and add to their earnings that day. In addition, she introduced them to various smaller monsters that were not listed on the wiki.

"Gah. You'd think they'd mention there were leeches here too," Arthur complained as he waited for her to burn off the latest one gripping his calf.

The thing was about the size of his hand, having fed on his blood for the last few minutes until its presence had been pointed out by Jan.

"Not magical, though" Karen said, watching the leech fall to the ground as it tried to escape the burning hand. She killed it by stepping on the monster, sending a squirt of blood to splash outwards and making Arthur grimace. "No stone."

"Still, that's disgusting..." Arthur grumbled, staring at his still-bleeding leg. "Also, won't they make me—

or anyone they eat—a mark for the roaming boss?"

"The Lemur?" Karen nodded. "On other levels, yes. It doesn't come down here often, though."

"Often," Arthur said, grimacing. He'd stop bleeding soon enough; his healing technique was already working on the anti-coagulant in the leech's bite. At the least, this damn floor was going to give his healing techniques quite the workout.

"Nothing's ever for certain. Now stop complaining." Jerking her head, she led them down the deer trail she'd found, heading back.

The sun was already setting, the group having been out longer than the previous days. With an actual guide, Arthur was willing to stick around longer to increase their returns over the next few days. Getting lost and having to spend the night in the forest, while potentially quite lucrative, was less than desirable.

Eventually, though, they'd have to get to it.

In the meantime, as Karen continued to explain her thinking, Arthur watched her. Deeper considerations passing through.

He did, after all, need a second-in-command on this floor.

Chapter 124

Arthur leaned back, days later, cups of alcohol before him. He stared at Karen—the woman alone for once, her daughter having managed to sneak away to hang out with others more her age—while Arthur asked his question. He had received word just this evening that Boss Kim from the fourth floor was finally ready to join him, along with some of her people, and that meant he had run out of time to ask his question.

"Why me?" Karen said, eyes fixed on his without fear.

"Why not you?" Arthur smirked, then cut her off before she could protest the non-answer. "You're smart. You train well, even if a little sadistically, and you have reason to stick around for a little while longer. You aren't in a rush at the least and you don't back down."

"You barely know me."

"More than I do your boss."

"That's not a selling point."

"Needs must."

Again, Karen shook her head. "This is a slipshod organisation. You'll introduce a lot of spies, a lot of slackers and individuals intent on nothing but their own good."

"I know." He nodded at her. "That's why you're in charge of helping." He opened his hand, gesturing around. "Someone who has managed to come this far but doesn't offer us much?" He shrugged. "Well, you'll be able to take care of them." Then, Arthur hesitated before adding, "After this, on the sixth floor and maybe even seventh… I don't know how many others I might find that are appropriate. Might not even leave anyone in charge on the sixth. Seventh might be... viable."

"Depending on who?"

"Exactly." The seventh floor had the most numbers, being a rest floor and having a place much like the fifth where individuals could gather. If anything, it was even more peaceful—at least from monsters—since the extended area around the portal stone on the fifth floor still received waves of monsters as the fifth floor attempted to recapture its original starting area. On the other hand, the fact stood that the Thorned Lotuses had never been a powerful group, and its members who managed to make their way up did so by virtue of luck or determination, alone without much aid.

Who he might find on the seventh floor was entirely unknown. Even the sixth floor would likely have few options for him to build a clan hall, so it was best for him to confirm what he could here. Which meant Karen.

"Look, it's not great. I know that, you know that. But none of the clans were great in the beginning. It's why so many of them fail or never really rise far." He shrugged. "The way the Towers are built, it makes it hard. But later on, if we grow enough, fast enough, I'll have more controls."

"A shaky foundation."

"Do you want the job or not?" Arthur said, suddenly fed up. "I promised her this floor, nothing else. You on the other hand…" He shrugged. "Well, you have options."

Karen sat back, fingers drumming against the table as she kept one arm extended. The knock-knock-knock of acrylic nails on wood made Arthur grit his teeth but he knew better than to interrupt her thoughts. He did wonder, idly, how she even managed to keep those nails. Not like you wouldn't break nails at some point. Or even outgrow those you arrived in.

So did she take them off before she went out? Because he was certain he would have noticed acrylic nails on their trips otherwise. If so, how? Didn't they glue it or something? Idle thoughts, to fill the time as he waited for an answer.

"Fine. I'll take it. But I've got some suggestions and some requirements," Karen said, leaning forwards. "Let's start with your bookkeeping system."

Arthur's eyes widened, alarmed at the change of topic. He looked around, spotting Mel and pointing at her. Then, he switched, turning the finger point to a gesture for Mel to sit down. He could ask her to deal with this, to discuss numbers and rules and other aspects of putting together—and keeping together—a clan. But that kind of attitude was how you could get backstabbed.

"Mel has been keeping the books and she's my second-in-command. So we should have this talk with her here," Arthur explained, leaning back in his seat a little more as he glanced around. "We're going to have to be short though, because we've got a lot of cultivating to do."

"I'll be brief." Karen said. "But this has to be done."

Done indeed. Rubbing his head later that evening, Arthur wondered why it hurt as much—if not more—to deal with such administrative things than pouring pure energy through one's veins. Meridians. Same thing in some was entirely different in others. Outside, multiple governments had attempted to ascertain exactly what these meridians were, tapping into age-old knowledge and running numerous tests. Some a little less ethical than others.

He knew that every other month or so, new announcements came along, decrying the sudden explosion of knowledge that a particular study had arrived at. Some new shocking revelation. Almost always followed by a new scam purporting to help individuals toughen meridians or make them cleaner or shinier or something.

It reminded Arthur of the diet craze, when nutrition information—always more nuanced than the journalists' take on the results—would flood the airwaves. All followed by fitness gurus and the latest health craze, such that true information about cultivation and meridians and the actual data was hard to find.

Arthur could not help but wonder if business information was like that. Certainly not as much about Guilds or Clans since the creation of those were half luck and half planned circumstance. But, if Karen was to be believed, it shared many of the same traits. Though why she thought a robust harassment policy was required seemed amiss even now. After all, women still consisted of the majority of his members. Surely they could handle things themselves?

Or was that sexist and patriarchal? After all, men could be harassed.

Either way, she had, eventually agreed to work with them. She would be the second in command, keeping the Gui Hin Kim in check till someone else of equal strength could come along. Then she'd move up, doing the same for the sixth or seventh floors as necessary. In time, Amah Si would send up others from the first floor, reinforcing whatever was done and fixing problems on the floors in between as well.

Energy from the monster core pouring into him, Arthur turned his mind to his other problem. Casey had grown quiet, only going so far as to deposit a pouch of beast stones for him to utilise as part of their agreement. He knew she was fighting her own battles, and it might still impact him. He hoped not, but her cousin had looked less than happy the last time Arthur had seen him.

Worse, though, was that Arthur had a feeling the problems that might occur would happen afterwards. When he had left the Tower, when he was at his weakest. Not physically, of course, but in terms of allies and infrastructure. The Chins and Prime Group, the other organisations and the triads, all had ways of passing on news.

By this point, it would not surprise him if they had gotten news all the way outside. What he might face, when he exited, was a little concerning. His family or his sifu taken hostage? Obligations and debts taken out on his name perhaps. Or, just as bad, individuals and corporations and guilds and clans getting ready to bully him into alliances.

Perhaps not getting more involved with the Chins was a strategic mistake. Getting Casey further on his side might have given him some protection. Or tied him further.

He had no way of knowing, but the pressure of time and crises outside of his control pressed upon him.

Damn it all and back.

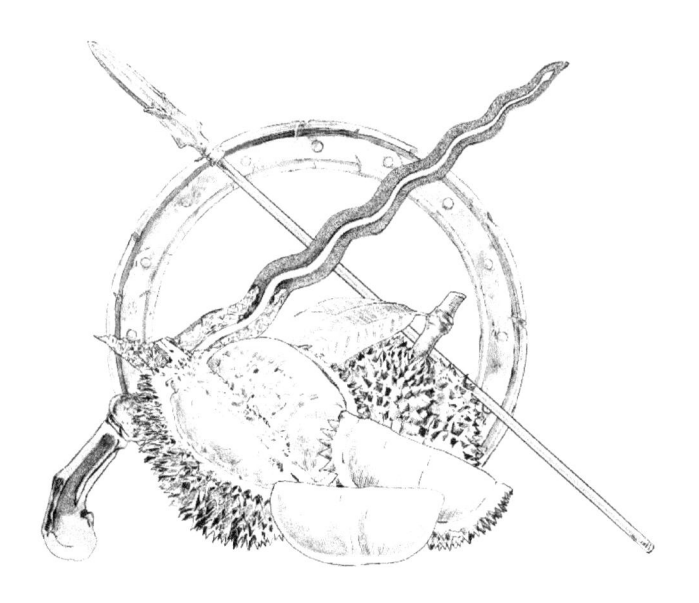

Chapter 125

"Biggest spider I've ever seen," Yao Jing said, the spear he was using for this battle held casually in his hands. The big muscular man knew his job. After all, they had discussed what needed to be done days ago when they started this expedition, but facing their foe in the flesh, so to say, was another thing entirely.

If nothing else, the fact that they would have to make their way through the webbed undergrowth to get anywhere close to harming the spider was telling. If not for the fact that previous groups had undertaken some of the necessary preparations, he might even have chosen to run away.

"It is," Arthur said, looking at the sprawl of webs that lay between the shattered stumps, the fallen logs and that reached upwards to the cocooned bodies of fallen climbers, and other foodstuff propped around to offer additional cover in the solitary grove where the spider lay. Beyond, at the end of a slope was the ritual site where individuals could collect the mark that would allow them to teleport home.

This area had returned to its default state. That meant a lot of webs and the lurking platform boss in the center of the grove. Previous attempts had seen that grove cut down, but that had resulted in the Tower simply reproducing the trees everywhere. As such, the teams had worked out a rough spacing that did not trigger the Tower and then cleared that area. Leaving the spider only this grove to rest its truck-sized body. American-sized truck.

You'd think that, with the general ban and high prices for gasoline and diesel, Americans would have shrunk the size of their vehicles. If nothing else, due to how much it decreased the distance electric vehicle range. Instead, they'd demanded for large, if not larger, trucks and that their corporations fix the charging problem.

And, credit due where it was gained, the companies had capitulated to both demands. Now, the world made do with more efficient batteries all over, even if the majority of those sold were from stolen and improved tech being made in low-cost countries in Africa and the Indian sub-continent.

"Oi. Ready or not?" Jan asked, hefting the pair of torches she held higher. Standing a distance to the right, she was one of two people in charge of starting the blaze. The other, of course, was Karen with her flaming hand on the other side.

"Let's do this," Arthur said. He could have started the attack by blasting the spider, but previous attempts at finishing the battle at range had almost always ended in failure. The creature was smart enough to hide behind webs and move rock or stone in the way or, worst case scenario, add additional webs.

In the end, it always came down to this.

The flames raced along dry spider web, catching against the edges, warming his face. He winced a little at the heat, swearing he could feel the sweat and moisture in his skin wicking away. The fire plunged deeper, reaching for fuel with its grubby little hands and coming across more tendrils of spider silk. Flames raced across the webs, burning merrily as Jan set fire to those nearby and then tossed her torches aside.

Together, the group stepped back, watching. At first the spider boss waited, as though it hoped the flames would go out. Then, it acted, loosing webs from its behind, spinnerets working overtime to coat the land. They doused some flames upon contact, but caught fire moments later.

"It's coming." Arthur spoke, softly. Energy coursed through him, the Heavenly Sage's Mischief giving him strength for when it was needed. A trickle of power gathered not at his hand but at his third eye. He had shifted the spot of the Refined Exploding Energy Dart once again to his forehead, confident now that his experimentation was stable. Bad enough, to lose a hand. He wasn't about to lose his head if he was jostled wrongly.

"Loose!" Mel barked out, and slings rotating at speed released. Stones arced through the air, even as they were replaced. They struck, hard, powered by the full strength of the climbers and shattering skin and bark. One hit so hard, the tree itself exploded, portions falling and only to be caught as webs pulled tight, holding them aloft.

No scream, for the spider had not a voice box. Instead, it moved, crossing the flames, crossing the ground between them. At the last moment, before it plunged deep into the box, it spun around and released a large net. Arthur looked up as the arc of web flew overhead, striking a tree, and then tugged tight.

And suddenly, a giant spider was flying through the air, the web pulled tight as a creature the size of an SUV was yanked forwards. Through and over flames, tiny hairs on its body crisping.

Mel, acting fast, and Jan—having finally gotten her sling working—released their stones. Mel missed, but Jan's stone cracked a spider leg, forcing it to dangle wildly.

Then, no more time for such things, as the spider was falling down among them, behind their lines. Rick stumbled backwards, the sawed-off shotgun he had pulled out for this particular exchange letting out a single bark, a loud thump that saw the slug tear a hole deep in the creature. It shrieked, but such was its size that the shot was insufficient to kill it.

Or perhaps it was a mortal wound, but one that would take a while. It mattered not, as the spinning grey-black spider with white feet and eyes and tendrils caught Rick in the side, sending him tumbling through the air.

Yao Jing was next, jumping through the air, spear slamming into the twisting body, sliding downwards as the spear plunged deep within the body. It caught, his body jerking to a stop moments later. He struggled, forcing himself upwards, legs scrambling to find purchase as he hung from the spear dug deep within.

Karen and her daughter, ducking in now, their paired swords slicing fast and thick, cutting at legs and deflecting attacks. Those legs were thick, protected at the bottom half against easy damage, easily able to pierce body and armour if caught unawares. The pair battled, even as the spider spun, loosing web to catch and grab, no flames in play. Not unless they wanted to get caught in the flames themselves, and no one wanted that.

Least of all Arthur. He came in fast, unable to catch a moment to unleash his own ranged attack. Not daring to fire into the melee and accidentally hit Yao Jing or the girls. Instead, he moved fast with his spinning spear, slicing a leg off with the empowered attack. Slipped under, stabbing upwards and popping his spear head through a joint and driving it further through.

No boar spear this, no cross-guard to stop the spear from sliding upwards, to kill. He had no chance at a one-hit kill, but it didn't matter. It wasn't what he was going for anyway. He knew not the anatomy of the spider, not well enough to end it with a single strike.

This was a battle of attrition then, and so he shoved harder, staying in motion with the creature. Timed it so that he ducked low, crab-walking for a moment as he yanked the kris out and stabbed. Keep moving the blade upwards as he cut, and cut, and cut into the softer underbelly.

Watching, sensing the kris' curse drive deep into the creature. A twisting movement and the spider was gone, and he was struck himself, losing grip of his weapon as lancing pain ran across his back and shoulder. He rolled aside, coming up and panting desperately. He wondered if perhaps leaving both his weapons behind was a bad idea.

Only to see the kris float upwards on a tendril of shadow and plunge forwards, flung ahead by a shadowed arm as Uswah came alongside him, hand held outwards as she controlled the shadows.

"Showoff..." Arthur grumbled. The creature was fleeing, Yao Jing on the forest floor, knocked off when the spider escaped. As it scrambled upwards, feet on groaning trees, he focused.

Released.

The Refined Exploding Energy Dart missed it, by mere feet. Close enough to send splatters of bark and sap into its face. But as it kept going, the already-straining tree broke, shattered under the weight. The boss spider fell, only to catch itself with its web. It held, for a moment, before wood snapped again, the creature plunging the rest of the way down.

Only for it to be intercepted. Mel, Karen, Jan, and even Rick and Yao Jing rushed in, weapons held aloft. They swung and blood splashed the air. A leg went first, and then another, the end of the spider damaged and gummed up. The creature fought and attempted to flee, but the kris' poison was slowing it. Marginally at first, but that was all that was needed.

All that was required amongst warriors as great as these. Arthur smiled, as he trotted in after the group, snatching his kris from the shadow tendril as he passed it by and joined them. Ready to finish off a battle and then, afterwards, to acquire the first of their platform teleportation tokens.

First part of the fifth floor done. And only two more to handle.

Sometimes, it seemed, handling the humans in the Tower was as much, if not more trouble than these mere monsters.

Chapter 126

"Good to have you back," Arthur said to Casey.

She offered him a wan smile in reply, the entire party ready to teleport over to the next platform. He knew, as did she, that that feeling was not entirely unanimous. If nothing else, because she and Lam Kor had joined the rest of the scavengers, making use of the marker to get their own tokens while the boss was waiting to respawn.

He cared not. And he understood she had her own battles to fight, and the cut along one cheek and the disheveled appearance she had shown him last night was more than evidence enough of that to him. But not everyone, namely Yao Jing and Rick, were accepting of such things.

As for what Mel thought, she kept it close to her vest.

"Best to learn the dangers from your guide," Casey said at last. They were about to leave for the longer expedition to the second platform. Breaking their way through the first platform would be tough but not impossible.

There were even marked routes, though how dangerous those were depended on your status with the local gangs.

As always.

"The second platform should be interesting," Arthur said, nodding back at Boss Kim as she waved the group on. He kept pace effortlessly, letting his gaze shift around with studied ease. Not looking down more than once or twice, a flick of his gaze to check for footing before moving on.

That was the mistake they made, the novices to hiking. One reason his sifu had taken them out quite often, to walk and then beat them till they stopped looking down. Forcing them to keep their heads up, to watch for problems. Walking in the woods was different, for there were no paved paths, no flat and easy steps. Because of that, many looked down, more worried about falling on their faces than getting their face eaten by a falling spider or other monster.

Of course, by the fifth floor, those who failed to understand the dangers of such Tower floors were dead. Everyone had learnt to look up, through hard lessons or the kind words of others.

"When we came in, the most recent shift was just coming in, wasn't it?" Casey said. "We had a few detailed reports, but I'm still amazed. Lizard humanoids, giant salamanders, and those komodo dragon variants." She shuddered. "I looked up the human variants, you know. What they did."

"Eating people alive, poisoning and infecting everyone?" Arthur muttered. "Yeah, Kim says the Tower variants aren't much better. Other than the fire variant. That one just burns you when it bites, rather than infecting you. Unless you're really unlucky."

Arthur twitched as he heard the snap of a bowstring. The flicker of an arrow passing nearby, pinning a spider before they even neared it, caught his attention. Lam wandered over, jumping upwards lightly as he used a movement technique to reach the heights of the spider and yank the arrow out. He gripped a nearby branch with one hand as he finished dealing with the corpse and beast stone before dropping down, avoiding the webs with casual ease.

Waste not, want not, especially in the middle of a Tower.

"You both seem to have improved," Arthur said, casually. He could see traces of it, in the way she moved, in the way Lam moved. The pulse of energy that was sheathed in her body as she ducked back and forth, utilising movement techniques even as the team spread out to beat back the monsters around.

"I had time to train and cultivate," Casey said, easily. "Even practise a little." Again, his gaze slid to the wound on her face, the slight darkness appearing above her hip. A wound, not closed as yet. After all, she did not have his healing technique bolstering her Tower-upgraded recovery speed. "Did you?"

"My team's been working hard at it," Arthur confirmed. He tapped his pouch where a handful of stones still lay, remnants of the stones from the last expedition that he had not sold off or used in the meantime. "Though there's never enough time, as we all can chime, in."

A flicker of a gaze, a slight roll of her eyes. But she swiftly changed topics. "So, that woman that moved in... your new floor boss?"

"Yes. A new friend," Arthur nodded. "Same with the two who came with her." Which he did want with him, but his training-hall seniors already had their second-floor teleportation marker. No point in them coming along to get it again, not when they could spend time reinforcing themselves further.

"Your seniors," Casey corrected, mildly.

"Yes." He wondered how she'd learnt, not that he was trying to hide it much. Still, always good to know how far she'd penetrated the confidences, how fast she learnt things. He might not like playing politics, but he was learning.

"Surprising how good they are. Or so I hear." She cocked her head to the side. "Lots of hidden tigers, eh?"

Arthur snorted. "Not that hidden. My sifu has a website."

Casey laughed softly at the rejoinder and then paused to help him deal with the incoming hornets. The group fought fast and furiously but not at all worriedly. Dealing with such creatures was simple enough, even if Yao Jing was clutching at his arm, hissing in pain as he dealt with the sting. He was shuffled inwards, a paste bandage slapped on his arm before the group moved on.

They picked up the conversation, not long after.

"Former Tower climber?" she asked.

"No. Never." Arthur shook his head to punctuate the point. "Sifu hates the Towers. Thinks they're a distortion, a curse, upon us all. Thinks that it lets people ignore the now, the real world, instead of fixing it."

"But he trains you all."

"Yeah." Arthur grimaced. "Let's just say he's not happy about it." He didn't explain the agreement they all made to pass his sifu's final test before they tried for the Tower. Not just a variety of other skills they had to showcase, like hiking or camping, but the final fighting test. A *kumite*—free sparring—with weapons and facing his Master as the final opponent.

Luckily, he didn't make them have to beat him, just survive.

Old memories. Good ones too. Though…

"He understands what we have," Arthur said. "But we all promise to help out. Get jobs for those who don't make it, pay for the food and meals of the others."

"He could get sponsorships." Casey offered.

"With you?" Arthur shook his head. "You all have your own masters. Your own trainers. Sifu would never consider himself better than them. Or take their places. Anyway, he likes what he does."

She nodded again. Noted how he never actually named the man or the school itself. Cautious. A flicker of regret that she had while turned away. Neither one was directly looking at the other. Her attempts at drawing him close might have backfired, and she regretted it. A little.

Even if she wasn't sure she would have changed things. He kept adding complexity, new allies. If she didn't get him as a close ally before he exited, there was no guarantee he would be one after. And that kind of failing was one that she might not survive, when her grandfather looked into it.

Well, survive at least in terms of standing. Her own family wasn't actually going to kill her, unlike some of clan and guild families that had cropped up, from what she'd heard. Scary, really, how much some people took to the Towers. She was glad her family wasn't like that; they just tossed you aside if you failed them.

"I'm sorry, you know," she said eventually as the day started waning. They'd talked, about other things, inconsequential matters. A lot of complaining about accounting and numbers and logistics and her own pithy comments. A little light on details on his part, though she wondered if he knew how much of a picture he'd painted for her... But then they'd fallen silent. Fighting and keeping watch had a way of bringing even the most talkative to silence.

"What for?" Arthur asked.

"For trying to draw you in. But you have to know, it wasn't because..." She trailed off, shook her head. "I did, I do, need the help. And it wasn't just for me. He's going to cause trouble for you. Make it harder... His side of the family, they control the media companies. The sponsorships."

"I'll survive," Arthur said. "We'll survive. I can't... I won't start now. Too much rests on this, and I'll not get caught up in a proxy war." He sighed. "We might end up growing slower, but that's fine."

"Is it?" she asked. "You know who else will want you, right?"

"Everyone and their dog?"

"The government."

Arthur hesitated, looked over, and she turned her gaze to meet his. Serious, all too serious. She wondered if he had thought of it, and seeing his eyes, she thought he had. Fear, worry, dread. No surprise, that.

After all, no one wanted to deal with the government. Wanted to face the kind of pressures they could apply, when they wanted something. Entire corporations, families had disappeared or been forced apart.

If he had further thoughts, he kept them to himself. Just offered a nod. And in that way, the rest of the night passed.

Chapter 127

It took them just over two days to cross the first platform and reach the edge of the second, cutting through jungle and utilising some of the common paths that had been carved out. It wasn't much safer, but even the minor aid was enough to allow the group to speed up. It helped, of course, that in a few cases they even had paid for the access beforehand, such that the Double Sixes and the Ghee Hin on this floor weren't going to cause problems.

It did, of course, highlight the path they were going to take, but for the sake of expediency Arthur's group was willing to take the risk. Of course, they only made sure to make payment the moment they were leaving, taking along the simple chit that showcased payment to offer to the gang members when they came across them later.

For all their precautions, they actually missed Double Sixes entirely. Either the gang had taken time off, or the team's slipping on and off the marked trail had let avoid any encounters. But that choice was mostly to avoid trouble geography or to locate batches of herbs, roots, and the occasional monster nest—a choice that was dictated by Kim and the slowly developing map that Yao Jing had bought upon entering the fifth floor.

Still, they were here, before the ivy-filled wall that led to the second platform. No gentle slope, just a straight wall which made up the entirety of the second geographic change. It was not unsurprising, though annoying, for the group as they took to climbing. Arthur stayed at the bottom, watching over his team as did Rick.

"Contact!" Rick roared, pistol pointed upwards. He did not fire, though, for the forty or so feet between him and the movement in the bush was too far for him to hit. Even perfect aim did little for the minor variations that pistol movement might cause, especially with a barrel that short.

He would fire if needed, but first…

Arthur was bounding forward, leaping towards the wall and kicking upwards again and again. He used the ivy that was present to give him footholds to carry him up a few feet each time, till a foot struck wrong and he pushed off further than he could recover. Away from the wall but still travelling upwards, he conjured the first cloud, striking it and using his cloudy step to throw himself up again and towards the wall. He could have done this earlier, but uncertain of where the monsters might be, he had elected to wait till the team was higher up.

Or a monster appeared.

The second-floor platform's first monster poked its head over the edge, hands held above itself. Between its clawed fingers it clutched a large rock, the creature ready to toss it at the climbers. What it did not expect was the soaring Arthur, coming in hot to grip the wall with one hand and swing his long spear with the other.

A jerk, a twisting pressure, as the spearhead exited the creature's mouth. The lizard humanoid thrashed and died, its held stone landing on the ground even as Arthur hauled himself upwards with one last surge. Screams and hisses greeted his appearance. Four-foot-tall lizard monsters pelted him with the stones they had begun hauling over.

Shielding himself with a hunched shoulder and twisted body, he swung his weapon to launch a series of attacks. One after the other, Arthur battered and broke limbs, striking at the smaller creatures. He felt rocks strike him, but the creatures lacked the muscle mass to truly injure him.

No, the rocks were not the danger. The problem was...

There!

He leapt and twisted, utilising the cloud steps that had reappeared again and pivoted before he could be bitten by the komodo dragon pet owned by the lizards. In the air, he struck downwards and to the side, piercing the back of the creature's skull and plunging his spear within. He felt the cloud he had formed begin to dissipate and he threw himself away, leaving the wounded dragon to mis-strike at the crowd of lizards.

Another stone, striking his leg, caused him to stumble as he recovered his footing. Individually, the lizards were not strong, though their claws could leave infection and poison behind. However, it was their swarm tactics that they utilised right now that endangered him, the creatures abandoning their ranged attacks to approach.

"*Cepat lah!*" Arthur cried, encouraging his team to move faster. He was providing a distraction, but not all the lizards had come to attack him, leaving some still at the cliff edge tossing rocks. He could hear the curses and cries of pain echoing up from below, even as he sought to keep the monsters back.

However, spin though he might, the lizards were fast and they only required a brief moment to strike. Some were even willing to risk death to land their attacks, leaving Arthur's lower legs bleeding where the armour did not cover them properly. Knees, back of legs, along his buttocks...

Cursing the lack of full armour, and yet knowing he'd die of heatstroke if he had worn it, Arthur fought on. He spun his spear, cut and battered lizards, or kicked them away when he had no other choice. He never stopped moving, even if it was by a few feet each time, because stopping was death.

And then, finally, finally the rest of the team managed to make it up. The first to rise was Karen, body blazing with flames, her aura pouring off her for a moment. She could not contain it for long, the technique exploding outwards to sear and scare the lizards. Then, she sat there, panting, exhausted.

Vulnerable.

Only for her daughter and Mel to arrive moments later, one cursing at her singed hair. Both drew their weapons from their backs, working to guard the recovering Tower climber. They lunged forwards, and the screaming, hissing lizards attempted to take at least one of them down.

One even managed to slip between the two and sink fingers deep into a raised arm. Then Karen took it down, gripping scaled forearm and pushing needle-toothed mouth into the dirt before she pounded fist into the back of its head, again and again till it stopped moving.

Then the others. Yao Jing and Lam , rising up from different sections. Yao Jing shrugged off the creatures clambering over him, the bronzed skin of his technique protecting him briefly even as he cast the monsters onto the land below. He struck, not with his weapons but with his fists as he preferred, knuckle dusters cracking open skin and breaking bones beneath with each impactful strike.

More komodo dragons arrived, some breathing ice which caused Lam to slip, to scramble and flail on his back as he tried to clear the cliff face for his employer. He struck and kicked a few off, turtling and spinning on the ground until a komodo dragon lunged and he had to hold it off from biting, holding tight to its neck.

Arthur cursed, feeling the poison course through him. The damn needle-point nails couldn't deliver a lot of hurt, but they didn't need to when the poison constantly kept adding to it. It numbed the skin around the injuries which was great, but it also stopped him from clotting and, most of all, it made his movements slower.

Death by a thousand cuts, as they said. The numbness was not just in his feet, though it was making him stumble now. Arthur moved to put his back against a tree and give himself more security. His fingers struggled to hold on to his spear.

It was in his hands, in his lungs. Enough of it, and it would stop a person from being able to move, to breathe at all.

A bad death.

But then, the bark of a gun. More cries of pain, as Uswah and Jan arrived, the pair of women tearing through the monsters surrounding him. They fought hard, giving him a break, nearly decapitating one of them completely. Drove dozens of lizards away, sent them scrambling back to their forest.

The group, finally, victorious. And on the second platform at last.

Chapter 128

All around him, Arthur could feel his companions and teammates moving around. Setting up for the evening, sortieing into the surroundings to deal with threats and hunt down monsters. Setting up traps in a few cases, just in case some of the threats chose to try for their camp late at night. Getting tents and a small fire going.

He sensed Mel talking to the second group that had come up their way, drawn by the fire reflecting off cloudy skies and luring them in like flies to a trap. Except, of course, they were not about to kill anyone. Just give them good warning not to bother others, trade a few pointers, and maybe ask for a little gift for clearing the way.

Nothing at all questionable. Arthur could sense them all, but his eyes were closed as he split his mind across two different and difficult scenarios.

The first was the flow of energy coming from his clasped hands on the knees of his crossed legs as he sat in a meditative pose, as he drew refined energy from the monster core. Replenishing energy as he worked it through his meridians and shoved it into his core, building up the reserves there.

And the other, a drawing of such energy out. Gradually, because he was more focused on the use of the energy. Wielding the refined energy to his own purposes, in combating the inflammation and deadness in his limbs, the poison that had swept through his body and was trying to stop his breathing.

Not that it was that bad—he hadn't been injected with enough venom that it was impossible to breathe. Just hard. The natural healing functions of the Tower and of his Accelerated Healing technique were working in his favor; removing the poisons. However, it was in fact working against Arthur's own desires. Because what it was doing was forcing him to try to keep up, to solve the issue and increase the technique's effectiveness against poisons and toxins by altering the flow of the technique itself.

He could see what was happening, and a study in basic biology had helped. Blood pumped and carried the poison through his body, where the chemicals leached into his cells and sat there, unwilling to separate themselves. Causing trouble with each breath, each heartbeat. Further down, deeper within his body, the liver and kidneys worked, breaking down the poisons, cleansing them from the body. Only a small portion at a time, normally.

Normally.

He could feel the technique bolstering the energy, washing the toxins away. Could feel his heart, beating faster than normal, washing blood over and over again in the infected area, trying to extract and dilute the poisons even as it dragged them to other portions of his body. He could feel cells and chemicals and Tower energy warring against the foreign chemicals, breaking them down in the parts they infected.

Moment by moment, refined energy and natural Tower energy were working together to heal him. He understood now why the healing technique needed refined energy in an active mode, whereas it subsisted on Tower energy every other moment. In the passive mode, in the background, it just made his altered body's method of healing more effective. Opening up channels, increasing the flow and refinement of the energy that his modified body managed.

On an active level, however, the refined energy pounded through his veins and arteries and meridians, pouring through his body and soaking in. It was like the turbo-charged version of plain Tower energy, throwing his body into overdrive in its haste to heal things. Patching and regenerating without careful co-ordination or consideration of what actually needed renewal.

Each level of upgrade, thus far, had him refining this use of energy. Fixing it, by altering the amount of energy required, improving the overall process. This time around, though, he was trying something different, something he had a feeling was an entirely different step.

He was guiding the movement of energy on a minute level. Not just shoving it into a hand or arm or a general wounded area and then letting the background processes of the technique work, letting his body close cuts and scab over before skin and scars formed. No, what he did now was the equivalent of attempting to redirect the energy on a tiny level, to pull at the portions of his body that worked best at clearing out these toxins, the entirely unnatural healing processes of the Tower energy and amping those up.

It was difficult. Kind of like threading a needle, except you were doing it with gloves on and at full hands-length distance. While watching yourself through a mirror.

Which made it all the crazier that he was doing it with only half his mind. But he had picked up all these traits, not just the ability to split his mind, but also Sticky Energy, Fast Learner, all of the various methods to speed up how fast he learnt. He would be damned if he didn't make the most of it, even if slipping occasionally meant he stabbed himself in the finger with the needle and did the spiritual and physical equivalent of pricking himself with a dagger. A very thin and sharp dagger.

That was, of course, the reason why he was shirtless and sweating. Not just sweat or the various toxins that made the air around him curdle, but also because of the occasional upwelling of blood. It hurt, but the advantage of a poison that dulled one's senses, especially bodily senses, was that it made for a very, very good painkiller.

Better even than morphine. Which Arthur had only tried once, after he'd been hit so hard in a sparring match that he'd damaged his liver permanently and had been peeing blood for weeks afterwards. Oh, and been sent to the hospital. Though that had also been for the various other bruises and cracked bones and ribs.

Sparring was serious business—when they were allowed to go hard.

Good times. Old times. Entirely different from now, where he was once again priming the energy within his body, trying to make the thread go through the needle, and why did he want to say needle through thread, and aaargh! He broke out spitting and coughing, blood leaking from his mouth, energy still redirecting through his body as he pulled it from the beast stone.

"Oh, that's why." His chest ached, his lungs ached. It felt like he'd been stabbed in the chest, and in that sense, he was the thread being stabbed by the needle of his own energy.

"Boss?" Yao Jing, leaning next to him, asked carefully, "You good?"

"No." Carefully removing one hand, he wiped at his face, cleared the blood, and then took the cloth from Yao Jing to do a better job. Handed it back and slipped hand back into position so that he could continue to draw energy without interruption. "This sucks."

"And we proud of you, boss!" Yao Jing said, cheerfully. He even went so far as to give Arthur a thumbs up.

A slight snort escaped Arthur before he dove back into his body. Better to stay focused, or try to. He had maybe an hour of practice left. After that point, his body would have cleansed enough of the poisons involved, and there would be nothing left to heal. And while there might be something to be said about practising, even when there was nothing to practise against...

He just wasn't that much of a masochist.

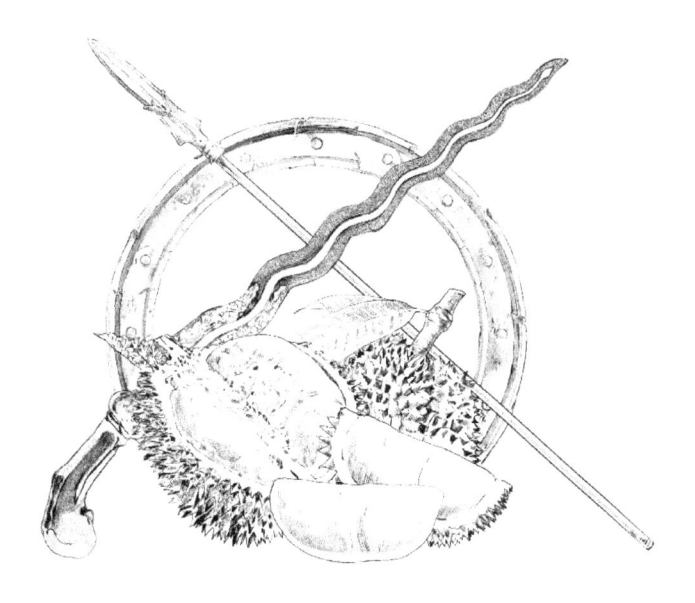

Chapter 129

The next day, the group moved into the depths of the jungle that hid the lizards. Arthur had to admit, this one felt different. Not just because of the various different monsters, even plant monsters, but also because the vegetation itself was just unusual. To his eyes, if nothing else. He assumed that was because he was more used to Southeast Asian rainforests, rather than these more... well, different ones. If he was pushed, he'd call it a South American one, but the only reason he'd say that was because of commentary on the wiki. And even then...

Well, not as though many of the commentators on the wiki and the forums had actually gone to South America, wended their way through the Amazon, and then come back to make clear pronouncements. Not more than a few, anyway, and even those had mixed results since they were relying on old memories to fit one or the other.

Or to deal with what was, Arthur believed, entirely alien plant matter. Like the creeping vines that were purple and draped all across tall softwood trees, climbing and twining their way upwards. Incredibly strong and quite useful as rope once dried out. In fact, that was one of their quests at the moment, though they'd take only the needed portions when they were ready to leave rather than haul it around.

But the vines also had the advantage of letting the four-foot lizards to sneak up on them, by clambering down or rappelling off the ground or just swinging in, using their claws extended to strike someone's face or neck or arm and then keep going until they were out of range.

Annoying, and you could kill one or two, but if there were a half-dozen of them swinging down one after the other, things got interesting. Which was something Arthur was finding out, about an hour and a half in.

"Form up, get close to a tree. Let their vines get tangled!" Karen was screaming out orders and instructions. The team froze at first, then some were shuffling over to stand next to one another, others darting to the nearest tree.

Arthur grimaced, realising she had messed up on her orders, even as he hunkered low and stabbed upwards. He chose not to listen to the conflicting orders, even as he sensed his bodyguards take flanking positions near him and copying his motion to lower their bodies. It caused the lizards some trouble as he had guessed.

Some swung over, too high up to do damage to Arthur's group but were still getting struck by his stabbing spear. Some tried to slide down, one sliding too far and landing on its ass and bouncing right into Yao Jing's fist. Others bounced into the group or missed their catch entirely, falling hard and smashing themselves into the ground.

The trio struck, again and again, until Yao Jing's spear got caught in the vines. It was yanked sideways, but the man's grip was strong enough that all it did was cause the vine to wrap around it, along with a couple of other vines in short order. That, with the swinging weight, forced him to drop the spear eventually, only for the entire thing to spring upwards on the backend and swing around dangerously.

Rather than stick around and get stuck, Arthur rolled out of the way, keeping hold of his own weapon and coming up near Uswah. The woman was using a novel method of dealing with the vines, utilising her shadows that jutted out of tree branches above her to grab and tangle the vines themselves, so that a group of lizards were struggling.

At the same time, the bark of a gun went off. Rick had risen and was firing with a single pistol. He kept the second one holstered, firing with a two-handed grip as he tried for accuracy against the moving objects. Next to him Casey and Lam dealt with those that were coming near him from other directions, striking with spear and sword.

As quickly as the attack began, it was over. The lizards on the ground tried to scamper away, only for the team to jab and cut at them till they fell over. Then, it was just a process of looting. Easy peasy.

Not like dealing with the trio of komodo dragons that they ran into a half-hour later. Sniffing the ground and then detecting his group, the creatures raised thin, triangular heads and charged forwards without care for their lives. Their mouths were open with forked tongues hissing; clawed hands tore up mossy soil as they approached.

Arthur wasn't the only one who looked worried at their appearance. Rick and Arthur loosed their ranged attacks at the same creature in the front. Both the shotgun shell and Refined Exploding Energy Dart tore holes into the stone-aspected komodo dragon, but didn't kill it—just left it bleeding.

Immediately, the pair got ready to launch their second attack, Rick beating Arthur's slower charge-up time with his shotgun. The second blast didn't dissuade the stone dragon though, the monster continuing its charge and splintering Mel's spear as it flexed and then cracked on the body, the woman barely dodging the snapping mouth.

Only a moment of valor by Yao Jing, throwing his body into the side of the creature and tackling it away, risking tearing claws as he charged it into a nearby tree, saved the group from being broken up.

Didn't stop the other two komodo, hiding behind their larger brethren, from closing the range. The first was a plain dragon, smaller, no bigger than maybe a large deer. It hissed and snapped as a shadow tendril reached out to grip it, and as Jan stabbed at it with her spear and Mel circled to the side to gut it. The other was the more dangerous of the two, a creature that lit up the surroundings with a radiance that caused everyone to squint and fouled their attacks. A light-based komodo dragon—not fire, for there was no heat. But it was so bright it was nearly impossible to tell where its body actually was.

Arthur had no time to worry about the creature, nor the others who were dealing with it. Karen and the rest of the team were fighting it, lunging into the brilliance, thrusting spears where they thought it might be, even as long tail and biting mouth chased them about.

For Arthur, all he could do was chase after Yao Jing and Rick. He brought his hands up, slammed into the first smaller dragon with his arm and spear held against his side to push its biting face away from the muscular idiot that was his bodyguard. He couldn't do much about the claws that tore at both of them, glancing off armour or the needle-like teeth that tore at his arm between gaps in his armour as he held the head away.

"Kill it!" Arthur roared, focused on holding the creature still. Focused on letting Rick get his shotgun right up against the body and then pull the trigger, angling it so that the shot didn't hit his teammates. Not so close that he pressed it against the scaled hide, no reason to risk blowback. But close enough, and painful enough, what with the heat and flame and hot air that erupted next to Arthur and Yao Jing.

Painful, loud. But the attack was effective. Tore into the creature, caused it to jerk and twist a few times, but then it weakened enough for him to grab his kris and slide it up along scales and into the monster's brain. He twisted the kris and sliced it out of the dragon head, ending the creature.

He got up and gripped his spear, heading to search for the other monsters. No surprise, Jan and the team had the basic komodo sorted, stabbing it again and again to end it. On the other hand, the last one...

Harder to kill. They couldn't tell if they were injuring it, and what would surprise people who have never gotten into a fight is how hard it could be to kill something fast. A slash was a slash; it could open up skin and muscle and maybe even cut through bone, which, by the way, is a lot softer than you'd imagine. But you had to hit the right parts to actually kill. You had to cut things that mattered, because otherwise, a creature could keep thrashing, keep fighting, keep tearing.

Until the damage, the shock, took over and it died. Didn't matter, of course, by then if it was five or fifteen minutes later, in a fight that could be a long time. And that was without consideration for things like adrenaline and other chemicals pouring through the body. Though, of course, that also meant that most battles ended fast.

Longer, with Tower bodies, but faster than most TV or movies would make you expect.

Which meant: not being able to actually target the komodo dragon was going to be a problem.

And problems often meant someone was going to get hurt. Or die.

Chapter 130

The salamanders, giant or not, were almost a footnote to the troubles the next monsters on the second platform caused for the team. They found themselves fighting through, slowly, forced to heal and sortie from embedded and fortified positions. Arthur knew that part of the reason for their glacial progress was his fault, for he had focused even more on attempting to improve the toxin and poison resistance in his techniques.

To his greatest surprise, Casey did not complain much. Instead, she and Lam focused on killing monsters as they arrived or on their own cultivation, building up their strength. It only took him a little to realise part of the reason why: for all their need for haste, the truth was that they were behind the curve too, like him. Rushing ahead meant they had less time to cultivate and strengthen their bodies, and while the use of monster cores and efficient cultivation methods might have allayed some of that, it could only affect so much.

In the end, time was what they all struggled with.

It was on the sixth day on the second platform, as the evening drew to an end that Arthur felt the click inside his mind that he had been searching for. With it came the insistent prodding of Tower information, notifications, and knowledge pouring in as he allowed the Tower access. It coursed through his mind, deepening his understanding of concepts he had been struggling towards on his own, altering minor scripts in his mind to refine the process.

It happened in the blink of an eye, and then Arthur's eyelids snapped open even as a grin spread across his lips. No one, however, was around to watch his triumph and he sighed moments later, closing his eyes as he allowed others to continue to cultivate or stand watch.

Variant Skill Created: **Accelerated Healing – Refined Energy (Grade III) -> (Grade IIIb)**

Passively increases base Tower healing rates by 73.1%.

Active use of technique increases base Tower healing rate by 218.4%.

Healing may now be directed.

Variant technique increases resistance against toxins and poisons by 38% (P)/ 114%(A)

May not replace lost limbs or other permanent injuries.

Active Cost: 0.1 Refined Energy per ten minutes

"About time," Arthur muttered to himself as he stared at the information. He waited, prodding at the Tower, wondering if there was any further update but could find nothing. He growled in frustration, trying desperately not to scream in anger or throw a tantrum as all his hard work failed.

Instead, he pulled at the Sigil information.

Sigil: The Flame Phoenix

Sigil Bonus (Clan Head): Accelerated Healing – Refined Energy (Grade IIIb)

Sigil Bonus (Clan): Cultivation Exercise – Accelerated Healing – Refined Energy (Grade Ib)

"YES!" Arthur shouted, jumping up. He lost control of the pull of energy he had been conducting while working on his Accelerated Healing skill, and the refined energy in the beast stone caused a backlash as he lost control of it. It made him drop the stone even as he felt a shock run through his body. He screamed a little, dropping to his knees and flexed the scorched hand.

"What?" Yao Jing jumped up, the man clenching his fist as he readied himself to fight. Unlike the others who were slow to come out of their cultivation, he had been only wielding Tower energy, making it simpler for him to exit the state of meditation and control he had been in.

"Nothing..." Arthur waved a hand. "Bad feedback."

"Oh...." Yao Jing relaxed, rocking back on his heels as he forced himself to calm.

"Wait!" Arthur said, eyes widening as he remembered. "I also got the refinement on the healing technique. Check your sigil!" He almost wanted to prance around, but the ache in his hands and along his arms stopped him. He could feel his healing technique working, fixing the problems and he gently guided energy over.

"Sigil?" Then Yao Jing realised what he was talking about and scanned within. While the man was reading it over, Arthur could not help but wonder if the sigil had changed for him. Perhaps it had. Hopefully it did... "*Wah!* Nice, boss!"

Arthur grinned, offered a thumbs up, and then winced as the pain from doing so shot through him. He shifted gingerly back into his seat and leaned against the tree, sprawling his feet out as he waited for his body to finish the healing process. The greatest problem with meridian burns and backlash from a bad cultivation session was that it was impossible—or at least, highly inadvisable—to use his healing technique to fix it. Pulling more energy into already strained meridians just added to the damage.

He needed to wait, and so he sat there, watching as Yao Jing proceeded to tell the rest of the team of the new boon. Arthur almost wished to talk but realised moments later that he was truly exhausted. Pushing, splitting his mind, forcing himself onwards for hours, days, on end suddenly came rushing in and he realised...

No. He was good just sitting here quietly.

Of course, that moment of peace and tranquility lasted just about twenty minutes before Mel came over and sat down beside him. He opened his eyes, noted her glance down to his arms still held before him in clawed fashion and waited for the chastisement. Yet, she didn't say anything. At least, not about his arms.

"You're at what? Version 3?"

"Yeah."

"Why didn't we get version two?" Mel asked.

Arthur grimaced and shrugged in answer.

"You should find out."

"Sure. I'll hit the library when I get back," he drawled.

Mel snorted, then glanced over to where Casey and Lam were watching the excited conversations going around them. The only ones not taking part were Rick, who was laid up and utilising the new technique's benefits to clear the infection in his arm from the latest komodo dragon bite, and Jan who was on watch.

"You want me to ask them," he said.

"Who else?"

No good answer there, but... "Asking means we owe them. If they have an answer."

"Not among friends."

"Are we, though?" Arthur muttered.

Now she shrugged and he had to admit she had a point. He sighed, pushing himself up to his feet with minor difficulty and wandering over to Casey. At her greeting, he smiled and nodded, then squatted beside her.

"That looks like it hurts," she said, before he could say anything.

"A little. Backlash," he explained.

"You shouldn't do two things at once," she rebuked him, but gently.

"So, do you know how sigils work, ah?" Arthur said, switching topics.

"A little. Why, ah?" She added the final intonation with a slight twinkle in her eyes, noting how Arthur had switched to Manglish.

"Tell me?"

"They're sort of a Clan's version of Titles. Wider-aspected but limited, unlike Titles. They're harder to get, but individually more powerful." She cocked her head to the side. "You have the phoenix. There's trickster, warrior, elemental, even animal sigils. Based off what the sigil means, you can tie in specific aspects, make it more powerful and prominent. Like the phoenix, you've got it for healing. But someone else might make it about the fire. Or longevity. Or even flight."

"Huh." Arthur frowned. "Only one aspect?"

Casey glanced over at Lam who stared ahead, stone faced. Arthur blinked, realising her non-answer was answer enough. "So, how do I make it more powerful?" He didn't want to mention it didn't tie in fully, though he wondered if she'd picked that up by now. After all, hard to miss how fast he healed compared to everyone else.

"No idea." Casey answered immediately, making him blink. "Not something I studied." Then she paused and added, "One interesting thing, though, is that it's a joint thing."

"What?" Arthur sad.

"Unlike Titles. Or maybe exactly like. You can get a World First Title, right, but most of them are for things the Guild wins or does, something big and important."

"Like clearing a Tower first, or killing an unkillable boss. Or finding a new, hidden aspect of a floor or Tower," Arthur said, confirming what she said.

"Right! But Sigils are things that, well, link to the entire Clan. So everyone can improve it. Might be that a majority are needed to make it possible."

"But it linked to my skill!"

"To start. You're always going to be the benchmark, but... the rest have to do their work too."

"So, everyone got the poison resistance improvement because… there's enough people poisoned?" he muttered, surprised.

"Close enough, I think." She shrugged. "A large enough majority. Or enough of you got poisoned regularly or... something."

Arthur shook his head. He knew the various floors had mild poisons, anything from the local equivalent of poison ivy to actual, dangerous poisons and toxins. But the entire clan had gotten injured enough that it was sufficient? It boggled the mind. Then again, it might explain why the sigil hadn't improved. If he was the only one with improvements in the technique, then there was no way for the others to push ahead.

Annoying but understandable.

"Oh, here." Seeing him quiet and thinking, Casey had dug into her pouch and come up with a foil-wrapped item. She handed it to Arthur who looked it over, frowning.

"Chocolate. Wait, durian chocolate?" he said, surprised. At the wide grin on Casey's face, he laughed softly and tore it open, careful not to send the chocolate flying and took the slightly melted mess into his mouth. Unlike what most might believe, durian chocolates weren't a horrid combination. The mix of sweetness and bitterness in both the durian and the chocolate complimented one another, though they were subtly different.

After all, Malaysia made a business of selling this to unsuspecting foreigners as tourist gifts. Couldn't scare them off with something that truly reeked.

Mouth full of chocolate, Arthur nodded thanks and wandered back to his seat, feeling the oils spread across his tongue, the warm smoothness fill his mouth. He sat back, closed his eyes, and tried to enjoy the treat.

After all, now they were really going to get moving.

Chapter 131

Three days later and Arthur was back in his clan hall, eyes half-closed and meditating. The last battle for the second platform had been a non-battle, the group stumbling upon the replenishing portal area half a day after another team had gone through it. They had taken the mark anyway, choosing to teleport back and turn to the Tower administrative center with the myriad items they had collected to complete some quests.

Arthur could still feel the chime of Tower notifications in his head, so numerous were the quests they'd finished.

Tower Quest Completed!
Deliver 12 bundles of Kava Roots

Tower Quest Completed!
Deliver 4 Pristine Ivory Leg Flowers

Tower Quest Completed!
Deliver 12 Monster Shards from Floor 5

Tower Quest Completed
....

And on and on. Of course, with all those quests came the piddly contribution point rewards, but he didn't even get to savour those. They all just went straight into the money pit that was his armour. The debt kept decreasing, though, which was good—and the armour was even already made. It just was being held till he could actually pay off his debt.

The good news was that he was close. Another run and he figured he'd be done. He might even be done now if he was willing to take a loan out, but he figured he owed enough people things that doing so was a bad idea. At least for now. Like most Asians, he had an instinctive dislike for debt, for owing others large amounts of money.

Oh, he knew there were things like leveraging and taking out loans to make your money work for you. Ways to be rich and grow richer without actually owning anything, or whatever the latest guru was talking about. Of course, most of those idiots preyed on individuals richer and more fortunate than him. But he'd hung out, at bars and nightclubs and the occasional house party, to overhear those conversations.

Never mind the endless streams of videos showcasing their amazing lives... Or what was supposed to be their lives.

No one, of course, talked about what happened when you failed. Or how much of those lives were lies. Doing 4:00am deliveries to people halfway up a mountain where they were waiting, carefully, with a dozen other "influencers," all for the right lighting. Sweaty and hot and grumpy, just to get a few videos. Or finding these beautiful and luxurious rooms were only clean in that one angle; clothing and discarded waste were everywhere else.

Of course, he'd also made a few extra tips helping pack up bundles of dirty food and taking it downstairs, doing garbage runs when he didn't need to. Mostly because it offended his sense of good order.

Lives were rarely as interesting or good as it seemed through a crystal screen.

Case in point, being the Clan Head of the Benevolent Durians.

"We need to finish up more copies of these rules and post them up," Mel said, head bent over the piece of paper where she was copying down the ruleset they had agreed upon. It was rather simple, not even ten points long so far, and most of it started with conceptual rules like "Hang together and support one another" and "No stealing, blackmail, or anything that'll get you put in jail in the real world." There were also more specific or pragmatic rules like "Clan techniques and cultivation methods are secret."

Penalties and the other sections weren't listed there, though a small book of recommended penalties was being created. They'd started most of this on the first floor with Amah Si, borrowing much of the Thorned Lotuses own ruleset to begin with and then elaborating on them further for the Durians.

Always with the belief that anything that was truly valuable was going to become public. Arthur figured they were leaking information like a sieve, what with the lack of controls of who was coming in or what they were saying. Which was the really important things were secrets, information only passed on to a small number.

And even then, the things Arthur didn't want others to know, he just didn't speak of. Like his Traits, like his speculation on how Aspects and Traits might improve further.

"I know. And I know you don't like me adding to this, but if Casey's right..."

"She isn't sure."

"No, but it won't hurt if we get more people working on actually learning the Accelerated Healing techniques," Arthur said. "If the Tower considers it a percentage number, then the time to do it is now. Before we grow too big."

"What if it's a fixed number?" Mel challenged. "What if we need like, fifty people with Accelerated Healing Grade II?"

"Then we're arsed, but at least the ones with the upgrade are doing better," Arthur said.

"Won't hurt," Uswah muttered, poring over the technique document that Arthur had written out. He'd even gone and spent more money to get it replicated and improved, so that they had a Tower-enabled document for both Uswah and Boss Kim to read. Together, the pair could work on upgrading their techniques.

"And you're sure I'll be able to buy the upgrades when you upgrade?" Kim asked, once again.

"Not sure, but pretty confident," Arthur said. "I recall it being possible. I just need to break in and through, and learn it further before the rest of you can purchase it. Or, you know, enough of you upgrade the rest of the way."

Kim frowned but turned away, focusing once more on the document. Arthur breathed a little sigh of relief when she turned back, for she had been less than impressed when he'd explained what he had learnt. Having her hope of getting her eye healed and finally leaving the place snatched away so soon after had nearly cost him his eye. At that thought, he reached out and touched his left eyelid, imagining that he could feel the knife that had nearly gone into it.

If not for Jan...

He shuddered but then pushed it away, suppressing his emotions before he broke the pull of energy from the beast stone he still clutched in his other hand. Learning to draw or refine energy while moving or talking would save him time. He was doing it carefully, only where he knew he could stop at a moment's notice and he didn't have to risk backlash.

Because doing it anywhere else but in the clan hall would be insane.

"I'll get it done. We could have this copied, maybe see if we can have a runner push it to the first floor before we leave?" Mel said, tentatively. "Be expensive but the Chins..."

"Maybe." Arthur rubbed his temple. "Though, we might not need it."

"Clan unlocks?" Mel muttered, softly.

"Yeah, at the end of this Tower climb, I think."

"Then...." Mel nodded after a moment, dropping the topic. No need to explain not wanting to take on more debts, not right now. They were too young, too small, but desperately needing to grow.

The Durians. Arthur forced himself not to sigh, to scream. It never felt like they had enough time, and so he took shortcuts, tried dangerous things like cultivating while talking or reading over the documentation of the other techniques that he was supposed to study. Even if he had not the time or money to buy them.

A dangerous thought was bubbling up, one that he had briefly considered and then discarded. But sometimes, when he felt the need to squeeze more time out, even when he was refining and training one of his other techniques, well, he considered it.

What would happen if he tried to cultivate Tower energy from the surroundings and refined energy from monster cores at the same time?

Chapter 132

"There are cultivation techniques like that, yes."

Arthur searched the speaker's face, looking for hints. Some clue about the quality of the cultivation technique, the difficulty. In the end, he found nothing, which wasn't surprising. The Tower administrators rarely gave away information, at least on things that were important.

"How much?" he asked.

"Depends on the technique." Again, that same droll answer.

"Right, right..." Arthur drummed his fingers, and then had to ask. "The cheapest?"

"One moment." The administrator stopped looking at Arthur directly, instead accessing some invisible screen. Or maybe just recalling things. Annoying that he wasn't using the slate before him, but that would have been too easy, too easy for Arthur to spot the name, to see how many or any other details. No hints for him. "Two hundred and fifty contribution points."

"*Celaka*," Arthur groused and stopped leaning. Well, he certainly did not have the contribution points, even after the short run they'd done to drop off their latest acquisitions and pay down his debt. In two days though... in two days he'd get enough, if everyone kept up their jobs and paid him their share of the clan tax.

Sucked that he had to take it, but it was either that or, well... not have armour. And considering the third platform, and the fact that when they got there, they weren't coming back...

Yeah, it'd do.

On his way back to his clan hall, Arthur pondered the piece of information he'd acquired. It was important confirmation, that what he wanted to do was possible. Now, the question was this: was it worth potentially causing significant damage to himself by testing it out? After all, he also confirmed it was a full cultivation method by itself. If he pulled Tower energy and refined energy into his body, were there specific ways the energy had to flow to make sure it didn't clash? Were there things he had to do, to make sure he didn't harm himself?

Or could he muddle his way through? Was he over complicating things?

If he was the protagonist of a story, he might try it and not concern himself. Consider it his cheat method—and the gods knew, he had quite a few now for himself, though nothing that stood out. Just work the energy through him and come out stronger than anyone. But he wasn't in a bad anime, and so messing around with a cultivation technique like that would likely damage him. Maybe not permanently, since this wasn't like those cultivation stories that had been popular once, where you could cripple yourself forever.

The Tower didn't have such limitations. They'd fix you, eventually, assuming you didn't blow out an arm or something. Eventually, even damaged meridians could be healed, for the most part. So he wasn't worried about that. But if he was laid out for a month, unable to cultivate, he was definitely going to break his agreement with Casey.

And that was a big danger.

So, Arthur pondered and turned over the options, considered if he could, perhaps, buy the really cheap option. He considered it while he had the clan get itself ready for his departure, while he talked matters over with the two Ks—Kim and Karen—hoping they could hold his fifth floor. He debated testing it, until it was time to go and his new armour came.

Because when he saw his armour, most other thoughts fled.

"Damn, but I look good..." Arthur couldn't help but say, as he stood in front of the mirror after dressing.

The hide was a beautiful dark brown after the treatment and hardening. It was built using a series of simple straps, a mixture of modern-day technology and old-school techniques so that it was all adjustable. Gorget, breastplate, pauldrons, and cup and more. A full set so that it covered the entirety of Arthur's body, protected him from harm from most angles unless you managed to sneak a blow in between the overlapping leather plates.

Hot, too, or should have been, but the magic kept things to an agreeable level. Not enough to actually make Arthur comfortable, but the comfort runes embedded in the armour were part and parcel of the package and would adjust temperatures up and down five degrees. Celsius, of course. It wasn't a lot, but it did mean that he wasn't sweating his ass off, even with the light gambeson he had to wear to ensure it didn't pinch.

Mostly though, Arthur had to admit, he looked like a medieval fighter, a serious one. Or a Tower climber in a TV show, maybe Tower Climber Ed or The First Climber in season one. You know, the hero. Except, of course, he wasn't Caucasian with a square jaw and stubble, he wasn't blonde or light brown hair and perfectly studly. Or with a deeply angsty backstory.

He was just him.

Still...

"This will do, nicely." Grabbing his spear, Arthur stepped out, heading down the hallway and the ladder. It was time to test out the armour, make sure he could move in it and the best way to do that was sparring. He also wanted to keep testing out some of his new techniques, and practice was about the only way to do it.

There might, also, be a couple who he needed to try his hand against.

"Wah! So nice, ah." Leia teased, leaning against the post that marked one corner of their impromptu ring. A couple of other posts and cheap ropes hung around the area marked off the ring, mostly so that others didn't randomly wander in and get smacked.

"Funny," Arthur said. "You ready?" He slipped between the ropes with ease, guiding his spear between the two and walking to the center. He had the training cap on it, just in case of accidents.

"Of course, *lah*." Leia kicked her spear into hand, the much shorter weapon shifting as she wandered forwards.

Arthur never did get that, her using a short weapon despite her short height, but she'd made it work for herself. On the other side, Eric continued to glower at everyone, a piece of straw stuck in his mouth as he chewed on it rather than a toothpick.

"Ready—" Arthur never finished, easily blocking the spear head that shot forwards to his chest. That was not a trick that he or anyone else who trained with their sifu was going to miss. Nor was Leia expecting him to, since she kept coming.

Holding his spear in two hands, Arthur blocked high and low, pushing his spear to keep her away from him even as he retreated under her relentless barrage and quick footwork.

Jab, disengage under, pull the backhand close and pivot the front of the spear to smack against the spear coming in. Sent it off-line just an inch at point of contact, which meant that by the time it reached his body it was off by a foot or more. Keep moving, raising the backhand up even as you pulled the front hand back, shuttling the spear backwards so that the point kept in-line and threatening. Then, push down with the backhand, send the shaft striking outwards at knee and thigh and in between, even as you pivoted.

Movement, always movement.

Even as he fought, Arthur found himself falling into the old rhythm. It was different, very different, fighting humans rather than monsters. The techniques one used against someone wielding a weapon were different compared to a raving monster with four legs instead of two and intent on eating your face.

With monsters there were no groin strikes, you could cut and tear open arms that came searching for you. Even pin them on your spear head, slam the tip of the staff butt into eyes that were lower to the ground or kick and hop backwards at the same time to catch leaping monsters. Sweeps were less useful, but knees became much more interesting as were elbows that dropped in close to strike heads.

Spinning staves that could strike and move, block attacks coming from behind, catch leaping monkeys in the air or lizardmen swinging from vines were less useful against a fighter that was smart enough to shorten their spear, slipping their attack in moments after your block was finished.

Or that wanted to target your poor fingers.

"Aaargh!" Arthur cursed, fingers going numb as she clipped his forehand. He let the spear drop rather than try to grip it, shifting close so that her next attack could not stab him, eating a jab into his ribs that he didn't even feel and he struck with his elbow. Slam into the cheek, splitting skin as she staggered backwards, only for him to kick the dropped spear, sending the edge hopping upwards and smacking her own hand and spear.

Then, shift, using a single hand, push as it dropped. Control it, just enough that it struck her inner thigh.

A crippling blow, for the inner thigh rarely was hit enough to toughen up.

She cursed, fell. And then, a hand streaked. Across the air, coming to a stop at the edge of her neck. Knife hand strike to throat, potentially fight ending. Probably not...

But school rules. No fatal blows. And the fight ends when it is landed.

After fifteen seconds.

Which was why Arthur struck, pulled back, and defended against a wildly swinging spear before he skidded to a stop.

After all, sometimes, people or monsters took a bit to realise they were dead.

And wasn't that another useful life lesson.

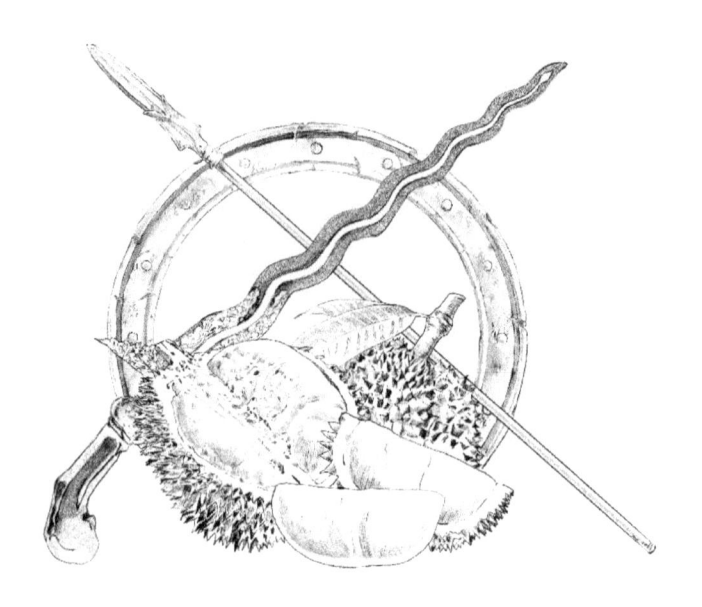

Chapter 133

It was not, after that, enough. Not for Eric, not for Leia, though Eric had insisted on having his chance to play with Arthur now while he was still fresh. Or as he put it, "Let me *lah*, before he becomes too big head."

Arthur, of course, snorted at that rather uncharitable view of him. He also felt he needed to remind them, "I was always better than you two. At least when it came to spears and weapons."

"Good you said that," Eric said, flexing a little. "Otherwise, we'd have to grapple."

"Mmmm..." Arthur muttered, rotating his ankles a little and bouncing before shifting to the side, gesturing for his senior to start. They might be his seniors in terms of how long they'd been training with their sifu, but he was still better than them. Even when it came to grappling, Eric was only marginally better. Mostly because the man had been categorically stronger, and no matter what they might like to tell you, it did matter.

Stronger is stronger, and while techniques could make a difference, all else being equal, stronger and faster was better.

"So." Arthur tapped and struck, feeling his friend out with the staff as they tested each other out at range. He wanted to get an idea of how fast the other man had grown, what kind of traits he might have gained. Each little tap, each thrust that was blocked, and each step was an answer. "You managed to get to your Second Transformation yet?"

A flicker, a flurry of strikes that pushed Arthur back as he finished his question. He guarded himself, battling the attacks as he watched his opponent for a tell, wondering if Eric had gotten rid of it, that little preceding motion he did. So minor that if you had never duelled him before you'd never notice, that shift of grip as he tightened his fingers.

So minor.

That was the thing that duelists forgot, that watchers of things like the Olympics or high-level combat matches the world over never realised. You could study your opponents, in video replays, in high definition and in live matches, over and over again till even the most minute tell could be picked out.

Oh, most fighters had the big tells worn away, taught out of them. The rocking, the head bob, the way the eyes shifted or the hands that dropped. Big tells, that told a tale of movement and intention. But once you ironed those away, got rid of them, then you got to the smaller ones. And smaller. And smaller.

Till you carved a perfect fighting robot—that mattered little in a real battle. In that flurry of combat you engaged someone and walked away from the battle thirty seconds later, when your opponent was—if you did it right—dead and not coming back. Then, a subtle tic no longer mattered, because they would never have the time to figure it out.

Or exploit it.

"I'll take that as a no," Arthur said, sliding out of the flurry of attacks. Another series of stabs and ripostes, the spear shafts knocking one against in a series of klacks. A common rhythm, formed from repetition and a specific form. Drilled to such an extent the pair could have done it with their eyes closed, muscle memory taking over even as both blazed through the motions, the spear shafts themselves straining to keep up with the attacks.

But repetition and muscle memory meant that you left openings, created a routine that might be exploited by the smart. He saw it, the slight tightening of a grip, the shift in body. He intercepted the attack, long before it began, stepping in close and blocking it tight, riding the motion forwards.

Forcing his friend, his opponent, to choose anew.

Grunting, the snap of cloth as they moved, the whistle of spears as they crossed. Arthur could smell the dust rising from the packed earth floor, the sweat pouring from his body. He had lost track of time, the pair no longer feeling one another out but fighting at range.

A dozen passes, some strikes that were glancing, injuring but not fatal. School rules had you fight on, ignoring the throbbing pain, ignoring the potential fractures and the definite bruises. Only a fatal hit would end it, a properly placed one.

Throat, head, heart, lungs. Or, if you managed it, a direct strike to an arm or leg that dropped the opponent, at which point they were no longer allowed to use it, even if sensation returned.

Arthur had to admit, as he lay gasping moments later, that he never saw it. The attack was unusual, a cut kick that he had dodged with ease, but the slip forward and the trip that followed the attack pulled his ankle to upset his balance. Then, the spear, pushed upwards so that Arthur's arm moved upwards, Eric guiding the attack before he threw an elbow upwards. Right into his chest, catching him lightly.

That he understood, that he noticed. What he didn't was the way that same energy pushed through him, cast him backwards as though it had exploded within him. He staggered back, holding his chest, trying to get his lungs to breathe again. He was so disturbed by the sensation that he only realised he'd dropped his guard when the spearhead tapped the top of his head.

"What was that?" Arthur hissed, stepping back till he hit the edge of the ring, the back of the ropes pushing into his skin, blocking his attempt to flee. He shifted the spear, forgotten in one hand, to the side and let it rest against the ropes, watched it slide down and clatter even as he kept rubbing at his chest.

"Think you're the only one who learnt something?" Eric said with a smirk.

"No, but..." He didn't know what else to say beyond that as he waited. Waited for an answer.

"New trait. Vibrating energy. Combined with a projection," Eric said, grinning as he leaned on his spear now as he grounded it. "Can't project it through my weapon just yet, but in contact, it does that."

"Triggers projected energy that disrupts my own energy and the muscles and bones in me," Arthur said, wonderingly. The vibrating slowly went away, leaving him uncomfortable as he rubbed at it once again and sighs. "Smart. And if you can project it..."

"Like your Refined Energy Dart, yeah. Or through Focused Strike. It'll bypass a lot of armour," Eric said with a smirk. "Nice, eh?"

Arthur nodded in agreement, then sighed. He bent down, grabbed his spear and raised it.

"1-0. Let's try that again."

His answer was only a grin from Eric as he set himself.

A dozen passes with each of his seniors. It was enough to leave Arthur panting over in the corner, sweat pouring off him as he wiped at his face and tried to catch his breath. He had pushed until he couldn't fight any longer, barely giving himself time to rest between bouts. Now, the pair were both in the ring, fighting in a group battle with Yao Jing and Jan. This was the second round, with the pairings changing each time.

Good training, even though his seniors were tired already. Just like him. On the other hand, at least he was gaining a good understanding of what the pair could do. And the truth was, they were both stronger than him. Not all the way to Second Transformation but a decent amount of the way there.

A good addition to his team, even if they did cause their own problems.

Chapter 134

Arthur hefted his bag, looking around. He nodded to Kim and Karen, the two Ks who were now bosses of the fifth floor, and the myriad members of the newly formed Benevolent Durian Clan there, many of them either members of the Suey Ying or the Thorned Lotuses. Which was, Arthur noted, causing its own tensions. He could see the way they looked at one another, the way the two disparate groups kept their distance.

"You guys going to be good?" Arthur said, looking between the two with a slight frown on his face.

"Don't worry, *lah*," Kim said with a wave of the hand. "I'll just beat them till they good."

"That's not the best method of ensuring compliance," Karen said, frowning.

"That's why your daughter doesn't listen to you," Kim said, turning to Karen with a sniff.

Said daughter glared at Kim, opening her mouth to protest but eventually shut it as Arthur focused on the pair. "Work together. I'm trust you all to. If you can't...." He trailed off for a second before he shook his head. "If you can't, well, someone else will fix it for you when they arrive."

"Wah, so serious ah!" Kim grinned, reaching up to rub at her eyepatch.

"You don't think this is?" Arthur grimaced, then waved a hand before she could reply. "Just, get it done, eh? You all know what you need and what we can offer. And it'll only get better."

"So long as you survive," Karen said now, eyes narrowing and flicking over to Casey and Rick. The pair were chatting, Lam hovering in the background as usual, the two scions of the rich relaxed as they waited for the group to go. "You sure of this?"

"As sure as I can be."

He offered the group one last nod, turned and waved goodbye to the rest. No speeches—he hated them—and it'd mean little to the group who barely knew him. He wished, he wished, he could do something about that. But if wishes were fishes, he'd have the ocean.

※

The armour made its effectiveness known within the first day as they waded through jungle to reach the first platform. Arthur felt not the usual random pricks and thorns that made up the undergrowth. Pity it didn't have an overall protective enchantment or a reinforcement of his aura that he'd heard the higher-end enchantments offered. One reason so few of the most powerful climbers didn't even bother with helmets.

He wasn't bothering with one either, though he did have a skullcap attached to the back of his backpack in easy grabbing distance. Hated the heat, the way it made him feel wearing it. Overheating was harder with a climber's constitution, but it could happen. And in the muggy weather, sweating under his armour was bad enough. Especially since the ability to actually dry off and wash was much harder.

Something that people who had never actually tried hiking in muggy rainforests never understood. It was also, partly, why so many natives went bare-chested or with a minimal amount of clothing. Arthur would have leaned that way too, if not for the constant monsters, the minor comfort runes of his new armour, and his increased constitution.

Misery was smelling days-old, damp cotton t-shirts that just never truly dried, having to put them on after a night of sleep, never feeling truly comfortable because of the grime that clung to you. Even hanging it near the fire didn't help much, often because finding dry wood to burn was a chore and a half—and making you smell of mildew and wood smoke wasn't that much better.

For the most part, all that discomfort was worth it when, for example, you had to survive getting stung by giant hornets because you'd accidentally wandered into a giant swarm of them, cracking open their nest.

Arthur swatted one of the hornets aside, felt the impact of a stinger going right through his backpack and against his armour. He snarled and dropped his spear at this point, instead using his kris and a long fighting knife to strike and protect himself, so swarmed was he that he couldn't even take the time to put on his helmet or gain space.

More than one impact of the hornets' stingers slammed into him, bouncing off armour as he focused on keeping them away from his neck and head and slicing off limbs, stingers, and the occasional wing. Those that fell to the ground he booted aside or just hopped away from, always moving forwards. Bark Skin helped against the occasional tearing of skin from serrated feet or the glancing blow of stingers, his body turning before they could penetrate more than an inch deep most times.

Even so, his face was bleeding from numerous cuts and punctures. His vision was clouding, poison injected into him sending waves of crippling pain through his body, causing muscles along his neck and face to clench, teeth gritted so tight he feared he'd crack them. Yet, he could not pay attention to anything but the fight, the movements, and the striking.

So many hornets, so damn many. He couldn't see otherwise, even as he waded forwards, even as he conjured the occasional Refined Exploding Energy Dart to send into the buzzing swarm, to throw monsters aside and give him breathing room, even as his ears throbbed and a metallic taste invaded his tongue.

Around him, he could hear, feel, the others fighting. Yao Jing with his fists, throwing jabs and sweeping attacks, his aura coated with flame now. A technique he'd purchased, mimicking Karen. Of course, he left smoking footprints behind him, burnt body parts and smoking leaves as he fought. A fire hazard that they'd have to watch for.

Mel and Jan on the outside, stabbing inwards with their spears, smashing away the swarm that concentrated on Arthur. The loud bark of a shotgun, dozens of pellets flinging themselves forwards to tear up corners of the swarm as Rick took his time to fire, ensuring he didn't catch anyone by accident. He was sweeping away large chunks of the group, nearly as far back as Uswah who did her best to back up Arthur using her shadow tendrils.

Not that she could help that much, what with the swarm blocking views. But the occasional tendril that grabbed and tore a wing off or blocked a hornet sting helped.

Everything did, everyone. Eric and Leia were on the other side, the man sweeping and striking with bare hands, with every single hornet he managed to strike properly falling to the ground. Leia's own attacks were quieter, less flashy, her techniques all subtle, passive movements, but she was doing as much, if not more damage as they dealt with the second swarm. Backed up by Casey and Lam, who were on the edges of the entire fight.

Vision faded, and Arthur struggled to keep Bark Skin working. He knew he shouldn't have been the one to charge in, but no one else had a full set of armour. At the least, he should have put on the skullcap. Would have protected him a little, especially when the damn things kept trying to sting his head and neck.

Maybe he should have gotten a Hardened Bones trait or something.

Or something…

Staggering around, attacking just by sight, by feel, Arthur swung and swung and swung. Until he couldn't move anymore, until he realised that someone was gripping him and screaming into his face.

And then he sagged, released his hold of Bark Skin. He breathed, tried to fill his lungs, force himself to breathe slowly.

And wonder, exactly how bad the damage was.

Chapter 135

Arthur lay slumped against a tree, one hand working on his side as he extracted the hornet stinger. It had burrowed into him nice and deep, bypassing his armour through a small gap as he'd lifted his arm to strike. Luck or skill, it didn't matter when he chopped the damn creature apart moments later. It didn't, however, mean the damn stinger hadn't stuck in him and caught at something within.

Wiggling the stinger out, trying to get the barbs around whatever organ or part of him it had caught within was an exercise of white-knuckled, tight-breath agony.

"You're just making it worse," Uswah said, crouched beside him. She eyed the occasional welling blood that pooled at the corner of his armour, shaking her head. "Just pull it out."

"Hurts..." Arthur groused. "More. Damage."

"And this isn't?" she raised an eyebrow. "Pretty sure you've squeezed all the poison into your body."

"Toxin." But he was sure she was right by now. He closed his eyes, a surge of pain running through him as his hand, trembling from the pain, twitched it in the wrong direction. Moving his spasming hand aside, he hissed as Uswah stopped asking and grabbed and yanked. He let out a breathless scream, curling up on his side and wincing further as his arm was grabbed and pushed upwards by a rough hand and knee combo before a poultice was slapped on his open wound.

"Hold still, hold it there." Now his hand was lowered, forcing him to grip and push against the welling blood. "Heal yourself."

Grunting, Arthur tried to focus on engaging his cultivation, on healing himself. At the same time, he split his attention such that he could go over the damage the swarm had done to the group. Wandering into a full nest like that was a party-ending story, in many cases. Too many groups had done that early on that the cultivators on the fifth floor had joined together to push back these nests, at least to a safe distance.

Unfortunately, the Tower had a tendency to repeatedly add them back, which meant the occasional unlucky group got the chance to find out what happened what a swarm of angry, oversized hornets could do. If not for the size of Arthur's team, they would have ended up taking actual casualties.

As it was, everyone had been stung at least once. Some, like Casey, only once, but most had two to three stings. Blood welling, limbs puffy, the group was doing their best to handle the surging toxins and the resulting pain and bleeding. While Arthur was not the most stung—armour was armour after all—he was still one of the worst off other than poor Jan. She'd managed to get three striking her at the same time, one burrowing into a calf muscle, another into her upper arm, and a third most dangerously at the point where shoulder met neck. She was struggling to breathe, the light gorget she wore already stripped away as neck muscles and skin inflamed and swelled.

A death sentence, without the anti-toxins they were using, without the resistance that had been passed on to her as a clan boon. As it was, she was still letting out little gasps of air as she struggled to bring in enough oxygen. Worst, this was only the first platform. Without thought, his gaze slid sideways to fix on Eric and Leia, who had both managed to make it out with minimal damage. He continued to glare at the pair, specifically Eric, till the man looked over.

"What?" he asked, hunching in a little at the look Arthur sent him.

"You," Arthur hissed.

"I didn't do anything!"

"Black. Hand." Another hissing breath and accusation. He could not do much, not without damaging himself but he felt the need to say this.

"Come on, it was your scout!" At Uswah's glare, he hunched even more. "Really! I didn't lead us here."

"Unlucky." Another pause, then two more words. "KL River."

"Now, see, that was just... unusual." Eric looked hunted now, glancing over to Leia who was refusing to meet his gaze. He waved both arms around, as though warding off their accusations. "I'm not bad luck!"

"What happened at the KL River?" Mel, hunched over the corpses and stripping them of their larger-than-normal beast stones, asked curiously. She was sweating profusely, working in the heat, but she had only managed to get a few minor stings and scrapes and was one of the few able to keep moving and not on watch.

"Idiot was leaning against the metal railing. Somehow, the brand new railing gave way and tumbled him into the river," Leia said. "Nearly dropped half—"

"Quarter at most!" Eric corrected, or tried to at least.

"—of the class in with him. The ground gave way too. Someone said it was bad concrete later on. A few people were injured. Bruises, cuts, even a few broken bones."

"But we got a payout from the contractor, right? Kept the lights on for nearly a year!" Eric said.

"Three years later," Leia said, shaking her head. "That was painful at best. And wasn't the only time, was it? We don't let him play Dai Di."

Uswah frowned. "Dai Di?"

"Big 2." Arthur clarified.

"Ohhh!" Uswah got it. She wasn't that sheltered, though Casey looked puzzled. It was a popular card game, a mix of trumps and poker and was named after the eponymous "biggest" card in the deck, number 2. Alongside mahjong, the game was highly popular, what with the ease of transportation.

Pushing himself upwards, Arthur focused on the myriad corpses around, many of which had been pulled apart for cores. Then, he turned to the nest that had been shattered somewhat, though a lot of it still lay intact. Reminded of the weird coincidences and one other issue, he raised his free hand and pointed at the nest.

"Break it down." He made sure to pull his kris out and lay it on his lap as he added, "And don't get us stung."

"You sure?" Leia said, staring doubtfully at the nest.

"Yes. Loot inside. Maybe."

Leia nodded, grabbing Rick and pulling him along. Together, the pair moved forwards, Uswah backing off and starting her sling spinning just in case. It wasn't the most effective method of killing creatures, but for the few that might still be left behind, it should work.

Or so they hoped at least.

The group, many healed enough at least that well-wrapped bandages could stem the blood flowing, gathered around the gathered loot. Not the monster cores, which had already been sorted and divided into pouches to be carried by Mel, Casey, and Arthur. Here now was actual loot they had found within the cracked and split hornet nest. Loot worn by the corpses of dead climbers.

"Dead bodies save me," Casey whispered, grimacing as Eric and Leia tore into aforementioned corpses with gusto, peeling off shredded clothing and armour with nary a care. "Don't you people have manners."

"Nah." Leia said. "Arthur's like us. We learnt not to care, a while ago. Bodies are bodies, you know?" She shrugged. "They're dead and don't need any of this."

"Not the loot, but—" Casey winced as Eric cracked some ribs just so he could extract the armour faster. Thankfully, the bodies were all mummified and stripped of flesh, something in the way the hornets had utilized the corpses for food and building materials leaving them mostly dry. The couple of still-rotting corpses in the distance had been left behind, after being stripped of course. "—the care. We could do this slower, maybe not break any bones…"

"What? You want to bury them afterwards?" Leia rolled her eyes. Eric snorted beside her and then paused when he looked around to see none of the others were laughing with the pair.

"Shit. Seriously, Arthur?" Eric said, looking at the man.

He shrugged, ignoring the byplay. Different clashing cultures now, and he had no intention of getting in the way of either. Instead, his focus was more on the things they'd extracted.

Broken armour, most of it not much better than what they had. Not a bad thing, overall, and probably salvageable if they had the time and skills to do so. He pushed most of that aside, not caring to worry about that. He was hoping to see the climbers still had pouches of monster cores— Yao Jing was sifting through the nest for them. Those they found were passed to Mel to keep track of. As their main bookkeeper, overseen by Uncle Lam, she'd sort out the split later.

Random equipment, camping utensils, clothing pieces, Tupperware, and ropes, all that was pushed aside. None of it pulsed or gave indication it was magical. The few that might be Arthur set aside for others to peruse; but at their level it was unlikely they'd find anything immediately useful. After all, that was the kind of thing you'd expect at higher levels.

Except for...

"That parang enchanted?" Arthur asked Mel, who was turning the weapon over and over.

"No. Not enchanted but... good material?" she muttered, unsure. "Water steel, see?"

Also known popularly as Damascus steel, even though the entire process of making water steel likely originated from India. Some also called it Wootz steel, or so Arthur vaguely recalled. Of course, these days, with the exceptional smelting process of modern-day presses, the addition of the popular markings was a matter of show rather than practicality.

Except, you know, with mass manufactured works like parangs, many which might not even have good steel used for their construction. Or, if a proper blacksmith had taken their time to prep the material and included monster cores within, such that the material could actually be enchanted later on.

Much like his spear.

"So, enchantable."

In answer, she handed it over long enough for him to sense the Tower pulling information for him. As usual, not much, but enough.

Water Steel Parang

Effects: Unknown

"Keep it. Let's keep looking," Arthur said.

When they were done, the group had found only two more items of interest. Quite the haul, if you included the monster cores. The first was a bracelet that glinted and, surprisingly, provided detailed information after Casey had handled it. The fact that the bracelet looked similar to the one she carried might have been answer to why.

Bracelet of Energy Gathering

Effects: Increase passive energy gathering by 0.01 per hour

Not much of a bonus, but it was passive. Which meant that even if you were sleeping, you'd still be gathering energy. Taking into account the way they all lost a little Tower energy each day, it helped offset the need for constant cultivation. After some quick debate, they passed the bracelet to Uswah for now.

The other item was even more interesting, though Arthur knew that it was going to cause even greater arguments in the future.

Chapter 136

Considering the injuries involved, the group chose to rest a little before making their way deeper into the platform. However, considering the amount of damage, churned earth, and spilled blood in their vicinity—along with the slow-to-dissolve corpses—the group were trudging a short distance away to a nearby stream. It was not far at all and was where Uswah had gone, bypassing the main hive in her search as she had scouted out the stream while the group followed the deer trail.

Bad luck overall, that she had pulled away at the moment when she should have been ahead. It was perhaps why the nest had managed to last so long—either teams stumbled right onto the nest or were distracted as they went towards the stream, skipping around the hidden nest.

"Eh, boss, *bagi sini lah*. I need a distraction," Jan was whining as she limped along beside Arthur. Arm slung around Yao Jing's body, she was mostly being carried by the bigger man as she'd otherwise pull open her barely-clotted wounds. Still, she reached for the document in Arthur's hands.

"Maybe focus on the walking," Arthur said, refusing her grabby hands. Not that she was trying very hard.

"Come on, *lah*, boss," Jan continued to whine.

"Yeah, if you aren't reading it, let one of us," Leia chimed in.

"You all know we're still in the middle of a platform, right? Keep watching for trouble," Arthur growled. "Do you want to be attacked?"

"I'm watching, I'm watching," Rick drawled. "But got to admit, I'm mighty curious."

"Children," Arthur huffed.

He could understand their feelings though. He barely had time to scan over the document, but the new cultivation technique was something he certainly wanted to delve deeper into.

Eleven Pagodas of Thought and Defense

A memory and mental defense technique, the Eleven Pagodas create a mental fortress within the mind of the cultivator, defending important pieces of information, control and intentions from outside influence and control.

Cost: Passive / Variable

Arthur knew that mental defense techniques were uncommon, same as with mental attack techniques. The ability to read minds was considered a near impossibility, outside of a few unique individuals who had lucked out. Emotional manipulators, those able to read micro-expressions or covertly influence individuals via body language and other subtler methodology was, however possible. It was not, of course, mind control or mental reading; but it sometimes felt like it.

However, just because cultivators were not able to influence others did not mean that monsters were as limited. It was well known that techniques like fear, enraging, freeze, and even certain stealth techniques influenced cultivators directly. Some of these were not, of course, mental manipulation directly, just emotional. The line between direct mind control and thought influence and emotional alteration and influence was thin at best.

"At least tell us, is that a one-use document? How complete is it?" Casey asked, curiously. Arthur looked over and just gave her a side-eye, at which point she shrugged. "Got to try."

"Even if I knew, I can't say right now," Arthur said eventually with a sigh. "Need to read it over more. But it didn't feel like a Tower technique."

She grunted at that. "You know, we haven't really discussed distribution of such things…"

"We're keeping the technique," Arthur said firmly. "Your family probably has something just as good, if not better." He hesitated, then added, "Also, frankly, there's a lot more of us. But the other items we picked up, we might be willing to give you. For a higher share."

"Don't need it," she said and held up her own arm, waggling a bracelet for Arthur to see. Lam on the other hand cleared his throat. "Well, okay. Maybe…"

Arthur couldn't help but grin. He, of course, wanted the bracelet too. Who wouldn't. Any edge was better than nothing, but a single piece of equipment wasn't a huge advantage and it was only individual-use. The cultivation technique, on the other hand, if he was right, would allow their whole clan to progress further. Even if they restricted who could study the cultivation technique—and they would have to work out restrictions at some point, depending on the strength and refinement of the techniques—it was still going to benefit more than one person.

Never mind the fact that Arthur really, really liked the idea of being able to control how much information was being taken from his brain and protecting himself against any outside influence. If it helped with those social manipulators out there, it could be a very powerful technique when he was out.

If.

"We're here," Uswah said, popping out from the side of the tree and making Arthur jump. He growled a little, though she just flashed him a grin before pointing to a nearby tree with a comfortable and convenient branch. "I'll be watching."

Arthur paused and stared at her a little, trying to read her face and intentions. As expected, there was a trace of guilt there, for missing the hive. She hadn't merely missed a single, stray animal that wandered in from the sidelines; nor was the nest something she could trust the team to handle. But the hive was something she could have, should have, noticed.

And so the guilt was eating away at her.

"Mel…" He looked around, only to find her looking at him. There was a look on Mel's face, one that he had trouble reading, but after considering it for a moment, he realized what it was. Expectation. And then, disappointment when he mentioned her name.

He realized, belatedly, that perhaps there were things that he should not just pass on to her without thought. Things that he should at least try to do as clan head. Managing the feelings and emotions of his subordinates, at least some of them, was probably part of that.

"Yes?" she said, arching a single eyebrow.

"Ah hell…" Exhaling, Arthur reached for his pack. Then, realizing it might take a little longer, tossed the entire thing to her, wincing as he pulled his wounds open a little. "Here. Check it out, report on it, will you?"

"Sure, boss."

Ignoring Casey's look, he turned around, spotted Rick and pointed to him and the watch area that Uswah was headed to. "You're on watch. Uswah, with me."

She tensed then, probably expecting to be told off. He chose not to clarify the matter just yet though, knowing that the conversation they'd have was better off done in privacy. He led her up the stream, walking for about five minutes before he finally found a comfortable spot to slump against.

"So." Arthur started off, then winced, mostly internally. Wasn't the best starter for a conversation.

"So."

He found himself annoyed by her follow-up but pushed it away. A part of him wanted to tell her it was fine, mistakes were human. However, instinct told him that might not be the best method with her. After all, that was the kind of thing you said to children. That mistakes were made, but it was fine. Everyone made mistakes.

"You missed the nest."

"I did." She hesitated, then lowered her head. The pink-flowered tudung she now wore was a little grimy after all this time, one of three that she had stored and patched rather sloppily with thread. "I'm sorry. I'll do better."

"I guess you will," Arthur said. "Or you'll try." He saw Uswah flinch at that, the guilt increasing. "But how?"

"Huh?" she replied, surprised by his change of direction.

"How are you going to do better?" Arthur chuckled softly. "Sifu used to say, it was fine to screw up, because everyone did. Everyone needs to improve. But just wanting to improve isn't enough. You need more than want. You need a plan."

"I'll work harder."

"Wrong," Arthur said, firmly. "Not harder. Smarter." He raised a hand before she could interrupt him again, already knowing that she was getting annoyed with the vagueness of his comments. Which, truthfully, was fair enough. "What did you do wrong?"

"I left the trail because I was looking at the stream."

"Why?"

"Because that's where monsters sometimes congregate. We also hadn't reached any water in the last few hours, and we needed to refill our water skins."

"So it wasn't a mistake to move off the trail, right? Your job is to scout and that means sweeping the area around and finding things that might be of interest," Arthur said.

"I... but I missed the nest."

"Right, because you weren't here. But what you chose to do wasn't wrong, it was just bad timing."

"I should have ranged out further, then doubled back," Uswah said, waving a hand forward and then curving it as though to demonstrate the area she'd be moving through.

"One option, for sure. Sounds like a tiring one, though."

"What else could I do?"

"We could have more scouts out," Arthur said, slowly, thoughtfully. "Or keep one scout dedicated to our pathway and another roaming. That way, we wouldn't be reliant on you entirely."

"I..." She frowned. "But..." She stopped talking and started thinking, considering their newly expanded numbers. "I guess. Who?"

"It'd have to be either Leia or Eric." Arthur rubbed his chin. "I'd lean towards Eric."

"Why?"

"He's more likely to make things more interesting." At her look, Arthur shrugged. "He's… lucky. That's the immediate problem solved. What else?"

"I… don't know." But she said that automatically, though her brows were furrowed as she considered the problem. She kept going over it, again and again, till she nodded slowly. "I think I need to expand my sensing skills. Maybe my traits."

"Don't you already have a trait like that?"

"Just one. But something wider," she said as she stared at her feet, at the shadows pooled there, and then nodded. "If I can sense through the shadows better, maybe use them to map the surroundings. I think I'd be a better scout."

"I'd think so too," Arthur said. "So, do that. Save up points for later." As Uswah began nodding, looking not less guilty but at least happier with a plan of action, that was when Arthur figured he should complicate matters. "That is, if you want to be our scout still."

"What?" she said, startled.

"I never asked. I know you took it on, but I never asked. And basing more of your techniques around scouting, well…" he shrugged. "Might limit you."

"I can't do much else, now can I?" Now she held up her missing hand, waving it around.

Arthur let his gaze fixed on it briefly before he turned to look back at her face. Ah, that was the other reason Mel wanted him to speak with her. That bitterness, that exhaustion and pain and anger and grief, that could be dangerous.

"Bullshit." He held his hand up, forming a Refined Energy Dart. He let it form there, hover before him before he pulled the energy back. "You could learn ranged attacks with Tower energy. Train to blast people from a distance. Increase those shadow tendrils of yours, so that they become a second, third, fourth limb. You're not crippled. It's just a hindrance."

"Not what you said to Kim."

Arthur flinched, then shook his head. "I didn't say it. She did. Or acted like it. She decided her lack of an eye was her problem."

"Mmm…"

Guilt flickered through him, and he wondered if he really had done that. If he had chosen to exploit someone's self-loathing for his own good. For the clan's good. Perhaps he had. But… "It doesn't mean I'm wrong about you. I don't need an answer, but perhaps you should be thinking about what role you want to play in the future."

With that said, he stood up. He could have said more, but he figured it was good enough. At least for now. After all, she had a lot to think about.

And perhaps, so did he.

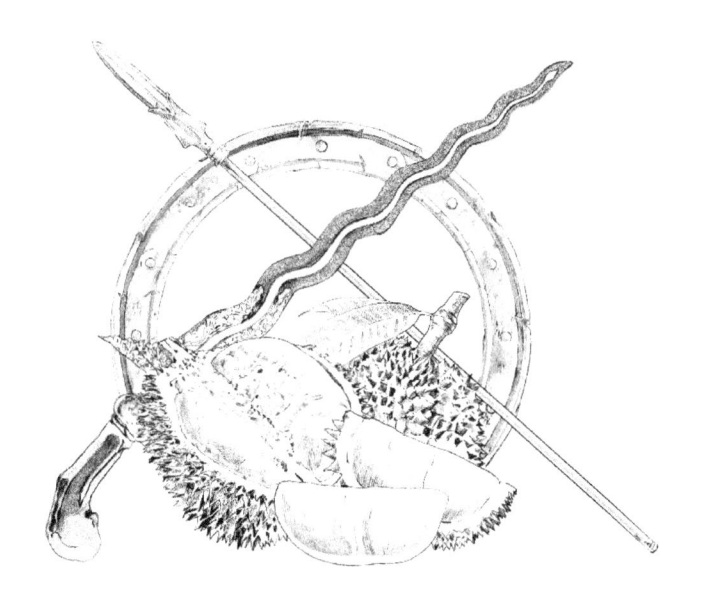

Chapter 137

Exiting the first platform did not take them long, their journey only stymied by the speed of their journey and the need to watch out for attacks. Thankfully, they didn't have to participate in any other major battles, at least none that slowed the group down significantly. Using the cleared paths, paying the minor tax to the two groups they ran into who kept the place clear, helped a lot with that.

Ascending to the second platform of the fifth floor and dealing with the gathered lizardkin tribe that had tried to ambush the first three of their climbers to ascend was a rough moment. Thankfully, they had packed the first three ascenders with their heaviest hitters: Rick with his shotgun, Arthur with his Refined Exploding Energy Darts, and Mel, whose ability to extend her spear and sweep it around to strike those at a distance kept the lizardkin away. When that didn't work, she would trigger the fiery elemental energy that coursed through the spear to explode upon impact, sending her victims flying into the distance.

Once the rest of the team had managed to climb up, the lizardkin had predictably fled once again. Not before leaving a number of their corpses behind. As the group dismembered their corpses for the monster cores, Rick had time to grouse about ammunition for his shotgun.

After that, it was just a matter of finding the most recent trail that had been broken and following that, keeping an eye on the direction they were moving in, of course. The second platform's trails were less well kept, what with the fewer number of teams that managed to make their way to this platform and were attempting to get through the third. Most that did traverse the second platform often did so to collect monster cores or to complete random gathering quests rather than with the intention of making it to the third platform.

Like Arthur and his team, few intended to spend more time than they needed on the third platform. Once they pushed through to the third platform, it was often time to break into the next floor, especially since the third platform was more dangerous than the first two and but the monster cores weren't significantly better. If not for the fact that there were decent quests for picking up on the second platform, it probably wouldn't even have been as trafficked.

That didn't mean they didn't have to spend at least a few nights on the second platform, though.

"What's the first thing you're going to do when you're out?" Rick asked, late at night after the group had a quick bite. Nothing too sumptuous, but the fruits that could be picked from trees and supped on led to a pleasant meal, even if it was an unnecessary one for the Tower climbers.

"*Chee chap chuk!*" Yao Jing said immediately, conjuring memories of pork porridge for everyone else who'd ever eaten it. "The one close to Masjid

Jamek. And I'll get some of the beef noodles there too. And maybe the chicken."

"The chicken is very good," Arthur said. "I prefer the noodles, though."

"Visit family, *lah*." Jan shook her head at both Arthur and Yao Jing. "They been waiting for us so long, why you don't go see them first?"

Yao Jing waggled a hand. "If during the day, they're all working, what."

"Let's not talk about family," Rick said with a sigh. He glanced at Casey as he said that, the pair of family heirs sharing a moment of mutual understanding. "What do you want to do, if you didn't have to deal with family or obligations?"

"Irresponsible," Uswah said. Then, after a moment, she added, "I'd visit the mosque."

"I said no obligations!" Rick said.

"It's no obligation." Uswah smiled briefly. "Some of us actually believe."

Rick opened his mouth, then at Arthur's warning look, shut it. He turned to Casey then, expectantly.

"A spa. I feel like I haven't been able to get clean in months." She stared at her nails which had soil underneath them and had chipped a little. "A hot stone massage, a facial, exfoliants and scrubs and a hot soak..."

"Sounds expensive," Arthur muttered.

"Oh, and what would you do?" she challenged him, glaring at Arthur as she hugged herself defensively.

"Sorry, sorry. I just..." Arthur paused now, as he considered what he would do. What he wanted to do. "I guess, I don't know what I'd do. If I didn't have obligations. I mean... that's all I have. Out there."

Beside him, Mel nodded. She went next. "I have family, brothers and sisters to meet with. My father is in the hospital, I need to make sure he's fine." She sighed. "Pay for his bills, sell whatever I can." She glanced over at Arthur, then added. "Help set up the clan outside."

"Oh yeah, that," he grimaced.

"So boring," Rick said. "And don't worry about the clan, my parents will take care of it."

Casey opened her mouth, as did Arthur to reject the high-handed offer of help. Only for the pair to be beaten by Eric.

"Arthur's always like this," the big man drawled.

"Like what?" Arthur said, dangerously.

"Boring! Always training and working, *lah*. We had to drag him out to go drinking, his first time. Then he complained, complained, all night about how it affected his training. Why, if we didn't tell him, he'd never see how little Yew wanted to—owww!" He grunted, rubbing his side where Leia had elbowed him hard in the side.

"Sweet *lah*," Leia said.

"Sweet or stupid."

"Oh, and you guys are much better?" Arthur groused.

"I am. Someone owes me a proper date," Leia looked over at Eric, who offered a half-smile and shrug.

"*Tsui*. Really, ah?" Arthur said, looking between the two. Sure, he'd had hints but still... "You know he still picks his toes with his fingers, right?"

"Not anymore." Leia looked inordinately proud of that. "He doesn't dare. Or else I won't sleep with him."

Eric growled a little but then stuck his feet out and waggled his feet side to side. Not that anyone could see his toes, what with his boots still on. Eventually, they'd pull them off and put on some boat shoes; the simple plastic of the slipper and straps meant they held up well. No one with any sense hiked through the undergrowth and floors with open-toe shoes though. Even toe shoes were considered a bad idea, since you never knew when someone might want to stab your foot. Steel-toe boots or the equivalent were the most popular form, closely followed by simple sneakers for their affordability and comfort, and then boots.

"Too much information," Arthur said, sticking fingers in his ears.

The group laughed quietly, before their attention turned to Lam Kor. The man had been silent all through this, and he shrugged. "I'm with Ms. Jan. I will visit my family. It will have been many months since I saw my children."

"What?!" The shouts and exclamations from the group were loud, so much so that a creeping salamander that had been closing in on them chose to flee instead.

"You're married?" Arthur said.

"How come you didn't say?" Jan demanded.

"How many?" Uswah asked, more importantly.

"I am. And three," Lam replied, serenely. The man eyes glittered with amusement at their surprise, though Casey at least did not look surprised. Which was for the best, Arthur figured, what with him being her closest employee.

"Your poor wife," Mel said, touching her stomach. Probably thinking about the pregnancy, though Arthur figured the whole process of bringing up three children alone was difficult. It did, however, explain his presence here. Having three must have cost quite the penny. And he must be making quite the penny, risking his life for the Chins.

"If you die, they get paid ah?" Yao Jing seemed to have jumped to the same conclusion as Arthur, asking curiously.

"My salary is guaranteed for a period of ten years," Lam confirmed. "We have enough savings that that should be sufficient for my family—all of my family—to find jobs or some form of education or hobby."

"Good deal," Yao Jing said approvingly and nodded to Casey, who smiled at that. Many others nodded too, though Arthur, Leia, and Eric shared a long look before turning aside. In the silent communication, they replayed old discussions about the value of a life, the price one put upon freedom and, finally, the undeniable separation of Tower climbers. A discussion their sifu had held with them again and again, because to do otherwise was to fail his students.

Yet, none of the three chose to speak. After all, that was a conversation for outside the Tower. Here and now, the choice had been made. There was nothing they could do, for Lam, for themselves, for any who were here. They could only accept their new lot in life, the railway path that led them from Tower to Tower and, finally, oblivion.

Or success.

And none of the trio ever expected to see the final Tower. After all, twenty years in, and not a single Tower climber had managed that.

Chapter 138

"Think we can find anyone to clear those salamanders for us?" Arthur asked, staring down into the distance where a trio of salamanders lay. Mini-boss monsters, all of them, meant to stop individuals from crossing over to the third platform. Not that they had to fight them; they'd just have to make it to the right or left of their current position and they'd find someplace to ascend. Even if it was harder, Arthur's Seven Cloud Stepping technique was quite useful for that.

"And let someone else take the stones?" Rick snorted. "Don't even think about it. I can handle one." He patted the stock of the shotgun he'd slung over his shoulder. "Though I'm running out of slugs."

"Use your pistols then."

"Too many bullets, it'll take quite a bit before they die," Rick objected. "Better to use a few slugs."

"What happens when you run out of bullets?" Lam asked, from the side.

"I won't. Seventh floor, there's someone waiting for me with reloads." Rick tapped his chest. "I planned ahead, you know."

"If they aren't there?" Lam asked.

"I'll figure it out," Rick replied, sweeping a hand through his floppy hair. "We ready?"

Mel, standing to the side, brusquely said, "Uswah, Jan, and I on the right."

"Rick, you're on the left." A breath, and then Arthur pointed. "Everyone else, middle. We take them down fast and help the others. Be careful of their breath attacks."

Earth, fire, and metal in respective order. Arthur started forming the Refined Exploding Energy Dart in his third eye, confident enough by now that he wouldn't blow his own head up. Casey, on the other side, was pulling back the bow, empty of an arrow. As she did so though, an arrow formed of energy.

"What is that?" Arthur said, surprised.

"Arrow of Seeking," Casey said. "Variation on the Dart of Seeking we used." Arthur could recall that it had a similar starting point to his own Refined Energy Dart. But it was more refined in terms of having the advantage of actually tracking the opponents to some degree, though it could not chase them around.

"You learnt that recently?" Leia asked, curiously.

"Recent enough," Casey said. "Wasn't confident in it till now." Even as she spoke, the arrow's form wavered a little, as though she was struggling to keep it contained. "You going to talk or...?"

The others had begun their own ranged attacks. In Jan and Mel's case, of course, that meant using slings and spinning up the stones to such speed that when they were unleashed, they'd strike and break open scales and wounds alike. Of course, after all this time, the group had found ways to spice up their attacks. In Mel's case, she went with the simple, infusing Focused Strike into the stone so that it could pierce and damage the creature easier. For Jan, she'd infused a portion of explosive fire energy within her stone.

Of them all, Yao Jing was the only one without a ranged attack.

Arthur counted the group down from three, all of them releasing an attack on the "loose." A part of Arthur noted that they probably should figure out timing, since certain attacks—physical stones and arrows—were slower by noticeable levels compared to more magical and explosive attacks.

The only person who hadn't fired was Rick, though by now, even Arthur knew why. Range on a shotgun was a lot shorter than their own, so Rick would be waiting till the Metal Salamander was close. It was for the same reason the Fire Salamander hadn't been picked for him—no one wanted that creature anywhere close to them. Burning energy dancing all across its body, the flames hot enough to leave ash behind, and small flames in the clearing were testament to the danger involved.

The hiss and grunt of pain, the staggered movement of the blinded Fire Salamander as the first arrow went into its eye, closely followed moments later by the explosion of the Dart that tore scales off the body all echoed through the clearing. Then, the impact of stones, the first with an exploding flame that consumed scale and skin, and then after that, Mel's that pierced the body with the power of Focused Strike.

More arrows, a spear of darkness shooting up from beneath the salamander to dig into its flesh and tear at hamstrings and slow the monster down. Yao Jing, crouched low and waiting, the spear he was holding shifted towards the back. Arthur knew he was going to try to throw it, rather than actually engage with the Fire Salamander, though it'd be best to end it before it came close enough to be speared.

Certainly, the Metal Salamander was the slowest, trundling forward ever so slowly, even as Rick shifted sideways so he could potentially run out to deal with it.

"Again! On your own mark." Arthur was already forming another Exploding Energy Dart, his own sling spinning up now that he could see it doing some damage. Not much, maybe bruising, maybe even crack a bone at best. But something was better than nothing, he figured. It didn't take much effort at all or slow down his formation of the darts.

Though, surprisingly, Casey was faster even than him. She had her arrow fitted and loosed by the time he was ready to send out his own. This time around, it curved and struck the other eye - or tried to. A last minute twist of the head sent the arrow skirting along the face, tearing a furrow and causing the salamander to hiss.

As Arthur released his own Energy Dart, he was surprised to notice that the creature had changed colour. The flames seemed to darken around the body, brighten and focus around its forehead. Intuition had him screaming, even as he threw himself down beneath a small rise.

Moments later, a gout of superheated air washed overhead, crisping his eyebrows and his hair. He cursed, patting at his head to make sure nothing was on fire even as the crackle of newly born flames behind him in the trees and the hiss and snap of branches breaking spoke to him from behind, telling a tale of overheated woe.

"Move, move, move!" Arthur said, scrambling to his feet. "Don't stick close together."

He checked around, made sure everyone was still alive and not cooked. Only to be caught by surprise moments later as the earth rumbled and his footing went haywire. He automatically hopped upwards, standing on a cloud as he tried to get away, even as the team on the right were thrown around—and in Jan's case, impaled in the upper thigh.

"*Tiu!*" she cried, twisting in agony and screaming louder as the stone refused to give way. Yao Jing bounced over, his body darkening as he hardened his body and shattered his way through the spikes.

In the meantime, the remaining two not injured were attacking the Earth Salamander. Uswah scrambled away, her only hand waving as she formed and wrapped a giant shadow tentacle around the creature's head, blinding the monster. At the same time, Mel ran forward, unslinging the spear from behind her back as she charged. Her sling was gone, lost somewhere in the mad scramble.

"Keep attacking!" Leia cried, releasing another ball of uncompressed energy. Arthur knew that attack, since it was the basic ranged attack one could purchase that did not utilise Refined Energy. It had the advantage of making use of basic Tower energy, which was easier to cultivate, but it was not compressed or as damaging.

Eric on the other hand was waiting, charging up the throwing knives he worked with. They were small and didn't have quite the same range, but he could still get a good fifty or so feet with them, between his increased cultivator strength and the technique he utilised. It pierced all the way through the Fire Salamander's body, the trio of knives forcing the monster to duck to the side and still get stabbed in the middle of its eye. Not particularly nice, but effective.

Popping upwards, Arthur waited. He saw the tic, the motion he had been expecting and he released his attack, aimed at where he judged it would move its mouth. Timed nearly perfectly, the flashing dart went into its open mouth and exploded within upon contact with the tongue, causing a gout of blood and skin to flood from its body.

Rather than face continued attacks, the Fire Salamander turned tail and ran, no longer content to be attacked or take further injuries. That didn't stop Casey from sending an arrow into a leg or Lam sending an arc of energy from his swung spear. It tore into the back leg, crippling the creature and leaving the others to continue their attacks.

"Switch!" Arthur roared, waving Yao Jing away to deal with the Earth Salamander. It had finally freed itself from the shadow tendril, and Uswah fell back panting as her energy stores ran out. The rest of the group turned to attacking it, except Rick who finally engaged the Metal Salamander. The heavy thump and roar of shotgun shells being fired at close range into the side of the Metal Salamander was interspersed with ringing, meaty explosions as the shells impacted the creature.

"Focus on the open wounds," Arthur called out to Casey, pointing towards the fleeing Fire salamander. "Bleed it out, don't try for an outright kill."

She and Lam nodded, taking the cue to keep attacking rather than give up. Not that Arthur figured it would matter, as he switched out for his spear and rushed the Earth Salamander.

Outside of the surprising ranged attacks from the salamanders, they'd managed this fight relatively well. Even as his friends were thrown off balance—a leg broke with a snap as Eric had his foot caught between two split pieces of stone that then twisted—Arthur knew they still had this in the bag.

The real question was how much they'd be slowed. And what the third platform had in wait for them.

Chapter 139

"Idiot," Leia was grumbling at Eric, as she waited for Arthur to finish resetting his shin bone and strapping everything into place. The muffled groaning as bone was manipulated back into place, before the flesh could swell too much and cause first aid difficulty, was just a little distracting for Arthur.

Then again, he deserved it.

"Why didn't you take to the sky?" Arthur asked.

"Can't. Still... learning," Eric said.

"You've had weeks," Arthur pointed out. "Have you been lazing?"

The glare that Eric turned on him was answer enough. Leia saved him too, adding softly, "Not that easy, boss. We have our own movement technique too. Can't use both of them, don't want to get rid of one entirely. So we're trying to integrate and not break it, you know?"

Arthur knew. You could, theoretically, learn multiple techniques; but the increased chance of mixing up energy flows could cause real problems, especially when one was in the middle of a fight. It was the same way people had preferred martial styles or movements, why someone who was good at hip-hop might not know ballet well, and learning both could be troublesome. The body remembered, and when stressed, had a tendency to revert.

Unlearning old habits was tough, refining old techniques even harder. It took time to work out bad habits, to relearn new ones.

"Whatever." Finishing the strapping down with the ivy, he stood up. "Cultivate and get it sorted. We can't wait forever, you know?"

Of course, saying it was one thing. The simple fact was that they'd need to wait a bit, since Uswah was out of refined energy entirely and so were a number of the others. He was doing okay, having kept a decent amount of reserve but only because he was moving towards another point allocated.

Abandoning the pair, Arthur checked on Jan who was being watched over by Yao Jing, then the rest of the team. Most were fine, Casey already seated against a tree with the latest monster core acquisition already being sucked dry. Lam was doing the same, though with a smaller core not far away, as was Uswah.

"Huh. Who's on guard duty?" Arthur said, looking around. It took him a moment to spot Rick, the man walking a circuit and checking out the undergrowth on the third platform.

Arthur had to admit, there was a lot to check. The foliage was tinted a weird purple, almost like eggplant, but along the wood and shading the leaves just a little. It made for a strange sight and led to even weirder colored fruit and flowers. The undergrowth crackled with every step that Rick took, and the occasional buzzing insect and hanging spider or lizard that scurried around were also weirdly shaded to fade into the surroundings better.

Straightening up after poking under the foliage, Rick caught Arthur's gaze. He raised an eyebrow in enquiry and Arthur found himself strolling over, sweeping his gaze about for problems as he did so. Finding nothing, he spoke immediately as he neared the other. "You need a break?"

"I'm fine," Rick said. "Just trying to do my part, you know?" He tapped the barrel of his pistol against his leg, finger off the trigger even if he was carrying it with him. Arthur idly noted that instinctive fear he had on seeing the weapon had died off a little, the concern about it accidentally firing and killing him, of ending his life, had faded. Maybe getting stabbed, bitten, gutted, and punched around had made him more callous. Maybe just knowing and being familiar with the weapon, watching it used over and over again, had made it as familiar as his own kris and spear.

"I can see that." A slight pause, then he added, "Thank you. For everything."

"Not done much."

"Which is a benefit, when you've got troublemakers in the clan," Arthur said. He carefully did not turn around to stare at his seniors or Yao Jing and Jan. "But you've also made offers and not pushed on it."

Rick grunted, then glanced over to Casey and Lam, who were meditating. He opened his mouth and then shut it, choosing to be silent for now rather than pursue that line of conversation.

"Exactly. Later."

Arthur waved after that, pointing to a nearby tree where he took a seat underneath, after carefully inspecting the ground and surroundings. After all, you only needed to sit on one *wong mama* ant nest, the big red soldier ants with pincers a centimeter across, to remember not to do that again.

Extracting a monster core of his own, he got to cultivating and refining. They'd run into the monsters on the third platform soon enough.

Spitting toads. Purple and green, hidden in the mushy ground that littered the floor. Once they managed to make it a few hundred feet, the footing underneath had gone from firm ground to a mixed marshland. Not the mangrove swamp of before, where they'd had to wade through water at knee or waist height, but mushy flooring that was a mixture of sucking mud and overgrown moss.

The toads loved sitting in the water, waiting for someone to get close enough before they spat acid and poison, striking with unerring accuracy. The spit stung a little when it touched open skin, burnt and inflamed underlying layers, and even made breathing difficult if one breathed it in too much. Their favorite tactic was to aim for the eyes, striking around the mouth if one dodged. Those struck had to wash the spit away as quickly as possible or be left blinded as their eyes watered, leaving them prey for a second assault, where long tongues darted out and pulled the struggling creature into the mud while more toads launched poison. In the end, suffocated as the lungs closed out and the heart over-exerted, their victims would be dragged over and consumed.

Or at least, that was the plan. The reality was that with such a large party, the group more often only suffered some minor splattering and stinging eyes before the toads were murdered. It did slow the group down though, as they waited for eyes to heal and breathing to steady before moving on.

Which, of course, left them open to the next monster.

The bondegezou really came as a package, a nasty paired package, but since they always came first, Arthur figured they deserved their own little addendum. In particular, the brown-black furred creatures with a pale tummy and snout-like faces snuck along the tops of trees, often passing slowly from branch to branch before crawling down the trunks, their curved and elongated claws sunk deep into the bark. Once they reached a sleeping or resting climber, they struck, claws sinking into neck and ears and scalp and tearing away.

The monsters were tiny, relatively speaking. Just about a foot and a half tall, but their claws were sharp, and their ability to sneak up on Tower climbers and camouflage made them dangerous opponents. Luckily, there were never more than one or two of them at a time; and if the bondegezou failed to make a lethal strike, they fled.

If not for the fact that the team moved in groups, they might have been outright lethal. A single successful attack, when someone was blind and suffocating, would have ended a climber's journey. Which was, of course, why everyone moved in groups. You couldn't stop them from sneaking up on you, not without elaborate precautions, but having an extra set of eyes to watch out for one another or an extra pair of hands to kill and pin one of the creatures left them as annoyances, not fatalities.

All fair and well. Of course, while you were dealing with the bondegezou, their handlers came along. Monkey-men, grey-furred, about four and a half to five feet tall. They wielded crude weapons, clubs, and sticks roughly sharpened to a point, stones strapped to the end sometimes. Plus loose stones, used to throw and cause chaos as they entered the fray, while their "dogs" were killed or were killing.

For every bondegezou, there were four or five of these *orang monyet*. Colloquially known for their similarity to the local legend of Bukit Timah Monkey Men, they were better known as timah monyet. Once they engaged, they never chose to back away. Despite their small size and lack of cultivation techniques or skills, they were theoretically a difficult, if not impossible, fight for most solo cultivators.

The wiki had large warning signs that groups of at least three climbers were recommended to engage timah monyet. Three, because if one or two were taken down or otherwise engaged by the previous monster threats, there was at least one more Tower climber that could handle the final monsters.

Of course, the more the better.

All of which was to say, with the entire team consisting of nine members, the Benevolent Durians and their allies were overpowered.

It still didn't mean they were moving fast through the floor, though. Just steadily.

Chapter 140

"Safe, but not very profitable," Arthur muttered his thoughts, about two weeks after their first ascent to the third platform. The problem, of course, was that the exit for the fifth floor to the sixth was never in the same place. There were a total of eight teleportation platforms, but which one was active at any one time was entirely random. So, the team could either trek around, searching for the latest one, or wait about.

Waiting was theoretically the smartest option, except for the fact that the teleportation platforms and access points never activated if someone camped by them. You had to wait until the final guardians reappeared at the location—which they would only do when it was empty—defeat them, and then use the teleportation gate that appeared to journey to the next floor.

Camping just outside the vicinity of the teleportation platform and boss formation area was theoretically possible, but no one had taken the time to test exactly how far away the optimal direction was. Also, if no one was going to the next floor and weren't killing the boss, you could be stuck waiting for weeks, if not months, hoping the boss would appear.

All things considered, most people just chose to kill their way upward, trekking their way through the marshy land.

"Yes." Mel was staring at the monster cores distributed to her. It had been long enough, and the breaks between fights wide enough that tonight they'd taken a moment to combine and then separate the cores gathered. It unfortunately left the team with just over two dozen each, not including the cores that they'd used as needed to keep energy levels up.

Perhaps one of the biggest issues of journeying through the third platform—or any floor, really—was the management of energy. Refined energy in particular, especially in fights. The need to use that energy to empower your body meant that the less you used up for fights, the faster you could grow your attributes. Which was why passive techniques that used Tower energy instead of refined energy were in high demand and ranked with quite a few more stars.

Unfortunately, not only were such techniques rare, but they were also limited to a significant degree. There was a reason his own Accelerated Healing utilised refined energy for the active healing process rather than Tower energy. There was a reason the majority of the powerful attacks were refined energy attacks, and why monster cores were utilised by climbers in other Towers. Though, supposedly, as one progressed through Towers, the density of even Tower energy increased, such that it was easier than ever to combine and integrate that energy.

"Should we split the team up?" Arthur said. "Not now, of course. But when we hit the next floor."

"The Chins already do," Mel pointed out.

"Seven is still too many." Arthur shrugged. "Five was fine, if a bit much, but now..."

"We need you with people we can trust," she said, eyes narrowed, as though guessing where he was going.

"I trust them. They're my seniors!"

"I don't."

Lips compressed, Arthur shook his head after a moment. "I won't argue. Anyway, four and three isn't a bad ratio. I would prefer more stones than less, but more safety isn't a horrible idea. So you or Jan or Yao Jing can rotate in when needed."

"Not me?" Rick, seated a short distance away, acted hurt.

Arthur paused, ran what he said without thought through his mind and realised what he'd done. Then, shrugged. "I guess not?"

"And here I thought we were becoming friends."

"We are," Arthur replied. "But... we aren't yet."

"Well, tell me when then." Rick turned away, leaving Arthur to stare at him and frown. The others were idly listening, most in the process of putting away their beast stones already or just cultivating them.

Mel cocked her head to the side, watching the pair interact before she spoke up. "Not a bad decision, but you might want to figure out why soon enough. You know?"

"Yeah..." He hoped it wasn't a racial thing. Just because he didn't have many Indian friends didn't mean he was prejudiced against them. Or so he thought. They just didn't run in the same social circles, mostly. Even his sifu's place had mostly been Malaysians who were ethnically Chinese. It was just the way things were, back in the real world. The Tower was a little different, the population here being a smaller group and forcing interactions.

At least, he didn't think he was being prejudiced. But the problem with swimming in the muck was that sooner or later, you swallowed some of it. You could try for cleaner water, purer thoughts, but at one point or another, you still got stained. Though, sometimes, he figured the blatant racism you saw was at least easier to deal with than the various micro-aggressions they talked about in the West.

"Eh, at least rich boy's not crying. All the *cronies* always think they can get what they want," Yao Jing said, rolling his eyes. However insulting the words were, though, he slapped Rick's arm to show he didn't mean it that much.

Not that Rick didn't roll his eyes a little. "Whatever."

"Hey," Arthur called out to Rick after a moment. "I know you got your movement skill. And I know you intend to do more with your guns. But… you know we aren't really able to help with that, right?"

Rick blinked, and Arthur noted that Casey had perked up. Her breathing had hitched just a little, though she was doing her best not to look over.

"Yes. It doesn't matter. My parents can help buy me what I want. We have contacts in the US, you know?" Rick said.

"Tower-enabled techniques?"

"No." Rick shook his head. "It'll be harder, but it was always going to be harder, not being there."

"So why not go back?" Mel could not help but ask. "I know your family's here now, but…"

"But why stay in Malaysia? Or South-East Asia?" Rick shrugged. "I don't think you all will be here too long. Not like Malaysia has many Towers."

"Two more," Arthur said. "One Beginner Plus. The other locked."

"And Singapore has its Intermediate one," Rick said.

Not that the terms they were bandying around were actual terms. The Climbers Association might have a document that they pushed, trying to get everyone to agree, but so did individual countries and even the net had different ways of measuring Towers. After all, this was a global phenomenon, with details still locked away half the time, and new information still coming to light, and Towers reconfiguring themselves.

Generally, though, the Towers were ranked based off two factors. How many prior Towers you needed to clear before you could enter them and the difficulty of the monsters within. Difficulty was based off the number of climber fatalities. Some more complex measures were used at times, like the mean and median number of days it took for a climber to exit a Tower, the loot factor in a Tower, the number of beast stones your average climber came out with, and even the kind of techniques available within, but those were generally just used on Tower wikis and the like. No one really talked about them in casual conversation.

"So, lots. And then Thailand, Indonesia..." Arthur said.

"You really want to do Indonesia?" Rick raised an eyebrow.

Arthur grunted. He did not look over at Uswah, who might have her own thoughts about the current state of that country. Even if she was Malaysian, you never knew who might have family over the water. Unlikely, of course, like thinking an American might have Canadian family just 'cause. But not impossible.

"Still quite a few places in this region. Be a while before I expand," Arthur said. "And probably for the best." He grimaced, thinking of having to deal with the Western guilds. Even if the Japanese, Chinese, and Indian subcontinent clans had long fingers and liked to get involved, the truth was, it was only at the Intermediate Towers or higher that they were a problem. "So why stay?" he asked Rick again.

"Told you, I want to grow your guild. Clan." He corrected himself before Jan could. "This is a hell of an investment opportunity, a way to really break the Tower." He leaned forward, saying firmly, "I do believe, the only way to climb the final Tower is via an organisation like yours. One that starts from the beginning."

"What makes you think there's a final Tower?"

"Ya *lah*," Yao Jing said, cracking one eye open as he cultivated. "No sign or anything."

"Faith."

Yao Jing snorted, and Arthur was not much better in his skepticism. Then again, Rick had stated he was a "real climber" on first meeting. You had to have faith, at least, to call yourself one. As for himself...

"I don't intend to do that," Arthur said, firmly. That got a smile from Mel. "A stable clan is all I want."

"Sure, sure…" Rick said.

"No, seriously. I don't."

To Arthur's chagrin, Eric was nodding along with Rick as they smiled skeptically at him.

Why did no one ever believe him?

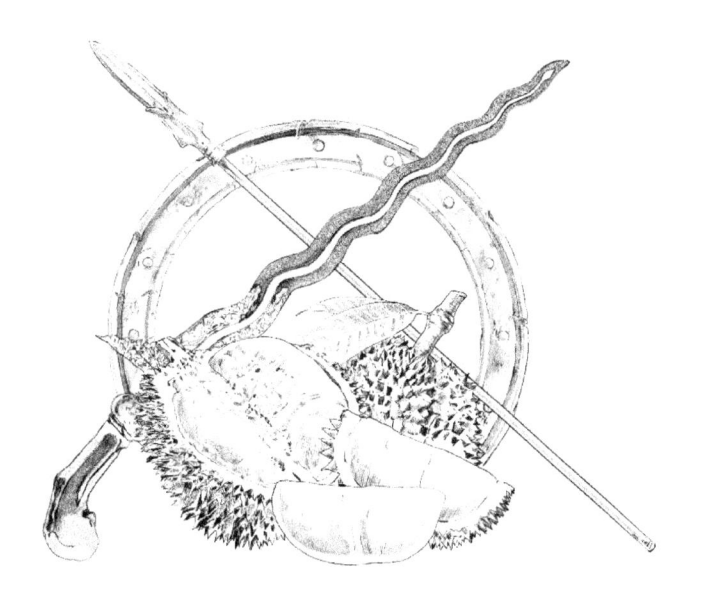

Chapter 141

The final boss on the fifth floor was a coin toss of who'd you get. It drew from any of the previous monsters on each platform and floor that a climber had traversed, so that you never knew exactly what combination you'd fight. A single boss—or a series of mini-bosses—was not even guaranteed. A few times before, there had been hordes of lower-grade monsters instead of a tough boss, though such instances were much rarer and only likely when no climbers had crossed over in some time. As though the floor had backed up and needed to release its creatures after the latest boss monster had not died in time.

In such instances, almost invariably, the climbers had fallen or been forced to flee. Twice, they had fled and led the horde all the way back to the starting zone where a pitched final battle was conducted. Numerous buildings and people had fallen during that period, with the culprits then blackballed for their actions. The few that still lived, that is.

It was because of this that Arthur's group travelled across the perimeter of the third platform searching for the teleportation platforms, charting their way by utilising the maps they had purchased, and approaching landmarks with some trepidation. Keeping in view the arc of the towering mountains in a distance, the land that sloped up steeply and delineated the end of the third platform to their right, they traversed the marshy platform battling monsters in search of their final victim.

When they finally reached that encounter, having made their way nearly halfway around the floor, it was to meet the most dreaded of groups: a hive of deadly, overgrown wasps. In sight were only a half dozen in number, hovering over the open ground of the teleportation platform, the worn stone that marked where it was located, and the standing columns that would host the gate. However, only a fool would think that those six, human-child-sized wasps were the only ones to watch out for. Especially not when the nest, built between the gate columns, had a large opening.

"Shit, shit, shit," Arthur muttered when he was informed of the danger. "Do we know if anyone else is trying to go up?"

"None," Mel said immediately.

"We can't wait!" Casey interjected at the same time.

"Those are the worst to fight. You know that. These might not kill us with a single sting. But the boss is almost guaranteed to end any of you." He grimaced. "I probably could survive one. Maybe two. Probably not, though. And I definitely don't want to test that idea."

"We can't wait. We've lost too much time," Casey repeated. "We have to push ahead."

"I know, but..." He waved at the stone platform. "This is bad. This is dangerous, to the nth degree."

"C'mon, boss. Don't be a chicken, *lah*," Jan said. "We can do it!"

"I liked you better when you were pessimistic," Arthur growled.

"Seriously, Art. We just need to take out their wings. If we hit them from range, it'll be fine," Leia said. "We got quite a bit of ranged attacks, right? Fire, all of that."

"Slingstones aren't great." Mel muttered. "Casey might be okay. We really need Karen..."

"Aura of Fire." Arthur said, softly. "Too late to go back for her."

"You're the one wanting a way out," Casey pointed out, before she waved a hand and cut him off. "So how are we doing this?"

Arthur sighed but stopped complaining. He turned to Uswah who detailed the surroundings to him. Not that there was much to explain. The clearing around the teleportation gate was clear, beyond the gate itself and the flying hornets. The ground around it, though, was made up of the same trees and marshland as the rest of the forest, which meant occasional low-hanging vines, a lot of thorny shrubbery, and not a lot of cover otherwise. Most of the hanging vines weren't that large and they were few enough that the hornets likely could either dodge through them or break through as they flew in.

They could, if they wanted, surround the location. So long as none of them were spotted, the hornets weren't exactly flying out of the base to hunt down climbers, which left them easy to ambush. Of course, they still were missing a few important factors, like how many of the creatures there were within the large nest, how far they'd chase if they had to break off, and how fast they'd react to an attack. Did they have to kill a certain number of hornets or would they leave the nest regardless?

"Alright, if we're doing this, we're doing it smart. We need a breakaway location." He frowned, thinking. "I remember a stream leading towards a pond a half-hour back. We never checked how deep the pond was."

"Why... Oh, you want to jump in," Mel corrected herself before she finished. "Not large enough for all of us."

"Yeah. It'll fit like maybe three unless it's a real sinkhole." He held a finger up. "Let's call it three, we'll check. That's one group. That leaves at two more groups then, that we should find places to run to." Thinking, he added, "Maybe a spitting toad base? I doubt they're friends..."

"And get attacked on both ends?" Rick said, doubtfully.

"Maybe not. But I don't think a lot of ponds or the like are around," Arthur pointed out.

"I can scout." Uswah offered.

"Me too." Leia stabbed her finger in the opposite direction of the pond that they'd marked with a stone. "I'll head this way. Even if it's a clearing or a particularly dense set of bush, it might be enough if it's far enough away."

"They track," Lam pointed out.

"Splitting up the forces still isn't bad," Eric said, jutting his chin out as he defended his sister.

"Didn't say it wasn't," Lam said.

"Okay. Three forces, our scouts check out for places to run to. If things go bad, we retreat. Each group moves independently for the retreat, because the hornets are going to chase them back anyway, so that'll be fine," Arthur said, firmly so as to avoid the burgeoning argument. He really didn't want to get involved in that, though the constant chaffing between his two seniors and the rest of the team was annoying to him. "We hit the first group with as many ranged attacks as we want. Question is, do we want to deal with the nest at all?"

"Deal with?" Casey said. "You mean destroy it."

"Yes. Fire and torches, light it up. Maybe see if we can maybe put some flames right in front of the openings to encourage the hornets not to come out, you know?" Arthur said.

"Might wake all of them up instead," Lam cautioned.

"I know."

"What?" Uswah asked.

"Other option is we wait around, hope they don't come out to kill us. It'll be tricky, especially because there's no guarantee the big boss won't come out immediately. Even if it does, there's also going to be someone who needs to be targeted to deal with it." Arthur hesitated, then sighed. "That's probably going to be me. If I keep it busy, you guys can finish the rest that come out."

"You lazing around then, ah?" Yao Jing said, teasingly.

"Why not me?" Rick asked, touching his shotgun.

"Firstly, we've seen how fast they move. You might miss," Arthur said. "Secondly, you don't have armour. I do. Thirdly, I can survive getting stung, you can't." He hesitated, then added, "But you should take a shot, when you get it. After I engage."

"Fine," Rick said.

"Why does no one want to live?" Arthur grumbled.

"We're climbers. None of us are exactly stable, you know?" Rick said with a grin.

Yao Jing snorted. "I don't wanna die. I won't *lah*."

"Nor do I," Mel said, softly.

"And I know I'm getting out," Casey said, firmly. "This is just a necessary step to taking control of the company and rising in its ranks."

Arthur opened his mouth then shut it after a moment. He never did get how the need to be a Tower climber and getting higher up on the Chins' ladder—or any major corporation in Asia—tied together. After all, climbers had a short shelf-life overall, the need to enter Towers driving them on as their body broke down and they lost energy outside of the Tower. Without Tower energy, they would eventually die if they didn't reenter it, even with a large surplus of stones.

Well, that was the theory. He guessed if you were the Chins or a large enough group, they could supply the increasing amounts of stones needed, lengthen the amount of time before it was necessary for you enter the next Tower. Then again, he also knew that a Beginner Tower was just the first, like what a Bachelor's degree was in the past. A starting point for the professionals.

If you wanted to go higher, you often needed to dip into other Towers, get better qualifications. Some of that, he knew, was because the big companies played dirty, fought and killed one another when necessary. Not always, of course, but when violence was something that you learnt as you climbed a Tower, the habits didn't necessarily go away.

Sometimes, it felt like they'd devolved with the appearance of the Towers. Gone back to the time of the Romans or the eighteenth or nineteenth century, when commerce was still being run by savages.

"Whatever," Arthur said. "We good for this?"

He checked around, scanning the group for objections. Noted none, because they didn't have that many strategies to use. Not here, not with the information they had or their abilities. Maybe another time, with more skills and techniques. For now, it was simple.

Hit them, hit them hard, and get out.

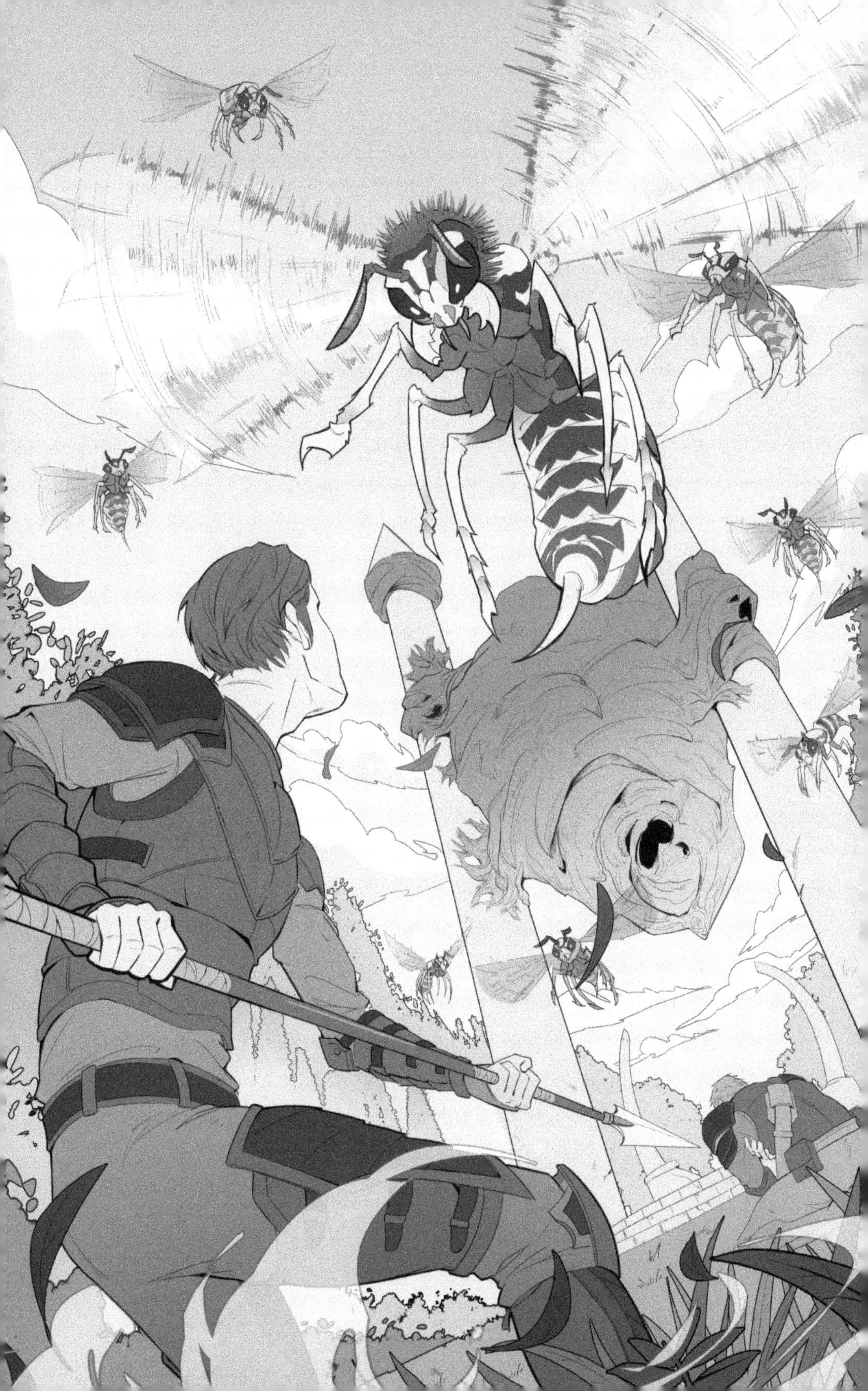

Chapter 142

It took them nearly to evening before they were ready to get going. Rather than start the entire battle at night, the group chose to pull back a little and rest. The evening was spent cultivating, drawing in energy to top up before they headed for the teleportation gate and the wasp bosses.

Split into three groups, the team slowly pulled forward to the edges of the clearing. Yao Jing, Rick, and Jan were with him as one group, Casey and Lam with Mel were another group, and his pair of seniors in the final group. His team was slightly oversized, mostly because they were meant to start the battle. More importantly, Arthur was meant to keep his own attacks contained until the big boss arrived. His Refined Exploding Dart was the most likely to damage, and certainly anger, the damn boss.

Crouched in the brush, just outside of view of the teleportation gate and the hornets waiting for them, Arthur was pulling energy into a Refined Energy Dart. He wasn't going to go with his more damaging attack right now, not with the possibility of angering the other hornets behind them in the nest.

The others were readying themselves, Yao Jing ready to use his spear, Rick with his pistols out and the shotgun loaded and by his side. Jan wasn't ready to start spinning her stone yet, needing enough space to do so.

"How long?" Arthur asked, softly.

"About ten minutes."

"Then it's time," Arthur said. "On three."

He counted them down, Jan stepping aside and beginning the spin of her sling as he started. He stepped forward on the last, pushing through the foliage. The low drone of beating wings sped up, shifted as the wasps noticed him. Arthur didn't give them time to react, releasing the Refined Energy Dart immediately.

He watched it shoot forward, striking the closest wasp on its yellow striped body. It tore through the cylindrical bottom, ripping a hole and causing it to jerk about in pain, twisting its body and leaving its stinger half-attached, blood falling to the ground and spraying the stones.

The other wasps were turning too, only for the bark of pistols firing to interrupt them. One after the other, the bullets entered their bodies, soft-shell bullets piercing through and mushrooming so that the exit was much larger. Using two hands, firing one after the other at the creatures still caught by surprise, Rick had no problem tagging them with the majority of his shots. His targets dropped, leaving five, moments before an exploding fire stone struck.

That creature flew backwards, wings buzzing, flames and shrapnel tearing through the air. It struggled for a moment, one of its wings torn and shredded, licks of flame dancing along its body before darting forward.

Now they were coming for them, so Yao Jing stepped in to strike the first to arrive.

A sudden movement saw the first hornet rise, dodging the spear for the most part, scraping its underside. The man shortened the spear, trying to keep up, but the hornet was faster, darting in close and curling up its body to launch its stinger. Yao Jing flinched, managed to strike it with the haft long enough to avoid the attack before he snarled. "Enough!"

Dropping the weapon, he switched to his preference, hands clenched tight as he threw a series of jabs and crosses at the flying monster, the pair dancing as twisted, colored light formed around Yao Jing's fists and body.

Then Arthur no longer had time to worry about anyone else. His attention was drawn to the two wasps coming after him, two more than he should have to deal with. He stepped back, dodged the buzzing of the first, while he beat to the side with his spear the injured wasp whose half-attached stinger. The creature flinched, twisting sideways and in pain as skin tore.

By this point, the second wasp had come in, higher than the first. It dropped low, darting forwards. No time to dodge, so Arthur hunched up, taking the attack on his armour, watching it bounce off the side of his arm as stinger met good hardened leather. The creature didn't stop with just one attack though, retreating and striking a second, a third time before Arthur managed to retreat and a spear pushed the monster away as Jan came to save him.

Rick was dealing with his own problems, the now fast-moving remaining wasp not willing to stick around for him to hit it. He had to be careful too, knowing that there were others in the background, emerging from around the clearing. Couldn't afford to shoot downwards, not if he didn't want to risk hitting them. Thankfully, the Tower-enhanced and monsterized wasp or not was not smart enough to plot all that out.

At the same time, the nest was buzzing and bulging. The hardened spit and clay and twigs that made up the nest was stretching, bursting apart as wasps crept outwards, taking to the air. The first to manage its way out caught a glowing blue arrow in the side, tearing through its body and pulling it away. Other attacks landed moments later, a large burst of yellow power catching another creature in the way and sending it tumbling to the ground.

Relieved of his own battle, Arthur struck at the wasp he had been fighting, pushing it back. It retreated high, dodging out of the way of his spear strikes, forcing him to pay attention to not only the creature above and the nest but also the formation of a large, expansive Refined Exploding Energy Dart.

He still remembered his goal, he knew he'd need to unleash it when the time came. Now, if he could just get some time to pay attention...

"Die, die, die!" Jan was chanting, swinging her spear around, trying to get to the damn wasp that had escaped her attention. She jumped a little, only for the creature to dart away and then, as her spear retracted, darted forward. It caught her arm, stinger tearing long furrows as she jerked away, blood welling up and the woman cursing as she struggled to keep grip.

"Got you!" Rick snarled, kicking the monster that landed beside him, one side torn up badly from a shot that managed to land. The body was sent tumbling away and he led its movements with more shots, tearing its body up as it twisted and tumbled aside. The man stepped back, sliding a gun back into its holster as he cried out. "Reloading!"

Arthur grunted, ignoring the fight, ignoring the cry. More attacks were landing from the other side, shadowy tendrils having gripped one wasp as it emerged and were in the process of playing a deadly and cruel game children all took part in in Malaysia. Pulling wings off the body, plucking them to make sure their victim could never fly again.

A twisted, cruel game against a most hated enemy. Wings, delicate and large, tore as they were pulled from the body, the creature falling to the ground, injured. Another, hurt, crawled along the ground, heading for the new groups of attackers. Eric, crouched low, spear aimed.

Waiting.

More creatures emerged. A flash of red, not the yellow and black of the other wasps. A decision reached faster than he could think, Arthur loosed the gathered Refined Exploding Energy Dart as the mini-boss variant made its way out. Not the actual thing, not at all, but the attack still struck and exploded. The maelstrom of energy it released caught another wasp on the way out, threw it against the nest that had its main exit widened further, even as insect bodies were cast aside.

"*Bodoh!*" Rick shouted, finishing with his reloading. He looked up, aimed at the creature buzzing around Arthur's head. Hesitated. "Shit, they're regenerating!"

Then Arthur looked up, realised the man was right. The one that had its stinger almost torn off was no longer bleeding. Long scar tissue had formed at the edges, its movements no longer as erratic from pain. It sought blood, only to get caught in the side by the fusillade thrown by the gunfighter.

It did nothing for those creatures that weren't entirely dead, many just gravely injured. Some were seeming to come back to life from the dead, though Arthur assumed it was a last-minute effort at regenerating the damage before things came to an end. More wasps poured out of the enlarged main entrance, the red mini-boss coming up as well, injured and its stinger entirely torn off but alive. Alive and angry.

Instead of six that began, now there were at least a dozen on the ground, littered around the clearing, coming in trying to strike one another. A triumphant cry saw another down, Yao Jing's fist sending shockwaves through the clearing.

Only for a pause in exits, as something larger and nastier tried to emerge.

The final boss. At last.

And no one ready to pick it up.

Chapter 143

The Boss Wasp was huge. The size of a human, about five and a half feet tall, from head to tip of its stinger. Hard to tell as it was curled up a little, and he wasn't even taking into account those long antennae that stuck out. Black and yellow stripes running down its body like a particularly deadly racing car. It moved like one too, breaking free of its nest to explode outwards, zipping upward to dodge a floating ball of unrefined Tower energy that struck the nest, moments later.

Arthur cursed, stepped back to give himself a second and focused. The Refined Exploding Energy Dart he had been building flew forwards, cutting through the air to target the creature as it flew upwards. To his anger, but not to his surprise, a slight twitch of the creature's body was enough for it to dodge the attack.

Damn it.

His attack had a lot going for it. Speed, conservation of energy, explosive power. But it was, at the end of the day, a single-shot, blind attack. Once released, it could not home in on its target, it could not change course. A monster moving this fast could easily dodge his attack.

As though dismissing Arthur, the boss flickered forwards, buzzing down so quickly it brushed by one of its own wasps, sending it spinning around as it struggled to deal with the turbulence. It struck at the last moment, pulling upwards from its dive to hover and stab with its massive stinger, the damn thing so big it might as well be a sword. One that dripped with poison.

Its minor hesitation was all that saved Yao Jing from immediate death; the big fighter crossed his arms before his body to take the attack. He managed to slip it just above the striking stinger, slowing its plunge even as it dug into his body and then ripped upwards. Stomach cleaved open by sheer force, throwing him upwards and backwards, skin already blackening from poison.

A bark, a bullet striking the creature in the side. Rick had no time to switch guns, and so he reacted by firing with his pistols. The bullets tore into the creature's body, the first one managing to hit, the second missing as it darted away. It buzzed higher, dodging the bullets as it twitched in the air, reorienting on Rick.

"Shit!" Arthur cried, trying to break free from his own attacker. No time to get around it though, with the damaged wasp focused and in his way. He blocked the latest sting, cursed as it got into his face and forced him back again and again. Always, he tried to get around to striking it, even as Rick stopped firing for a moment, his gun clicking empty.

Arthur could see the future in his mind's eye. The Boss Wasp flying in, plunging its stinger into Rick. The man wasn't as fast as Yao Jing, and Arthur could imagine the attack impaling the man entirely. See it shake the body off, even as Rick died. Then, it would pull back and the wasps that were already becoming a problem would turn on them, finish it off.

Energy that he had been pulling towards him was poured into the Heavenly Sage's Mischief. Too slow, he knew, as he watched the Boss Wasp dart in.

Perhaps Rick knew what was coming too, for he had thrown himself backwards, abandoning trying to reload his weapons as he brought his hands up to guard himself. Even as the wasp came to a hovering stop, shadows emerged from the ground. Some to slam upwards, to slow down and block the striking stinger, others to grip Rick and pull him back further.

At the same time, more attacks landed. An arrow, fired from the distance, buzzed through the air, slamming into one wing and then tearing out through the other. It caused the Boss Wasp to stutter in its flight, to tumble downwards, its attack marred as it scored Rick's bracers and glanced off them. The creature fell to the ground, even as shadows tried to wrap themselves around its limbs, pulling at stick-thin legs as it scrambled on its back.

Not that that was the only battle, for a bottle of oil landed on the nest. It went up in flames, the dried clay and spit and twigs and whatever other materials the wasps had used were now burning merrily. It caught at the thin hairs of the wasps that still struggled to exit, spread as droplets fell, as another keening stone cracked open heads and a blast of condensed Tower energy struck.

Eric ran towards the nest, holding his spear close to him, stabbing down at wasps that had been grounded. Killing them before they could crawl over to do more damage. Mel, by his side, fighting desperately against a pair of uninjured wasps trying to strike him down. Yao Jing was desperately trying to stem the flooding blood of his wound.

Then, time sped up again, as future prediction shattered and the cultivation technique snapped into place. Arthur felt the surge of energy coursing through him, Heavenly Sage's Mischief empowering his body. When he next blocked the wasp before him, it found itself thrown backwards further than expected. A moment's hesitation as it tried to reorient its body, instinctively trying to find altitude. Instinct betrayed it, for now it was far enough away for the spear point to find its body.

A single thrust, empowered and using Focused Strike, plowed through the body, leaving it pinned. Arthur didn't even bother trying to retrieve the spear that had punched all the way through, instead dropping it to the side as he snatched at his kris and dashed over to the boss.

He wove another technique, knowing he had only a little time before it broke free from Uswah's tendrils. Gambled, on Murphy, on expectations as he chose which of his many techniques to use, knowing he still needed the Heavenly Sage's Mischief to do battle.

The Boss Wasp broke free, tearing itself out of the gripping shadows, pulling itself upwards. Damaged wings or not, the mixture of magic and physics was more than sufficient to empower its rise. A foot, two feet, four. It rose upwards in a blink, rising almost vertically.

Grinning, Arthur engaged his Seven Cloud Stepping technique, kicking himself higher off on the cloud that he leapt onto, getting above the creature. He came crashing down as it rose, arms extended with the kris leading the way. Blade plunged into body, one arm fouling around the tip of a wing and bearing the creature down as he let go of the qinggong technique, giving the Boss Wasp his full weight.

Something burned along his body, drawing a streak of pain that dug into his side and nearly causing him to let go of the wasp he bore down on. The bark of a bullet came nearly at the same time. Eyes wide, even as he twisted and turned the kris in the bucking, twisting wasp.

"You shot me!" Arthur cried. He'd glare at Rick, but his face was buried next to the creature's flesh, his skin tickling as tiny hairs brushed at his skin with each jerk of the monster.

"Shit! Don't just jump without warning me," Rick cried.

"Don't just shoot!" Arthur snarled, continuing to twist and dig in. He could sense the kris' Yin poison entering the creature's body, even as it thrashed around. If he could just hold on, he'd win. Of course, that was a big if.

After all, it wasn't as though the Boss Wasp was not moving around desperately, twisting and turning even as they fell to the ground, bouncing the pair of them on the earth as they thrashed around. His grip was slipping. His legs hurt, his face was battered again and again by flapping wings, the stinger stabbing open air and batting at his legs, seeking an opening in the armour.

Tiny feet, pushing against his body, barbed and tearing at his flesh. It was like holding onto a rotating skewer of meat, one filled with poison and malice. Each drop of poison that fell from the stinger wafted into the air, causing Arthur's eyes to burn, his breathing to tighten. He felt his strength being robbed with each moment in close contact.

Still, he was winning. He was sure of it. He just had to hold on. None of his friends could help him, but he could win.

As the drumming increased, Arthur realised it was not the pulse of his heartbeat juddering in his ears. No, it was the drone of more wasps as they emerged.

He could hold on. Now, if his friends could do the same, they might just win.

Chapter 144

Twisting, turning, bucking. Wings rapidly beating a tattoo on the ground, on his arms, in the air. Stinger dripping poison, the fumes themselves choking the air, causing Arthur's eyes to turn red, for his breathing to tighten and himself to wheeze. A kris embedded in the body, threatening to slip out with each juddering movement, sent its own ethereal poison into the creature. Large as it was, the Boss Wasp was fighting it off, though blood, sticky and pale yellow, spilled out from the growing wound.

A nasty stalemate, as Arthur struggled to hold onto the body, one that he might lose. But more worrying was all that happened around him.

Arthur caught a glimpse of it in flashes, as he saw sky, ground, and fleshy body as they thrashed, side-to-side, and he tried not to get stabbed by the massive stinger. Even then, his legs were torn up, the barbed sides of the stinger tearing at exposed flesh and cloth, leaving surface wounds that spilling poison could enter.

No, not a worry except for the battle as dozens of massive wasps took to the air. The shuddering, percussive blast of a shotgun tearing into the sky. Wrong shells loaded though, meant for the monster Arthur clutched tight. The slugs shredded each wasp they hit.

In the meantime, the team was battling the creatures individually, using swords and spears and the occasional arrow from a bow. Lam, keeping them off Casey, his metal spear blocking and striking. The tip of it was a little longer, the head meant to help tear into creatures with a twist, rather than a simple cone like most of their weapons. Better made too, as befitted the Chins. In the meantime, Casey drew and loosed, her brows furrowed with concentration. Each arrow blasted through a wasp, and then curved a little to hit a second and sometimes third.

Not killing blows, but damaging enough that often the creatures would falter, fall to the ground. Forced to crawl towards them, their ire undiminished.

Leia and Eric were in the middle of the clearing, doing their best to try to near them. The pair fought together with casual ease, covering for one another in a display that would have movie producers salivating in the olden days. Even now, they were more like choreographed fighters than scrambling madly for survival like the others. Years of fighting together, of training, and a deep connection kept them from being overwhelmed.

Barely.

Over there, Jan and Mel, backed off fighting near one another. Working together, though neither had the skill or synchronicity of his seniors. Uswah was over by Yao Jing, trying to patch him together, a bubble of shifting darkness wrapping itself around them as it fended off four wasps.

He needed to get back into the fight, but releasing the creature he held was a guarantee of them dying too. Not that he had a choice, moments later, when a sudden and unexpected curl and rotation had the creature pop free, the kris torn out of the wound. It popped free like a seed squeezed from a mango, blood slick as it flopped around and climbed upwards.

Movement lethargic, even as Arthur managed to roll over. He released the attack he'd been holding back, the Boss Wasp too slow to dodge the Refined Exploding Energy Dart this time, the Yin poison having caught up to it. The eruption of energy as the dart struck along its back tore out wings, sent gobs of flesh and dust spiralling outwards, and blinded Arthur due to his proximity.

"Aaargh!" Backwards, backwards, he scrambled on his butt, one hand covering his eye. He desperately tried to blink, to shake his head to reorient himself, to get the ringing to fade away, and failed. A buzzing noise, an impact along his chest. Something digging into the armour around his shoulders, surging pain as flesh was torn and poison seeped in. Then the stinger was withdrawn as he swiped at the air with his kris ineffectually.

Backwards, he scrambled, till a hand gripped the back of his armour. It hauled him to his feet and he halted his attack halfway towards the body, realising it was help.

"Careful!" Rick snarled, stepping back. The bark of his pistols, quieter than the shotgun, erupted around Arthur. Instinctively, Arthur froze, scared to move and get shot. Forcing his eyes open, he began to see around him again, the world a watery haze.

"Kill the Boss!" Arthur said, when he realised that Rick was shooting the wasps around him, not the finally grounded Boss that was struggling forwards. It was healing, he knew it was healing.

"I... have... trouble! *Bevkoof*" Rick snarled. "You. Do. It!" Then, one last bark of his pistols. "Reloading!"

Instinct had Arthur moving forwards, putting himself between the man and the wasps. He jabbed his kris outwards, catching a wasp as it came forwards with its stinger. Felt the impact of the stinger as it struck his bracer, nearly tearing it off as his own kris ripped along the body. A line of fiery pain coursing along his arm, as he struggled to keep hold of his weapon and swing at the random moving bits.

Even then, he was working on cultivation techniques, kept building the necessary energy for his next attack. Arthur knew what he needed to do, as the Refined Exploding Energy Dart formed at his third eye and he dropped the Heavenly Sage's Mischief and attempted to accelerate his healing.

The Boss had to die, because unless they managed to kill the other wasps or did enough damage that they would expire anyway, the fight would never end. Instead, they needed to kill the one monster that was offering them a boost. At least, Arthur hoped it was an overall boost and not just the natural nature of these mini-bosses.

If not, this was really going to suck.

His eyes began to clear up. The big body, moving and struggling upwards. He swung again, a creature ducking in close, stinging him. It tore at his pauldron, glanced off it just enough that it missed plunging deep inwards. A tap on his left arm and he instinctively stepped away, towards the creature that had tried to sting him.

Moments later, the bark of pistols firing again as Rick let out a series of attacks. The creatures hovering around them fell, and in that moment, Arthur had a chance to focus. He released the Refined Exploding Energy Dart, watched it fly through the air. Only for a wasp to dodge in the way, detonating the attack moments before it could hit the Boss.

Again, dust and bodies and gobs of flesh, even as Arthur felt his eyes finally clear up. He glared, trying to pull at the energy for another attack, knowing he was already running low. Healing himself, the Energy Darts, Cloud Step and all, it was just energy down the drain. He knew he had to be careful, but finishing the fight was more important.

"Cover me!" Arthur snarled, as he ducked low and underneath Rick's line of fire. He dashed forward, keeping close to the ground, spotting the Boss Wasp already rising upwards. Over his head, he could feel the passage of bullets, moments before he slammed into the creature.

Kris plunged into soft, yielding flesh. Stinger entered the foolish, human body.

A lightning bolt of agony coursed through him, nerves on fire as they clenched around the stinger that had managed to find the gap between his ball cup and the bottom of his breastplate. The curved movement of the creature plunged it upwards, tearing open his stomach muscles, pumping poison into him.

His own kris went deep in, angled downward between bulbous eyes. It pierced chitin and flesh, tore into the brain and pumped Yin poison, even as the wavy dagger sawed at skin and flesh. As the wasp retracted its attack, Arthur pulled forwards, tearing the kris downwards towards him, pulling the wasp together.

Face and shoulders battered by weakening wings, he hunched over the creature, shoving with all his strength to push the wasp onto the ground. He fell onto it, bearing it to the floor as his legs gave way, blood pouring from under the armour as his legs gave way to the poison.

Unable to move, Arthur could feel another sting strike him between the shoulder blades, hard pressure bouncing off his armour. Again and again, before it fell, the hard bark of a pistol. The corpse bounced on his body, moving feebly, even as Arthur rolled off the Boss Wasp. It hd stopped moving at last, poison and wounds finally causing it to succumb.

Now, they just had to deal with the rest of the wasps, all of which were still hovering around them, angered even more at the loss of their leader.

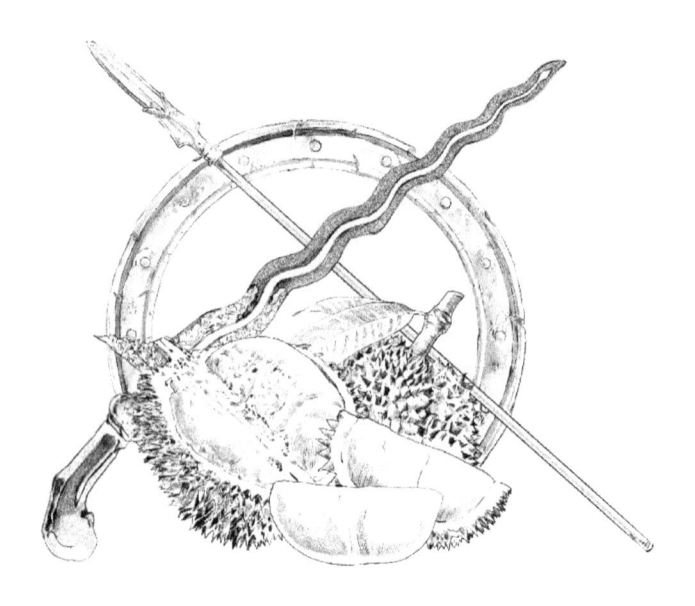

Chapter 145

Hand raised, Arthur released the Refined Exploding Energy Dart from it, watching the attack slip past the flames to embed itself inside the wasp nest that was merrily burning away. It exploded, sending shards and burning goblets of compressed dirt and twigs through the air. Moments later, the flames swept into the now-open insides, burning the eggs, half-formed wasps, and one last, trapped creature. They struggled, their bodies lit by lurid flames that crackled, a wordless shriek echoing through the air. A louder shriek came from the bigger wasps caught by the fire.

None of the Climbers moved to put an end to the creatures' suffering though. Most were too tired, too injured after their last pitched battle. Unable to retreat due to the injured among them, the group had been forced to stand and fight to the end. That had left more of them injured and hurting, such that nearly half the group was down, attempting to heal their injuries.

Funnily enough, Arthur was one of those best in shape, even with the poison coursing through his veins still and the hole in his stomach. That had clotted, and while he was not standing up and doing a jig, he had managed to pull himself over to a tree to lean against. Running the Accelerated Healing technique and forming a Refined Exploding Energy Dart simultaneously, he was on the lookout for potential problems.

Leia and Uswah were the only two not injured, the pair moving around the corpses and tearing out monster cores before they disappeared. Thankfully, after pulling out its core and chopping off the stinger, the Boss Monster had faded almost immediately, leaving the poison sack and stinger behind as well. That, they knew from previous documents, was one of the advantages of breaking into the higher levels. The chances of drops, of parts left behind by monsters, increased.

"*Sakiiiit*," Yao Jing groaned in pain, clutching his body. At least, now he was actually well enough to complain after finally managing to heal enough of his body. He was all kinds of sweaty though, his eyes still a little unfocused. None of the others were doing well, but the worst off was Casey.

"She going to be fine?" Arthur asked Lam. The man had been hit in his thigh and was grim-faced in dealing with it by putting a tourniquet around his leg, compressing the meat such that only a small trickle of blood could flow through it. It wasn't the best option, but at least it allowed him to function somewhat. And he needed to, since he was dealing with Casey.

"She will be," Lam said, firmly, as though he refused to believe otherwise as he pressed down upon the wound in her torso. The wasp had managed to slam into her hard enough that it pierced the overlapping plates around her abdomen, embedding its stinger inside Casey's body. She'd managed to kill it soon after, but the creature's stinger continued to be stuck within, refusing to come out till Lam had ripped it clear. That had left an open wound and also a ton of toxins.

Not a big issue, if she had a healing technique. However, she was not part of the Durians and thus did not benefit from their Clan Seal. All she could do was struggle through the pain, using the anti-toxin pills that the pair had taken from the Chins' compound, and wait for passive Tower healing to take effect.

"Alright." Arthur lifted his hand, having formed it there rather than at his third eye because he was a little too woozy to risk having his conjuration explode in his face. He shifted it around, searching for trouble and then dropped his hand, keeping the formed Energy Dart there while he waited. "This was a mess."

"Yes," Rick grated out by his side. He was carefully trying to reload his guns, but his hands were trembling so badly he dropped more bullets than he did managed to slip into the magazine. Still, he stubbornly persisted at it, as though he needed the distraction. "We should. Have. Run."

"Yeah," Arthur replied. "My fault. I should have ordered it." He'd gotten focused on handling the Boss Wasp, to keep it from attacking anyone else, that he forgot to order everyone else to flee. Perhaps if they had done that, they might have managed to get away.

"Too fast," Mel said, then coughed and spat. She was, surprisingly, not one who had been stung. Instead, she'd managed to injure herself by falling over, after catching her foot in the wrong place. The break at her lower leg was nasty-looking and was still healing, and the process of setting it had nearly caused Leia to throw up. "It would have caught us."

"Maybe..." Arthur admitted. He had not considered that. Certainly, he hadn't had time to try to kill it more than once, before it had targeted Rick. "Should have had nets. Or something."

"Would've been nice, yeah. Or a fire aura, like Karen said."

"Maybe the Karens have a point, eh?" Rick said. The joke fell rather flat, since it was not only a little out of date but had never really transferred over to Malaysia that well. Not to say they didn't have their own busybodies or loud-voiced females, but it certainly was not as much of a cultural touchpoint for their generation.

"Still, lots of stones." Leia said, wandering back over to prod Eric with her toe. He did not stir, lying on his back and meditating. She bent low, eyeing the hastily packed and bandaged wounds, nodded to herself as she noted they'd stopped leaking blood and left him to continue his healing. "So, when does the portal form?"

"Have to wait for the fire to go. And the nest to be cleared," Arthur said, gesturing. "We'll want to check the nest. There's possibly something in there too."

"Possibly?" Leia said, frowning.

"Reports vary. Not sure why, but sometimes there are things inside." Arthur grimaced and added, "Also, Tower tokens and the like."

"Ooooh." Avarice glimmered in Leia's eyes and even Jan stirred from where she lay, before they subsided into weariness.

Now attention turned to the merrily crackling fire as they waited for it to burn down. One way or the other, they weren't going anywhere till it did.

By the time the fire had burnt down, the Durians were mostly on their feet. Arthur was back to normal and had even had time to pull energy from one stone, refilling a portion of his reserves. Using his spear, he was breaking down the last of the smouldering nest, shoving it around rather than sticking his hand into the still hot detritus.

The others were doing much the same, either with spears or broken-off branches. They swept the various pieces of the nest and wasps aside. Some of the eggs and the half-formed juveniles had yet to disperse. Perhaps they might not. The point at which the Tower considered something part of the biome and what was a monster corpse that needed to be removed was still a question, a wavy gradient that much smarter and more bookish people than Arthur spent their time studying.

For his part, he was mostly considering whether some of the less burnt eggs could be traded in.

"No one wants them," Leia said, firmly. "Don't even think about packing some away."

"You sure? I mean, the Tower might make them into pills or something..."

"If they did, it'd be on this floor. And no one asks for it." More firmly, she added, "So, stop it. It's disgusting."

Arthur snorted, rolled his eyes and bent low as he spotted a glint. He pointed it out and Mel managed to hook it over with some leaves and branches, sweeping it clear and touching it quickly to check for warmth. She eventually picked it up, tentatively, and turned the Tower token over in her hand.

"So, someone died." Mel said, slightly sad.

"Nice!" Jan said, making grabby motions for it, only for Mel to glare at her. "What!? They're dead. Not as though we killed them."

Mel just shook her head, while Arthur firmly said, "Mel keeps them all. We'll share the spoils later." A beat, then he added again, "Later!"

"Yes, sir!"

Another ten minutes and the group had the pillars clear, which resulted in a familiar-looking inky black opening in the air forming. They'd also managed to find three other Tower tokens and one broken one that they'd hoped could be reused. With five tokens total, it was clear that there had been at least one group that had died trying to make their way through. The question was...

"Where's the bodies? Their gear?" Rick said the question out loud.

No one had an answer and even after they checked the surroundings, sweeping the area nearby for the missing bodies, they were not able to locate anything.

"Tower ate them?" Jan made a face at the thought.

"Did something else to the bodies?" Eric asked, more pragmatically.

No clues on the past, and Arthur found himself waving it off. Tower mysteries like these were all around, and finding the answer would waste time. Though...

"You okay?" Arthur said, looking at Casey who was sitting up, though she looked all too pale, exhausted and sweaty.

"Healing..." Casey looked at outwards, stared at the portal then shook her head slowly. "Can't. Got to wait."

"Yeah, I figured." Arthur sighed and waved the team off. They were ready, they were good to go for the sixth floor. But his team was still slightly injured and Casey needed at least a day. Maybe two. And while it might make some sense for them to test the next floor themselves, they might as well heal up more and cultivate. It would make little difference in the end. But might keep her safe.

One more night, one more day. And then, the sixth floor and the last of the weird platform biomes.

Almost there.

Almost.

The End of Book 2

Want to continue Arthur's adventure now?

Read the next chapter in the free web serial on Starlit Publishing

https://starlitpublishing.com/blogs/climbing-the-ranks

Author's Note

Thank you all for continuing to read Climbing the Ranks. I know it's not exactly what most people expect from a tower climber or cultivation series, especially if you'd read A Thousand Li. On the other hand, I hope the addition of the Benevolent Durians has added some interesting new aspects of the world, as we'll be seeing more of them in book 3 and, importantly the second arc (4+).

I recently took up a spear workshop, that taught a bunch of new spear techniques to me. It's fascinating learning about various martial arts, and how the length of a spear and just general intended use has changed styles and training philosophies.

Not surprisingly, Arthur's mostly trained in Chinese spear techniques, and the shorter spears rather than the long ones. Extra long spears are great for working in an army, shoulder-to-shoulder with another; but not as useful when you're alone. Short spear techniques are similar, somewhat, to staff techniques with more stabs, quick direction changes and methods of extracting stuck spears.

I'll probably bring more detailed spear fighting techniques in future books. Not surprisingly, the next few chapters are going to feature the final climb; including what I hope to be somewhat interesting biomes and a real 10th floor challenge.

Once more, thanks for reading everyone. Do check out Starlit Publishing if you want to get ahead of the curve, as we push more chapters out on the site ahead of the general release.

~Tao

About the Author

Tao Wong is a Canadian author based in Toronto who is best known for his System Apocalypse post-apocalyptic LitRPG series and A Thousand Li, a Chinese xianxia fantasy series. His work has been released in audio, paperback, hardcover and ebook formats and translated into German, Spanish, Portuguese, Russian and other languages. He was shortlisted for the UK Kindle Storyteller award in 2021 for his work, A Thousand Li: the Second Sect. When he's not writing and working, he's practicing martial arts, reading and dreaming up new worlds.

Tao became a full-time author in 2019 and is a member of the Science Fiction and Fantasy Writers of America (SFWA) and Novelists Inc.

If you'd like to support Tao directly, he has a Patreon page - benefits include previews of all his new books, full access to series short stories, and other exclusive perks. www.patreon.com/taowong

Want updates on upcoming deluxe editions and exclusive merch? Follow Tao on Kickstarter to get notifications on all projects.

www.kickstarter.com/profile/starlitpublishing

For updates on the series and his other books (and special one-shot stories), please visit the author's website: www.mylifemytao.com

Subscribe to Tao's mailing list to receive exclusive access to short stories in the Thousand Li and System Apocalypse universes!

For more great information about great LitRPG series, check out the Facebook groups:

- GameLit Society
  www.facebook.com/groups/LitRPGsociety
- LitRPG Books
  www.facebook.com/groups/LitRPG.books
- LitRPG Legion
  www.facebook.com/groups/litrpglegion

And join my Cultivation Novel Group for more recommendations and to talk about the Thousand Li series:

www.facebook.com/groups/cultivationnovels

About the Publisher

Starlit Publishing is wholly owned and operated by Tao Wong. It is a science fiction and fantasy publisher focused on the LitRPG & cultivation genres. Their focus is on promoting new, upcoming authors in the genre whose writing challenges the existing stereotypes while giving a rip-roaring good read.

For more information on Starlit Publishing, early access to books and exclusive stories visit our webshop. www.starlitpublishing.com

You can also join Starlit Publishing's mailing list to learn about new, exciting authors and book releases: www.starlitpublishing.com/newsletter-signup/